kissy kissy,

. No sexo!"

bit his lip to hold back the laugh that wanted to escape him. He suspected she wouldn't see what was so amusing here, but really, he'd imagined their first meeting repeatedly over the last fifteen years. But not once in any of them had she been a feisty little bit of goods in a sexy as hell see-through gown telling him "no sexo!"

"Got it?" she repeated.

Domitian nodded mildly, allowing a smile to curve his lips. "As you wish."

Sarita straightened to prop her hand on her hips as she looked him over. Reluctant concern entering her expression, she asked, "How are you feeling?"

Domitian couldn't hide his surprise at the seeming change in attitude.

"I mean are you full or what?" she explained, and then apparently not wanting him to think she was actually concerned about his health, added, "Full enough not to bite me if I unchain you?"

"I will not bite you," Domitian assured her solemnly, and then just because he felt quite sure it would annoy her, added, "Until you ask me."

By Lynsay Sands

LYNSAY SANDS

IMMORTAL UNCHAINED

AN ARGENEAU NOVEL

AVONBOOKS

An Imprint of HarperCollinsPublishers

"Bliss" was published as an e-book in July 2010 by HarperCollins Publishers.
Excerpt from *Bliss* copyright © 2001 by Lynsay Sands.

IMMORTAL UNCHAINED. Copyright © 2017 by Lynsay Sands. All rights reserved. Printed in the United States of America. No part of this book may be used or reproduced in any manner whatsoever without written permission except in the case of brief quotations embodied in critical articles and reviews. For information, address HarperCollins Publishers, 195 Broadway, New York, NY 10007.

First Avon Books mass market printing: April 2017
First Avon Books hardcover printing: March 2017

ISBN 978-0-06-246884-0

IMMORTAL UNCHAINED

Prologue

"**I** begin to think they are going to be late," Domitian murmured, hefting his duffle bag higher on his shoulder so that the microphone hidden in his sleeve would catch his words.

"Perhaps it is a sign." Lucian Argeneau's voice was surprisingly clear. The earpiece they'd given Domitian was so small that it was unseen once inserted, but the sound came through loud and crystal clear. "We should scrap this now and—"

"Still trying to talk me out of going, Uncle?" Domitian asked with amusement, and then suddenly impatient, added, "I do not know why you are so resistant to my doing this. Especially with Uncle Victor, Lucern, Decker, Nicholas, Aunt Eshe, Mirabeau La Roche, and Santo Notte now among the missing. I would think with all of them having been taken—"

"That is precisely why," Lucian growled. "This is dangerous. We have already lost several hunters, people armed and trained to handle situations like this. You, Domitian, are going in there unarmed, and you are *not* a hunter."

"True, but I was a warrior once. I can handle myself," Domitian argued. "Besides, none of your hunters were invited, I was."

"Yes, but was it because you are a chef and Dressler wants you to work for him? Or because you are an immortal he wants to add to his collection?"

"I told you. He does not know I am an immortal," Domitian said slowly and firmly, stressing each word. They'd had this conversation several times already, but it seemed they would have it again. "If Dressler knew, he could have taken me at any time. He has been a regular in my restaurant for five years. He obviously does not know."

"Or perhaps he did not wish to kidnap an immortal so close to home," Lucian countered. "It might have led us straight here to Venezuela."

Domitian shifted impatiently at the suggestion. "One immortal missing in Caracas would hardly have brought you here when so many have gone missing in the United States."

"Perhaps. Or perhaps we would have—"

"Is that helicopter headed this way?" Domitian interrupted, raising a hand to shield his eyes from the sun as he watched the vehicle approach. It was flying low and seemed to be headed straight for where he stood at the base of the large dock . . . which was where he'd been directed to wait for his ride. He'd expected a boat, but—

"Are those pontoons?" Lucian asked sharply in his ear.

Domitian knew that Lucian and the others wouldn't have as good a view from the small boat where they waited farther along the docks. On top of that, they were staying out of sight in the small cabin in the bow, which had only tiny windows that were glazed and screened. Their view would be highly obscured compared to his.

"Yes. The helicopter has pontoons," he confirmed, his gaze on the skids with the floatation devices affixed to them. It was fitted out to be an amphibious helicopter so that it could set down on water or land, which made Domitian suspect that this *was* his ride. Apparently he wasn't the only one to think that, he realized, wincing as a loud curse sounded in his ear.

"You are not to get on that helicopter!" Lucian ordered firmly. "Make an excuse. Tell them you have changed your mind. We did not plan for this. The boats out in the bay might lose the helicopter. Do you hear me?"

His thoughts racing, Domitian watched the helicopter slow and begin to drop by the end of the dock. To get on board or not was the question. If he said he had a fear of flying, Dressler might send a boat for him and then Lucian's men could follow from a safe distance to find the island. Then again, he might not. Dressler might suspect something was afoot and simply cancel the job offer altogether . . . and Domitian couldn't risk that. He had to get on that island. His life mate was there and could be in danger.

"Domitian? Can you hear me?" Lucian barked sharply, and then his voice faded as he asked someone else, "Is this thing working? Why is he not answering?"

"Perhaps the noise from the helicopter is drowning you out," another voice responded. Domitian was pretty sure that voice belonged to the young hunter Justin Bricker and was grateful for the suggestion. He would pretend it was true and he couldn't hear his uncle. He *was* getting on that helicopter. He might be risking his life doing it, but not getting on risked his chance of any kind of a happy future.

"Dammit! Domitian! Do not get on that helicopter! Domitian?"

Ignoring the voice in his ear, Domitian watched the helicopter set down, not on the water, but on the end of the dock. He then started forward.

"Domitian Argeneau!" Lucian's voice roared in his ear.

"It's Argenis, Uncle. Not Argeneau," Domitian reminded him gently before unobtrusively plucking the earpiece from his ear and tucking it into the front pocket of his tight jeans. It didn't matter what anyone said. He was going, Domitian thought as he watched the passenger door of the helicopter open.

Instinctively ducking, he rushed quickly under the rotors to the entrance. A man in a suit was waiting with his hand out to take his duffle bag. Domitian handed it over with a nod of thanks and then grasped the door frame and climbed in. The window seat was the only one available, so he settled into it and pulled the door closed without having to be told.

Domitian then started to turn to get a better look at the other men in the helicopter but stiffened in surprise as he felt a sudden sharp pain in the side of his neck. He lost consciousness almost at once.

One

Sarita closed the book she'd been trying to read and tossed it impatiently aside. It was a horrible book. Or perhaps she just wasn't in the mood to read, she acknowledged with irritation, getting restlessly to her feet. As a police officer, her life at home in Canada was usually a busy one, full of activity and even urgency. But here . . . all this sitting around waiting to be able to visit her grandmother was beginning to fray on her nerves. Sarita was anxious to see for herself how her grandmother was doing after her accident. It was why she was here, after all. Instead, she'd spent her time since arriving in Venezuela, stuck on this island, alternating between pacing and trying to read books that simply couldn't hold her interest. It was driving her crazy, sitting here, waiting for Dr. Dressler to return to the island and instruct his men to transport her to the mainland. Unfortunately, he hadn't been here when she'd arrived, and they wouldn't take her there without his orders.

Clucking impatiently under her tongue, she left the library, her mouth tightening as her gaze slid to the two men standing guard inside the front double doors of the house. They stood one on either side, eyes straight ahead, faces expressionless, hands loosely at their sides within easy reach of the sidearms she knew each wore.

And that was the only thing they were doing right as far as she could tell. She'd been told the ridiculous level of security on the island was because kidnappings had become so rampant in Venezuela and "el Doctor" wanted to ensure his safety as well as that of his family, his employees, and visitors like her. But if that was the case, then he should have all of his security on the outside, watching for the approach of would-be kidnappers, not inside, watching the goings-on in the house. Although he had that too, she acknowledged. There were two men standing guard outside the double doors as well, and a dozen more walking the grounds as far as she could tell. "El Doctor" was obviously paranoid about kidnappings. But since her own mother had been kidnapped and killed when she was young, Sarita supposed she should probably appreciate his efforts to ensure their safety. Instead, she just found the men posted everywhere something else to be annoyed about today.

Knowing she was in a foul mood from a combination of boredom and frustration, Sarita turned on her heel and headed up the hall toward the kitchen. She'd get a drink and maybe one of Aleta's yummy cookies, and see if the cook had something for her to do to help pass the time. At that point, even something as mundane as washing dishes would be welcome . . . which told Sarita just how bored she was.

Grimacing at the depths to which she'd sunk after three short days of inactivity, Sarita pushed the kitchen door open and stepped inside. The rich aroma of something delicious rolled over her as she entered, and her nose twitched as she inhaled the scent. Spotting Aleta stirring a pot simmering on the range in the center of the island, she moved closer to peer at the contents with interest. There were chunks of vegetables and meat in a thick juice. It smelled like heaven.

"Hola," Aleta greeted her softly, a shy smile curving her lips.

Sarita smiled at the woman. *"Hola.* That smells good. I swear, Aleta, you're an angel. Everything you make is delicious."

"Gracias," Aleta said, flushing with pleasure.

"What is it?" Sarita asked, leaning across the island to inhale more deeply.

"El estofado de ternera," she answered.

"Mmm," Sarita murmured, again inhaling the scent coming off the beef stew.

"Is not quite time for dinner, but it is ready," Aleta said, watching her practically drool over the pot. "If you are hungry, you can eat now."

"Oh, yes please," Sarita said at once.

Aleta chuckled at her eagerness. "Go out to the dining room and I will bring it in."

Sarita shook her head. "I can eat here. It would be nice to have some company," she added when Aleta frowned.

The woman's expression softened then and she nodded. "Here then. Sit down," she added, gesturing to the stools on the opposite side of the island from where she was cooking.

Sarita wanted to insist on getting her own food and drink, but suspected if she tried Aleta might change her mind about letting her eat in the kitchen. So she sank obediently onto one of the stools and watched as Aleta fetched her a bowl and spoon and served up the stew.

"Que quieres tomar?" Aleta asked as she set the bowl before her.

"Water is fine," Sarita answered and then said *"Agua"* as well. Aleta seemed to speak English well, but the way she slipped back into Spanish at times—as she had when she'd just asked what Sarita wanted to drink—suggested the cook might not be fully fluent in the language. She had no desire to embarrass the woman by making her admit it.

Picking up her spoon, Sarita scooped up some of the stew, blew on it briefly, and then slipped it into her mouth. It was as good as it smelled, better even, and she moaned with pleasure as the flavor burst on her tongue.

Chuckling, Aleta set a glass of water and a plate with a large *tequeno* on it next to her bowl, and then turned back to her stew.

Sarita picked up the fried breadstick with cheese inside and eagerly took a bite. She loved Aleta's *tequenos*. Honestly, she loved everything the woman had made for her since her arrival on the island three days earlier. Sarita was seriously considering trying to lure her away to Canada with a job. She was just trying to work out if she could afford it. Her apartment didn't have enough room to house the two of them. She'd need to buy a house, and then there was the whole immigration issue to worry about.

Sarita was just finishing her stew and *tequeno* when Aleta set her spoon aside again and retrieved a blender from the cupboard. The cook set it on the counter, plugged it in, and then moved to the refrigerator. A moment later she walked back to the counter with an armload of cleaned and precut greens and vegetables.

"What are you making now?" Sarita asked with curiosity as Aleta dropped a good portion of the vegetables into the blender and then moved to the pantry.

Aleta backed out of the pantry a moment later with a jar of some kind of powder. Carrying that to the blender, she murmured, "El Doctor's *bebida nutritive.*"

The doctor's nutrition drink, Sarita translated and stiffened on her stool as she watched Aleta measure out a portion of the powder. Voice sharp, she asked, "El Doctor's back?"

"Back?" Aleta frowned at the powder in her measuring cup and added a bit more, shaking it to level it out as she did. "Back from where? He has not gone anywhere for weeks. He is always down at the labs since he took the *ano sabatico.*"

Sabbatical, Sarita translated. Dr. Dressler had told her he was on sabbatical from the university when he'd called her about her grandmother's falling and injuring herself. And apparently he'd been spending all of his time since then down at his labs . . . not on the mainland as she'd been led to believe. After Dr. Dressler's call telling her about her grandmother's accident and his fears for her well-being since falls could be deadly for older women, Sarita had immediately booked a flight to Venezuela to check on her. She'd been met at the airport by the head of Dr. Dressler's security team and flown out here by helicopter only to learn that her grandmother was still in the hospital in Caracas and had not yet returned to the island. She'd immediately requested to be transported back to the mainland so that she could see her, but had been told that neither the boats nor the helicopter could be used without first gaining Dr. Dressler's permission and he was not here.

Sarita had assumed that meant he wasn't on the island and had been waiting impatiently for his return, but it seemed he was on the island, just not at the house. She frowned now at this news, furious that Dressler's man hadn't made that clear. Had she known, she could have sought out Dressler himself to get the needed permission, and been at her grandmother's bedside days ago.

Scowling, Sarita stood and quickly carried her empty bowl and plate to the sink.

"Leave it. I will do that," Aleta said when Sarita started to rinse them.

"*Gracias,*" Sarita murmured rather than argue and turned off the tap. She'd finished rinsing them anyway. Turning to head for the door, she added, "And thank you for the dinner. It was delicious."

"*De nada,*" Aleta said absently as she concentrated on her measuring.

Sarita was halfway up the hall before she recalled the men at the front door. Not wanting to be questioned and possibly stopped from going down to the labs, she turned as she reached the entry and jogged up the stairs that led to the second floor. Sarita moved quickly along the hall to the room she'd inhabited since arriving and slipped inside.

A cautious glance out the French doors in her room showed her that the sun was setting. In the dying light she could see men moving toward the house from every direction. While it had not quite been dinnertime when she'd arrived in the kitchen, it was nearly that time now and she was not the only one who appreciated Aleta's cooking.

She watched until all of the men had moved around the house and out of sight. They'd be heading to the door of the kitchen to fetch their food, she knew. It would leave a skeleton crew of two men at the front door as well as the men on the towers and at the gate to the fenced-in labs. Those men would then be relieved so they too could eat. Or perhaps food would be taken to them. Sarita had no idea, she'd never cared enough to find out.

She didn't really care now either, Sarita decided as she slid out onto the balcony. Finding the yard empty, she climbed over the balcony rail, lowered herself until she hung from the bottom of the white-painted metal, and then let herself drop lightly onto the terrace below. A little grunt slid from her lips as her bare feet slapped on the stone. After a quick glance around, she hurried along the side of the house to the front corner.

A quick peek around the corner showed Sarita that even the men at the front door had gone in search of their meal. She'd always assumed that because the men inside waited to eat in the second shift, that the men outside would too, but it seemed not. Pondering that, she broke away from the house and hurried across the lawn, heading for the path through the trees to the labs.

Sarita expected to be stopped at any moment, but she made it all the way to the tree line outside the fence without encountering anyone. Pausing just inside the trees, she eyed the fenced-in buildings that made up Dr. Dressler's labs. From the air the half a dozen long low buildings had made her think of army barracks.

Now, as her gaze slid over the towers on each corner of the high fence surrounding the buildings, she decided it looked more like a prison.

She looked at the men in the towers again, this time checking each one more carefully. Sarita couldn't be sure in the dying light, but it seemed to her that their attention was focused inside the fence rather than out. As if they were guarding against someone escaping rather than intruders. Thinking that could only be good for her, she straightened her shoulders and approached the gatehouse at the fence entrance.

Sarita prepared herself for a verbal battle as she crossed the short distance, expecting whoever was guarding the gate to refuse her entry. But she was determined that she would at least make them call Dr. Dressler out to the gate. She *would* get him to tell his men to take her to the mainland in either the helicopter or a boat so that she could see her grandmother. It was why she was here in Venezuela. And Sarita was pretty pissed about being made to cool her heels here on the island for three days when her grandmother was in a hospital on the mainland.

In the end, Sarita didn't have to argue with the man in the gatehouse. She walked up to the window, opened her mouth to explain herself, and then closed it without saying a word as she noticed that the blond man inside wasn't even looking her way. He was sitting with his back to the window and gate, earbuds in his ears as he watched a movie on the computer on the counter in front of him.

A porno, she saw as her gaze slid to the computer screen.

So much for security, Sarita thought dryly and glanced

to the gate. There was a large gate, presumably for vehicles, and a smaller one for people to pass through. Sarita walked to the smaller gate. When she found it wasn't even locked and opened easily, she shook her head with disgust and slipped through, then pulled it gently closed. She headed for the nearest building at a quick clip and was more than halfway to it before a shout sounded. It was followed by another, and then another as others heard the call and noticed her.

Sarita ignored them and kept going, but she did move a little faster. She made it to the door, and a glance around as she slipped inside showed her that while one or two men were climbing down the ladders on the towers, the man in the gatehouse still had his head down as he watched his porn. Apparently, he hadn't yet noticed anything amiss. She suspected he'd be in a heap of trouble for it.

Pulling the door closed, Sarita turned to survey the room she'd entered. It was a lab, all white with upper and lower metal cupboards on two walls, a large industrial refrigerator as well as a large industrial freezer along another and a desk against the last wall. Two small, wheeled tables sat a little distance apart in the center of the room, and those caught and held her attention at once.

Having trouble accepting what she was seeing, Sarita moved slowly across the room to the first table and stared down at the top half of the corpse lying strapped on it. It was a man who was probably about twenty-five. His hair was short and blond, his face handsome but bloodless, and his upper body was in perfect shape . . . except for the fact that it ended just below his belly button where he appeared to have been cut in half.

Sarita stared at him blankly, noting that there were a couple dozen metal straps rising out of the table, crossing over his body, and then disappearing through slots in the table surface. There was one across his forehead, and then at his throat, his shoulders, under his armpits, and another every couple of inches down his torso after that for the length of the table. There were also half a dozen smaller metal straps holding his arms down from his armpits to his wrists.

Sarita turned her head to peer at the second small table where the lower half of his body lay. A small towel was draped over his groin, and there were even more straps running over his lower body, with a great gaping wound where his body had been separated. It looked as if he'd been sawn in half like a tree.

As she studied the open wound on the lower half of the body, and the one on the upper body, Sarita had to wonder why she wasn't freaking out.

Probably because of the lack of blood, she thought . . . and because it didn't look real. Or perhaps because it reminded her of Body Worlds, an exhibition of preserved human bodies that showed the anatomy of the inner body. Her father had taken her to see it at the Ontario Science Centre back in 2005. This reminded her of it, a bloodless display of inner workings. It looked like one of those. It was obviously a cadaver from the university or something.

That made sense, Sarita thought. After all, Dr. Dressler was a professor at one of the universities in Venezuela. Mind you, universities didn't generally let professors take cadavers home that she knew of.

And why both halves of the body were strapped to the table like that was a complete mystery to her.

The sound of approaching voices caught her attention and Sarita turned her head toward the door as someone said, "I will handle it. You get back to your posts . . . and do your jobs this time."

The door opened then and an older man stepped inside. Dressed in dark pants and a white doctor's coat, Dr. Dressler was tall, with a full head of snow-white hair parted at the side and brushed away from his face in waves that suggested he was a little overdue for a haircut. He had a mustache and goatee to match, but his eyebrows were a mix of snow-white and a darker brown or black that suggested he'd been a dark-haired man when younger. The skin on his neck was saggy and a little crepey and his face had the wrinkles and lines age eventually carved in everyone's face, but they were much less pronounced than she would have expected from someone she knew to be in his eighties.

"Dr. Dressler?" she asked uncertainly, before glancing to the woman who followed him into the room. Also wearing dark pants and a doctor's white coat, she was much younger, perhaps in her thirties. Her hair was blond and pulled back in a tight bun, revealing a face that was untouched by makeup but still beautiful.

At least it would have been beautiful if she didn't have such a sour expression on her face, Sarita thought.

"Sarita, my dear. What a pleasure to finally meet you," Dr. Dressler said, drawing her attention back his way as he led the blonde across the room. He clasped her hands in his and used his hold to shift her to the side as he added, "Unfortunately, you have arrived at a rather inconvenient moment. This experiment is time sensitive, so please just stay here out of the way while we do our work and we shall talk afterward."

Staying by the wall where he'd urged her, Sarita watched silently as he then joined the blonde and helped her roll the two tables together so that the upper torso of the corpse met the lower torso perfectly.

"Fetch the blood, Asherah," Dr. Dressler ordered as he then moved to flip latches on each side of the tables where they joined, turning the two short tables into one long one.

The blonde immediately moved to a refrigerator at the end of one wall of cupboards and opened the door, revealing stacks of bagged blood inside.

Sarita stiffened in surprise. The bags looked like something you'd see in a hospital or blood bank, but the number of them was staggering. She would have guessed there were at least a hundred bags stacked on the refrigerator shelves. A ridiculous amount for anyone to have.

Asherah carried the bags to a wheeled tray of surgical instruments, dumped them on it, and rolled the tray up next to the table, then moved off to collect two IV stands without being told. The moment she set them next to the table, Dr. Dressler collected one of the bags of blood from the tray and began to set up one of the IVs. Hanging the bag of blood from the hook, he quickly affixed the tubing before inserting the needle in the corpse's left arm. Once finished he grabbed another bag of blood off the tray and dragged the second IV around to the right side of the body to do the same. He then glanced up expectantly.

Following his gaze, Sarita saw that Asherah had gone back to the cupboards to collect something else. She was now returning with what looked like a ball gag, but with more straps. There was also a funnel where the ball would be, she noted as Asherah got closer to the table.

"Two minutes," Dr. Dressler warned, eyeing his watch as Asherah strapped the harness into place, with the funnel in the corpse's mouth.

Asherah straightened and moved quickly back to the refrigerator to collect another half a dozen bags of blood. She dropped most of them on the wheeled tray with the others when she returned, but kept one and picked a scalpel from the surgical items on the tray before moving up to the table where it was joined. She peered down at where the two halves of the body were pressed tight together and simply waited, seemingly at the ready.

Shaking her head with bewilderment, Sarita asked, "What—?"

"Shh," Dr. Dressler hissed. "You'll understand in thirty seconds."

Sarita closed her mouth, but shook her head again at the madness she was witnessing. Offering indignities to a corpse was an indictable offense in Canada and what they were doing seemed to fit that description. Unfortunately, this was not Canada and she had no idea what the laws were here in Venezuela. She'd certainly be looking into it the first chance she got, though, Sarita decided.

"Time!" Dr. Dressler snapped and quickly opened the roller clamp on the IV next to him, before rushing around the table to do the same on the second IV. Blood immediately began to race down the tubes toward the corpse's arms, but Sarita hardly noticed that—she was too busy watching with horror as Asherah poked a hole in the bag of blood she held, and allowed the crimson liquid to gush out over the body where the two halves were now pressed together.

"Dear God," Sarita breathed with a disgust that only increased when Dr. Dressler now grabbed a second scalpel and another bag of blood off those remaining on the wheeled tray and punctured it over the corpse's face. Blood immediately began to flow into the funnel fixed in the corpse's mouth.

Clenching her fists, Sarita stood to the side, revulsion curling her stomach as she watched the pair's actions. She was starting to wish with all her heart that she was a police officer in Venezuela instead of Canada and could arrest the mad doctor and his equally crazy assistant. She had no idea what they thought they would achieve with this lunacy, but—

Sarita's thoughts died abruptly as the corpse's eyes suddenly popped open and he began to shriek. Or tried to. What came out was a raspy gurgle as he tried to scream around the liquid pouring down his throat. It forced some of the blood back out in a small spurt that splashed over Dr. Dressler.

"You forgot the tube, Asherah," Dr. Dressler accused harshly, but quickly added, "Don't stop what you're doing!"

Asherah had started to lift away the bag of blood she was holding over the wound at Dr. Dressler's first words, but stopped at once when he ordered her not to.

"Sarita, there should be a length of tube on the counter along the wall behind me. Fetch it for me," Dr. Dressler ordered sharply as he continued to let the blood pour down the throat of the man she'd thought was dead, but who was now screaming his head off and shooting the blood back out of his mouth as he did.

Stunned now by what was happening, Sarita did as asked, found the mentioned tubing and took it to

Dr. Dressler. When she reached his side though, he nodded toward the tray. "Grab another bag of blood."

Turning, she picked up the bag and offered it to him. He took it with one hand, waited a heartbeat for the one he already held to empty, then tossed it aside and moved the fresh bag over the mouth.

"Hold this," Dr. Dressler commanded once he'd punctured the new bag as he had the first.

Sarita hesitated, but then moved around to the opposite side of the table and took over holding the new bag of blood. Her hands were trembling, she noted, but she did her best to hold the bag steady and ground her teeth together as the corpse continued to scream, sending most of the blood shooting back up through and around the funnel and onto her and the doctor both now. But a moment later Dr. Dressler was feeding a tube through the funnel and down the man's throat. The tube, apart from ensuring the blood got to his stomach, also appeared to hamper his ability to scream. The moment several inches had been fed through the funnel, his screams stopped.

Quite sure the action was only adding to the man's pain, Sarita had to look away and shifted her gaze down to Asherah rather than watch. The assistant was tossing aside the first bag she'd cut open, but quickly grabbed and opened another over where his body was split in half. Sarita shook her head, unable to believe what was happening.

Dr. Dressler finished inserting the feeding tube, but didn't then take back the bag of blood she held as Sarita expected. Instead, he hung two fresh bags from the IV stands next to the ones already in use. It drew her attention to the fact that both bags were already half-empty. IVs usually didn't work that quickly in her experience. All she could think was that the catheter must be larger than the standard. She had no idea what it might be doing to the corpse's veins though.

The very thought made Sarita give her head a shake. The man obviously wasn't a corpse. Corpses didn't move and scream. But he *should* be a corpse. He'd been cut in half for God's sake. That thought kept running through her head as she held bag after bag over his mouth while Asherah did the same over his wound and Dr. Dressler manned the IVs and fetched fresh blood from the refrigerator as needed.

Sarita was holding her sixth bag and beginning to think this would go on forever when Asherah suddenly growled, "Time."

Dr. Dressler immediately glanced at his wristwatch, nodded, and then beamed at Sarita. "Very good. Asherah will clean up the worst of the blood, and then take over with that last bag you're holding. I have to make a note of the time and then we can talk."

He hurried away to the desk she'd noticed earlier, and Sarita turned her attention to Asherah as the woman reached under the table and retrieved some kind of nozzle. It was only when she pushed a lever and water began to run out over the midriff of the body that Sarita realized what it was.

Careful to keep her hand in place over the funnel, Sarita bent slightly to look under the table and saw that the top half of the table was fixed in place, only the bottom half was movable. Two pipes ran up one table leg, one pipe ending at a hose with the nozzle on the end, the other to a drain on this side of the table. Straightening again, she checked to be sure the bag of blood was still over the funnel, and then looked over to see that Asherah had already rinsed away most of the blood from the body.

Finding the spot where the upper body had been separated from the lower half, Sarita saw that they were now joined, with just an angry red scar where they had once been separated.

"Madre de Dios," she breathed, unable to believe her eyes.

"Move."

Glancing around with surprise, she saw that Asherah had finished with the hose and moved up beside her. Even as she noted that, the woman took over holding the bag and urged her away. "El Doctor wants to talk to you."

Sarita stepped back, her eyes returning to the scar where the body had once been cut in half.

"Move," Asherah repeated coldly. "You are done here."

Noting the dislike on the woman's face, Sarita reluctantly turned to walk to the desk where Dr. Dressler was scribbling furiously in a notebook.

Apparently finished making his notes, he raised his head as she stopped in front of the desk, and he smiled at her widely as he stood up. "Thank you, Sarita. Your help was invaluable."

"What exactly did I help with?" Sarita asked with a frown as Dressler moved around his desk. "That man was dead."

"Not dead," he assured her, crossing the room to the cupboards and retrieving a couple of syringes before moving to the refrigerator. "And not a man."

Eyebrows rising, Sarita peered back to the table. "He looks like a man to me."

"Yes," he agreed, bending to retrieve two ampoules from the refrigerator. "But he's not. He is an immortal."

"Immortal?" Sarita asked, following him back to the table. When he didn't answer, but concentrated on preparing a shot for the man, she glanced to Asherah as she tossed the now empty blood bag away. When the woman then moved around to the wheeled tray and grabbed another bag of blood, Sarita thought she intended to keep feeding it into the funnel. Instead, she replaced one of the now empty IV bags before grabbing another bag and replacing the other as well.

"Immortals are scientifically evolved mortals," Dr. Dressler announced, drawing Sarita's attention back to him. "This man is full of bio-engineered nanos programmed to keep his body healthy."

Finished filling the syringe, he set the ampoule on the wheeled tray and then simply held the shot and peered down at the man he called an immortal as he explained, "These nanos fight disease, repair the ravages of sun and time, and—as you saw—repair injuries."

Sarita shifted her gaze back to where the body had once been separated, and was quite sure the scar was smaller and less angry-looking than it had been just moments ago.

"After enough blood there won't even be a scar," Dr. Dressler announced. "The blood is what powers the nanos you see. They apparently use it to replicate themselves as well as to make repairs and so on."

"Blood," Sarita murmured, glancing toward the empty blood bags now littering the floor.

"Yes, they need a lot of it when injured," he said with a nod. "But even if not fighting illness or repairing an injury, the nanos need more blood than their host bodies can produce to keep them young. The nanos have forced their host bodies to evolve to make up for that need. In effect, making them scientifically created vampires."

When Sarita turned to him with disbelief, he glanced to Asherah and said, "Show her."

Asherah unhooked the harness from around the man's head and began to slowly remove it, pulling the feeding tube out with it.

Sarita half expected the man to begin screaming again, but other than a weak moan he was silent. Once Asherah had set the harness and tube aside, she picked up one of the disposed blood bags and sliced it open, then wiped up the little bit of blood left inside. It amounted to a couple of drops at best, but she waved it under the man's nose and despite his seeming to be unconscious, two of his upper teeth shifted and slid down in his open mouth, becoming fangs.

Gasping, Sarita took a step back.

"It is fine. We are safe," Dr. Dressler assured her. "Although if those straps were leather instead of titanium it would be a different matter. Aside from giving them fangs, the nanos make their hosts incredibly strong and extremely fast. They also have astonishing night vision. And they can read and control minds," he added grimly, finally bending to inject the man with the shot he'd prepared as he said, "Which is why we have to keep them drugged."

"Them?" Sarita asked with a frown.

"There are eighteen here in my labs," Dr. Dressler said, straightening from giving the shot.

"Why?" Sarita asked with dismay as he put the used

shot on the wheeled tray and set about filling the second syringe. "Surely they're dangerous?"

"Not normally, no," he assured her. "As a rule they consume bagged blood. In fact, it's a law among their kind, now that blood banks exist. They are forbidden to bite us mere mortals."

Sarita relaxed a little. If they stuck to bagged blood that wasn't so bad.

"And even before blood banks, they apparently weren't allow to kill anyone they bit. It's how they've managed to live among us with no one the wiser all these millennia."

"Millennia?" Sarita narrowed her eyes on the doctor, but he merely shrugged.

"Apparently they were a people isolated from the rest of the world who advanced technologically much more quickly. The nanos were a result of one of those advancements." He pursed his lips and considered the man. "They claim their home was Atlantis, and that when it sank into the ocean, only those with the nanos survived and crawled out to join the rest of the world. They also say that in Atlantis they had doctors and hospitals as we do today, and were given blood transfusions to combat the nanos' need for extra blood. But when Atlantis fell it was an end to those transfusions. Technology in the rest of the world was far behind that in Atlantis, and the nanos forced fangs, speed, and the other abilities on them so that they could gain the extra blood they needed to survive."

Sarita surveyed the man on the table and shook her head. "If I'd passed him on the street, I never would have known he wasn't human."

"That's the beauty of it. He *is* human," Dr. Dressler assured her. "He and others like him have children and families and live, laugh, and love just like the rest of us. Only they get to do it longer and don't suffer illness while they do. He's no different than you or I except for those nanos. Without them, he would be merely mortal, and with them, *we* could be *immortal*."

Sarita stiffened, something in his voice as he said that last part disturbing her. "You cut him in half," she said slowly, putting it together in her head. "You want the nanos and cut him in half to try to get them."

"No," Dr. Dressler assured her. "That would be a waste. The nanos are programmed to remain in the host body. Even bleeding them dry doesn't work. The nanos apparently move into the organs and skin to avoid leaving with the blood. You might get a couple from your efforts, but those disintegrate quickly once out of the body."

Sarita was about to ask how he knew that, and how the man *had* got cut in half if he hadn't done it, when Dressler continued, "I know the nanos must be transferrable, though. They have to be for them to turn their life mates."

"Life mates?" she echoed, briefly distracted.

"Hmm." He nodded thoughtfully. "Apparently while immortals can read and control most mortals, there are a few instances when they can't. One is if the mortal is mad. Apparently, that makes it difficult. The other is if the mortal is a life mate to them. In fact, that is how they recognize a life mate."

Sarita opened her mouth to ask what a life mate was, but closed it again as he said, "Anyway, I didn't cut him in half in an effort to retrieve nanos. I did it as part of an experiment to see how long his upper and lower body could be separated and yet still repair itself if pressed back together. We started with thirty seconds, and have been working our way up from there. This time it was two hours. Of course you have to void them of blood before doing it or else the nanos try to use what blood they have to try to repair the body at once while separated. The two halves start to seal, the bottom half dying from lack of blood long before it finishes the job. But as long as there is no blood, it's as if the nanos force the body into a sort of stasis. Once you put the two halves back together and add blood though, they kick into action and heal the body. It works if you just cut off a finger, hand, foot, or limb too. And the faster you give them blood, the faster they heal."

"Dear God," Sarita breathed, peering down at the man on the table. She was horrified that Dr. Dressler had actually deliberately inflicted this kind of pain on a living, breathing human . . . vampire or not.

"I have made it my business to find out all I can about their kind but must confess I'm growing tired of this experiment. I think we'll move on to removing a limb and destroying it, and then see if the nanos can build a new limb in its place."

"You—" Sarita broke off in shock when he suddenly raised the second syringe he'd prepared and shoved it into her neck, pressing the plunger home. It happened so quickly she didn't get a chance to react or try to stop him. By the time she started to raise her hand, he was already pulling the needle out and setting it on the wheeled tray.

"Wh—?" She stared at him in horror, unable to form the question she was trying to ask. When she swayed on her feet, he caught her arm to steady her, and then glanced toward the ceiling as the sound of a loud engine reached them.

"That will be the helicopter returning with your life mate," Dr. Dressler murmured and then offered her a smile as he let her sink slowly to the floor. "The two of you are going to be a great help to me, Sarita. I can't tell you how much I appreciate it."

Two

Sarita stirred sleepily, slowly realizing she was on her back in bed. She never slept on her back. She was a side sleeper and always had been. Being on her back with her hands resting just below her breasts . . . well, frankly it made her think of her father in his coffin.

Grimacing as that thought pulled her the rest of the way from sleep, Sarita promptly turned onto her side and let her eyes open. She then froze for a heartbeat before jerking to a sitting position in bed.

"What the hell?" she muttered, staring around at the alien room.

It was not her bedroom in her sunny little apartment in Toronto, Ontario. This room was decorated all in white. It was also at least three times the size of her room at home. Three large ceiling fans hung overhead, spinning in a desultory fashion and stirring up a nice soft breeze, and they, along with the three sets of French doors that lined the wall to her left seemed to parcel off each section of the room without the need for walls. In front of the doors at the far end, a couch, loveseat, and two chairs made up a sitting area, all were wicker with white cushions. In front of the middle set of doors was a small, glass-topped wicker dining table for two. The final set of French doors was right next to the bed she was sitting in, which was a sea of white bedclothes. Sarita had never seen a bed so big. It was bigger than king-sized, certainly. It was also terribly romantic with gossamer white curtains pulled back to drape at each post of the four-poster bed.

All in all, it looked like she'd been dumped in the middle of an advertisement for a honeymoon retreat in a tropical paradise, Sarita thought, peering out at the plants and palm trees she could see through the doors next to the bed. There was a stone floored terrace just outside the doors, but beyond that was a wall of jungle that would offer privacy to any honeymooners making use of the four-poster. It was a lovely room, and a lovely setup . . . but she had no idea how she'd got there or what she was doing there.

Pushing the soft white sheets aside, Sarita slipped her feet to the hardwood floor on the same side as the French doors, and then noticed the white nightgown she was wearing and paused to finger it with bewilderment. This was definitely not hers. She was the kind of gal who slept in an overlarge T-shirt and cotton panties. This too was straight out of an advertisement for honeymooning in paradise. Spaghetti straps dropped down to make up a piped and gathered neckline that barely reached above her nipples, and even then didn't cover them well. The material was thin and sheer, offering cover to her breasts only because of the way the material gathered there. The silky material wasn't presently gathered on her legs, however, and she could clearly see her tan legs through it and even the mole on her upper right thigh.

Standing abruptly, Sarita glanced around, relieved when she spotted a robe draped over a wicker chest at the foot of the bed. She hadn't noticed it on her first scan of the room. Moving to the end of the bed, she snatched up the material and quickly shrugged her arms into it. A grimace claimed her lips, though, as she wrapped it around front and used the sash to tie it closed. The robe was as light and sheer as the night-gown, the neckline piped and gathered too and just as low as the neckline on the gown. They were obviously a set but weren't meant for covering anything.

Muttering under her breath, Sarita took another look around the room in search of actual clothing, prefer-ably her own. But there was no sign of luggage or even drawers that might hold her possessions.

Aside from the French doors leading outside, there were also three solid wood doors in the room, all painted white to match the walls. One of the doors was in the wall opposite the bed, beyond the wicker furni-ture. For some reason Sarita suspected it was the one that led out into the rest of the house or hotel this room was in. She turned away from it for now, unwilling to leave the room dressed as she was.

Her gaze slid between the other two remaining doors. Both were in the wall the bed butted up against, one on either side of it, in fact. The one on the side she stood on was open, and Sarita found herself looking into a large white bathroom.

Moving to the doorway, she glanced around and saw

that the honeymoon theme continued here with a tub built for two and a large glass-walled shower you could have fit most normal-sized bathrooms into . . . or two people having crazy monkey sex. There was also a long white marble counter with two sinks, a separate smaller counter with a chair and large lighted mirror for doing makeup, and a door leading to an entirely separate small room that turned out to hold nothing but a toilet and a bidet.

Sarita peered at them and was suddenly aware that she had to relieve herself. Sighing, she quickly slipped inside to use the facilities, her mind racing. A plethora of questions were chasing each other through her mind. Unfortunately, she had no answers and her mind was just running around in circles in her head. Where was she? What had happened? How had she got here? Whose clothes were these? And how had she got into them?

Sarita wondered about that as she noted that even the panties she wore weren't her own. A silky white thong was the only thing under the nightgown. Sarita did not wear thongs. She'd tried them once because they were so sexy-looking, but hadn't been able to bear the feeling of having a constant wedgie. What the hell was going on? That seemed to be the question that kept drumming through her head. The last thing she remembered . . .

Actually, her memory was pretty fuzzy just now. She had some vague recollection of a lab and a corpse and some nonsense about vampires, but it was all so disjointed and surreal in her mind that she felt sure it was some fragmented nightmare she'd had. She also had something in her mind about worry for her grandmother, but, again, it was so fragmented and fuzzy she wasn't sure whether it was real or a dream. For all she knew, what was happening right now was a dream too. Certainly she couldn't afford a vacation in a place like this.

Panic tried to climb up inside her, but Sarita forced it down. She was a police officer, trained to control her automatic responses and assess situations before deciding the best way to respond to them. So . . . she would assess, Sarita decided firmly as she finished in the water closet.

Stepping back out into the large bathroom, she caught a glimpse of herself in the mirror over the sinks. The sight made her blink. Her black hair fell in wild abandon around her face and over her shoulders. It and her tan skin were an amazing contrast to the sheer white, flowing gown and robe. She looked like she'd stepped out of a gothic novel . . . or a porno, she thought with dismay, noting how her tan skin and the white thong she wore were revealed through the sheer cloth as she moved. Fortunately, the way the material gathered at the neckline helped hide her breasts . . . mostly.

Clucking her tongue with irritation, Sarita quickly washed and dried her hands, using the soap and fluffy white towels provided. Their presence made her start opening drawers and cupboards in the bathroom to see what they held. She found loads of soap, shampoo, conditioner, towels, and washcloths in the cupboards under the sink.

Lifting the makeup tabletop next, she found more cosmetics than a woman could use in a lifetime. There seemed to be every shade of lipstick, blush, and eye shadow ever created, all brand-new and with their wrapping intact. There were also various eyeliners, mascara, tweezers, nail files, and clippers, and so forth in the same packaged state, along with a hair dryer, several different curling irons, from flat to huge curls, and hairspray as well as various hairbrushes and combs. Basically, anything a woman might need to make herself pretty for any occasion.

Sarita stood still for a moment, simply staring at what was available as she tried to understand what all of this meant. The sheer sexy nightgown, the makeup, the big bed . . .

"No," she muttered and then let the makeup tabletop drop as she whirled away to hurry out of the bathroom. The bedroom was still empty—that was all Sarita noticed as she rushed around the bed to the door on the other side of it. Her breath left her on a relieved sigh as she opened that one to find a walk-in closet stuffed with clothes and shoes.

Thank God! She could put on some real clothes and go find out where the hell she was and what was going on, Sarita thought. Her relief was short-lived, however. Within moments she was standing in the middle of the closet, forcing herself to breathe slowly.

The confusion that had assailed her on first waking had given way to anger as she'd gone through the closet. There wasn't a scrap of her own clothing here, or at least, nothing she recognized as her own. Every single item hanging up was a negligee or nightie. There were various colors and lengths, from short skimpy blue baby dolls to long see-through crimson peignoirs, but every hanging item of clothing was some revealing nightwear suitable only for a honeymoon.

As for the drawers, they were full of thongs, stockings, and bikinis. There wasn't even one bra. And those shoes she'd noticed on first entering? They were all stilettos, a rainbow selection of them, one to match every peignoir hanging up. They were sexy as hell and useless in her current situation.

Letting her breath out slowly, Sarita turned and moved back into the bedroom and then paused, unsure what her next move should be. Her gaze slid to the door she suspected led into the rest of the building . . . and possibly to answers, but Sarita found herself moving away from it. She had no idea what was beyond that door and after discovering all the negligees and baby dolls in the closet, she wasn't sure she wanted whatever answers were waiting for her. But staying where she was didn't seem a good idea either, Sarita decided as she bumped up against something and turned to stare down at the bed.

Her gaze slid reluctantly to the unknown door again, but then quickly shifted to the French doors instead. At least there she could see what she was stepping out into, Sarita thought and moved around the foot of the bed to the first of the three sets of French doors. Pausing, she peered out at the terrace and jungle, and then glanced as far to each side as she could from her position.

The terrace stretched out in both directions, left and right, the jungle bordering its length like a privacy fence. She also saw that there was wicker furniture outside, but she didn't see any people around.

Sarita reached for the handle of the right door and turned it carefully, trying to be as quiet as possible. Once it unlatched, she eased it open and then poked her head out far enough to get a better look around. There wasn't really much more to see than that the terrace ran around both corners of the building. Sarita couldn't tell what might lie around the corner of the building to her left, but to her right she spotted the rounded end of an in-ground pool sticking out just past the building.

After a brief trip back to the bedroom to unplug and snatch up the bedside lamp, Sarita slipped out onto the terrace and began to creep along the cold stone tiles toward the right. She slowed as she passed the last set of French doors of her room and neared another set. Hand tightening on the lamp, she leaned forward just enough to peek inside.

Her gaze slid over a large open living room. It stretched the entire length of this end of the building. Again there were ceiling fans, hardwood floors, and white walls, but there were also throw rugs, and pillows adding splashes of color. The furniture was of the large overstuffed variety rather than the wicker used in the room she'd woken up in. The room was empty of any human inhabitant.

Relaxing a little, Sarita continued to the corner of the building to survey the pool and its surroundings. The jungle bordered this area too, running around the teardrop-shaped pool and back on the other side of the building. There was a waterfall at the top end of the teardrop where water spilled lazily over rocks stacked twelve feet high before dropping into the pool. It was beautiful.

Unfortunately, she wasn't in a position to enjoy it, so Sarita moved along the terrace to the next corner of the building. This one led to the front of the house, where the jungle fell away, leaving sand to border the terrace and run twenty or thirty feet down to the shore and an empty dock. She looked out at the ocean briefly and then considered the solid front double doors of the house under the shady porch before turning to retrace her steps to the open door of the bedroom.

Sarita didn't stop there, but continued on to the next

corner to peer around it. More terrace and French doors awaited but there was no sign of an actual person. Sarita moved to another set of French doors and repeated her cautious peeking routine. What she found this time appeared to be an office, also uninhabited. Her gaze slid over a dark wood desk and bookshelf-lined walls, and then she continued on to a small window. Knowing this would be a new room; she slowed and peeked cautiously through the high window at . . . another bathroom. Much smaller than the one off the bedroom, it was just a toilet and sink.

A guest bathroom, she supposed, and moved cautiously forward to the first of two sets of French doors beyond the bathroom. Sarita wasn't surprised when the first set of doors gave her a view of a kitchen, while the second revealed a dining area. She *was* surprised however that both rooms were just as empty as the rest of the house.

Pausing at the front corner on this side of the house, Sarita stared out over the sand and water again and then frowned and peered at the front doors. None of this was making sense. She was dressed for sex in the middle of a honeymoon paradise, but there didn't seem to be anyone here but her.

Unless there was a second floor, Sarita thought suddenly. She hadn't seen any stairs in her exploration, but . . .

Sarita walked quickly out onto the beach and then swung back to peer at the house. No second floor. She was alone. Which made absolutely no sense at all. Despite her embarrassing state of undress, she still would have preferred to find someone who could have explained things to her . . . like why she was here, and where here was.

Shaking her head, Sarita turned away from the house and next made her way out to the dock. She walked out onto the end of it and peered first one way and then the other along the beach, noting that it didn't stretch far on either side before curving away. So this house was on a tip of the island, or some body of land, she reasoned and glanced down, noticing what appeared to be brand-new rope on two of the dock posts. One on the post at the very tip of the dock, and one on the second one from shore, they were a good ten or fifteen feet apart, suggesting the boat that usually docked here wasn't a large one.

Sarita turned to look at the house. There was nothing but jungle around the building, no sign of a road. It could only be accessed by water. But there was no sign of a boat and she appeared to be the only person here.

For now.

That last thought had her heading for the house again, this time moving quickly. She appeared to be alone. But someone had brought her here. The empty dock suggested that whoever that was had left for some reason. But they hadn't just dumped her in a house in the middle of nowhere for no reason. They would certainly be back and she needed to prepare herself for that. She needed to find a weapon or a phone or something to help get her out of this situation.

Whatever this situation was, Sarita thought grimly. Considering all the negligees and skimpy swimsuits she'd found, and that they were the only form of covering available, she suspected sex had something to do with her presence here. If that was the case . . . well, Sarita had no intention of being anybody's sex slave.

Mouth tightening, she used the front doors to enter the house. The entry was a large area between the dining room and living room. She could see into both rooms from there and quickly ascertained that they were as empty as they'd appeared from outside. After a hesitation, she turned into the dining room. It held a large glass-topped table and six chairs. There was a large vase in the center of the dining table with a huge, riotous bouquet of flowers. Sarita barely gave the flowers a glance as she continued on through the large arched entrance separating the dining room from the kitchen.

The kitchen seemed the most likely place to find a better weapon, so Sarita started there and was surprised to find she didn't have to search every drawer and cupboard to obtain one. There was a wooden block on the island with a set of chef's knives in it. Long sharp knives, short sharp knives, and a cleaver were on display.

Setting the lamp on the kitchen counter, Sarita moved to the wooden block and pulled out the butcher knife. After testing the feel of it in her hand, she set it on the island and pulled out two of the steak knives as well, thinking they would be good for throwing. Jerking up the ridiculous robe and nightgown, she slid the two blades under the strap of the thong. When the strap held and wasn't dragged down by the weight of the knives, she grabbed two more and added them. They did pull a bit at the strap, but it stayed up, so she let the frothy white material fall back into place and snatched up the butcher knife again.

Okay, she was armed. Now what? Find a place to hide where she could ambush her captor on his return? Or—

Phone! Sarita thought suddenly, and clucked her tongue with irritation as she recalled her earlier intention to find one. A quick glance around the kitchen didn't reveal a phone, so she moved back through the dining room to the living room, but a survey of that room proved there wasn't one there either.

Fingers crossed, she used the door from the living room to slip into the office and walked to the desk. Sarita wasn't terribly surprised not to find one there either. It had been a bit much to hope for, she supposed. Kidnapped and left alone with weapons *and* a phone? Not likely. She was lucky the knives were even available, or that she'd been left alone, Sarita thought and frowned. Really, what kind of kidnapper kidnapped you and then left you alone with weapons so readily available? You'd think he would have cleared out anything and everything she might use to defend herself. Unless whoever it was hadn't expected her to wake up so soon from whatever drug they'd given her, she thought. Or perhaps they'd been unexpectedly delayed in returning. Maybe she'd got lucky and their boat had blown up.

That would be karma, Sarita thought and was smiling at the idea when she noticed the envelope leaning up against the desk lamp. Smile fading as she saw that her name was on it, she snatched it up and started to sit in the desk chair only to be pointedly reminded of the knives she'd sheathed in the strap of the thong she wore. Literally. A quick poke from a couple of the blades was enough to make her straighten and decide to remain standing.

The envelope wasn't sealed. Setting down the butcher knife, Sarita lifted the flap and pulled out the letter inside, then unfolded and read the message on the fine vellum paper.

Dear Sarita,
Your clothing was blood encrusted. Asherah cleaned you up and put you to bed.

Sarita sagged against the desk as those first words sent memories washing over her. Dr. Dressler's lab. The poor man cut in half. Dr. Dressler and the woman arriving. Blood splashing over her as that poor immortal tried to scream and—Immortals? Bio-engineered nanos? Her head spun briefly as everything Dressler had told her washed back into her mind, and then she recalled the shot he'd given her in the neck.

"Bastard," she muttered with a disgust that was directed at herself as much as him. While it seemed obvious he was a scumbag, she should have been more alert. She should have noticed the movement when he'd reached out to inject her, and she should have batted his hand away or something.

Taking a deep breath, she counted to three and reminded herself that she wasn't Wonder Woman. No one was. She did the best she could and regret was a waste of energy that could be directed toward more useful endeavors.

"Right," she muttered. "Let's get on with it."

Raising the letter, she started again.

Dear Sarita,

Your clothes were blood encrusted and ruined. Asherah cleaned you up and put you to bed.

It occurred to me once you'd lost consciousness that I didn't explain the importance of your being a life mate. From what I can gather it appears a life mate is chosen by the nanos in their host, and are rare creatures that the immortal cannot read or control, and can live happily with throughout his or her life. They are also few and far between. Some immortals apparently wait centuries or even millennia to find theirs. While some have been fortunate enough to find one, lose them, and later, usually much later, find another, there are other immortals who never find even one life mate. So life mates are valued more than anything else in an immortal's life.

It seems immortals—like gibbons or wolves— mate for life. Not because of any moral standard, but quite simply because another mate would not satisfy their needs. What I've been told is that life mates suit each other in every way, and that life mate sex is like no other—powerful and overwhelming to the point where both parties faint or pass out at the end. I suspect that the nanos must cause this by releasing a rush of the relevant hormones.

I also understand that life mates find each other irresistible, and in fact often spend weeks or even months in bed on first meeting. I tell you this so that you know there is no reason to believe I will think less of you if you find yourself doing

*the same thing, or even let the man bed you on
your first meeting. I expect that.*

Sarita snorted at the comment. She didn't give a crap
what a whackjob like Dressler thought of her. She'd
sleep with whoever she wanted whenever she wanted.
Although, frankly, she wasn't a one-night-stand kind of
gal or one likely to "drop trou" on first meeting someone either. Sarita's father had been an old-fashioned
type of man; he'd also been overprotective and insisted
on meeting every male she'd ever dated. She knew
without a doubt that he'd given every one of them the
*"hell hath no fury like a father whose baby has been
groped by some horny teen"* speech, quickly followed
by the *"I have a big backyard to bury you in"* speech.
She was lucky she'd got laid at all.

Shaking her head, Sarita turned her attention back to
the letter, quickly finding where she'd left off.

"Yada yada first meeting," she murmured as she
found the spot.

*Now, do not be alarmed. You are in the home
my wife and I first inhabited on moving to Venezuela. We lived there for a year as we waited
for our house on the island to be built. I had it
renovated and updated some months ago in an-
ticipation of this eventuality. I hope you find it
comfortable and to your liking.*

*Everything there has been supplied for your
use.*

*The refrigerator and cupboards in the kitchen
are stocked full of food and will be refilled as*

*necessary. The wine rack in the dining room is
full of vintages I thought you might enjoy.*

Sarita's mouth tightened. It was sounding like he expected she would be there for a very long time. He had
another think coming.

*You have met your life mate, although it was
long enough ago that you may not recall. Apparently you were thirteen when you first entered his
restaurant in Caracas. He recognized that you
were his life mate, but was gentleman enough not
to claim you while so young. Instead, he decided
to let you live your life and grow up first and put a
private detective on your tail who, for the last fifteen years, has fed him monthly reports on your
life.*

"What?" Sarita gasped with dismay. Thirteen? That's
how old she was when her mother died. It was also when
she and her father had moved to Canada. She tried to
think of any restaurants they'd visited here in Venezuela before moving to Canada, but it had been fifteen
years. Besides, with the trauma of what had happened to
her mother, that year was kind of a blur in her memory
anyway.

Sighing, she glanced back to the letter, reading the
part about this life mate's *deciding* to *let* her live her
life and grow up. Big of him, she thought with disgust.
As if she didn't have a say in it? As for putting a private
detective on her tail for the last *fifteen years* . . . well,
that was just creepy. Stalkerish even. But just because

Dressler said it, didn't mean it was true. Not once in fifteen years had she noticed anyone tailing her around town or anything, and she was a cop, trained to observe things.

Sarita frowned briefly, but then continued on with the letter. "Yada yada, reports on your life . . . there it is."

His name is Domitian Argenis. He is below.

"Below what?" Sarita muttered, and then read the next line.

I left the refrigerator downstairs stocked with blood for him.
For your own safety, I suggest you wait for him to wake up, feed him at least four bags of blood, and ensure he understands that you are not responsible for his being chained to the table, and that you are a victim and as helpless as he—

"Helpless my ass," Sarita growled.

—before you unchain him.
Good luck. I expect to learn a lot from your stay at my home away from home.

Dr. Dressler

"*Before I unchain him?*" she muttered with disbelief. Some poor guy was chained in the basement? At least she assumed he was in the basement. "El Doctor" had said he was below and then mentioned a refrigerator in the basement, so she was guessing below was the basement.

"But where the hell is the basement?" Sarita muttered, scowling at the letter for not adding that bit of information. She hadn't seen stairs anywhere in her tour of the house.

Dropping the letter, Sarita started around the desk, thinking she'd have to go through the house again. But she paused as she noticed a bookshelf at an angle in the opposite corner of the room. The edge of it was out an inch or so past the shelf next to it.

Eyes narrowing, Sarita walked over to the bookshelves, grasped the side of the one sticking out and pulled.

"Eureka," she murmured as the shelf swung out like a door. "Hidden doors. Just what I should have expected from Dr. Whackjob."

Stepping into the opening left behind, Sarita eyed the set of stairs leading down into darkness and scowled. "Cozy."

A glance to the wall on either side did not reveal a light switch. Feeling along the wall on either side of the door frame itself didn't either. It seemed she was expected to creep down blindly into the dark like an idiot.

Sarita stared briefly into the black hole, wondering about the man chained up down there. She wasn't buying this life mate business Dressler had written about, but she was curious to find out what this supposed life mate looked like.

With her luck, he'd be some cross-eyed drooler with a cowlick, Sarita thought and then shrugged. Whatever. It didn't matter. She wasn't interested in being some vampire's vampiress. She *was* curious to see him, though. But there was no way in hell that she was creeping down into that darkness without some sort of light.

Spinning away from the hidden entrance, Sarita headed back to the kitchen to search for a flashlight. But, of course, there didn't appear to be one.

Slamming the last cupboard door with an irritated bang, she hesitated, and then sighed and moved to the drawer beside the sink. Opening it, she retrieved the box of matches she'd spotted there during her search. It was one of those big boxes of wooden matches with a striking strip on the side, and it was full, she noted, opening the box.

Taking them with her, Sarita walked out to the living room. She had a vague recollection of spotting candles in here on one of her trips through and—

"Aha!" she said with triumph, hurrying to the fireplace mantel where there were four large candles in holders lined up with some sort of brass decoration in the middle as the centerpiece. Snatching up one of the candles, she returned to the office.

Setting the candleholder on the desk, Sarita quickly lit it, and then tucked a couple of extra matches between her lips just in case her candle went out. She then snatched the candleholder and her butcher knife and headed for the secret door.

The stairs were tight and steep she discovered with the first step, and Sarita caught up as much of the cloth of the nightgown as she could in the hand holding the knife and raised it above her knees. She would never admit this, but she had been known to be a bit clumsy at times, and tangling her feet in the gown and taking a fall was not something she wanted to experience.

Sarita took a couple more steps, candle held out in

front of her, and squinted against the flame while trying
to see beyond it. She then slowed as a scene from an old
black-and-white movie she'd once seen came to mind.
A lone woman in a long white nightgown descending
stairs into darkness with only a candle to light her way.
Meanwhile the evil Dracula waited in the darkness
below, ready to pounce on her.

*Yeah, good one, Sarita. The perfect thing to think of
at this moment*, she reprimanded herself mentally as
she continued down. Her Dracula was supposed to be
chained up down there, but what if he'd got loose?

Sarita quickly pushed that thought away as unhelpful
and continued down. She couldn't see any more than a
couple steps ahead, and didn't need old movies to help
her imagine what lay ahead. Still, other scenes from
movies were suddenly sliding through her mind. All of
them were just different versions of that one scene in
every horror movie where the stupid chick did something incredibly idiotic that got her stabbed or horribly
beheaded.

That thought made Sarita stop abruptly on the stairs
as she realized she really was being like that idiot broad
from every horror movie. The big-haired twit with
large bouncy boobs and no brains usually in something
skimpy and—Cripes! *She* had big hair, big boobs, and
was wearing a see-through negligee! She *was* that girl!

Nah, her hair was long, not really big. It wasn't curled
to within an inch of its life and hair-sprayed to death.
And yeah, she had big boobs, but that was hardly her
fault. They were natural not bought, and truly, her
large breasts had been the bane of her existence since
they'd popped out on her chest when she was thirteen.
Their presence had not gone unnoticed by the boys in

her school and what had followed was teasing, taunting, and attempts to cop a feel by the more skeevy of
her schoolmates. They were the reason behind her first
punching a male in the face. She had punched many
more since then, both on and off the job, which was
why her partner at work called her Rock'em Sock'em
Reyes, or just RSR for short.

Sarita smiled crookedly at the thought of Jackson, her
patrol partner. He was a good guy. Newly married and
madly in love with his wife, he often treated her like a
little sister. He was the closest thing she had to family
now and just thinking of him made her straighten her
shoulders. Big-boobed twit or not, she was going down
there. Besides, unlike the idiot chicks in movies, she
was armed with more than double Ds. She had a knife
and knew how to use it. Mind you her gun would have
been more reassuring, but . . . Whatever, Sarita thought
as she stepped down onto a cold hard floor and paused.

She stood still for a moment, just listening, but there
was no slight shuffling as someone moved in the darkness, no hiss of a vampire about to launch himself
on her.

Nothing, she thought, and let go of the breath she'd
been holding to suck a draft of fresh air into her eager
lungs.

Okay, not so fresh, she corrected herself, wrinkling
her nose at the stale, damp scent that assailed her.
The basement definitely had a moldy odor to it. Sarita
shifted one bare foot along the floor and then lowered
the candle until she could see that it was indeed concrete and not simply hard packed earth.

Straightening, she glanced around, hoping her eyes
might have adjusted enough for her to make out some-

thing in the dark. They hadn't, though, so she shuffled forward several feet until the candlelight revealed a wall with a door in it. Releasing the hold she'd had on her gown, she reached for the doorknob.

The clank of metal on metal as the knife handle banged against the knob made her wince, but Sarita turned it and pushed the door open.

The candle flickered wildly in the draft created by the opening door. Terrified it would go out, Sarita instinctively drew it closer to her chest and raised her butcher-knife-holding-hand to try to shelter the flame. She didn't know if that helped, but after a moment the candlelight settled again and she let out the breath she'd been holding on a relieved sigh that blew the damned thing out.

"Crap!" Sarita muttered into the darkness, nearly spitting out the two matches she'd placed between her lips. Reaching up instinctively to remove them, she poked herself in the cheek with the butcher knife and was so startled she dropped the candle, holder and all. Sarita then immediately froze as the dark seemed to crowd in on her, sending a prickly sensation along her skin.

Trying to ignore it, Sarita took a deep breath and reasoned with herself. The candle had gone out and she'd dropped it and now it was dark. Not a big problem. She had matches. She'd light one, find the candle, and light it again. *Boom*, problem solved, she told herself.

The minute Sarita reached up with her now-empty candle hand and took one of the matches from her mouth she felt a little better. Even the match would give off light. All she had to do was strike it on something. It would light and she'd use it to find the candle. Everything would be fine, Sarita reasoned . . . except that she hadn't brought the matchbox with its striking strip on the side.

Not a problem, she told herself again, the concrete floor was rough, and she could use that. It sounded easy enough. Unfortunately, Sarita had forgotten the knives tucked into her thong. She was reminded forcefully of them when she dropped quickly into a kneeling position and the knives stabbed into her skin, her hunched position pressing her stomach against the top of them and basically forcing them into her legs.

The match in her mouth was spat out on a curse as Sarita quickly straightened again. Ignoring that for now, she felt the top of her thighs to see how much damage she'd done to herself. But it was dark, and the cloth of the nightgown and robe didn't help any.

Muttering over her stupidity, she yanked up the material of both gown and robe and felt around again. Sarita's fingers encountered what she assumed was blood on the front of her upper legs, but there didn't seem to be too-too much of it. At least it wasn't gushing or anything, so she didn't think she'd done herself too much damage. Which was a relief.

Sighing, Sarita put the hilt of the butcher knife between her teeth to hold it, caught the material of the gown and robe between her chin and chest and used both hands to retrieve the knives from her thong. She then raised her chin, letting the material drop back into place and took the butcher knife out of her mouth as she considered her options. She only had two—find the matches or at least one of them, light it, and find and light the candle, or go back upstairs and retrieve another candle and more matches.

Sarita glanced over her shoulder toward the stairs, relieved to see the light spilling down from the open door above. Actually, now that the candle was out, her eyes were adjusting and she could see a little more than she had with it. Or maybe it was because the light wasn't between herself and what she was trying to see. Whatever the case, she could see darker shapes in the gloom around her. And what looked like a long chain or string dangling from the ceiling at the foot of the stairs.

Forgetting about the matches and candle, Sarita crossed back to the stairs, caught all of her knives between one hand and her chest, then reached up to feel the item with her free fingers. It was a string with a tiny bell-shaped weight on the end. She gave it a tug and then squeezed her eyes shut when a click was accompanied by an explosion of light in the room. Easing her eyes cautiously open after a moment, she saw that the source of light was a bare bulb in a fixture on the ceiling.

Lowering her head, Sarita turned to peer around at what appeared to be a storage area. Old wicker furniture was stacked along the wall to her right, and several boxes filled the space on the left, the stairs were in front of her, and—

Sarita turned and stared at the opposite wall where more items and boxes were stacked on either side of the door she'd opened. The light didn't reach far into the next room, but she could see the corner of a metal counter just inside. She could also see her candle and its holder lying in the doorway with the matches not far away.

Sarita crossed the small space, set her knives on the counter just inside the door and knelt to gather the dropped items. She collected the matches and set them and the candle on the holder, picked it up, and started to get back to her feet, but she paused as she looked at the room before her.

Enough light was spilling through the doorway that she could make out shapes, and one in particular had caught her attention. There was a table in the center of the room . . . and there was a body on it. Sarita immediately thought of the last man she'd found on a table. Well, two tables really, at least at first.

Stomach clenching, she straightened slowly and reached blindly to the side with her free hand to feel along the wall for a light switch. Her fingers encountered a cool metal upper cupboard, and then just below that she found what she thought was a light switch. Relieved, Sarita flicked it upward, and was blinded all over again when overhead florescent lights buzzed to life at least ten times brighter than the room with one bald bulb.

Blinking rapidly, she caught snapshots of the room as she tried to force her eyes to adjust more quickly. Blink. The lab was very similar to the lab in the fenced-in area on the island. Blink. There was the metal table in the center of the room to her left. Blink. There *was* someone on the table. Blink. He was unmoving and naked and— Blink. Damn he was hot.

Three

Sarita wasn't sure just how long she stood in that doorway gaping at the man on the table. But he was worthy of the time given. Because he was definitely not a cross-eyed drooler with a cowlick.

Well, actually, his eyes were closed and he was unconscious so she couldn't be positive about the cross-eyed drooler part, but frankly, with a body like that, she could overlook a few flaws, Sarita thought and then blinked and gave herself a slap.

"Snap out of it," she muttered. "He's a vampire . . . scientific or not. And if Dressler was telling the truth, he's been having you followed around for years like some creepy perv," she added for good measure, because really, that bothered her. It wasn't that she trusted Dressler and what he said all that much, but really, why would he lie about something like that? Still . . . how could she have been tailed by a private detective for fifteen years and not have known it? Crazy. Impossible. "God, look at that chest."

Sarita rolled her eyes as that last part slipped out. She had no idea where it had come from. But seriously, he had an amazing chest. At least what she could see of it above the chains that were wrapped around both the table and his body from just below his elbow to his upper thighs. It was a lot of chain.

There was also an intravenous catheter taped to his inner elbow on this side, she noted. And strong, muscular legs were revealed below the chain skirt, tapering down to nice calves before chains began again at his ankles, covering several inches and then stopping at his feet.

Dr. Dressler had mentioned that these immortals were stronger than mortals, but this just seemed like overkill, Sarita thought and finally started forward. She stopped after only a couple of steps when she realized she was still carrying the candle. Pausing, she swung back to set it on the counter by the door, making a mental note not to forget it when they went back upstairs. They might need it again.

That thought gave her pause. When *they* went back upstairs? *They* might need it? Was she really planning to free the naked vampire on the table? Originally she'd just been curious to see him. She hadn't intended to free him necessarily. Now though . . .

Turning back to face the room, Sarita let her gaze drift over the chains binding the man. He was supposed to be stronger, faster, and whatnot. He might come in useful in helping her get out of this place. And yeah, he was a vampire, but he had also been drugged and dropped here by Dr. Dressler just as she had. They had a common enemy. What was that old saying? The enemy of mine enemy is my friend?

Damned right I'm unchaining him!

Maybe, Sarita added, moving back to the table.

She glanced over the chains, but not seeing the end of it anywhere on top, started to bend to check under the table, only to pause as she spotted a drop of blood on the floor. Straightening again, she looked more closely at the chain around his lower arm. It was just above where the spot of blood was on the floor and she, at first, thought he must be wounded under all that chain. A more thorough examination didn't reveal any evidence of blood on the table or chain, though.

Perplexed, Sarita glanced back down to the floor again to see that there were now two drops of blood, side by—

Three, she corrected as she stepped back, revealing another drop lying between where her feet had been.

She was the one bleeding, Sarita realized and quickly began to tug up the material of the negligee and robe she wore. She'd forgotten all about stabbing herself with the knives earlier. Her worries about getting the candle lit and being able to see again had pushed it from her mind. That worry was gone now, though. She had lots of light and took the opportunity to get a better look at the wounds.

A grimace claimed her lips once she got her nightgown and robe out of the way and could see the four slices along the tops of her thighs. Two of them were very shallow and already scabbed over with dry blood. Two, one on each leg, were bleeding freely. Not a lot, but enough that blood was dribbling down her legs in slow rivulets.

She'd clean them up and bandage them later, Sarita decided as she let the gown and robe drop back into place. They weren't so deep as to be a major concern, but cuts could get infected and that was more likely in the tropics than anywhere else. It wasn't just spiders and slithery creatures that thrived here. Bacteria enjoyed the wet, hot climate too.

Assuring herself that she'd tend to them the first chance she got, Sarita peered at the face of the man again and then reached out to gently pat his cheeks in the hope of waking him. There was no reaction at all, not even a stirring, so she tried again, patting his cheek more firmly. When that had no effect either, she flat out slapped him. Nothing.

Leaning over him, Sarita pressed a thumb against his eyelid and pulled it open. The man's eye was the most beautiful blue she'd seen in her life. Seriously, it was gorgeous, as blue as the sky on a sunny day, but with streaks of silver shot through that almost seemed to shimmer. She was so taken with the color that it took a moment for her to remember why she'd opened his eye in the first place, but then Sarita forced her attention to the pupil and nodded solemnly.

"Drugged," she muttered, releasing his eyelid and turning to look at the intravenous bag. His being immortal and all, she'd assumed it was an empty bag of blood. Now she saw that there was an inch of clear liquid still in the bag. Well, mostly clear, she noted, narrowing her eyes at the milky quality of the liquid inside.

Not just saline then, Sarita thought.

Turning her attention to the catheter in his arm, she ripped the tape away and slid the apparatus out. She let it drop to swing free next to the table, and then gave the insertion point a quick look to be sure all was well. A bead of blood had bubbled to the surface, but when she brushed it away Sarita couldn't even see a pinpoint to show her where the needle had gone in. He healed that quickly.

Shrugging, she released his arm and peered at his face again, wondering how long it would take for the drugs to wear off. Probably a while, she decided and debated what to do next.

Sarita glanced around the room, spotted the refrigerator along the wall to her right, and walked over to open it. Blood. Lots of it. Not as much as had been in the refrigerator she'd seen in Dr. Dressler's torture chamber, but a good thirty or forty bags.

Another sign that Dressler expected them to be here a while, Sarita thought and felt her mouth flatten. That was not going to happen. She was getting out of there as quickly as she could. She had things to do. She had to find her grandmother, and that could be a problem in itself. She hadn't seen her in Dressler's house or in the labs, but that didn't mean she wasn't there. Certainly, Sarita no longer trusted that the man had told her the truth when he'd called with the news that her grandmother had been injured in a fall. Wherever she was, Sarita had to find her and get her away from the crazy old geezer the woman had worked for since before Sarita was born. And then she fully intended to report the bastard to the Venezuelan police and see that charges were laid against him before she went home to her little apartment and her job. She'd have to take her grandmother with her, Sarita thought now. The woman would have nowhere to go here.

Her mind immediately crowded with worries about

how she could do that. Would she need a visitor's visa? How did you go about getting one? Did her grandmother even have a passport?

Shoving those concerns away for now, Sarita pushed the refrigerator door closed and turned to lean against it as she considered how to get away from this place. Dr. Dressler had said in the letter that this was where he and his wife had lived as they'd waited for the house on the island to be built. She supposed that meant this house was on the mainland. That was something at least. There was a dock and no road so they were obviously on the coast and a good distance from the nearest village or town.

They'd have to walk out, Sarita supposed. Try to find help. Hopefully they wouldn't have to travel too far to find it. But there were plenty of provisions here that they could take with them just in case it took them a while to find civilization.

Sarita didn't like the idea of having to walk out of there dressed as she was, though, or in any of the ridiculous concoctions in the closet upstairs. Which was probably why that was all there was available to her. Dr. Dressler had probably hoped that would keep her here.

"Not gonna happen," Sarita muttered and pushed away from the refrigerator to walk out into the next room. She'd quickly check the boxes while she was waiting for sleeping Dracula there to wake up. Maybe she'd find something useful, like old clothes. They'd probably stink of mold or mothballs, but she could deal with that, and at least she'd have some protection against being eaten alive by bugs.

Stopping by the boxes along the one wall, Sarita

began opening them. The first appeared to be stuffed with plain brown paper, but when she grabbed a handful and pulled it out, it unraveled and something tumbled to the ground and shattered.

Frowning, Sarita stepped back and peered at the broken china on the floor. A teacup, she realized, spotting a delicate handle still attached to a broken bit of china. The box was full of china, she realized after feeling the paper-wrapped items still inside. Setting that box aside, she moved on to the next, but it too held china, as did the third. The fourth box had a bunch of old board games in it. The next two boxes had books. Most were paperbacks, old romances and pulp fiction, nothing that would be helpful to clothe herself or the man in the next room.

Sarita barely had the thought when a jangling noise drew her head sharply around. Recognizing it as the sound of chains clanging against each other, she forgot about the boxes and turned to rush for the door. Unfortunately, while she'd been conscious of the broken teacup on the floor and been careful to avoid the shards of porcelain while she'd searched the boxes, she didn't think of them as she turned to sprint for the door. At least, not until a sharp pain had her gasping and reaching for the nearest box for balance as she jerked her foot up off the floor. The box didn't offer much stability. The minute her fingers brushed it, the damned thing and the two boxes it rested on toppled away, crashing to the floor.

Holding her sore foot off the floor, Sarita stared at the sea of broken glass now covering the ground between her and the door and couldn't hold back the explosive string of curses that slipped from her lips.

Domitian had just woken up and realized he was chained to a table when someone began calling their duck. At least he thought they were calling a duck. His thinking was a little slow and fuzzy, his vision blurry, and his hearing might be off too, but he was sure what he heard was "Duck! Duckity duck duck duck! Duck!"

Although why anyone would name their duck Duck was beyond him, and really, no animal would answer to the fury in that voice, he thought. And then another "Duck" rent the air, only this time he realized it wasn't *duck* he was hearing at all, but *fu*—

"You're awake!"

Domitian turned his head and stared blankly at the vision standing in the doorway. And she *was* a vision. Long dark hair tumbled over the woman's shoulders, flowing out behind her, and beautiful dark eyes peered at him over her presently puckered lips as she peered at him with displeasure. He wondered over her expression briefly, but then she began to hop forward, the movement causing the long, sheer flowing gown she wore to play peek-a-boo with the tiny white panties and beautiful olive skin it was doing a poor job of hiding.

Damn, the woman was a gorgeous little bundle. Short, curvy with large breasts and in the most sinful nightgown it had been his pleasure to see, Domitian decided, letting his gaze slide over the see-through white gown with red ribbons. It was almost enough to make him forget he already had a life mate, he thought as he watched her breasts bounce with every hop.

Hop? he thought suddenly. Yes, she was hopping, Domitian reassured himself as she continued forward. It was not a result of whatever had left him so fuzzy-headed where he lay. The woman was hopping on one foot and leaving a trail of blood on the concrete floor as she made her way to him.

"I didn't expect you to wake up so soon," she said as she reached the side of the table and grasped it to balance herself. Her eyes slid over his face. "I only took out the IV maybe ten minutes ago. I figured you might be under for another hour or better."

"IV?" Domitian queried, his voice surprisingly gruff. His throat was dry and scratchy. His head hurt too. He was obviously dehydrated and in need of fluids, he thought as he tried to ignore the scent of blood coming from the woman, but it was hard to ignore and made his stomach rumble.

"Yeah." She reached to the side and dragged an IV stand with an almost empty bag hanging from it closer so that he could see it. "Dr. Dressler left you all trussed up here on a saline drip with a little something extra added to keep you in la-la land. I took it out when I got down here."

Releasing the IV, she turned and hopped away.

Domitian immediately turned and tilted his head, trying to see where she was going. She hopped to a refrigerator behind him. He saw her open the door, but couldn't see why until she let the door slide closed and turned to hop back, now with half a dozen bags of blood in her arms. His eyes widened incredulously.

"What is that for?" he asked warily.

"For you," she said, her tone all business. Reaching the table, she dropped the bags on the metal surface next to him. "You're an immortal."

It wasn't a question. She sounded pretty sure and Domitian's eyebrows rose. He wasn't used to mortals knowing about his kind, but she was somehow connected to Dr. Dressler, who knew. Which was a damned shame, he decided, his gaze locking on her breasts as he saw that her activity had made the cloth of her gown gather between them, leaving the lovely full globes as good as bare with just a veil of sheer cloth over them.

Domitian had a terrible urge to reach out and touch them, but the chains restrained him . . . which was a good thing, he told himself with a frown. He had a life mate, or would once he claimed his Sarita. He had no business noticing other women's breasts.

"You work with Dressler?" he asked and scowled at both the possibility and the fact that the words didn't come out as strong as he would have liked. Damn, his throat was dry and sore. He needed blood.

"The hell I do," the woman growled, sounding insulted at the suggestion as she turned and hopped away toward the door.

She picked up something and turned, but it wasn't until she was halfway back that he saw that what she'd gone to fetch was a long butcher knife. And she was hopping around with it, apparently oblivious to the fact that she could skewer herself with it if she fell. Not a rocket scientist then, he thought dryly.

"Dressler's a whacked-out sadist," she huffed out as she reached the table again and picked up one of the bags. "He drugged and dropped me here too."

Domitian frowned. "Why would he—?" The words stopped on a gurgle as she suddenly held the bag over his mouth and punctured it with the knife, sending a torrent of the thick liquid splashing into his open mouth and onto his face.

Swallowing the mouthful he'd first got, he turned his head to the side to avoid the flow and snapped, "What the hell are you doing?" as the liquid now continued to pour out over the side of his head.

"Trying to feed you," she said with exasperation. Catching him firmly by the chin, she tried to force his head back to its original position. "Open your mouth."

Domitian resisted at first, but then conscious of the wasted blood, let his head roll back and opened his mouth for the blood to flow in. The liquid was running too swiftly though. He tried to keep up with it, but ended up choking and coughing, sending a good portion of the liquid shooting out over the woman's face and chest.

"You guys are messy eaters," she muttered with disgust, tossing the bag aside the moment it was empty and reaching for another.

Domitian ground his teeth and growled, "This is not how we feed."

"Oh?" She stopped with the bag and knife over his mouth and raised an eyebrow. "How do you feed, then?"

"Unchain me and I will feed myself," he said at once.

That brought a snort from her luscious lips. "Yeah, right, buddy. *If* I unchain you, it isn't gonna happen until you've had at least four bags of this stuff. I have no intention of being your breakfast."

Domitian scowled. "We do not feed on—"

"Yeah, yeah," she interrupted. "You have rules against feeding off mortals and yada yada. Well, forgive me, but I'm a cop and know a lot of rule breakers. I have no intention of taking chances here. So tell me how to feed you properly or I'm gonna slice this bag like I did the last one and feed you that way."

They glared at each other briefly and then Domitian sighed. "I let my teeth out and you pop the bag to them," he said grimly, and then reluctantly cautioned, "But not too hard or the bag will rupture and splash everywhere. And not too lightly or my teeth won't puncture it."

"Right. Not too hard, and not too light," she said with a roll of the eyes. And then she lowered the knife and said, "Okay, so get your fangs out. We don't have all day here."

Domitian spared a moment to glare at her. He had no idea who she was, but she was definitely a bossy bit of goods . . . and ridiculously sexy in that damned nightgown. Cursing under his breath, he opened his mouth. His fangs had been trying to slide out since she'd entered the room, bringing the scent of blood with her, but he'd forced them to stay where they were. Now he let them slide forward. The woman watched with fascination, and then slapped the bag to his mouth.

They both released a relieved little sigh when it landed properly, sliding onto his fangs without bursting. Domitian relaxed then, his gaze sliding over her as he waited for his fangs to drain the bag. There were splashes of blood on her cheek and neck now, but it pretty much coated her pretty breasts both above the gown's neckline as well as through the frail cloth itself. He found himself wishing he could lick it away for her. The thought was a rather shocking one for a man who hadn't thought about sex in centuries, at least not in regards to anyone but the life mate out there waiting for him to claim her.

Shocking enough in fact to clear Domitian's thinking a bit and make him realize that he should have taken control of the woman and made her unchain him the moment she'd entered the room. That had his gaze rising to her forehead so that he could focus on her thoughts and take control.

Only he couldn't.

Coming up against a blank wall in her mind, Domitian regathered himself and tried again, but it was no good. He couldn't read this woman.

For a moment Domitian was too shocked to think anything, but then his brain began to screech.

Dear God! She was another life mate! After all these millennia alone, he now had two women to choose from; his sweet little Sarita and this . . . creature.

Domitian's gaze skated to her breasts again as a surfeit of possibilities began to fill his mind. The most interesting one was the thought of two life mates in his bed. He had some trouble picturing his sweet Sarita naked and in his bed at that moment, but he could see this one there, her hair a wild mass on the pillow, her eyes sleepy with desire, her mouth open on a moan rather than pursed with irritation or displeasure and her breasts glistening with blood as they were now.

If the bag hadn't been in the way, Domitian would have licked his lips as he gazed at them. They were lovely. Large and full like ripe melons waiting to be plucked from the vine. And her nipples, he breathed out slowly through his nose as he focused on her nipples, noticing that they were growing hard before his eyes.

Curious, he glanced back to her face and saw that while he'd been ogling her, her own eyes had been busy traveling down his body. They were now focused on the chains across his groin.

"Are you wearing anything under that chain skirt of yours?" she asked suddenly, her voice slightly husky.

Apparently not pleased by that, she scowled and lifted her gaze back to his face. "Are you?"

Domitian merely peered at her over the bag in his mouth. It was hard to speak with a mouthful of bag.

Seeming to realize that, she said, "Blink once for yes and twice for no."

Unsure of the answer, he stared back unblinking.

"I'll take that as an I don't know," she announced dryly and ripped the now-empty bag away.

"What's your name?" Domitian managed to get out just before she slapped another full one to his teeth.

She arched her eyebrows at him. "You should know. You're the one who's had a private detective following me around for *fifteen years*."

Domitian stilled at this irritated announcement, his eyes examining her face. Sarita? No it couldn't be, he thought. But now that he was looking at her face and not her breasts, or the rest of her body in that seductive nightgown she was wearing, there was something . . .

As she'd said, the private detective he'd hired had been sending him monthly reports for fifteen years. The reports had told him what she was doing and with whom. He'd read about her doing well in school, her taking martial arts, her part-time jobs as a teenager, and the large group of friends she'd had. He'd been proud as could be when she finished high school and went on to university to get a bachelor's degree in criminology. He'd always planned to wait until she'd grown up and worked at her chosen career for two years before going to claim her. So, when she'd graduated, he'd started to plan his trip to Canada, where he'd intended to arrange to "bump into her" and then woo her as she deserved. But then Sarita had applied to and been accepted into the police college. At the time he'd been disappointed at the delay in his being able to claim her. But he'd stuck to his guns and waited.

She was well worth the wait, Domitian decided as his gaze slid over her again.

While the reports he'd received had been pretty thorough, even at first mentioning the boys she had dated, the one thing they had not included was pictures of Sarita. That had been by Domitian's choice. He had wanted her to experience a little life before he claimed her, and it had been easier for him to resist doing that so long as he thought of her as the child she'd been when he'd first seen her in his restaurant. Domitian had feared he might not be able to resist going to her sooner if he got pictures of her at eighteen, nineteen, or twenty. So in his mind she'd remained the skinny, flat-chested child he'd first met, and while he'd often imagined what she might look like now, none of his imaginings had equaled the seductive and lush woman bending over him, feeding him blood. Damn, she'd grown up fine.

So, not two life mates, Domitian realized, and wasn't at all disappointed. Fantasies aside, it would be difficult to please two immortal life mates in bed when you passed out after pleasuring the first. Besides, he could only turn one and would have had to choose between them if there were two.

Now he didn't have to, Domitian thought, his eyes drifting back to her breasts. God he couldn't wait to get his hands on them. He would feast on them, lick the blood away, and suck those perfect little pebbles between his lips, lash them with his tongue, and nip at the buds as he thrust into her and—

The clank of chains drew his attention from her

breasts and Domitian peered down to see that he'd definitely been affected by his thoughts. He'd managed to work himself up to the point that he now had an erection pressing against the chains across his groin. He hadn't thought there was a lot of give in the chains, but judging by the bulge now noticeable between his legs he supposed there must be.

Apparently he wasn't the only one to notice his present state. Sarita said dryly, "If you have enough blood to spare it for erections, you've definitely had enough."

Domitian shifted his gaze back to her, his eyes getting caught on her jiggling breasts as she tossed the empty bag aside.

Sarita turned back, scowling when she saw where he was looking and snapped, "Hey! Eyes up here, buddy!"

He jerked his eyes up to meet hers, and she scowled and shook her head. "Look, we have to get something straight here. Dressler said we're life mates or some such thing and mentioned a bunch of twaddle about great sex and yada yada, but I'm not interested. Got it? There will be no kissy kissy, gropey gropey . . . or sex. *Entender? No sexo!*"

Domitian bit his lip to hold back the laugh that wanted to escape him. He suspected she wouldn't see what was so amusing here, but really, he'd imagined their first meeting repeatedly over the last fifteen years. But not once in any of them had she been a feisty little bit of goods in a sexy-as-hell see-through gown telling him *"no sexo!"*

"Got it?" she repeated.

Domitian nodded mildly, allowing a smile to curve his lips. "As you wish."

Sarita's eyes narrowed, his words hitting on some

memory in the back of her head. When she couldn't access it, she just let it go and straightened to prop her hand on her hips as she looked him over. Reluctant concern entering her expression, she asked, "How are you feeling?"

Domitian couldn't hide his surprise at the seeming change in attitude.

"I mean are you full or what?" she explained, and then apparently not wanting him to think she was actually concerned about his health, added, "Full enough not to bite me if I unchain you?"

"I will not bite you," Domitian assured her solemnly, and then just because he felt quite sure it would annoy her, he added, "until you ask me."

"Yeah, well that'll be when hell freezes over then," Sarita muttered and suddenly ducked out of sight.

Startled, Domitian lifted his head and strained against the chains to glance over the side of the table, relaxing when he saw that she'd merely dropped to sit cross-legged on the floor so that she could examine the chains under the table. But he frowned when he noticed the smears of blood on the floor where she'd been standing. And those red ribbons he'd thought were part of the gown? They were crimson rivulets of blood trailing from her upper thighs down, he saw.

Domitian had just opened his mouth to ask if she was all right when she announced, "There's a padlock holding the chains together."

"Are you—?"

"It's okay. It's a number lock padlock," she growled.

Forgetting his question, Domitian let himself lie flat again and asked, "Why is that okay?"

"It's one of those padlocks with four number wheels

on it. You have to enter the right numbers to open it," she explained and he heard her moving around and the jangle of chain.

"And that's good because?" His tone was dry this time. It didn't sound all that good to him. If the padlock was on the top of the chains around his waist, he could have just broken it and got himself free. But not being able to reach it made that a problem and he knew without a doubt she wouldn't have the strength to simply break it herself.

"It's good because I had a boyfriend in high school who showed me how to crack these suckers," she informed him. "I think he was trying to impress me," Sarita continued dryly. "But really, all it did was convince me that he'd be one of the guys I'd have to arrest one day when I became a cop, and that I should never use these kind of padlocks again. At the time, I had one for my bike," she explained absently, and then added irritably, "You'd think Dressler would have left the combination in his letter."

"Hmm," Domitian murmured, but he was wondering if the boyfriend in question was one he'd received reports on. After her first couple of boyfriends in high school, he'd told the private detective not to bother reporting on them in future. While he'd wanted her to grow up and have all the usual experiences a young woman had, Domitian had found he had a terrible jealous streak. Every mention of a spotty teenage mortal taking her to a dance or film had made him want to get on a plane and go claim her. Fortunately, he'd restrained himself.

"So," he said when the silence drew out with just the

clanging of chains, "you wanted to be a police officer even in high school?"

"Since I was thirteen," she answered, her voice growing husky and sad.

Domitian merely grunted. Thirteen was when her mother had died. He didn't doubt for a minute that was the reason she'd decided to become a police officer. It was a subject that obviously still hurt her, though, and he found he didn't like her sad. He preferred his "feisty Sarita," so, knowing it would annoy her, he suggested, "Perhaps you should look around and see if he left a combination somewhere here in this room."

"I don't need a combination," she ground out with obvious irritation. "All you have to do is pull firmly on the shackle and spin each of the wheels from the farthest one out, to the one nearest the shackle. As each wheel hits the right number, it locks in place and the shackle slides out a bit and you move on to the next. It's easy and—" she gave a hoot of success and then finished "—done!"

Her fist flew up with the removed lock in it and then Sarita popped back into view. Her air was triumphant, but he didn't miss the wince that crossed her face as she straightened next to him. A determined expression took over almost before he'd registered the pain, and she quickly began to unravel the chain from around him and the table.

"I'm not sure where we are," Sarita said as she worked, drawing the end of the chain across his body, letting it drop under the table and then reaching across him to grab the now-longer length of chain and pull it across him again. "Dressler said it was his first home here in Venezuela. Where he and his wife lived while they waited for their island house to be built. We're on the coast, but I'm not sure where, and there's no road access, just a dock and no boat. We're going to have to walk out of here to find help."

"You're bleeding," Domitian said the minute she stopped speaking. "He hurt you?"

"What?" She paused in removing the chain to look down at herself. Her gaze stopped on her bloody chest and she shook her head. "You're the one who got me all bloody. While I was feeding you. Remember?" she said, trying to prod his memory.

"Not your beautiful breasts," he said solemnly, and was surprised to see her flush and appear a little flustered. Apparently, she was not used to compliments like that. A situation Domitian intended to change. "I was referring to your shapely legs and feet."

When she peered down at herself again, he craned his head to get another look at her blood-streaked lower body and feet.

Sarita scowled at her injuries and shook her head again as she returned to unraveling the chain. "That wasn't Dressler."

"Then what happened?" Domitian asked at once.

"I stepped on broken glass," Sarita said with a shrug as she drew the chain across his body again and let it drop.

That explained the bloody footprints and her hopping, he acknowledged. But—"What about the blood on your legs?"

Sarita was silent so long he didn't think she was going to answer, but finally she grimaced and admitted, "I stabbed myself with steak knives."

"What?" he asked with disbelief. "Why?"

"Well, I didn't do it on purpose," she said with irritation. "It was an accident."

"How the hell do you accidentally stab yourself with a steak knife?" Domitian asked with disbelief.

"Four steak knives actually. Well, a paring knife and three steak knives," Sarita corrected and then explained, "I had them tucked into my thong, forgot about them, bent to pick up something, and—" She ended with a shrug, and then suddenly stopped working to glance toward the door. In the next moment she'd grabbed the knife she'd set on the table and started to hop away toward the door.

"What are you doing?" Domitian asked with concern. "Stop that, you will hurt yourself. Finish unchaining me and I will see to your wounds."

"You aren't seeing to anything," she assured him sharply. "And I'm just getting my knives in case you go getting ideas once you're unchained."

"Do not be ridiculous," he growled, and then watched with dismay as Sarita reached the counter by the door and began to gather several knives off the metal surface. No doubt the paring knife and three steak knives she'd mentioned. Much to his dismay, she clutched them by the handles, pressed close to her chest along with the butcher knife, and began to hop back to the table.

"Stop!" Domitian bellowed with horror, visions of her falling and stabbing herself dancing in his head.

"Stop yourself," Sarita barked continuing forward.

It was all too much for Domitian. Positive she was about to tumble to the floor and impale herself on all five of the damned knives, he sat up abruptly, snapping the remaining chain surrounding him. Some part of his mind noted that he hadn't been left completely naked, he still had his boxers on. But most of his concentration as he lunged off the table was on getting to his life mate before the foolish woman killed herself with those damned knives.

Sarita released a startled curse when he swept her off her feet and pressed her to his hard chest. But she didn't protest, merely clutched her knives against her bosom, and scowled up at him as he carried her out of the room.

Four

Domitian carried Sarita upstairs before slowing and then it was only to look around the office they were now in. The moment he spotted the open door into what appeared to be a living room, he headed that way, only to stop once through it.

"A bathroom?" he asked.

Instead of answering, Sarita glowered at him and demanded, "Put me down."

Snorting at the suggestion, Domitian glanced around again. This time he spotted a door farther along the wall and instinctively headed that way. He didn't bother to ask Sarita to turn the doorknob for him when he reached it. Half-suspecting she'd refuse anyway, he released the hold he had on her legs and reached out to open it himself, leaving her weight to balance on his arm without his hand to hold her in place. It only took a second and then he was carrying her into the room.

As his gaze slid over the sitting area, table for two, and bed, Domitian at first thought he'd made the wrong choice. His footsteps slowed, but then he spotted the long counter with double sinks through the door to the right of the bed. He continued forward more quickly now, carrying her into an opulent white bathroom and right up to the sink counter where he set her down between the two sinks.

Sarita hadn't said a word since demanding to be put down. She'd merely glowered at him, her hands tight around her knives, her expression suggesting she'd like to plunge the lot of them into his face.

Half-afraid she'd do just that, he tried for a soothing tone. "I will not harm you."

A snort slid from her lips and her fingers tightened around the knives. "Damned right you won't."

"I am just going to remove the glass from your foot and tend to your injuries," Domitian continued, ignoring her rude response. Raising his eyebrows, he asked, "Okay?"

"I can do it myself," she snapped.

"It will be easier if I do it," Domitian argued and dropped to kneel in front of her. He took her foot in hand to examine it.

"It's the other one," Sarita said at once, her tone dry and sharp.

"Of course," he muttered and quickly switched feet. Raising it so he could better see the bottom, Domitian tried to concentrate on the job at hand and ignore the sweet smell of her blood. It was hard, though, when all he wanted to do was lick if off her, and that desire had nothing to do with hunger, at least not the hunger for blood. He'd had enough blood to fight whatever had been used up trying to combat the drugs he'd been given. His hunger now was purely for the woman before him. She was independent and feisty and sexy as hell sitting there in that damned gown.

His eyes wandered from Sarita's bloody foot to the trails of blood on her legs and followed one up under the gossamer cloth of her nightgown. It led all the way up her calf to her thigh, and up it to the sliced skin just below the strap of the thong she wore.

She may as well be wearing only the thong for all the protection the gown offered, he thought with disgruntlement. But he found himself licking his lips as his gaze slid between the blood trails and that pure white triangle of cloth, the only thing preventing him from having a perfect view of her—

"There are tweezers in the makeup table."

Domitian's eyes immediately shot to her face and he could tell she'd noticed where he'd been looking.

"I will tend to the cuts after I see to the foot," he announced as if that's what had held his attention. He suspected she wouldn't fall for the ruse, though. His voice had been raspy with a desire he couldn't hide.

Domitian set her foot down and stood to move to the makeup table she'd mentioned. A quick search produced tweezers still in their packaging, which he broke open as he moved back to Sarita.

"I will try not to hurt you," Domitian promised as he knelt in front of her and reclaimed her foot.

Sarita merely nodded, but he couldn't help noticing the way her hands tightened around those knives of hers again. It made him release her foot and straighten.

"What are you doing now?" she asked suspiciously.

"I would rather not be stabbed should I inadvertently

hurt you while removing the glass," Domitian said simply and then waited.

When Sarita stared at him suspiciously, not setting down the knives, he found a little exasperation of his own.

"They are really quite useless to you as a weapon anyway. It would not kill me if you stabbed me."

"Maybe, but I bet it still hurts," she said grimly.

"Yes. Which is why I would rather avoid it," Domitian said pointedly, and then added stiffly, "You are my life mate, Sarita. Dr. Dressler may not have told you this, but an immortal would never willingly harm a life mate. However, unless you want to continue to hop around like a crazed bunny, I need to get that glass out of your foot, and may unintentionally hurt you doing so. I do not wish to be stabbed for my efforts. Please put the knives down."

Sarita scowled, glanced down at the weapons she held, and then sighed and set them on the counter next to her with obvious reluctance.

"Thank you," he said softly, and set down the tweezers to pick up the knives and quickly move them to the other side of the sink and out of her reach. When he then went to grab the tweezers again, they were gone.

Sarita had them, Domitian saw. She had also raised her injured foot to rest on her other knee so that she could see the bottom of it. Smiling at him widely, she shrugged. "No need to thank me. I couldn't hold them and take the glass out at the same time anyway."

Domitian opened his mouth, but then simply closed it again and leaned against the counter next to her. Waiting. There were three pieces of white porcelain in her foot, one large piece and two smaller. She could manage the large piece, but he knew the smaller ones were going to be difficult and painful to remove, which was why he'd suggested removing her knives.

Ignoring him, Sarita plucked out the larger of the three pieces first as he'd expected. She then turned her attention to the small pieces just visible under the skin and Domitian winced as she began to poke around the no-doubt tender flesh, trying to force the glass to the surface.

"Let me help," Domitian said, straightening when she sucked in a hissing breath of pain.

"I don't need help," Sarita said stubbornly and continued to poke and dig, causing herself unnecessary pain.

Losing patience with her, Domitian snatched the tweezers from her hand and knelt in front of her again. "Give me your foot."

"No," she growled. "Give me back the tweezers."

"No," he responded at once, and then took a breath before saying in a more reasonable tone, "I have better eyesight. I can remove it quickly. Let me help you."

For a moment he thought she'd refuse, but then Sarita released a pent-up sigh, and snapped, "Fine," as if she were doing him a favor and stuck out her foot. She then crossed her arms and glared at him.

Domitian found a smile creeping across his face at her attitude and quickly ducked his head to examine her foot so she wouldn't see it.

Apparently he hadn't been quick enough, however, because she growled, "Go ahead and snicker, fang boy, but you walked right through a floor full of that broken china on your way up here and I get to dig at your feet next."

"Why do I get the feeling you would enjoy causing me pain?" Domitian asked wryly, leaning in to remove the first small piece of glass from her foot. She hadn't responded by the time he removed the glass, so after tapping the tweezers on the edge of the sink to remove the fragment, he asked mildly, "What have I done to make you so angry?"

A glance up showed her looking dissatisfied and as mulish as a twelve-year-old boy. When he simply held on to her foot firmly, and waited for her answer, Sarita finally shrugged unhappily. "I don't like the idea that someone has been following me around for fifteen years."

"Ah." Domitian turned his attention back to her foot. "I apologize for that. But I did not wish to disrupt your life by insinuating myself into it while you were so young. I wanted you to have a normal childhood and experience everything other girls do—school, friends, even boyfriends," he added, his mouth tightening around the word. "However, I didn't wish to lose track of you either. I wanted to be able to approach you once you were old enough and woo you in the normal fashion. But I needed to know where you were when the time came, so I hired a private detective."

"That's all?" she asked suspiciously.

Domitian shrugged as he worked on the last sliver. "Pretty much. I got monthly reports letting me know that you were alive and well. Sometimes they included little details like the school you attended, or that you had friends and were attending parties and dances or whatnot. But I told him not to give me names or to be too intrusive in gaining his information."

"Why?" Sarita asked, sounding a little more curious and less angry.

"Because I did not wish to know who you were dating," he admitted gruffly.

"Why?" she repeated with real interest now.

Domitian raised his head and peered at her briefly, but then admitted, "Because you have been mine since the moment you entered my restaurant with your father at thirteen and I realized I could not read you," he admitted solemnly.

Sarita's eyes widened slightly at this announcement and the possessive way he said it and she was suddenly aware of both his hands curved around her heel, and his breath blowing softly over her foot. Swallowing, she closed her eyes and struggled not to curl her toes as Domitian returned to his efforts, adding, "I did not want to know another male might be kissing you."

Sarita bit her lower lip and dug her fingernails into her hands as she not only felt his words breathed across her toes, but suddenly had an image in her mind of this man kissing her, his arms tight around her, his fingers pulling her head back, his hips grinding against her as his tongue swept through her mouth. Frightened by the wave of need that rolled over her, Sarita forced her eyes open, banishing the image.

"Or caressing your luscious breasts," Domitian continued. His fingers shifted, brushing over the sensitive skin of her instep, but it was Sarita's breasts that tingled in response. Her nipples even hardened as if he was doing what he was speaking about and she closed her eyes briefly again, only to be assailed by a sudden vision of Domitian peeling her nightgown down away from her breasts and covering them with his hands.

"Or stripping your clothes away and exploring your hidden depths with his lips and tongue and body."

Sarita shook her head and forced her eyes open to see that his gaze was sliding along her leg, following an invisible path to her core. It was just a look, but she could almost feel his touch there, and she foolishly closed her eyes again as a shudder ran through her. This time the vision that filled her mind was of his kneeling between her legs, tugging her forward until she perched on the edge of the counter and then kissing a trail up one thigh to the strip of white cloth between her legs.

"Oh God," Sarita gasped, startling herself. She blinked her eyes open with confusion just in time to see Domitian getting to his feet and setting the tweezers on the counter.

"All done," he said lightly, turning back to her. "That was not so bad, was it?"

Sarita stared at him blankly, her body throbbing with need, and then raised a hand to her forehead and shook her head. "I don't—"

She closed her eyes again and sucked in a breath as the imaginary Domitian was immediately there, tugging the silky cloth of the thong aside and burying his head between her thighs so that his tongue could rasp across her sensitive flesh.

"Sarita? Are you all right?"

She opened her eyes to find that Domitian had bent toward her as he asked the question. His face was directly in front of hers, his lips just inches away, his breath sliding over her lips and setting them tingling too.

Growling, Sarita caught him around the neck and tried to pull him closer, wanting—no, needing—to kiss him. But Domitian resisted and reminded her, "You said n—"

"Shut up and kiss me," Sarita snapped, and much to

her relief he did. His mouth immediately shot down to cover hers, his tongue sweeping out to slide between her lips just as it had in her mind moments earlier.

His kiss was hot and deep and so sweet that she almost didn't notice his hands sliding under her bottom and lifting her as he straightened. She did wrap her legs around his hips, though, when his hands shifted to her upper legs and he urged them up and apart. Sarita groaned into his mouth as their groins rubbed against each other, the action sending a wave of liquid fire rolling through her body.

Trembling in its wake, Sarita kissed him desperately and shifted her hips to bring about the sensation again. She felt Domitian's hand tugging at the neckline of her robe and gown and briefly broke their kiss to lean back enough to allow him access. She then watched as he quickly tugged the material of both items down, freeing her breasts. Her nipples were hard and excited, eager to be touched, and Sarita breathed "yes" on a groan when his hand covered one. But she then tightened her arms around his neck and pressed forward, trapping his hand there as she covered his mouth again, silently demanding another kiss.

Domitian answered the call, whipping her into a frenzy with his tongue even as he squeezed her behind and the breast he held. When he then caught her nipple between thumb and finger and rolled and pinched it gently, she cried out into his mouth and broke their kiss to throw her head back as she arched into the caress. She also tightened her legs around his hips and shifted, grinding against the hardness that had grown between them.

Domitian's response was a string of curses through

clenched teeth, and then she felt the edge of the cold counter under her bottom.

Blinking in surprise, Sarita stared at him with confusion, and then uttered a startled gasp as he dropped to his knees before her and simply tore off the hated white thong she wore. When he then buried his face between her thighs, Sarita cried out, her feet slapping against the front of the cupboards and her arms moving back so that she could brace herself on the countertop as she arched, her butt partially lifting off the counter as he set to work.

Domitian didn't just rasp his tongue across her flesh as he had in her imaginings, he devoured her. Holding her legs firmly apart, he used teeth and tongue and lips as he explored every inch of her most sensitive flesh.

Within seconds Sarita was lost. Legs thrashing where he held them pinned open, bottom bouncing, she clawed at his head and shoulders and moaned over and over. And every time she moaned, Domitian groaned in response, his mouth vibrating against her skin and increasing her pleasure twofold and then twofold again.

Just when Sarita was sure she couldn't stand a moment more, Domitian broke off what he was doing, and stood up between her legs. He jerked his boxers down, freeing a truly impressive erection, and then clasped her by the hips and thrust into her.

Sarita wasn't sure what she'd expected, but it wasn't to explode into orgasm with just that first thrust. But she did. She dug her nails into his shoulders and threw her head back on a long scream as wave after wave of pleasure exploded over and around her, drenching her in it, drowning her, until it finally pulled her down with it into the soothing darkness that waited beyond consciousness.

Domitian woke on the bathroom floor with Sarita draped across his chest. He didn't remember passing out and falling back, taking her with him, but he must have. He reached up to feel his head. There was no cut or bump, but there was dried blood. He'd obviously taken a good head banging as he hit the floor. It made him glad he hadn't been awake for it.

Domitian peered down at the top of Sarita's head, glad she had landed on top of him. He never would have forgiven himself if she'd got hurt. Life mate sex could be damned dangerous for a mortal, at least when it ended, and was therefore best performed only on soft surfaces. He knew that, but had got carried away in the moment.

Next time he'd take more care, Domitian vowed silently, and ran a hand gently over Sarita's hair. She'd been even more passionate and responsive than he'd expected when he'd sent those images out to her of what he wanted to do to her. Domitian had merely hoped they would excite her and soften her attitude toward him, so he'd been more than surprised by her reaction. Pleasantly surprised, but surprised. The woman was a powder keg of passion.

And she was his, Domitian thought with satisfaction. Finally, his patience had been rewarded and he was here with his life mate in his arms and all was right with the world.

Well, not all, he thought suddenly as he looked around the room.

Domitian hadn't been thinking very clearly since waking up chained to the table in the basement. He'd like to blame it on whatever drug had been used to keep him asleep, but he knew that wasn't the case. He'd been suffering a bad case of life mate–head; the inability to think past his desire to possess the woman presently lying unconscious on his chest. It had passed for now, but he knew it would be back, and probably at the most inopportune time. Which meant he had to think while he could, and now that he was doing that, several questions were coming to mind.

Where the hell were they?

And why were they there?

His gaze dropped to Sarita and Domitian had a vague recollection of her saying something about Dressler drugging and dropping her here too. Why? What was the man up to? Why had he kidnapped them and then put them together in this house? For that matter, why had he kidnapped all those other immortals? Were they each in other houses, wondering the same thing?

Domitian didn't know, but he was pretty sure that as pleasant as things were at that moment, whatever plans Dressler had for him and Sarita didn't include an ending he would like. They needed to get out of there.

And he needed blood, Domitian thought, becoming aware of the gnawing in his stomach.

Glancing down to Sarita, he gave her a gentle shake to wake her. When that had no effect, he eased her gently off him and to the side to lie on the cold tile, then got quickly to his feet and bent to scoop her up off the floor. She didn't even stir as he carried her into the bedroom and set her in the bed.

Domitian stared down at her for a minute, taking in her sweet face in repose. You'd never guess how prickly and stubborn she could be from how she looked now, he thought wryly. And then his gaze slid down to her body and his thoughts turned to her passion. Her breasts were still exposed above the neckline he'd tugged under them, showing that her nipples were no longer hard. And her legs had fallen open a bit when he'd set her down, leaving a perfect view of what he'd been so eager to taste.

Domitian licked his lips, suddenly hungry to taste her again. He almost did just that, almost crawled onto the bed with her to lick away the dried blood as he'd wanted to do earlier and then taste her essence. It was the licking away the dried blood that kept him from climbing into bed for round two. Domitian would have had no compunction about licking fresh blood from her body should she have freshly cut herself, but dried blood was something else. It was just nasty. Even thinking about doing that told him how much he needed to feed.

Sighing with regret, Domitian turned away and left the room to make his way to the office and downstairs. It wasn't until he reached the bottom of the stairs that he recalled the glass everywhere.

Domitian paused, briefly considering just walking through it again, but that and his head wound were the reason he needed blood again so soon. The nanos had forced the glass from his foot as he'd knelt to remove her splinters. They had also repaired the small cuts from the china as well as his head injury and now needed more blood. There was no sense adding to their need.

Turning on his heel, he returned upstairs to fetch a broom and dustpan from the kitchen.

Sarita stretched happily and rolled onto her back in bed. She felt great. Awesome. Incredible. She hadn't felt this good in a long time, if ever, and she owed it all to—

Her eyes blinked open and she stared blankly up at her own reflection. It told her that she was alone in the bed, but—*Dear God, the ceiling is mirrored above the open bed frame!* How tacky was that? And how had she not noticed *that* when she'd woken up here earlier?

Obviously, she hadn't looked up. Tilting her head, Sarita wondered what it would have been like to have watched her and Domitian having sex. Probably not that great, she decided. Watching herself writhe and moan while Domitian had done the things he'd done . . . well, frankly, it would have taken her right out of the moment.

Which would have been a shame, because she hadn't had her pipes cleaned like that in a heck of a long time, Sarita thought with a grin and then quickly groaned and closed her eyes.

"Snap out of it," she ordered herself grimly, but it wasn't easy. He was *sooo* hot, and man, she'd never experienced sex like that, hadn't even imagined it was possible. Unfortunately, her Catholic upbringing was warring with the woman she'd grown into, an independent female cop who had no qualms about going after what she wanted. It was all leaving Sarita an extremely confused woman. One part of her brain was telling her she had been very naughty and should head to the nearest priest for confession. The other part was suggesting if she was going to have to do penance anyway, she really should find Domitian and jump him again.

Dear God, she'd really done that! Sarita shook her head at her reflection with dismay. After her grand lecture to him that there would be no kissy, kissy, gropey, gropey and *no sexo*, she'd gone ahead and started it herself! *She'd* kissed *him*.

Oh, the shame! Oh, the humiliation! Oh . . . she wanted to do it again.

Opening her eyes, Sarita met her gaze in the reflection above and said solemnly, "You are obviously a very confused woman."

And God, what a mess she was, Sarita thought as she noted the dried blood everywhere. It was on her face, her chest, her hands, legs, and feet. And her nightgown? That was a tangle around her waist leaving everything else bare.

She looked like a two-bit whore whose last John had been a slasher.

"Ugh," Sarita said with disgust and forced herself from the bed. She needed a shower and a good stiff drink. Alternately, she needed a shower and a good stiff Domitian, she thought. And then she shook her head.

"You are incorrigible, Sarita Reyes," she muttered to herself as she headed into the bathroom. "Your father is up there somewhere in heaven, his head hung low with disappointment and shame, and all you can think about is . . ."

Sarita stopped talking to herself as she reached the shower and quickly turned on the taps. But her thoughts didn't stop there, because all she was thinking about as she fetched a towel, shampoo, and soap was just how mind-blowing and hot sex with Domitian had been.

Dressler had said life mate sex was like no other and she couldn't agree more. He'd also said it was over-whelming and stuff, and he hadn't been kidding. If what she had experienced was all due to those nanos he'd mentioned, then damn! They were one fine invention and she was all for them, Sarita thought as she stripped off the ruined nightgown and robe and stepped into the shower to begin shampooing her hair.

Unfortunately, or perhaps fortunately, thoughts of Dressler were enough to dampen her wayward desires and Sarita's mind turned instead to what El Doctor wanted as she rinsed the shampoo from her hair. Why had he put her there with Domitian? Sarita wondered as she began quickly scrubbing the soap over her body, removing the dried blood.

In the letter he'd said he hoped to learn a lot from her stay here. What exactly was it he hoped to learn? He'd already known about life mate sex, so that wasn't it. Unless he had cameras here and hoped to see it for himself.

Sarita stiffened at that thought, and then raised her head and turned in the shower. She spotted one almost at once. It was in the corner of the shower, recessed in the wall, but a tiny lens was just visible if you were looking for it.

Resisting the urge to cover her private bits, Sarita lowered her head, turned her back to the corner, and then stepped under the spray to rinse off. The moment she'd finished, though, she turned off the water and grabbed the towel she'd collected. Rather than dry herself with it, she simply wrapped it around herself toga-style.

Sarita glanced around the bathroom as she stepped out of the shower, spotting three more camera lenses as she did. There was one in each of the other three corners of the room.

"Nice," she hissed under her breath.

Pretending not to have seen them, Sarita walked over and snatched up a hand towel off the rack to dry her hair as much as possible, then ran a quick brush through it before slipping out of the room.

A stop in the closet proved that it wasn't magic and hadn't suddenly produced real clothes for her. Heaving a resigned sigh, she went through what was available and chose a short, red-and-black lace-and-satin night-gown that at least had substance to its very short skirt.

"And that's all it has," Sarita grumbled once she had it on and saw that the lace top showed as much as it hid. She could clearly see the outline of her breasts, but at least a couple of strategically placed lace flowers mostly hid her nipples. Shaking her head, she didn't bother with shoes, but hurried out of the bedroom in search of Domitian.

A search of the living room, dining room, and kitchen did not turn up Domitian. Though, she did spot more cameras, four in every room. She should have checked the bedroom too, but now supposed she needn't bother. If the bathroom wasn't sacred, the bedroom definitely wouldn't be.

The office was empty too but also had cameras, Sarita noted as she rushed through it to make her way quickly downstairs. She didn't, however, spot any in the room at the bottom of the stairs. Probably because the walls were stone and cameras couldn't be recessed in them. Possibly also because the room was unpleasant, damp, and smelly. He wouldn't imagine they'd do anything there.

Sarita was halfway across the floor before she noticed that the glass had all been cleaned up, but barely gave it a thought as she hurried into the abandoned lab.

"Domitian." She scowled when she spotted him by the refrigerator. She'd started to worry that he'd been removed while she'd slept, and here he was chowing down on more blood, she thought with irritation as he removed an empty bag of blood from his mouth. The last of four, she saw, counting the empty bags already on the counter.

"Mi Corazon," Domitian greeted with a smile as he tossed the empty bag next to the others and moved to meet her. As he walked his eyes dropped with appreciation down over the nightgown she wore.

Noting that his blue eyes grew more silver with each step and recalling that they'd burned a brilliant silver as he'd made love to her upstairs, Sarita began to back warily away. Putting her hand up, she said *no* firmly, her gaze skating around to find the cameras in the corners. Not in the walls this time, but recessed in the trim on top of the upper cupboards.

Eyebrows rising, Domitian paused and Sarita hesitated. She wanted to talk to him about Dressler and why they were there, but not around the cameras. She didn't doubt for a minute that they recorded audio as well as video, and she didn't want Dressler knowing what they were talking about.

"Not here," Sarita said finally, and then tried on a

pouty moue for the cameras that she suspected looked more like a grimace and said, "The floor is too hard."

"Ah," Domitian breathed, moving forward again. The silver had receded a bit in his eyes at her *no* but came surging back now, and Sarita's body responded, producing liquid like Pavlov's salivating dogs. Only her salivating was much lower and warmer.

"Come. We will go upstairs," Domitian breathed, slipping his arm around her and urging her toward the door.

"Yes," she muttered, unable to resist leaning into him as his hand ran down her side from her waist to her hip and lower, before sliding up under her nightgown to clasp one round cheek. It was only then Sarita realized she'd forgotten to hunt for a thong to wear under the skimpy gown.

"Oh boy," she breathed, and then slipped away from his caressing hand and stepped determinedly in front of him as they reached the bottom of the stairs. Whispering so the cameras in the other room wouldn't pick up her words, she said, "We need to talk,"

Misunderstanding her whispering, Domitian stiffened at once and glanced up the stairs. "Is someone here?"

"No," Sarita assured him, patting his chest reassuringly. At least it started out a reassuring pat, but turned into a pawing pat. He had such a lovely chest she just couldn't resist touching it.

"*Mi tresoro?* What is it?" he asked softly. Unfortunately, he also clasped her arms and then ran his fingers lightly up and down them as he waited.

The simple touch was very distracting and Sarita found herself shivering as it sent tingles slipping through her again. She didn't even really notice herself inching closer to him until her nipples brushed against his chest through the lace top of her nightgown. Already semi-hard, they turned to stone then as excitement raced through her, and a little *ahhh* slid from her lips.

"Ah, Sarita. *Besame,*" Domitian breathed the demand that she kiss him, his head lowering toward her.

"No!" She turned her head abruptly away, scowling again with irritation at how distracting the damned man was. It was bad enough fending him off without her own body betraying her like this. "No kissing. I need to talk to you," Sarita added quietly. "We have to get out of here."

"Si," he agreed. "Talk. I will listen." Domitian began kissing her cheek, since that was all that was available to him, and then trailing his lips to her ear.

Sarita snapped her mouth closed to keep from moaning at the sensations his actions sent washing through her. She raised her hands to his shoulders, intending to push him back. Instead, she found herself clutching at him and arching as he nibbled on her tender lobe.

"Mi Amante," Domitian breathed, his arms slipping around to cup her behind and lift her up against him so that he could pepper kisses down her throat. *"Tu eres la mujer mas bella que he visto. Tue eres mi luz en la oscuridad."*

You are the most beautiful woman I have ever seen. You are my light in the dark, Sarita translated in her head and then shook it to try to force the love words out and concentrate. "I really—we need to talk," she said breathlessly.

"Si," he breathed, easing her back to her feet. "Talk."

"Good," Sarita said with relief and tried to gather her thoughts again.

"I like this nightgown," Domitian murmured, one hand rising to toy with a nipple through the lace.

"That's not very helpful," Sarita growled as he caught the excited tip through the cloth and pinched it between thumb and finger. When his other hand then slid under the skirt of the nightgown again and clasped her bottom, Sarita was sure she was lost . . . until his fingers began a lazy meander around in front and along the top of her tender thigh. It was the first time she'd felt pain since cutting it. All she could think was that he'd unintentionally caught the skin of the cut and pulled it slightly. Whatever had happened, it was enough to help her fight off her attraction to him and pull back. When Domitian tried to follow, she slapped him sharply across the face and hissed, "Snap out of it! We have to talk about Dressler."

Five

Domitian gave his head a shake and peered down at the little spitfire in front of him. Her face was flushed with desire, her lips full from his kisses, but her eyes were on fire with fury, passion, and despair. It was the despair that reached through his surprise and anger at her slapping him and brought on immediate calm.

They were in a tenuous position and needed to find a way out. The desire and need they were both obviously experiencing was playing havoc with their ability to do so, and they *were* both suffering under that desire and need. He could see it in Sarita's face. But she was trying to fight it while he had followed his growing erection across the room, thinking only of plowing it deep into the woman presently trying to come up with a way to save them both.

Letting his hands drop away, Domitian straightened and took one slow step back. He nodded and then, voice flat, said, "You are right. We should talk."

He saw regret flicker briefly across her face, but Sarita took a small step back and simply asked, "Do you know why we were kidnapped?"

After a hesitation, he said, "I was kidnapped because I am immortal. Dressler has been collecting immortals for the last couple of years."

"Do you see any other immortals here?" she asked dryly and then pointed out, "And I'm not immortal."

Domitian shook his head slowly, and then eyed her with curiosity and asked, "You have some idea why we are both here?"

Sarita sighed, and nodded unhappily. "Dressler has been experimenting on the immortals he took."

"Experimenting how?" Domitian asked at once with concern.

"I only know about one experiment, but it was absolutely awful," Sarita said grimly and quickly told him about the experiment she'd interrupted and then inadvertently helped with.

"At the end he explained about the nanos that made your kind immortal, and mentioned that my life mate was coming." She frowned and then added, "Before that though, he said he'd made it his business to find out everything he could about your kind. I'm quite sure this experiment was just one of many. I wouldn't be surprised if every one of the immortals he has is strapped to a table with different limbs or pieces missing. The man is sick."

"Madre de Dios," Domitian breathed. His stomach was now churning at the thought of what the one immortal Sarita had seen had suffered and what the others might even now be going through. The worse part was he knew some of those immortals. Hell, he was related

to four of them. Glancing at her sharply, he asked, "What color eyes did the man you saw have?"

She appeared surprised at the question, but then thought briefly before saying, "He only opened his eyes once and it was quick, but I remember thinking they were the most beautiful silver-green eyes I'd ever seen."

"Green," Domitian breathed with relief.

"What is it?" Sarita asked with a frown. "Do you know one of the immortals on the island?"

He wasn't surprised she'd guessed that. The woman was smart and a police officer. She was probably trained to put clues together.

"*Si*. Or at least I know five men who have gone missing and suspect they are on the island," he admitted, but he didn't mention that one was his uncle Victor and another three were his cousins Lucern, Nicholas, and Decker. The fifth man, Santo Notte, was related only by marriage and very loosely at that. He also didn't mention his aunt by marriage, Eshe Argeneau, or her partner Mirabeau La Roche.

"I'm sorry," she said solemnly and Domitian winced as her words made him realize that while none of his relatives could be the man cut in half, they were probably being subjected to other, equally horrible experiments as she'd suggested.

Concern and guilt battled within Domitian as he realized that while his relatives were suffering unknown horrors, he'd been dropped into a tropical paradise and was mating with his life mate. Shaking his head, he paced away, and then returned, growling, "Why am I here? Why am I not in a lab being cut up? Why is he not experimenting on me?"

"I think he is," Sarita said quietly.

Domitian stopped midstep and whirled on her. "What?"

She shrugged and gestured to the nightgown she wore and pointed out, "He put us here in this honeymoon haven, left only skimpy gowns for me and boxers for you, along with lots of food, wine, blood for you, and a *very* big bed."

"Si?" he said, not seeing how that could be an experiment.

"He said he'd made it his business to learn everything about immortals," Sarita pointed out. "I think that must include seeing firsthand the life mate sex he's heard about. There are cameras all over this place. At least inside. I didn't look to see if there are any outside."

She frowned briefly and then shrugged. "I suspect this is part one of the experiment—watching us mate in a natural habitat. The next part is probably to force us to mate in a lab with electrodes all over us to measure heart rate and whatnot, and then take blood tests before, during, and after to check for hormone levels and such."

"El es el Diablo," Domitian breathed with horror.

Suffering the physical pain this man was likely putting the others through was bad enough, but while Sarita tried to hide it, he could see that the idea that someone had filmed and watched their private moments upset her. He couldn't imagine how being forced to perform sexually in a lab with electrodes and whatnot would affect the petite woman before him. And he wouldn't have it, Domitian thought grimly. They would not be making love again until they were away from here and safe.

"Of course," Sarita said now, a scowl on her face, "he could have taken our blood after we . . . you know . . .

banged upstairs in the bathroom," she said, flushing a bit. "I lost consciousness. He said that happens, but I woke up in bed instead of on the floor and he could have—"

"I moved you to the bed when I woke up," Domitian assured her and then said stiffly, "And we did not *bang*, we made love."

Her eyebrows rose slightly. "I'm pretty sure you have to love someone for it to be making love, and I don't love you. I don't even know you."

Domitian knew he shouldn't be hurt by her words, but he was. It reminded him that while he'd known for a decade and a half that she was his life mate and had followed her life, coming to admire, respect, and care for her over the years, she'd never even heard his name until just hours earlier. He put that issue aside for now as another cropped up in his mind. "Wait, this cannot be an experiment. There is no way Dressler could know that you are my life mate."

"He does," Sarita assured him. "He told me in the lab, and then he talked about how hot life mate sex is and stuff in the letter he left."

"The letter. Where is it?" Domitian asked at once.

"It's on the desk in the office," she admitted, but caught his arm as he turned toward the stairs and reminded him in a quiet voice, "There are cameras everywhere up there, and in the lab down here too. We need to watch what we do and say."

Domitian's expression tightened. Giving a short nod, he caught her hand and led her back upstairs.

The letter was on the desk where she'd left it. Domitian urged her into the desk chair, and then settled on the corner of the desk and quickly read the message.

Unlike her, he only paused to comment once while reading it and that was to curse.

"What?" Sarita asked curiously.

"He knows my name," Domitian said on a sigh.

"Okay," she said, narrowing her eyes. "Was he not supposed to?"

He shook his head. "I have lived under the name Diego Villanueva for the last five years, and that was the name he hired me under."

"Hired you?" Sarita asked with surprise.

"*Si.*" Domitian supposed she'd assumed that he'd just been abducted off the street or something like the others, so he explained, "Dressler has been offering me a job for years and I always refused. But when this kidnapping business was tracked to him, I accepted his offer. The bastard played me from the start," he added grimly. "He knew my real name all along."

"What job did he hire you for?"

"Chef at his home on the island."

Sarita nodded slowly. "Yeah, he played you. Aleta is the cook there and she's amazing. He wouldn't replace her," she said with certainty.

"I am a master chef, trained at all the best European schools," Domitian said a little stiffly.

Sarita shrugged that away as if all his training and skills were of little import and then asked curiously, "So why have you been living under the name Diego Villanueva for five years?"

"Immortals live a long time and do not age. We have to move every ten years to avoid mortals noticing."

"Ah," she murmured with understanding. "What was your name before Diego?"

"My true name, Domitian Argenis," he answered

promptly. "And when I leave here I will be Domitian again. Diego the chef has left the restaurant and moved on to greener pastures."

"And no one will recognize that Diego is Domitian?" Sarita asked dubiously.

Smiling faintly, he explained, "I have several restaurants. I will not return to the same one. The manager there will continue managing and reporting to me for another ten years and I will move on to another restaurant or start a new one."

"Right," Sarita murmured and then turned the subject back to where it had started and asked, "So how do you think he knew about me and this life mate business then?"

Frowning, Domitian turned his attention back to the letter and read the rest, but mostly it was just Dressler saying he hoped to learn a lot from their stay in his "home away from home" before he signed off.

Domitian shifted his gaze back up the letter to the part about Sarita being his life mate and that while she didn't know him, they had met when she was thirteen and he'd kept track of her ever since using a private detective. The man seemed to know everything regarding him and Sarita, he noticed with bewilderment.

"I do not know how Dressler knows," Domitian said finally, tossing the letter on the desktop. Meeting her gaze he assured her, "I told no one you were my life mate."

"What about this private detective you hired?" she asked. "Could he have—?"

"No," Domitian said at once. "He is mortal. He knows nothing about immortals and life mates and I did not educate him in the matter."

Sarita accepted that, but then tilted her head and asked, "So what reason did you give the detective for why you were having me followed?"

"Ah." Domitian shifted uncomfortably, grimaced and then admitted, "I told him that your mother was my sister, but that your father and I had a falling out and he would not let me see my only living blood relative anymore. I said I wanted him to keep track of you so that once you were an adult and could make your own decisions I could contact you and you could decide whether you wished to see me or not."

That seemed to shock Sarita. Eyes wide with disbelief, she asked, "You told him you were my *uncle*?"

"Well, I could hardly tell him the truth," Domitian pointed out, defensively. Scowling, he added, "I do not see why it would bother you anyway."

"Hmmm, I don't know," she said dryly. "Why would it bother me for people to think I was playing patty cake with my uncle?"

"Patty cake?" he asked with bewilderment.

"Bumping fuzzies," she said and when he still looked blank added, "Shaboink."

Domitian just shook his head with bewilderment. He had no idea what she was talking about.

"Never mind," Sarita muttered and then sighed and pointed out, "Anyway, we still don't know how Dressler knew you thought I was your life mate."

"I do not *think* you are my life mate, I *know* it," he said firmly. "And you should know it too after what happened in the bathroom."

"Yeah, yeah, it was mind-blowing sex and I fainted," she admitted. "Whatever. That still doesn't explain how Dressler knew."

"No, it does not," he admitted and pondered that briefly and then shook his head. "I have no idea how he found out."

"Well, I guess we can ask him when he comes to get us for part two of the experiment."

Domitian peered at her silently. While her words were light and slightly sarcastic, he could see the fear in her eyes. She was terrified they would not escape and would be forced to take this experiment, if that's what it was, to the next level. He wasn't going to let that happen, however.

"I think we need a swim to relax," he announced suddenly, catching her by the arm and urging her toward the door. He actually got Sarita halfway across the room before she jerked her arm free and spun on him.

"A swim? Are you kidding me?" she demanded.

"I think better after a swim," Domitian said mildly, but jerked his eyes toward the nearest camera as he added, "Trust me. Go get changed and I will fetch towels."

Judging by the way Sarita suddenly calmed and turned toward the door, she'd got his message. "Fine. I'll meet you by the pool."

"Yes," he breathed with relief and waited until she left. Domitian then said, "Towels," and turned toward the French doors. He slid out onto the side terrace and headed for the French doors to the kitchen. A quick glance ahead, and another back the way he'd come as he slid into the kitchen proved that there were no cameras mounted on the side wall of the house.

All Domitian could find in the half bathroom off the kitchen were a couple of hand towels. Shrugging, he took them, and then slipped back outside through the French doors again. He walked around the house to the pool so that he could check the front of the house and the side the pool was on as well. No cameras outside then, he noted as he paused and glanced along the back of the house where the bedroom and en suite bathroom were.

That was something, at least, Domitian decided and carried the towels over to drop them on one of the lounge chairs. At least they could talk out here without the fear of being listened to. It was why he'd suggested a swim. Also, a quick dunk in the cold pool would hopefully help keep their minds on track if they got distracted from their objective.

That thought in mind, Domitian walked over and dipped a toe in the water to test the temperature.

"How is it?"

Glancing around he saw Sarita approaching in a hanky torn into three tiny triangles that were taped over her important bits. At least that's what it looked like. The bikini bottom had less material than the thong she'd worn earlier, and the bits of cloth over her breasts barely covered her nipples let alone her breasts.

"Dios," Domitian breathed and thought with horror that Dressler was a diabolical bastard.

Sarita slowed as she noted Domitian's expression. The bathing suit she had on, if it could be called that, was the biggest one available. Not big in size—they were all her size—but this one had offered the most material, covering more than the others would have. It still covered very little.

Sarita kept in shape for work. She did a hundred sit-ups and push-ups every morning and night, and then did an hour of cardio every evening after dinner to stay fit and in good running order to chase down perps. She was extremely fit.

Unfortunately, she also liked to eat, and the combination left her fit but still overly curvy. She had thighs and hips she felt were too big and a muffin top that made her groan with despair. However, her body was her body and after a quick grimace on seeing herself in the bikini and noting what it exposed, she'd shrugged and headed out with her head held high.

Now, on spotting the horror on Domitian's face, though, Sarita narrowed her eyes and stopped, almost daring him to say something insulting about how she looked in the swimsuit.

She didn't have long to wait.

"How is a man to think with his woman looking like this?" Domitian exploded, waving at her as if she were a nightmare. "Look at you! Your beautiful breasts overflowing those little patches of cloth. You might as well not even be wearing the top! And those little straps that make up the bottoms. They just draw the eye to your luscious hips and your shapely legs. *Oh Dios!* Your legs! I just want to lick and kiss my way up their gorgeous length. No! I want to lick and kiss every part of your beautiful body, and then—" He broke off, almost gasping, and then turned and plunged into the pool to start swimming toward the waterfall.

Sarita stared after him rather blankly, her mind slow to understand what she'd just heard. She'd thought him horrified because of how she looked, and he was, but not in the way she'd expected. Good God, the things he wanted to do to her. Domitian would give good phone sex—that was for sure. His words alone had left her standing there wet and aching for the pleasure she already knew he could give her. And she couldn't do a damned thing about it. They had to work out a plan to get off this island, and she was guessing that was why Domitian had suggested the "swim." He had been thinking that there were no cameras here.

She glanced around the pool, eyeing the forest suspiciously. There could be cameras in there that they couldn't see. It didn't matter, however. Being overheard was the main concern and the sound of the waterfall would cover any conversation they had so long as they kept it down. The problem was controlling themselves long enough to talk and come up with an idea to get out of there, and that was starting to seem impossible.

"God, I need a drink," Sarita muttered and glanced over her shoulder toward the house, but turned back quickly at the sound of splashing.

Domitian had surfaced after one lap and was now walking up the pool stairs, the water falling away with each step to reveal his gorgeous shoulders, his wide chest, his flat stomach, and—

Good God, he'd said she might as well not be wearing the top, but he might as well take off his boxers. Soaking wet, they clung to him like a second skin, and were doing nothing to hide the amazing erection he was sporting. It was pointed straight at her, and he was following it she noted, taking a wary step back.

"I need you, *mi Corazon*," Domitian said helplessly.

"No," Sarita said firmly, taking another step back. "We need to figure out how we're going to get out of here."

"We will walk out at nightfall," he announced, continuing forward.

"But how? If Dressler knows we're trying to leave,

he could send men after us. Hell, there could be a fence around this place a mile into the woods where his men are waiting to stop us."

"We will worry about that after I make love to you," Domitian assured her soothingly. "But now . . ." He shook his head helplessly, and gestured toward his penis. "I cannot think like this, *querida*. I need you. I need to fondle and kiss your sweet breasts and suckle your nipples with my lips. I need to feel and taste your wet heat on my tongue, and then bury myself in your warm, hot body and feel you squeeze and milk me as I thrust into you until we both scream our pleasure."

"We'll faint," Sarita protested weakly, continuing to move back.

"*Si*, but it is only midafternoon, we have time."

"The cameras," she protested with a little more strength, and her face went grim as she recalled them. Her voicing that worry had been a desperate attempt, but now that they were in her head, they were an issue. She had no desire to be a porn star for the likes of El Doctor.

"The cameras are inside. We are outside," he said gently.

"There might be cameras out here," Sarita pointed out stubbornly, not backing up anymore, but staying put and crossing her arms forbiddingly. "But even if there aren't, we could be seen by the cameras in the living room."

Domitian paused, a frown furrowing his brow as he considered the problem and then he brightened. "The pool."

"We'd drown when we passed out at the end. At least I would," she pointed out.

"Oh, *si*," he muttered and considered the problem

again, and then said, "Come. I have an idea." Catching
her arm, Domitian turned and tugged her to the nearest
lounge chair where he released her and dropped to sit
halfway up, his legs on either side and feet flat on the
stones that made up the terrace floor.

"What are you—?" she began with confusion and
then gasped with surprise when he caught her by the
upper legs, turned her, and tugged her down to sit in
the V his legs made.

"There. See?" Domitian murmured, brushing her hair
out of the way so that he could press kisses along her
neck.

"No, I don't see," Sarita muttered, trying to get back up.

"All the cameras in the living room see is my back,"
he whispered by her ear before giving it a nip.

"True," she said and her attempts to remove his
hands from her waist and get up weakened a bit, but
only a bit before she said, "What if there are cameras
in the trees?"

"They will see nothing I promise. Watch."

Sarita had no idea what she was supposed to watch
until one of his hands left her waist. She glanced
around curiously to see that he'd reached behind him
to retrieve a . . . towel? She blinked at the tiny hand
towel and shook her head. "*Those* are the towels you
brought for us?"

"It was all I could find in the small bathroom off the
kitchen," Domitian said with a shrug and opened the
towel to rest it on her chest and stomach. Sarita stared
down at it with bewilderment until he slid one hand
under the towel, and then up under the ridiculously tiny
bathing suit top she wore.

Gasping, she pressed back against him with her

shoulders while her chest arched upward into the palm that suddenly covered her breast.

"You see? No one will see anything."

Sarita gave a breathless laugh. Her voice was equally breathless as she writhed between his chest and fondling hand and gasped, "So you're . . . just going . . . to grope me . . . to orgasm."

"Oh, much more than that, *mi amor*," he assured her, sounding a little breathless himself, and then his other hand slid under the towel and down between the cloth of the bikini bottom to cup her between the legs.

Sarita jumped in his arms and gasped as he slid a finger smoothly inside her.

"Much more," Domitian assured her on a groan as his thumb began to slide around the nub above where his finger was plundering her.

Sarita groaned in response, but started to shake her head. Turning to try to glare at him, she said, "You can't—"

Her protest ended abruptly when his mouth covered hers, his tongue slipping in to silence her own.

Sarita shuddered, her hips moving of their own accord to the dance he was leading, her tongue tangling with his. She lifted one hand to cover his where it remained at her breast, encouraging him as he began to pluck at and toy with the nipple of first one breast and then the other. The combination of everything he was doing was driving her to a fever pitch. Whoever said making out and just hitting first, second, and third base without making it to fourth wasn't very satisfying, had obviously never had an immortal life mate running those bases. The man was driving her wild. One more minute of this and she would—

Sarita's thoughts died abruptly as he slid a second finger in to join the first and her body went off like a rocket. Grabbing for his hands, she tore her mouth away to cry out, vaguely aware that he was shouting as well, and then sunset came early for her as Sarita's mind shut down.

She woke up some time later to find herself reclining on Domitian Argenis's chest as he ran his fingers lazily up and down her arms. He might be a great lover, but he made for a lumpy bed, she decided and immediately sat up. This time he hadn't carried her to the bed. They were still on the lounge chair by the pool.

Sarita caught the hand towel as it started to fall, but on checking to see that her bathing suit was in place and covering as much as it had before this little side excursion, she let the towel drop away and turned to scowl at Domitian as he sat up. "That wasn't fair."

His eyebrows rose in question. "What, *mi amor*?"

"First you made a meal out of me in the bathroom and now you . . ."

"Pleasured you?" he suggested.

Sarita flushed and turned away. "Yeah, that, here. Meanwhile, you haven't got a thing from it," she muttered, and tried to stand up, only to have him catch her shoulder and keep her on the seat.

"*Si, mi Corazon.* I have."

"What?" she asked with disbelief. "You—"

"I got great pleasure from both joinings."

Sarita clucked her tongue with irritation and tried to remove his hand from her shoulder so she could get up. "There was no joining. Well, I suppose there was for half a second the first time," she added dryly. "But there was no joining this last time. You just—" Her words died abruptly as Domitian released her shoulder to slide down to catch her hand and drag it back to cover the front of his boxers. He was already semierect, or perhaps still semi-erect, she guessed, but at her touch, began to grow. Sarita didn't notice at first, she had frozen, shocked and confused by the excitement and pleasure that jolted through her the moment her hand touched him.

"That is how we joined," Domitian said, his voice gravelly with passion.

Sarita turned slightly on the end of the lounge chair to look at him, and then glanced to where her hand was touching him as her movement accidentally shifted her hand, sending another thrill of pleasure through her.

"It is called shared pleasure," he said, growling now. "It is something only life mates enjoy." Covering her hand to keep it still, Domitian added, "I felt every moment of your pleasure, experiencing it as if it were my own. And at the end, my shout of pleasure joined yours and we both lost consciousness."

"Really?" She glanced to his face with interest.

"*Si*. Really."

"That's a pretty nifty perk," Sarita admitted, and slid her hand inside his boxers to pull him out. He was surprisingly sensitive, she found. Just doing that had jolt after jolt of pleasure riding through her.

Domitian bit back a groan and tried to remove her hand. "*Si*. Now let go, turn around, and let me—"

"No," she said, shifting to kneel on the concrete in front of the chair instead, never releasing her hold on him as she did.

Domitian groaned, but then caught her hand to stop

her and asked, *"No?"* with bewilderment. "But I want to touch you."

"Too bad," Sarita said with a shrug. Offering him a wicked smiled, she added, "You've already done that. And I've always wanted to know how good I was at BJs."

"BJ? That is—Ah yes, that is what I thought it was," he said faintly as she leaned onto the end of the lounge chair and took him into her mouth.

Startled by the tsunami of pleasure that swept through her then, Sarita closed her eyes and nearly bit him, but managed to stop herself at the last moment. Once she felt she was prepared for what was going to come, Sarita began to move her mouth over him, moaning along with Domitian as pleasure immediately began rushing through her again. The vibration from her moan merely added to the pleasure, causing her to moan again, which brought on more pleasure and more moaning. It was like a circle without end, the pleasure building and building with each go-round until she could barely breathe.

"Madre de Dios, you are good," Domitian gasped, his butt rising off the seat slightly as he tried to follow her mouth.

Sarita couldn't agree more. Literally, she couldn't agree with him with her mouth full. But she was rather impressed with herself as she drove them both crazy with her lips, teeth, and tongue. She was vaguely aware of Domitian tangling his hands in her hair and clutching her head a moment later. Sarita knew he was saying things, but he wasn't making much sense. Beautiful words in Spanish were followed by the filthiest demands, but she didn't pay them much attention. She was listening to her own body's dictates, applying more pressure now, moving faster, slowing, speeding up, nipping lightly to increase the pleasure she was experiencing. And the entire time, Sarita was moaning, her body trembling on that very edge of the freedom release offered her, and then . . . *bang*! Something snapped and pleasure shot to every corner of her body, filling her and blocking out the light as she sighed and slid into unconsciousness.

Six

Sarita woke up this time to find her head on Domitian's thigh and his exhausted member passed out in front of her.

It was a heck of a thing to wake up to, she thought wryly as she eased carefully away from him to sit up on the stone floor at the end of the lounger. He was still asleep this time, she noted, which was kind of weird. Domitian had woken up first the last two times today, she thought, and she glanced along his body to his face to see that not only was he still unconscious, but he was also extremely pale.

Sarita glanced up toward the sun and frowned as she tried to figure out what time it was. The sun was making its downward journey, but was still high in the sky so she supposed it must be mid to late afternoon, somewhere between 2 and 4 P.M.

That realization was somewhat staggering. She hadn't even know Domitian a full day yet. It felt like forever.

And really, how stupid was the man to be messing about out here with her where he would pass out under the hot sun? Not once, but twice, mind you. This life mate sex obviously made idiots of its victims. And had it really not even been twenty-four hours since Dressler had knocked her out in his lab with that shot? *Really?* It felt like a week.

Sighing, she got to her feet and then paused in surprise as a wave of dizziness swept over her. Domitian wasn't the only one who'd had too much sun, apparently. While Sarita had grown up in Venezuela, she wasn't used to such concentrated sun and for so long anymore.

She probably needed water, Sarita told herself. She would get some before she went down to get blood for Domitian. She glanced down at him and changed her mind. He looked like death warmed over. She'd get the blood first and then fetch water for herself, she decided, moving cautiously away from the lounge chair and toward the house.

Sarita felt better the moment she stepped inside the shaded house. It was a good twenty degrees cooler than it was outside, the ceiling fans turning slowly and pushing the cooler air around. She actually shivered at the difference as she pulled the door closed and headed for the office and the hidden door to the basement.

Her gaze swept the boxes in the room at the foot of the stairs as she passed through it, and Sarita recalled that she hadn't finished her search of them. She'd return to do that after getting blood for Domitian, she decided as she continued into the old lab to retrieve the blood.

Sarita had four bags in her arms and was backing out of the refrigerator when she felt something brush her elbow. Glancing to the refrigerator door, she saw that there was a piece of tape sticking out with a bit of paper on the end. It looked like something had been taped there but had been torn off.

Letting the door close, Sarita glanced around and spotted a balled-up piece of paper on the floor. Curious, she carried the blood bags to the table and set them down, then hurried back to pick up and smooth out the paper. On one side there were four numbers and Sarita grimaced as she recognized them. They made up the combination for the numbered padlock she'd had to pick to free Domitian.

It seemed Dressler had left the combination after all. He'd probably put it in the refrigerator to make sure she did feed Domitian the blood before she freed him. Too bad he hadn't put it on the bags where she might have noticed it rather than taping it to the inside of the door where she'd overlooked it.

"Men," she muttered to herself, and in the next moment silently apologized to men in general for the insult. Dressler was a monster not a man.

There were a couple of words under the numbers and she read them with interest.

This combination is for you to use to free Domitian AFTER YOU FEED HIM AT LEAST FOUR BAGS OF BLOOD. However, the letter inside is for him. Please be sure he reads it.

It was a piece of paper, not an envelope, but it still had the crease where it had been folded in half, closing the letter to Domitian inside when taped to the door. Eyebrows rising, Sarita turned the paper over and read the message on the other side.

Domitian Argenis,

This blood is clean and unsullied. It is safe to consume. I offer it as a way to ensure you do not hurt our little Sarita. I know how important life mates are to your kind.

Obviously there is something I want from you. I will contact you soon to let you know what that is. In the meantime, please enjoy my home away from home.

Dr. Dressler

Sarita read the note at least three times before balling it up and tossing it on the floor where she'd found it. The message didn't really say much. The blood was obviously fine. At least it hadn't harmed Domitian, although, frankly, she hadn't even considered that it might not be fine.

And Domitian had already told her that life mates were important to an immortal. As for the "obviously he wanted something from Domitian" part, that wasn't really news either. They'd already decided he'd put them there for a reason. But that line troubled her anyway. As did the mention that he would contact Domitian soon to let him know what that something was. He didn't say he'd contact them, just Domitian.

Frowning, Sarita gathered up the blood she'd come down for and headed back upstairs. She was crossing the living room to the doors to the terrace before she realized what she found most bothersome about the letter. It was the fact that Domitian hadn't mentioned it to her.

Why was that? she wondered, pausing by the doors.

Several possibilities filled her mind. Perhaps he had thought it would upset her, which suggested he thought her weak. Or perhaps he hadn't told her because he didn't want her to know Dressler was going to contact him somehow. Or perhaps because he'd already contacted him and told him what he wanted. Perhaps Dressler had told him about the cameras and that he wanted them to have sex. Maybe he'd promised Domitian freedom or something if he performed often and enthusiastically.

Sarita glanced to where Domitian still lay, apparently unconscious on the lounge chair. She briefly considered not taking the blood out to him. She even considered leaving him out there in the sun to fry, grabbing several bottles of water from the refrigerator upstairs, and trying to leave right now on her own. But then she pushed the door open, stepped out, and kicked it closed before walking to the lounge chair.

One glance was enough to ascertain that Domitian was still unconscious and incapable of feeding himself. Sarita dumped the bags of blood on the chair next to his body and then gave him a good slap to try to wake him up so he could feed. When that had no effect, she straightened to consider what she should do.

After a moment, Sarita hurried back into the house and through the living room and bedroom to the en suite bathroom where she retrieved one of the steak knives still lying on the counter. She then fetched a large bath towel as well before hurrying back out to the pool.

Moving quickly now, she covered Domitian with the bath towel from the neck down to prevent further damage from the sun, then grabbed a bag of blood and held it over his mouth. Sarita was raising the knife to puncture the bag when she recalled what Asherah had done in the lab to bring on the immortal's fangs. Pausing, she set the bag down and punctured the tip of her finger instead. It was just a small jab, enough to bring on a bead of blood that she then waved under Domitian's nose.

His nose twitched, and then his mouth fell open and she watched as two of his upper teeth shifted and then slid down, becoming pointy little fangs. Sarita stared at them for a minute, marveling that they looked just like normal teeth when in their resting position, but then she grabbed the bag of blood again and popped it to his fangs. Once she was sure it was fixed in place, cradled in his open mouth, she let go and slowly removed her hand, ready to grab it again if it rolled or shifted and fell off. When that didn't happen, Sarita straightened with a sigh and then left him there and went back inside to get her water. She was quite sure he'd wake up before the first bag was empty and would be able to then feed himself the rest of the bags she'd left him. It hadn't seemed to take much for the corpse guy to come sputtering back to life and he'd apparently been drained.

The bottled water was ice cold when Sarita pulled it from the refrigerator. Hot as she was, she didn't open it at once, but instead pressed it against her forehead and then her cheeks, sighing as it cooled her heated flesh. When she finally opened it and began to drink, she gulped half of it down in one go. Sarita then tossed the cap in the sink and grabbed a second bottle from the refrigerator to take with her before heading for the basement again. She was determined she would finish her search of those boxes this time . . . and the cupboards in the old lab too.

Actually, perhaps she'd start in the lab, Sarita thought suddenly. There might be an old lab coat stashed away in one of the drawers or cupboards that she could wear when she left this place. Even an apron would cover more than anything in the closet upstairs did.

Heck, if there were curtains on any of the windows here, she'd be sewing herself a gown a la *Gone with the Wind*, Sarita thought dryly and then paused at the bottom of the stairs as she thought of the sheets on the bed. She wouldn't even have to sew that, she could just wrap it around herself toga style.

Sarita almost turned to run back upstairs, but then continued on into the lab. It would only take a minute to check the cupboards for a lab coat, and that would be much less cumbersome than the large sheet from the bed.

She started her search with the cupboards along the wall next to the door, quickly opening and closing cupboards and drawers one after the other as she walked along. All Sarita found was dusty old—and probably outdated—lab equipment, a couple of pencils, a stapler, an empty whiskey bottle, and blank notepads.

Disappointed with her results, she moved on to the floor-to-ceiling cupboards along the wall with the refrigerator and freezer. The first cupboard was an old broom closet with a tin dustpan and a broom and mop, both disintegrating with age. The other two cupboards were empty except for hooks, which had no doubt at one time held lab coats.

Sarita almost gave up her search then to go out to the waiting boxes in the next room. But she'd been trained to be thorough in a search, so she continued on to the row of upper and lower cupboards along the wall opposite the door. She didn't expect to find anything of much interest in these cupboards either, though, so was startled to open the first door and find herself staring at several large liquid-filled jars with bizarre shapes floating in them.

Sarita eyed them briefly with bewilderment, and then stepped forward and picked up the center jar of three on the lower shelf. She then drew it closer to her face to examine the contents. For one whole minute she had no idea what she was looking at. Her mind simply couldn't make sense of what she was seeing.

Here was a tiny fist. Here a tiny foot attached to what could be a tiny, malformed leg. Here another tiny foot with a perfect leg, and between the two a tail of some sort. A fish tail, Sarita realized, turning the jar slowly until she could see the head of the bent figure. But instead of a baby's head, some kind of large insect head peered out at her through the clear glass. The sight so startled her that Sarita nearly lost her grip on the jar.

Tightening her fingers at the last moment, she caught the lid of the jar, then quickly set it on the counter and backed away, her instinct to get as far away as possible from the monstrosity.

Sarita stopped after just a couple steps, however, her gaze sliding to the other jars in the cupboard. There were two rows of three, or had been before she'd removed the one she'd just set on the counter. Now her gaze slid over the other jars with a sort of sick fascination. Each held a mutant fetus, what she presumed were partially human babies with atrocious deformities or mutations. There was a perfectly formed fetus with skin that made her think of a salamander. One with a misshapen head and what looked like fur running down its back. Another with no limbs, just a head and trunk, the skin so see-through the organs inside were visible, though those didn't appear to be quite right. Another fetus was almost perfectly formed, but with only four toes and fingers and those sporting long curved claws. The last was just a jellied mass with nothing human about it.

"Dear God," Sarita breathed. She stared at the jars on display for a moment, her stomach turning, and then moved almost without thinking to the next cupboard and opened that door as well, and then the next and the next and the next. Her gorge rose with each door she opened and each set of six jars revealed, until Sarita was gagging on her horror and disgust as she opened the last.

Covering her mouth, she backed away then and simply stared at the varied monstrosities on display, hardly aware of the silent tears spilling from her eyes and running down her cheeks.

These were not naturally occurring malformations. They couldn't be. She was sure they had been engineered. Human DNA spliced with various animal and fish DNA to create atrocities she'd never imagined could exist. It was horrifying. She couldn't imagine how it had been done. What kind of sick psycho could do something so monstrous?

Dressler seemed the obvious answer. It seemed immortals weren't the only thing he liked to experiment on. He liked to play with human DNA too. The real question was why? Why would he do this? What did he hope to get from it?

Footsteps coming down the stairs in the next room caught her ear, and Sarita quickly dashed her tears away. She wasn't a crier by nature. She'd only cried three times in her life; when her mother died, when her grandfather died, and when her father died. Her tears now were an aberration, and one she wasn't willing to share with anyone.

"Sarita?"

Taking a deep breath to steady herself, she turned to see Domitian crossing the room toward her.

"I woke up and you were not—" He paused halfway across the room, concern suddenly flooding his face. "What is wrong? Have you been crying?"

"No," Sarita snapped, and then rolled her eyes with irritation. So much for her attempt to look normal, she thought, but added in a calmer voice, "There is nothing wrong. I was just . . ." She turned, gesturing to the open cupboards and frowning at the jars.

"Ah . . ." Domitian continued forward to stand at her side, his face grim as he looked over the jars. "I saw them earlier."

"I didn't," Sarita responded, her voice hollow.

"Then this must have been a shock," he murmured, slipping a comforting arm around her shoulder.

Sarita didn't respond. She also remained stiff under his arm, unable to relax. It wasn't because of the jars, though. It was that damned letter and his not telling her about it, and her worry that Dressler already had contacted Domitian somehow.

"My uncle said that one of Dressler's men mentioned a host of creatures on the island," Domitian announced now. "Fish people and bird people, and a centaur I think."

"What?" she asked with disbelief, but then she glanced back to the fetus with the fish tail between its legs before letting her eyes slide over the other mutations. She shook her head. "I didn't see anything like that on the island."

"Perhaps they are kept in the labs you mentioned," Domitian suggested.

Sarita nodded slowly. "There were several buildings. I only saw the front room of the first building, though. I suppose he could have had any number of people and things locked up there."

"Speaking of locked up, Dressler did leave you the combination to the padlock on my chains," Domitian announced suddenly.

Sarita stiffened up just a bit more. "Oh?"

"*Si*. It is around here somewhere." He glanced around the floor briefly. "It was taped on the inside of the refrigerator door. It had the combination on the outside and a brief note on the inside saying the blood was unsullied and he would contact us later to tell us what he wanted from us."

Turning back, Domitian grimaced and admitted, "I meant to tell you about it, but when you came down in that little red-and-black nightgown I am afraid I forgot. I can find it, though, if you want to read it. I think I tossed it on the floor somewhere."

"No," she breathed and felt herself relax. He'd meant to tell her and got distracted. That was all. He hadn't been hiding anything from her.

"He is a monster."

Sarita glanced to Domitian to see that his attention was on the jars again. She peered at them herself, and felt a lump forming in her throat. These creatures Dressler's man had mentioned must be his successes, the mutations that had survived. Fish people and bird people, and a centaur? Why would he create such beings? What kind of life could they have in this world? Not that he was allowing them out into the world. At least she hadn't encountered any while on the island. She wouldn't be surprised if they were locked up in his labs, probably being dissected and experimented on just like the immortals.

Suddenly unable to bear it anymore, Sarita stepped forward and closed the cupboard door in front of them. The moment she did, Domitian began to close the others to the left of it and she started to do the same to the ones on the right.

"We have to leave here," Domitian said quietly as they worked together.

"Yes," she said simply.

Once the last door was closed, he moved back to clasp her arms and turned her to face him. Peering down at her solemnly, he said, "Thank you. For the blood. And for covering me. For taking care of me."

"It was nothing," Sarita said, shrugging his hands as well as his words away and turning to lead the way out of the room. And it really had been nothing. It certainly hadn't been taking proper care of him in her book. That would have included staying to feed him bag after bag until he woke up and then making sure he was okay. Not just popping one to his fangs and leaving. But she'd been too angry to do that, angry and suspicious about the letter and his not telling her about it.

No, that wasn't the truth, Sarita acknowledged. She *had* been angry, but it had been because his not telling her about the letter had frightened her. She'd feared what it might mean. She'd thought they were a team trying to escape together up to that point, but the letter had raised doubt in her, and fear. Most anger was based in fear, she knew.

"The sun will be setting soon. I think we should collect some bottled water and some canned goods and leave as soon as possible," Domitian said quietly once they were out of the old lab.

Sarita paused and turned back to point out, "He'll see what we are doing on the cameras and might send men to hunt us down."

"There is nothing we can do about that. We will just have to be quick about gathering things and hope to get out before he can get men here to stop us," he said firmly.

When Sarita frowned and looked uncertain, he pointed out, "We either take a chance and leave now, or wait here for whatever he has in store for us next. What do you prefer?"

"Leave now," she said without hesitation. Putting it that way rather made it obvious that it was the only choice.

Domitian smiled and relaxed a bit. "I am glad to hear it. I was not happy at the thought of having to knock you out and drag you out of here like a caveman."

Sarita snorted and turned to start upstairs, saying, "Knock me out? In your dreams."

"Trust me, in my dreams knocking you out is the last thing I would do to you," Domitian assured her, following. "Unless you count—"

"Don't say it. Don't even think about it," Sarita warned, knowing he was thinking about their postcoital faints.

"It is difficult not to think about it when I am following your perfect behind up the stairs in that ridiculous swimsuit," Domitian assured her. "Why do bikinis no longer have a back on them? Why even wear them at all, if all it is, is a strip of cloth up the crack of your bottom leaving your cheeks on display?" he complained, and then added, "Do not mistake me, it is a beautiful behind you have, but most distracting and—"

"Domitian?" Sarita interrupted as she stepped off the stairs and into the office.

"*Si?*" he asked.

"Stop looking at my butt," she ordered firmly.

He remained silent as they left the office, but as they entered the living room, murmured, "As you wish."

The words made Sarita whip around to eye him suspiciously. The last time he'd said that was in response to her lecture about no kissy, kissy, no gropey, gropey, and *no sexo.* And look how that had ended. She suspected the man wasn't as agreeable as he'd like her to believe, and that "as you wish" from him didn't mean what it would from everyone else. She just hadn't figured out what it did mean from him yet.

"Why do you not go take a shower and change into something a little less distracting? I will prepare a picnic for us while you do and we can eat out on the beach," Domitian said loudly, adding a wink in case she didn't understand that he was trying to buy them some time before Dressler would realize they were making an escape attempt.

"Sounds good," Sarita said just as loudly, but turned toward the kitchen instead, adding, "I'll just grab the first aid kit so I can put some antiseptic on the cuts on my legs after I shower."

"There is a first aid kit?" Domitian asked, following her.

Sarita nodded. She'd spotted it on one of her earlier

searches through the kitchen. There was a sewing kit too, and she decided she'd take that to the bathroom with her as well. Sewing a sheet onto herself might be the only way for her to have something that would help her cover up against mosquitos and the other bugs here. She wasn't running through the jungle in a bikini or one of those ridiculous negligees.

"All set?" Domitian asked when she straightened from collecting both kits.

"Yes." Sarita headed for the door adding, "Can you throw some bottled water in the picnic too? I'm pretty dehydrated after spending all afternoon in the sun."

"My pleasure," Domitian said, but he was beaming at her, and she knew he was pleased she'd just given him an excuse to pack the water. It might help keep Dressler from realizing too quickly what they were up to. She could only hope, anyway, Sarita thought.

The moment she stepped out of the kitchen, Sarita's mind turned to what they might need for this escape. The problem was they hadn't discussed how they meant to travel. Did he plan for them to traipse through the jungle or follow the beach?

Following the beach away from here would be easiest and probably safest, at least from whatever animals, reptiles, and insects might inhabit the jungle. On the other hand it left them out in the open and exposed should Dressler realize what they were up to and send men to search for them along the shoreline.

Then again, while heading straight out into the jungle might make for a shorter trip and one where they were less likely to be found again by their kidnapper, it also meant they might be walking into unknown peril. Sarita had lived in the city as a child here, she and her parents living in Caracas before moving to Canada. She had no idea what animals could be found in the jungle around this house, but knew there were tigers and jaguars in Venezuela's Amazonian jungle as well as bushmaster snakes. Yeah, the jungle didn't sound a good bet to her.

Hurrying back through the bedroom to the bathroom, Sarita turned on the shower taps and then went to fetch towels. She meant to grab one, but quickly changed her mind and grabbed four instead, tossing three on the makeup table before taking the other with her to sling over the shower. It had occurred to her that the large towels could come in handy. They could be useful just as towels, but could also be used to bundle everything up in and carry slung over their shoulders like Santa's sack. That was the reason for two of them. The third one was because she was considering turning it into a toga rather than using a sheet. The towels were quite big and should reach well below her knees. They were also thick, offering more protection from bugs and snakes. But aside from that it would demand the least effort. She could wear a swimsuit, wrap the towel around herself and then use one of the large safety pins in the sewing kit to pin the towel closed. She could even use a second one to secure it to her bikini top so that there would be no risk of the towel dropping and tripping her up.

Satisfied with that idea, Sarita stripped off her bikini and stepped quickly under the water.

She took care in washing the cuts along her upper legs as well as those on her feet. And was careful to scrub every last inch of her body to be sure she removed every trace of the dried blood she'd missed during her earlier shower. She even shampooed her hair again to ensure she removed any drops of blood that may have splattered there. With all of that, it still didn't take her more than three or four minutes to shower.

Turning off the water, Sarita tugged the towel off the panel where she'd placed it. She scrubbed her hair with it to dry it as much as possible and then simply wrapped it around herself, toga-style. Grabbing the other three towels as well as both the first aid and emergency sewing kits, she then left the bathroom.

Sarita entered the closet a moment later and quickly went through the swimsuits in the drawers again. She retrieved and donned the most decent of the remaining bikinis, a black number that she hadn't noticed earlier. It actually had more than a thong back unlike most of the others, and the top actually looked like it might at least cover her nipples.

She opened the first aid kit next, considered the contents, and then set to work smearing her injuries with antiseptic cream. Once that was done, she slapped a fabric bandage over each wound, including the ones on her feet.

Satisfied she'd done all she could, Sarita set the first aid kit next to the sewing kit and grabbed one of the large towels. She wrapped it around herself, and then opened the sewing kit to retrieve a couple of the large safety pins to pin the towel into place.

Satisfied, she then turned her attention to the shoes in the closet.

Seven

Domitian closed the last box along the wall and shoved it away with irritation. He'd come downstairs to finish searching the boxes and see if he could find anything to wear besides the boxers he presently had on. It was a sensible idea. He could hardly go traipsing into the jungle in just boxers. Well, really he could, but Sarita couldn't in a negligee and high heels, and she had mentioned that those were the only clothes available to her here besides bikinis.

Unfortunately his search had turned up nothing. Not only were there no clothes in the crumbling old boxes in the room at the bottom of the stairs, but there wasn't anything else they might use when they left this place either.

Turning away from the boxes, Domitian started for the stairs. He would check on Sarita and see if she was nearly ready. He had set out some things in the kitchen for their supposed picnic, but they would need more than he had out. He just didn't want to bring the rest out until Sarita was ready to go. The more time they had to get as far away as they could from the cottage before Dressler sent his men out to stop them, the better.

He headed to the kitchen first, hoping she might be done with her shower and waiting for him there. Domitian didn't find Sarita, but he did find proof of her recent presence. It looked as if someone had ransacked the place and he was quite sure that neither Dressler nor any of his men were responsible for it the moment his gaze slid over towels, canned food, and a first aid kit.

That was all he bothered to catalog before hurrying to the bedroom. They had to get moving. If Dressler was watching the camera feed, all that stuff on the island would tip him to the fact that a simple picnic wasn't their intention.

A muffled thudding reached Domitian's ears long before he reached the bedroom. Frowning at the sound, he pushed through the door and spotted Sarita almost immediately. There was a closet to the left of the bed that he hadn't noticed before. The door was open and Sarita was sitting on the floor, wrapped in a towel . . . trying to beat a shoe to death with a . . . can opener?

Slowing, Domitian walked to the door and peered down at her.

"Hi," she said, not bothering to glance up.

"Hi yourself," he responded. "What are you doing?"

"Trying to get the heel off this shoe," she answered, and then gave the heel another whack with the can opener before explaining, "I'd rather not go traipsing through the jungle barefoot if we have to go that way."

Sarita paused to examine the shoe she'd been pounding. "The leather feels soft. It might flatten out a bit with a little wear. I just need to get the heel off—"

Her words died as Domitian bent, plucked the shoe from her hand and snapped the heel off with little effort.

"Huh," Sarita muttered, taking the shoe when he handed it back. Pursing her lips, she examined it briefly and then muttered "Thank you" as he bent to pick up the second shoe and snapped off its heel as well.

"We have to go," he said, offering her a hand to get up.

"Yeah. I know." Ignoring his hand, she got to her feet and moved past him into the bedroom. Grabbing two large bath towels off the bed in passing, she led the way to the door.

Domitian followed, his gaze on her legs below the towel she had wrapped around her body. She'd obviously taken a shower as suggested. Her hair was still wet, he noted.

"I gathered together some things we might need before I thought of the shoes," Sarita announced as she led him through the living room.

"That would not be the pile of stuff on the island in the kitchen would it?" Domitian asked with a frown.

"Yes. I thought we could load it all into these two towels and carry it Santa-style." She held up the bath towels she'd grabbed as she spoke.

"Santa-style?" Domitian echoed with bewilderment. What the hell was Santa-style?

"Like a sack," she explained. "We put the items in the middle, gather the ends, and hoist them over our shoulders to carry them."

"Dear God," he muttered with dismay.

"What?" Sarita asked over her shoulder and he could

hear amusement in her voice. "You're a big strong guy. You could probably carry it all by yourself if you had to."

"Yes, but Sarita, we cannot possibly drag everything you have piled in the kitchen with us," he said reasonably. "I do not think everything will even fit in two towels. We would probably need six to fit it all. Surely we do not need all of it?"

They had reached the kitchen by then and Sarita considered the stack of items on the island and snatched up a pile of towels. Tossing them onto the stove, she said, "I suppose we don't need those. The supersized bath towels can do double duty as Santa sacks and towels if necessary."

Domitian raised his eyebrows. That was all she didn't think they'd need? His gaze swept the stack of items and he picked up a plastic box about the size of a ream of paper. "What about this?"

"It's a sewing kit," she explained, taking it away from him and setting it back on the island with the other items.

"You intend to get in a little sewing around the campfire at night?" he asked dryly.

"Not me, but those boxers of yours look kind of flimsy. Catch them on a branch or something else and you might be as good as naked if we don't have something to sew them up," she pointed out, and then shrugged and added, "But I was thinking more along the lines that the sewing kit might come in handy if one of us gets badly injured and needs sewing up. The first aid kit has antiseptic and bandages and such, but nothing to close a deep wound."

That gave Domitian pause. Considering the cuts in her upper legs and the glass in her foot, Sarita was proving almost more dangerous to herself than Dressler was so far. If she continued as she was going, he might very well have to sew up some wound or other at some point. Still, they could just take a spool of thread and a needle. It wasn't necessary to drag the whole sewing kit along with them, he thought and was about to say so when Sarita spoke up again.

"Besides, while it's larger than I'd like, it's a nice flat surface and might come in handy for cleaning fish on, or setting things on that we don't want to get dirty, like bandages. *And*," she added, picking it up again and hefting it. "It's pretty light, so won't add to the weight."

"Very well." Domitian gave in. Her arguments were actually pretty good, but there was still way too much for them to be carting around, so he turned to the island and snatched up a pile of white cloth, only to frown as it unraveled and he recognized it. "Is this your night-gown?"

"It *was* the nightgown I was wearing," Sarita corrected, apparently unwilling to claim it as her own. Picking up a second ball of cloth, she said, "And this is the robe I was wearing. But—" she pulled the hem of the robe over her head and grinned at him through the gossamer material, "—now they're mosquito netting to keep the bugs out while we sleep. I washed the blood out of both of them," Sarita added and then examined the material as she removed it and pronounced, "They're both almost dry already."

It was actually a pretty clever idea, but Domitian didn't say so. He was troubled by the fact that she seemed to think they would have to walk for more than a day to find civilization and help. Or perhaps he was more distressed that he couldn't assure her that wouldn't be the case. Turning to the items on the island, he pulled out a racket next and pursed his lips as he spun it in his hand.

"A tennis racket? Really?" Domitian shook his head. "Where did you even find it?"

"It's a badminton racket," she corrected, taking it from him. "And I found it in one of the wicker storage boxes on the terrace. There was a badminton net too and I considered bringing that, but it's far too big and bulky, so I decided that the racket and stockings would do instead."

"Do for what?" he asked with bewilderment.

"As a fishing net," she said as if that should be obvious. When he merely stared at her blankly, Sarita sighed with exasperation and picked up one of a pair of stockings. Holding the racket up, she explained, "We slice out the strings of the racket so it's a hoop, loop the top of the stocking over the hoop and sew it on, and voila, a net to catch fish." Peering at the silky cloth Sarita smiled wryly and added, "A shame they aren't fishnet stockings, huh?"

Domitian smiled faintly at her joke, but merely said, "That is brilliant." He took a moment to enjoy the satisfaction his compliment brought to her face, but then asked quietly, "But you have canned food and water here too. Do you really think we will need to find fish for supper? Just how long do you think it is going to take us to find help?"

Sarita's pleasure faded at once. Turning back to the island, she set the racket and stockings down and then quietly admitted, "I don't know. But Venezuela's coastline is more than 1,700 miles long. A lot of it is inhabited, but not all, and there are at least four national parks along the coast too that aren't inhabited. I really don't think Dressler would have put us here if it was close to help. Do you?"

"No," Domitian acknowledged solemnly. He'd planned to just pack up Sarita and a few items and charge out of here like a bull charging a red cape. He hadn't considered that it might take longer than he hoped to reach help. Now he considered that and realized this might be more dangerous than he'd first thought. He hadn't considered the effects of trekking for days through the woods without blood to top himself up, or that he might become dangerous to Sarita if that happened. And that was just as a result of the passage of time. It didn't take into account the exertion of the trek, the effects of the heat and sun, or the possibility of injury. Any of those could quickly leave him in serious need of blood and dangerous.

Once those issues were factored in, Domitian began to wonder if this was such a good idea. But they really had no choice.

"Right," he said aloud, straightening and turning on his heel.

"Where are you going?" Sarita asked with surprise.

"I shall be right back," he said instead of answering. "But then we are going to sort through every last item here and get rid of anything that is not absolutely necessary. We cannot possibly take all of this with us."

Domitian didn't wait for her response but made his way quickly to the office and then down into the basement. He'd top up before leaving. Not too much, the nanos would just work to get it out of his system. But Domitian wanted to start out with as much blood in his system as he could safely consume to ensure he lasted as long as possible. He didn't want to harm Sarita.

Trying to distract himself from that worry, Domitian started running through a mental list of the items he'd taken note of upstairs, trying to decide what they could leave behind.

"What time do you think it is?"

Domitian glanced toward Sarita, his mouth twisting with displeasure when he saw how she was flagging under the weight of the "Santa sack" she carried over her shoulder. Despite his determination that they wouldn't take everything she'd collected, in the end they had.

Oh, he'd tried to whittle down the contents, but Sarita had a reason for every item she'd chosen, and her reasons were good. At least they sounded good when she explained them. So they'd ended up piling everything onto the two towels and then gathered the ends making a "Santa sack" each.

While Sarita had teased earlier that he was a big strong guy and could probably carry all of it on his own, her bag was as big, bulky, and heavy as his was. He had tried to take the heavier items in his own bag to lighten her load, but she had refused to allow it, insisting on dividing the items evenly between them and carrying "her share."

The woman was stubborn as a mule, Domitian thought but found his mouth curving into a slight smile at the knowledge. He kind of liked that about her. Oh, not that she was stubborn, really, so much as that she wasn't acting like an entitled princess, expecting him to take care of her and carry the load alone. He liked that she was independent and determined to take care of herself. Still, he hated to see her struggling under the weight of her Santa sack when he could easily carry both without much effort. The problem was finding a way to get her to let him take more of the burden. She was proud and independent. It was tricky.

"Domitian?"

"Hmm?" He dragged his mind from his thoughts and glanced at her face inquisitively.

"What time do you think it is?" she asked, sounding a little annoyed that she had to repeat the question.

Domitian turned his gaze to the darkening sky over-head. In Caracas, the sun rose between five minutes to six and about ten or twelve minutes after six every morning, but it set eight minutes after six pretty much every night. He didn't think the house they'd been put in could be far from Caracas if the doctor had lived in it while first teaching at the university. Shrugging, he said, "Probably a little before six o'clock."

"Dinnertime," Sarita muttered.

Domitian frowned. They'd only been walking for about an hour, but while they'd started out at a quick clip, Sarita had begun to fall behind a bit after the first half hour. It had surprised him. She was a fit woman. But then she was carrying that ridiculously heavy Santa sack. And trudging through the sand took more energy than walking on the hard-packed earth of the jungle would have.

Domitian had wanted to take the jungle route ini-tially, but had quickly changed his mind. It wasn't be-cause of Sarita's argument that they could get lost too easily in the jungle, where they wouldn't be able to see the sun's position to ensure they traveled in a straight line, or that it was likely to be full of poisonous snakes and other dangerous animals. It was more because she didn't have any proper clothes or shoes.

Domitian had been a little stunned when he'd suggested she go dress before they leave and she'd announced that she *was* dressed. And then she'd pointed out that she had the bikini on underneath, that she'd pinned the towel to it, and that it certainly covered her more decently than any of the nighties in the walk-in closet would. He supposed it did. Although he suspected one of the long negligees, while sheer, would have at least protected more of her from insect bites. And that was the only reason he thought that perhaps she should have worn one of those instead. It had absolutely nothing to do with the fact that he was recalling, and missing, the view he'd had of her breasts, stomach, and thighs, not to mention the sexy little thong she'd had on under the gauzy white nightgown he'd seen her in. At least that's what he told himself, but even he wasn't buying it.

As for shoes, even without the heels, the ones she'd chosen made walking awkward for her. The leather may have seemed softer and more likely to flatten out than the other shoes she'd had to choose from, but the soles were not flat. The shoes had retained their form, only now without the heel to offer its little bit of support. The moment she'd put them on and staggered across the kitchen, Domitian's mind had been made up. She couldn't possibly wear the shoes as they were. They would have to take the beach. At least at the start. He planned to soak the shoes in the sea for a while on their first stop to see if he couldn't flatten them out after that for her. In the meantime, he hadn't been willing to risk the jungle with her barefoot. So they'd set out along the beach, determined to keep an eye peeled for approaching boats in case Dressler sent men after them.

Now, though, her comment that it was dinnertime made Domitian glance to Sarita with concern and ask, "When did you last eat?"

Sarita was silent for a minute, and then reluctantly admitted, "Supper last night. If it was last night that Dressler drugged me."

Cursing, Domitian turned to head for the trees that bordered the beach.

"What are you—Hey!" Sarita protested when he snatched her "Santa sack" in passing and slung it over his shoulder with his own makeshift bag.

It said a lot that Sarita didn't protest further, but trudged along after him. That alone told him that she must be on her last leg.

As an immortal Domitian didn't have to eat so long as he consumed blood. Sarita, however, had to eat for energy, and while he'd fed countless times that day and even taken in extra blood before they'd left, Sarita hadn't eaten at all.

He hadn't seen her drink anything today either, Domitian thought with a frown. Here she'd taken care of him, fetched him blood and popped it to his mouth when she woke up on the terrace and he still slept, and he hadn't bothered to even ask if she'd eaten. And he was a chef!

Upset at himself for his lack of consideration, Domitian glared at Sarita when she dropped to sit on the sand with a weary sigh.

"It was foolish of you to go without food," he growled, though he was more upset at himself than her.

"I often do foolish things," Sarita informed him, not

sounding concerned. "It's part of my charm. My father used to say so," she added, and flopped back to lie in the sand.

"He did, did he?" Domitian asked, a reluctant smile tugging at his lips and forcing his anger back. Setting down the bags and dropping to sit next to her, he began going through their contents in search of something healthy for her to eat.

"Yes," Sarita assured him and suddenly sat up to lean past him and snatch a can from the pile of items in the nearest bag. Waving it in front of his face, she added, "Besides, you haven't eaten either."

"No, I have not," Domitian agreed. The difference was he didn't need food if there was blood available. There wasn't blood available to him right now, however, and eating would reduce the amount of blood he would need. Not by that much, but every little bit helped when you were without. Besides, it would lighten the load in their sacks if they ate some of it, but Domitian frowned as he read the label on the can she was waving at him. "Canned fruit?"

"Nourishment and liquid too," she said simply and dropped the can in his lap before reaching for another as well as the can opener. Sarita made quick work of opening her own can, and then handed him the opener and sat back to begin picking fruit out of the metal tin and popping it in her mouth.

Domitian watched her briefly, but then opened his own can and began to eat the fruit inside. It actually wasn't bad, considering, he decided. It wasn't that good either, though.

"So, you are a chef," Sarita commented after they'd eaten in silence for a few moments.

Catching the wistful tone in her voice, Domitian glanced over to see her eyeing the label on her can with dissatisfaction. It seemed she wasn't completely happy with her meal. He couldn't blame her, Domitian decided as he chewed a piece of what he thought might be peach. The can label said mixed fruit, but while the pieces inside were of varying shapes and colors they all seemed to taste the same. He should have made her a meal before they'd left the house, he thought. Something hearty and filling and as delicious as he found her. He would like to cook for Sarita, Domitian thought. He wanted to satisfy all her appetites. Unfortunately, at the moment they didn't have the time for him to satisfy even one.

Deciding to distract them both from what they couldn't have, Domitian picked another piece of fruit out of his can, and commented idly, "Dr. Dressler is your grandmother's employer?"

"Yeah. She's worked for him for . . . God, I don't even know how long it's been," Sarita admitted and then tilted her head skyward and tried to work it out aloud. "Forty-some years, at least," she guessed finally. "My father was a little boy when she started to work for Dr. Dressler," Sarita said. "She apparently worked for him and his wife for eight or nine months before leaving my father and grandfather to move to the island."

"So she lived at home and came here to the house where we were placed at first, and then once they moved to the island she left your grandfather to live on the island permanently?" Domitian asked with interest. This was news to him. The reports from his private detective had only covered the fact that her grandmother still lived in Venezuela, worked for Dr. Dressler, and that Sarita wrote to the woman weekly. It hadn't covered the history of the grandmother. That hadn't been important to Domitian. At least, not until his uncle had arrived in Venezuela with several hunters in tow, claiming Dressler was behind the recent rash of immortals that had gone missing.

"Yes. Well, I don't know if it was just for the job. Maybe my grandfather was abusive or something. I don't know the whole story. It's the one thing Grandmother is reticent about. But, Dad—" she shook her head sadly "—he never forgave her for abandoning them. She apparently tried calling to speak to him, but he wouldn't take the calls, so she started sending weekly letters that he tore up and threw out."

Domitian's eyebrows rose. "Then how did you end up in contact with her?"

"My mother," Sarita said simply.

"How?" he asked. "Did she insist you write her?"

"No." She frowned at the suggestion, and explained, "Grandmother didn't know that Father was throwing out her letters. She must have suspected when she never got a reply, but she kept writing anyway and was still sending weekly letters when he and my mother married. Mom said he never mentioned the letters to her while they were courting, and when the first one arrived after their wedding, she was the only one home to receive it."

"She said she didn't think much of it until she gave it to Dad and he just tore it up and threw it in the garbage, and then left the room. She said he was grumpy the rest of the evening, which was unusual for him, and then was fine after that until the next letter about a week later, and the next. Mother said four letters came in four weeks that he just tore up and threw out, and each was followed by a night where he was angry and miserable to live with. By that fourth letter she'd had enough. She waited until he had slammed from the room as usual, retrieved the letter, and hid it away.

"After he left for work the next morning, she fetched the letter. Then she sat down at the table, taped it back together, and read it. She was shocked when she realized it was from his mother. There had only ever been my grandfather in my father's life since she'd known him and Father had always refused to talk about his mother, so Mom had assumed Grandmother was dead and talking about her was just too painful for him."

Sarita fell silent for a minute and picked up her can again to pluck another piece of fruit out of it. After chewing and swallowing, she shook her head and said, "I don't know what was in that first letter, but my mother decided to write her back herself. Her first note was just to let my grandmother know who she was and that Dad didn't read her letters, but just ripped them up and threw them out."

Sarita smiled faintly. "Mom said she was just hoping that once the woman knew she was wasting her time writing, she'd stop sending letters and upsetting Dad. But a week later another letter arrived, this time addressed to her."

"Whatever was in that letter apparently touched my mom," Sarita said solemnly. "She answered it and every week another letter came addressed to her, and every week my mother answered. She told Grandmother about herself, my father, their life together, and then about me when I was born. She said Dad never asked if he'd received his weekly letter, and she never explained why he wasn't getting them anymore. It became the only secret she ever kept from him."

"When did you find out about the letters?" Domitian asked when she fell silent.

"I was about eleven," Sarita said with a small reminiscent smile that fascinated Domitian. It suggested a softer side to her she seemed determined to keep hidden most of the time.

"I was snooping and came across a box stuffed full of letters," Sarita explained. "Mother had kept every one in case my father ever had a change of heart and wanted contact with his mother. He could read the letters. Instead, I found and read a bunch of them before she caught me. Mother explained how she had come to correspond with Grandmother and made me swear not to tell my father. It became our secret then."

"And you started to write her too," he suggested, but Sarita shook her head.

"No." She peered down into her can of fruit, and swallowed, before saying gruffly, "That didn't happen until my mother died when I was thirteen. When the first letter arrived from Grandmother after that, I wrote her to explain that mother was dead and could not answer her letters anymore. The next letter was addressed to me. We've been writing ever since."

"And your father never knew?" Domitian asked.

"Are you kidding?" she asked with dry amusement. "That man knew everything. He pretended not to know though."

"What makes you think that? Perhaps he did not know."

Sarita shook her head. "There were many times when he got to the mail before Mom or I could. He must have seen the letters. He would have recognized the handwriting, but he never said anything."

"Hmm," Domitian murmured, but asked, "Did your mother ever take you to meet her?"

"No." Sarita shook her head. "Grandmother never left the island or invited us to it."

"Until now," he said.

Sarita frowned now, her lips pursing as she shook her head again. "Actually, she didn't invite me this time either. Dr. Dressler did."

Domitian stilled.

"Dressler called me last weekend," she explained. "He introduced himself as Grandmother's employer, said she'd taken a tumble on the stairs and hurt herself. He said he was concerned. She was older and injuries like hers could lead to complications in the elderly. He felt that a visit from me might help perk her up and ensure her recovery. He asked me to come to the island to surprise her." Sighing, she added, "I had two weeks of vacation coming up. I asked for it off and was on a flight two days later."

"So you got to the island . . . three days ago?" he guessed.

"Four," she corrected. "He called Saturday. I flew out Monday, and then wasted three days kicking up my heels before Dressler knocked me out and brought me here. Today would be the fourth day since I flew here to Venezuela. Unless I was unconscious more than just overnight as I assumed when I woke up here, this is Friday."

Domitian nodded. It had been Thursday when he'd gone to meet the helicopter that he'd thought was to take him to the island. She was probably right that it was Friday. Unless, as she'd said, he too had been unconscious for more than just a night. Pushing that worry away, he asked, "Did you think it odd that it was Dr. Dressler who invited you and not your grandmother?"

"Yeah." Sarita nodded and then shook her head and said, "But no. I thought she'd taken a bad spill and was weak and sick. I thought it was good of him to call me," she added bitterly.

They were both silent for a minute and then she said thoughtfully, "You know, my grandmother rarely mentioned Dr. Dressler in her letters, but when she did it seemed obvious she didn't care for him at all and didn't consider him an "honorable man" as she put it. I should have realized there was something up when he called. Barring that, I should have realized at the airport, or when I got to the island."

"Why at the airport?" Domitian asked with curiosity.

"Because when I landed here I didn't even go through customs," Sarita told him grimly. "We landed on the tarmac. They rolled up one of those portable stair thingies for us to disembark, and when I got to the bottom of the stairs, this big beefy guy in a suit stepped in front of me. He asked if I was Sarita Reyes. I said yes I was and, while everyone else continued into the airport and to customs, he just took my arm and steered me to this jeep. My luggage was already waiting there," she added, and when Domitian's eyebrows rose, she explained, "My seat was on the back of the plane. I was one of the last to disembark. Everyone's luggage was out and on this big metal shelf on wheels on the tarmac when I came out. Well, except my luggage, which, as I said, was already in the jeep."

When he nodded, she continued. "Anyway, the minute the big beefy guy had me in the jeep, it took off and drove farther down the tarmac to where a helicopter was waiting. Big Beefy Guy loaded me and my luggage in, plopped himself down beside me, and we took off and flew to the island. I didn't go through customs or immigration or *anything*," she said and then shook her head. "Jeez, I knew crime and corruption were bad here, but seriously, skipping customs and immigration? Who does that?"

Domitian merely shook his head and didn't bother mentioning that immortals did that on a regular basis. It wasn't germane to the conversation. Besides, Dressler was not immortal, although he had several at his disposal. Immortals he'd kidnapped. Perhaps the man had coerced one of them to handle things at the airport, he thought. If not, it must have cost him a lot of money to ensure Sarita's arrival in Venezuela wasn't recorded. That didn't suggest that his plans for her included her leaving, he thought with concern.

"Anyway, once we got to the island, Big Beefy Guy ordered two men to bring the luggage and then showed me up to my room. I thanked him and asked when I could see my grandmother and he said she wasn't on the island. She was in the hospital on the mainland. But would be home soon."

"I am surprised you didn't demand to go to the mainland to see her," Domitian commented.

"I did," Sarita said grimly. "But Big Beefy Guy said he couldn't authorize that—he said that I would have to wait for Dr. Dressler to return. He was the only one who could give permission for use of the helicopter or boat to take me to the mainland. In the meantime, I should just relax and *enjoy my stay*," Sarita finished with disgust.

"That must have been frustrating," Domitian murmured.

"Yeah, you could call it that," Sarita said dryly. "Actually, I was super P.O.'d. Especially when I found out that Big Beefy Guy had misled me. He made it sound like Dr. Dressler wasn't on the island and there was no way to contact him. Meantime, Dressler was there on the island all along, just down at his labs."

"How did you find that out?" Domitian asked.

"Aleta."

"The cook?" he asked, recognizing the name.

Sarita nodded and quickly told him about her early dinner in the kitchen and Aleta's having made El Doctor's nutrition drink. "That's when I snuck down to the labs and saw the immortal cut in half."

They were both silent for a minute, and then Sarita frowned and said, "You know, my grandmother started out as a cook and housekeeper for the Dresslers, but as she got older they brought in more help. She mentioned that someone was hired to cook, and then later someone to help with cleaning house, and I got the feeling that now she's more a companion to Mrs. Dressler."

"*Si?*" Domitian murmured, wondering where she was going with this.

"But none of the names matched up," Sarita said now. "I mean, I can't remember the name she mentioned—it was only the once—but I'm pretty sure the cook she named wasn't Aleta."

"Perhaps the first girl left and was replaced with this Aleta and your grandmother just didn't mention it," Domitian suggested.

"Yeah, that's what I thought too, but she also only mentioned one girl being brought in to help with house-keeping and there were at least three at the house," Sarita continued. "And before you say it, yes I know they might have hired more help over the years that Grandmother didn't mention, but on top of that, I didn't once encounter Mrs. Dressler or their son even once while I was there."

"Son?" Domitian asked with surprise. His uncle hadn't mentioned that Dressler had a son.

"Hmm . . ." Sarita nodded solemnly. "Grandmother mentioned him several times over the years. I got the feeling she thought he was the perfect son. His name is Thorondor."

"Thorondor?" Domitian asked, wincing over the un-usual name. Life would be hell for a boy with a name like that. Children could be cruel.

Sarita shrugged. "I guess Mrs. Dressler was a Tol-kien fan. They call him Thorne for short."

Domitian nodded, but suggested, "Perhaps this Thorne and his mother are staying in their apartment on the mainland so that Mrs. Dressler could visit your grand-mother daily." He knew his uncle had sent men to check the apartment on the mainland and found it empty. But Mrs. Dressler and this Thorne fellow could have been at the hospital at the time, he supposed.

"I didn't know they had an apartment on the main-land," Sarita said slowly. "I did think maybe she was on the mainland, though, to visit Grandmother, but . . ."

"But?" he prompted.

She hesitated, and then admitted, "During the three days I was on the island, I wandered pretty much ev-erywhere in that house. Every door was open except for Dr. Dressler's office door and I looked into every room I could." Shaking her head solemnly, she added, "There was no sign of Mrs. Dressler or Thorne. I didn't see either of them, and there were no pictures or personal items to suggest either they or my grandmother ever lived there. Every room, even what was obviously the master bedroom was . . ." Sarita frowned, searching for the words to explain what she'd found. "They all looked unlived in. They were like empty hotel rooms. Furnished and ready for occupancy, but unused at the moment."

"And when I asked Aleta where Dr. Dressler's wife and son were, she just gave me this blank look as if she'd never heard that he had a wife. Then Big Beefy Guy came into the kitchen and told me to stop bothering the staff with questions that were none of my business. He suggested I go out in the garden or otherwise amuse myself."

Domitian shook his head, not sure what to say, or even what to make of this information. He'd never really given Senora Dressler much thought. Ensuring his life mate was safe and finding out the location of the island as well as what Dr. Dressler was up to had been his only concerns when he'd agreed to go.

"As we were walking here I started to wonder if Mrs. Dressler, Thorne, and my grandmother didn't live in the small house," she added thoughtfully.

"The small house?" Domitian asked at once. "What small house? You never mentioned a small house."

"It never came up," Sarita said with a shrug.

"It is up now. Explain," he requested firmly.

She seemed amused by his stiff voice, but said, "When we flew in on the helicopter I got to see the whole island. The fenced-in area with the labs was on the tip of the island as we approached, there was a bit of jungle and then the big house came next with an open area around it. After that there was a large expanse of jungle, but at the very tip of the far end of the island there was a smaller house on the beach with a pool beside it."

"A small house with a pool?" Domitian asked, straightening from where he'd relaxed back against the base of a palm tree. His voice sharp, he added, "Like the house we just left?"

"Yeah. I considered that myself as we were walking," Sarita admitted, sounding unconcerned. "But then I thought about not encountering Mrs. Dressler or her son at the big house and decided they—and my grandmother—probably live in the little house instead. I mean, who would want to live with Dressler? The man's a monster.

"Of course," she added with a frown. "Now that I know about the apartment, I suppose that could be where they are. The big house could be like a cottage. Where they usually stay on the weekends and in the summer when Dressler isn't teaching. That could explain the hotel air to the place." Following that through, Sarita continued slowly, "But if they normally stay in the big house and just aren't there now because they returned to the mainland to stay close to Grandmother, then the little house isn't where they live . . . which means it *could* be the little house that we woke up in after being drugged."

Domitian couldn't have been more stunned if she'd pulled a hammer out from under the towel she was wearing and suddenly hit him with it. For a minute his thoughts were in such chaos, he couldn't even hold on to one.

He'd rushed them out of the house to get her as far away as possible to somewhere she'd be safe from Dressler, and instead might be walking her straight into his arms.

Cursing under his breath, he leapt to his feet.

"Where are you going?" Sarita asked with alarm, getting up as well.

"It is okay. I just want to go a little farther along the beach and see if you are right and we are still on the island," he said reassuringly.

"But what if you're seen?" she asked with concern.

"I will be careful. But I have to see if you are right, *mi Corazon*. If we are on Dressler's island then we have to find a way off it, and quickly. And walking up to the house and asking for a ride is not the way to go about it. Just sit and rest for a bit. I will be back before you know it," he said and then turned and hurried away before she could argue further.

Sarita watched until Domitian followed the curving beach out of sight, and then turned to glance out toward the water. She'd been keeping an eye out for anyone approaching in a boat as they walked, and even if they were on the island with the house and labs as she suspected, she still had to because water was the only way to approach the house.

From the helicopter, Sarita had thought she'd spotted a road disappearing into the jungle in the direction of the little house, but if that's where they were, apparently it didn't go all the way to it. They'd double-checked before setting out and hadn't found even so much as a dirt path to walk on.

Movement out of the corner of her eye drew Sarita's head quickly around, but she relaxed when she spotted Domitian jogging toward her. Her first reaction was relief, until she noted the vexed expression on his face.

"What's wrong?" she asked as he stopped and simply gathered the ends of first one towel and then the other.

Domitian didn't really answer her question. He merely slung both Santa sacks over his shoulder as he straightened. Turning back the way he'd come, he then said, "Come with me," and started walking at a quick clip.

Sarita frowned and hurried after him, but his legs were longer, allowing him to take larger strides. The shifting sand underfoot didn't help either. It had made walking difficult even when they'd been moving at the slower pace they'd settled into on leaving the house, which was why they'd moved down to walk in the wet and more solid surf despite the risk of being spotted by an approaching boat. Domitian had matched his stride to hers then so as not to leave her behind, but he wasn't now. He seemed to be in the grip of some strong emotion and eager to get to where he was taking her, so Sarita bit back her protest at his speed and tried to move a little more quickly.

With her focus on Domitian and keeping up with him, Sarita didn't notice the dock at first when it appeared before them. Or anything else really, until he stopped and turned back to peer at her.

Slowing, Sarita took in his inscrutable expression and finally glanced around at their surroundings. Her heart stuttered with anxiety when she spotted the dock a little ahead on their left, and her head quickly jerked to the right even as her feet stopped moving altogether, but then she just gaped at the house above the beach.

Sarita didn't know what she was expecting to see. The dock was much smaller than the one in front of Dr. Dressler's house. Still, the last thing she expected was to find herself peering at the same house she'd woken up in that morning, and which they'd left behind a little more than an hour ago.

"But—" She glanced back the way they'd come, briefly wondering if they'd somehow got turned around and come back the way they'd left, but even as she did it, she knew that wasn't what had happened. She had been wrong. This wasn't Dr. Dressler's island. At least not the one where the houses and labs were. It was a different, much smaller island . . . and they'd just walked all the way around it and right back to the house they'd been trying to escape.

Eight

Sarita surfaced in the pool and ran her hands over her hair, pushing the water back along the soaking strands and away from her face. Letting her hands drop into the water, she then peered toward the waterfall with a little sigh. It was as beautiful at night as it had been during the day. There were lights in the pool as well as along the edges of the waterfall. They were also on the house, brightening the terrace. So, even at night it was a truly beautiful spot, a little bit of paradise in the middle of the ocean.

Too bad it was like that Eagles' song, Sarita thought, you could never leave. At least, that's how it seemed to her, because as far as she could tell, they were stuck there.

Sighing again, she leaned back to float in the water and stared up at the night sky overhead. By her guess, perhaps half an hour had passed since Domitian had led her to the beach in front of the house. After getting over her shock at finding herself there again and realizing the ramifications, Sarita had glanced at Domitian. He'd noted her expression and then had turned silently and led her back into the house.

They hadn't said a word to each other since. Domitian had simply set down the bags on the floor in the entry and then had disappeared into the office. Sarita had briefly considered unpacking the bags and putting everything away, but then had thought, *Why bother?*

She'd headed for the bedroom and the bathroom beyond. Their excursion, short as it had been, had left her hot and sweaty and covered with sand; a shower had seemed a good idea. But once she'd got there, she'd simply stood in the bathroom and looked around at the opulent setting, her stomach churning. It was part of a prison. A pretty prison, but a prison just the same and Sarita suddenly couldn't bear even being inside.

Turning, she'd retraced her steps and made her way back out to the living room where the pool had caught her eye. The cool water had seemed to be calling out to her, offering to soothe her stressed body. The next thing Sarita knew she was moving to the doors. By the time she'd reached them, she had undone the two pins fastening the towel to her bathing suit top. She'd opened the door and stepped out to walk to the edge of the pool, undoing the last pin, the one that kept the towel closed, as she went. Then she'd simply let the pins and towel drop and made a shallow dive into the pool.

Now she lay in the cooling water, surrounded by the soothing sounds of nature. The whisper of the breeze through the trees of the jungle surrounding the pool. The twitter of night birds. The splash of water traveling over the rock waterfall at one end of the pool . . .

It should have been a little slice of heaven—instead, it was a kind of hell.

"Sarita?"

Straightening in the water, she turned toward the house, spotting Domitian at once. He'd come out of the dining room and was moving through the living room toward the door to the bedroom as he searched for her. She called out to him and he paused at once and glanced her way.

Spotting her through the glass doors, Domitian used the one she'd left open and slipped outside to stand by the pool. He then just stared at her.

Sarita stared back, wondering why he'd gone to the office.

"Are you okay?" he asked finally.

"As okay as a cockroach in a Roach Motel," she said sarcastically. When confusion covered his face, she realized he wouldn't understand the reference and explained, "They are cockroach traps. The cockroach goes in, but is caught and can't get back out."

Domitian didn't smile at her poor joke. Expression serious he said, "We are not trapped, Sarita. I promise I will get you off this island and take you somewhere safe."

"You shouldn't make promises you can't keep."

"I can keep it," he assured her.

"You're forgetting that Dr. Dressler could be back at any moment. He could be pulling up to the dock in a boat right now," she pointed out.

"He will not come here so soon," Domitian assured her.

"You can't know that," she said.

"His letter said he had this house renovated and up-dated for just this eventuality," he reminded her and pointed out, "He would hardly go to that trouble and expense for one day's use."

"True," Sarita said thoughtfully. She'd forgotten about that part of the letter. "But why did he do it? What the hell does he want from us?" she asked, and heard the frustration in her own voice.

"I do not know," Domitian admitted, and then announced, "I made us a meal."

Sarita almost snapped that she wasn't hungry, but she actually was, and taking out her temper on him would not get her the answers she wanted. Shaking her head, she moved to the stairs and walked out of the pool.

Domitian was waiting with a towel held open.

"Thank you," Sarita murmured, when he wrapped it around her shoulders. Clutching the ends under her chin, she moved past him, saying, "I'll just go change. I'll be quick."

If he responded, she didn't hear it as she hurried back inside.

Two minutes later, Sarita had removed the damp towel Domitian had wrapped around her and was glancing from it to the somewhat lacking wardrobe that was available to her. She briefly considered pulling on a dry swimsuit and pinning a fresh towel to it, one that wasn't damp, but really all the remaining swimsuits had thong bottoms that were just plain uncomfortable. She wasn't eager to wear any of them. Besides, the towel she'd worn as a toga that day was a dirty heap by the pool, the one she'd just removed was damp and would be uncomfortable, and between their using them after showers and swimming, and her raiding them to carry their items, the stack of towels was shrinking quickly. They'd soon be out of clean towels if she kept using them as clothing.

Dropping the damp one, she turned resolutely to the clothing supplied to her and wondered with disgust who had picked all these ridiculous nightgowns. Muttering under her breath, she settled on a black one with a short, sheer skirt, but lace on the top that would mostly cover her breasts. She'd have to wear a thong with it for it to be anywhere near decent, but the top was what Domitian would see sitting at the table and that was her main concern. Most of the other gowns were sheer there too.

She pulled it on quickly, found a black thong, donned it with a grimace and then hurried into the bathroom to run a brush through her wet hair. Her gaze slid briefly to the makeup table as she did, but then slid away. This wasn't a date. The last thing she needed was to make herself attractive. They already had trouble keeping their hands off each other and she didn't want to end up splayed on the dining room table and howling for the cameras as Domitian—

Sarita cut that thought off quickly as she felt heat pool in her groin. Honestly, she was like a bitch in heat around the man. Just thinking about him made her . . .

Rather than finish the thought, she threw the brush on the counter and hurried from the room.

Domitian was in the dining room, standing behind a chair that he politely pulled for her when she entered.

Sarita glanced at his face as she approached, caught the way his eyes started to glow that strange silver as his gaze slid over her latest ensemble and just managed not to shake her head as she took her seat. Much to her relief, Domitian didn't so much as touch her shoulder, but eased her chair in and then immediately moved around to claim the seat opposite.

Sarita glanced down at her plate and then stopped and said with surprise, *"Lomito en salsa de mango!"*

"Si." Domitian smiled faintly when she glanced to him with amazement. "It is what you ordered each of the three times you were in my restaurant, so when I saw we had the ingredients to make it, I did."

Sarita smiled crookedly. "Well, now I know which restaurant you own. Buena Vida was my father's favorite. But expensive—it was only for special occasions," she said with a reminiscent smile. "Before my mother died, Papa took her there every year on their anniversary. The first time I got to go was the night before we moved to Canada. He wanted 'our last meal in Venezuela to be memorable,' as he put it, so he took me there."

She smiled faintly, and then her expression turned sober and she said, "We went again five years ago when Grandfather died. We came back to arrange the funeral and see him buried, and the night before we left for home, Papa took me there again . . . the last time I was there was two years ago when Papa—" Much to Sarita's horror her voice cracked, and she bowed her head quickly and stared through eyes suddenly glazed with tears at the sirloin in mango salsa on her plate.

"When your father died and you brought him home to be buried between your mother and grandfather," Domitian finished for her solemnly.

Sarita nodded once, but was concentrating on her breathing. She was taking in repeated deep breaths that she then let out slowly, the whole time thinking, *Dammit, I never cry!*

"You ate in my restaurant the night before you flew back to Canada," he added. "This time alone."

Sarita closed her eyes as that last word cut through her. *Alone*.

She'd thought she'd lost everything when her mother died and her father moved her away from her friends and grandfather to live in Canada. But Sarita hadn't felt truly alone until the day her father had a heart attack and left this earth. Oh, she still had the friends she'd made in Canada, and the other cadets who had been in police training with her at the time. But she alone had flown home to Venezuela with her father's body, and she alone had seen him buried.

Even her grandmother hadn't been there, which was Sarita's fault. It had all happened so quickly and there had been so much to do to arrange to fly her father's body back to Caracas as well as make the funeral arrangements long distance that she hadn't thought to contact her grandmother until the morning of the funeral. By then it was too late. She hadn't had a phone number for the woman then. They'd only ever written. So she'd seen her father buried, and then she'd written and mailed a letter to her grandmother with the news of his death. That night she'd followed tradition and eaten at her father's favorite restaurant, alone.

"I wanted so much to comfort you that night," Domitian confided quietly and then admitted, "I got the latest report from my detective just that morning. I knew your father had died and that you had flown home with his body to see him buried. The moment I got the lone order for *Lomito en salsa de mango* I looked out. I could not see your face, you were sitting with your back to the kitchen, but I knew it was you. You looked so lost and alone sitting there all by yourself. It was a struggle for me not to go to you."

"Why didn't you?" she asked, her voice sharper than she'd intended. But she had really needed comfort that night. Sarita raised her head to peer at him through watery eyes.

"To you I was a stranger," he said simply. "You would not have wanted comfort from me. And had the natural attraction between life mates overwhelmed us, I feared you would hate yourself for whatever happened between us at such a tragic time."

Sarita gave a short nod of understanding, then peered down at her plate and breathed out slowly again. Sirloin in mango salsa. She would never look at it again without thinking of her father . . . and she simply couldn't eat it.

"I'm sorry," she murmured, pushing her chair back. "I think I just want to go to bed."

Domitian didn't protest or point out that he'd worked hard to make the meal that she wasn't eating. He simply murmured in understanding and let her go. Sarita was quite sure he couldn't know how much she appreciated that.

Sarita wasn't sure how long she'd been asleep or even what woke her up, but suddenly her eyes were open and she was staring into the dark, listening to a soft rustling sound somewhere at the bottom of the bed. Ears straining, she tried to figure out what it was without giving away that she was awake. When she couldn't, she reached slowly for the bedside lamp, only to pause as her hand encountered material.

Frowning, Sarita slid her hand first to the left and

then to the right, but the material appeared to be hanging there like a wall. Easing silently up the bed a bit, she ran her hand along the cloth until she found the end, and then reached around it, felt for the lamp on the other side and turned it on.

Of course, she was immediately blinded by the light, but her eyes quickly adjusted and Sarita noted the wall of white cloth along the side of the bed, hanging from the top frame. Another ran along the bottom as well and Domitian stood on a chair, even now affixing a third swath of white cloth along the frame on the opposite side of the bed.

"Sheets?" she asked with amusement.

"Si." Domitian continued his work, stepping off the chair and onto the edge of the bed to string the cloth farther along the frame without having to move the chair now that she was awake.

Sarita watched the play of muscles in his arms and chest until she noted that she had an interesting view up the bottom of his boxers from her position. Clearing a suddenly full throat, she asked hopefully, "Are we going to have sex?"

"No."

"No?" Sarita squawked with disbelief. "Why not? What's all this for then?" she asked, gesturing toward the curtain of sheets now nearly surrounding the bed. She'd assumed it was so they could have sex without worrying about the cameras in the room capturing it . . . *Apparently not*, Sarita thought and scowled at him.

Domitian chuckled at her outrage as he continued his work, moving farther up the edge of the bed until she could have reached out and touched him. "First it's *'no sexo!'* Now it's *'What? No sexo?'"* Glancing at her, he arched an eyebrow. "I have plans for you, you will see."

"Hmm." Sarita muttered, but resisted the urge to touch him and sat up in the bed. She shifted back to lean against the headboard, but didn't bother tugging the sheets up to cover her lap despite the fact that she was now nude under the sheer black nightgown. The last thing Sarita had done before climbing under the sheets and duvet was to strip away the latest hated thong she'd donned earlier to wear under it. They really were uncomfortable. She wouldn't have been able to sleep with it on. Now, she was as good as naked to him from just under the breasts down.

"Oh," Domitian sighed. "You are going to make this difficult, *si*?"

"I don't know what you're talking about," she said with a shrug, straightening her shoulders and thrusting her breasts out as she pretended to examine her nails.

Domitian chuckled under his breath but continued to work. It seemed to take forever for him to finish, though, mostly because he kept casting furtive glances over her rather than paying attention to what he was doing.

"Finally."

Sarita glanced up at that to see that the sheet now reached all the way to the wall on this side as well, and frowned when she noticed that he was now outside it. She was about to lean over and tug the sheet aside to see what he was doing when he did it himself.

Pulling the sheet back with one hand, he climbed in to join her, balancing a tray on his other hand like an expert waiter.

"What's this?" she asked with interest as he let the sheet slip closed again and settled cross-legged next to her.

"Food. You must eat," Domitian said firmly. "You have had little more than a couple of pieces of fruit all day."

"Oh." Sarita peered with interest over the tray he set on the bed between them. There was a selection of meats and cheese, crackers, olives, two glasses of juice, and one glass of wine.

"Who gets the wine?" she asked suspiciously.

"You," he answered easily. "Wine is no good for us."

"Us being immortals?" she asked with interest.

Nodding, Domitian picked up an olive and popped it into his mouth.

"How is it no good for you?" Sarita asked at once, picking up a cracker and piling cheese and meat on it.

"The only effect it has on us is to make the nanos work hard to remove the alcohol from our system. It means consuming more blood."

Sarita wrinkled her nose at that, placed a cracker on top of the meat and cheese, making a mini sandwich and ate half of it in one bite. Flakes of cracker immediately sprinkled down on her breasts and thighs and she made a face. Thinking they were going to have crumbs in bed, she raised a hand to brush away the ones on her chest, but Domitian caught her hand.

"I will lick them off later," he assured her, urging her hand down.

A slow smile spreading her lips, Sarita said with satisfaction, "So there will be *sexo* later."

"No," Domitian answered promptly and built a cheese, meat, and cracker sandwich for himself.

Sarita stared at him for a moment, half confused and half annoyed, but then just shook her head and popped the second half of her own cracker sandwich into her mouth. She was hungry. More like starved really. She would worry about the "sex or no sex" thing later.

They ate in silence for a bit, and then Sarita glanced at Domitian and said, "So you're a chef with your own restaurant. Why would you accept a job cooking for Dressler?"

Domitian blew a breath out and shrugged. "It is a long story."

"Yeah, well, it doesn't look like we're going anywhere for a while, so spill."

Nodding, he said, "Several immortals have gone missing from the United States over the last couple of years. No one noticed at first, because it was only one or two and they were spaced far apart. But the number has grown and the time between kidnappings grew shorter recently and it was noticed."

Sarita's eyebrows rose slightly, but she nodded to encourage him to continue.

"I knew that my uncle had the Rogue Hunters looking into it from a phone conversation I had with Drina, and—"

"Who's Drina?" Sarita asked sharply, surprised at the different emotions whipping through her at the mention of another woman. Possessiveness, worry, and even jealousy were suddenly tugging at her emotions, which was kind of unexpected for Sarita since she wasn't clear on her own feelings for the man.

"My sister," he explained gently. "She is a Rogue Hunter in Canada. She used to live and work in Spain where my family lives, but found her life mate recently. Since he lived in Canada, and Uncle needed more Rogue Hunters there, she moved to be with her mate."

"You have family?" she asked, unable to hide her surprise.

Domitian arched his eyebrows. "You thought I had been hatched?"

"No, of course not. I just—" Shaking her head at her own stupidity, Sarita said, "Dr. Dressler mentioned that your kind were like us, with families and everything, but I guess I just—I mean Dracula didn't have family, you know? I guess I just keep mixing you up with him." Seeing from his expression that she'd managed to insult him, she quickly said, "I'll try not to do that. So what are Rogue Hunters?"

Domitian stared at her narrow-eyed for a moment, but then slowly relaxed and explained, "Basically, they are the police for immortals. They hunt rogue immortals, those who are breaking our laws and feeding on or harming mortals, or turning them in numbers, and so on."

Her eyebrows rose. "You have your own police force?"

"Well, mortal police could not manage our kind what with our ability to read and control minds," he pointed out gently.

"Right. Dr. Dressler mentioned that you guys were able to do that," she said with a frown. Tilting her head, she added, "But he said you couldn't read or control me?"

"No. It is how I knew you were my life mate," he said solemnly.

Unwilling to talk about that, Sarita lowered her eyes and tried to think of something to say that would steer the topic away from this life mate business. She wasn't sure how she felt about the man sitting across from her. He was sexy as hell, and she'd never had sex like they shared, but really he was still a stranger to her . . . and he was different. Not mortal.

Sarita was no longer horrified by the fact that he was a vampire. Or perhaps it was closer to the truth to say she'd stopped worrying about that for now. However, while she needed to work with him to get off this island, Sarita wasn't sure she would be able to accept what he was once that was done. She certainly wasn't ready to think about what he might want from her or if she could give it.

"So is your uncle the head of these immortal police then?" she asked, finally, as that question occurred to her.

"*Si*. But no," Domitian said and grinned at the face she made in reaction to the confusing answer. Taking pity on her, he explained, "A man named Garrett Mortimer is supposed to be the head of the Rogue Hunters, but he answers to Uncle Lucian who was never good at delegating."

"So two cooks in the kitchen?" Sarita suggested.

He smiled with appreciation at her choice of words and nodded.

"Why does this Mortimer guy have to answer to your uncle? Who is he?"

"My uncle Lucian is the head of the North American Council of Immortals. They make the laws, and basically govern our people there. He also used to run the hunters before he put Mortimer in charge of them."

"Right, okay." Sarita nodded, sure she understood the basics now. "So, your uncle had this Mortimer guy put his Rogue Hunters on the job."

"*Si*. They were to find out if the disappearances were connected and, if so, who was behind them. Immortals were disappearing from several areas, but the last three disappeared from bars in Texas, so they concentrated there and hunters and volunteers were sent out to act as bait. But something went wrong. A couple weeks ago two of the volunteers—twin brothers I understand—were kidnapped together."

"Twins," Sarita murmured recalling Dr. Dressler's "experiment." Scientists had a thing for twins and experiments, didn't they? She couldn't even imagine what he was doing to them. Maybe cutting them in half and then seeing if once blood was applied Twin A's bottom half would reattach itself to Twin B's upper half and vice versa? The very thought made her shudder with disgust.

"Fortunately, both men escaped," Domitian added finally, and would never know how close he came to getting punched for not saying so right away and sparing Sarita her distressing imaginings.

"A handful of Dressler's men died," he continued obliviously, "but not before our people found out some vital information. One, the intent was to fly the two captured men to Caracas, and then on to an island, and two, that the man in charge was a Dr. Dressler."

Sarita nodded.

"So Uncle Lucian rounded up as many Rogue Hunters as he felt he could spare and flew down here to try to find Dressler. They quickly realized that he was a university professor here in Venezuela. But he must have caught wind that they were coming, or perhaps he suspected they might when he didn't hear from his men, because by the time the hunters landed in Caracas, Dr. Dressler had gone on sabbatical."

"During their first week here, all they were able to

learn was that Dressler had both an apartment in the city where he stayed while teaching at the university, and a residence on an island somewhere that he went to on weekends and during summer break. No one seemed to know the name of the island, though, or where it was, although it was mentioned that he had a helicopter as well as several boats that he used to get back and forth. So Uncle Lucian decided they would have to check every island within five hundred miles of Caracas."

Sarita blinked and asked with disbelief, "Five hundred?"

Domitian shrugged. "He was being conservative in the hopes of speeding up the hunt."

"You think five hundred miles is *conservative*?" she asked with a disbelieving laugh.

"*Si*," he assured her. "The apartment in the city might have been necessary only for the nights he had evening classes. But it may also have been because the island was too far to travel to and from daily so that the island house was like a cottage would be to an American or Canadian. Helicopters can travel at speeds of one hundred and forty miles an hour. Five hundred miles would only take three and a half hours or a little more to travel to."

"Hmm," she murmured with a nod. A couple of guys at work had cottages up north in the Muskokas, a good three-hour drive away or more depending on traffic and coffee stops. One of them had invited a bunch of their coworkers out to the cottage one weekend last summer. Sarita had been one of those invited and she'd been chatting with the people in the neighboring cottage. They lived farther south and drove five hours to reach their cottage every weekend. Driving up Friday night and leaving Sunday afternoon. If the island house *was* used as a cottage for Dr. Dressler, three or four hours wouldn't be that far to go she supposed.

"Anyway," Domitian continued, "Uncle Lucian divided the areas up into four quadrants and sent two teams of two hunters out to each."

"What happened?" she asked at once when he paused.

"Nothing at first," he answered. "They were using boats, not helicopters, in the hopes of making a stealthy approach, but it was a lot of area to cover."

"And?" Sarita prompted when he fell silent.

"The third day two teams from two different quadrants did not report in," Domitian admitted solemnly. "Two women, Eshe, my aunt by marriage, and Mirabeau La Roche McGraw made up one team, and my cousins Decker and Nicholas made up the second team."

"Oh," Sarita breathed softly. She'd known he knew some of the missing immortals but hadn't realized they were family, and she asked, "Your aunt and cousins are Rogue Hunters too like your sister?"

"*Si,*" Domitian murmured, and then cleared his throat and continued, "Anyway, when the two teams didn't turn up by dawn, Uncle Lucian tried to have their phones tracked, but they must have been disabled. So he pulled everyone off the other two quadrants, and split them up between the two quadrants the teams had gone missing from. But now they were looking for the missing hunters as well as the island Dressler owns."

"Did he check the land registry office?" Sarita asked and then frowned. "That's what it's called in Canada, I don't remember what it is called here, if I ever even knew, but they must have some record of who buys what properties."

Domitian nodded. "They checked. There is no property listed to a Ramsey Dressler in Venezuela."

"Ramsey," Sarita muttered. She'd never known Dr. Dressler's first name. Her grandmother had never mentioned it. Shaking her head, she said, "He must have used another name then."

"*Si*, that is what is suspected, but we have no idea what name he might have used."

"Right," Sarita breathed. "So, I gather from the fact that Dressler is still out here torturing people with his experiments that they didn't find the island?"

"No, and another four hunters went missing. This time one from each team of two."

"What?" she asked with amazement. "How?"

Domitian shrugged helplessly. "No one knows. With each team it was the same story. The other hunter was there, and then suddenly was not."

Sarita stared at him blankly and then shook her head. "Well, the ones who came back had to have seen or heard *something*. They were on boats, right?"

"*Si*, but the hunters who returned were all piloting the boats. In each case they said they were skimming through the water, glanced around to say something to their partner, and they were gone. They did not hear or see anything to suggest a struggle. And whatever happened was quick. In two cases the missing man was holding a conversation with the pilot when it happened. They said something, the pilot responded, glanced back to them, and they were not there."

"Oh, that's just spooky," Sarita declared after a moment.

"*Si,*" Domitian murmured.

"None of them were related to you this time, were they?" she asked with concern.

Domitian nodded slowly. "My uncle Victor, and Lucern, another cousin, were among those taken. My sister, Drina, was on one of the teams, but fortunately, she was piloting the boat. She returned, but the man partnered with her, a man named Santo Notte, did not."

"Your sister is here in Venezuela?"

"*Si.* Uncle Lucian called in all the Rogue Hunters in North America after my aunt and cousins went missing. There are several civilians down here now too trying to help, which has Uncle Lucian furious," he added wryly.

"Why would that upset him?" Sarita asked with surprise.

"Because he's lost so many hunters who are skilled and trained for situations like this. He considers it far too dangerous to have nonhunters here and fears they will just be cannon fodder."

"But he let you help," she pointed out.

"Actually, he refused my help when I first offered it," Domitian admitted with a crooked smile, and explained, "When I learned he and the others had flown in, I went directly to the villas they'd rented and offered to help, but he said no, it was too dangerous and I was not a hunter." He shrugged. "So I returned to my restaurant and helped the only way I could."

"Food?" she guessed at once.

Domitian nodded. "I cooked large batches of food four or five times a day and sent it to the villa."

"I'm sure they appreciated that," she assured him.

He shrugged, and continued, "I offered my assistance

again when my aunt and cousins went missing, but again was refused."

Sarita reached out and covered his hand sympathetically. He seemed perfectly calm about it all, but she could sense the frustration and anger simmering under the surface at not being allowed to help search for his missing family members.

Domitian stared at her hand briefly, then turned his own over and clasped her fingers gently, his shoulders relaxing somewhat.

"So," she said, clearing her throat, "what changed? Why did he let you help in the end?"

"You," Domitian said squeezing her fingers lightly.

"Me?" she asked with surprise.

"*Si*," he said solemnly. "Dressler has been a regular in my restaurant for at least two years and has offered me a job as his personal chef every couple of months during that time. But two days ago, he called and offered it again. This time, though, he mentioned that Sarita, the granddaughter of one of his employees, was coming for a visit and he wished to offer her more than the slop his regular cook served."

"Aleta doesn't serve slop," Sarita said, snatching her hand away and scowling at him for the insult to the woman.

"He said it, not me," Domitian assured her solemnly. "And now that I know he knew all along that you are my life mate, I am sure it was just an excuse to mention your name and let me know you were here."

"Oh . . . yeah, it probably was," she said, relaxing.

"Anyway," Domitian continued, "I could hardly refuse the offer this time, not when I knew you were on the island and quite possibly in danger. So I accepted the job—as Dressler no doubt expected—and then I went straight to the villa to give Lucian the news." He smiled wryly. "I expected him to be pleased. After all, Dressler had no idea I was an immortal so I would not be in danger, and my uncle could have my phone tracked and find out where the island was."

"I gather he didn't see things that way?"

"Hell no. According to him I was throwing myself in harm's way. Dressler probably *did* know I was an immortal, and this was just a trap to add another one to his collection, and Dressler would incapacitate my phone and myself quickly to prevent their following. Which he was right about as it turns out," Domitian said on a sigh.

"And yet he let you come," she said.

Domitian snorted. "He had no choice. This is South America, the North American council has no power here or over me. Once I pointed that out, he had no choice and started making plans on how best to track me and keep me safe and so on."

Sarita nodded, but was now frowning as she considered what he'd said and then asked, "I'm surprised that wasn't a problem."

"What?" Domitian asked.

"Well, this isn't North America," she pointed out.

"No," he agreed.

"Mortal police can get pretty testy about jurisdiction and whatnot," she said with a grimace. "Don't the South American Council mind that your uncle has come into their jurisdiction in pursuit of a perp? Or did your uncle contact them and coordinate with them on this operation?"

Domitian made a face, and then admitted, "Actually, I assumed they knew, but when we were on the way to the docks, a call came from the villa that the South American Council were there and wanted to see him. Uncle Lucian just said he'd be back soon and hung up, but one of the men, Justin Bricker, said, 'Uh-oh. They've found out we're here.'"

"Hmm." Sarita bit her lip. If immortals were anything like mortals, she suspected there might be a mini turf war happening on the mainland about now and wondered what that looked like between vampires. A duel at dusk with stakes? Shaking her head, she reached for another cracker, intending to make another cracker sandwich, only to pause as she realized they were all gone. They'd eaten every last crumb of food from the tray Domitian had brought as they'd talked. There wasn't even an olive left.

"Time for dessert," Domitian announced, grabbing the tray and slipping quickly out of their sheet-wrapped cocoon. When he didn't reappear again right away, Sarita frowned and crawled across the bed to tug the sheet aside and see what he was doing.

Setting the tray aside and stripping off his boxers maybe? she thought hopefully. He would make a lovely dessert. But when Sarita looked out she saw that the room was empty. Domitian had left.

Releasing the sheet, she dropped back to lie on the bed with disappointment. The man was sending mixed messages. Saying no he didn't plan to have sex with her, and then saying he'd lick the crumbs off her later. Now he had apparently gone off to find them dessert. She had no idea what he had planned.

Nine

Domitian cut the last profiterole in half, filled it with ice cream like the others, and then retrieved the chocolate sauce he'd left to stay warm on the range. Tipping the pan, he drizzled it slowly over the profiteroles he'd arranged on the plate, and then set the plate on the tray with the wine and small dessert plates. He took a moment to go over the items on the tray, making sure he had everything, and then picked it up and headed back to the bedroom.

Sarita had chosen bananas flamée as her dessert the three times she'd eaten at his restaurant, but after her reaction to the sirloin in mango salsa, he wasn't making the mistake of serving her the dessert she usually ordered too. He was hoping the profiteroles would be better received.

"More wine?" Sarita asked with amusement as he pulled the sheet aside and climbed back into their cocoon.

"It is a muscat, perfect with profiteroles, but I made cappuccinos too. You can have one or both as you wish." He settled on the bed and let the sheet drop back into place as he set the tray on the bed between them.

"Profiteroles?" she asked with interest and leaned over to look at them. Her eyes widened. "Did you *make* these?"

"Of course," he said with amusement.

"I've never had freshly made profiteroles," she confessed. "I've had the frozen ones they sell at the grocery stores in Canada, but—"

"Garbage," he assured her as he slid two onto a small plate and offered them to her with a fork. "These will be much better."

Sarita smiled slightly at his bragging as she took the plate and fork. She cut off a piece of ice cream–filled profiterole and slid it into her mouth as Domitian busied himself pouring her a glass of the muscat before pushing the sheet aside and leaning to set the wine bottle on the bedside table and out of the way.

"Mmmmmmmm."

Domitian let the sheet drop back into place and turned to smile at Sarita as she moaned over her first bite of profiterole. "Good?"

Sarita nodded and swallowed. "Oh yeah. Heavenly," she assured him. "You're a keeper."

"I am glad to hear you say that," Domitian said solemnly, and recognized the moment when she realized what she'd said by how she stilled and then flushed with embarrassment. When Sarita followed that up by gulping down a mouthful of wine, Domitian sighed to himself and picked up his own plate to eat.

The woman hadn't yet accepted that they were life

mates, and he knew he shouldn't rush her, but couldn't help himself. He had waited more than two millennia to find his life mate. Fifteen years ago he had found her, but had forced himself to wait for her to grow up and become her own woman. The plan had been to wait until she had worked for a couple years in her chosen profession and then find and woo her, but Dressler had cut some time off that goal with his actions. Still, to his mind, Domitian had been incredibly patient. However, it seemed he would have to be patient a bit longer. He could do it. One did not live this long without learning patience. But that didn't mean he would enjoy it.

Glancing at Sarita, he noted the tight, uncomfortable expression on her face and sighed inwardly. The woman was as closed up as a turtle in its shell. He needed to open her up a bit before she would even see the possibilities before her. Swallowing the bit of profiterole in his mouth, he said, "Tell me about yourself."

Sarita glanced up with surprise, and then arched an eyebrow. "I would have thought your private detective had told you everything there was to know."

Domitian shook his head. "Those were just cold hard facts written on pristine white paper. I want to know more than the facts. I want to know you," he said firmly. "I want to see the past through your eyes. The present too. I want to know your dreams, your wishes, your heart. I wanted to know the real Sarita, not the facts behind her existence."

Sarita stared at him wide eyed for a moment, and then lowered her head and peered down at the ice cream melting and sliding out of her profiteroles. She was silent for so long he began to think she wasn't going to respond at all, but then she said, "I had a pretty normal childhood until I was thirteen."

Domitian exhaled slowly, realizing only then that he'd been holding his breath, unsure she would respond to his request.

Sarita shrugged. "Happy loving parents, good in school, lots of friends, and a grandfather who spoiled me rotten and who I adored . . . and then my mother was kidnapped."

She took a bite of profiterole and ice cream, chewed, and swallowed and then chased it with a sip of wine before adding, "Although, I suppose that was pretty normal too when you think about it. Kidnapping in Venezuela is practically a national pastime and there were more than a couple of kids in my school who knew someone who had been kidnapped."

Domitian nodded solemnly. Kidnapping had become rampant in Venezuela. It was visited on everyone, the rich, the middle class, and even the poor. In fact, it was so commonplace that people had begun forming groups with friends, coworkers, and neighbors, joining together to put money into funds to pay off kidnappers and get back the loved ones of the people in their groups.

"My father loved my mother dearly and did everything the kidnappers told him to do. He didn't contact the police, he didn't tell anyone, and he gathered together the demanded money and went to the meeting place they instructed him to, to deliver it. He'd expected my mother to be there and to be exchanged for the money, but they told him it didn't work that way. That once they were safely away and sure that the *policia* weren't there somewhere waiting to jump them, they would send my mother to him."

"But they did not," Domitian said softly, sorry he'd made her relive this sad part of her life.

"Oh, they did," she assured him, and then added bitterly, "in pieces."

Domitian winced. The kidnapping had happened three months before he'd met Sarita and learned he couldn't read her. The detective he'd hired had mentioned in his first report that her mother had died in a kidnapping gone wrong, and her father was moving her out of the country because of that, but hadn't given specifics. Domitian hadn't asked for any.

"I am sorry," he said softly.

Sarita acknowledged his words with a nod and turned her gaze back to her plate as she scooped up another bite of profiterole. After swallowing, she said, "After my mother's death, my father was afraid the same thing would happen to me, and decided he had to get me out of Venezuela. He worked for the Royal Bank of Canada here. He was the assistant manager at their branch office in Caracas and, with the bank manager's help, was able to get a transfer to a branch in Canada." Her expression turned thoughtful. "I think the bank helped to speed up the paperwork needed for us to move, visas and whatnot. It still seemed to take a while, though, several months I think."

She paused, apparently trying to recall, and then shrugged. "Anyway, off we went to Canada. We settled in a little town just south of Toronto where it would be easy for my father to commute into the city to his new bank. Fortunately, it was summer and school was out. Well, for everyone else," she added wryly. "My father wanted me to get a good start once school began, and he wanted me to be able to protect myself, so he signed me up for martial arts two nights a week, and then hired me a teacher to teach me English. I spent that first summer learning English eight hours a day, every day. It was English, English, English with the occasional martial arts break at night."

"Your father found a teacher willing to work seven days a week?" he asked with amusement.

"Oh no, the teacher only taught me during the week-days, my father taught me on Saturday and Sunday . . . and usually for a couple of hours on weeknights after work. My whole life was mostly English. By the time school started, I was sick to death of contractions and the order of adjectives and nouns." She rolled her eyes and then sighed and shrugged. "But I had learned enough that I was able to go to a normal high school."

"Were you already in high school at thirteen?" he asked. It seemed young to him.

"Fourteen," she corrected. "My birthday is—"

"July seventh," Domitian finished for her with a nod. "Yes, of course. You would have been fourteen by the time school started."

"Right," she said slowly, eyeballing him. "Your private dick would have told you my birth date."

"Yes," he said simply.

"Hmm," she muttered, and then continued, "Anyway, my life was pretty normal again after that. High school dances, going to the mall with friends, bush parties, making—"

"Excuse me," he interrupted. "Bush parties? This is what?"

Sarita shrugged. "Just what it sounds like, parties in the bush."

Domitian pursed his lips briefly and then said, "That would be a very small party."

"Heck no, tons of kids went. Like I said, it was a small town. There wasn't much to do unless you drove to the city, and the first two years of high school there was no driving anywhere. But even after my friends and I all started turning sixteen and getting our licenses, none of our parents were willing to let us take the family car into the city. I don't think anyone's did really. The older kids were at the bush parties too."

"In a bush?" he asked with disbelief. "Lots of you? In a bush?"

"Yes," she said, not seeming to understand his confusion, and then her eyes widened. "Not the bush like a plant, not *arbusto*. Bush like a small woodland area or forest, *bosque*."

"Ah . . ." Domitian nodded, a wry smile curving his lips. "I learned English centuries ago and still cannot get it right. I am impressed you mastered it in a summer."

"I wouldn't say I mastered it that summer," she assured him, seeming amused. "I still struggled my first year of high school, but I knew enough to get by. Besides, you speak English perfectly. New words and terms or slang pop up all the time. Even speaking it daily it's hard to keep up sometimes. The kids are always coming up with something I've never heard before."

Domitian smiled softly. She was trying to make him feel better as if he might feel stupid that he'd made a mistake. His self-esteem wasn't that weak, but it was sweet of her to be concerned for him.

"Anyway, like I say, everything was pretty normal after that. I finished high school, went to university to get a criminology degree, went through police training, and—" she shrugged "—now I'm living the dream."

Domitian's eyebrows rose at the tinge of sarcasm in her voice. "Your dream was not to be a police officer?"

Sarita made a face. "Yeah, it was, but—" she shook her head "—I wanted to be a police officer to *help* people. To make sure no one else lost their mother the way I did. Instead, I'm scraping drunks up off the sidewalk, stopping speeders, and arresting shoplifters. And none of them take responsibility for why they're in trouble. Do they just say, 'Thank you, Officer, for not leaving me to freeze to death on the sidewalk' or 'Sorry, Officer, you're right. I was speeding' and take their ticket or whatever? No. They're always trying to give excuses. The drunk we pick up every night like clockwork never drinks too much, someone must have roofied him. The speeder was unfamiliar with the road and thought the speed limit was higher, or their speedometer must not be working, or everyone else was doing it, or they were speeding because they had to pee. And the shoplifter? Oh no, they weren't shoplifting, they just absentmindedly dropped it in their purse or pants and forgot to pay."

She puffed out a breath of exasperation. "And when those excuses that we've already heard a hundred times don't work? Then they start cursing and shouting at us, and kicking out at us and struggling so that we have to wrestle them to the car. And the whole time they're yelling at their friends to videotape this. 'It's abuse! It's abuse!'

"It gets pretty fricking depressing at times, I gotta tell you. I became a police officer to help people, but they don't want the help when it's directed at them. Oh yeah, they're happy when it's directed at someone else but—For instance, a couple months ago Jackson and I pulled this guy over for speeding and weaving. He—"

"Speeding and weaving?" Domitian interrupted. "I understand speeding, but by weaving you do not mean—?"

"Weaving all over the road," she explained.

"Ah." Domitian nodded. "Sorry. Proceed."

"So, he blows over the limit and—I mean on the breathalyzer," she stopped to explain. "It reads how much alcohol they have in their system."

Domitian nodded.

"Right, so he blows over the legal limit, and then freaks out when we arrest him. Starts cussing us out and even took a swing at Jackson. Fine. Nothing new there, right?"

Apparently it was a rhetorical question, because she went on, "Fast forward to two weeks ago. We're called to a traffic accident. This cute little six-year-old was hit crossing the road from her house to her neighbor's across the street. Turns out the driver was speeding and over the limit."

"And it is the man you arrested two months earlier," Domitian guessed.

"No. *He's* the kid's father. *This* drunk is a neighbor. But the father, who let the kid cross that busy street without supervision, and who wanted to kill us both just a month and a half earlier for arresting *him* for doing the same thing, *and on the same damned street*, starts shouting at us now about how we don't do our jobs and stop speeders and drunk drivers in his area.

"Ack!" she exclaimed with disgust. "I wanted to plow the guy. But no, I had to be polite and take his abuse. And the whole time he's yelling at me, I'm trying to comfort the little girl with a shattered pelvis and broken leg as we wait for the ambulance."

When she sat back with a little exasperated grunt, Domitian said gently, "It sounds a very thankless job."

"It is," she assured him, and then added, "And it isn't."

"Which is it?" he asked with a faint smile.

Sarita smiled crookedly back. "Sometimes you can make a difference and really help someone. And sometimes they even appreciate it, and those days—" she blew out a long breath "—those days make up for all the crap days. But man, they are few and far between. I've only been on the job for a year and already feel like I've aged ten. Seeing the things people do to each other?" She shook her head sadly. "Sometimes I'm ashamed to be human."

They were both silent for a minute. Sarita was peering thoughtfully down into her cappuccino cup. He was peering just as thoughtfully at her, thinking that her job sounded incredibly thankless and stressful. Most police officers no doubt got into it because they wanted to help people. But he suspected the things she'd described probably wore them down pretty quickly. He didn't like the idea of her being worn down. And he wondered how much of the hard outer shell she presented to the world had been there before she'd become an officer. Perhaps they trained them to be that way. She was expected to be strong on the job, and in control in emergency situations. It would mean being tough he supposed.

Once he'd persuaded her to be his life mate, perhaps he should talk to her about changing her career and—

Domitian stopped his thoughts there and gave his

head a little shake. If all he'd wanted was a Barbie doll to do as he thought best, he might as well have picked any mortal who caught his fancy. But part of the reason life mates were so special was because they could not be controlled. And the entire reason he'd left Sarita to grow up rather than claim her when he'd found her while so young was so she could grow into her own woman and hopefully wouldn't be led by him.

No. He wouldn't try to convince her to change her career. He would let her make her own decisions and simply support her in those decisions the best he could.

Sarita drank the last of her cappuccino, and set the cup back on the tray with a little sigh, then straightened her shoulders and glanced at Domitian. Judging by his expression, she'd depressed him as much as herself with her little rant. Time to change the tune of this conversation, she decided and said, "So, that's me. Your turn. Let's hear about you."

Domitian jerked his head up and eyed her with surprise. "Me?"

She chuckled at his expression, and then teased, "What? A pretty boy like you has never had a gal want to stare into your dreamy eyes and hear all about your life?"

"Not that I recall," he said with a smile.

Sarita snorted with disbelief. "Yeah right."

"I am telling you the truth," he assured her.

Sarita eyed him suspiciously, and then arched an eyebrow. "So what do you do on dates then? I mean most people at least tell a little about themselves."

"I do not date."

"Right," Sarita said slowly and then shook her head. "Sorry buddy, no one gets as talented as you are in the bedroom, or should I say bathroom and lounge chair," she added dryly before finishing, "without a couple thousand sexual experiences under their belt."

"Ah." Domitian murmured, and then shrugged mildly. "I have had sex, of course."

"Of course. You just didn't bother to first talk to the women you bedded," she said with disbelief and then sat up straight as she realized that was how it had gone with her. She hadn't known a damned thing about him other than his name and that he was an immortal when she'd jumped him in the bathroom.

"I undoubtedly did speak to the women I bedded as you so charmingly put it," he said with amusement. "However, it was so long ago I don't recall if they asked about my life first."

That was sufficiently distracting to pull Sarita away from fretting over what she feared might be considered slutty behavior, and she eyed him now, wondering how long it had been since he'd slept with a woman. He was immortal—he could be two, maybe even three hundred years old. Had it been ten years? Twenty? Maybe even fifty years since he'd slept with a woman? As her father used to say, the only way to know was to ask, so she did.

"How long has it been since you slept with a woman? Before me," she added quickly in case he tried to avoid the answer by naming the incident on the lounge.

"Hmm." Domitian tipped his head, apparently having to think back a bit to remember, and then he nodded and said, "I believe it was when Auletes succeeded Alexander II."

Out of cappuccino but still thirsty, Sarita had just

reached over to pick up the glass of wine he'd poured for her. Straightening with it in hand, she glanced to him with confusion. "Who? What now?"

"Sorry," Domitian said with a wry shrug. "I should have said when Ptolemy XII Neos Dionysos succeeded Ptolemy XI Alexander II as King of Egypt."

Sarita stared blankly, and then simply said, "Huh?"

Domitian frowned and offered, "Neos Dionysos was also known as Auletes or Nothos, does that help?"

"Are you kidding me? Hell no, it doesn't help! What are you talking about?" she asked with exasperation. "Egypt has presidents not kings, and right now it's some guy named el Sissy or something."

"El-Sisi," he corrected with amusement. "And yes, they have presidents now, but the leaders were kings when I lived there. Or Pharaohs."

"Pharaohs?" she gasped. "Seriously? *Pharaohs?*"

"*Si.*" He nodded, seeming fascinated with the expressions flittering across her face.

"But Pharaohs are—That was back before—Christ, you—"

"*Si*, pharaohs reigned before Christ," he said with a nod. "Then the Romans invaded in about 30 B.C. and they carried the title of emperor for—What is the matter? Are you all right? Why are you gulping your wine?" he asked with concern.

Sarita just shook her head and downed the rest of the wine in her once-full glass. By the time she finished, she was gasping for air. Setting the empty glass on the tray, she gave her head a shake and then glared at Domitian for a minute as she regained her breath, before saying, "Please do not tell me that you are trying to tell me that—you're telling me—"

"Concentrate, *mi Corazon*," he encouraged. "You can get it out."

"You are *not* telling me that you were born in 30 B.C.," she said firmly.

"No," Domitian agreed, turning to tug the sheet aside and grab the wine bottle off the bedside table.

"Thank God," Sarita muttered, her body relaxing.

"Thirty B.C. is when I last enjoyed copulation with a female . . . other than yourself of course," he explained, letting the sheet drop back into place and turning with the bottle. "I was *born* in 260 B.C."

"No, you weren't," she said at once.

"*Si*, I was," he assured her and began to pour more wine into her glass.

"No, you—Just give me the bottle," she muttered and snatched it from his hand when he stopped pouring and glanced to her with surprise at the request. Ignoring that, Sarita raised the bottle to her lips to drink straight from it.

"The detective I hired did not mention a drinking problem," Domitian said dryly as he watched her chug.

Sarita glared at him around the bottle, but then stopped chugging and lowered it. She held on to it, though, and simply stared at him for several moments.

Ignoring her, Domitian slid another profiterole onto a plate and offered it to her.

Sarita was so annoyed with him she almost refused out of principle. But the profiteroles were so good, and it wasn't their fault she was annoyed with him. It seemed unfair to take out her anger on them so she took the plate, muttering a very short "Thank you."

"*De nada*," Domitian murmured, watching her cut off a large piece of profiterole and pop it in her mouth.

In her irritation, she wasn't paying much attention to what she was doing and the piece was much larger than she'd intended. Not dangerously so, but it meant a lot of chewing and moving food around in her mouth before swallowing to be sure she didn't choke. The entire time she did, Sarita glared at Domitian.

"I do not understand your distress," he said as he watched her chew. "You said that Dressler had explained about the nanos and our being immortal and such."

Sarita swallowed the food in her mouth, took a drink of wine from the bottle to clear her throat, and then nodded. "Yes. Immortal. But I was thinking—you know—a hundred years old, maybe two . . . *not* two *thousand!*"

"Two thousand, two hundred and—"

"Oh my God!" The words exploded from Sarita's mouth and her eyes went as big as saucers. "Two thousand years?"

"Two thousand, two hundred and—"

"In Egypt?" She interrupted his second attempt to give her his exact age.

"*Si.* I lived in Egypt two thousand, two hundred and—"

"So you wore those little white skirts and stuff?"

"What I wore was a shendyt not a skirt," he said stiffly.

"If that means little white skirt, that's what I'm talking about," she said with a grin and then started to raise the bottle to her lips again, but stopped as a thought occurred to her. "Were you still there when the Romans took over?"

"*Si.*"

"Oh God!" Sarita gulped down some more wine, and then lowered the bottle to say, "Please don't tell me you had to trade in your skirt for those ridiculous long togas and those silly-looking leafy things they wore on their heads."

"I fear so," Domitian said with amusement as she raised the bottle again for another chug. "Although as a gladiator, I had to wear a subligaculum and—"

"Oh my God! You were a gladiator?" she asked the minute she could get the bottle down and swallow what she'd taken in. "Oh, I bet you were super hot as a gladiator."

"Er . . ." Domitian said, unsure how to respond to that. He had a healthy ego, but it seemed kind of egotistical to agree with her that he had looked hot in his subligaculum.

"Tell me what it was like?"

"Wearing a sublig—?"

"No, no," she interrupted. "What was it like being a gladiator?"

Domitian shrugged. "Up early, good food, hard training, the most amazing massages I have enjoyed in my life, and—"

"Wait, wait," Sarita said with a frown. "You're a vampire."

"Immortal," he corrected stiffly.

"Whatever," she said, waving one hand. "But as a gladiator you'd have to be out in the sun all—"

"No. I can control minds, remember?" he said gently. "I just made sure our *doctores* always placed me in the shade for practice."

"Doctors decided where you would fight?" Sarita asked with surprise.

"Not doctors, *doctores*," Domitian corrected her gently. "It is what the trainers were called."

"Oh." She shrugged. "Okay, so you got to train in

the shade, but you couldn't gladiate in the shade. That would have been out in the coliseum, in the open."

"*Si*, but each gladiator only had to fight three or four times a year, five at the most," he said with a shrug.

"What?" she gasped with disbelief.

Grinning Domitian nodded. "*Si*. The rest of the time it was just good food, training, massages, baths, and willing women. Life was good."

"Hmm. Sure," Sarita muttered, suddenly seeming annoyed. "If that's all you want from life."

"I was young then," Domitian said with amusement. "It *was* all I wanted from life."

"Um, no," she said dryly. "You said Rome conquered Egypt in 30 B.C., so if you were born in 260 B.C. you were . . . er, let's see, we have to go backward, right, so two hundred and thirty minus thirty . . . two hundred and thirty years old," she said, and then arched an eyebrow at him. "Two hundred and thirty years old is not young."

"Actually, I was only one hundred and fifty. I was a gladiator in 110 B.C. while I still enjoyed food and sex," he explained. "And it was in Rome, not Egypt that I was a gladiator."

"Oh," Sarita frowned. "For some reason I thought you were born in Egypt."

"I was. My family was from Egypt, and I lived and worked there for my first thirty years."

"Worked as what?" she asked curiously.

"I was trained to be a *sesh*—a scribe," Domitian explained. "That was what my mother wanted me to be, and I did try, but it was terribly boring to me and when I was about twenty-five I ran off to be a soldier. I thought that would surely be more interesting, and it was at times, but in peacetime it was just hard labor, helping to move stones for pyramids and such. I only stayed with it for five years or so."

"Really? You helped build a pyramid?" Sarita asked with fascination.

Domitian smiled faintly at the question. "I think calling what I did 'helping to build a pyramid' a bit of an overstatement. I helped move a few large blocks, but that was about it, and it was backbreaking work, even for an immortal," he assured her. "Anyway, I soon grew tired of that and landed in Ostia, where I was a *urinatores* for a decade."

"Er, what is a urinator?" Sarita asked, wrinkling her nose.

"*Urinatores*," he said on a laugh. "A salvage diver. We dove down as far as thirty meters with nothing but a diving bell with air trapped in it that we could breathe out of as we worked. Once it ran out we had to surface and trap fresh air to go back down. A dangerous job for mortals, but not for me, which is why I made out so well monetarily."

"From there I landed in China where I ended up becoming a *praegustator* for a decade for Emperor Qin Shi Huang. I pretasted food to test it for poison," Domitian explained, and then added, "Another very dangerous job had I been mortal since the emperor wasn't well liked. But I was immortal, so . . ." He shrugged. "I was well paid while there, which is part of the reason I stayed a full decade, but it was also because I found I quite liked food."

"You didn't like it before that?" she asked with amusement.

"Oh, yes. Well, sometimes. Soldiers did not exactly

eat gourmet meals, and I was not much of a cook myself so my time as a *urinatores* was not very educational in that regard, but the emperor had proper cooks and he did like his food. And so did I. The food there was new and different. I decided I wanted to travel around and try food from other cultures. So, despite being offered a great deal of coin to stay, I left and started my wandering, looking to try different foods and such. At least until I started to lose my taste for food."

"When was that?" she asked at once.

Domitian sighed and thought back. "I guess it started when I was about a hundred and eighty or so. I began to eat less and less frequently, and five years later at the celebration of Ptolemy XII's accession was the last time I actually enjoyed food."

"And the last time you had sex," she said.

Domitian nodded. "The two appetites often dwindle away together."

"Why?" she asked at once.

Domitian shrugged helplessly. "It happens to all immortals eventually. I actually held on to my appetites longer than some of my kind. I think because I traveled around and tried various and exotic foods."

"And various and exotic women?" she suggested sourly.

"Si," he said unapologetically, and then added, "All of whom are long dead and turned to dust so no longer worth your jealousy."

"I'm not jealous!" Sarita protested at once, but wasn't sure she was telling the truth. She'd certainly felt the pinch of something as she'd brought up his exotic women. *Damn, I am jealous*, she realized and took another drink from her bottle.

Lowering it, she squinted at him and asked, "So what else did you do besides urinating and gladiorating?"

"*Urinatores,*" Domitian corrected on a laugh, and then added, "I do not think *gladiorating* is a word."

"Eh . . ." Sarita waved that away with unconcern. "So, what else did you do?" she demanded.

Domitian shrugged. "Once I lost my appetites, I bounced between farming, traveling as a trade merchant, and opening and running pubs or hostels, with the occasional mercenary work thrown in to keep practiced in defense."

"What kind of mercenary work?"

"I was a dragoon for a while," he said after thinking for a moment.

"What? You guys suck blood *and* blow fire?"

"Dragoon, not dragon," he said on a laugh. "A dragoon is a musketeer on horseback."

"Ooooh," Sarita breathed, impressed. "Musketeers are cool. I bet you were hot with long hair and those froufrou hats."

"Froufrou hats?" he asked, sounding affronted.

"Well, you know, with the wide brim and the feathers all poking out of it," she said, waving her hands around her head to show him what she meant. "Most guys wouldn't be able to carry it off, but I bet you did. Just like I bet you carried off that Egyptian skirt thing nicely too."

When Domitian merely stared at her with a bemused expression, Sarita asked, "Were you ever a pirate? I could see you as a pirate. All tight black pants and billowy shirt and long sword."

Domitian nodded slowly. "*Si*. As it happens I did do a brief stint as a pirate."

"No!" Sarita breathed with amazement. "Oh, you were *naughty!*"

"In my defense it was only for a year or so to aid my sister, Alexandrina. She was short a couple men on her ship, so I put in with her for a while to help out."

"Your sister was a pirate captain?" she asked, eyes wide.

"Well, technically, Drina was a privateer," Domitian admitted.

"Ah, pirating with permission," Sarita said, nodding wisely, and then asked, "Any other jobs that were exciting? Were you ever a knight?"

"I was knighted three or four times," he admitted, and then explained, "In a different country each time."

"What else?" she asked.

Domitian shook his head apologetically. "I am afraid there is nothing else of much note I have done. Other than that, I farmed, and—Oh, I almost forgot, I was a Bow Street Runner for a while. They were—"

"I know what Bow Street Runners were," Sarita interrupted on a laugh. "I'm a police officer, and those guys—well, I had a teacher who considered them London's first professional police force." She smiled. "So that means, you were a sop too at one time."

"I think you mean cop," Domitian said with amusement. "Yes, I guess I was or was as good as, and I think you are tipsy."

"Me? Never," she assured him. "I don't drink."

"Which would explain why you might be tipsy now," he said dryly, taking the half full bottle from her lap and pushing the sheet aside briefly to set the bottle on the bedside table again.

"I'm sure I don't know why you'd think that," Sarita said, sitting up straight on the bed and trying for a serious face, which just made her want to giggle.

"I think that—" Domitian let the sheet fall into place as he turned back to face her again "—because you are laughing and smiling and completely relaxed. I suspect those are three things you do not often allow yourself to do."

"Oh, so now you're saying I'm a stick in the mud too," she accused teasingly.

"Never," he said solemnly. "But I am saying that you have a beautiful smile and if a glass or two of wine makes you relax enough to share it with me, then I think I shall serve you wine at every meal."

Sarita swallowed, her smile wavering. Sobriety dropping around her like a cape, she said, "I don't want to eat any more meals here, Domitian."

After a hesitation, he leaned forward and cupped the back of her head to draw her close so that he could whisper, "Just two or three more meals here, *mi Corazon*. I plan to get us both off this island tomorrow night."

"Tomorrow?" she asked with surprise. Drawing back slightly, she peered at his face as he nodded. "How?"

The word was barely a whisper, but he heard and drew her back to say, "I am going to swim for the mainland."

Her eyes widened with shock. "You're going to leave me here alone?"

"Hush," Domitian whispered and placed his forehead on hers. "No, *mi tresoro*, I would never do that. I will take you with me . . . on my back."

Sarita gaped at him briefly, and then opened her

mouth to tell him just how crazy an idea that was. But Domitian trapped the words before they could even be formed by simply kissing her.

Startled, Sarita raised her hands to push him away, determined to tell him his plan was completely insane. But by the time her fingers reached his shoulders the thought was lost and she found herself clinging to him as she kissed him back.

Domitian's arms closed around her at once, his hands spreading on her back and pulling her tightly to his chest, molding her upper body to his. Sarita groaned into his mouth and shifted to her knees to move closer. The action put her at the same height as he was sitting, she noted and then was distracted when his hands slid under the sheer black nightgown and skimmed up her legs.

When one hand cupped her bottom and the other slid up to brush teasingly between her legs, Sarita gasped and broke the kiss.

"You have been driving me mad with this all night, *mi Corazon*," Domitian growled, releasing her bottom to tug at the sheer cloth of her nightgown. "Take it off for me. I would lick and suckle your breasts."

Sarita groaned as the hand between her legs teased her again, and then quickly caught at the material of the nightie and tugged it up and off. It wasn't even over her head before Domitian closed his mouth on one excited nipple and began to draw as his fingers stopped teasing and slid smoothly along the warm, damp flesh between her legs.

"Oh!" Sarita gasped, tossing the nightgown aside. Clutching at his shoulders, she panted, "I thought you . . . said . . . *no sexo*."

Letting her nipple slip loose he raised his head to meet her gaze and agreed, "*No sexo*. But I will make love to you."

Sarita's eyes widened, but she went willingly when he eased her back to lie on the bed.

Ten

Sarita woke up abruptly and with the certain knowledge that she had to get up at once and visit the bathroom. Too much wine was her personal assessment of the situation. The good news was at least her head didn't hurt, she thought and glanced around to see that Domitian was unconscious on the bed next to her.

Smiling, she started to sit up, but paused as she realized that his arm was across her waist. Sarita carefully lifted his hand up and to the side so she could sit up. The man didn't even stir as she crawled to the top of the mattress to tug the sheet aside and get out of bed. Letting it drop back into place, she hurried into the adjoining bathroom.

She snatched up a bath towel on her way in, tossed it over the shower's glass panel and then reached in to work the taps. Leaving them on to allow the water to warm, she then slid into the water closet to handle more pressing issues.

Moments later, feeling much relieved, Sarita left the water closet to check the temperature of the shower. The water was perfect and she stepped under it with a little sigh that died in her throat as she tipped her head back and spotted the camera lens.

Mouth tightening, Sarita lowered her head and pretty much raced through her shower after that. She then turned off the water and quickly wrapped the towel around herself sarong-style as she got out. Moving to the counter she ran a brush through her damp hair and brushed her teeth as she debated whether to go back to sleep or not. Sarita wasn't tired anymore, but if they really were going to try to leave the island that night, she should probably sleep as much as possible today.

Grimacing, she met her gaze in the mirror and shook her head slightly. There was just no way they were going to be able to swim to the mainland. First, they had no idea what direction the mainland was. Secondly, there were sharks and other predators out there in the ocean, and she didn't fancy playing Jonah in the belly of a whale. And then there was the distance. She hadn't seen even a hint of land in any direction as they'd walked around the island. They could be ten miles from the mainland or a hundred. Neither of them had any idea.

No. Sarita just couldn't see swimming for the mainland. But maybe they could build a raft or something. Turning off the taps, she dried her hands and then leaned against the counter to think. They might not be able to leave tonight if they went by raft, but at least there was a better chance of surviving.

How long would it take to build a raft? She pondered that now. Cut down some trees, tie them together using sheets maybe. Make some kind of shelter to keep Domitian out of the sun, and make some paddles or something so they didn't end up getting pulled out to sea by currents.

That thought was alarming enough that Sarita pushed away from the counter and moved back into the bedroom. She glanced toward the bed, but all there was to see was the sheet wall Domitian had created. Leaving him to sleep, she slipped into the walk-in closet and grabbed another swimsuit to put on under her towel. Once she was as decently dressed as she was able in this place, Sarita headed for the office with its shelves of books.

When she didn't know something, Sarita researched it. At home she would have been checking the internet, Googling "how to make a sturdy raft" and "how to navigate unknown waters by the stars" and "what you should take if you expect to be stranded on the ocean." Unfortunately, there was no internet here. Hopefully the office had something useful on one of its many bookshelves.

It didn't take Sarita long to see that the books in the office wouldn't be much help. There were a couple of shelves of novels, but the rest were old scientific journals on genomes and DNA splicing and whatnot. If she'd wanted to create one of the poor creatures in the jars in the basement, she probably would have been all set, Sarita thought grimly. But there wasn't a single book that looked like it could tell her how to navigate by the stars or build a raft.

She was turning away with frustration when her gaze landed on one of the novels on the shelf, an old classic, *Robinson Crusoe*. Figuring it was better than nothing and might have at least one or two useful bits of information, Sarita grabbed it, cursing when the book next to it tumbled off the shelf and fell to the floor.

Muttering under her breath, she bent to pick it up, reading the title as she straightened. It was *The Hobbit* by J.R.R. Tolkien, Sarita saw, and there was a bit of paper sticking out at the top. Curious, Sarita opened the book and stared at the folded pages inside. It looked like a letter. Carrying everything to the desk, she set the books down, settled on the chair and opened the letter.

Dear Margaret,

Sorry this letter is so long in coming, but life has been a bit chaotic of late. And I apologize but this will be a short letter because it's nearly bedtime and Ramsey will be home soon.

First the good news; Ramsey and I are expecting our first child! Oh, Maggie, I wish I could have told you this face-to-face. I know you'd be as happy for me as I am about it, and we'd be hopping up and down and squealing like schoolgirls.

I did try to convince Ramsey to bring me home for a visit so I could tell you this in person. Sadly, he says there is just no way we can make it back to England before the baby is born. As disappointed as I am, I know he's right. There is so much to do!

I mentioned in my last letter that we were living in a charming little house on its own island, but that we were looking for a larger home nearby.

We found several nice houses, but none of them seemed to have everything Ramsey needed, so he determined to build a new house instead, and bought a nearby empty island.

The new island is five times bigger than the little one we're now living on and, as far as I can tell, Ramsey is having a house built that is also five times bigger. He's building labs too, which is good if it means he won't have to stay at the university so late working in the labs there.

Fortunately, the new island is only half an hour away in the little fishing boat Ramsey purchased to motor back and forth. Well, it is when he pilots it anyway. I'm afraid I don't go as fast as he does and it takes forty or forty-five minutes if I'm alone. I prefer it when Ramsey takes me, but he's so busy preparing his classes and overseeing his student's labs that most of the decisions about the new house have fallen to me. That means that more often than not I have to make the trip myself to meet up with the contractor on the bigger island.

The big island isn't visible from the little island except on the clearest of days and even then it's nothing more than a shadow on the horizon, easily missed if you didn't know it was there. You can't imagine how nervous I was about piloting the boat my first time alone. I was sure I would miss the island and end up out in the middle of the ocean and out of gas. But Ramsey was so sweet and encouraging about it. He was sure I could do it, and did everything possible to make it easier for me. He marked the boat's compass at a point just between the twenty and thirty degree points and said to keep the boat headed in that direction and I would reach the island fine. And he was right! I could and did do it, and was ever so proud of myself afterward. Mind you, I still prefer him at the helm, but needs must and in this case we need the house done and ready before the baby comes and if it were left to him that would never happen.

Speaking of that, Maggie, I don't mean to complain, and I know he has to work, but I just didn't realize how much time Ramsey's work would take up. Most of the time I'm left alone out here on this little island with no one but our maid, Mrs. Reyes, to talk to and I'm afraid she doesn't know much English. On top of that, she is only here during the day when I often am not. Ramsey pays a local fisherman to bring her out and take her back to the mainland every night and some days I see her only in passing as she arrives and I leave or vice versa. But the nights are lonely. Ramsey often doesn't return from the mainland until bedtime and then he's too exhausted to do more than grunt "goodnight." It makes me long for home. I miss you so. I miss all my family and friends and I miss England. This isn't nearly the exciting adventure I thought it would be when I agreed to marry him and move here. But I'm hoping everything will change once the house is done and the baby is here. Then he can work in his own lab and spend time with the baby and me. I'm sure things will improve then. In the meantime, I—

Sarita lowered the letter with a frown. It ended there, rather abruptly too, obviously midthought. She supposed Dressler had arrived home from the university then and Mrs. Dressler had probably shoved the unfinished letter in the book, intending to finish it later, but never getting back around to it.

Slipping the pages back into the book, Sarita closed it and tapped her fingers on the cover, her mind churning.

Domitian rolled over and reached for Sarita, but found only sheets. Frowning, he opened his eyes and peered around the cocooned bed. He was alone. Turning onto his back, he stared up at the ceiling, only to find it was himself he was looking at. The ceiling was mirrored.

Damn, he hadn't known that was there, Domitian thought and examined his reflection. His short hair was spiked in spots, probably from Sarita pulling on it last night, but other than that there was nothing much to see. The scratches and hickies he was quite sure she'd given him were gone now, the nanos having erased every trace of what had happened in that bed last night, three times.

Well, unless you counted the mess the bed itself was in, he supposed. The duvet was gone, probably lying somewhere on the floor next to the bed, and the upper sheet was bunched up at the bottom of the bed. As for the lower sheet, it had come off on both upper corners and curled in toward his head and shoulders. That was all there was to see. Now if Sarita was there, he would have had a perfect morning view. He could kiss her awake and then if he laid on his side next to her, he could watch her face in the mirror as he caressed her body and gave her pleasure.

That idea was rather appealing, Domitian decided, sitting up. He'd take a shower, brush his teeth, run downstairs for a quick blood top-up, and then find Sarita and lure her back to bed.

It was a solid plan, and worked right up to the point where it came to luring Sarita back to bed. Domitian showered, used the razor he found in the drawer to shave, and then brushed his teeth before heading downstairs to suck back some blood. He heard banging from the kitchen as he passed through the living room from the bedroom door to the office door, and wondered what Sarita was doing but didn't stop to check. After draining four bags, he went back up, though, and straight to the kitchen, his nose twitching. There was a heavy stench of something burning in the air, and his footsteps slowed warily as he passed through the dining room to the kitchen.

"There you are!" Sarita greeted him in a tone he would have said was a cross between "I'm super annoyed and trying not to show it" and "June Cleaver's got nothing on me" good cheer. In other words, it was super fake and tinged with the threat of violence. One glance around the chaos in the kitchen told him why. His Sarita was brilliant, beautiful, sexy, and he was sure she had many talents . . . but cooking obviously wasn't one of them, he decided as she announced, "I made us breakfast."

"*Si*. I see that," Domitian murmured, his gaze sliding over burned toast, bacon that was raw on the ends and burned in the middle, and eggs so underdone the tops of the whites were clear. No, the woman could not cook, he thought and sat down in the chair at the island when she indicated it, determined to eat every last bite if it killed him.

"I'm not as good a cook as you," Sarita announced as she settled next to him. "But you made me dinner last night, so I thought I'd handle breakfast." Shrugging, she confessed, "Breakfast for me is usually cereal or toaster strudels, though, and they didn't have those here, so I did the best I could."

It was such an unapologetic apology that Domitian was hard pressed not to chuckle. The woman had no problem acknowledging her few flaws or failings and even seemed to accept having some as inevitable. He really liked that about her. Too many people tried to be perfect at everything, or made excuses for not being perfect. Sarita just shrugged as if to say "I did my best. Take it or leave it."

He was more than happy to take it, Domitian decided and picked up his knife and fork, then paused to glance at Sarita when she began to make choking, gagging sounds.

"Oh God," she muttered after spitting out the piece of toast and egg she'd apparently combined to put in her mouth. "Oh, ick. No, put those down." She slapped at his hands, making him put down his fork and knife, then snatched up both her plate and his and stood to carry them around the island, saying, "We can't eat this. It's awful. Those eggs are *raw*." Opening the cupboard under the sink, she tossed both meals into the garbage, plates and all, and kicked the door closed with a shudder. "Ugh. I hate raw eggs."

Exasperated, Sarita walked to the refrigerator, opened

it to peer inside, and asked, "How about a cheese sand-wich instead? I can manage that."

Shaking his head, Domitian stood and walked up behind her to catch her by the shoulders and urge her back toward the chair she'd just left. "How about you sit down and relax and I make breakfast?"

"Oh, but you cooked last night," she protested. "I could try again. Maybe French toast or something. That's just toast dipped in eggs and milk then fried, right? Al-though, I'll have to see if they provided any maple syrup here first. Do you guys get maple syrup down here or is that a Canadian thing? I don't recall ever having it when we lived here."

Sarita had escaped his loose hold and made a dash for the cupboards, but he caught her and turned her back toward the stools at the island. "Sit. It will be my pleasure to cook for you. I enjoy it. In fact you are the reason I learned to cook."

"What?" she asked with surprise, dropping onto the chair and turning to look at him.

"It is true," Domitian assured her, opening the refrig-erator to pull out more bacon and eggs. "If you will recall, I lost my appetites back—"

"Before Christ was born," Sarita finished for him dryly. "Yeah, I remember." Frowning now, she said, "Speaking of which, if you didn't eat before meeting me, why did you own a restaurant?"

"I like them," he said simply. "It is where people go to celebrate happy events. Besides, I do not only own restaurants. I have a couple of hotels and a nightclub too. In fact, prior to encountering you I had always spent more time overseeing the nightclub than at any of the restaurants. I usually left those up to the managers I hired to run them."

"So why were you at the restaurant the night my father took me?" she asked curiously.

"That was pure luck," he assured her as he pulled out a clean frying pan and set it on the range. "The previous manager had left rather abruptly due to health issues. That was not the lucky part," he added dryly, before continuing. "The lucky part was that I hired a replacement for him, but had to train him myself. And then you walked in." Smiling, he shook his head. "Suddenly I was much more interested in the food than in the management end of the business. Meeting you reawakened my appetites," he explained.

"All your appetites?" she asked, her eyebrows rising. She'd only been thirteen. Surely his interest in sex hadn't—

"All of them," he admitted solemnly as he began to lay the strips of bacon in the pan one after another. Turning the flame on under the frying pan, he added, "Of course, there was nothing to do about the reappearance of my physical desire. You were far too young. But food . . ." He shook his head. "Not only did I rediscover my delight in it, but I found I had a great desire to learn to cook the meal you ate that first time. You seemed to enjoy it so, and I wanted to be able to make it for you. So I had our chef teach me how to make it, and found I enjoyed cooking as much as eating."

"So you learned to cook?" she asked, watching him turn the bacon.

"*Si*. I hired a manager to oversee all the businesses for me and flew to Europe to attend the best culinary schools available. I spent ten years training."

"Ten?" Sarita squawked with surprise as he turned the bacon.

"*Sí*. I had time to fill while I waited for you to grow up," he said with a shrug. "And I wanted to learn it all. I wanted to be able to make anything your heart desired. I wanted to ply you with delicacies no one else could."

"Ten years," she said thoughtfully. "Were you here then the second time we ate at your restaurant? The night before we returned home after Grandfather's funeral?"

"*Sí*. I had returned just three weeks before," Domitian admitted and smiled as he recalled that day. "You cannot imagine how shocked I was when my manager came to tell me someone had asked him to thank the chef for such a lovely meal and I glanced out to see you and your father just making your way to the door to leave my restaurant."

"Your private detective hadn't told you I was here in Venezuela?" Sarita asked a bit archly.

Domitian shook his head. "His report came the day after you left. Which," he added, "was probably a good thing in the end."

"Why was it a good thing?" she asked with amusement.

"Because you were no longer a child," he said wryly. "You were twenty-three, a fully grown woman." He dropped some butter in the empty pan to melt and began cracking eggs into a bowl as he recalled the wash of emotion and desire that had rolled over him at just knowing she was near. "You were leaving, your back was to me, and I could not see your face. For a moment, I just stared at your back, hoping you would turn so that I could see your face. But you did not. Once the door closed behind you I did not think, I just rushed after you. But it was a busy night and there seemed to be a waiter or customer in my way every couple of feet. By the time I got outside you and your father were gone.

"I struggled that night," Domitian admitted solemnly. "When I first found you at thirteen, I had determined I would not claim you until you had worked at your chosen career for at least two years. At the time you returned to my restaurant you had returned to university to get your master's degree in criminology after taking only one year off to work."

"My father had paid my way through university to get my bachelor degree, but I felt I should pay my own way for my master's, so I worked for a year to get the money together and continued to work while getting my master's," Sarita explained softly.

"*Si . . .*" Domitian nodded as he eased the raw eggs from the bowl onto the second frying pan. Glancing to her then he grinned and said, "You cannot know how sorry I was to learn you had chosen a career that needed such long schooling. Although," Domitian added dryly, casting her the stink eye. "I understand a master's degree is not necessary to become a police officer, so you took longer than absolutely necessary."

Sarita laughed at his expression and shrugged. "I want to be a detective someday. So I went for a master's in criminology with a minor in psychology."

"And then it took forever to get accepted to the police force," he said grimly.

"Yes, there's a pretty lengthy selection process," she admitted. "There are three stages of assessment with tests and whatnot at each stage. It takes a while, and then once you're accepted, you still have to go to the police college for training."

"*Si.* I know this," Domitian assured her. "I found it out when I learned what you wanted to do. I was trying to judge how long it would be before I could come and woo you," he admitted, and then shook his head. "However, when I saw you that night in my restaurant, my good intentions flew out of the window, and if I had caught up to you, my noble plans would have been meaningless."

"Noble, huh?" Sarita asked with amusement.

Glancing up from the bacon he was turning again, Domitian eyed her seriously. "Believe me, waiting was noble. A sacrifice. I had already waited more than two thousand years to find you when I first saw you. They seemed to me to pass so slowly, but these past fifteen years?" He shook his head. "They seemed longer than the two thousand that came before."

Turning, he pushed the button to start the bread toasting and then grabbed two plates and butter. As he set them next to the toaster, Domitian admitted, "I searched for you that night. I called every hotel in the city looking for where you and your father were staying."

"We stayed in my grandfather's apartment," Sarita said softly.

"*Si.* That was also in the report I got the next day, but by then you were on a plane back to Canada." He fetched another plate, lined it with paper towel and shifted the bacon strips from the pan to the plate one at a time. "I forced myself to calm down then. I told myself it was fate making sure I stuck to my original plan, and I would wait until you had graduated and worked two years in your field."

Domitian glanced over to see Sarita watching him with an indefinable expression. She looked serious, but her expression was uncharacteristically soft at the same time. Wondering what she was thinking, he set the plate of bacon before her and turned his attention to removing the now perfect sunny-side-up eggs to two plates.

"And when I came for my father's funeral?" Sarita asked, walking around the island to begin buttering the toast when it popped.

Domitian almost sighed inwardly. He'd planned on skipping that trip, not wanting to upset her as talk of her father had last night, but it seemed fate was pushing them that way anyway, so he admitted, "I struggled then too, but a little less. You were in the police college. Once done I would only have to wait two years to come woo you."

"So, you were planning to come to Canada this summer?" she asked with curiosity.

"I already have the plane ticket," he admitted with a shrug. Turning off the heat under both frying pans, Domitian carried the plates with the eggs on them around to set on the island in front of their seats.

"And how did you plan to approach me?" Sarita asked, following with the toast.

Domitian held her chair for her as she sat down and set the toast on the island, then claimed his own seat before turning to her and saying solemnly, "I was going to walk up to you and say, 'My name is Domitian Argenis . . . You are my life mate . . . Prepare to be loved.'"

Sarita blinked at him several times, and then recognition bloomed on her face, and she cried, *"The Princess Bride!"*

"Si." Domitian grinned, pleased she recognized it.

"As you wish!" she said suddenly and shook her head. "I knew it reminded me of something when you said that, I just . . ." Sarita shook her head. "I can't believe I didn't pick up on it at once. I love that old movie. It's a classic."

"It is not that old," he protested.

"It was made before I was born," she said dryly.

"*Si*, but you are still young," Domitian said, and she grinned.

"Yeah, and I always will be to you . . . because you're *so old*," Sarita taunted.

"You do enjoy reminding me of that," he said wryly.

"Hey," she said with a shrug. "I find amusement where I can. Life is short."

"It does not have to be," he said solemnly.

Sarita had turned back to her plate, but seemed to freeze at his words. The moment she did, Domitian could have kicked himself for saying them. It was too soon. He was rushing her and would scare her off if he wasn't careful.

"Orange juice," he said abruptly, and got up to go fetch glasses and the juice.

"Domitian."

He just managed not to hunch his shoulders as if against a blow as he heard the solemn tone to her voice. Forcing himself to remain calm and relaxed, he smiled at her inquisitively as he carried the glasses and orange juice back to his seat, trying not to look like he knew she was going to say something that would alarm him. *"Si, mi tresoro?"*

"I've enjoyed our time together," Sarita started carefully, and he heard the *but* coming before she said,

"But once we are off this island and I'm sure my grand-mother is safe, I am returning to my job and home in Canada."

Domitian forced himself to nod mildly. "*Si*. And I will follow."

She frowned. "You'd follow me to Canada?"

He shrugged. "I have family there. It would be nice to be closer to my sister."

Her eyes widened incredulously. "You mean you'd *move* there? But what about your restaurants and—?"

"*Mi Corazon*," he interrupted gently, "you are my life mate. I will not rush you. I will remain patient and give you the time you need, but I will follow you to Canada and woo you as you deserve."

He saw Sarita's throat move as she swallowed, but then she turned her face down to her plate and he wasn't sure how she was taking his words. Domitian supposed he'd hoped she'd throw her arms around his neck and declare him the most wonderful man in the world and vow to be his. He knew that was a ridiculous hope, however. Life never went that easily.

They ate in a mostly companionable silence, and then cleaned up together. Domitian was about to finally get to his plan to lure her to the bedroom when she suddenly took his hand and led him from the kitchen. Thinking he wouldn't need to lure her to the bedroom and that she was leading him there instead, he followed easily. However, he frowned with confusion when instead of turning toward the bedroom, Sarita instead led him across the living room and outside.

"Er . . . Sarita?" Domitian asked finally as she tugged him toward the pool. "What are we doing?"

"We're going in the pool," she announced, releasing

him to reach up and undo the towel wrapped around her torso. Letting it drop to the ground, she stepped over it and dove into the water.

Domitian stared after her with bemusement for a minute, his mind frozen on the view he'd got of her in the tiny, pale pink bikini she was wearing today. It was smaller even than the white one he'd first seen her in and contrasted beautifully with her tan skin.

"Hey! Come on. Hurry up."

Blinking, he forced the image of Sarita that was still frozen in his mind's eye away and peered at the real woman to see that she was by the waterfall and appeared to be waiting for him. That was when he got the idea she might want to talk about something that she didn't want overheard by the cameras. Kicking himself into action, he walked to the edge of the pool, dove in, and swam toward her, surfacing just a foot or so in front of her.

"I was thinking when I woke up," Sarita announced.

"Okay," Domitian said warily and waited.

"Well, we have no idea where we are and no clue what direction to go in to get to the mainland," she pointed out. "And the ocean is full of sharks and whales and other unfriendlies."

"Unfriendlies?" he asked with amusement.

Sarita shrugged, "I just didn't want to say creatures that want to eat us," she admitted with a crooked smile. "Anyway, the point is I got thinking that maybe we need a raft, and maybe there'd be something in one of the books in the office that could help with this escape of ours, so I went and took a look. There wasn't really," she added quickly. "I mean the closest thing I found to useful was Daniel Defoe's *Robinson Crusoe*. But—"

"Sarita," he interrupted gently. "It will be fine. We may not know where we are, but it has to be north of Venezuela, so if we go south we will find the mainland."

"Yeah, but we have no idea which way is north and which way south," she said at once.

Domitian raised an arm and pointed toward the front of the house and the dock. "That way is south."

She blinked, glanced in the direction he was pointing and then turned back to him and raised her eyebrows in question.

"I am more than two thousand years old, *mi Corazon*. I learned long ago how to navigate by the stars."

"Oh." Sarita looked nonplussed, and then glanced toward the beach again, but followed that by turning to peer toward the jungle behind the house. "So north would be that way."

"Si," he agreed patiently.

"Okay, well see, that's good to know, because the big island is north of this island," she announced.

Domitian stiffened. "I thought you did not know where this island was? Yesterday you thought we might *be* on the big island."

"I found a letter," Sarita said, suddenly practically bursting with excitement. "It was from Mrs. Dressler to a friend of hers back in England, and she was saying that they were living on this island but building a new bigger home on an island not far from here. Half an hour by one of those little fishing boats with an outboard motor. Well, half an hour when Dr. Dressler piloted it, but forty-five minutes when she did," she corrected herself. "Elizabeth Dressler said she was nervous about driving it there on her own, but he marked the compass at a point between twenty and thirty degrees north and said to keep the boat heading that way and she would reach the island."

"That is good news, *mi Corazon*," Domitian said smiling at her widely. "It means when we get to the mainland, we can tell my uncle where the island is."

Sarita frowned at him. "Yeah, but I was thinking . . ."

"What were you thinking?" he asked, wary again.

"Look, I don't especially want to go to the island, but—"

"No," Domitian interrupted firmly. "I am not taking you anywhere near that island. The idea is to get you as far from Dressler as possible, not to deliver you and myself into his arms."

"I know," Sarita said with understanding. "But just listen to me. I was awake for the helicopter ride to the island and it was quite a long ride. Unfortunately, I didn't check my watch when we left and arrived, but I'm guessing it was a good hour, and the helicopter wasn't puttering along like a fishing boat, it was going really fast. I don't think we can make it to the mainland."

"I can swim for a very long time," he assured her.

"Pulling me?" she asked. "Because I suspect you'll have to. At least part of the way. I can swim, but not all night and day. And that's the other thing," Sarita added. "What if it does take twenty-four hours or something to get there? You're the one who said five hundred miles was your uncle's *conservative* estimate of where the island might be. You aren't swimming that far in a night. We'll be swimming during daylight too, without blood for you to top up on. I don't particularly want to be a walking blood bank."

Domitian frowned. "We do not have to make it to the mainland. I am sure we will encounter another island—"

"What if we don't?" Sarita asked. "And what if we are attacked by a shark? What if you're injured?"

He was more concerned about *her* being injured by a shark, but before he could say so, she added, "Without blood to help you heal, you might be more dangerous to me than a shark."

Domitian opened his mouth to assure her he would never harm her, but paused as he realized he couldn't make that promise. If he were badly injured in a shark attack . . . Well, immortals had been known to lose their heads and attack mortals in that state. The nanos could cause terrible agony and a blood lust when they needed blood. Sarita might be right. He could be more dangerous to her than a shark in that case.

"And then there's my grandmother," she said now.

Domitian focused on her with confusion. "Your grandmother is on the mainland."

"Do you really believe that?" Sarita asked dryly. "Think about it. Dressler wanted us both here for some reason, and he is the one who called and told me that my grandmother needed me. What are the chances that she just *happened* to fall down the stairs and hurt herself at the exact time when he apparently wanted us here? Hmm?"

Domitian shook his head. That hadn't occurred to him. "But you said she wasn't on the island. We thought perhaps they live on the mainland in the apartment and use the island house as a cottage."

"I said there was no sign that she lived in the *big* house," Sarita said firmly. "But I was thinking about Grandmother's letters, and according to everything she's ever written me, she definitely lives on the island with Mrs. Dressler and her son year round. I'm pretty sure Dressler is the only one who stays in that apartment in town. They have to be in the little house. There is nowhere else that they could be."

"Okay," he said reassuringly. "We will give that news to my uncle and they can be sure to—Why are you shaking your head?" he interrupted himself to ask, but suspected he already knew why.

"I am not going to the mainland," she announced, proving he had known why after all. "I don't think we'll make it if we head that way. And I'm not leaving my grandmother stuck out there on that island with Dr. Demento while I follow you to my death in the middle of the ocean."

"Sarita," Domitian said patiently.

"I'm not," she said firmly. "But I won't stop you if you want to try it. Your chances are probably better without me to slow you down. You might even make it. And I'll even tell you everything I know about the big island so you can tell your uncle."

"And what then? You will try to make it to the big island by yourself?" he asked with disbelief, and then said grimly, "I don't recall any of the reports I got saying you were suicidal."

"I'm not," she assured him. "And while I'm not a marathon swimmer, I did take lessons as a kid, and I'm a good floater. I can swim, then float for a while to rest, then swim again."

"Sarita," he said, running a hand wearily through his wet hair.

"It's closer than the mainland," she pointed out firmly. "I know I can't make the mainland, but the island is closer. I'm sure I can manage getting there, and I don't even have to build a raft. There are some blow-up lounge mattresses in one of the wicker chests that will do for a shorter journey."

Domitian scowled. "I think you probably could reach the big island, but we would be swimming directly into Dressler's waiting arms."

"We?" she asked.

"Well, I am not letting you swim anywhere on your own. There are sharks out there," he said gruffly.

Sarita smiled widely, but then responded to his comment about swimming directly into Dressler's arms. "El Doctor and his men will be watching for boats, not someone swimming to the island."

Domitian considered that.

"Actually, this might work out better all the way around. After we check the little house on the north end of the island to make sure my grandmother is okay, we can sneak around and find out all we need to know to help your uncle and his Rogue Hunters attack the island."

"Si," he agreed. "But how do we get that information to him?"

Sarita shrugged. "There is a phone in the big house. If there isn't one in the little house, then we can sneak into the big house and use that one. We could call your uncle, give him the location and all the pertinent info, and coordinate with him."

"Coordinate?" Domitian asked with alarm.

"Yes. Find out what time he expects to attack the island so we can help. We can even try to get in and free the kidnapped immortals so they can help from on the island," she added thoughtfully.

"No," Domitian said firmly. "You will wait some-where safe while I—"

"Domitian," Sarita interrupted patiently.

"*Si?*" he asked warily.

"Please don't go all Ramsay on me."

"Ramsey?" he squawked, seriously insulted. "I am nothing like Dressler."

"Gordon Ramsay, not Ramsey Dressler," she said dryly. "I know you're a chef, but that doesn't give you leave to go all Gordon Ramsay and start trying to boss me around," she explained. "I'm a police officer, trained for confrontation, and I've also studied martial arts since I was thirteen. As I mentioned, that was the first thing Dad signed me up for in Canada. Of the two of us, I'm more equipped to deal with this."

"I am more than a chef," he said indignantly. "I have been a warrior, a knight, a pirate. I can handle myself in battle, Sarita," he finished stiffly.

"Oh yeah. I guess you can help then," she said, turn-ing to head for the stairs. "Come on, we should get as much sleep as we can today so we're well rested to-night."

Domitian turned, but didn't start moving right away. Instead, he stared after her with suspicion, wondering how his trying to protect her had somehow turned into his having to justify his involvement in the battle that would come.

She'd turned the tables on him, he realized. And quite neatly too. And was now prancing off thinking he was going to let her risk herself by helping on the island.

"Sarita," Domitian said sharply. "We need to—" He'd meant to say they needed to discuss this further, but his voice died in his throat when she reached back to undo the top of her bikini and let it drop into the water as she mounted the stairs.

Turning once she stood on the terrace, Sarita faced him. Her hands were on her hips and her head was held high and proud, he noted before his gaze fell to her beautiful bare breasts. God, he loved her body.

"Hurry, Domitian. You need to make love to me so I can sleep," she said huskily. "I think we should stay in bed all day to be sure we are well rested for later."

He was across the pool and out, scooping her into his arms before she quite finished the last word.

"As you wish," Domitian growled as he strode toward the house.

Eleven

Eyes narrowing, Sarita scanned the island in the distance, looking for any movement that might tell her someone was patrolling the beach and might notice their approach when they got closer. In truth, she wasn't worried about Domitian being seen, he was mostly under water with only his head bobbing up once in a while as he took in air.

Sarita, however, was presently lying on her stomach on an inflatable pool lounger and was much more visible. She knew they'd have to pop the mattress and let it sink soon, but that was okay with her. She hadn't really wanted to bring it anyway. She would have taken it willingly if she'd been trying to reach the island alone, just for safety's sake. But with Domitian to help her, she hadn't expected to need it. She'd insisted she could alternate swimming and floating and make the distance without the air mattress when he'd brought it up as they ate their last meal on the island in the cocooned bed. He'd insisted they bring it, however, arguing that her resting would slow them down and they needed to reach the island before dawn. With the lounger, she could rest on it when she wearied and he could tow her as he swam.

Sarita had given in and retrieved the air mattress from the wicker chest where she'd seen it earlier. Leaving Domitian to blow it up by the pool, she'd gone to collect scissors, and had taken them with her to the bedroom. She'd made the rope to pull the air mattress in the privacy of the cocooned bed in the hopes of not giving away what they were up to any earlier than necessary. It was the sheets actually on the bed she'd used, cutting thin strips that she'd then braided together. Fortunately, it hadn't taken too long. Still it had been later than they'd wanted when they'd taken the mattress and rope and headed for the beach.

Unfortunately, as Sarita had feared, she'd spent a good portion of the trip on the air mattress. Oh, she'd swum more than half the distance under her own steam, but Domitian was a much faster swimmer than her and she'd found herself having to climb onto the mattress to rest more often than she'd liked. It was humiliating each time he'd noticed her flagging and had relegated her to the mattress to be towed along like a sick whale pulled out to deeper water by a boat.

That thought made Sarita cast a quick glance around at the moonlit water for any sign of a shark or anything. They'd been fortunate and not encountered anything like that so far, but how long could their luck hold out?

Movement below her made Sarita glance down through the clear plastic window in the center of the lounger's headrest. She half expected to see the shadow of a fish swimming along under her. She'd seen that once or twice in the bright moonlight, the darker shadow of a fish in the dark water, or even a flash of color if it was right beneath the mattress. This time, though, she was shocked to see a human figure swimming past under the mattress. She saw the clear outline of a head, chest, and arms moving quickly through the water headed toward Domitian.

Cursing, Sarita immediately lunged off the mattress after the figure.

Domitian was just thinking they were getting close enough to the island that they should stop, pop the air mattress, and leave it behind when the makeshift rope tied around his waist suddenly seemed to go slack. Stopping, he turned swiftly in the water to look back and saw that while the lounger was still there, Sarita was gone.

Frowning, he quickly reached under water, grabbed the rope at his waist and gave it a tug. Pain seared his back as the cloth dug in before the makeshift rope snapped, but he ignored it and dove under water. The ocean was dark, but Domitian had no problem spotting Sarita some fifteen feet away. Still, it took him a second to accept that she appeared to be struggling with something. Not something, *someone*, he realized. It was a man, and he was dragging Sarita down deeper in the water and away from the air she needed to survive.

Growling in his throat, Domitian shot forward, swimming hard to reach them as quickly as possible. Sarita couldn't survive long under water without air. She already appeared to be flagging while the man showed no signs of having the same problem. Swimming up behind the man, Domitian didn't even hesitate, he simply snapped his neck, then caught Sarita by the arm and kicked for the surface, pulling her with him.

He'd feared she was unconscious on first grabbing her, but Sarita started coughing and sputtering the moment her head broke from the water. It was music to his ears. Relief racing through him, Domitian dragged her to the air mattress, and lifted her to lie across it, then held on to it with one hand as he patted her back to help her spit up the water she'd swallowed.

"Are you okay?" he asked with concern as she gasped for air.

Sarita nodded, but simply continued to suck in great drafts of air. When she'd recovered enough to speak, she turned a stark face to him and gasped, "His face."

Domitian frowned, and then glanced around for the man, but he hadn't floated to the surface. A sliver of concern slipping through him, he said, "Wait here," and released the mattress to dive under water again. He spotted the man right away, motionless in the water where he'd left him some fifteen feet away.

Bewildered, he swam to the figure and stopped to look him over. While Domitian was having to work hard to keep from rising to the surface thanks to the air in his lungs, the dead man was just floating there about ten feet below the surface, neither sinking nor floating upward. He appeared dead, though.

Catching one of the man's hands, Domitian kicked for the surface, dragging the body behind. He wasn't surprised to see that Sarita hadn't listened, hadn't rested on the lounger as he'd instructed. She was halfway between him and the mattress, looking around worriedly when he broke the surface and pulled the man up next to him.

"There was something wrong with his face," she told him, swimming closer to peer at the man now lying facedown between them. "And he seemed to be breathing under water."

Domitian nodded and pulled the man closer. It was as he started to turn him in the water that he noticed something behind the man's ear. Pausing, he pulled the ear forward to get a better view.

"They look kind of like gills," Sarita said with amazement, stopping next to him.

"Yes," Domitian muttered, running a finger along one of the six four-inch flaps that ran around the man's ear and curved down his neck.

"Does he have a tail too or just legs?" Sarita asked tightly, no doubt thinking of the fetuses in the jars back at the lab. "I couldn't tell while we were struggling."

"Legs," he answered.

"His fingers are webbed, though."

Domitian glanced to the hand she was looking at and saw that the skin between the fingers was indeed webbed.

"Probably his feet too," Sarita said thoughtfully, releasing his hand. "He was moving pretty fast in the water. If I'd been any slower I wouldn't have got him. As it is, I barely dove in quick enough to grab his foot as it whipped by."

"*You* attacked *him*?" he asked with surprise. He'd assumed the man had pulled her off the mattress.

Sarita nodded. "I saw him swim under the mattress. He was heading for you at speed. I was sure he was going to attack you so I dove in and grabbed him. It wasn't until he jerked around that I saw the knife," she added with a grimace and then glanced to the man. "He could have stabbed me right then, but didn't."

Domitian turned his gaze back to the man as well, wondering if he'd allowed his worry for Sarita to make him kill someone who had really meant them no harm.

"He seemed to be trying to half drown me, though," Sarita added. "Yet he wasn't overly rough while he did it." She frowned and then glanced to Domitian and said, "Dr. Dressler still needs something from us. Perhaps he's given orders that if we came around they weren't to harm me, but could do whatever was necessary to subdue you because you'll heal. Maybe he wasn't really trying to kill me, just weaken me to make me easier to handle."

Domitian nodded and relaxed a little. Sarita was probably right about that. Dressler would know by now that they hadn't just gone for a swim in the ocean and were headed somewhere. He would have warned his people to keep an eye out in case they somehow ended up near the island. Which meant there were probably other hybrids like this one in the water.

"We have to move," Domitian said, releasing the man and taking Sarita's arm to urge her back toward the air mattress.

"I wanted to see his face," she protested. "What I could see of it while we were struggling seemed odd."

"No time. There could be others out here," he pointed out grimly. "We need to move."

"Oh, yes of course," Sarita murmured and stopped trying to turn back.

When she started to swim, Domitian released her and followed the rest of the distance to the air mattress.

"We should pop the lounger," she said as they stopped next to it. "I can swim from here."

Domitian merely nodded, let his fangs slide out and bit down into the mattress. But he was wishing it was a bag of blood. His body had used up a lot of energy to get this far and keep his body heat high. He was starting to cramp with the need for blood.

"Handy," Sarita said with a wry smile as she watched him puncture the mattress twice more to speed up the release of air.

Domitian grunted. "Let's go," he said softly. They'd both instinctively been talking quietly. Voices carried across water.

Sarita nodded and struck out at a steady pace he could have easily outstripped, but didn't. They still had a distance to go to get to the island and then they had to make their way around to the north end. It was better to go at a steady medium pace than to go fast and wear Sarita out. Besides, he wanted to keep an eye out for any more gilled people that might be out there with them. Fortunately, they needn't rush. Either the big island wasn't as far from the little island as he'd thought, or they'd made good time. By his guess it was still a good couple hours until dawn.

Sarita kept expecting Domitian to overtake her and surge ahead to urge them to a faster pace, but he didn't. He stayed behind her as they approached and then swam around the island where Dressler had his labs. They were just turning to curve around the end of the island where the little house she'd seen should be when

Sarita realized why he hadn't overtaken her. He was watching her back in case there were more gilled creatures out there like the one now floating in the water on the other side of the island. Which was nice, but there was no one watching him and she twisted her head and glanced back toward him as she turned her face up out of the water to get her next breath. It was something she'd done every other breath since they'd left the air mattress behind, and he was there just as he had been each time she'd checked. But this time, he was swimming sidestroke instead of freestyle, obviously watching for her to look back, she thought when he noticed her looking and stopped swimming to gesture at her to stop as well.

Sarita obeyed at once and turned in the water to face him. As she waited for him to move up next to her, she cast a glance toward shore. They were much closer now than the last time she'd tried to scan the island. Back then it had been little more than a black blob with lights shining out from behind black shadows here and there. But they'd cut in closer as soon as they reached the end of the island, and in the dark shadows, she could make out the general shape of the beach and where the jungle that bordered it started. She couldn't see the house yet, but suspected they were close.

"Am I right in guessing the house is just around that cliff?" Domitian asked in a hushed voice as he paused beside her to tread water.

Sarita glanced to the outcropping he was talking about and nodded her head. "I think so."

"Then I think we should go ashore here and move through the trees instead of approaching by water."

Sarita glanced along the beach. There might be someone in the trees inside the jungle, but it was easy to see that the beach at least was empty. The same couldn't be said for the water around them. There could be a dozen gilled creatures hovering nearby under the surface, watching them, and they wouldn't know it until they were attacked. She nodded.

"I will follow you," Domitian said, glancing around the calm surface of the ocean.

Turning, Sarita struck out for shore, actually relieved to be able to do so. She stayed fit for her job, but while she hadn't had to swim the entire way like Domitian had tonight, it was obvious to her that she wouldn't have been able to. By her guess, she'd only been swimming for an hour or a little more since they'd left the mattress, and not quickly, yet was trembling from the effort. Those nanos obviously made Domitian and others of his kind superhuman.

The thought made her worry about how he was doing on that count. Were his nanos using up blood like crazy to keep up his speed and stamina? Was he now in need of blood? She had no idea what they would do if that was the case. They'd left the blood supply back on the island. Although, she knew there was a large refrigerator full of it in Dressler's lab. The problem was getting to it.

The first scrape of sand against her fingertips as she performed her next stroke made Sarita push those worries from her mind and lift her head from the water to look around. They were still quite a distance from where the water lapped at the beach, but it seemed it was shallow here, she realized as her feet drifted down to touch the sand her fingers just had.

Sarita stood up in the water and staggered to the

side before catching herself. Sighing, she stood still for a minute, surveying the trees as she gave her legs a moment of rest before forcing them to move.

"Are you all right?" Domitian asked in a voice that was almost a whisper as he waded up beside her.

Sarita nodded. "Just checking to be sure there's no one in the trees," she said softly.

Nodding, Domitian surveyed them himself. When he let out a little breath and relaxed a moment later, she knew that he hadn't seen anything. Since his eyes were undoubtedly better than hers thanks to those nanos, Sarita gave up looking as well and started forward. With every step she took she was sure her legs were going to give out, but they held her up and carried her to shore.

"Let us move up by the trees and sit down," Domitian suggested, taking her arm to urge her forward. "I think we should rest for a minute before we continue on. I want you able to run if there is trouble when we get to the house."

"What kind of trouble are you thinking there might be?" Sarita asked with a frown, briefly forgetting her shaky legs.

Domitian shook his head. "Could be anything— guards on the house, guards inside the house. Or your grandmother might not even be here. Dressler might have given the house to his head of security as part of his income."

Sarita considered the possibility, but shook her head. "That can't be. My grandmother and Mrs. Dressler have to live somewhere here on the island. And other than this house and the big house, all there is are the labs."

"I am sure you are right," Domitian said mildly. "I

just want to be sure you can move fast if you have to. Now sit down and rest your muscles."

Sarita glanced around to see that they'd walked all the way to the edge of the jungle while she was distracted. Relieved, she dropped to sit in the sand facing the water and drew her knees up to rest her arms on top of them. Resting her chin on her crossed arms, she peered out toward the horizon, noting that it was lightening. Dawn wasn't that far away. They couldn't rest long and should be inside before the sun brightened the sky and made them easily visible. There might be guards here.

"I will be right back."

Sarita glanced up with a start, but before she could ask where he was going, Domitian had slipped into the trees and disappeared.

"Probably going to the bathroom," she told herself in a mutter and glanced nervously along the shore, watching for anything moving. There was nothing that she could see.

Sighing, Sarita turned to scan the spot where Domitian had disappeared. Not seeing anything, she shifted her gaze back along the shore again to give it another quick once-over and then repeated the two actions, looking for Domitian, then checking the silent beach. Sarita had just done that for about the twentieth time and was looking along the shore when a crackling sound brought her head sharply around toward the trees behind her.

Sarita peered into the dark mass of trees, straining to see and thought she saw branches moving in a tree behind and to the left of her. And then a sound behind her on the right had her turning her head sharply to look that way. She sagged with relief when she saw it was Domitian slipping back out of the woods.

"Come," he whispered, holding a hand down to her.

Sarita took his hand and allowed him to haul her to her feet. Her legs were no longer trembling, but her muscles protested at being forced to move again so soon. Ignoring that, she followed Domitian into the jungle, asking, "Shouldn't we use the beach?"

"It is shorter this way," he replied quietly.

Sarita nodded to herself as she forced her legs to follow him up a winding path. He hadn't gone to relieve himself in the woods then, but had been checking out the house to be sure it was safe to approach. The man seemed to forget she was a police officer and could take care of herself. They'd have to talk about that some time, she thought, and then glanced up and leaned to the side, trying to see how much farther they had to walk. Her calf muscles were burning like crazy.

Unable to see around Domitian's wide chest and shoulders, Sarita simply put her head down and continued forward, reciting song lyrics in her head as she went as a way to distract herself. It worked so well that she was completely unprepared when Domitian suddenly stopped. She plowed right into his back, nearly knocking him over.

"Woah," he whispered, reaching back to steady her as he regained his own balance.

"Sorry," Sarita muttered and clasped his arm to lean out and try to peer around him again. This time she managed the feat, and her eyes widened as she saw that they were there. A small English-style cottage sat not ten feet in front of them. Two stories, it was cross-gabled with steeply pitched roofs and tall, narrow, lattice windows. Her gaze slid over the chimney and gabled entry and she nodded solemnly. "Oh yeah, Mrs. Dressler lives here."

"What makes you say that?" Domitian asked in a whisper.

"She was missing England in her letter, and this is definitely a little bit of England in the middle of the tropics," Sarita pointed out. "It looks like it could have been scooped up out of the Cotswolds and dropped here or something."

He nodded agreement. "Yes, I suppose it does."

"Come on . . ." Sarita started to move around him, but he caught her arm.

"Wait," Domitian rasped, pulling her close to his side. "What is the plan?"

"We knock on the door and ask to see my grandmother," she said simply.

"Just like that?" he asked with disbelief. "What if Dressler has some of his security detail in there?"

Sarita glanced at the cottage again and shook her head. "It's too small for that. My guess is there are three tiny bedrooms upstairs, a living room, bathroom, kitchen, and dining room downstairs. There can't be much more than that," she said with certainty.

"I did not say his men had to be living there," Domitian said grimly. "What if they are posted at the doors?"

Sarita sighed with exasperation, but supposed it wasn't impossible. "Okay, we'll look in the windows first and then knock on the door if there's no sign of Dressler's goons."

"And if there are goons in there?" Domitian asked.

"Then we come back here and make another plan," she said patiently. "Come on."

He didn't stop her this time when she started toward the house, but did mutter, "You are entirely too used to being a police officer."

Sarita scowled at him over her shoulder. "What does that mean?"

"It means you seem to think you can just walk up to the door and knock and no one will take a shot at you or anything."

"I agreed to check the windows, didn't I?" Sarita pointed out. "Besides, I suspect Dressler needs us alive for whatever nasty little experiment he has in mind for us, so we aren't likely to be shot. Now hush or we'll wake someone up before we want to," she warned, slowing as they approached the front window on this side of the house.

"Too late for that, children. Do come in. We're all awake."

Sarita stiffened and peered at the window as the voice of what she thought was an old woman drifted out to them. Only then did she see that the window was open. Mouth tightening, she peered in at the dark shapes inside.

"The door is unlocked," the voice said now and Sarita thought it was coming from a chair across the room where she could just make out what looked like a seated figure. The voice was definitely an old woman's and it had an English accent to it.

"Mrs. Dressler?" she asked.

"Yes, dear. And you are Maria's granddaughter, Sarita. Come in, dear, she'll be down in a minute."

Sarita turned at once and moved around the corner to the front of the house. Domitian was hard on her heels. When she got to it, the front door wasn't just unlocked, it was half-open. They both slowed cautiously as they entered. Sarita half expected someone to leap out and attack them, but nothing happened and she paused a couple of steps inside to glance around. They were in a tiny entry. A door on her left led into a small kitchen cast in shadows from a light that had been turned on in the room behind it. A set of stairs were directly in front of them, leading to the second floor, a narrow hall led past the stairs to a door at the back of the house, and a door on their right led into a small sitting room.

"Come in," Mrs. Dressler said again, sounding a bit impatient now. "And close the door, dear. Ramsey has a man stationed on the beach, and if he sees the door open he might decide to investigate."

Sarita turned back, but Domitian was already closing the door.

"The guard on the beach is also the reason we can't turn on any lights yet. So we'll just have to sit in the dark and talk until the sun rises," Mrs. Dressler added now as Domitian took Sarita's arm and led her into the room. While she couldn't see a thing in the unlighted space, he seemed to have no trouble navigating the dark. But then Dressler had mentioned night vision as one of the improvements the nanos gave their hosts, she recalled.

"Your eyes are glowing, young man," Mrs. Dressler said quietly. "Are you one of the hybrids my husband created and enjoys torturing?"

"No," Domitian murmured and Sarita glanced around to see that his eyes were indeed glowing. Rather like a cat's did at night, she thought. But that didn't disturb her as much as the fact that the woman's question suggested she knew what Dressler had been up to all these years.

Sarita had rather hoped that wasn't the case. She'd been hoping Mrs. Dressler and her grandmother had been both ignorant and innocent all these years, and that was why they'd never turned him in or done anything to stop him. It seemed that wasn't the case, though, and it worried her that their lack of action might make them accessories. They might even approve of his actions, she thought now and turned back toward the chair where Mrs. Dressler sat. Using her best constable's voice, Sarita asked, "So you know what your husband has been doing, ma'am?"

"Oh, yes, child. I know better than anyone what that bastard is up to."

Sarita relaxed a little. There was no way to mistake the tone in Mrs. Dressler's voice as anything but loathing. The woman hated her husband and didn't approve of what he was doing. It didn't get her, or Sarita's grandmother, off the hook for not trying to stop it. But at least they weren't accomplices.

"This way," Domitian said quietly, taking her hand now and leading her the rest of the way to what turned out to be a couch. When he sat and tugged at her hand, Sarita settled next to him and squinted toward the woman in the chair across from them, but couldn't make out much more than a silhouette.

"You said my grandmother was coming?" she asked politely.

"Yes. My son went to wake her after he got me up and about," Mrs. Dressler said softly. "That was just before you started chattering outside the window. She won't be too long. But not too quick either, I should imagine," she said wryly, and pointed out, "We're not as spry as we used to be."

"Of course," Sarita murmured and then just sat there like a bump on a log, completely at a loss as to what to say. The situation seemed somewhat surreal to her in that moment. Fortunately, Elizabeth Dressler didn't appear to have the same problem.

"My son thinks the pair of you swam here," she announced abruptly. "Is he right?"

"Yes," Sarita answered.

"Where from?" Mrs. Dressler asked at once.

"From the little island you first lived on when you moved here from England," Sarita admitted.

"All that way?" she asked with amazement.

"Yes," Sarita assured her and then admitted, "Well, really Domitian swam all that way, I spent a good deal of the night lounging around on an air mattress, watching him do all the work."

"And tackling men with gills who planned to stab me from behind," Domitian put in at once, apparently not appreciating the picture she'd just painted of herself as a useless female.

"Ah. One of Ramsey's hybrids," Elizabeth said and sounded weary now. "Most of them are victims who want nothing more than to be left alone. But some suffer a sort of syndrome—What do they call it when kidnap victims start to side with their kidnappers?" she asked, a frown evident in her voice.

"Stockholm syndrome, I think," Sarita murmured.

"Yes. That's it," Mrs. Dressler said at once. "Well, some of his hybrids suffer from a version of that and simply live to serve him. They are extremely dangerous," she warned. "Like Charles Manson's followers, they would do anything for him, even kill. Bear that in mind."

Sarita opened her mouth to say she would, only to close it and glance around as she heard a creak from upstairs.

"That is your grandmother leaving her room. She will be down here soon," Elizabeth commented and then added, "I feel I should warn you . . . she will not be pleased that you are here."

"What?" Sarita asked sharply, her head jerking back toward her. "Why not?"

"Because you have stumbled right into the heart of hell here, child," Mrs. Dressler said unhappily. "People that come to this island rarely leave. At least not alive. My husband sees to that."

"And you allow it?" Domitian asked, his voice deep in the darkness.

"Allow?" Mrs. Dressler asked with dry amusement. "I have nothing to do with it. I am as much a victim and prisoner as those poor hybrids he's created. So is Maria."

Sarita's eyes were beginning to adjust, or perhaps it was just growing lighter in the room as the sun crept closer to the horizon, but she was quite sure she saw Mrs. Dressler's head turn her way as she added, "Did you really believe your grandmother wanted to abandon the husband and young son she loved more than life itself? Or that she wouldn't have done anything to meet her only grandchild? No," she said firmly. "She had no choice. Her one joy all these years has been the letters first from your mother and then from you. These last fifteen years, she has consoled herself with the knowledge that you were at least safe in Canada, far away from this horror. So," she added grimly, "no, she will definitely not be pleased that you are here. Neither am I, for that matter."

"You?" Sarita asked with surprise. "Why would you care?"

"Your grandmother was kind enough to share her letters with me, Sarita. First your mother's, and then yours when your mother died. She'd read them to me and then write you back, speaking her response aloud as she wrote and I would often suggest she mention this or that. It made me feel a part of it," she admitted. "Those letters have been the only bright spot in a very dark world for both of us over these many years. I've come to feel I know you as well as your grandmother does. I've grown to care for you. And it breaks my heart to see you sitting here on this island within Ramsey's reach."

"Elizabeth?"

Sarita glanced behind her at that call and heard someone shuffling down the stairs.

"In the sitting room, dear," Mrs. Dressler called softly.

"Thorne said there was someone here to see me. Who could—Why are you sitting in the dark?" The question was accompanied by a click and light suddenly burst from overhead.

Blinking, Sarita stood and turned to look at her grandmother for the first time in her life. What she saw was an elderly woman in a cotton nightgown and a fluffy white robe that she was clutching to her throat. She had silver-white hair, startled dark brown eyes, and a kind, wrinkled face that was presently filled with confusion.

"Who are you?" she asked uncertainly, her hand tightening on the bit of robe she clutched at her throat as she glanced to Mrs. Dressler. "She looks like—"

"Yes, Maria. It's Sarita," Mrs. Dressler said, sounding sad.

"What?" the woman said with bewilderment and turned back to Sarita, who nodded.

"*Si, abuela*. It's me," she said almost apologetically.

"Sarita?" she asked, her voice high. She took a couple of unsteady steps into the room and then just collapsed.

Twelve

Sarita rushed around the couch toward her grand-mother, but Domitian was faster. He even managed to get there and catch her grandmother before she hit the floor, saving her what would undoubtedly have been a good knock to the head. The moment he scooped the fragile old lady up into his arms, her eyes fluttered open.

Grandmother peered around with confusion, but her gaze sharpened as it landed on the face of the man in whose arms she lay, and she demanded, "Who are you?"

Sarita moved closer, drawing her attention and offered a reassuring smile. "It's okay, *abuela*. He's my . . ." She hesitated and then finished with "friend," frowning even as she said the weak word. It should fit, but Domitian had already become more than that to her. The problem was she wasn't sure what that more was.

"Sarita, dear, turn out the light before Ramsey's man sees it," Mrs. Dressler ordered.

She glanced toward the woman, and then stepped over to the wall and flicked off the light her grandmother had just turned on. But a vision of Elizabeth Dressler was burned into the back of her eyes as she did. The woman was in a wheelchair, not a seat, and there was a terrible scar down the side of her face. A face that otherwise seemed familiar to Sarita despite never having seen her before even in pictures. While she'd sent pictures every time they were requested by her grandmother—which was several times a year— when Sarita had requested one in return she'd been told her grandmother didn't have a camera.

"Set me down. I can stand!"

Sarita bit her lip at her grandmother's cantankerous order and turned to look to where the two had been before the lights went out again, but she couldn't see a darned thing. She was completely blind now after the intrusion of the bright light. Her eyes needed to adjust again, she supposed, and then frowned as she realized Domitian hadn't responded to the demand and her grandmother hadn't repeated it, yet she could hear movement. Guessing he'd used some of that mind control business to soothe her grandmother and prevent further protest, he was probably now carrying her around to set her on the couch. Sarita decided to find her own way back to the couch.

Reaching forward tentatively and finding nothing in her path, she moved forward, sure the back of the couch wasn't far away.

"Look out the window, Thorne dear, and be sure your father's man didn't notice the light going on and off. He might come to investigate," Elizabeth Dressler murmured and Sarita stilled, her ears straining for the sounds of movement. She hadn't seen anyone else in the room when the lights had gone on, but she hadn't really looked anywhere but at her grandmother and Mrs. Dressler.

Something brushed against her arm, and Sarita stiffened and turned her head. She smelled a hint of sea breeze and jungle and then a shadow moved in front of the window to the left of the front door, and she caught her breath at the misshapen silhouette revealed. Instead of a head and shoulders, it looked like Thorne had three heads, or a head and two humps, she thought. She glanced around with surprise when someone touched her arm.

"This way," Domitian said softly, drawing her to the right and in front of the couch again. He steered her along the couch and then urged her to sit. "Your *abuela* is on your left."

"Thank you," Sarita murmured as she settled on the cushions and then felt a hand on her arm. Knowing it was her grandmother reaching for her, she covered the hand with her own, but glanced back to the window only to see that the silhouette was gone.

"He doesn't appear to have noticed anything amiss," a voice as deep as Domitian's announced near where Mrs. Dressler sat.

"What are you doing here, Chiquita?" her grandmother asked unhappily as Sarita felt Domitian settle on the couch next to her.

"I came for you," Sarita said apologetically, squeezing her grandmother's hand in the darkness.

"Oh, such a good girl," her grandmother crooned sadly and Sarita caught a whiff of roses and then found herself pulled into the soft embrace of a much shorter

and rounder woman as she added, "But I don't understand. Why?"

Sarita hugged her back, closing her eyes as a wave
of emotion rolled over her. It had been two years since
she'd had the love and comfort of family. Forcing back
the overwhelming feelings, she cleared her throat and
explained, "Dr. Dressler called and said you fell and
hurt yourself."

"Fell?" her grandmother asked, pulling back as if she
were trying to see her face to verify she'd heard her
right.

Since Sarita couldn't see her grandmother, she doubted
very much that the old woman could see her, so she
said, "Yes. He said he was worried that there could be
complications and felt my visiting might help you get
through this."

"But I haven't fallen," Maria Reyes said with a confusion that soon turned to vexation as she added, "The
old *bastardo*! What is he up to now?"

"Nothing good, I'm sure," Elizabeth Dressler said
wearily and then asked, "But if he invited you to
the island, why did you have to swim from the little
island?"

"You were on the little island?" her grandmother asked.

"*Si*," Sarita answered, squeezing her hand and then
said, "I was here first. When I arrived I was told you
were in the hospital and would be back on the island
soon and I should wait. But the third day I was here,
he knocked me out and I woke up on the little island
with Domitian. We think we were supposed to be part
of some kind of experiment," she admitted, but didn't
explain that she thought it had to do with sex. It was her
grandmother after all.

"Then you *are* one of the hybrids," Elizabeth Dressler growled, sounding furious. "And you were probably privy to what was going on the whole time."

Sarita stilled, at first thinking she meant her, but then the woman added, "What did Ramsey want you to do to our Sarita?" The question had barely ended before she snapped, "Thorne, restrain him."

"No," Sarita barked, practically throwing herself across Domitian's lap. "He's not with Dressler, he's here to catch him."

"What?" Mrs. Dressler gasped.

There was suddenly absolute silence in the room as if everyone had frozen and Sarita frowned with frustration, wishing there was some light so she could see where everyone was and what they were doing. Especially Thorne.

Hoping the stillness meant they would listen and leave Domitian alone, Sarita straightened to sit next to him again and explained, "People have been going missing from North America. Enough that it was noticed, and a—" she hesitated and then said "—a special policing team was put together to find out who was taking them, why, and where they were taken to. This team tracked the disappearances to Caracas and Dr. Dressler, but by the time they got here, Dressler had taken a sabbatical from the university and retreated to the island. They were able to find out he had an island, but not where it was. Apparently there's no record of his owning an island."

"He bought it under my maiden name," Mrs. Dressler said. "Elizabeth Salter. I didn't understand why at the time, but it was probably for just this sort of eventuality. The man is always thinking ten steps ahead of everyone else," she finished bitterly.

"Oh," Sarita breathed and glanced instinctively to Domitian. She couldn't see his expression, but when he squeezed her hand, she turned back. "Well, they didn't catch that, so sent teams out in boats to scout the islands. But eight of their people went missing during the searches and they were no closer to finding the island, so Domitian agreed to accept a job from Dressler to be a chef on the island to help them locate it. The plan was for them to track his phone to find the island, but Dressler didn't really want Domitian for the chef job. That was apparently just bait to get him here. The moment he got on the helicopter to fly here, he was knocked out. He was then dumped on the little island with me. That was the day before yesterday. Or maybe it was the day before that now," she added uncertainly, exhaustion slowing her thinking. Finally she stopped trying to work out the day count and simply said, "This is the third morning since both of us woke up on the island."

There was silence for a minute and then Thorne asked, "This special police force is going to storm the island?"

It was hard to tell if he was glad or concerned, Thorne's voice seemed to hold both emotions and again Sarita wished the light was better so she could see his face. As the sun rose, lighting in the room slowly got brighter, but it was still full of shadows and Thorne seemed to be in the darkest shadow in the room.

"They want to," she said firmly. "But they can't until they figure out where it is. As I say, they were hoping to track Domitian's phone, but Dressler must have destroyed or disabled it or they'd already have stormed the island, taken Dressler into custody, and freed the people he's taken."

"But why would El Doctor put you on the little island with this man, Chiquita?" her grandmother asked.

"Probably to harvest eggs," Mrs. Dressler said grimly, saving Sarita having to answer.

"He wouldn't need the man for that. Just Sarita," Thorne said, and the familiarity with which he used her name startled her. He spoke her name as if he had known her for years. But then, perhaps he too had been there for the letter readings, she thought. Perhaps like Mrs. Dressler he felt he knew her from her writings.

A crooked smile claimed her lips. It seemed like everyone in this room knew all about her life and had known of her and felt connected to her for years, Domitian with his private detective reports, and the rest of them from her letters. She was the only one who didn't or hadn't known much in return. She hadn't known about Domitian at all, and other than mentioning their names, her grandmother hadn't said much about Thorne or Elizabeth Dressler, and hadn't revealed much about herself either . . . like that she'd been a prisoner here all these years.

"Perhaps he was hoping for some fertilized eggs," Mrs. Dressler said into the silence.

"He couldn't have expected my little Sarita to have sex with a stranger," her grandmother protested at once. "She's a good girl."

Sarita winced at those words, and felt Domitian squeezing her hand gently.

"I wouldn't put it past Ramsey to have put drugs in whatever food and water he supplied to get whatever he wanted," Elizabeth said gently in response and then turned her head back toward Sarita and Domitian and added, "It's good you left the little island. Whatever reason he had for putting you there could not be good. But why come here?" she asked almost plaintively. "This is even less safe for you than the little island."

"That is my fault," Sarita admitted. "Domitian wanted to swim for the mainland, but I found a half-written letter from you, Mrs. Dressler, to someone named Margaret. It was tucked in a book in the office. In it you mentioned that this island was about half an hour or forty-five minutes north of the little island by fishing boat. That seemed manageable, whereas we weren't sure how far the mainland was.

"Besides, I was worried about you, Grandmother," Sarita said, addressing the woman next to her. "I saw one of his experiments in that lab of his, and after Dressler knocked me out, and then I learned about all the people he's been taking and experimenting on, I was worried about you. I thought this way we could check to be sure you were all right, get the exact co-ordinates for the island from you, use your phone to call the mainland, and pass along the information. And now I can tell them to be cautious, that there are hybrids and humans who are not on Dressler's side, but some who are."

"Oh, Chiquita . . ." Maria Reyes squeezed her hand firmly with one of her own, and patted it with her other. "We have no phone. El Doctor would not trust us with one. We could not even seal any letters we sent from the island. They had to go through him and he read them first."

Sarita wasn't terribly surprised by this. It actually explained the odd tone of the letters over the years. They were affectionate yet reserved at the same time.

A curse from Domitian brought her from her thoughts

and Sarita turned his way and assured him, "It is all right. There is a phone in the big house."

"Are you sure?" he asked with concern.

"Yes. The office door was open one day and I rushed to it thinking Dr. Dressler must be back, but Big Beefy Guy was inside talking on a phone."

Rather than relax at this news, she could actually see him frown. The room was getting lighter quickly. In fact, she could see him well enough to notice that he was extremely pale.

"Getting into the house might be tricky," he said now with concern. "I do not like your taking that risk. I will do it myself and—"

"Yeah right," Sarita said and snorted rudely at the suggestion. "Not gonna happen. Besides, it isn't *that* risky. Dressler's security is a joke," she assured him. "All we have to do is wait until dinnertime and we can practically walk in."

Domitian shook his head. "I do not want you taking that risk."

"And I am not going to be left behind like some helpless creature who can't take care of herself," she snapped impatiently. Honestly! She was trained for this stuff. Well, not exactly *this* stuff, Sarita acknowledged, but she wasn't some—

"Perhaps it would be better to try to steal a boat," Domitian said now. "That way we could take every one in this room and get them safely away from the island before the raid." Glancing to where Thorne stood hidden in the shadows, he asked, "He has more than one boat here, *si*?"

"Yes," Thorne answered. "But the keys are kept else-where and he keeps both the keys and the boats well guarded. He makes sure that no one can leave the island without his say so. As for the security on the house," he added and Sarita thought his head turned slightly her way. "While most of the men leave their posts at dinnertime. There are still some on duty, and the cameras do not turn off. They are on all day every day. The minute you entered the house someone would know."

Sarita pursed her lips as she considered the situation and then said, "His office has French doors. We'd have to go in that way. I could barricade the doors to the hall while you made the call. You'd have to be quick, just tell them the island is owned by Elizabeth Salter, and warn them to be prepared for a large security force and then get off. Hopefully that way we can get out before they stop us."

"And if we don't?" Domitian asked solemnly.

"Then we get caught and hold on until help comes," she said with a shrug.

"You don't seem to understand," Thorne said now. "The cameras are everywhere around the house, labs, and dock. They are also in trees on the border of the jungle so that Dressler can see every inch of shoreline and yard."

Sarita stiffened and looked to Domitian with alarm. "He'll know we're here then."

"No," Thorne said, drawing her gaze his way again. "Fortunately for you I couldn't sleep last night and was out . . . walking. I noticed you in the ocean long before you neared shore and took care of the cameras on the cove where you came out."

"Took care of them how?" Domitian asked.

"I snapped a branch above one, so that it hung in front of it obscuring its view. No doubt they'll send someone out to check on it, but hopefully they'll just assume an animal landed on the branch and snapped it."

"You said you took care of *them*," Domitian pointed out.

"I positioned myself in front of the other one until you left the cove," Thorne admitted reluctantly. "They won't think much of my being there."

"In the tree?" Sarita asked, recalling the sounds she'd heard and the moving branches in the tree. If this man had caused it, he was one hell of a tree climber, she thought. The branches she'd seen move had been at the top, some thirty feet in the air at least.

Thorne grunted in the affirmative and then added, "There are no cameras in the jungle itself, just in the trees along the border. There were at one time but they kept getting damaged or destroyed by animals, so Dressler didn't bother replacing them. He felt watching the approach to the jungle was sufficient. So once the two of you had started up the hill, I hurried ahead to wake mother and warn her you were coming. Once I had her situated out here, I took care of the cameras along the side and front of the house as well, and then went up to wake Maria."

"Will he not think it odd that all the cameras on the front and side of the house were destroyed?" Domitian asked, a frown in his voice.

"No. I destroy them regularly," Thorne said with a shrug.

"And Ramsey repairs them regularly," Mrs. Dressler added dryly. "It is a silent battle of wills between Thorne and his father."

"Do not call him my father," Thorne said stiffly. "He is a sperm donor, nothing else."

"Wait," Sarita said now, sitting up straight and trying to pierce the shadows around Thorne with her eyes as she asked, "How did you know who we were, or that we were headed here to the house?"

"You were talking when you came out of the water," he said with unconcern. "But even if you hadn't mentioned wanting to see your grandmother, I would have recognized you at once from your pictures," he said quietly. "Except for the color and style of your bathing suit, you could have stepped out of the one you sent Maria of you and your friends at the beach celebrating your getting into the police college."

"Right," Sarita said and sagged back on the couch, reminded of the skimpy suit she was wearing. She was suddenly grateful the light wasn't that great in here. Forgetting that her grandmother had already seen her, she said, "Don't have a heart attack when you see my swimsuit, *abuela*. It wasn't my choice, it was what Dressler left at the house for me." She grimaced and added, "Although I suppose I shouldn't complain—at least I had a change of clothes, even if I don't care for how revealing they are. Poor Domitian has been wearing the same boxers for three days."

"Oh dear, well we can do something about that at least," Elizabeth Dressler said, and suddenly wheeled her chair around the couch and toward the kitchen. "Come along Sarita, Maria, we'll raid my closet and see if we can't find something a little more suitable."

Sarita stood when her grandmother did, but glanced uncertainly to Domitian.

"Thorne," Mrs. Dressler said then. "Will you see if you have something Sarita's 'friend' can wear?"

"Of course," he murmured.

Mrs. Dressler nodded with satisfaction and then smiled at Sarita's grandmother when she took up position behind her chair and began to wheel her from the room. "Thank you, Maria," she murmured and then said again, "Come along, Sarita."

"Go. I will be fine," Domitian said when she still hesitated.

Nodding, Sarita turned to follow the two women. It turned out she'd been wrong. There might be three bedrooms upstairs, but the room she'd assumed would be a dining room turned out to be Mrs. Dressler's bedroom on the main floor. Still, Sarita suspected it had originally been a dining room, but had been converted to accommodate the elderly woman in her wheelchair.

"Here we are. Now, let's see . . ."

Mrs. Dressler's words drew her attention to the closet the woman had opened. It was a good size, running the length of the room, but the clothes all hung high enough that there was no way the woman could reach them. Sarita had just decided her grandmother must fetch the clothes she wanted for her, when Mrs. Dressler snatched up a long rod hanging amid the clothes and used the hook on the end to lift down a lightweight cotton peasant blouse.

"What about this?" she asked, holding it out to Sarita.

"It's beautiful," Sarita assured her, taking the top.

"Oh, yes that would look lovely on you, Chiquita," her grandmother said happily. "I have just the skirt for you to wear with it. And it is new, I just finished making it. Wait here and I will fetch it."

Sarita watched the little woman hurry from the room with a smile that faded slowly as she thought of what Mrs. Dressler had said earlier. Turning back to the woman, she said, "You suggested you were all prisoners here. Including my grandmother?"

"Yes," the woman said simply.

"Why?" she asked with a frown. "From what I understand when she was first employed by you, Grandmother came to work in the mornings and was allowed to leave at night. At least she did while you lived on the little island. Why did that not continue here?"

"It did for the first couple weeks after we moved here to the big house," Mrs. Dressler said, hanging her hooked pole from the clothes rod again. Sitting back in her seat then, she sighed and added, "But then I went into early labor with Thorne." Mouth tightening, she explained, "I had made arrangements to move to the mainland for the last month of my pregnancy in case there were complications. Ramsey was going to fly me out the next day, but suddenly I was in the throes of it. What I didn't know then was that Ramsey had no intention of letting me have my son on the mainland and had put something into my drink at lunch to induce labor."

Sarita's eyebrows rose at that. She was surprised he'd take the risk with his own child. If complications had occurred he might have lost both his wife and child.

Huffing out an angry breath, Mrs. Dressler continued, "I should have realized something was amiss when he cancelled his classes for the day and was home in the middle of the week. He said it was because he wanted to spend time with me, and I thought it was sweet and even fortunate that he was there when I started having contractions. I hurried to him, sure he'd put me in the helicopter and fly me straight to the mainland, but he said everything was fine. It was too early, these were probably just Braxton Hicks contractions. He said I should just relax and breathe, and they would surely go away. He kept saying that right up until my water broke."

Her mouth tightened and anger crossed her face. "And then he showed his true colors. The sweet man I thought I'd married became a cold hard monster. He flat out said he'd never had any intention of my going to the mainland to have the baby. He'd brought the labor on early to ensure that didn't happen, so I might as well resign myself to the fact that I was having the baby here on the island, and stop whining and crying at him. I'd be in labor for hours. Go lie down and leave him alone. He'd check on me later and help if necessary."

"I was young then," Mrs. Dressler said sadly. "And I was shattered by his behavior. I burst into tears and stumbled back to my room and locked the door. And then I decided I wanted that man nowhere near my baby and stuck a chair under it to make sure he couldn't get in." Clucking her tongue she shook her head and added, "And with that one action, I sealed your grandmother's fate."

Sarita's eyebrows rose at the words. "How?"

"Because Maria was in the room," she explained quietly. "I didn't realize it until I finished jamming the chair under the door and turned to see her frozen with the bed half-made, her eyes wide."

Mrs. Dressler shook her head sadly. "If I'd known what my actions would mean for your poor grandmother, I would have moved the chair and ordered her out at once. But I didn't know, and I was grateful to have her there. I was scared and feeling more alone than I had in my life and she was all I had." Smiling wryly, she said, "We weren't exactly friends back then.

While your grandmother knew a few words of English, I knew not a single word of Spanish. There was a bit of a communication barrier there, but Maria was kind and gentle and supportive and helped me through the darkest hours of my life. She is the one who saw Thorne into this world." Mrs. Dressler sighed. "And the moment she laid eyes on him, Maria was doomed to remain on this island for the rest of her days."

"Why?" Sarita asked with confusion.

"Because she saw what I am."

Jerking around, Sarita peered toward the doorway at that grim comment and got her first really good look at Thorne Dressler. The man was breathtaking. With high cheekbones, a chiseled jaw, pale golden eyes, and hair so fair a blond it was almost white where it lay flat against his head. Towheaded, she thought, that was what they called it because it was the color of tow—flax or hemp fibers.

Sarita stared at him blankly for a minute and then shook her head slightly. "I don't understand why seeing you would—"

The words died in her throat as he stepped into the room and out of the shadow that had hidden the humps at his back. Still staring at his face, she'd barely noted the humps when he suddenly swung his arms out and up. Immediately, the two humps dropped and swung out into two huge chocolate-brown wings. They stretched out at least six feet to each side of his back, touching the walls at either end of the room.

"Dear God," she breathed.

Thorne's mouth tightened as if at a blow.

"They're magnificent," she finished and he blinked, looking suddenly uncertain.

"Did you find some clothes for Domitian?" Mrs. Dressler asked gently.

Clearing his throat, Thorne nodded and looked at his mother as he said, "Yes. That is why I came. I thought to tell you he is all set and changing." He hesitated and then said, "I will put on some tea and wait with him in the kitchen for you ladies to finish."

"Thank you, son," Elizabeth Dressler said affectionately.

Sarita watched him leave, her gaze sliding from his pale golden eyes, the sleek, white cap of what she now thought might be feathers not hair, and then as he turned to leave the room, she examined the chocolate-colored wings that had folded back into place behind his back. She also saw that there was no back on his shirt below his shoulders. It had been specially made to accommodate his wings.

"Bald Eagle?" she asked softly once he'd left the room.

"Yes." The word hissed out of Mrs. Dressler on a sigh. "My husband—" the word sounded like a curse from her lips "—apparently drugged me and harvested my eggs on our wedding night. He fertilized them with his sperm and then injected them with various concoctions of mixed DNA from animals he considered valuable. At least I think that's what he told me." She waved a hand irritably and added, "I was a tad distressed at the time."

"I can imagine," Sarita said sympathetically.

"Anyway, while I don't pretend to understand what he did, he did mention gene splicing or something when I confronted him." She shook her head, and then added, "He apparently drugged me again about a week after our wedding and planted one in my womb. My Thorne."

She glanced toward the door where her son had been and then back to Sarita. "The eagle in him shows up the most because of the wings and his eyes. Ramsey always had to wear glasses, so the exceptional vision eagles are known for appealed to him. But Ramsey says there is other DNA in him too. Jellyfish because they age backward. Salamander because they can regenerate limbs, ears, even their hearts, and so on. We don't know what all he has, or what it could mean. Ramsey wanted to test him over the years to see what DNA had taken and what effect it had, but I refused to let him anywhere near my son," she said grimly. "I couldn't protect all those other children he made, but I kept him from Thorne and refused to even live in the same house with him. I threatened to live in the jungle if he didn't build a small cottage for me, Maria, and Thorne to live in, and I would have. I couldn't bear that house after realizing the kind of monster I'd married. I think I would have killed myself long ago if not for Maria and Thorne."

Sarita peered at Mrs. Dressler's face. While she obviously loved and was proud of her son, she was also furious and probably hurt that the husband she'd thought loved her had done such a thing. And she was probably hurting for her son too, because the man could never have a normal life. Were he to show up on the mainland, she had no doubt he'd soon find himself in a lab somewhere, being poked, prodded, and experimented on as doctors and scientists tried to sort out just what he was.

"Here we are."

Sarita glanced to the door as her grandmother rushed back in, and she thought about what Elizabeth had said.

Maria Reyes had been kind and comforting and had been doomed to remain here the moment she'd helped bring Thorne into this world.

Of course, now that she'd seen Thorne properly, Sarita understood. She was quite sure everything Dressler had done was illegal. From harvesting his wife's eggs without her permission to the genetic game of Scrabble he'd played with them and so on. He couldn't risk her grandmother leaving the island and telling anyone what she'd seen.

So all these years, her grandmother had been kept here against her will, while her husband and son had thought she'd abandoned them. Sarita could have wept for her . . . for all three of them really. If her father and grandfather had known the truth, she had no doubt they would have moved heaven and earth to bring her *abuela* home. Not knowing the truth, though, they'd thought she'd abandoned them and had hated her for it instead.

"Do you like it?"

Sarita forced her attention to the skirt her grandmother was holding out and smiled with surprise. It was a lovely slate-blue peasant skirt. Touching the soft material, she nodded. "Yes."

"Are you sure?" her grandmother asked and frowned down at it. "It's probably ridiculously old-fashioned, I know, but we don't have patterns here to make the clothes. We are lucky Ramsey brings in cloth for us at all, and—"

"*Abuela,*" Sarita said firmly, tugging the skirt from her and hugging her tightly. "Peasant skirts will never go out of style. It's beautiful. I love it."

Releasing her, she added dryly, "And I will be ever so

glad to be wearing something more than—as Domitian put it—a hanky ripped into three tiny bits and pasted on."

Her grandmother looked her over in the minuscule bikini she wore and smiled wryly. "I am surprised he complained. You are gorgeous, Chiquita."

Sarita chuckled. "He was complaining that he found it distracting when we were trying to sort out a way off the island."

"Now that I can believe," she said with a grin, and then tilted her head and asked, "He is a good man, *si*?"

"Yes," Sarita answered without hesitation. "He is a very good man."

"How?" she asked at once.

Sarita blinked in surprise, but didn't have any trouble answering. "Well, he's strong and smart and brave. He's considerate too. And he can cook," she added, that was pretty important since she couldn't. "And I think he must be the most patient man I've ever met, and—" Sarita paused and glanced at her grandmother uncertainly when she released a little sigh. "What's wrong?"

"Nothing," her grandmother said quickly.

It was Elizabeth Dressler who said, "I'm afraid your grandmother and I have allowed ourselves to dabble in fantasy a bit more than we should to relieve the boredom here. We had rather built up the hope that someday perhaps Ramsey would die, and we would be free to invite you here. We were sure once you met my Thorne, the two of you would fall in love and we could live happily here with the pair of you producing several grandbabies for us to spoil."

"What?" Sarita gasped, her eyes wide with shock. Turning on her grandmother, she said, "You didn't!"

"Well, Thorne thought you were pretty when he saw

your picture . . . and he enjoyed your letters as much as we did," her grandmother said defensively. "And he is a good man, Chiquita. He is so good to us, but he is so lonely. He deserves to be happy too." She sighed and shook her head. "But if you love this Domitian then . . ." She shrugged.

"I never said I love Domitian," Sarita squawked with alarm, feeling her cheeks heat up with embarrassment. "We hardly know each other. We only met a couple days ago on the little island. I can't possibly love him."

"The things you said about him suggest you know him well, and they sounded like love to me," her grandmother said and then glanced to Elizabeth Dressler. "Did you not think so, Elizabeth?"

"Yes, I'm afraid so."

"*Si.*" Her grandmother glanced back and shrugged. "But if it is not, then *bueno*. There is a chance still for you and Thorne."

"Er . . ." Sarita said weakly.

"Come on, Maria," Mrs. Dressler said, sounding amused. "Thorne was making tea. Let's go see if it is ready and leave Sarita to dress."

Nodding, her grandmother moved around behind the woman's chair and wheeled her out.

Sarita watched them go and then blew out her breath and shook her head.

"Unbelievable," she murmured. The pair had been marrying her off to Thorne in their fantasies before she'd even met them, let alone the man in question. Wow. So this was what having a grandmother was like?

The thought made her smile faintly. Sarita's grandparents on her mother's side had died while she was quite young. Her memories of them were fuzzy at best.

They consisted of a grandfather who always had a smile on his face and a cigar in his hand, and a grandmother who had smelled of lavender. That was it. It looked like having a grandparent was going to be interesting.

Shaking her head, she began to pull the borrowed clothes on over her swimsuit.

Thirteen

"You must be tired after swimming all night."

Domitian tore his eyes away from the closed door to Mrs. Dressler's room at that comment from Sarita's grandmother and turned his attention back to the people seated at the tiny kitchen table with him. Mrs. Dressler, Maria Reyes, and Thorne. The table seemed almost too small for the three of them to eat at. He hadn't thought they'd fit five chairs around it. They'd managed it, though. It was tight, but would serve for having tea.

"Yes, I am a bit tired," he said finally, mostly because they would expect any normal person to be tired after such a trek. But while Domitian was tired, he was also in pain. He'd definitely used up a lot of blood with the swim here and needed more. However, he wasn't going to feed off any of the people here at the table. The women were both in their late seventies by his guess, and fragile. Feeding off them could cause a heart attack. As for Thorne—

His gaze shifted to the man. Thorne looked to be in his early thirties, but there was no way he was that young. This house was old and the walls thin, Domitian had had no trouble hearing what Mrs. Dressler had told Sarita about her marriage and her son's birth. If he'd been born eight months after she and Dr. Dressler married and moved to Venezuela, then he knew Thorne was in his fifties.

It wasn't Thorne's age, however, that removed him from consideration as a blood donor. It was the fact that he wasn't wholly human. Domitian had no idea how the DNA splicing had affected Thorne's blood, or how his blood would affect him. He wouldn't risk it.

"Oh well—" Sarita's grandmother began, and then paused as the bedroom door opened and her granddaughter stepped out.

Domitian was on his feet at once, and moving behind the empty chair next to his own. He'd fetched it for her from the living room as they'd arranged the table. It was a straight-backed cushioned chair and he now pulled it out slightly, his eyes sliding over Sarita as she approached in a pure white peasant blouse with a slate-blue peasant skirt. She looked beautiful and he smiled and murmured, "Lovely," as she approached.

Sarita smiled at the compliment as she settled into the chair he held for her. "Thank you."

"My pleasure," he murmured, easing the chair in.

"Domitian was just saying that he was tired from swimming all night," Sarita's grandmother commented as he reclaimed his seat.

"Yes," Mrs. Dressler agreed. "And actually I could do with a little rest myself. I'm not used to getting up this early."

"Neither am I," Maria Reyes admitted and then confessed, "I seem to sleep in later and later the older I get."

"Then I think we should all go to bed after tea," Mrs. Dressler announced. "Sarita, you can have the guest room upstairs. It used to be my room until . . ." She gestured to her wheelchair with distaste.

"Domitian can have my room," Thorne said. "I'm not tired, and someone should keep an eye on the guard on the beach anyway. Make sure he doesn't come up to the house."

"Well, good then. It is all decided," Sarita's grandmother said brightly. "We will finish our tea and then all get some rest. That way we will be bright and well rested when we decide how best to get the needed information to the police waiting to raid the island."

Domitian eyed the old women, noting their satisfied expressions and got the distinct impression they had planned this between the two of them. They obviously didn't want Sarita doing anything as risky as accompanying him to the house to use the phone, and he agreed with them. In fact, they'd just made things easier for him. He could pretend to go to bed, wait until he was sure Sarita was sleeping, and then slip out and go make the call himself . . . stopping along the way to feed on one of Dressler's security men of course. *Or two*, he added, and then noticed that Sarita was eyeing him with concern.

No doubt she'd noticed his pallor, Domitian thought with an inward sigh. Unfortunately, the sun was now climbing the sky and streaming through the windows and there was no way she would miss it. The woman didn't miss much of anything from what he could tell.

"Yes, sleep sounds a good idea," he said now, smiling at Sarita's grandmother and Mrs. Dressler.

Much to his relief, Sarita nodded in agreement and her grandmother then asked her if she'd received her last letter before leaving for Venezuela. As she turned to answer her, Domitian considered his plan. Telling his uncle that the island had been purchased under the name Elizabeth Salter would be helpful in getting them here, but it certainly wouldn't prepare the Rogue Hunters for what they would encounter once they arrived. Part of his coming had been to get as much information as he could about the security on the island and whatnot.

Turning to Thorne, he asked, "Do you know how many security men and domestic workers Dr. Dressler has on the island?"

The man hesitated, but then shook his head regretfully. "Other than a couple of trips to check out where the cameras were and to see if I could not take one of the boats and get my mother and Maria away from here, I stay away from that side of the island as much as possible."

"At my request," Mrs. Dressler said solemnly. "The last thing I want is Ramsey to get his hands on Thorne and experiment on him as he has the others. So he stays here at the cottage for the most part."

"We all do," Maria Reyes said sadly, breaking off her conversation with her granddaughter. "Our whole life is this cottage, the garden, and the beach below the cliff."

Domitian nodded with understanding, but wished it was otherwise. Some information about what the Rogue Hunters would be facing would be helpful, and so far he had very little.

"He has a fair number of people here," Sarita said

quietly, drawing his attention as she began to tick them off on her fingers. "In the house there was the cook, Aleta. She rarely leaves the kitchen so shouldn't be a problem. But there are at least four other people inside the house who help with cleaning and whatnot. There were also three or four men and women working outside in the gardens." She paused briefly and then said, "That's it for domestics. At least at the house."

"And security?" Domitian asked.

"There was a ton of security," she admitted. "He had four men at the front door, two inside and two out, and two more at the back door out to the garden, one in and one out. But I saw a good twenty of them coming from every direction at meal times, so I think there must be a lot of them who walk the beach, the yard, and the jungle. And that's not including the guys in the towers and gatehouse down by the labs."

"Towers and gatehouse?" he asked with interest.

Sarita nodded. "Aside from the guy in the gatehouse, there were four towers. One on each corner of the fencing around the labs," she said succinctly. "There were two men in each tower. But they were more interested in staring at the buildings inside the fence than anyone coming from outside." She paused, and then said, "Now that I know about the people they've kidnapped, I suppose their job is really to watch for possible escape attempts rather than intruders getting in." Her mouth twisted slightly. "I did think when I saw it that the setup looked more like a prison than labs."

Shaking her head, she said, "But while there are lots of men around, like I said, his security is a joke. At least by the labs. The guy in the gatehouse was watching porn. I just walked right past him. And the guys in the towers didn't notice me walking to the buildings until I was halfway to the first one. I was inside before they could climb down the ladder to the ground." She paused and said, "He may have more people inside the buildings, though. In fact, I know he has at least one other person working with him. His assistant, Asherah," Sarita said and then added, "She was a tall blond Amazon, cold as a fish and snarky. Didn't seem to like me much."

"Impossible," Domitian said softly and Sarita grinned at him in response. He smiled back and then said, "Tell me about Dressler's labs."

Sarita nodded. "I only saw the first room of the building closest to the gate. But there are several buildings. From the helicopter I counted six in the fenced-in area and one outside of it. They look like army barracks, long low, narrow metal structures with only one door each on the end facing the gatehouse. No windows that I saw," Sarita added grimly and then said, "I think the one outside the fence is probably the barracks and mess hall for the security guys. A bunch of them would come up at meal times to collect the food, but they took it back to that building to eat and then returned the pans and stuff after."

She paused, thought for a minute, and then shrugged. "That's all I know."

Domitian nodded on a sigh. It would have to be enough.

"But we can't forget to mention the gilled man to your uncle," Sarita added suddenly. "There might be more like him out there. In fact, now that I think about it, there most likely are. That is probably how your uncle and that Santo fellow as well as the others were dragged off the boats and disappeared without your sister and the other pilots seeing."

"Si." Domitian nodded slowly. That made perfect sense. They could easily have been shot with a dart and dragged over the side, pulled down into the depths and dragged away by one of the creatures he'd killed on their way here. They could have dragged the immortals all the way to the island without surfacing and not killed them. The nanos would simply have gone into a sort of stasis and then activated again to repair things once oxygenated blood was available again. He doubted that had happened, however. Some of them had been taken so far from the island that traveling back and forth would take too long. There must have been boats around, out of sight, waiting for them to bring their quarry.

"Warn them about winged hybrids watching from the air too," Thorne said.

Domitian glanced to him sharply, but he wasn't being sarcastic.

Raising an eyebrow, the man asked, "Did you think I was the only one?"

"Actually, I did," Domitian admitted with a wry twist to his lips. "There are others, though?"

Thorne nodded. "They only fly at night. Probably because El Doctor doesn't wish them to be seen, but sometimes they fly out quite a distance over the ocean."

"Are there other hybrids I need to warn them about?" he asked.

"I'm sure there are many variations," he said grimly. "However, since I do not go to the other side of the island . . ." He shrugged. "I'm afraid I can't help you."

"Of course," Domitian said and nodded thoughtfully. He'd just have to warn them to keep their eyes open.

"Well, I don't know about the rest of you but I'm ready for bed," Mrs. Dressler announced brightly.

"Me too." Sarita's grandmother stood, hesitated and then bent to kiss Sarita's cheek shyly before saying, "You should sleep too, Chiquita. You have been up all night."

"Yes, *abuela*," Sarita said softly, her hand rising to touch her cheek where her grandmother had kissed her.

"I'll walk up with you after I see Elizabeth to bed," Maria Reyes added with a smile.

Domitian saw the way Sarita's eyes softened and realized quite suddenly that she hadn't had the softer influence and affection of a female in her life for a very long time, not since she was thirteen. This must all be a bit overwhelming for her in some respects.

"Goodnight, Sarita," Mrs. Dressler said, reaching out to squeeze her hand affectionately. "Sleep well."

"You too," Sarita said and then stood to kiss her cheek, before straightening to hug her grandmother and kiss her cheek too.

Both women beamed at her for the affectionate display, and then Mrs. Dressler smiled at Domitian and said, "Thorne's room is the first door on the left at the top of the stairs. You should run along to bed. You look ready to drop."

Domitian nodded politely and stood as Sarita's grandmother began to wheel the woman away. When the ladies disappeared into the room and Sarita turned back, he kissed her cheek gently. "I'll leave you to your grandmother and go get some rest. Sleep well."

"Goodnight," Sarita whispered, and he saw her earlier concern flicker across her face. "Are you okay?"

"I am fine," he assured her and then turned and slipped away before she could ask anything else that might force him to lie.

"Well, this is Elizabeth's old room," Sarita's grandmother said, a little breathless from mounting the stairs. She gestured to the door on their right as they stepped into the upper hall.

"Oh." Sarita glanced at it and then said, "I'll just walk you to your door."

"Don't be silly. It's only a couple feet. Go on in and go to bed. I know you must be tired." She patted her shoulder, then turned her cheek up and Sarita bent to kiss her again, which made the woman beam once more. Turning away, she headed for the door at the end of the hall and said, "Goodnight, dear."

"Goodnight," Sarita murmured and watched her, but then she opened her door and slipped inside when her grandmother reached her own door and glanced back.

Sarita eased the door closed and then simply stood there listening until she heard her grandmother's door open and close. Letting her breath out on a little sigh, she then eased her door open again and glanced out into the hall. Finding it empty, Sarita hesitated, her gaze sliding to the door across the hall where Domitian was. But finally, she slipped out and tiptoed across to his door.

She started to raise her hand to knock, but caught herself at the last moment and rolled her eyes. Someone would hear. She was definitely tired. Giving her head a shake, Sarita turned the doorknob slowly and carefully and then slipped inside.

Domitian was lying on top of the bed, fully clothed and wide awake. He sat up at once as she entered, but remained silent as she eased his door carefully closed. He didn't say anything after that even, but simply watched silently as she approached the bed, Sarita noted as her gaze slid over him.

He was wearing jeans and a backless shirt. She'd noticed that when he'd walked away to go upstairs. But then she supposed she shouldn't have expected anything else. Thorne wouldn't have shirts with backs in them. Still it had startled her and she'd had to bite back a laugh.

She wasn't laughing now. You couldn't see that the shirt was different from the front and this was the first time she'd seen him in anything but boxers. He was sexy in boxers, but she found him just as irresistible in clothes. Domitian wasn't as pretty as Thorne, she supposed, if you took him feature by feature, but there was just something about him that appealed to her.

"Sarita," he growled in warning and rolled off the other side of the large bed as she started to sit on the edge of it beside him.

Straightening, she frowned and walked around to the bottom of the bed as he did.

"You should not be here," Domitian whispered, catching her arms as if to hold her back. "We need to sleep."

"Yes we do," Sarita agreed. "But you need blood too."

"*Si,*" he admitted grimly. "Unfortunately, there is none to be had just at the moment."

"There is," she said solemnly and shifted her long hair away from her neck. Pushing it over her shoulder to trail down her back, she bared her throat to him. Sarita didn't say anything, simply tilted her head to the side, offering him her neck.

"So," the word came out on a hissed breath, and then Domitian pressed a kiss to her throat and murmured, "the impossible has happened."

"What?" she asked with confusion, shivering as his lips ran along her throat.

"Hell has frozen over," he whispered, reminding her

of her words on first meeting him. Hell would freeze over before she let him bite her, she'd claimed.

Before Sarita could respond, his teeth sank into her throat. She stiffened at the sharp pain it caused and then relaxed as that was suddenly gone and pleasure slid through her, a warm wet sensation that settled low in her belly.

Moaning, she pressed closer, her arms sliding around his shoulders, her hands cradling his head as he drank from her. Somehow one of his legs was between both of hers and she gasped as it rubbed against her, and then she shifted, rubbing back and adding to her pleasure as he—was suddenly gone.

Blinking her eyes open, Sarita glanced around with dismay as a loud crash sounded and she saw Domitian slamming to the floor with Thorne on top of him. She gaped briefly as the two men began to roll on the floor, grappling to get their hands around each other's throat, and then some of her good sense returned and she hurried around the pair to reach their heads. Bending, she grabbed each man by an ear and twisted.

"What the hell are you doing?" Sarita hissed when they both froze, their eyes shifting sideways to take her in.

"I did not start this," Domitian pointed out stiffly. "I was just . . . er . . . and then he suddenly knocked me away from you."

"Er?" she asked dryly.

"Is that what you call biting her?" Thorne growled and started to struggle with him again, but froze at once when Sarita gave his ear another twist.

"Dammit, woman, stop that," he growled. "I am trying to protect you from this vampire."

"He is not—"

"Hello?" Her grandmother called through the door, knocking. "I heard a ruckus coming from in here. Is everything okay?"

Sarita bit her lip, and then looked to Domitian and said, "Control his mind and make him tell her everything is fine."

Domitian turned to Thorne and concentrated on his forehead.

"Hello?" her grandmother called again, more loudly.

"What's going on, Maria?" Mrs. Dressler's voice sounded from downstairs. "Is everything okay?"

"I don't know, Elizabeth. No one is answering me."

"I cannot read or control him," Domitian whispered finally, sounding both surprised and worried.

Sarita's eyebrows rose. "Another life mate?"

Domitian gave a start at the suggestion, but then shook his head. "He's not wholly human. Perhaps that is why I cannot read him."

"Hello?" Her grandmother started pounding on the door.

"It is all right, Maria," Thorne said suddenly. "I was just moving my chest for Domitian and dropped it."

"Oh, all right, Thorne dear," her grandmother said, sounding relieved. "Well, don't stay in there too long. Domitian needs his rest after swimming all night."

"Of course," he said grimly and then arched his eyebrows at Sarita.

"It's okay, Elizabeth," they heard her call now. "Thorne just dropped his chest."

"Oh, good. Okay, well sleep well, old friend," Mrs. Dressler called.

When Sarita heard her grandmother's answer sounding farther from the door as she apparently left, she released both men. Backing up she watched warily as Thorne got off Domitian and stood up. He didn't offer Domitian a hand to rise, she noticed, but crossed his arms and watched them both warily in return as Domitian got up as well.

"Let me see your neck," Domitian murmured with concern, immediately moving toward her.

Thorne stiffened and took a step forward, but Domitian cast him a glare and growled, "I am concerned some damage might have been done when you tackled me. If there is tearing she could bleed to death."

Thorne looked concerned at the comment, but didn't try to interfere as Domitian examined her throat. He looked relieved when Domitian said, "It seems all right. I retracted my fangs quickly enough it would seem."

Relieved herself, Sarita nodded, and lowered her head when he released her. She glanced to Thorne then and sighed when she saw his expression. He was going to need explanations.

"I will handle this," Domitian said quietly, taking her arm and attempting to usher her to the door.

Sarita stuck her ground and shook her head. "I don't trust you won't fight."

"We will not fight," he assured her and then glanced to Thorne and said heavily, "Will we."

"Not if she tells me she's okay with you biting her," Thorne growled.

"I wouldn't say I'm okay with it," Sarita admitted wryly, keeping her voice low. "But I came in here of my own free will and without being invited and told him to do it. The swim here obviously left him in need, and there is no bagged blood here like on the island where we were staying."

Thorne shifted his gaze to Domitian. "So that's why El Doctor wanted you? You're a vampire. I didn't think they truly existed."

Frowning, she said, "He's not—"

"Mi Corazon," Domitian interrupted. "Please. Go to bed. Thorne and I will talk."

Sarita hesitated, but then sighed and nodded. She was tired, and didn't really want to go through the explanations of what Domitian was and so on. This time when Domitian tried to urge her to the door, she went without protest.

"I will see you when you wake up," he murmured, and pressed a kiss to her forehead before opening the door.

Smiling crookedly, Sarita nodded and slipped out to tiptoe back to her own room, leaving Domitian to explain things to Thorne. She didn't know if it was his taking some of her blood or not, but she was so exhausted that Sarita didn't bother to strip off her borrowed clothes or even crawl under the sheet and duvet. She simply dropped onto the bed, asleep almost before her head hit the pillow.

The moment Domitian woke up, he knew he'd messed up. He'd only lain down for a minute, intending to wait half an hour or so to be sure Sarita was sleeping before slipping out to make his way through the jungle to the big house. His thinking had been that he'd rather take the risk of making the attempt in daylight than take Sarita with him and put her at risk. Fortunately, after he'd explained everything to Thorne, the man had agreed to help by making sure the cameras were out along the back of the house so he could slip into the woods that way. Trying to go the way he and Sarita had approached the house before dawn this morning would have left him visible to Dressler's goon on the beach now that the sun had risen.

Unfortunately, the swim last night had left him exhausted and the little bit of blood he'd taken from Sarita before Thorne had knocked him away from her hadn't been enough to make much of a dent in his appetite. He'd dozed off and the moment that had happened he'd been lost.

Sitting up, Domitian ran a hand through his hair and then rubbed the base of his neck. Shared dreams were common among life mates. While this was his first experience with the phenomenon, he'd heard about them. They never happened when the mates were together and had made love, but when they were near and hadn't sated their needs, the dreams often kicked in.

He'd been told that both parties contributed to the dream whether consciously or unconsciously, and either party could change the dream's setting and what was happening at the drop of a hat. He'd heard that the dreams were hot and all consuming, but differed in that there was no loss of consciousness after sex in the dreams, probably because they weren't conscious to begin with. He'd also been told that, in a way, they could be better than actual life mate sex because the overwhelming need that made life mate sex so fast and frantic was lessened, and life mates could often do those things they never got the chance to do while conscious.

Domitian had found all that he'd heard to be true. He'd apparently joined Sarita in a dream she was already having when he'd fallen asleep. He'd found himself standing on the edge of an outdoor skating rink, watching her whirl and whiz around the ice, leaping and spinning. From the reports he'd received, he knew she'd taken skating for several years after moving to Canada and had watched with fascination, wondering if she could actually perform the moves in real life. It was something he'd have to ask her, he'd thought and then she'd spotted him and stopped to stare with surprise.

As he'd walked toward her, Domitian had consciously changed the setting. By the time he'd taken her into his arms, they were in a wooden lodge with a fire burning to keep them warm and a soft fur rug where he could lay her back and do all the things he never got the chance to do when in the grip of life mate urgency. Of course, Sarita had soon turned the tables on him and he'd found himself tied to a bed while she'd driven him wild with her beautiful mouth and hands, and then his chains were gone and he'd rolled her beneath him and made slow, passionate love to her. And so the day had passed, with him lost in dreams of being in Sarita's arms.

Getting out of bed, Domitian headed out of the room, relieved to see that the door to Sarita's room was closed. Hoping that meant that she was still sleeping, he moved silently down the stairs.

"You're awake."

Domitian stepped off the stairs and glanced toward

Thorne as the other man appeared in the kitchen doorway.

"I was afraid it would be Sarita and you'd have missed your chance," he said dryly.

"She is not up yet then?" Domitian asked with relief. She'd been in his dreams right up until he'd opened his eyes, but might have woken up at the same time and slipped down before him.

"No," Thorne said and then glanced toward the ceiling and said, "but I suspect it won't be long before she is."

"What makes you say that?" Domitian asked with a frown.

"Because she was moaning and groaning like crazy all day, but has finally gone silent. I suspect that means she'll be up and about soon too." He glanced back to Domitian and considered his expression briefly before saying, "You both were. It alarmed the ladies. Maria went up to check on Sarita several times and said she was thrashing around and hollering fit to die and the nightmares she was suffering must be horrible." He quirked an eyebrow. "She made me check on you too. Didn't look to me like you were having a nightmare."

"Why did you not wake me?" Domitian asked with irritation.

"You didn't ask me to," he said with a shrug.

Domitian scowled at him and then turned and headed up the hall next to the stairs, asking, "Did you take care of those cameras for me?"

"I said I would, didn't I?"

"Yes, you did," Domitian murmured. "Thank you."

Thorne gave a grunt of acknowledgment.

"Where are the ladies now?" Domitian asked as he

reached the back door. He was turning the doorknob when Thorne answered.

"All that screaming unsettled them so much they decided to sit out in the garden."

Domitian froze, and then heaved a resigned sigh and pulled the door open. He stepped outside, wholly expecting the women to come at him with a barrage of concerned questions. Instead, a glance around revealed the garden was empty.

"I guess they must have gone around to the pool or out front," Thorne said with unconcern when Domitian glanced back to him.

"Right," Domitian said, heading for the trees that lined the garden. "Keep Sarita here if she wakes up before I get back. And if something happens to me, don't let Dressler get his hands on her."

They had reached the tree line by then. Domitian didn't wait for Thorne to agree, but set off into the woods at a run. He already knew the man would do his best to keep Sarita safe. He had no doubt that Thorne had been there for the reading of Sarita's letters every week too, and that, like the ladies, they had been the bright spot of his life in this gilded prison. Domitian suspected Thorne had been half in love with Sarita before she'd ever set foot on the island. Once he'd seen how vital, brave, and beautiful she was in real life though, Domitian had no doubt the man had lost the rest of his heart to her.

Fortunately, Domitian wasn't the jealous type, and the pinching he'd felt as he'd entered the kitchen and overheard Sarita in Mrs. Dressler's room, saying Thorne was magnificent . . . well that hadn't been jealousy. Nor had the tightness he'd suffered in his chest each time Sarita had smiled at the man while they'd had tea that morning. She'd smiled at all of them several times as they'd had their tea. There was nothing to be jealous of. But it did occur to him as he made his way through the woods that if anything happened to him, Sarita might be stuck on this island for a long time, hiding in the cottage with her grandmother, Mrs. Dressler, and Thorne her only comfort.

"Bastard," Domitian muttered, but it wasn't jealousy.

Fourteen

Sarita stepped out of her room and frowned when she noted the open door to Thorne's room, where Domitian was supposed to be sleeping. He'd obviously woken up before her, she realized, and she headed toward the stairs just as her grandmother's voice sounded, calling Thorne.

"Coming," she heard him say and the word was followed by his heavy footfalls. Sarita reached the top of the stairs in time to see the man slip outside and pull the front door closed. Frowning, she jogged down to the entry and peered out the window in the door to see that her grandmother, Mrs. Dressler, and Thorne were all out front, talking as they eyed Dressler's goon on the cliff.

Goons, Sarita corrected herself as she followed their gazes to the two men now on the cliff. Dressler had doubled the guard. Did that mean they'd found the gilled man Domitian had killed last night and now suspected they might have come this way? Probably. The gilled man had probably rolled right up on the beach, pushed there by the tide, she thought with a frown. They should have weighed him down or something. Although, they hadn't actually had anything to weigh him down with, she thought with a sigh and turned away from the door.

A glance into the living room didn't reveal Domitian. Neither did a look in the kitchen. Sarita even crossed the kitchen and took a peek into Mrs. Dressler's room, but no luck. The main floor bathroom was the last place he could be, and Sarita didn't even have to open the door to see he wasn't in it, the door was already open.

She started to turn back up the hall, but paused and eyed the back door. Stepping up to it, she tugged the curtain aside and peered out to see a path leading through first a small patch of grass and then a garden before it disappeared into the jungle. It must have rained at some point that day—the path was muddy, and she could clearly make out two sets of footprints heading away from the door. And one returning.

He'd left without her. Sarita knew it as surely as she knew her own name. Domitian had gone ahead without her.

Cursing under her breath, she pulled the door open and slipped outside. She was entering the jungle before it occurred to her to worry about the cameras.

Too late now, she told herself and burst into a run. Sarita was determined to catch up to Domitian. Actually, she *had* to. He didn't know the layout of the house and yard, the routine of the men patrolling the grounds, the path they took to approach the kitchen at dinnertime, or even which set of French doors led to Dressler's office. He needed her.

As desperate as she was to catch up to Domitian, Sarita soon found she had to slow down. While it had still been relatively light when she'd left the house, with the sun setting it quickly became much darker in the jungle. Afraid she'd trip over something and break a leg or that she might even wander off the path she was trying to follow, Sarita slowed down to a quick walk and cursed the need to. She knew without a doubt that Domitian wouldn't have to slow down. The man had great night vision thanks to those nanos of his. He had increased speed as well. Her only real hope of catching up to him was if she arrived at the edge of the woods before the men headed around to the kitchen to get their dinner. He would have to wait inside the woods for that to happen before making a run for the house. At least that was his best bet of success.

The trek through the jungle was longer than Sarita had expected. Long enough that she wasn't surprised to find it was full dark outside the jungle too by the time she reached the edge of the grounds. A quick scan of the area proved she'd missed Domitian.

As well as dinnertime, Sarita saw, stepping quickly behind the trunk of a palm tree as two men drew near, patrolling the edge of the property.

"I don't know why he wants the patrols doubled," one was complaining. "I've already done my shift. Hell if I want to be out here holding your hand while you do yours."

"Hey, I hear ye," the other one said. "And believe me I'd rather be doing this alone."

"Yeah?" the first man asked. "You're not afraid of those vampires?"

The second man gave a short laugh. "I'm not stupid.

I know they're dangerous, but I've got El Doctor's special juice in my gun same as you. Hit him with one of these puppies and it's '*hasta la vista*, baby,'" he said with satisfaction. After a moment, he added, "And frankly I'd rather let the bastard drain me dry than have to listen to you whine and cry about having to walk around a little longer."

As the first man told the other one to do something anatomically impossible, Sarita eased away from the tree and crept along the tree line to get nearer the house. The path came out about two hundred feet in front of and to the side of the house. She wanted to get up about even with it. It would put her in a better position to help Domitian when he tried to leave the house.

He had to still be in there. Sarita had neither caught up to him, nor passed him on the trail. Unless she'd missed another trail that branched off from the main one, he was still in the house. Hopefully, that meant he was on the phone, giving as much information as he could to that uncle of his, and not that he'd been caught in the house and was now unconscious or wounded or just chained up somewhere.

Sarita had just about reached a spot that was even to the front of the house when she spotted movement at the far corner of the terrace. Stilling, she watched, her eyes straining. A moment later Sarita was assaulted by a combination of excitement and concern. She was happy because she was quite sure the head that kept poking around the corner of the house was Domitian. He hadn't been captured or injured. Her concern, though, was because he was obviously considering trying to run across the front yard, despite the two men on front-door duty who would surely see him.

Holding her breath, Sarita watched him change focus and stare at the two men by the front door. Much to her amazement, first one suddenly turned and faced the wall beside the door he was guarding, and then the other did. It was as smooth as clockwork . . . and rather shocking to see, Sarita acknowledged, letting her breath out. She was suddenly very glad the man couldn't read or control her.

Sure that Domitian was going to make a break for the jungle path now, Sarita glanced toward the yard, noting that every man she could see appeared to be looking away from where Domitian was. She glanced up the side of the house next and then sucked in a horrified breath. Two men were just coming around the corner from the back of the house, headed along the side wall toward the front.

Sarita wasn't sure how this mind control business worked, but suspected Domitian had to concentrate to do it. If he were unexpectedly tackled by the two men he couldn't see approaching, he would no doubt lose his focus, and then he would have every man in the yard converging on him. And apparently the men had some special "juice" in their guns. She was guessing a high tech bullet or something. Whatever it was, it would apparently be game over for Domitian.

Sarita considered the situation briefly, and then cursed under her breath and hurried along the edge of the trees until she was about halfway along the side of the house. Now even with the men Domitian couldn't see, she swerved out and charged them. While one of the men appeared deep in the middle of telling a tale about something that needed big hand movements, the other one did glance up and see her just before Sarita reached them. She saw him raise his gun to aim it at her, but it was too late, she was already in the middle of a flying kick. It hit him hard across the face, spinning him and sending him to the ground.

The second man couldn't help but notice her then. He immediately raised his own gun.

Grabbing the barrel of the rifle, Sarita moved her head to the side to avoid getting shot and rammed it back into the man's face as he tried to aim. When he looked dazed but didn't go down, she slammed it into his face again. This time the man's eyes rolled back and his body followed the motion so that he landed flat on his back in the grass.

The third man came out of nowhere. Sarita saw a large shadow out of the corner of her eye and then an iron band was around her throat, lifting her off the ground as the sound of large wings flapping told her it wasn't a human she was dealing with, but one of the hybrids. One who was winged like Thorne.

Gasping for air, Sarita struggled to free herself, clawing at the arm that was around her throat and choking off any access to oxygen. She was also kicking wildly, but dangling under the man as she was, her legs were kicking nothing but air. Desperate to be able to suck in a breath, she redoubled her efforts at clawing up his arm, but he seemed impervious to the deep trails she was gouging into his skin.

"Keep it up," her captor suggested lazily. "If I drop you now, you're dead."

Sarita glanced down then to see that they had gained height quickly and were already above the treetops.

Darkness was just beginning to crowd in at the corners of her eyes from lack of oxygen when she spotted Domitian below. He had reached the trees unhampered and was disappearing into the woods completely oblivious to the fact that she was flying high above him.

"Good girl," the man holding her said approvingly when she stopped struggling. The pressure around her neck eased as he shifted his hold. Sarita found herself suspended in the air with one of her captor's arms across her ribs under her breasts and the other now across her shoulders at the base of her throat rather than choking her.

Too aware that he could decide to drop her at any moment, she merely held on to his arm with both hands and stared out over the island.

"My father will be happy to see you," he announced, turning them toward the labs. "You and that vampire of yours rather ruined things leaving the island when you did. We were on the way to the island to put Father's plan in motion when MacNeil radioed us with the news that the pair of you had left the island, swimming south, and towing an air mattress behind you. He thought you'd headed for the mainland, and we spent many hours last night crisscrossing the water trying to find you."

Sarita didn't comment. That had been her idea. She'd suspected that a man who had so many cameras inside, probably had them outside as well and had suggested leaving by the beach in front of the house and swimming around it to the north after they'd first swum south for fifty feet or so away from the island. Apparently it had worked for a while.

"But when MacNeil radioed in that my brother's body had washed up on shore with his neck broken, we knew you'd come here, so we all headed home."

Yep, should have found some way to sink the gilled man's body, she thought, since that could be the only man he was speaking of. Even dragging it along with them would've been better, she thought grimly. Domitian could have tied the rope from the air mattress around the man's waist and pulled him along, and then they could have dragged his body on shore and into the jungle and left him there under some leaves. At least there was less likelihood he would have been found that way, Sarita thought and then frowned.

"He was your brother?" she asked as what he'd said sunk through her thoughts. Her voice was raspy, Sarita noted with a frown.

"One of many," the man answered indifferently, and then asked slyly, "Afraid I'll want revenge and drop you?"

Sarita stiffened in his arms.

"I could," he said with amusement. "Claim you were struggling and I lost my grip on you."

Sarita peered down at the trees below, wondering what crashing through them would do to a body.

"Fortunately for you, I didn't like my brother," the man added.

Sarita was silent for a minute and then asked, "How do you feel about Dressler?"

He chuckled. "Hoping I hate my father too and could be convinced to help you escape?"

"You might want to consider it. I'm sure the Rogue Hunters will go easier on you if they know you've helped me."

"The Rogue Hunters?" he said thoughtfully. "You don't mean those idiots on the mainland do you? They won't find us here."

"They will as soon as they look up which island Elizabeth Salter owns," Sarita said grimly.

"Problem is they'll never know to look up Elizabeth Salter," he said with amusement. "Is that what you were trying to do at the house? Call the mainland and tell them that? I suppose the vampire was there somewhere and you think he managed to make the call. He didn't," he said with a certainty that struck at her heart.

"The minute MacNeil radioed that my brother had washed up on the beach, Father told him to have the satellite phone removed from his office in the house and locked up in his office in the labs. There's no one coming for you, little Sarita. Your life is here now."

Sarita's mind rebelled at the suggestion and she was about to tell him that her life sure as hell wasn't here now, but snapped her mouth shut when he suddenly swooped downward, dropping quickly toward land. For one moment she thought they were going to crash into the ground between the fence and the labs, but at the last moment he pulled up, swinging his body down and forcing hers with it as he flapped his wings against the wind to slow them. They landed rather abruptly, but on their feet, and then he took her arm in a steely grip and started walking toward the first building.

Sarita glanced around at the yard inside the fence. The towers were all manned with armed men as they had been the first time, but this time they had noticed their arrival at once and were watching them.

"They'll shoot if you make a break for it," the winged man said idly.

Sarita snorted at the suggestion. "I doubt it. Dressler wants me for something. Some kind of experiment."

"Yes, he does," he agreed easily as he marched her toward the first building, the one where the immortal had been cut in half and put back together. "But you don't have to be in good shape for what he wants. Just not dead. They can shoot you in the leg without angering him."

When Sarita glanced at him narrowly, trying to decide whether he was telling the truth or not, he added, "What do you think we were headed to the island for? It wasn't to bring you fresh linens."

Sarita faced forward again, her mind racing, and then asked, "What does he plan to do with me?"

He hesitated and then shook his head. "Father wouldn't like it if I ruined his surprise. You'll find out soon enough. But let me give you a little advice," he said as they approached the lab. "Don't fight him. You can't win and he'll just make things unpleasant for you. On this island my father is God."

They had reached the door and on the last word, he pulled it open and shoved her in ahead of him.

Sarita stumbled inside and glanced swiftly around the lab, relieved to see that the table was empty this time and there wasn't some poor tortured immortal on it cut in half or missing limbs. She was less happy to see Asherah sitting at the desk Dressler had used, writing something in a notebook. The woman glanced up with a start at their entrance.

"I have a gift for Father, Asherah," the winged man announced, pulling the door closed. "Where is he?"

"Sleeping," Asherah said, eyeing Sarita with an odd expression on her face.

"Well, wake him up. He'll want to know we have the girl."

Asherah shook her head and closed her book before standing. "He said not to wake him unless we had them both."

"But—"

"That's what he said, Caelestis," Asherah said firmly, coming around the desk.

"Don't call me that—you know I hate that name," the man holding Sarita snapped.

"Fine. That's what he said, *Cael*," she said impatiently and then arched an eyebrow. "Better?"

"Yeah, but—"

"No, buts," Asherah interrupted irritably. "You know how miserable he gets when he's woken up from sleep. We don't wake him up until the vampire's caught too."

Cael released a resigned breath. "Fine. What do we do with her, then?"

"Lock her in the cells until the vampire is found," Asherah said with a shrug, retrieving a large set of keys from her pocket.

"I thought the cells were full?" Cael commented and Sarita turned slightly, getting her first good look at him in the light. He was almost a dead ringer for Thorne. He had the same high cheekbones, the same full lips, the same pale gold eyes and the same coloring to his wings. He was also just as gorgeous as the other man. But he was on the wrong side.

"They *are* full. I'll have to put her in with Colton," Asherah said absently as she led them toward the refrigerator, sorting through the keys on her chain.

"Is he still alive?" Cael asked seeming surprised.

"Just," Asherah said and paused next to the refrigerator to unlock . . . a door, Sarita saw when Cael urged her closer. She hadn't noticed it the last time she was here because it was hidden by the protruding refrigerator. She should have expected it existed, though. This lab didn't take up a fifth of the building. There had to be a door to whatever lay behind this room, which, as it turned out, were cells from what these two had said.

Sarita glanced around curiously the moment Cael marched her through the door. All there was to see was a hallway with white walls and white tile on the floor like the lab they'd just left. There were also five white doors off it. Two on either side and one at the end. Asherah led them to the end door, unlocked it and stepped in, flicking on a light switch next to the door as she went.

Sarita got halfway through this door and then froze. The white walls and white tile floor were gone, replaced by metal walls and a bare concrete floor. There were also six barred cells here, three on either side, all of them occupied. A wide aisle ran down the length between them, leading to a door at the far end of the room. Since the lab, the hallway, and these cells probably only took up half the length of the building, Sarita suspected the far door led to more cells and more prisoners.

She slid her gaze over the occupants of the first two cells. There were two women in the one on the left. They stood as still as statues, faces expressionless as they watched them enter. A lone man was in the cell on the right. He was huge. Even sitting slumped against the wall, Sarita suspected he was almost as tall as her. Standing, she doubted she'd reach halfway up his upper arm. He was also bald and extremely pale, almost blue. His eyes were closed, his head down, his chin resting on his chest. She wasn't sure he was breathing.

"Move." Cael shoved her forward with his hold on her arm and Sarita reluctantly followed Asherah down the aisle past the first two cells, aware that the women tracked them with narrowed eyes.

"You should have moved Colton to the front cell instead of leaving him surrounded by these monsters," Cael said tightly as Asherah stopped at the second cell on the right and began searching through her keys again. "At least then he would only have had them on one side of him."

Asherah shrugged. "They can't reach him in the center of the cell and he's not moving until we carry him out."

"What about her?" Cael asked, thumbing toward Sarita with his free hand. "They might bite her."

Asherah selected a key and stuck it in the cell door. As she turned it, she glanced at Sarita and her mouth twisted. "Judging by the footage from the island, she seems to like vampires. She'll be fine."

Sarita felt heat rush into her face at the woman's words as she realized Asherah had obviously watched the camera footage of her and Domitian. They'd been careful to not do anything outside the cocooned bed once Domitian had created the little shelter, but before that there had been the incident in the bathroom that first day. There was also their interlude by the pool. It was possible that a camera had been placed in the trees by the waterfall and caught that action. Though she'd been covered by the towel when Domitian had given her pleasure, it wouldn't have been hard to tell what was happening. And there had been no towel covering Domitian's erection afterward, just her mouth.

Her soul shriveled at the thought of this bitch witnessing those intimate moments between her and Domitian, but as Asherah opened the cell door, Sarita raised her chin and asked sharply, "Did you enjoy the show? Or were you jealous?"

Growling, Asherah caught her by the arm, nails digging deep into Sarita's forearm as she dragged her from Cael and shoved her through the open door. Sarita stumbled several steps, nearly stepping on a figure on the floor before catching herself. Freezing, she stared down at the boy she'd nearly trampled. He was young, perhaps six, and he was lying on the cold concrete with only a blanket wrapped around his bulky shape, leaving just his thin face visible.

"Let's go," Asherah snapped as the door clanged shut.

"No. We can't leave her here. If they drain her dry, Dressler will be pissed," Cael said and Sarita glanced over to see him eyeing the inhabitants of the other cages warily.

"Fine," Asherah snarled and pulled a gun from her pocket.

Sarita took an instinctive step back, pausing when she stepped on something. As she glanced down to see that she'd stepped on the boy's blanket, not any part of him, she heard two soft *pffts* of sound, and glanced back to the woman. She then followed the gun point to the cell next to the one she was in as the two men inside suddenly dropped like puppets whose strings had been cut. There were darts sticking out of each of them now, she saw.

"Happy?" Asherah asked Cael tersely.

"What about him?" Cael asked, nodding his chin toward the man slumped against the wall in the first cell on the other side of Sarita.

"He's bloodless. Can't do a thing. Now let's get out of here," she said, heading back up the aisle toward the door they'd entered through. "These guys give me the willies."

Cael hesitated, but then turned and followed Ash-erah out.

By Domitian's guess he was little more than a couple of minutes away from the cottage when something large swooped out of a tree on the side of the path and landed on the trail in front of him. It brought him up short, and he started to crouch into a fighting stance, and then recognized the man in front of him.

"Thorne," he said with surprise, straightening. "What are you—?"

"Did you call your people?" he interrupted, trying to glance around Domitian as if expecting there to be someone behind him.

"No. They moved the phone," Domitian admitted, his voice heavy with disappointment at having failed.

"Did you search for where they moved it to?" Thorne asked with a frown.

"Of course, I searched," Domitian said impatiently. "And then I read the mind of one of the men guarding the front door and learned that Dressler had it moved to the labs the minute he realized we were on the island."

"How did he know you were on the island?" Thorne asked with concern. "I thought I took care of the cameras . . . unless the bastard has some I don't know about."

Domitian shook his head. "I do not think you need worry about that. Unfortunately, the man with gills washed up on the shore today. They deduced that his broken neck meant he didn't die of natural causes," Domitian said dryly, and then frowned as he noted that

Thorne was trying to look around him again. Shaking his head, he continued, "They put one and one together and made two. Two being we had made it here."

Thorne cursed violently.

"Yeah. That means a change of plans. I'm going to take Sarita and swim for the mainland or another island, whichever we reach first. I need to get her away from here. From there I'll get the information to my uncle at the villa."

"Your uncle?" Thorne growled. "I thought some special police force was after El Doctor. What is your uncle doing here?"

"Uncle Lucian heads up the special force," Domitian said soothingly. "He's rented a couple of villas in Caracas and taken a couple more on Isla Margarita in the Rancho de Chano area for himself and the rest of the hunters while here."

Thorne grunted and then tried to look past him again.

Growing tired of the game, Domitian turned sideways on the edge of the path so he had a clear view. "What the hell are you looking for?"

Thorne stared up the dark, empty path and then asked worriedly, "Where is Sarita?"

"What?" Domitian asked with alarm. "She's supposed to be at the cottage. You were supposed to be keeping her th—"

"She's not there," he interrupted on a growl.

"What do you mean she's not there?" Domitian snapped. "You were supposed to be watching her. You—"

"I *was* watching her. I sat in the living room almost the entire time you were gone."

"Almost?" he asked grimly. "*Almost* the entire time?"

Thorne winced. "I only stepped out for a minute.

Maria called me, I thought perhaps there was a problem, but she just wanted to tell me that the guard on the beach had been doubled. She feared El Doctor suspected something. The women were upset. I took just a moment or two to calm them and then went back inside to continue waiting. I thought Sarita was still in bed until MacNeil and a bunch of his security men showed up."

"What?" Domitian hissed, glancing down the path toward the cottage.

Thorne nodded. "They barged in, scaring the hell out of mother and Maria and started searching the place. I ran upstairs to try to warn Sarita, but when I opened the guest bedroom door, she was gone."

"Wh—?"

"Just shut up and listen," Thorne snapped. "MacNeil was right behind me and saw the room was empty. He started cussing and swearing and then someone called him on his radio. I didn't hear what was said, MacNeil pushed me out of the room and told his men to take me downstairs to the living room with the women while he took the message and then slammed the door. But he came downstairs a few moments later and said to tell you that they have Sarita and if you want her to live, you are to give yourself up by midnight."

"What?" Domitian gasped with dismay. He then shook his head. "Well, then why the hell did you keep looking behind me? Why did you think she was with me?"

"I was sure he was bluffing," Thorne said on a sigh and then rallied and said, "And I still half think he is. Aside from being a trained police officer, Sarita has years of martial arts training under her belt. Her father made her learn to defend herself after her mother's murder. He was afraid to lose her like he did her mother."

"I know," Domitian said quietly. Aside from it being in his reports, she had mentioned the martial arts training herself.

"And she's smart," Thorne added firmly. "I just cannot see her getting caught on her own. It must be a bluff. She is probably on her way back here right now. You just missed each other on the path. Where are you going?" Thorne finished when Domitian turned abruptly to head back the way he'd come.

Domitian did not pause or slow down, he simply said, "To turn myself in."

"Wait." Thorne hurried after him. "You have a little over four hours before you have to do that."

Domitian paused and thought briefly, and then sighed and nodded. "*Si.* I will look for her first. If I find her I will free her, but if not, I *will* turn myself in at midnight."

"What about getting word to your uncle?" Thorne asked with dismay.

"I have no way to call him and have no idea how long it would take me to swim to Isla Margarita. I will not risk trying to swim there and return with a team in time to save Sarita. I must be here at midnight to turn myself in. We are on our own."

Fifteen

"Your name is Sarita."

Sarita turned from watching Asherah and Cael leave and glanced warily at the men in the cell across from the one she was in. She was quite sure the man who had spoken was one of those three, but had no idea which one. They all looked very alike. All of them wore identical black leather outfits as if they belonged to a biker gang. They also all had dark hair and similar facial features. They were obviously related, but the two on the ends were a little smaller than the man in the middle. Not a lot, they were all big men, but the two on the ends just had very muscular shoulders, while the one in the middle had *incredibly* muscular shoulders. Sarita dubbed them Biker #1, Biker #2, and Biker #3 in her mind.

"Sarita Reyes," the man in the middle, Biker #2, said now.

"You are Domitian's life mate," the man on the left, Biker #1, said with interest.

"You sacrificed yourself for him," the one on the right, Biker #3, added.

"You—"

"Okay, let's just slow our ponies here, boys," she said finally, interrupting Biker #2. Propping her hands on her hips and using her best constable scowl, she said, "Yes, my name is Sarita Reyes. Yes, Domitian thinks I'm his life mate. But no I didn't sacrifice myself for him." Raising her eyebrows she suggested, "Now how about you guys mind your own business and stay the hell out of my head? Hmm?"

"Domitian does not think you are his life mate," Biker #2 said solemnly. "He knows it . . . and so do you."

Sarita scowled at the suggestion, but before she could comment, Biker #3 said, "And you did sacrifice yourself. Knowing he could not see them, you tackled the men coming up along the side of the house . . . sacrificing yourself so that he could escape."

"I'll take that as a 'no, we won't mind our own business and stay out of your head, Sarita,' shall I?" she asked dryly, and then snapped, "And I did not sacrifice myself." Scowling, she added, "I mean, it wasn't *supposed* to be a sacrifice. I was supposed to kick their butts and join Domitian to head back to the cottage. And I did kick their butts. I just didn't expect Bigbird to fly in and carry me off like an eagle snatching up a bunny," she finished irritably, because, really, that hadn't been fair at all.

"You're more a porcupine than a bunny, lass," one of the two men in the cell on the right of the one holding the bikers commented with a thick Scottish accent. Sarita scowled at the blond man for his trouble.

"Quinn," Biker #2 growled in reprimand.

"What?" the Scot asked innocently. "Ye have to admit she is, Victor."

Sarita stiffened at the name Quinn used to address Biker #2. She was pretty sure the uncle Domitian had mentioned being taken was named Victor. Could this be him?

"Bunnies are soft and fluffy," Quinn continued. "This woman's thoughts are sharp and pointy." Turning to Sarita, then, the Scot smiled charmingly and added, "It's no' an insult. I like sharp and pointy. A lot."

"Dial it down, Quinn," Victor suggested dryly. "Try to romance this woman like you do every other mortal female and Domitian will kill you. She is his."

"I am not!" Sarita protested at once, resenting the way they made her sound like a possession.

"Really?" Quinn asked, waggling his eyebrows.

"Oh, stuff it, Romeo. I'm not interested," she growled, and then glanced down at the boy at her feet when he moaned in pain.

Frowning, Sarita dropped to her haunches to get a better look at his face. While Asherah had turned on bright lights when they'd entered, she'd also turned them off on leaving. The only illumination in the room now came from weak bare bulbs overhead that cast a dim glow. It was enough to see by, though, and she peered at the child's pale face with concern and then felt his cool forehead.

"He doesn't have a fever," she mumbled to herself as she looked him over. The boy was panting slightly, and there was a bluish tint to his lips and ears. Intending to check his fingernails to see if his nail beds were blue too, she tugged his blanket away and then froze.

"Madre de Dios," she breathed, staring at what she'd

revealed. The boy had the head, arms, and chest of a little boy, but from the waist down he was all pony, right up to the tail.

Another one of Dressler's experiments, she thought grimly, brushing the tips of her fingers lightly over one of his legs to feel the coarse horse hair. The boy moaned and shifted restlessly, and Sarita glanced back to his face and frowned. He didn't look well at all.

Sighing, she covered him again, and then brushed the human hair back from his face and peered at him sadly as she asked, "What's the matter with him?"

"He is dying," Victor said solemnly.

"What from?" Sarita asked, glancing around at the man and noting the compassion on his face as he looked at the boy.

"I cannot be sure, but judging by the rapid heartbeat, his shortness of breath, and the blue of his lips and ears, I would guess that he is not taking in enough oxygen to support his body so it is failing."

Sarita glanced back to the boy and thought that was a pretty good assessment of the situation. At least it did match the symptoms. "Do you think it's pneumonia or something? Shouldn't Dressler be giving him antibiotics or other meds?"

"I suspect if that were the case he would," Victor said solemnly. "Since he is not, I would guess the problem has more to do with the boy's physiology than illness."

"His physiology?" she asked, with a frown, lifting the blanket again, a horse's body to the neck where a human upper body began. A whole human torso, head, and arms rather than just a horse head.

"It could be anything," Victor said sounding weary. "Perhaps he was born with only human lungs. They would not be able to supply enough oxygen for the body he has. Or perhaps it has something to do with the fact that he has a human nose and sinuses. Horses have much bigger nostrils and their sinuses run the length of their head. Human sinuses may not be large enough to accommodate his body's needs." He shrugged. "I do not know."

"But if it was physiological rather than an illness, wouldn't he have died shortly after being born?" Sarita asked, not wanting to believe the boy couldn't be saved.

"Perhaps," Victor said. "But from the boy's memories it would seem he has always been weak and gasping for breath. He could manage a sprint for a brief distance, but had no endurance so was unable to run and play with the others. And then as he aged he could no longer sprint or even walk far, and then not at all without losing his breath. He has apparently grown weaker over time as his body grew."

"You can read him?" Sarita asked glancing over with surprise.

"Yes."

"Domitian couldn't read the gilled man we encountered. I thought perhaps they were all unreadable."

"Most of them are," Victor said with a shrug. "I haven't been able to read or control any of the other hybrids we've encountered. Just this boy, which is what made me wonder if from the waist up he is not completely human."

Sarita turned to look back at the boy. He was lying on hard concrete with just the thin blanket beneath him. It didn't look comfortable, she thought. Sitting down, she drew his head into her lap and brushed the hair back from the boy's face as she silently cursed Dr. Dressler to hell.

Knowing that was a waste of time, Sarita glanced to Victor and the other two men in the cell across from her, noting that they'd all moved to the front of the cage and were now leaning against it, watching her. This time when she looked them over, she noted that they not only looked similar to each other, but that many of their features, especially their eyes, were very similar to Domitian's.

"So?" she asked, zeroing in on the larger man in the middle. "You're Victor Argenis? Domitian's uncle?"

"I am Domitian's uncle Victor," he acknowledged, but then added, "However, it is Argeneau, not Argenis."

That made Sarita frown. "But Domitian's last name is Argenis not Argeneau."

"Both are just a variation on our ancient name Argentum," Victor explained. "In old times there were not really last names. It was basically Bob the baker or Jim the smithy. For us it was a first name plus silver, because of the silver in our eyes. As the family grew and spread, different variations of Argentum occurred, Argenis in Spain, Argeneau in France, and so on."

"I see," Sarita murmured, but wasn't sure she did. Whoever heard of someone changing their name to match the country they lived in or moved to? And just what kind of person did that?

"Someone who wishes to not draw attention to themselves," Victor said quietly, obviously reading her thoughts.

Sarita bit her tongue to keep from snapping at him for obviously piddling about in her thoughts again. Though, judging by the amusement that suddenly curved Victor's lips, she suspected he knew she was peeved. Sighing, she shifted her gaze to Biker #1.

"My nephew, Nicholas Argeneau," Victor announced, gesturing to the man she was looking at. Turning next to Biker #3, he added, "And another nephew, Decker Argeneau-Pimms."

Sarita nodded in greeting, recognizing the names of Domitian's cousins. She then glanced to the men in the third cage on the opposite side. Eyes settling on the Scot, she said, "And I know you're Quinn . . . also Argeneau?"

"Sadly no. We are no' *all* Argeneaus, lass," the man said in a tone that suggested he was glad to have avoided that fate. "Fortunately, I'm a MacDonald through and true. And pleased I am to meet ye, m'lady."

He gave a gallant bow, waving his hand around as if doffing a hat, and then straightened and pointed to the second man in the cell with him and announced, "And me cellmate is one Ochoa Moreno, the most recalcitrant Latino I've ever had the pleasure o' meeting. We suspect he and his partner are both hunters for the South American Council, because they did no' come with us. But he'll no' tell us a damned thing about how he and his partner landed here. His partner by the by is Enrique Aurelios, the dark-haired fellow lying unconscious on the floor over there."

Sarita turned to glance toward the slumped fellow in the front cell next to hers.

"No, not him. That fellow is bald, and his name is Santo Notte," he said dryly. "I said the *dark-haired*—Oh, you recognize the name Santo," Quinn interrupted himself to say. "Ah yes, Domitian told you about his disappearing from the boat he was on with the fair Drina."

Sarita turned a glare at the Scot. "Do you think you could just stop reading my mind?"

"I'm afraid not," he said, not sounding very apologetic. "In truth, none of us has to read you. Like all new life mates you're kind of shouting your thoughts at us."

Sarita narrowed her eyes on Quinn and then turned to Victor Argeneau inquiringly.

"He is telling the truth. We are not reading your thoughts so much as receiving them."

Sighing, Sarita shook her head, and glanced to her right now, at the two men Asherah had shot. Enrique Aurelios, he'd said. She eyed the man, noting his dark good looks, and then glanced to the second man lying unconscious on the floor with a dart sticking out of him.

"That is Lucern," Quinn informed her dryly and then added, "Yet another Argeneau cousin of your life mate's."

Sarita merely nodded, recognizing the first name. She then turned her gaze to the last cell, the first one on the other side, across from Santo's cell where the women were. Victor took over the introductions again, saying, "The lovely lady with flame-colored tips to her hair is my sister-in-law, Eshe Argeneau, and the woman with pink-tipped hair is Mirabeau La Roche McGraw."

Eshe Argeneau snorted with amusement. "You could have just said the black chick and white chick, Victor. We wouldn't have taken offense and it would have been simpler."

"I would never deign to define you as simply black, Eshe," Victor assured her.

"But you'd define me by my hair tints?" she asked with disbelief.

"Our skin color is merely something we are born with,

like our hair color and eye color," he said with a shrug. "However, the fiery tint you apply to your hair actually does reveal a great deal about you, and better reflects your personality."

"He's good," Mirabeau—the white chick—said, nudging Eshe's arm.

"Yeah, those Argeneau boys," Eshe said with a slow smile. "All smooth talk and sex appeal."

"Spoken like a woman mated to one," Mirabeau said on a laugh.

"And I'm not the only one here who is," Eshe pointed out and smiled at Sarita. "Welcome to the family, kiddo. I don't know Domitian well, but if he's anything like his uncles, you're in for one hell of a ride."

Sarita felt the blush that suddenly swept over her, but before she could even think of how to respond, the man Quinn had called Santo Notte suddenly issued a roar of pain. Turning sharply, she watched as he suddenly jerked upright and clasped his right wrist in his left hand. It was only then she noticed with some horror that his right hand was missing, cut off at the wrist.

The scream ended as abruptly as it had started, as if the sound had woken him from sleep, and now conscious, he could silence the sound of suffering. He sat panting for a minute, and then leaned back against the wall and took several long deep breaths one after the other.

Sarita swallowed the bile that had risen up in her throat at his suffering and watched with pity as he mastered his pain. She couldn't imagine what he was going through. Wanting to help if she could, she eased the little boy's head back to the floor and stood to move toward the bars between their cells.

"Stop!" Victor barked. When she paused and glanced around with surprise, he added, "Do not go any closer, Sarita. Santo might lose his head and attack if you get close enough for him to grab you."

"I will not attack her." Santo's voice was a weary growl. "But I would appreciate it, Sarita, if you would move back to where you were. Your scent is strong and, frankly, more of a torment than Dressler's pitiful attempts at torture."

"Pitiful?" she asked with disbelief. Cutting off body parts seemed pretty horrific as tortures went to her, Sarita thought as she surreptitiously bent her head to sniff herself by the shoulder and armpit.

"*Si*. Pitiful. I have been tortured by men far better at it than him," Santo said solemnly.

Sarita frowned, both at his words and at the fact that she didn't smell that bad. She wasn't fresh as a daisy, but—

"He means you smell delicious," Victor said, sounding amused.

"*Si. Delizioso*, like Momma's Swordfish a la Siciliana," Santo said on a sigh, and then lifted his head and inhaled deeply.

Her brow furrowing with concern, Sarita ducked her head again, this time sniffing her other shoulder and armpit. She didn't smell anything fishy, but she *had* been in the ocean all last night swimming here and she hadn't had a chance to shower or anything since. Sighing, she moved back to sit down next to the little boy again.

"Is Santo the only one of you that Dressler has experimented on so far?" Sarita asked as she eased the boy's head onto her lap again.

"Experiment? Is that what he calls it?" Victor asked, his voice stiff.

Sarita nodded. "Apparently he's been subjecting the other immortals he has to various and sundry experiments."

"And here we thought he just cut off Santo's hand because he wouldn't tell him how to turn a mortal," Decker said dryly.

"Turn a mortal?" Sarita asked, glancing up with surprise. "Can you do that?"

Victor gave one slow nod.

"And Dressler wants to know how?" she asked sharply. The ramifications of that happening rushed through her mind. The man was brilliant, and as Mrs. Dressler had said, he thought ten steps ahead of everyone else. That was how he had got away with torturing his hybrids, holding people against their will, kidnapping immortals, and probably killing people for fifty years on this island without detection. The one bright spot her grandmother and Mrs. Dressler were looking forward to was the day he died and they would be free. But what if he discovered how to become an immortal and turned himself? God save them all then. The man could continue torturing and maiming people and immortals on this island indefinitely. The thought was a horrific one.

"But no one has told him, right?" Sarita asked anxiously. "Not even the guy he cut in half?"

"He cut someone in half?" Victor asked sharply.

"Who?" Decker gripped the bars of their cell. "What was his name?"

"I don't know," Sarita admitted with a frown.

"What did he look like?" Nicholas asked.

Sarita tried to think back. All she could remember

was his open wounds and how gray he had looked. She couldn't envision his face at all.

"Did you see what color his eyes were?" Victor asked.

"Green," Sarita said at once. Domitian had asked her the same question and she remembered the man's eyes opening as she had when he'd asked. "And he had fair hair, and—"

"It is all right, we can see the memory in your mind," Victor said quietly.

Sarita raised her eyebrows. Domitian hadn't been able to do that, but then he said life mates couldn't read each other's minds.

"It was Davies," Decker muttered with disgust.

"Yes," Nicholas agreed. "Christ, he's just a pup. Barely a hundred years old."

"But he was one of the first to go missing," Victor pointed out. "So if he yet lives, the others might still be alive as well."

"It wasn't the first time Dressler did that to him," Sarita said with a frown. "He said he'd cut him in half and left him for only ten seconds the first time and had worked his way up to two hours. If what Dressler truly wanted was to know how to turn a mortal, well . . ." She shook her head. "Frankly, I'm surprised anyone could withstand that torture and not tell."

"Hmm," Victor murmured, looking troubled, but then he asked curiously, "Would you let Dressler know how to live forever?"

"God no," Sarita said at once. "I'd rather die."

Victor nodded with approval, but said, "The problem is, Domitian wouldn't."

"You don't think he'd die rather than tell him?" she asked with surprise, because frankly, Sarita couldn't see that. She was quite sure Domitian would agree with her and die before giving such information to the man.

"I am sure he *would* die before telling Dressler," Victor said solemnly. "But I do not think he could stand by and let *you* die for any reason. Even that one. He will do whatever it takes to save your life if it comes to that."

Sarita shook her head.

"He is right, Sarita," Decker said solemnly. "All of us would give anything for our life mates. It is our greatest weakness."

Sarita lowered her head, her mind suddenly whirling. These people thought that Dressler's experiments were just an excuse to torture information out of immortals on how to turn a mortal. Or how he could be turned, because that's what Dressler no doubt wanted it for. But she didn't totally agree with their assessment.

Dressler was a scientist, he needed to know how things worked, and she had no doubt he'd want to know how the nanos would affect him once he was turned. She suspected many of the experiments were to see what he could survive, or how long certain injuries might incapacitate him. The man did things ten steps ahead after all. He must know that becoming immortal wouldn't stop the others from hunting him. If anything they'd probably look harder. Knowing what he could withstand and the fastest way to heal, and the like would certainly be useful to a man like that.

But what of her and Domitian? She'd thought they were put on the island as part of an experiment. But this business about turning a mortal and how protective immortals were of their life mates put a new slant on things. The birdman, Cael, had said Dressler was headed to the small island when MacNeil had called with the news that she and Domitian had left it. What had he and his men been coming to the island for? Nothing good she was sure, but . . .

"Dressler probably intended to force Domitian to tell him how he could be turned by threatening your life," Victor said quietly.

Sarita glanced at him, for once not annoyed that her mind had been read. "But why put us on the island at all? Why didn't he just try to force him to do it here? In his lab?"

"Perhaps he thought Domitian would be more likely to give up the information if the two of you had bonded," Decker suggested and then said, "Apparently you did not know Domitian before being thrown together on the island?"

"No. I didn't know him from Adam," she admitted. "But he knew me. He'd known I was his life mate and had been getting reports on me for fifteen years. So are you saying that Domitian would give up that information now, but might not have before our time on the island?"

"No. I am saying Dressler no doubt believed that was the case," he said gently. "You have to remember that he has kidnapped and tortured several immortals in the last couple of years, yet none of them would reveal the information, even though it probably would have saved them from future torture and might perhaps have gained them their freedom. For a man like Dressler, who has no concept of what it means to be immortal or the value of a life mate or even how to love, it would be beyond his understanding as to how a man would not give up that information to save his own life, but would for a woman he had never interacted with. He was probably hedging his bets. Making sure Domitian wanted you badly enough before he carried out his plan."

"So I am the bait," Sarita said grimly. "He'll make Domitian reveal your secret by threatening my life?"

"Undoubtedly," Victor agreed solemnly. "And Domitian will not hesitate to give him what he wants to save you."

Sarita thought about that for a minute, and then glanced to the women and asked, "But Domitian and I are the only life mates he has, right? None of you—"

"You are the only life mates that are both here," Eshe agreed. "Fortunately for us, Lucian would not allow life mates to work together on this hunt. He felt it too dangerous."

Sarita nodded, then eased the boy's head to the floor again and stood to approach the bars between her cell and Santo's again.

"Sarita," Eshe said with concern. "I can see what you are thinking, but there is no need for this."

"Christ, she's going to sacrifice herself," Decker muttered, sounding dismayed.

"Domitian called Lucian with the information about this island, Sarita," Nicholas reminded her urgently. "He will be here soon bringing the other men with him and—

"Santo," Victor growled suddenly in warning when the other man turned his head abruptly, spearing Sarita with silver eyes rimmed with black.

Dressler had said the nanos went into the organs and whatnot to remain in the body when an immortal had been drained of blood, and it seemed a lot of them were in Santo's eyes. Pausing at the bars, she slid her hands through to his side and gestured to Santo like he was a puppy and she had food.

"Come. Feed," she encouraged. "Drain me dry. I don't want Dressler to hurt even one more person."

Domitian was creeping through the strip of jungle between the bluffs over the beach and the fence around the labs when he heard a *pssst*.

Pausing, he peered around until he spotted a woman in a white lab coat, crouched about ten feet ahead, behind a tree. He was sure he'd seen her come out of the labs several moments ago and walk down to the gatehouse to talk to the guard there. Apparently, she'd made her way around here afterward.

Domitian eyed her warily, but when she gestured for him to go to her, he considered his options. He'd searched the jungle for Sarita first. He hadn't been surprised when she wasn't there, but he'd had to make sure and glancing around as he moved through it hadn't slowed him much. He'd reached the edge of the jungle to find the men all gathered on the lawn getting instructions on searching the island for him. Using their distraction to his advantage, he'd moved along the inside edge of the jungle until he was parallel to the back of the house and then had quickly snuck across to the back corner.

A glance through the window in the first door had shown him a kitchen with a woman pottering around, apparently oblivious to or unconcerned by what was happening outside. Domitian had moved on without disturbing her and used a set of French doors that had led into an empty games room. Other than the woman in the kitchen, the house had seemed completely empty. Domitian had searched it quickly, but there had been no sign of Sarita. As he'd feared, she'd been taken to the more secure labs with their towers and gatehouse. He'd spent the last hour or better, moving through the woods that lined the back and sides of the fence, looking for a weak spot, or a place he might enter without anyone noticing. But while he could control the guards in the corner towers and make them look away, the cameras everywhere ensured his approach would be seen.

He'd just been taking one last look around, hoping for inspiration on how to save Sarita before resigning himself to giving himself up to Dressler, when he'd heard that *pssst*. Now he crept to the woman, hoping against hope that the angels had sent a solution to his problem.

"You have to save Sarita," the woman hissed the moment he stopped in front of her. "I can help."

"Who are you?" Domitian asked, eyeing her warily. "And why would you help?"

"I'm—My name is Asherah."

He stilled at the name, recognizing it. Sarita had said the woman had been present when Dressler had injected her with a knockout drug. This woman had done nothing to help her.

"Again," he said coldly. "Why would you help?"

"Because if you don't get her away from here, El Doctor is going to use her to make you turn him immortal," she said grimly.

"And you do not want that?" he asked dubiously.

"Damned right I don't," she snarled, glancing resentfully toward the labs. "He's tortured us long enough. You need to get Sarita out and away from here to somewhere he can't get his hands on either of you."

Domitian glanced toward the buildings again, debating whether to trust the woman or not. Sarita had said Asherah hadn't seemed to like her much, but she might have mistaken the rage obviously boiling under the surface of this woman as dislike of herself. Either way, it didn't really matter. He didn't see a way to get in without help. If the woman betrayed him and delivered him to Dressler, than she was simply doing what he'd just about decided he'd have to do anyway and turning him in.

"How?" Domitian asked finally, still eyeing the grounds inside the fence. "I can control the guards and make them look away, but I cannot control the cameras."

"There's a blind spot between two of the cameras," Asherah said at once, and he turned sharply to look at her.

"Where?"

"Right here," she answered, nodding toward the fence. "If you stay on a straight line from this tree to that third light on the building, the two cameras on this side of the lab will not pick you up."

Domitian eyed the light she was talking about and then glanced at first one camera and then the other on the corners of the building and thought it might be possible they were angled in such a way as to miss a three-foot-wide strip of the grounds. But then he glanced to the next building behind this one and frowned. "What about the cameras on that building? Won't the one pointed this way catch me?"

"It's not angled right," Asherah assured him and then added, "I use this blind spot to slip away from the labs and go down to the beach for a swim when El Doctor makes me stay all night to watch over one of his horrible experiments. I've never once been caught."

Domitian nodded slowly and then eyed the path she was talking about.

"How do you manage the fence?" he asked after a moment. He could climb it quickly and easily, but Sarita might have difficulty with it on their way out.

"There's a slice in the fence that goes up about five feet. I tied a bit of wire around it in the middle and at the bottom to keep it closed between uses."

"And the men on the security team have never noticed?" he asked with disbelief.

"The men on the security detail are useless," Asherah said acerbically. "They don't even patrol along here. I don't know why El Doctor wastes his money on them. Although, I suppose I shouldn't complain since I wouldn't be able to slip away to swim if they were on the ball."

Domitian glanced to the towers. The two men in the tower to his right were talking and laughing as they smoked. The two in the tower on his left looked like they were playing a game of cards. It seemed none of them were too concerned about the search the other men were involved in.

"Once we get to the wall, plaster yourself against it and follow me to the door, but then just wait there. I will get Sarita out to you."

"I will come in with you and get her myself," he announced grimly.

"You can't," she rasped. "El Doctor is working in the

lab. He'd shoot you with a dart the minute you entered and it would all be over."

Domitian's eyes narrowed. "Then how did you get out?"

"He sent me to tell the guard at the gatehouse to gather the men in the towers and go aid in the search. He thinks their absence will encourage you to walk in and give yourself up," she added. "I saw a flash of movement as I came out and felt sure it would be you, so after I passed along the message, I just slipped around to talk to you."

"The gatehouse guard doesn't appear to have listened," Domitian pointed out, motioning to the two towers on their side of the fenced-in area.

"Yes he has," she said and pointed to two men approaching the gate from the other side of the buildings. "He's just slow and lazy. And he probably got talking to one of the men when he called them. Once they all make their way out, we can slip through the fence and hurry to the building. But follow me. If you step outside the blind spot and the cameras pick you up . . ."

Asherah shrugged helplessly, not stating the obvious, and Domitian nodded silently and then glanced again toward the guard towers he could see, noting that one of the men playing cards had stopped to take a phone call. Moments later the man ended the call, said something to his partner and the two men began to descend the ladder to the ground.

Domitian's gaze shifted from them to a third pair of men as they appeared from the other side of the buildings, headed for the gatehouse. That left only—he glanced toward the tower on their right to see the men had stopped talking to each other and one had a phone pressed to his ear. He watched the man end the call and then those two men began to descend their ladder as well, heading to ground. He followed them with his eyes as they trooped toward the gatehouse, wishing he could shout at them to hurry up. It seemed to take forever, although it was probably only five minutes or so. Just long enough for Domitian to come up with another concern.

Spearing Asherah with cold eyes, he asked, "If Dressler is inside, how do you intend to get Sarita out?"

"I have a plan," she assured him.

"What plan?" he insisted.

"She can tell you all about it once she's out. We need to move now," she said and then rushed from the tree to the fence to crouch down and begin removing her ties.

Tense and suspicious, Domitian followed, arriving just as she undid the second tie. Before he could ask his question again, she turned and handed the ties to him. "Make sure you do it up before you follow me. If someone sees the fence torn open they might investigate and block your exit."

Asherah was almost through the hole before she finished speaking. Frowning, Domitian followed, and then paused to do as she'd instructed, slipping one tie through both edges of the fence at about the midpoint in the cut, and twisting it twice to seal the fence loosely, and then doing the same at the bottom of the fence.

When he turned toward the building, Asherah had already reached it and stood with her back flat against the wall, waiting for him. Seeing that she was directly below the light she'd mentioned, Domitian headed straight forward.

Asherah waited until he'd nearly reached her, and

then started to slide along the building with her back still flat to it. Following her example, Domitian turned his back to the wall and did the same.

They paused briefly at the corner of the building while Asherah peeked out to be sure the coast was clear, and then they slid around the corner to approach the door. They were nearly to it when Asherah glanced back and whispered, "Wait here. Sarita will be out in five minutes. Maybe ten. And make sure you take the long way back. Follow the edge of the jungle around the labs and house. They are searching the beach by the boats, expecting you that way."

Continuing forward then, she slipped through the door into the lab and disappeared, leaving him to eye the now-empty gatehouse and the path beside it worriedly.

Sixteen

Sarita watched as the silver in Santo's eyes completely obliterated the black of his irises. It was as if the nanos were eagerly responding to the offer, but then Santo turned his head away in refusal.

"Goddammit," Sarita snapped furiously. "I don't want to be responsible for Dressler becoming immortal. I couldn't live with knowing he was out there hurting others because Domitian couldn't let me die. Don't force him to make that choice."

"Has it occurred to you that perhaps Santo could not live with knowing he had taken an innocent's life?" Victor asked, his voice sharp. "You are asking him to kill you."

"He's an immortal. You all feed off innocents all the time," she said impatiently.

"To live," Eshe snapped. "But we do not murder people to survive any more than an accident victim or hemophiliac would to get the blood they need. We are not animals, Sarita. He will not feed on you. You are just torturing Santo right now, and for no good purpose. Leave him alone."

Sagging against the bars, Sarita withdrew her arms and then turned to scowl at Eshe and Victor. "I don't want to torture Santo or make him do something he might feel guilty about. But I would rather die than allow Dressler to succeed, and I would rather die than allow Domitian to have to live knowing he'd given Dressler the information he needed to become immortal, and feeling guilty for any deaths and torture that follow."

"I know, but—" Eshe began, and then paused and glanced sharply toward the door when it opened.

They all watched silently as Asherah entered, this time alone.

"Time to go," the woman said, unlocking the cell Sarita was in.

She hesitated, but then noticed the knife Asherah had in her hand and approached the cell door as the woman swung it open.

"Sarita," Victor growled.

"Do not," Eshe commanded hoarsely.

Ignoring them, Sarita stepped out of the cell, mentally preparing herself to kick out at the woman. The way she saw it, she'd either beat the crap out of Asherah, get her keys, and free everyone, or she'd fail and die, blowing Dressler's chances of forcing Domitian to give him the information he wanted. Either way, she won. Although, really, staging a breakout and surviving would be the better ending for her, all things considered.

Smiling wryly, at the thought, Sarita started to turn

toward Asherah and then stiffened and released a startled gasp at a sharp pain in her side. Lowering her head, she stared with amazement at the knife sticking out of her just above the waist.

Well, that was unexpected, she thought, vaguely aware of the shouts and curses coming from Domitian's family. She lifted her head to stare at Asherah blankly.

"You're not dying," Asherah said wearily as the others fell silent. Sliding the knife back out, she caught Sarita by the arm when her legs immediately gave out. Leaning close she whispered, "You should know by now that there are cameras everywhere on the islands. El Doctor heard your plans to sacrifice yourself and decided I should collect you early to make sure you didn't spoil his plans."

Asherah pulled Sarita's arm over her shoulder and turned to half walk and half drag her to the door, adding, "I'll try to get you out of here. But it won't be easy, and he'll kill me if he finds out I helped you."

"Help?" Sarita asked with surprise.

"Do you think I want that bastard living another year let alone hundreds?" she asked in a bitter whisper. "I'd kill him myself if I had the courage, but . . ." She shook her head and opened the door to the hallway, walked Sarita through, and closed it again.

As she helped her along the hall, Asherah added, "He only has months to live. He has cancer. That's why he stepped up his game. Not because he was worried about getting caught. No one will find this island and if they do, they won't make it ashore alive. The flying hybrids circle a two-mile area around the island, watching for anyone approaching. They would sound the alarm and it would be Armageddon on the water with the human security men and the various hybrids all joining in. So we can't count on help. We just have to hold out for a couple months and then we are all free . . . so long as he doesn't find out how a mortal is turned."

"Kill me," Sarita said at once. "That would stop him. Domitian would never tell him without proof I am alive."

Asherah tossed her an exasperated look. "If I can't kill that animal Dressler, what on earth makes you think I could kill you?"

"You stabbed me," she pointed out dryly.

"Yes, but not mortally. And it's just to ensure El Doctor thinks you're subdued and will not be difficult."

"Yeah, well, I'm afraid I believe it too," Sarita said weakly, aware that she was leaning more heavily on the woman with each step. She also felt lightheaded, dizzy, and she was starting to sweat, all bad signs she knew. "I think you hit something important after all."

"What?" Asherah asked sharply, and eased her to lean against the wall so that she could examine her side. "Dammit."

"That doesn't sound good," Sarita muttered, trying to keep her eyes open.

"I think I must have nicked an artery or something. Just hang on a minute. Don't pass out. I'll be right back."

Sarita nodded weakly, but her eyes were closed and she couldn't see the woman leave, although she did hear her walk quickly away. A door opened and closed, followed by silence and then the sound of a door opening and closing again. Sarita heard returning footsteps.

"Here. I'm giving you a shot of adrenaline and something to slow the bleeding," Asherah whispered just before Sarita felt a sharp pain in her thigh. "It should start working relatively quickly."

Sarita swallowed, and while she waited to feel better, asked, "How are we going to get out of here?"

"Not we, you."

She opened her eyes at that and peered at the woman with disbelief. "I won't be able to get out of here by myself. I can barely stand."

"You'll be fine once the shot kicks in," Asherah assured her.

"But—"

"Besides, Domitian is waiting outside," she assured her.

"He is?" Sarita asked with surprise.

"Yes. I saw him on the camera earlier, sneaking around the fence, trying to find a way in. So I distracted El Doctor until he was past the camera and then made an excuse to leave and went out to lead him safely through the cameras to the side of the building. There is a blind spot," she explained. "Only one and very small. He's waiting for you."

"What about the men in the towers?" Sarita asked with confusion.

"El Doctor sent them to help search the island for Domitian." Asherah eyed her with concern. "How are you feeling?"

Sarita hesitated and then straightened away from the wall, finding she could hold her own weight again. She wasn't feeling 100 percent or anything, but she could move under her own power at least.

"Good. Now listen, it has to look like you escaped and I had nothing to do with it, do you understand? El Doctor will kill me if he thinks I let you go or helped you in any way."

"How do we do that?" Sarita asked dubiously. "I'm injured and you're no weakling."

"There is a stereo dissecting microscope on the wheeled tray. I put it there earlier. When I walk you past the tray, you grab it and hit me on the head," she instructed. "Make it look good. If he doesn't believe it, I'm dead," she repeated. "Once you've hit me just run for the exterior door. Dressler is old, he won't catch you if you are quick, and you only have to make it out the door. Domitian will be there to get you away. Got it?"

Sarita nodded abruptly, her hands clenching, and then asked, "What is a stereo dissecting microscope and what does it look like?"

Asherah blinked and then cursed under her breath, and said heavily, "Just look for a big thing on the tray that looks heavy."

"Right," Sarita muttered, feeling stupid.

"Come on," Asherah said, pulling her arm over her shoulder again. "Lean on me and look weak. And keep your head down so your expression doesn't give you away. You have to fool El Doctor."

Nodding, Sarita leaned on her and lowered her head as they made their way up the hall the last five or so feet to the door.

"Good luck," Asherah whispered just before pulling the door open and urging her through.

"Ah, there you are. I was beginning to wonder what was taking you so long." Dressler sounded annoyed at the delay.

"I think I wounded her a little worse than I intended," Asherah said apologetically. "She's losing blood fast."

"No matter. It's nearly midnight now. I'm sure Domitian will turn himself in soon and save the day," he said dryly. "And a little urgency wouldn't hurt in helping him make the right decision. Lay her on the table and chain her up, Asherah, so she's the first thing Domitian sees when he enters," Dressler instructed. "I just want to start my notes before the excitement begins."

Asherah squeezed her uninjured side then, and Sarita glanced up to see that Dressler had turned his back to them to bend over the desk and write something in his book. She also saw that they were just approaching the wheeled tray. The only thing on it was something that looked like the microscopes they'd used in high school science class, but more sci-fi-ish to her mind.

Sending up a quick, silent prayer that this would work, Sarita snatched up the weighty microscope and swung it at Asherah. It was heavier than expected and, afraid she'd kill the woman, Sarita pulled back a bit at the end trying to lessen the blow. She still connected with a solid thump and wasn't surprised when Asherah cried out and fell to the floor.

Seeing Dressler straightening and turning toward her, Sarita wheeled the microscope at him and made for the door as quickly as she could. Which really wasn't that quickly, she worried as she staggered forward. Sure she would be stopped by the old bastard at any moment, Sarita put on a burst of speed and stumbled through the door unaccosted. But the effort cost her and she pretty much fell out the door as it swung open.

One minute the ground was rushing toward her face, and the next she was caught up in strong arms and pressed to a hard chest.

"Thank God," she whispered as Domitian's scent filled her nostrils.

"Mi Corazon?" Domitian whispered with concern when Sarita went still in his arms. She didn't answer, and the scent of blood was heavy on her. He took a moment

to listen for her heartbeat, his own heart stuttering with concern when he heard how weak and thready it was.

"Rest, *mi Corazon*," he whispered. "I have you."

Pressing her tight against him, he glanced around to be sure the way was still clear and the men had not returned from their search, and then he moved quickly around the corner and back along the wall. When he reached the light Asherah had pointed out, he hunched over and ran for the fence, making sure to stay within the dead zone between cameras as Asherah had instructed. Reaching the fence, he didn't bother untying the tie, but pushed his way through, careful to avoid any part of Sarita getting caught by the sharp and broken wire.

Once through he immediately ducked into the jungle outside the fence and then hesitated. It would be faster to cut back on this side of the island and Sarita was injured and needed immediate tending. However, Asherah had warned him that route was too dangerous.

Cursing, he turned and followed the longer route, rushing through the small strip of forest that ran between the fence and the bluffs over the beach, following them around the fenced-in labs and then behind and past the big house. He had to stop only twice to avoid being spotted by the few searchers in this area. As Asherah had said, it appeared they were concentrating on the other side of the island in front of the house, expecting him to try for one of the boats.

Domitian continued on a straight path along the cliffs until he was a good distance through the forest between the big house and the cottage where Sarita's grandmother and Mrs. Dressler lived. He then cut into the forest, avoiding the paths, but making a zigzag trail of his own toward the cottage. Domitian saw a pair of men to his left at one point, but both men were looking the opposite way and he continued on, moving as silently and swiftly as he could, hoping they wouldn't turn and look in his direction until he was well past. When no one shouted or started shooting at him, he was sure he'd avoided detection.

It seemed to take forever to reach the cottage, and Domitian spent the entire trip listening anxiously to Sarita's heartbeat, afraid it would stop at any moment. Nothing in his life had ever terrified him as much as the possibility of losing Sarita did during that interminable journey back to the cottage. He didn't slow as he reached the edge of the clearing, simply raced forward down the path. When the door opened before he reached it, he thought Thorne must have been watching for him, but it was Sarita's grandmother.

"Is she all right?" Maria Reyes asked with alarm as Domitian hurried inside.

"She will be," he assured her grimly in passing and rushed up the hall to the stairs.

Domitian carried Sarita straight up to the guest room she'd slept in earlier, kicked the door closed behind him and settled on the bed with her in his lap. He didn't think about what he was doing, or that he should lock the door or tie Sarita down first, or that he would need blood to help her with the turn, Domitian simply shifted his left arm under her neck so that her head dropped down to hang off it. When her mouth then fell open, he tore into his other arm with his own fangs and pressed the gushing wound to her mouth.

When the bleeding stopped, he repeated the action. Domitian was just finishing doing it for the third time when Sarita's grandmother finally caught up to him and bustled into the room.

"Is she—?" Maria Reyes drew up short halfway to the bed as her eyes telegraphed what they were seeing to her mind. She stared at the blood soaking Sarita's side and hip, the blood smeared on her lips and face, and the bloody wound now stretching from Domitian's wrist to his elbow, and then her eyes rolled up in her head and she just keeled over.

Domitian sat up slightly, craning his head to see the woman, worried he'd killed Sarita's grandmother, and then was distracted when Sarita began to scream and thrash in his arms. Obviously, she'd had enough blood. The turn had begun. Cursing as he realized how unprepared he was for it, Domitian scooped Sarita up, stood, set her on the bed and tried to hold her down.

He could hear shouting from below, recognized Mrs. Dressler's anxious voice, but didn't have time to answer her questions. He was in the middle of a battle royale with his life mate. Sarita was bouncing, thrashing, kicking, and hitting. She was also screaming her head off the whole time, in obvious agony and need and there wasn't a damned thing he could do about it. He didn't have any blood.

After taking a third kick to the groin and having her nails raked across his cheek twice, Domitian, out of desperation, threw himself on top of the wild woman, hoping to pin her down with his weight. It didn't exactly work as he'd hoped. Instead of pinning her down, Domitian found himself holding on for dear life as she bucked and bounced around on the bed like a wild bronco.

"Oh dear . . . What . . . ?"

Domitian wasn't sure if he actually heard those words over Sarita's caterwauling or if Maria Reyes was so distressed she was shouting her thoughts. Whatever the case, he glanced around then to see the woman sitting up on the floor, looking both dazed and horrified as she watched him and Sarita hump around the bed. At least until Sarita gave one great heaving hump and kick that sent them turning and tumbling off the bed onto the floor next to the woman.

Tightening his grip on Sarita, who was now on top, Domitian tried to offer the older woman a reassuring smile, but his head was bouncing repeatedly off the floor, sent there by Sarita's breasts as she thrashed on top of him, and he suspected what he actually managed was a rictus of pain.

Eyes wide, Maria Reyes dragged a golden cross out from the neckline of her dress, clutched it between her hands and began to pray. It wasn't until she started yelling "Out devil! Out foul demon!" that he realized she thought Sarita was possessed.

Domitian closed his eyes and began to pray as well, but he was praying that he would survive Sarita's turning with at least one testicle still intact. He was quite sure that one of them was ruptured.

"What the hell?"

Domitian opened his eyes with hope to find Thorne standing in the doorway to the room with a very alarmed-looking Mrs. Dressler in his arms.

"Oh, *gracias a Dios*," Maria Reyes cried and rushed to stand next to the pair in the doorway, chattering away in Spanish so quickly and frantically even he couldn't understand it, and Domitian had been speaking Spanish for centuries. When she finally wound down, the three of them just stood there watching in horror as Sarita continued to rock and thrash on top of him as if he were a rocking horse. With Domitian's hands locked around her waist, she was now throwing herself forward, smashing his head into the floor with her breasts, and then throwing her upper body back and bringing her knees down, pow, right between his legs. And they were just watching, he thought with disbelief. As if this was some WWF bout.

"Help," Domitian whimpered in a voice he was sure was too low to be heard. Fortunately Thorne seemed to understand. He glanced around a little wildly, and then set his mother on the bed. Maria had followed and settled beside her so that the two women could clutch each other's hands as they watched and prayed. At least he was quite sure Maria was praying, Elizabeth Dressler was shouting advice to her rather confounded son as he tried to sort out how to help Domitian.

"Quick, grab her around the chest when she swings up!" Mrs. Dressler shouted.

Thorne straightened his shoulders, straddled Domitian and Sarita and tried to wrap his arms around her chest as she threw herself up and back, slamming her knees into Domitian's much-abused family jewels. Stars exploded behind his eyes, a buzzing sounded in his ears and he closed his eyes on a groan as he waited for the agony to end. But when he could hear again, Elizabeth Dressler was saying, "Oh dear, Thorne, no I don't think—Oh, that isn't working at all."

Forcing his eyes open, Domitian saw that while Thorne had started out wrapping his arms around Sarita's chest, she was thrashing and bobbing around so much that he now had her only by the breasts, one hand clutching each. It brought a growl from Domitian just before the man muttered, "Sorry," and released her.

"Her legs, Thorne! Try her legs!" Mrs. Dressler suggested.

Nodding, Thorne stepped to the side, and then moved down to grab Sarita's feet as they flew up in the air. That was all Domitian saw before his head was smashed into the hardwood floor by Sarita's upper body. But he soon realized this was not going to work either. With her legs in the air, Sarita's mobility was restricted to a short up and down. Basically, her breasts were playing patty cake with his head on the floor.

"Oh, dear, no that isn't going to work either, Thorne," Elizabeth Dressler said with dismay. "Let go of her legs."

Domitian bellowed when Thorne listened to his mother, released Sarita's legs, and they promptly slammed down into his groin together.

"Out Devil! Out spawn of hell!" Maria Reyes roared in response.

Domitian closed his eyes in misery as he realized he wasn't going to get out with even one testicle intact. He'd felt the second one pop this time. God help him, but he was grateful to be low on blood in that moment. The thought of his testicles healing only to be crushed again . . . Well, it was really more than any man should have to endure, he thought.

"What the hell is going on here?"

Domitian blinked his eyes open and stared at the man now towering in the doorway, and then Sarita's breasts obscured his view. But when she rose up again, and the ringing in his ears ended, he opened his eyes and peered at his uncle once more. All he managed to get out was "She was dying," before Sarita's upper body slammed into his head again. Fortunately, it was a mere bounce this time, because Sarita was suddenly lifted off him.

Opening his eyes, Domitian saw that Lucian had grabbed her under the arms and was now holding her out in front of him as far as his reach would allow as if she were a child with a dirty diaper. Releasing a sigh of relief, Domitian scrambled to his feet, took one unsteady step, and then fell over as the world tipped.

He was quite sure he heard a sigh from his uncle and then the man began barking orders.

"Bricker, run back down to the boat and get the chain we brought! Jo, go with him and fetch the blood! Nephew, stay down!" he added when Domitian opened his eyes and tried to move. "The back of your head is hamburger. You need blood before you try to rise again. And, Basha, please control and remove these ladies so I can set Sarita down!"

"On it," three voices said at once and Domitian watched as the room burst into activity. Justin Bricker and a pretty young woman who must be Jo rushed from the room to fetch chain and blood, and Basha stepped in front of Maria Reyes and Elizabeth Dressler for a moment as Thorne looked on with concern. She then turned to say something to Thorne that Domitian couldn't hear over Sarita's continued screeching and then stepped aside to allow Thorne to pick up his mother. Taking Sarita's grandmother by the arm, she then led her from the room too.

Domitian stared after the woman, trying to focus, and then asked, "Is that—?"

"Yes. Your uncle Felix's daughter, Basha." Lucian nodded.

"I heard she was found," he muttered, closing his eyes again to avoid having to watch the room spin. "Is she a hunter now?"

"Yes. As is her husband, Marcus."

Domitian nodded and then winced when it caused him pain to move his head on the floor. He then pondered the fact that he could hear his uncle despite Sarita's screaming. And then realized the man probably wasn't talking at all, but transmitting his thoughts to him.

Justin Bricker was the first to return with his booty. The rattle of the chains brought Domitian's eyes open again, and ignoring his uncle's orders, he rolled onto his stomach and crawled to the bed as Lucian laid Sarita on it and began to chain her down with Justin's help. Halfway through the process Sarita finally stopped screaming and went silent.

Concerned, Domitian managed to pull himself up to kneel at the side of the bed, and then flinched in surprise when a bag of blood was slapped to his mouth, which was open on a breathless pant.

Domitian raised a hand in thanks, the best he could do with a bag of blood in his mouth, then watched as Jo carried a cooler full of blood around to the other side of the bed and set it down.

"Dani's sending someone with drugs to help with the turn," Jo announced as she straightened. "They found Nicholas and the others. She said most of them are all right, but Santo is in a bad way. His hand was cut off and is partially sealed over and they can't find the hand."

"And Dressler?" Lucian asked.

"No sign yet," Jo said grimly. "They're still searching."

Lucian finished chaining Sarita down, then straightened and considered her briefly, before asking, "Is she sending an IV?"

"Yes," Jo said, grabbing another bag of blood and moving out of his vision.

"Then all we can do is wait," Lucian said.

Domitian flinched as the now-empty bag was ripped from his mouth, but raised a hand to catch the next bag as Jo went to pop it on his fangs.

"How did you know where the island is?" he asked, and then popped the bag on himself as he waited to hear the answer.

"A little birdy told me," Lucian said dryly, bringing a snort from Justin Bricker as he finished locking the last chain on his side of the bed and straightened.

"A big damned bird, man," Justin said and then grinned. "Hey, get it? Birdman? Bird, man?"

"Please. Spare us," Lucian said dryly.

"No sense of humor at all," Bricker complained and then glanced to Domitian and grinned. "You should have seen Lucian jump when Thorne came swooping out of the air and perched on the rail of the balcony at the villa like a big damned vulture."

"He is part eagle not vulture," Lucian growled.

"Yeah. Whatever. You should have seen your face, though. That was the first time I've seen you surprised by anything."

"It is the first time I have been surprised in many centuries," Lucian admitted. "Are you saying you were not surprised?"

"Oh yeah, I was surprised all right," Bricker admitted and then glanced to Domitian and told him. "Lucian damned near killed him before we knew he was a friend. Fortunately, Thorne blurted your name and then explained everything. He led us back to the island as soon as we could round everyone up and arm them. About three miles out he made us stop and wait, said he could see hybrids in the air ahead. I thought he was kidding, but Jo pulled out the binoculars and sure enough, there were a couple of them flying around. They were far enough apart Thorne was able to take care of them one at a time. He flew up really high in the sky so he could approach unnoticed," Bricker said, raising a hand upward as far as he could reach. He then brought it swiftly down adding, "And then he swooped down and sucker punched the first one in the back of the head as he flew past." He slammed a fist into his palm with a smack. "The guy was still falling through the air when he swung around and gained height again to go after the next one."

Bricker shook his head. "When he flew out of sight around the island, we didn't know what was happening. Turns out there was one patrol on each side of the island. Ten minutes later he flies back around with a bird hanging from each hand. Literally," he added with a grin. "They were chicks. Both unconscious but alive. Lucian had them locked in the hold of the big boat, and then we picked up the two in the water. One had landed on his wings on his back and was unconscious, but still alive. One landed facedown, though, and drowned before we got to him."

"After locking them in the hold with the other two, we continued forward for another mile, but then Thorne made us stop again, and warned us he could see gilled hybrids in the water about a mile out from the island. Again, I thought he was kidding, but—" He paused to wait as Jo ripped the second bag of blood from Domitian's mouth and replaced it with a third. And then he continued, "Anyway, after some discussion, it was decided Thorne would take Basha up in the air with him. He held her around the waist and flew, and she picked off the gilled hybrids with one of our dart guns. We put them in the hold too, but aren't sure how they'll handle our darts. They're strong enough to knock out rogues, so . . ." He shrugged grimly, not needing to say they might be deadly to the hybrids depending on how strong their constitution was.

At least they'd tried not to kill them, Domitian thought. Although, if these were the ones that Mrs. Dressler had mentioned were loyal to her husband, he wouldn't feel too bad about their deaths. They'd been complicit in Dressler's activities, some of which had been directed against his own people.

"After that, Lucian sent the other boats to raid and search the house and labs, and we followed Thorne around to the cottage to make sure his mother and Sarita's grandmother were all right."

"Because of me." That comment came from Basha as she entered the room and joined the conversation.

"It was not because of you," Lucian said calmly. "Someone had to check on Domitian and Sarita and we had the blood on our boat. If anyone would have needed it, it would have been them."

"We did not even know they were here," Basha argued shortly. "And what we had on our boat was me." Holding up her hand to silence him when he would have argued, Basha asked pointedly, "When before have you ever delegated the battle to others and taken the safer task, Uncle? Never," she answered herself.

"Basha," Lucian began.

"Uncle," she countered, interrupting him. "You really need to let go of your guilt over what you think of as failing to protect me as a child, and stop trying to protect me from everything now. If you do not, I will suggest to Marcus that we move to Italy full-time to be near his family."

Turning on her heel, Basha left the room then and silence briefly reigned.

"Well," Bricker said brightly, avoiding looking at Lucian who appeared to have turned to stone. "Where was I? Oh yes, we followed Thorne back. Of course, flying, he got here faster and . . . well, you know the rest."

Domitian nodded slightly, wincing as the action sent pain radiating through his head. He stopped moving his head in the hopes of ending the pain, but instead it just built and grew, focusing mostly on the back of his skull. The healing had begun, he thought grimly just before he lost consciousness.

Seventeen

Sarita woke up in the guestroom she'd been given in Dr. Dressler's house and for one moment thought that everything had been a mad, mad dream. After all, who would believe in vampires and winged men? No one, of course, she thought, and then a warm arm slid around her waist, and the scent of the man now spooning her assured Sarita that it hadn't been a dream. All those wild memories crowding her mind had really happened. Including the first time when she'd woken up and Domitian had told her what had taken place after she'd stumbled into his arms outside the lab.

He'd turned her to save her life. Sarita didn't know how she felt about that. She wasn't keen on the whole blood thing. On the other hand, she was even less keen on the whole death thing, so blood won that round, she supposed.

Domitian had also told her that Thorne had taken out four winged hybrids alone, and then had taken an im-

mortal woman named Basha up in the air to use tran-
quilizer darts on the gilled hybrids. Sarita had much
less ambivalence about that. She was glad Thorne was
all right and had come through it safely, and while
she was sorry for the hybrids who had died, including
young Colton who had apparently slipped away during
the battle, she was even sorrier for the ones who had
fought against the immortals and survived, because
their future looked pretty bleak from what she could
tell.

Right now they were locked up in cells in the labs
where all the others who were now free, had been kept.
Rather ironic in her opinion. But there was talk of their
being judged by the council. The problem was, no one
seemed to be sure which council just yet. Apparently,
the South American Council, who had been none too
pleased with Domitian's uncle trampling all over their
turf, was now delaying talking to him about what to do
about the island and its inhabitants. It meant Lucian
and a good portion of his people were stuck here until
a decision was made. Something he apparently wasn't
too pleased about, according to Domitian.

And then there was the something Sarita wasn't too
pleased about . . . Dr. Dressler had escaped capture.
After Thorne had taken out the hybrids in the air and in
the water, the Rogue Hunters had attacked the island.
Dressler's security men had put up a bit of a fight and a
couple of immortals had been knocked out by darts. But
when the locked-up immortals and hybrids had been
freed to join the fray, the security men had soon given
up. The overriding consensus had been that Dressler
didn't pay well enough for them to risk their lives.

It didn't matter, though—it was too late. Dressler had

apparently already made his escape. Despite repeated questioning, no one seemed to know where El Doctor might be until hours had been wasted searching every inch of the island. Only then did MacNeil "suddenly recall" that Dressler had a boat in a hidden cave on the side of the island behind the house.

By that time, the boat was long gone, of course, as was Dressler, Asherah, and an immortal Asherah had apparently gone to fetch after assisting in Sarita's escape. The immortal was Davies, the man Sarita had first seen cut in half. And no one was sadder than her to hear that news. The man had surely suffered enough. What more could Dressler visit on him? No one knew, but Lucian had sent hunters out searching for the trio, hoping to capture Dressler and save Davies and Asherah.

Speaking of Asherah, Sarita was a bit confused when it came to how she felt about the woman. She'd seemed all right in the end. She'd even saved Sarita's life. Well, actually she'd stabbed Sarita and damned near killed her, but then she'd helped her to escape. However, there was something troubling Sarita about that whole escape thing. Domitian had told her that Asherah claimed Dressler had sent her out to talk to the guard in the gatehouse when she'd gone out to help Domitian. But Asherah had told her a different story. She'd claimed that she'd seen Domitian on the camera, distracted Dressler until he was safely past, and then made an excuse to leave and lead him safely to the building. They were two different stories, and Sarita had been trained to look for inconsistencies in people's stories. It was a clear sign of the unreliability of a witness and sometimes a sign of an attempt to cover up a crime.

Sarita was a little concerned about what Asherah might have been covering up.

Pushing that thought from her mind, she snuggled closer against Domitian and sighed with satisfaction. He was such a good man. While he and her grand-mother had sat at her bedside as she went through the turn, he'd apparently explained what he and now Sarita were to her *abuela*. Her grandmother had taken it better than Sarita had expected, although she did now wear three crosses and pray a lot for their souls. Other than that, she seemed fine, though.

Sarita stilled as Domitian shifted, his hand sliding to rest over her breast through the sheet. When he stopped there, his breathing deep, she decided he was still asleep and closed her eyes with another smile. As he'd promised, now that the danger was over, he was wooing her as he felt she wanted. She had only been awake a week, but he'd already brought her flowers and candy, and had even taken her on two actual dates . . . with her grandmother accompanying them.

It seemed Grandmother thought they needed a chap-erone. For the first date he'd taken them to dinner at one of his restaurants. Sarita had actually enjoyed her-self. Talking to Domitian was easy, and the three of them had laughed a lot as they ate. Sarita suspected she wouldn't have experienced that if they'd been by themselves. They wouldn't have lasted through the ap-petizers before they were rushing out of the restaurant to find the nearest safe spot to have sex and pass out. Instead, they'd stayed for hours, chatting and laughing before flying back to the island in the helicopter. After a chaste kiss under her grandmother's watchful eye, Domitian had left them at the cottage and departed for the big house where he, along with Lucian and some of the hunters, were staying until the situation on the island was resolved.

Their second date had been dancing, an overnight stay at his mainland home, and a trip to visit the graves of Sarita's father and grandfather the next day. It seemed Grandmother had mentioned to Domitian that dancing was the one thing she'd missed most besides her husband and son while a prisoner on the island. Domitian had decided that was where he would take Sarita on her second date . . . with Grandmother as chaperone. It seemed he wasn't above ingratiating himself with the old lady to win Sarita. But she hadn't minded. She'd actually enjoyed it. Her grandmother's presence had forced them to behave and Domitian had spent the night dancing with first one of them and then the other.

Her grandmother had truly enjoyed herself and so had Sarita. But, dear God, dancing with Domitian had been sweet torture. His body pressing against hers, his hands on her, his breath on her ear. He'd driven her wild and there hadn't been a darned thing she could do about it with her grandmother there. Not even once they'd got to Domitian's home afterward.

At first Sarita had been too stunned at the décor to think about her need for Domitian. She'd peered around at the potted plants, the overstuffed light-colored furniture, and the beautiful hardwood floors and had thought this was the home she'd always dreamt of. The one she'd planned to make for herself one day, and here Domitian had created it for himself. It had made her wonder about those nanos. Maybe they really knew their business. Domitian certainly seemed to suit her in a lot of ways.

Sarita heaved a little sigh and peered at the wall across from her as her mind whirled with the chaos that had claimed it for days as she considered all her options and all her wants and needs. She hadn't just been dancing and visiting graves this past week, she'd spent a lot of time helping her grandmother and Mrs. Dressler as they assisted the hybrids on the island. The two women had made it their mission to make sure that as many of them as possible could have normal lives.

For some that wasn't feasible. Like Thorne, their differences were too noticeable and would make their having a life approaching anything near normal unattainable. But for others it was possible, and the two women were determined to make it happen for those they could. It turned out they had the finances to do it too. It seemed the money Dressler had so happily been spending was his wife's. Elizabeth Salter Dressler had inherited a fortune from her grandparents before marrying Dressler, and later had inherited her parents' even more substantial fortune.

Now that Dressler was out of the picture, Elizabeth was taking back her power and her money. She'd reverted to her maiden name and had all her money moved so that El Doctor couldn't access it. She'd then placed nearly half of it in an account for Thorne, and intended to use the rest to help the hybrids.

For Sarita just a week of helping these people had been more satisfying than a year as a police constable, and with not even 1 percent of the stress so far . . . And that was part of her problem and the reason for the chaos in her mind. When she'd first woken up to find she'd been turned, Sarita had felt a little lost and so had instinctively turned to her old life for comfort.

She'd determined she would stay for a week or so and then return to the safety and comfort of her home and job in Canada. Domitian had already said when they were on the little island that he would enjoy living closer to his sister and would follow her and woo her as she deserved, so she hadn't even considered him in the decision. But she had asked her grandmother to return and live with her, and her grandmother had jumped at the chance and seemed really excited.

But that was part of the problem. Now that she was adjusting to the idea of being an immortal, Sarita found she had less interest in returning to Canada and her job. She found helping the hybrids satisfying, and she liked spending lazy afternoon siestas in bed with Domitian. But she didn't want to disappoint her grandmother either, or make her stay on an island that had been a prison to her for fifty years.

A soft snore sounded behind her and she grinned to herself, acknowledging that the truth was, now that he was wooing her as he felt she deserved, Sarita didn't really need it. Something had shifted in her. Or perhaps it was just that everything was blending together to make her realize how much they suited each other, from his home being her dream home to how his sense of humor matched hers, how their taste in foods seemed to be always lining up, and how they had danced together as smoothly as if they'd been doing it their whole lives. While she knew she couldn't possibly love him already, she felt in her bones that she belonged with Domitian.

A soft tap at the door sounded and Sarita slipped quickly out of bed, tugging her clothes back into order as she rushed to answer it. That was one benefit of life mate sex—it all happened so fast and furious they rarely managed to get all of their clothes off, she thought wryly as she reached the door.

"Hi," Eshe said softly when Sarita opened the door.

"Hi," Sarita responded with surprise. She hadn't seen the woman since they'd been locked in the cells. Eshe, along with the other hunters had been out searching for Dressler, Asherah, and Davies morning, noon, and night since they'd disappeared.

"Got a minute?" Eshe asked.

"Of course." Sarita slipped into the hall, easing the door silently closed and then followed Eshe up the hall, her mind whirling with curiosity as she tried to figure out what this was all about.

"It's beautiful here," Eshe commented a few minutes later as she led Sarita out into the gardens. "Hard to imagine the nightmare Dressler made it into for everyone when you look at such beauty."

"Yeah," Sarita agreed, peering out over the well-tended gardens.

"I wanted to talk to you about Domitian," Eshe said, leading her along a path with tall flowers growing on either side of it.

"Oh?" Sarita asked, suddenly wary.

"You know you love him, right?" she asked.

Sarita swallowed and glanced away, her brow furrowing. "I've only known him for—"

"Cut the crap," Eshe said not ungently, and Sarita blinked and turned back to her with surprise. Smiling, Eshe said, "Kiddo, I've been alive for a long time and—"

"How long?" Sarita asked with curiosity. Honestly, none of these people looked over thirty and most of them looked more like twenty-five. Yet Domitian was fricking ancient.

"I was born in 1446 B.C.," Eshe said matter-of-factly.

"Did people exist back then?" Sarita asked, trying to wrap her mind around that number. Was there any history back then? She didn't remember studying anything that old. Wasn't that the ice age or something?

"The last ice age was eleven or twelve thousand years ago," Eshe said dryly, obviously reading her mind.

"Right . . . and you were only born three thousand, five hundred years ago . . . give or take a couple decades," Sarita added sarcastically. "God!"

Eshe laughed at her expression and said, "Look. I just wanted to talk to you before I go because Victor was saying Domitian is worrying that you aren't letting him in and aren't acknowledging your feelings for him."

"I don't know what my feelings are," Sarita said with frustration. "They're all a jumble and I can't think straight when he's around. I mean I know I want him. He's like crack to my crack ho, but—" She shook her head helplessly.

"Hmm," Eshe murmured. "And yet you were willing to die for him in the cells."

"That was so Dressler wouldn't know how to become immortal," Sarita argued.

"No. Actually, what you said, and what I read from your mind at the time," she added firmly, "was that you would rather die than allow Domitian to *live knowing he'd given Dressler the information he needed to become immortal, and feeling guilty for any deaths and torture that followed.* That's dying for Domitian, so he wouldn't suffer guilt."

Sarita stared at her.

"What? You gonna deny it?" she asked and then said simply, "You love him, Sarita. This isn't earth-shattering news to anyone but you. As immortals we know that we'll love a life mate if we're fortunate enough to find them. It's a simple fact. And down deep you know you love him. It's just the mores and traditions of your mortal life that are hanging you up. According to them you can't love him yet and should wait to accept or admit it until a suitable period of time has passed."

Turning, she started walking again and added, "And you're free to do that. But I hope you don't, kiddo, because Domitian has waited a long time for you already and he deserves to be happy. As do you. And it pains me to know you're struggling with this when it's all so simple."

Sarita followed, thinking it really was simple. She had wanted to die that day to save Domitian a lifetime, a very *long* lifetime, of guilt. And she would die for him now to save his life if necessary. He was a special man, so patient and kind and passionate. She'd never met anyone like him. Never dated anyone she respected as much or cared as much about. She did love him, Sarita acknowledged, whether she'd known him as long as society would deem long enough or not.

"Anyway," Eshe said after a moment. "I just wanted to say that before we leave. And to again welcome you to the family, because you're a part of it now whether you admit it today or next year."

Sarita stopped walking and frowned. "Leave? I thought you were all staying until Dressler was found?"

"That boat has sailed, unfortunately," she said flatly. "We've got information suggesting that he's left the country. Lucian's arranging for a couple of Rogue Hunters to stay on the island in case he tries to come back here. They'll be working with a couple of Rogue Hunters the South American Council is assigning to the island and the island will be under both councils' purview, at least until Dressler is caught. But in the meantime, the rest of us are going home."

Breathing out a sigh, she smiled wryly and added, "I was looking forward to seeing my husband, Armand, but apparently that's not going to happen for a while yet."

"No?" Sarita asked curiously.

Eshe shook her head. "Some rogues took advantage of our absence and have caused a good deal of trouble back home while so many of us were away. We have a couple of messes to clean up and some fires to help put out." She shrugged. "Having been a mortal cop, you know how it is. While the cop's away, the perps will play, right?"

Sarita smiled faintly. She'd never heard that one. She'd have to remember to tell it to Jackson.

"Listen, that's something else I wanted to say," Eshe added now. "If you ever get tired of playing cops and robbers with the mortal miscreants, we have some real rotten rogues that need putting down. And every job saves lives. There's no dragging cats out of trees or slapping the wrists of shoplifters. Every rogue is a really bad dude who is killing or controlling mortals. And I already talked to Mirabeau about it. She liked you too and said you could ride with us. Just a thought," she added. "No pressure. And the job will still be there ten, twenty, or even a hundred years down the road if you'd rather stay and help out the hybrids for a bit."

"Did you read that out of my mind?" Sarita asked with amusement.

"Didn't have to," Eshe assured her. "You glow when

you're helping them, just like you do when Domitian is around. It's obvious it makes you happy."

They had walked full circle and were approaching the house again, and Sarita frowned when she saw her *abuela* rushing toward them.

"Looks like I'm not the only one who wants to talk to you today," Eshe said, eyeing her grandmother with interest. "I'll leave you two to it."

"Eshe?" Sarita said as the woman started away. When the older immortal turned back she said, "Thank you."

Eshe smiled. "Don't tell the boys we had this heart to heart. They think I'm a hard-ass and I like it that way."

"Oh please," Sarita said with amusement. "You *are* a hard ass."

"Yeah." She grinned. "But so are you. That's why Mirabeau and I like you. See you around, kiddo."

"Later," Sarita said with a smile and then watched as the two women passed each other. Eshe smiled at her grandmother easily, and Maria Reyes smiled nervously back, eyeing her a little leerily until she was well past her and had reached Sarita.

"She is one of those vampires, no?" her grandmother asked in a whisper, her hand going to the crosses at her throat as she glanced back at Eshe. She was wearing only two today, Sarita noticed. That was progress.

"She is an immortal, *abuela*," she said firmly. "Like me."

"*Si*. A vampire." She turned back to her and shook her head sadly. "So young and pretty to be a vampire."

"Again, not a vampire. And not so young either," Sarita said with amusement. "She's older than you."

"No," her grandmother said, turning to stare at the woman again. "No."

"*Si*," Sarita assured her. She almost told her Eshe's

age, but decided it might give the poor woman a heart attack, so asked, "Did you want to talk to me?"

"Oh, *si*." Maria Reyes turned back to her and said worriedly, "*Si*, Chiquita, I need to talk to you."

"What is it?" Sarita asked, her smile fading. "Has something happened?"

"No," she assured her quickly and then sighed unhappily and blurted, "I want to be a part of your life, yes? But I cannot come to Canada with you, Chiquita. Elizabeth would be alone and she needs my help. These poor hybrids, so abused and imprisoned so long. They need help. And you don't need help. You have your Domitian. But they have no one, and Elizabeth has only me and Thorne and—"

"*Abuela*," Sarita interrupted gently when the woman didn't show signs of winding down. "It's okay."

"*Si?*" she asked uncertainly.

"*Si*," Sarita assured her, and then took a deep breath and admitted, "I've been thinking I might like to stay and help with the hybrids too."

"Oh, Sarita!" She hugged her quickly. "That would be wonderful! I know Elizabeth will be so pleased. And then Domitian can stay and keep his restaurants and marry you like he wants and you can make babies for us to spoil and—"

"Yeah, Gran, you maybe want to slow your ponies there," she said dryly. "Domitian hasn't asked me to marry him or anything."

"He asked me for permission to marry you."

"He did?" Sarita asked with surprise. "When?"

"When he took us dancing. He is a true gentleman, that one. He asked for formal permission out of respect. A good boy."

"What did you say?" she asked with curiosity.

"I said yes, of course," she exclaimed as if that should be obvious. "He loves you and you love him and you will make me beautiful little grandbabies to spoil."

It seemed everyone "knew" she loved him, Sarita thought wryly. She was the only holdout . . . and she didn't want to be.

"Oh! There he is now. I will go. You tell him you are staying and will marry him. He will be so happy." Her grandmother rushed off before she could protest and Sarita watched her beam happily at Domitian in passing.

When all he managed was a weak smile in return, Sarita frowned. Something was obviously up, and it didn't look like this was the time to tell him anything. The moment he had passed her grandmother, his smile died and his expression became a combination of anger and concern.

"What is it?" Sarita asked, when he caught her hands and began to urge her farther into the garden.

"I was just talking to Lucian," he said and then announced abruptly, "Dressler went to his apartment when he left here."

"They found him?" she asked with surprise.

"No. They found what he left behind."

Sarita eyed him uncertainly. "Davies?"

"He is alive. He was in a bad way, but they have given blood and he is recovering and talking and told us all he knew," he said, rubbing the back of his neck. Raising his head, he added, "Asherah is dead, though."

"How?" she asked at once.

"Her throat ripped out," he said bluntly.

Sarita stiffened. "Davies didn't—"

"No. That is what they first thought when they got on the scene, but he said no and the information on Dressler's computer backs him up. El Doctor apparently left it in his rush to get out, and I guess it was rigged to record everything the cameras saw . . . *all* the cameras."

"Us on the little island?" she asked and then winced when he nodded. Well, that was embarrassing.

"And us on this island," he said quietly. "Including when I turned you."

"What? But—"

"Lucian sent someone down to search the cottage. There was a camera in every room in the house. The recordings started while Dressler's men were searching the cottage. They were planting and activating the cameras during their 'search.'"

"So he knows how to become immortal," she said with dread, and then realization struck and she glanced at him sharply. "That's why he took Davies."

Domitian nodded.

"He made him turn him," she guessed.

Domitian shook his head. "Apparently he turned himself. Nearly chewed Davies's arm off to do it too."

Sarita winced. "So Dressler killed Asherah."

"He drained them both dry, Davies and Asherah. She died, but most of Davies's nanos moved into his organs. He was suffering until help came, but alive. Poor bastard." He ran a hand through his hair and said, "As for Asherah, she made her own bed. She was never trying to help us when she arranged your escape. That was Dressler thinking his ten steps ahead as usual. His plan was to wound you mortally and let you go so I would turn you in front of the cameras he had placed in the cottage during the search. He did not even stick around until I turned you. Once I had you and was headed back to the cottage, he had Asherah grab Davies and take him to the boat in the cave. They were gone before the hunters made the island."

"Oh," Sarita said quietly.

"Davies says they were on the way to the mainland by the time I got you to the cottage and turned you. Dressler watched it on the boat, and the minute they got to his apartment in town, he attacked Davies. Bit his arm over and over to be sure "it took." I guess he didn't take bagged blood with him. The plan was that Davies would supply the blood he needed."

"But we aren't supposed to feed off immortals," she said quietly. Domitian had been giving her lessons on being immortal since her turn. That was the first point he'd stressed. No biting. Taking in immortal blood was bad. The influx of nanos meant the host's blood was used up at an accelerated rate. Drinking Davies dry would have just increased Dressler's need for blood, which was no doubt why he'd then drained Asherah dry.

"Yes, well, apparently that was one thing Dressler didn't learn from all his experiments," Domitian said dryly.

"I'm sorry," Sarita said solemnly.

He glanced at her with surprise. "For what?"

"That your turning me gave Dressler exactly what he wanted," she said simply. "The knowledge of how to turn himself."

"Oh, no no, Sarita, no," he said gently, taking her hands in his again. "He already knew how an immortal turned a mortal. Davies told him repeatedly in the hopes he would stop when he was cutting him in half.

They have it on the tapes from the lab. Dressler knew exactly how an immortal turns a mortal before he ever put us together on the island."

"What?" she asked with surprise, and when he nodded, she asked, "But then why did he need us? Why go to all that trouble of putting us on the island? And what was that escape nonsense all about?"

Domitian's mouth twisted slightly. "Because he wanted to see what exactly happened before he submitted himself to it. It seems Dressler enjoys inflicting pain on others, but does not care to suffer it himself. He wanted to know if it was painful, and if so, just how painful."

"You mean he had Asherah damned near kill me just to see a turn before he tried it?" she said with disbelief, and when he nodded, she asked, "Didn't Davies tell him it was painful?"

"*Si*. But he thought he was just trying to talk him out of doing it. So he had to see for himself and needed a pair of life mates to accomplish that."

"Us," Sarita growled angrily. "How the hell did he find us?"

"Pablo Guerra, my private detective," he admitted unhappily. "Dressler hired him, explained about our eyes, and said he would pay him a fee for every immortal he reported to him. Well, my eyes fit the description," Domitian pointed out. "So Pablo told him he'd been working for a client for thirteen years who had eyes like that. A strange man, who just wanted regular reports on a girl in Canada. She was thirteen and living here in Venezuela when he hired me, et cetera, et cetera."

"Dressler apparently asked the few immortals he had at that time why I would do that. They guessed, correctly, that perhaps you were my life mate and I was waiting for you to grow up to claim you. So he told the detective he would hire others to find the immortals— Pablo was just to send him copies of the reports I was paying for and put cameras in your apartment. And then he apparently waited for me to go to you, because surely I would do so soon now that you were grown-up."

"Only you were being noble," she said softly.

"Si," he said.

Sarita nodded, and then shook her head. "But why did he keep trying to hire you?"

"I am not sure," he admitted. "He only started eating in my restaurant about two years ago."

"About when he hired Pablo," she commented.

Domitian nodded. "He offered me a job the first night, but said it jokingly, and then repeated the offer every once in a while." He shrugged. "Perhaps he planned to lure you to the island if I did not claim you quickly enough and wanted to be able to use hiring me as an excuse to get us together."

"Which is what happened," Sarita pointed out and then commented, "I'm surprised he didn't wait to turn until he could get his hands on some drugs to ease the pain if he saw what I went through. From what everyone said afterward, it sounds like it was agony." Wincing, she added, "What I remember was agony."

"Ah . . ." Domitian made a face.

Sarita raised her eyebrows. "What?"

"Well, the camera in the bedroom was faulty. There was no sound, and the picture was a bit grainy, and according to Davies, Dressler thought I fed you my blood, held you for a minute and then we had wild sex, so it could not have been so bad."

"What?" Sarita gasped with disbelief. "He thought we had sex while I was in the turn?"

"Well, I was on top of you and we were very active on the bed," Domitian pointed out. He then added, "And apparently the camera angle was such that he never saw your grandmother enter the room. And then he only saw your upper torso rising up and down beyond the bed after you rolled us both to the floor. Davies said Dressler stopped watching when that business started, so . . ." He shrugged almost apologetically, apparently able to see how Dressler could misunderstand things so badly.

Sarita stared at him blankly and then closed her eyes and let her head drop into the palm of one hand.

There was silence for a minute and then Domitian asked, "Are you angry?"

She jerked her head up with surprise. "With Dressler? Of course, the—"

"No, with me," Domitian interrupted.

"Why would I be angry at you?" she asked with confusion.

"Because it was my detective who caused all of this to happen to us. If I had not hired him—"

"No," Sarita interrupted firmly. "You are not responsible for Pablo's actions," she assured him and then smiled wryly and said, "So I was worried you'd blame me for Dressler's learning how to become immortal because you had to turn me to save my life, and meanwhile, you were worried that I'd be angry because your hiring Pablo led Dressler to realize we were life mates."

"Si," he said with a crooked smile.

"Hmm . . ." Sarita murmured, then took a deep breath and said, "I guess it must be love."

Domitian stilled, his gaze locking on her face. "Do you think so?"

"I know so," she admitted quietly and then offered him a crooked smile and said, "Actually, everyone else apparently knows so too."

"*Si.*" He gave a solemn nod. "You are an intelligent woman, *mi Corazon*, but in this instance . . ."

"Yeah, yeah, I was the last one to the table this time," she muttered.

Domitian smiled, and then asked, "Does this mean that you will consent to be my wife as well as my life mate?"

Sarita swallowed, but then nodded. "Yes. But . . ." she added, raising her hand between them quickly to prevent him from kissing her when he bent toward her.

Domitian paused, uncertainty on his face. "But?"

After a hesitation, she slid her arms around his waist and pressed her cheek to his chest before admitting, "Grandmother doesn't want to move to Canada."

"I am sorry," he said sincerely. "I know you looked forward to having her with us there."

"About that," she muttered and then took a deep breath and admitted, "Actually, I have been thinking I might like to stay here too."

Domitian stilled and then pulled back slightly to peer down at her. "Really?"

Sarita nodded.

"What about your job?" he asked uncertainly.

"I wanted to help people, Domitian. That's why I became a police officer. But . . ." Shaking her head, she said, "I can't think of anyone who needs help more than the people here do. And I mean, we don't have to stay here forever. I'd just like to help as many as I can get on their feet. But I know you mentioned it would be nice to be closer to your sister and—"

"Sarita," he interrupted.

"Yes?" she asked warily.

"I love you. I am happy to stay here. I like your grand-mother and we will be close to her while she is with us. I can keep my restaurants running for now while you help here, and we can visit my sister in the summers. And if you later wish to move somewhere else, we can do that too. We have time."

Sarita snorted. "Yeah, we've got time. Like thousands of years apparently."

"It will pass quickly," he assured her.

"Yeah, I'm not too sure about that," she said dubiously.

"Mi Corazon," Domitian said solemnly, lowering his mouth to just above hers so that his breath brushed across her lips tantalizingly as he spoke. "If there is one thing I have learned in my long life, it is that life passes quickly when you are happy. And you make me very happy. Our life together will fly by in a heartbeat."

"That's so sweet, my love," she said softly and then, grinning, added, "You old guys know just the right thing to say."

Domitian closed his eyes, shook his head, and then silenced her laughter with a kiss.

Can't get enough of Lynsay Sands?
Look for her medieval romance BLISS
On bookshelves Summer 2017

Prologue

England, 1173

"Damn!" King Henry crumpled the scroll he had been reading into a ball and threw it to the floor in disgust. He spent a moment muttering about the soft hearts and interfering ways of women, then sighed with resignation and held his hand out to Templetun. "You may as well give me Lord Holden's message, too."

The other man's eyebrows flew up in amazement at the request, a touch of fear mingling with suspicion in his eyes. "How did you know?"

"It is not conjuring or anything, Templetun, simply experience. I never receive a complaint from Lady Tiernay that I do not receive one from Lord Holden as well. Besides, I saw his man ride in earlier and assumed he bore a message. There have been a few small uprisings in Normandy, and I asked Hethe to tend them for me. No doubt he is waiting to tell me he has done so."

"Ah." Relaxing, the older fellow handed over the document in question.

Henry opened the scroll a bit irritably, displeased at having to explain himself. Templetun had only worked in the capacity of his chaplain for the past couple of days—his usual chaplain was ill—but already Henry was wishing for the latter's speedy recovery. His replacement was entirely too nervous, superstitious, and seemed to be far too eager to lend credence to Henry's reputation of being the "Spawn of the Devil." Shaking his head, Henry focused his attention on the parchment he now held. A moment later, it was a crumpled mass on the floor not far from the first, and Henry had leapt up to pace before his throne.

As he had expected, Lord Holden had cleaned up the little revolts in Normandy and was on his way home. But he had also added a complaint or two about his neighbor. It seemed his chatelain was harassed mightily by the Lady of Tiernay and was beleaguering Hethe with letters regarding the woman. In his turn, the Hammer of Holden had respectfully requested that his king do something about the woman . . . or he, himself, would.

It sounded very much like a threat, and it displeased Henry greatly to be threatened by one of his vassals. In fact, if Hethe weren't such a valued warrior and had not aided him so often in the past ten years, he would have seen him punished. But, unlike his father before him, Hethe had been a great asset.

He grimaced at the thought of the previous Lord Holden, Hethe's father. Born the second son, Gerhard had expected to be allowed to join a monastery and live out his life amongst the musty old papal scribblings he so adored. Unfortunately, his eldest brother had died, forcing him to abandon those plans in favor of marriage and producing an heir. The man had taken out that displeasure on his son.

To be honest, in Henry's opinion, Gerhard had been a touch mad. Fortunately, Hethe had not yet shown the same tendency. Unfortunately—for Hethe, at least—he had not even shown the same love of learning his father had, and the two had not gotten along. Gerhard's hatred had driven the boy from his home and straight into Henry's service as soon as he earned his spurs.

Ah, well. Gerhard's loss had been his own gain, Henry decided. But that didn't relieve Hethe of his responsibility to show his king respect. "What the Devil am I to do with these two?" he asked in frustration.

"I am not sure, my liege. What appears to be the problem, exactly?" Templetun asked tentatively. "I do realize they are both complaining—and from your reaction, I would say quite frequently—but about what, exactly?"

Henry turned to scowl down at him, opening his mouth to explain rather acerbically that his question had been rhetorical, when he changed his mind. Instead, he said, "Each other. Lady Tiernay writes to 'warn me' of her neighbor's cruel and abusive behavior to his serfs and villeins, because she '*knows* I would not wish to see any of my subjects so sorely mistreated.'"

"Ah," Templetun said again, biting back a smile at his king's sarcastic imitation of a woman's high-pitched voice. "And Lord Holden?"

Henry gave a short laugh. "He writes to say that Lady Tiernay is a nosy, harping busybody who makes his life hell."

"Hmmm." The new chaplain was silent for a moment,

then murmured, "Did not Lord Holden's wife die several years back?"

"Aye. Ten years ago. In childbirth. And Hethe has been my best warrior since. Always ready for a fight, always away on campaign for me. I don't know what I'd do without him."

"Did Lady Tiernay's husband not die four or five years ago as well?"

"What?" Henry scowled briefly, then his expression cleared. "Oh, nay. That was her father. Lady Tiernay is not married and has not been. Her father neglected to see to that ere his passing."

"She is of marriageable age, then?"

"Oh, aye. She is beyond old enough to marry, I should think. Why, she must be . . ." Henry paused, doing the math in his head. "I think she may be twenty or thereabouts." Groaning, he walked over and wearily rested his hand on his throne. "And there is another problem. I shall have to marry her off soon. How the Devil am I expected to find a husband for a harping wench like her?" Again, he began to pace.

"Perhaps you already have one, my liege," Templetun offered with some trepidation. When the king turned on him sharply, he shrugged. "Mayhap the solution is to have Lord Holden marry her. It will solve both problems at once. She will be married, and they will be forced to work out their difficulties between themselves."

"They will kill each other within the week!" Henry predicted with disgust.

"Mayhap." Templetun paused innocently. "But still— both problems would then be solved, would they not?"

Henry considered him with frank admiration. "Damn, Templetun," he finally breathed. "You have an evil mind."

He rushed back to his throne and threw himself excitedly upon it. "You shall write two messages in my name . . . and take them forth yourself!" Then he turned to the chaplain with a dangerous look in his eye. "And, Temple-tun," he added. "Don't fail me."

One

No one was more surprised than Helen when she kicked the ball. She had only paused on her way across the bailey to watch the children play for a moment when the ball suddenly rolled toward her, and she impulsively kicked it. It was a mistake.

Goliath, who'd stayed dutifully by her side as always until then, took it as a sign that they were going to play. He was off after the ball in a heartbeat, barking gaily and running like the wind. Helen tried to call him back, but her voice was easily drowned out by the squeals of the children who raced after the huge wolfhound. The dog reached the ball first, of course. Unfortunately, he didn't understand the rules of the game and, as a hunting animal, he did not fetch it back right away. Instead, he picked it up in his massive jaws and shook it viciously side to side.

Helen couldn't hear the material tear, but she knew it had happened when feathers suddenly filled the air around the beast. Satisfied that he had killed his prey, Goliath strode cheerfully back through the dismayed children to drop the ruined ball at his mistress's feet. He then sank to the ground and rested his head happily on his front paws in what Helen considered the very picture of male satisfaction. Shaking her head, she bent to pick up and examine the damaged toy.

"My lady?"

Helen turned her attention from the slightly damp-with-dog-drool ball and glanced at the two women who appeared beside her. "Aye?"

"This is Maggie," Ducky said quietly. Ducky was Helen's lady's maid, but also a friend. If she had brought this other woman to her, there had to be something the two needed. Surveying the slightly warty but kindly looking crone, Helen decided she liked what she saw.

"Hello, Maggie." she greeted the woman, then tipped her head slightly. "You are not from Tiernay." It wasn't a question. Helen knew every one of her people; she made it her business to know them. This woman wasn't one.

"Nay, my lady. I come from Holden."

Helen's lips tightened at the news. It could only mean trouble of some sort. Her thoughts were distracted by a murmur of discontent as the children arrived to cluster around her. Their accusing little eyes moved unhappily from Goliath to their now-mangled toy.

"I shall repair it at once," she assured them guiltily, relieved when the promise seemed to appease them. "Come."

The order was for Goliath, who immediately got to his feet to keep pace at Helen's side as she headed for the keep, but the humans obeyed as well. Ducky and Maggie promptly fell into step behind her while the children trailed at the back. The group made a small parade as it crossed the bailey, mounted the steps, and entered Tiernay keep.

"I shall need some fresh feathers, Ducky," Helen announced as they crossed the great hall.

"Aye, my lady." The woman was off at once, heading for the kitchens where Cook had been plucking chickens all morning for that evening's meal.

"You children go wait at the table. I shall have Ducky bring you drinks and pasties while you wait." So saying, Helen led Maggie and Goliath over to two chairs by the fire. Seating herself in her usual spot, she gestured for the older woman to take the other, then began to search through the small chest nearby for her sewing needle and thread. Goliath settled on the floor by her feet.

Helen was aware of the way the woman hesitated, then perched uncomfortably on the edge of her chair, nervous and stiff as could be, but she ignored it as she sought what was needed. She had just gotten ahold of the necessary items when Ducky appeared at her side with a wooden bowl containing the requested feathers.

"Thank you." Helen accepted the bowl and smiled at the woman with appreciation. "Perhaps you could have someone fetch the children some refreshments and sweets while they wait?"

"Aye, my lady."

Helen began to thread her needle, her attention focused on the task as she asked Maggie, "So, you are from Holden?"

"Aye." The old woman cleared her throat and shifted uncomfortably on her perch. "I used to be in charge of the chambermaids there."

"Used to?" Helen inquired gently. She drew the thread through the needle's eye, then glanced up in time to note the bitterness that flashed across the servant's face.

"Aye. I was released last Christmastide," the woman admitted reluctantly. A moment later she blurted, "The lord wanted only young and pretty maids to serve in the chambers."

Helen's mouth thinned. Such news didn't surprise her. Very little could surprise her regarding the Hammer of Holden's behavior. Hard work and service were not often repaid kindly by the man. Cruel bastard, she thought with irritation, then forced herself to start mending the large jagged tear in the children's ball. After several stitches she felt calm enough to ask, "And what have you been doing for these last six months?"

The woman cleared her throat again. "Farmer White had been courting me up until then. He was a widow," she explained, blushing like a lass fresh out of a school-room. "When I was released, we married. I tended his home and helped on the farm." Her smile and blush faded, leaving her pale and weary looking. "He died these two weeks past."

"I am sorry," Helen said gently. Glimpsing the tears that sprang to the woman's eyes before Maggie lowered her head, she turned her attention back to her task. Deciding she had left just enough unsewn, she turned the ball back inside out and began to stuff it with feathers. She was nearly done with the chore when Maggie recovered enough to continue.

"I knew there would be trouble. I couldn't manage the farm on my own, of course . . . ."

"He evicted you and gave the farm to another couple,"

Helen guessed quietly. Such wasn't unheard of, but to her mind it was cruel to treat someone so shabbily when they had worked so hard and faithfully for so long.

Maggie nodded. "He sent poor young Stephen down as usual to do his dirty work."

Helen nodded. Stephen was Lord Holden's second, the man left in charge of Holden while the Hammer was away. Which appeared to be quite often. Lord Holden seemed forever off doing battle somewhere. But while Stephen was Holden Castle's chatelain, none of the decisions were his. Surely the Hammer kept up a steady discourse with the man, ordering him to do this or that—none of it very pleasant or kind—and from all accounts, young Stephen suffered horribly from being forced to carry out such wicked deeds.

"He had Stephen claim everything in the cottage for heriot," Maggie continued, drawing Helen's attention back to her. "Then he was ordered to burn it all before me and send me on my way."

Helen's eyes widened incredulously. Heriot was the equivalent of a death tax, a legal part of the feudal system. But claiming every last possession, then burning it all . . . well, that was just cruel. And deliberately so. "Did Stephen do it?"

Maggie grimaced. "Aye. He is a faithful servant. He apologized the whole while, but he did it."

Helen nodded solemnly as she stuffed the last of the feathers firmly into the ball and prepared to sew it closed. Of course young Stephen had done it. He would follow his lord's orders.

"His mother would have wept to see him forced to act so."

Helen glanced up questioningly at the woman's words

and Maggie explained. "We were friends when she lived in the village. This would have broken her heart."

"She is dead?" she asked politely, knowing the old servant needed the change of topic to help her maintain composure. If talking about Stephen's mother would help her distance herself from her recent losses, Helen saw no reason not to indulge her.

"Oh, nay. She is not dead. But when Stephen became chatelain and was forced to dole out such harsh punishments . . . Well, she could not bear to stand by and watch. She left the village. Most people think she is dead, but I think she is living on the border of Tiernay and Holden. Stephen often rides out this way for the afternoon. I think he is visiting her." She fell silent for a moment, then added, "He rode out here after seeing to burning my things. Probably went to visit her then as well."

Helen took in the lost expression on the old woman's face and the way she was slumping in her seat and said gently, "And so you came to Tiernay."

"Aye." Maggie sat a little straighter. "My daughter married the tavern keeper in the village ten years back."

Helen nodded. She knew the tavern owner and his wife, of course.

"And they have offered to take me in . . . but they must have your permission first."

Helen was silent for several moments. She was responsible for her land and everyone on it, and therefore, as the woman said, her permission was imperative before any new tenants were allowed to move in. Her first instinct was simply to nod and say certainly Maggie was welcome at Tiernay. But Helen had noted the woman's odd tone as she had spoken of her daughter's offer.

There was no doubt that Maggie had worked her whole life. Losing her position in Holden Castle must have been extremely demoralizing. Her marriage and position as a farmer's wife had saved her pride somewhat, but now she was reduced to accepting charity from her own child. Helen suspected it rankled the old woman greatly, and now, considering the matter solemnly, she shook her head. "Nay."

"*Nay?*" Maggie looked fit to burst into tears, and Helen mentally kicked herself for speaking her thoughts aloud.

"There will be no charity for you, Maggie. You are still strong and healthy. You can work. As it happens, I am in need of someone with your skills."

Maggie lost her tragic look, hope slowly filling her withered face. "You do?"

"Aye. Edwith used to be in charge of my chambermaids here. She died a month ago and I have yet to replace her. Ducky has had to fill that job as well as tend to her own duties. You would be doing both of us a service should you take Edwith's place. It would relieve a great burden on Ducky."

"Oh!" Much to Helen's consternation, the woman burst into tears. For a moment, she feared she had erred and Maggie wished to stay with her daughter. Then the woman positively beamed at her through her tears, and Helen relaxed.

"Oh, my lady. Thank you," the new mistress of chambermaids breathed, positively glowing at the idea of being useful again.

"Thank *you*," Helen said firmly, then smiled at Ducky, who had appeared suddenly beside her. "Perhaps Ducky could show you around and introduce you to the girls who will be under your guidance."

"Certainly." Ducky beamed at the other woman, then glanced back to Helen. "Boswell says there is a party approaching."

"A party?" Helen raised an eyebrow in inquiry, and Ducky nodded.

"Aye. They bear the king's standard."

Helen paused briefly, then smiled widely. "Good, good. If you should see my aunt on your tour, pray tell her the news." With that, she quickly slipped the last stitch through the ball, tied it off and broke the thread. Standing as the other two women moved away, Helen carried the ball over to the table where its owners were still eating and drinking.

"Here you are," she said cheerfully, setting the ball on the table. "Good as ever. Hurry up with your treats, then get you outside to play. 'Tis too nice a day to be indoors."

Moving away to a chorus of the children's agreement and thank-yous, Helen scurried to the door of the keep, brushing down her skirt as she went.

The travelers were riding through the gates of the bailey as she stepped out into the light. She waited for Goliath to follow her through, then pulled the door closed behind the dog and quickly smoothed down her hair. She felt nervous. This was a party from the king, Ducky had said, and Helen could see that her servant was right. Henry II's standard fluttered there for all who cared to look—and Helen was looking. This was a banner day. The king was likely responding at last to the many letters she had sent him regarding Lord Holden. That was the only explanation for this visit.

It did her heart good. Helen had been begun to fear that the king was entirely ambivalent toward the cold-hearted and even cruel behavior of her neighbor. She

had been left feeling frustrated and helpless by her inability to do more than to take in Holden's serfs and villeins who fled or made their way to Tiernay, and write
letters of complaint. Why, once or twice she'd even had
to go as far as to purchase Holden's prospective victims
to save them from his wrath. Lord Hethe, the Hammer
of Holden, was most certainly a devil in human guise.

But finally the king had sent someone to handle the
matter. At least, she assumed he had sent someone. This
entourage was far too small to count the king amongst
it. Henry's own traveling party could span for miles, as
it included his lords and ladies, his servants, his vassals
and everything he might need on his journey.

Nay. He had obviously sent a man in his stead to tend
the matter, and that was fine with her. This affair was
most likely beneath his attention anyway; it affected
only those whom the Hammer abused. Compared to an
entire country's hardships, this was a small problem.
In fact, the people of Holden were very fortunate King
Henry was looking into the matter at all.

That thought cheering her, Helen waited patiently
until the group of men reached the bottom of the stairs;
then she made her way down to greet them, Goliath at
her side.

"Lady Tiernay?" It was the oldest of the train who
greeted her, his expensive robes rustling as he dis-
mounted and faced her. He wore a hopeful expression.

"Aye. You are from the king." She stated the obvious,
and the gentleman nodded, a smile tugging at his lips
as he took her hand and bowed to press a kiss to her
knuckles. "Lord Templetun, at your service."

"You are welcome here at Tiernay, Lord Templetun," Helen said formally, then placed her hand on his

arm and turned toward the stairs. "Pray, you must be hungry and thirsty after your journey. Allow us to welcome you properly with a meal and drink."

Nodding, Lord Templetun started up the stairs with her, calling orders over his shoulder as they went. They had nearly reached the door to the keep when it burst open and the children poured out. Laughing and screaming one moment, they were wide-eyed and silent the next. At the sight of Helen and Lord Templetun, the group mumbled their excuses and moved solemnly down the stairs, only to burst into a noisy run once they were past. Headed back to the game she and Goliath had interrupted, Helen thought with amusement. She smiled and ignored the questioning glance Lord Templetun threw her.

Leading him inside, she urged the king's man to the table the children had just emptied. Helen saw him seated in the head chair that her father had always occupied, then excused herself for a quick trip to the kitchens. She returned moments later with a passel of servants trailing her, bearing the finest food and wine available in Tiernay keep, on its finest silver trays. After nervously supervising the serving of Lord Templetun, at last Helen seated herself beside him and sipped silently from a mug of mead while he ate. She was impatient to confirm his purpose in being there, but she knew it would be rude to do so before he had satisfied his hunger and thirst.

Fortunately for her state of mind, Templetun was not a man to waste time on savoring sustenance. He devoured a shocking amount of food—and even more of her finest wine—in a trice, then sat back with a satisfied sigh and beamed.

"I must compliment you on a fine table, my lady. That meal did you credit."

"Thank you, my lord," Helen murmured, wondering how to broach the subject of his purpose. Templetun soon put an end to that worry by tugging a scroll from his voluminous robes.

"I bring news from the king." He set the parchment before her, then began to dig at his not-so-shiny teeth with the longish nail of the baby finger on his right hand as he awaited her perusal of it.

Her hands suddenly shaking, Helen broke the seal and quickly unrolled the scroll, her mind racing over the possibilities of how the king intended to punish her neighbor for his rough treatment of his subjects. Appoint someone to watch over him? Fine him? Chastise him?

"Marry him?" The words seemed to scream out of the scroll at Helen as her eyes flew over its contents. "Nay!" Her head was suddenly light and fuzzy. Feeling herself sway, she shook her head determinedly and peered at Templetun. "Surely this is a jest?"

She was so upset, she didn't even notice that she was agitatedly tearing the scroll as she glared at Lord Templetun. Nor did she notice the sudden wary concern on the man's face as he slowly shook his head. "Nay, my lady. The king does not jest."

"Well, he must—He cannot—This is—" Helen's stumbling monologue died abruptly at the sound of approaching footsteps. She turned, relieved to spy her aunt entering the room. Aunt Nell was ever the voice of reason. She would know what to do about this . . . situation.

"Aunt Nell!" Even Helen was taken aback by the desperate tone of her voice as she launched out of her seat and rushed to greet the woman who had served as mother to her since her own mother's death some few years ago.

"What is it, my dear?" her aunt asked and caught her hands, her gaze sliding between the ripped and crumpled scroll Helen held and her niece's pallid face.

"The king, he sent Lord Templetun here." Helen gestured at the man at the table. "And he—" Unable to even say it, she shoved the remains of the scroll at her older relative, silently urging her to read it.

Taking the torn message, Lady Nell uncrumpled it and slowly read its contents. Helen watched as her aunt's eyes flew over the words on the page, then paused, went to the top, then flew over it again.

"Nay," the woman breathed with a horror as deep as Helen's own, then whirled on the man still seated at the table. "Is this a jest, my lord? Because if it is, 'tis a sad one indeed."

"Nay, my lady." The king's man shifted uncomfortably in his seat, looking oddly guilty. His gaze darted around the room, looking everywhere but at its occupants, then he said, "The king dictated that missive himself and ordered me to bring it to you. I am to take another on to Lord Holden and bring him back here for the wedding. The king thought it would be good to allow your people time to prepare for the celebration."

"But—" Helen paused and shook her head, trying to gather her rather scattered wits. "But, this cannot be. Lord Holden is an evil, horrid, *cruel* man. The king cannot expect me to marry *him!*"

When Templetun remained silent, his head lowered, refusing to meet her eyes, Helen began to realize that she was indeed expected to do just that. Numbness crept over her, softening her horror, and she sank back onto the trestle table bench. She was to marry that horrid, cruel bastard neighbor of hers. Hethe. The Hammer of Holden. The man who burned villeins out of their homes for no purpose. Dear God, what would he do when he was displeased with *her*?

"There must be a mistake," Aunt Nell announced firmly, drawing Helen from her miserable thoughts. "Surely the king would not be so cruel as to force my niece to marry *that* man. Perhaps he simply does not understand. We must travel to court and explain things to him. We must—"

"The king is no longer at court," Templetun interrupted solemnly. "He has gone to Chinon to see young Henry and remove some of the members of his court."

Helen and Nell exchanged startled glances at mention of the king's son. It was Helen who murmured uncertainly, "Remove some of his court?"

"Mmmm." Templetun's face was full of displeasure. "Aye. Henry wishes to arrange a marriage between the daughter of the Count of Maurienne and young John. The count seems interested, but wants to be sure John has prospects first. The king offered to invest him with the castles Loudon, Mirebeau and Chinon, but young Henry objects. He will only concede to this if his father allows him to rule either England, Normandy or Anjou in his own right."

"He wants more power." Nell sighed with disgust.

"Aye." Templetun nodded his head solemnly. "It was a mistake for the king to crown his son while he himself yet lives. The boy wants the power that goes with the title."

"But what has that to do with removing some of his court?" Nell asked impatiently.

"Ah, well, the king first thought to take Henry into custody as a warning, but he believes some of young Henry's courtiers are sparking these ideas in him and hopes that after the removal of their influence, his oldest son will settle down." He spoke candidly, then, seeming to realize that he was gossiping, frowned and changed the subject back to the matter at hand. "In any case, seeing him would make no difference. His mind was made up. He feels that you, Lady Helen, and Lord Holden should work your problems out between yourselves, and he wishes the wedding to take place at once. I am to see to it."

Helen lowered her head, her gaze landing on the scroll her aunt still held, proof of King Henry's intent in the matter. It had been written plainly in the message, but for a moment her aunt's words had given her hope. If she could but talk to the king, throw herself on his mercy—

Movement and a rustling just beyond her right shoulder drew Helen from her thoughts. Peering back, she spied Ducky. The maid was wringing her hands, grief and fear both twisting her face as she stared at her mistress. Obviously, the woman had heard enough to know what the message ordered, and she was no less horrified by the missive than her mistress. Straightening, Helen forced a reassuring smile to her face for the servant's benefit, then glanced around with a start when her aunt—the sweetest, gentlest of ladies—suddenly bellowed like the veriest fishmonger.

"Where the Devil did he get an asinine idea like this?"

Helen spared a moment to gape at her aunt briefly, then turned to hear Lord Templetun's answer. He did not appear eager to give it. In fact, he was looking quite reluctant. Guilty. The old man was nearly squirming in his seat with his discomfort. Helen was just starting to get the oddest inkling when her aunt suddenly spoke that suspicion aloud.

"You!"

Templetun froze abruptly, the expression on his face not unlike that of a child startled while raiding the pantry.

"It *was* you," Helen breathed in horror, unsure whether to ask why or simply go for the man's throat. Before she could do either, Templetun was on his feet and easing around the far end of the table.

"Well, I should be getting on now. The king doesn't like dawdling, and, while it is not a long ride to Holden, the day is waning and travel is so much more uncomfortable at night, is it not?"

The question was rhetorical, Helen was sure. At least, the man didn't appear to intend to stick around for the answer. He was sidling eagerly toward the main door now, moving fast, and talking faster still. She wished he'd choked on the food she had served him.

"I have been informed that Lord Holden is presently on his way home from performing a task for the king," he continued as Helen's aunt began to follow him slowly across the floor, eyes narrowed and furious. "So you will have plenty of time to prepare the celebratory feast. I would guess you should plan it for next week's end. That should be about right. I will send a messenger ahead, of course, so that you can see to any last-minute details." The last was said as he slid through the door.

"The little rat!" Nell said harshly once the keep door had slammed closed behind him.

Helen heartily agreed with the pronouncement, but

had other concerns more pressing. "Why would he suggest to the king that Holden and I marry?"

"Why, indeed?" Aunt Nell muttered, then moved back to place her hands on Helen's shoulders to comfort her.

"Surely you are not going to actually marry him?" Ducky gasped, moving forward to join them. "Not the Hammer?"

"I hope not, Ducky. Truly I do." Helen's shoulders slumped miserably.

"But what will you do?"

Frowning, Helen began to twist her hands together as her mind flew over the possibilities. Flee? To where? Beg the king? How? He was away and the wedding was to take place at week's end. Kill the prospective groom? A nice thought, but not very practical, she admitted with a grimace.

"My lady?" Ducky prompted anxiously.

Helen sighed. "I am not sure what I *can* do," she admitted unhappily.

Ducky's eyes widened in horror. "Can you not refuse him? Just refuse and—"

"And have the king send me off to an abbey? I would rather marry the man and kill him than do that! Who would look after my people if that happened? The Hammer, that is who. Tiernay would be forfeit to him as my dower should I refuse the king's orders."

Ducky bit her lip at that, then leaned closer to whisper. "Maggie knows this and that about herbs. Or Old Joan the Healer. She might know of something we could give him to—"

"Bite your tongue," Helen hissed, covering the maid's mouth with her hand and glancing nervously about the empty great hall. "I never want to hear such a suggestion from you again, Ducky. It could get you strung up in the bailey."

"But then what will you do?" The servant looked miserable as Helen removed the hand covering her mouth. "You cannot marry the Hammer."

Helen sighed again. "It appears I will have to. I cannot refuse a direct order from the king."

"Why not?" Ducky asked frantically. "The Hammer does it often enough. Why, he—"

"That's it!" Aunt Nell, who had stood silent and thoughtful throughout the last few moments, suddenly grabbed Helen's arms excitedly, unconsciously giving her a shake.

"What?" Helen asked with a glimmer of hope.

"*You* cannot refuse. But the Hammer *can*. He is too powerful a lord for the king to force him, should he really wish to refuse."

Ducky snorted. "And do you really think for one minute that the Hammer will refuse to marry her? Look! She's as pretty as her mother ever was. And sweet as honeyed mead as well. Then there is her land. Who would refuse a dower like Tiernay?"

Helen sagged slightly, some of her hope leaving her, but Aunt Nell merely straightened her shoulders and spoke staunchly. "Then we shall have to make you and Tiernay less attractive."

Ducky looked doubtful. "Templetun has already seen her for the pretty lass she is. You can't suddenly blacken her teeth and shave her head."

"Nay," Helen agreed slowly, a small smile teasing the corners of her lips as an idea flared in her mind. "But there are other things we can do."

HARD TIME
Sara Paretsky

P9-DNO-817

"V.I. WARSHAWSKI IS BACK . . . AND BOY,
WAS IT WORTH THE WAIT. . . .
This is Warshawski at her black-and-blue best."
—*The Miami Herald*

"In a crowded field of female detectives,
V.I. Warshawski rules."
—*Newsweek*

"REMARKABLE . . . ONE OF THE BEST
CRIME WRITERS IN THE BUSINESS . . .
a good old-fashioned thriller . . .
No major writer has done more to bring modern
Chicago lovingly to life on the page. In all its
brashness and chaos the city lives and breathes in
Paretsky's remarkable series of novels."
—*The Baltimore Sun*

"WELCOME BACK, V.I. WE MISSED YOU."
—*Chicago Sun-Times*

"THIS IS THE BEST WARSHAWSKI NOVEL
EVER AND WELL WORTH WAITING FOR.
Brilliantly plotted, full of heart-wrenching emotion,
packed with fast-paced action, and peopled with
richly complex characters, *Hard Time* packs a
powerful, unforgettable punch."
—*Booklist*

"HARROWING."
—*The Seattle Times*

*Please turn the page for
more extraordinary acclaim. . . .*

A V. I. WARSHAWSKI NOVEL

SARA PARETSKY

HARD TIME

A DELL BOOK

Published by
Dell Publishing
a division of
Random House, Inc.
1540 Broadway
New York, New York 10036

Copyright © 1999 by Sara Paretsky
Cover design by Tatiana Sayig

Dell® is a registered trademark of Random House, Inc., and the colophon is a trademark of Random House, Inc.

ISBN: 0-440-22470-5

Reprinted by arrangement with Delacorte Press

Printed in the United States of America

Published simultaneously in Canada

September 2000

10 9 8 7 6 5 4 3 2 1

OPM

For Miriam

The footnote Queen, without attribution,
in the year you weren't writing,
(Oh, except for this essay on Shanghai, that one on
Benjamin, a little piece on theory)

In the year you're writing,
Let me have one back

THANKS

As always, many people provided help in creating this story. Dr. Robert Kirschner of the University of Chicago gave me much helpful forensic advice—even if his facts forced me to abandon an early draft of the manuscript and start over. Professor Shelley Bannister of Northeastern Illinois University explained much about Illinois prisons to me, including the law regarding prison manufacture. Attorney Margaret Byrne was helpful with specifics on treatment of inmates in the Illinois prison system. She also suggested the unique structure of my mythical prison in Coolis. Angela Andrews kindly and bravely shared her personal experiences with me.

On other technical matters, Sandy Weiss of Packer Engineering gave me much useful information, especially on the various cameras V.I. makes use of in this story. Jesus Mata provided Spanish translations for me; Mena di Mario did the same for Italian. Rachel Lyle suggested what became the main impetus to writing this novel. Jonathan Paretsky as always was most helpful with details on legal matters.

This is a work of fiction, and no resemblance is intended between any characters in it and any real people, whether living or dead or never known to me. The combined prison-jail complex at Coolis in this novel does not exist in reality anywhere in America as far as I know, but I believe it is a plausible one. However, details on treatment of prisoners in Coolis were drawn from the Human Rights Watch report *All Too Familiar: Sexual Abuse of Women in U.S. State Prisons.*

CONTENTS

HARD
TIME

Media Circus

Lᴀᴄᴇʏ Dᴏᴡᴇʟʟ ᴄʟᴜᴛᴄʜᴇᴅ her crucifix, milky breasts thrust forward, as she backed away from her unseen assailant. Tendrils of red hair escaped from her cap; with her eyes shut and her forehead furrowed she seemed to have crossed the line from agony to ecstasy. It was too much emotion for me at close quarters.

I turned around, only to see her again, red hair artlessly tangled, breasts still thrust forward, as she accepted the Hasty Pudding award from a crowd of Harvard men. I resolutely refused to look at the wall on my right, where her head was flung back as she laughed at the witticisms of the man in the chair opposite. I knew the man and liked him, which made me squirm at his expression, a kind of fawning joviality. Murray Ryerson was too good a reporter to prostitute himself like this.

"What got into him? Or more to the point, what got into me, to let him turn my bar into this backslapping media circus?"

Sal Barthele, who owned the Golden Glow, had snaked through the Chicago glitterati packed into her tiny space to find me. Her height—she was over six feet tall—made it possible for her to spot me in the mob. For a moment, as she looked at the projection screens

on her paneled walls, her relaxed hostess smile slipped
and her nose curled in distaste.

"I don't know," I said. "Maybe he wants to show
Hollywood what a cool insider he is, knowing an intimate bar they never heard of."

Sal snorted but kept her eyes on the room, checking
for trouble spots—patrons waiting too long for liquid,
wait staff unable to move. The throng included local
TV personalities anxiously positioning themselves so
that their cameras could catch them with Lacey Dowell
if she ever showed up. While they waited they draped
themselves around executives from Global Studios.
Murray himself was hard at it with a woman in a silver
gauze outfit. Her hair was clipped close to her head,
showing off prominent cheekbones and a wide mouth
painted bright red. As if sensing my gaze she turned,
looked at me for a moment, then interrupted Murray's
patter to jerk her head in my direction.

"Who is Murray talking to?" I asked Sal, but she
had turned away to deal with a fractious customer.

I edged myself through the crowd, tripping on
Regine Mauger, the *Herald-Star*'s wizened gossip columnist. She glared at me malevolently: she didn't know
who I was, which meant I was no use to her.

"Will you watch where you're going, young
woman?" Regine had been tucked and cut so many
times that her skin looked like paper pulled over bone.
"I'm trying to talk to Teddy Trant!"

She meant she was trying to push her bony shoulders
close enough for Trant to notice her. He was the head
of Global's midwest operations, sent in from Hollywood when Global acquired the *Herald-Star* and its
string of regional papers a year ago. No one in town
had paid much attention to him until last week, when

Global unleashed its television network. They had bought Channel 13 in Chicago to serve as their flagship and brought in Lacey Dowell, star of Global's wildly successful romance-horror flicks, to appear on the first "Behind Scenes in Chicago" segment—with host Murray Ryerson, "the man who turns Chicago inside out."

Global was launching a "Behind Scenes" feature in each of their major markets. As a hometown girl made good and a Global star, Lacey was the perfect choice for the Chicago launch. Crowds of teenagers as excited as my generation had been by the Beatles lined up to greet her at O'Hare. Tonight they were waiting outside the Golden Glow to catch her arrival.

With the excitement of television and movies on hand, no one could get enough of Edmund Trant. Where he dined, how his mediagenic wife decorated their Oak Brook mansion, all were avidly covered by columnists like Regine Mauger. And when invitations were issued for tonight's party, everyone in Chicago's small media pond was anxious to find the silver-edged ticket in the mail.

Regine and the other gossip columnists weren't of much interest to Trant tonight: I recognized the Speaker of the Illinois House and a couple of other state pols in the group close to him and had a feeling that the man he was talking most to was another businessman. Regine, peevish at being stiffed, made a big show of inspecting the hem of her black satin trousers, to show me I'd torn them or scuffed them or something. As I pushed my way through the melee toward a corner of the bar I heard her say to her counterpart at the *Sun-Times*, "Who is that very clumsy woman?"

I edged my way to the wall behind Sal's horseshoe mahogany bar. Since my assistant, Mary Louise Neely, and her young protégée Emily Messenger had come with me, I knew I was in for a long evening. In her current manic state Emily would ignore any pleas to leave much before one in the morning. It wasn't often she did something that made her peers jealous and she was determined to milk the evening to the limit.

Like most of her generation Emily was caught up in Lacey-mania. When I said she and Mary Louise could come as the guests my ticket entitled me to, Emily turned pale with excitement. She was leaving for France next week to go to a summer language camp, but that was bore-rine compared to being in the same room with Lacey Dowell.

"The Mad Virgin," she breathed theatrically. "Vic, I'll never forget this until my dying day."

Lacey got the nickname from her lead in a series of horror flicks about a medieval woman who supposedly died in defense of her chastity. She periodically returned to life to wreak vengeance on the man who tormented her—since he kept reappearing through time to menace other young women. Despite the pseudofeminist gloss on the plot, Lacey always ended up dying again after defeating her agelong foe, while some brainless hero cuddled a vapid truelove who had screamed herself breathless for ninety minutes. The films had a cult status among Generation X-ers—their deadly seriousness turned them into a kind of campy self-satire—but their real audience was Emily and her teenage friends, who slavishly copied Lacey's hairstyle, her ankle boots with their crossed straps, and the high-necked black tank tops she wore off the set.

When I got to the end of the bar near the service entrance, I stood on tiptoe to try to spot Emily or Mary Louise, but the crowd was too dense. Sal had moved all the barstools to the basement. I leaned against the wall, making myself as flat as possible, as harassed wait staff rushed by with hors d'oeuvres and bottles.

Murray had moved to the far end of the bar from me, still with the woman in silver gauze. He seemed to be regaling her with the tale of how Sal acquired her mahogany horseshoe bar from the remains of a Gold Coast mansion. Years ago when she was starting out, she got me and her brothers to climb through the rubble to help her haul it off. Watching the woman tilt her head back in a theatrical laugh, I was betting that Murray was pretending he'd been part of the crew. Something about the shape of his partner's face or the full-lipped pout she gave when she was listening was familiar, but I couldn't place her.

Sal stopped briefly by me again, holding a plate of smoked salmon. "I have to stay here till the last dog dies, but you don't—go on home, Warshawski."

I took some salmon and explained morosely that I was waiting on Mary Louise and Emily. "Want me to tend bar? It would give me something to do."

"Be better if you went in the back and washed dishes. Since I don't usually serve food here at the Glow my little washer is blowing its brains out trying to keep up with this. Want me to bring you the Black Label?"

"I'm driving. San Pellegrino is my limit for the evening."

Murray maneuvered his way across the bar with his companion and put his arm around Sal. "Thanks for opening up the Glow to this mob scene. I thought we ought to celebrate at some place authentically Chicago."

He kept an arm around Sal in a protective hug and introduced her to his companion. "Sal Barthele, one of the truly great Chicago stories. Alexandra Fisher, one of the truly great Chicago escapees. And you know V. I. Warshawski."

"Yes, I know Vic." Sal extricated herself from Murray. "Stop showing off, Murray. Not all of us are swooning because you sat in front of a camera for fifteen minutes."

Murray threw back his head and laughed. "That's what makes this a great town. But I was talking to Alex. She and Vic were in law school together."

"We were?" The name didn't ring a bell.

"I've changed a little." Alex laughed, too, and squeezed my hand in a power shake.

I squeezed back, hard enough to make her open her eyes. She had the muscle definition of a woman who worked seriously with weights, and the protruding breastbone of one who survived on lettuce leaves between workouts. I have the muscles of a South Side street fighter, and probably matching manners.

I still couldn't place her. Her hair, dyed a kind of magenta, was cut close to her skull at the sides and slicked back on top with something like BrylCreem, except no doubt pricier. Before I could probe, a young man in a white collarless shirt murmured a few apologetic words to Alex about "Mr. Trant." She waggled her fingers at Murray and me and followed the acolyte toward the power center. The wizened gossip columnist, still hovering on the perimeter, stopped her for a comment, but Alex was sucked into the vortex and disappeared.

"So—what did you think, V.I.?" Murray scooped half the salmon from Sal's platter and downed it with a mouthful of beer.

It was only then that I realized he had shaved his

beard for his television debut. I had watched the beard go from fiery red to auburn to gray-flecked in the years he and I had collaborated and competed on financial scandal in Chicago, but I'd never seen his naked jaw before.

Somehow it made my heart ache—foolish Murray, anxiously decking himself for the media gods—so I said brusquely, "She has beautiful deltoid definition."

"Of my show, Warshawski."

I kept my eyes on the mahogany bar. "I thought you brought the same attention to Lacey that you did to Gantt-Ag and the Knife grinders and all those other stories we worked together."

"Sheesh, Warshawski, can't you ever give a guy a break?"

"I wish you well, Murray. I really do."

My glance flicked to his face. Whatever he saw in my eyes made him look away. He gave Sal another exaggerated grin and hug and headed in his companion's direction. As I watched him walk away I realized someone had been pointing a camera at us: he'd been embracing Sal for tape.

"Something tells me Murray picked the Glow to show all those Hollywood types he hangs around with black people," Sal said, frowning at his retreating back.

I didn't want to admit it out loud, but I thought sadly she was probably right.

"That Alex Fisher is part of Global's legal team," Sal added, her eyes still on the room. "They brought her out from California to mind the shop here. I had to deal with her a few times on liability questions about Lacey —I actually had to buy insurance to cover the event tonight. The studio wasn't even going to cover the cost of that until I told them the city health department was raising so many questions about food in the Glow that I'd have to shut down the event."

"Why'd they care? They could go anywhere."

"They're paying for the catering, and I only told them this morning. I hear they say in Hollywood that no one kicks Global's ball, but they're out-of-towners here." She laughed and disappeared into the minute kitchen.

Around midnight there was a flurry at the door. I hoped it was Lacey making her dramatic appearance so that I could collect Emily and leave, but it was only a couple of Bulls players—bore-rine to Emily Messenger and her friends. As the crowds shifted for them I made out Mary Louise and Emily, stationed where Emily could get an autograph as soon as Lacey cleared the entrance. Emily was in Mad Virgin uniform: the black tank top, stretch pants, and platform shoes that were sold through the Virginwear label Global owned.

Mary Louise must have worked something out with one of the officers assigned to cover the event. She had been a cop herself for ten years, and when she quit the force two years ago she'd done it in a way that didn't lose her any friends. The guy on duty tonight had placed Emily behind the velvet ropes set up to create the illusion of an entrance hall. He'd even found a barstool for Emily to perch on. I was envious—my calves were aching from hours of standing.

"Are you waiting for Lacey, too?"

I turned to find a stranger addressing me, a compactly built man several years younger than me, with curly brown hair and the hint of a mustache.

"I'm a friend of the groom," I said, "but I have a young guest who won't leave until she gets Lacey's autograph."

"A friend of—oh." His eyes twinkled in appreciation. "And I'm a friend of the bride. At least, we grew up in the same building, and she squeaked with excitement when she told me she was coming back to Chicago."

"Is she really from here? When actors say they're from Chicago, they usually mean Winnetka and New Trier, not the city."

"Oh, no. We grew up in Humboldt Park. Until we were twelve we hung out together, the only nerds in our building, so that the bigger kids wouldn't pick on us. Then she got a role on television and whoosh, off she went like a rocket. Now all those kids who used to corner her in the stairwell are trying to pretend they were her buddies, but she's not a fool."

"She remembered you?" I wasn't really interested, but even idle talk would help get me through the evening.

"Oh, sure, she sent me one of her fancy cards to this event. But she won't meet with me alone." He reached across the bar for a bottle of beer and shook himself, as if shaking off a train of thought. "And why should she? Which groom are you a friend of? Do you work for the television station?"

"No, no. I know Murray Ryerson, that's all."

"You work for him?" He grabbed a plate of tiny sandwiches from a passing waiter and offered it to me.

I don't like to tell people I'm a private investigator—it's almost as bad as being a doctor at a party. Everyone has some scam or some time that they've been robbed or cheated that they think you'll sort out for them on the spot. Tonight was no exception. When I admitted to my occupation, my companion said maybe I could help him. Something rather curious had been happening in his plant lately.

I stifled a sigh and dug in my evening bag for a business card. "Give me a call if you want to talk about it in a place where I can give you my full attention."

"V. I. Warshawski?" He pronounced my name carefully. "You're on Leavitt and North? That's not so far from me."

Before he could say anything else there was another stir at the entrance. This time it was Lacey herself. The waters parted: Edmund Trant extricated himself from his crowd and appeared at the door to kiss Lacey's hands as the cameras began to whir again. Murray used his bulk to barrel his way next to Trant in time for Lacey to kiss him for the cameras. The policeman at the door greeted Lacey and directed her to Emily. I watched while she hugged Emily, signed her book, and flung herself into the arms of another Global actor on hand for the event.

While I worked my way along the wall to the front to collect Mary Louise and Emily, Lacey moved her entourage to the center of the room. The guy I'd just been speaking to managed to position himself behind the waiter bringing her a drink. I stopped to watch. Lacey greeted him with enthusiasm, so he must have been telling the truth about their childhood. But he seemed to be trying to talk to her seriously about something—a mistake in a gathering this public. Even under the soft rainbows of Sal's Tiffany lamps I could see Lacey's color rise. She turned away from him in hauteur and he made the mistake of grabbing her shoulders. The off-duty cop who'd gotten Emily her seat muscled his way through the crowd and hustled him out the door. When we followed a few minutes later, the man was standing across the street staring at the Golden Glow. As we came out he hunched his hands down in his pockets and walked away.

"Vic, you've made me *blissfully* happy," Emily sighed as we walked past the line of Lacey's fans. "There they are, waiting for hours just to get sight of her, and she actually kissed me and signed my book, maybe I'll even be on TV. If someone told me two years ago that every girl in Chicago would be jealous of me, I'd never have believed them in a million years. But it's come true."

The Woman in the Road

EMILY CHATTERED WITH excitement all the way to the car, then fell deeply asleep in the backseat. Mary Louise leaned back on the passenger side and slipped out of her high heels.

"I stayed up all night to watch poor Diana marry Prince Creep when I was that age," she commented. "At least Emily got to touch Lacey."

I had wanted to go to O'Hare to join the vigil for Ringo and John, but my mother was desperately ill by then; I wasn't going to worry her by riding around on buses and L's after curfew. "Some guy was trying to get next to Lacey as we left. He said they grew up together in Humboldt Park. Is that true?"

"I'm glad you asked." In the sodium lights on the Inner Drive I could see Mary Louise's grin. "I have eaten and drunk Lacey Dowell facts for the last two weeks, ever since you called with the invite, and it's high time you shared the treat. Lacey's birth name was Magdalena Lucida Dowell. Her mother was Mexican, her father Irish; she's an only child who grew up in Humboldt Park and went to St. Remigio's, where she starred in all the school plays and won a scholarship to Northern Illinois. They have an important theater program. She got her first break in film twelve years ago, when—"

"All right, all right. I'm sure you know her shoe size and her favorite color, too."

"Green, and eight-and-a-half. And she still likes the chorizo from her home neighborhood better than any trendy food in L.A. Ha, ha. Her father died in an industrial accident before she started making real money, but her mother lives with her in Santa Monica in a nice oceanfront mansion. Supposedly Lacey gives money to St. Remigio's. They say she kept the cardinal from closing the school by shoring up its scholarship fund. If that's true it's worth something."

"A lot." The light at Lake Shore Drive turned green, and I swung into the northbound lanes.

"Come to think of it, you should have picked up some of these gems from Murray's interview. Didn't you watch?"

I grimaced at the dashboard. "I think I was so embarrassed to see him doing it at all that I couldn't focus on what he was saying."

"Don't be too hard on him," Mary Louise said. "Guy has to live on something, and you're the one who told me the Global team axed his biggest stories."

She was right. I knew Murray had been having a tough time since Global bought the paper. They hadn't stopped any of his digging, but they wouldn't print any stories they considered politically sensitive. "We have to pay attention to the people who do us favors in this state," Murray quoted to me bitterly when management killed a story he'd been working on for months about the new women's prison in Coolis. He mimicked his editor one night at dinner last winter: *Americans*

*have grown accustomed to sound bites. Sex, sports, and
violence are good sound bites. Skimming pension funds
or buying off the state legislature are not. Get the picture, Murray?*

What I'd somehow forgotten was how much of a
survivor Murray was. No one was more surprised than
me to get one of those prized tickets to Global's
postlaunch party—and maybe no one was more surprised to read on it that we were celebrating Murray's
debut as Chicago's "Behind Scenes" reporter. What
Murray had done to land the job I preferred not to
contemplate. He certainly wasn't going to tell me that—
or anything else. When I called to ask, I spoke to an
assistant who politely assured me she would give him
my messages, but he hadn't come to the phone himself.

I knew Murray had put out discreet feelers for reporting work around the country. But he was a couple
of years older than me, and in your forties companies
start looking at you as a liability. You need too much
money, and you're moving into an age bracket where
you're likely to start using your health insurance. Also
against him was the same thing that made it hard for
me to operate outside the city: all his insider knowledge
was in Chicago. So he had looked long and hard at
reality, and when reality stared back he blinked first.
Was that a crime?

At two on a weeknight, traffic on the drive was
sparse. To my right, sky and lake merged in a long
smear of black. Except for the streetlights coating the
park with a silvery patina, we seemed alone on the edge
of the world. I was glad for Mary Louise's presence,
even her monologue on what the sitter would charge
for looking after Emily's young brothers, on how much

she had to do before summer session started—she was going to law school part time besides her part-time work for me—was soothing. Her grumbling kept me from thinking how close to the edge of the world my own life was, which fueled my hostility to Murray's decision to sell himself on the air.

Even so, I pushed the car to seventy, as if I could outrun my irritability. Mary Louise, cop instincts still strong, raised a protest when we floated off the crest of the hill at Montrose. I braked obediently and slowed for our exit. The Trans Am was ten, with the dents and glitches to prove it, but it still hugged corners like a python. It was only at the traffic lights on Foster that you could hear a wheeze in the engine.

As we headed west into Uptown, the loneliness of the night lifted: beer cans and drunks emerged from the shadows. The city changes character every few blocks around here, from the enclave of quiet family streets where Mary Louise lives, to an immigrant landing stage where Russian Jews and Hindus improbably mix, to a refuse heap for some of Chicago's most forlorn; closest to the lake is where Uptown is rawest. At Broadway we passed a man urinating behind the same Dumpsters where a couple was having sex.

Mary Louise glanced over her shoulder to make sure Emily was still asleep. "Go up to Balmoral and over; it's quieter."

At the intersection a shadow of a man was holding a grimy sign begging for food. He wove an uncertain thread through the oncoming headlights. I slowed to a crawl until I was safely past him.

Away from Broadway most of the streetlights were gone, shot out or just not replaced. I didn't see the body in the road until I was almost on top of it. As I stood on the brakes, steering hard to the left, Mary Louise screamed and grabbed my arm. The Trans Am spun across the street and landed against a fire hydrant.

"Vic, I'm sorry. Are—are you okay? It's a person, I thought you were going to run over him. And Emily, my God—" She unbuckled her seat belt with shaking fingers.

"I saw him," I said in a strangled voice. "I was stopping. What could yanking my arm do to help with that?"

"Mary Lou, what's wrong?" Emily was awake in the backseat, her voice squeaky with fear.

Mary Louise had leapt out of the car into the back with Emily while I still was fumbling with my own seat belt. Emily was more frightened than injured. She kept assuring Mary Louise she was fine and finally climbed out of the car to prove it. Mary Louise probed her neck and shoulders while I fished a flashlight out of my glove compartment.

Assured of Emily's safety, Mary Louise hurried to the figure in the road. Professional training pushed the four beers she'd drunk during the evening to the back of her brain. Her stumbling gait on her way to the figure was due to the same shock that made my own legs wobble when I finally found the flashlight and joined her—we hadn't been going fast enough to get hurt.

"Vic, it's a woman, and she's barely breathing."

In the light of my flash I could see that the woman was very young. She was dark, with thick black hair tumbled about a drawn face. Her breath came in bubbling, rasping sobs, as if her lungs were filled with fluid. I'd heard that kind of breathing when my father was dying of emphysema, but this woman looked much too young for such an illness.

I pointed the light at her chest, as if I might be able to detect her lungs, and recoiled in horror. The front of her dress was black with blood. It had oozed through the thin fabric, sticking it to her body like a large bandage. Dirt and blood streaked her arms; her left humerus poked through the skin like a knitting needle out of a skein of wool. Perhaps she had wandered in front of a car, too dazed by heroin or Wild Rose to know where she was.

"Vic, what's wrong?" Emily had crept close and was shivering next to me.

"Sugar, she's hurt and we need to get her help. There are towels in the trunk, bring those while I call an ambulance."

The best antidote for fear is activity. Emily's feet crunched across broken glass back to the car while I pulled out my mobile phone and called for help.

"You take the towels; I'll deal with the emergency crew." Mary Louise knew what to say to get paramedics to the scene as fast as possible. "It looks like a hit-and-run victim, bad. We're at Balmoral and—and—"

I finished covering the woman's feet and ran to the corner for the street name. Glenwood, just east of Ashland. A car was about to turn into the street; I waved it on. The driver yelled that he lived there, but I took on the aura of my traffic-cop father and barked out that the street was closed. The driver swore at me but moved on. A few minutes later an ambulance careened around the corner. A squad car followed, blue strobes blinding us.

The paramedics leapt into efficient action. As they

attached the woman to oxygen and slid her smoothly into the ambulance, a crowd began to gather, the mixed faces of Uptown: black, Middle Eastern, Appalachian. I scanned them, trying to pinpoint someone who seemed more avid than the rest, but it was hard to make out expressions when the only light came from the reds and blues of the emergency strobes. A couple of girls in head scarves were pointing and chattering; an adult erupted from a nearby walk-up, slapped one of them, and yanked them both inside.

I took the flashlight and searched the street, hoping to find a wallet or paper or anything that might identify the woman, but was stopped by one of the patrolmen, who led me over to Mary Louise with the comment that searching the accident scene was police business.

Mary Louise kept a protective arm around Emily while we answered questions. The officers joined me in an inspection of the Trans Am. The fireplug had popped the hood and bent the front axle.

"You the driver, ma'am?" one of the cops asked. "Can I see your license?"

I dug it out of my wallet. He slowly copied the information onto his report, then typed in my name and plate numbers to see how many outstanding DUI's I had. When the report came back negative, he had me walk a line toe-to-toe—much to the amusement of the pointing, snickering crowd.

"Want to tell me how this happened, ma'am?"

I glared at Mary Louise but went through my paces: no streetlights, didn't see body until almost on top of it, swerved to avoid, impaled on fireplug.

"What brought you down this street to begin with, ma'am?"

Normally I don't let the police make my business their business, but normally I don't have a white-faced sixteen-year-old in tow. Poor Emily, her thrilling adventure in ruins around an accident victim—I didn't need to prolong her misery by fighting with cops over the Fourth Amendment. I meekly explained that I was running Mary Louise and Emily home and that we were taking a shortcut through side streets. A long cut as it turned out, but who could have known that? And at least our stumbling down this street might give the young woman a fighting chance at survival. All I really grudged was my damaged car. I felt ashamed: a young woman lay close to death and I was worrying about my car. But major repairs, or even a new vehicle, were definitely not part of this summer's budget. I thought resentfully of Murray, rolling with the punches and coming up roses.

"And where had you been with the young lady?" A narrowing of the eyes, what were two grown women doing with a teenager they weren't related to.

"We had an invitation to the Lacey Dowell event downtown," Mary Louise said. "I'm Emily's foster mother and I don't let her go to events like that alone at her age. You can call Detective Finchley in the First District if you have any questions—he was my commanding officer for four years and he knows how Emily and I came together."

After that the atmosphere thawed: one of the men knew Finchley, and besides, if Mary Louise was one of them she couldn't possibly be involved in anything criminal. The officers helped me push the Trans Am away from the hydrant so that it wouldn't be ticketed. They even gave us a lift home. I didn't mind being squashed between the cage and the backseat: it beat waiting for a slow ride down Clark Street on the number twenty-two bus.

As we pulled away from the curb the people on the street watched happily: a satisfactory end to the outing —three white women carried away in the squad car.

House Call

My father was lying in the road in the wasted final stage of his illness. He had left his oxygen tank on the curb and was gasping for breath. Before I could get into the street to pick him up, a squad car rounded the corner and ran over him. You killed him, you killed him, I tried to scream, but no sound came out. Bobby Mallory, my father's oldest friend on the force, climbed out of the car. He looked at me without compassion and said, You're under arrest for creating a public nuisance.

The phone pulled me mercifully out of sleep. I stretched out an arm and mumbled "Is it?" into the mouthpiece.

It was my downstairs neighbor, his voice rough with anxiety. "Sorry to wake you, cookie, but there's some cops here saying you was involved in a hit-and-run last night. They was hanging on your bell and the dogs were going crazy so I went to see what was going on, and of course Mitch bounces out to see who it is, and the one guy, he starts carrying on about Mitch, don't I know there's a leash law in this town, and I says, last I heard you don't need to keep a dog on a leash in your own home and who are you, anyway, disturbing the peace like this, and he whips out his badge—"

"Did he really say hit-and-run?" I demanded, pushing my sleep-sodden body upright.

"He holds out his badge and demands you by name, not that he could pronounce it right, of course. What happened, doll? You didn't really hit someone and leave them lay, did you? Not that I haven't told you a million times not to drive that sports car so fast around town, but you stand up to your mistakes, you wouldn't leave no one in the street, and that's what I told the one twerp, but he starts trying to act like Dirty Harry, like I'm scared of some tin-pot Hitler like him, when I beat up guys twice his size at—"

"Where are they?"

Mr. Contreras is capable of going on for a day or two once he's in full throttle. He's a retired machinist, and even though I know he worked some fancy lathe in his days at Diamondhead Motors, I can really only picture him with a hammer in his hand, out-driving John Henry, along with any mere mechanical device. "They're downstairs in the lobby, but I think you better get out of bed and talk to them, doll, even if they're pissers, pardon my French, not like the lieutenant or Conrad or other cops you know."

It was heroic of him to include Conrad Rawlings in the same breath as Lieutenant Mallory. Mr. Contreras had been unhappy about Conrad's and my affair, his usual jealousy of the men I know compounded by his racial attitude. He'd been relieved when Conrad decided things weren't working between us, until he saw how deep the feelings had gone with me. It's taken me a while to recover from the loss.

I hung up and shuffled to the bathroom. A long shower used to be enough to revive me after short nights, but that was when I was thirty. At forty-plus the only thing that revives me is enough sleep. I ran cold water over my head until my teeth were chattering. At least my blood was flowing, although not as much to my brain as I needed for an interview with the police.

While I was toweling myself I heard them leaning on the bell at my third-floor door. I looked through the spy-hole. There were two, a short one in a brown polyester suit that had been through the dryer a few too many times, and a tall one with an acne-scarred face.

I cracked the door the width of the chain and poked my head around so they couldn't see my naked body. "I'll be with you as soon as I get some clothes on."

The short one lunged forward, trying to push the door open, but I shut it firmly, taking my jeans into the kitchen to dress while I put my stove-top espresso-maker on to boil. It's one of those cheap metal ones that can't foam milk, but it makes strong coffee. I scrambled into my clothes and went back to the door.

The short one in brown polyester bared tiny teeth in a circle like a pike's. "V. I. Warshki? Police. We have some questions for you."

"Warshawski, not Warshki," I said. "My neighbor said you were with the police, which is why I opened the door, but I need to see some proof. Like your badges. And then you can tell me why you've come calling."

The tall one pulled his badge out of his coat pocket and flashed it for a nanosecond. I held his wrist so that I could inspect the badge. "Detective Palgrave. And your companion is? Detective Lemour. Thank you. You can sit in the living room while I finish dressing."

"Uh, ma'am." Palgrave spoke. "Uh, we don't mind talking to you in your bare feet. We have a couple of questions about the female you came on last night."

A door thudded shut at the bottom of the stairwell. Mitch and Peppy began to race upstairs, followed by Mr. Contreras's heavy tread. The dogs barreled past the detectives to get to me, squeaking as if it had been twelve months instead of twelve hours since we were last together. Lemour kicked at Mitch but only connected with his tail. I grabbed both dogs by the collars before anything worse happened.

When they finished jumping up and kissing me, the dogs, especially Mitch, were eager to greet Lemour. Peppy's a golden; Mitch, her son, is half black Lab and enormous. Like all retrievers, they are incurably friendly, but when they're pawing the air and grinning they look ferocious to strangers; our visitor wasn't going to try to muscle his way past them.

Mr. Contreras had reached the doorway in time to see Lemour kick at Mitch. "Listen here, young man, I don't care if you're a detective or a meter maid, but these dogs live here and you don't. You got no call to be kicking them. I could have you up before the anticruelty society, policeman kicking man's best friend, how'd your ma and your kids like to read that in the paper?"

The detective wasn't the first person to be rattled by Mr. Contreras. "We're here to talk to the lady about a hit-and-run she was involved in last night. Take your animals downstairs and leave us alone."

"It so happens, young man, that the lady owns the golden. We share looking after them—not that it's any of your business—so if she wants them up here it's fine with me. And as for whatever questions you got, you're way off base if you think she was involved in some hit-and-run. I've known her twelve years, and she would no more run over someone and leave 'em lay in the street than she'd prop up a ladder to climb to the moon.

So you got some accident victim claiming otherwise, you been totally misinformed. Be a good idea if you called your boss and made sure you got the right address or license plate or whatever, otherwise I guarantee you'll feel foolish wasting your time and everyone else's on this—"

"Uh, sir." Palgrave had been trying to cut the flow short for some minutes. "Uh, sir, we're not accusing her of hitting someone. We only want to ask her some questions about the incident."

"Then why didn't you say that?" Mr. Contreras demanded in exasperation. "Your buddy here was carrying on like she ran over the pope and left him to bleed in the street."

"We need to ascertain whether the Warshki woman hit the woman or not," Lemour said.

"Warshawski," I said. "Have a seat. I'll be with you in a minute."

I went back to the kitchen to turn the fire off under my pot; fortunately it had just reached the point where it sucked water up through the filter into the top, not the point where it started filling the house with the stench of scorched metal. Lemour, apparently fearing I might be going to hide or shred evidence, perhaps my car, followed me to the kitchen.

"It makes two cups," I said. "Want one?"

"Listen, Princess Diana, don't get smart with me. I want you to answer some questions."

I poured out coffee and looked in the refrigerator. I'd been in Springfield testifying at Illinois House hearings into contracting scams the last few days. The only thing close to food was a dried heel of rye. I looked at it dubiously while Lemour foamed at the mouth behind me. I ignored him and took my coffee into the living room. Detective Palgrave was standing stiffly at attention while Mr. Contreras sat in my good armchair, holding Mitch's collar.

"Detective, is there any word on the woman I stopped to help last night?" I said to Palgrave.

"She was taken to Beth Israel, but—"

His partner cut him off. "We ask the questions, Warshki; you give the answers. I want a complete description of the encounter you had in the road last night."

"It's *Warshawski*. It may be a sign of dyslexia when you can't pronounce all the syllables in a long word, but you can get over it with speech therapy, even as an adult."

"Uh, ma'am," Palgrave said, "could I just ask you to describe what happened last night? We're trying to investigate the incident, and we need to find someone who can tell us what happened."

I shook my head. "I don't know anything about the woman—she was lying in the road. The streetlights are out on that stretch of Balmoral, so I didn't see her until I was about ten feet from her. I stood on the brakes, swerved, hit a fireplug, but did not hit the woman. My passenger, who's a ten-year veteran with the Chicago police, summoned an ambulance. We could see that the woman had a broken arm, and her breathing was labored; the front of her dress seemed bloody. I don't know anything else about her. I don't know her name, how she came to be there, or whether she's still alive."

"How much did you drink last night?" Lemour demanded.

"Three bottles of mineral water."

"You're sure you didn't hit her and are trying to dress it up as a Good Samaritan act?"

"Uh, Doug, why don't we talk to the passenger. Get some confirmation of Ms. Warshki's—sorry, ma'am, what is it? Warshouski?—anyway, of her story."

"She took so long answering the door, she was probably calling to feed the other woman her lines," Lemour grumbled.

"You can talk to Ms. Neely," I said, "but the officers on the scene took a complete report last night. They even breathalyzed me. Why don't you look at that?"

Palgrave's face became more wooden. "Uh, ma'am, did your passenger witness the breathalyzing? Because we were told it didn't take place, that you refused."

I stared at him. "I signed that report, and it included a statement that I had not been drinking. Let me see it."

Palgrave shifted uncomfortably and said they didn't have the report with them. Lemour was all in favor of arresting me for manslaughter on the spot; I was trying to weasel out of a DUI charge, he said. Palgrave told him to tone it down and asked if it was really true that Mary Louise was a ten-year veteran with the force.

"Yes, indeed. You can talk to Bobby Mallory—Lieutenant Mallory—at the Central District. She was under his command for quite a few years," I said. "I'll get him on the phone for you now. Or Terry Finchley. He was her immediate superior."

"That won't be necessary, ma'am," Palgrave said. "We'll talk to this Neely woman, but if she witnessed your—uh—breathalyzing that's probably good enough. To be on the safe side, we'll take a look at your car, make sure it wasn't involved in the accident."

"Who is the woman I stopped for, anyway?" I demanded. "Why does it matter so much to find someone to take the fall for her injuries?"

"We're not trying to make you take a fall," Palgrave

said. "She's an accident victim and you were on the scene."

"Come on, Detective," I said. "I happened on the scene after someone left her lying in the road. I didn't put her there, didn't hit her, didn't do anything but wreck my car swerving to miss her."

"In that case a look at your car will get us out of your hair," Palgrave said. "We'll tow it to the police lab and get back to you about when you can pick it up. Where is it now?"

"It wasn't drivable. It's where the accident took place—you can look up the address on the report when you get back to the station."

That made Lemour start to boil over, but Palgrave calmed him down once more. When they finally left I felt limp. Who could the woman be to merit this much aggravation? But I couldn't worry about that until I dealt with my car. If the cops were determined to find a perpetrator, I wanted the Trans Am to have a clean bill of health before it got into police hands.

I called the mechanic I go to when I have no other choice. Luke Edwards is one of the few guys out there who still knows what a carburetor does, but he's so depressing I try to avoid him. He came to the phone now with his usual drooping tones. He identifies so totally with machines that it's hard for him to talk to people, but our relations have been particularly strained since a car of his I borrowed got totaled by a semi. Before I could finish explaining what I needed, Luke cut me off, saying he didn't want to hear my tale of woe, he'd known since I trashed the Impala that I couldn't be trusted behind the wheel.

"I spent three months getting every bearing on that engine purring in unison. I'm not surprised you wrecked your Trans Am. You don't know how to look after a car."

"Luke, forget that for a minute. I want a private lab to inspect my car and certify that it didn't hit a person. I'm not asking you to work on it today, just to tell me the name of a good private lab."

"Everyone thinks they come first, Warshawski. You gotta wait in line along with all the working stiffs."

I tried not to scream. "Luke, I need a civilian lab before the police get to my car. I ran into a fire hydrant swerving to miss an accident victim, and some cop is taking the lazy way out instead of running an investigation. I want to have a lab report to wave in his face in case he doesn't do the rest of his homework."

"Police after you, huh? About time someone called you on your reckless driving. Just kidding you. Calm down and I'll help you out. Cheviot is the lab you want, out in Hoffman Estates. They're pricey but they got a rock-solid rap in court. I and my friends have used 'em a couple of times—I can call for you and set it up if you want. Tell me where your baby is and I'll send Freddie out with the truck, get him to take the Trans Am out to Cheviot. He sees a cop, should he run over him?"

Luke being funny is harder to take than his depression. I pretended to laugh and hung up. Mr. Contreras, watching with bright anxious eyes, told me I'd done the right thing but wanted me to do more.

I didn't think there was much else I could do except call Mary Louise. She was trying to dress one of Emily's young brothers, who was protesting loudly. When she realized what I was saying she let the kid go and gave me her full attention.

"I don't know anyone named Lemour, but I'll ask

Terry," she promised. "I read that report last night before I signed it, and it made crystal clear the fact that we had not hit that poor creature. There shouldn't be a problem. I'll certainly tell them that when they come around here. I have to get Nathan to day camp, but I'll call Terry as soon as I get back."

Mary Louise could make that phone call more easily than I. Terry Finchley, her commanding officer her last four years on the force, was a rising star in the violent crimes unit. When Mary Louise resigned, she was careful to do it in a way that left him on her side.

I'd actually met Mary Louise on cases where Terry Finchley and I had crossed paths. I'd always liked him, but since the end of Conrad's and my affair he's been rather stiff with me. He and Conrad are pretty close; even though it was Conrad who broke things off, Terry thinks I treated his friend shabbily. Still, he's too honest a person to extend his stiffness to Mary Louise simply because she works for me.

"You gonna call the lieutenant and make a complaint?" Mr. Contreras asked, meaning my father's old friend Bobby Mallory.

"I don't think so." Bobby was much more likely to chew me out for interfering with a police investigation than he was to phone the Rogers Park station and complain about Lemour. He would probably say, If I wanted to play cops and robbers, I'd have to be ready to take the heat that comes with it.

Searching for Wheels

So WHATCHA GOING to do next, doll?" Mr. Contreras asked.

I frowned. "I'd like to find out who that woman is, so I can try to understand why the cops are so eager to find someone to take the fall for hitting her. In the meantime, I need to get hold of a car. Who knows how long it'll be before the Trans Am is fit to drive again, especially if it ends up as police exhibit A."

I called my insurance company, but they were useless. The Trans Am was ten years old; the only value it had to them was as scrap. They wouldn't help me with a tow, the repairs, or a loaner. I snarled at the agent, who only said blandly that I shouldn't carry property damage on such an old car.

I slammed down the phone. What was I doing sending good money to this idiot and the company of thieves he represented? I checked a few rental places, but if the Trans Am were tied up for weeks I'd be shelling out hundreds, maybe even a thousand, to rent something I'd have no equity in.

"Perhaps I should scrape together a few grand and buy something used. Something good enough that I could resell it when my car comes out of the shop. Or a motorcycle—you know—we'll see the world from my Harley!"

"Don't go buying a Harley," Mr. Contreras begged. "One of my buddies, before your time, old Carmen Brioni, he used to ride a big old Honda 650 around town, thought he was a teenager all over again, until a semi run him off 55 down by Lockport. After that he never talked again, lived like an eggplant for seven years before the good Lord was kind enough to pull the plug."

We studied the ads in the paper together, which left me more discouraged: anything roadworthy seemed to run three or four thousand. And would take a good day out of my life to hunt down.

"Why don't you leave car-hunting to me?" Mr. Contreras said. "I sold mine when I moved here because I figured I couldn't afford all that extry for insurance and whatnot on my pension. In fact, you know that's why I moved out of the old neighborhood when Clara died, besides, most of my friends had got scared and left the city, so it wasn't like I was missing my pals. Here I figured I'd be close by the L and walking distance to the stores. And of course it saves me all that parking aggravation, but I still can tell whether an engine runs good or not. What do you have in mind?"

"A Jaguar XJ-12," I said promptly. "There's one here for only thirty-six thousand. Standard shift, convertible, the old body before the Ford engineers got their hands on it."

"That ain't practical. Those ragtops don't have any backseat to speak of, and where would the dogs sit?" He startled me into laughing, which made him beam with pride.

"Oh, yeah, the dogs," I said. "You know, it's going

to have to be a beater. Unless I decide to junk the Trans Am. But I only want to buy something if it's a reasonable alternative to renting."

He started running a black fingernail down the page, whispering the words under his breath as he read, his eyes bright with interest. He has his own friends, and he tends a garden in our tiny backyard with painstaking care, but he doesn't really have enough stimulation in his life—it's why he gets overinvolved in my affairs.

I skimmed the news sections, trying to see if our accident victim had made the morning edition, while Mr. Contreras worked the ad pages. Commonwealth Edison's inability to provide the city with power got a tiny mention, as did wildfires in Florida, but Global's television debut took up most of the front page.

Murray had a byline, describing his interview with Lacey Dowell. It was the first time he'd been on the front page in ten months. First time in the paper in three. "Just haven't been covering the right stories until now, Murray," I muttered. First the paper spends four days hyping Global's new television network. Then the network makes its debut. Then they write up what they showed on television. It made a neat loop, but was it news?

Even Regine Mauger's column had been moved to a prominent spot because she was covering the television launch. *Teddy Trant was glowing last night, and not only from the soft lights of Sal Barthele's original Tiffany lamps,* she cooed. *With House Speaker Jean-Claude Poilevy on one side and Lacey Dowell on the other he has every right to be pleased with the impression he's making on Chicago.*

Regine went on to describe the other players, including members of the Illinois Commerce Commission, the mayor and his wife, whom I'd missed in the throng, and of course the denizens of the town's TV studios, whose feelings get hurt if they're overlooked.

Murray Ryerson, whose trademark red beard disappeared for the occasion, took to the camera like a duck to water. His chosen escort—or did she choose him?—was Alexandra Fisher from Global's front office, stunning in an Armani evening ensemble. But don't let that cleavage fool you: when she puts on her power suits she's as invincible as Dick Butkus.

Of course some problems always erupt at occasions like this. A bird tells us that Lucian Frenada, from Lacey's old neighborhood, finagled an invitation in the hopes of holding Lacey to a boy–girl romance, but Officer Mooney, on loan from Chicago's finest, muscled him outside before he could make a full-scale scene. Lacey had no comment, but Alex Fisher says the star is troubled by the misunderstanding. Other hangers-on, like Chicago investigator V. I. Warshawski, who used to be an item with Ryerson, probably were hoping for crumbs to drop from one of the richest tables to be set in town for years.

That last sentence jolted me out of my chair so fast that Peppy barked a warning. Damned scrawny bitch with her fifty face-lifts, annoyed because I'd tripped on her Chanel trousers. Me, hoping for crumbs from a Hollywood table? And still pining for Murray? I didn't know which suggestion offended me more.

It's true Murray and I once had a fling, but that was history so ancient there weren't even any archaeological remains to look through. Far from pining over him, I'd

realized after a few weeks that going to bed with someone that competitive had been a colossal mistake. Who
the hell had even cared enough to tell Regine Mauger?
Murray, out of spite toward me for not being enthusiastic enough about his debut? "Took to the camera like
fleas to a dog," I said savagely.

The story reminded me that Alexandra Fisher said
she'd gone to law school with me. While Mr. Contreras
continued his slow study of the ads, I went to the hall
closet and pulled out the trunk where I keep bits and
pieces of my past. On top, wrapped in cotton sheeting,
was my mother's concert gown. I couldn't resist taking
a moment to pull back the sheet and finger the silver
lace panels, the soft black silk. The fabric brought her
to me as intensely as if she were in the next room. She
wanted me to be independent, my mother, not to make
the compromises she did for safety, but holding her
gown I longed to have her with me, guarding me
against the great and little blows the world inflicts.

I resolutely put the dress to one side and rummaged
through the trunk until I found my law-school class
directory. We'd had a Michael Fisher and a Claud, but
no Alexandra. I was snapping the booklet shut when I
saw the name above Claud's: Sandra Fishbein.

The photograph showed a petulant, wide-mouthed
face with a mop of wild curls a good six inches thick.
She'd been number two in our class and what the
faculty called a rabble-rouser. I remembered her chewing me out for not joining her proposed sit-in over
women's bathrooms at the law school.

You're a blue-collar girl, she harangued me with a
speech she'd used before, *you should know better than
to let the establishment stand on your face.* I remembered the scene vividly—she came from the kind of

family where children got European travel as high-
school graduation presents. For some reason the fact
that I was a blue-collar girl, maybe the only one in my
class, made her feel she needed my support or approval
or respect, I was never sure which.

It's your establishment, and your face, I'd replied on
that occasion, which only wound her up tighter. *If
you're not part of the solution, you're part of the problem,* she'd snapped. Oh, all that old-time rhetoric. She'd
applauded my going to the public defender, while she
went off to clerk for a judge on the tony Sixth Circuit.

Well, well. Girl radical had gone to Hollywood, cut
her halo of wild hair close to her head, changed her
name—and conducted surgery on her politics. No wonder she'd given me that challenging stare last night.

I put away the directory. Emphysema had forced my
father onto long-term disability when I was in law
school. His illness affected everything about me then,
from my decision to marry in the hopes I'd produce a
grandchild for him before he died to my lack of interest
in campus politics. I'd taken the public defender's job
so I could stay in Chicago and be with him. He died
two years later. My marriage hadn't survived much
longer. I'd never had a child.

The dogs were pacing restlessly, a sign that they
badly needed a walk. I carefully rewrapped the silk
dress and pushed the trunk back into the closet. I promised the dogs I'd be with them as soon as I checked my
appointments on my Palm Pilot. I had a one o'clock
with one of my few really important clients—translate
that to read big retainer, big billing, prompt payment.
Thanks to Lemour and the ruckus he'd stirred up, it
was after eleven now. I barely had time to run the dogs

and get something to eat. Since my refrigerator held only an orange besides the stale bread, I leashed up the dogs and went out with my backpack to forage for food.

A cool spring had given way overnight to the oppressive mugginess of midsummer. There aren't any parks close to our building, but I couldn't make the dogs do three miles to the lake and back in air that covered us like a sock. By the time we reached the grocery store, even Mitch had stopped pulling at the leash and was glad to rest in the shade of the building. I pulled a collapsible drinking bowl out of my pack and bought a bottle of water for them before buying my own food, along with a cappuccino from the coffee bar across the street.

As we ambled home in the heat, I kept wondering about the woman in the road. In the dark street I couldn't tell what had happened to her, but that humerus sticking up like a branch from a swamp told some terrible tale of violence. The tall stolid detective had let out that the woman was sent to Beth Israel. That was fortunate, because Max Loewenthal, the executive director, was the lover of one of my oldest friends. With dogs in one hand and coffee in the other, I couldn't very well whip out my cell phone to call the hospital. I urged the dogs to a trot, bribing them with some bread.

As we rounded the corner at Racine, a brown Chevy bristling with antennas slowed down. Detective Lemour rolled down his window and called out "Warshki." I kept going.

He turned on his loudspeaker and broadcast to the neighborhood that those dogs better not be let off their leash. "You think you're smart, Warshki, flaunting your friends in the PD, but I'm going to be on you like your underwear this summer. If you so much as run a stop sign I'll be there, so watch your step."

A woman with a toddler in tow looked from me to the police car, while two kids on the other side of the street stared, slack-jawed. I stopped and blew Lemour a kiss. His face darkened with fury, but his partner seemed to restrain him; he took off with a great screeching of rubber.

Why did the cops care so much about the injured woman? Maybe it was only Lemour who cared, but his threat made me almost as nervous as he intended. I urged the dogs up Racine to my apartment. I was beginning to think having an outside lab look at the Trans Am was the smartest thing I'd done this year.

Mr. Contreras had left a note in his large unpracticed hand to tell me he was down in his own place, making phone calls to a few likely prospects, and would I drop the dogs off with him on my way downtown. I showered again to wash the sweat from my hair, then called Max Loewenthal's office while I dried off.

Max was in some meeting or other, which didn't surprise me. Fortunately his secretary hadn't gone to lunch and was glad to check on a Jane Doe for me. I gave her my cell-phone number and dressed at a record-setting pace, in a wheat-colored pantsuit, black top, and silver earrings. I could slap on a little makeup in the L.

I didn't have time now for breakfast. I grabbed an apple from my groceries, stuffed my pumps into a briefcase, and ran back downstairs with the dogs. Mr. Contreras stopped me with a status report, although I told him I was on my way to Darraugh Graham's.

"You'd better get going then, cookie," he said, following me to the hall and hanging on the door. "It don't do to keep the one guy who pays his bills on time waiting. I got a lead on a Buick Century with ninety-seven thousand on it, and a Dodge with some less, but maybe a whole lot more rust. What time do you think you'll get back? Want me to take a look at these without you, or what?"

"You the man, Mr. C. Pick out the car of our dreams and I'll drive you downtown to the Berghoff for dinner."

The dogs were convinced I was going to the lake and tried to leave with me. I shut the door on them firmly. Running the four blocks to the L got me sticky and sweaty again. I could have made time for breakfast by skipping the second shower.

I climbed the platform for the Red Line going south. The Red Line. In some moment of hallucination a few years back, the city had color-coded the trains. You used to know what train to take by where you wanted to go. Suddenly the Howard L, which I'd ridden all my life, became red and the O'Hare Line turned blue. It made Chicago look like Mister Rogers's neighborhood instead of one of the great cities of the world. And what if you're color-blind? Then how do you know whether you're even on the Brown or the Orange Line? And then, to make it worse, they'd installed these ticket machines. You have to buy a round-trip ticket even if you're only going one-way, the machines don't give change, and there aren't any human beings to assist you if you climb onto the wrong platform by mistake.

And the final insult: when a train finally arrived, the air-conditioning wasn't working. I melted into my seat, too hot to bother with makeup. I folded my jacket on my lap and tried to sit absolutely still for the fifteen-minute trip. I was riding the escalator up at Randolph Street when Cynthia Dowling called back from Max's office. "Vic, I'm afraid it's bad news about your Jane Doe. She died in the operating room."

Diving into the Wreck

A Dr. Szymczyk had been the surgeon on call. With
the broken arm and severe contusions on both legs,
they couldn't be sure what the main locus of her problem was, but when Szymczyk saw the X rays he'd decided her abdominal injuries were the most critical.

Cynthia read to me from the surgeon's dictation:
"*She had advanced peritonitis: the entire abdominal
cavity was filled with fecal matter. I saw already it was
late, very late for helping her, and as it turned out, too
late. The duodenum had ruptured, probably sometime
previous to the broken arm, which looked very fresh.
Forensic pathology will have to answer questions of
time and manner of inflicting wounds.* Is that what you
wanted, Vic?"

Not what I wanted, that death, those wounds. Poor
little creature, to meet her end in such a way. "I take it
they didn't find anything on her to identify her? Do you
know what time she was sent to the medical examiner?"

"Umm, hang on . . . yes, here it is. Dr. Szymczyk
pronounced death at seven fifty-two. The operating-
room administrator called the police; your Jane Doe
was picked up and taken to the morgue at ten-thirty."

So she was my Jane Doe now, was she? I came to a

halt in the middle of the sidewalk. I'd made a vow a few years back to stop diving into other people's wrecks: I only got battered on the spars without getting thanks— or payment. I didn't feel like jumping overboard one more time.

A woman hurrying toward State Street banged into me, jarring the phone and breaking the connection. "Do you think a cell phone gives you ownership of the streets?" she yelled over her shoulder.

Sidewalk rage, the new hip form of urban rudeness. I tucked the phone into my briefcase and went into Continental United's building. On the outside, the curved glass walls reflected the city back to itself; inside, it cooled the inhabitants with arctic efficiency. The sweat on my neck and armpits froze. I shivered as I rode the elevator skyward.

During a meeting to discuss the background of a candidate to head the paper division, and the unrelated problems dogging delivery trucks from the Eustace, Georgia, plant, I wondered what special insight fasting brought people. The apple I'd snatched on my way out the door was all I'd eaten since the snacks at last night's party. Far from feeling a heightened consciousness, all I could think of was food. I tried to keep a look of bright attention on my face and hoped the general chatter would cover my growling stomach. Fortunately I've sat through enough similar sessions that I could interject a cogent-sounding question or two, laugh at the human-resources vice president's dull jokes, and agree to turn around the investigation in three days, unless I had to go to Georgia.

When we finally broke, at four, I encountered Darraugh Graham himself in the hall. Civility—need—required me to chat with him, about his son, about the political situation in Italy where he had a major plant, about the assignment I'd just been handed. I was lucky that Darraugh continued to come to me, instead of turning all his business over to one of the big outfits like Carnifice. Of course Carnifice supplies the armed guards Continental United needs for transporting payroll. I think they handled Darraugh's security when he visited Argentina last winter. But he still gives me a significant chunk of work requiring more analysis than muscle; it behooves me to pay attention to his private chitchat.

He clasped my shoulder briefly and gave a wintry smile of farewell. I hurried to the elevator and fell into the frozen yogurt stand in the lobby. Extra-large chocolate and vanilla with nuts, fruit, and little waffle chips. Breakfast and lunch in one giant cup. I sat in one of the spindly chairs in the lobby to pry dress pumps off my swollen feet and slip back into my running shoes. Happiness lies in simple things, after all—a little food, a little comfort.

When I'd eaten enough to raise my blood sugar to the functioning point, I called Luke to get the word on my car. My better mood deflated rapidly: he estimated repairs at twenty-nine hundred.

"Freddie towed it to Cheviot for you, but he took a look at the damage when he unloaded it. You bent the front axle and stove in the radiator for starters. And when Freddie got there he found the neighborhood helping themselves to the battery, the radio, and a couple of tires, so I'll have to repair the dash. And before you squawk, let me tell you that a big shop would charge at least a thousand more."

I slumped in the hard chair. "I wasn't squawking. That gurgling noise was the last of my pathetic assets being sucked into the Gulf of Mexico. Does this esti-mate include the kind of professional courtesy I gave you when I drove those creeps away from your yard?"

"You didn't do anything for me I couldn't do myself, Warshawski, but I know you don't know what it takes to fix this car."

I bit back an acid rejoinder. "What about your fo-rensic buddies? What are they saying about inspecting the front end?"

"The earliest they can get to it is tomorrow after-noon. And I have a note here from Rieff at Cheviot. He says they need the autopsy report on the hit-and-run victim. And they ideally need the clothes she had on when she died. Their analysis is going to run you an-other grand, easy, probably more. Of course I won't start repairs until after they've finished. And until you give me the go-ahead. But tell you what, Warshawski, being as you helped me out with those kids, I won't charge you for the tow."

"Luke, you're a prince."

Irony was wasted on him. "One good turn deserves another."

I pressed the END key before I let my temper get the better of me. I'd spent three nights in his alley, nabbed a group of teenagers, put the fear of God into them suffi-ciently to make sure they didn't return, and then stu-pidly gave Luke a courtesy discount in the belief he would reciprocate on future repair bills.

Twenty-nine hundred in repairs plus another grand for a forensic inspection. And yet another thousand or two for a replacement? Maybe I'd be better off renting by the week. Of course, I could let the Trans Am go for scrap and buy a used car with more oomph than the ones Mr. Contreras was investigating, but I loved my little sports car.

I smacked the tabletop in frustration. Why can't I ever get ahead of the game financially? I work hard, I pay serious attention to my clients, and here I am, past forty and still scrambling at month's end. I looked with distaste at the melted remains in the cup. Soggy waffle and lumps of berry floated in beige sludge. It looked like an artist's depiction of my life. I stuffed the cup into an overflowing garbage can by the door and went out to catch the Blue Line to my office.

Since it was rush hour a train came almost as soon as I climbed onto the platform. Not only that, it was one of the new ones, air-conditioned and moving fast. It didn't make up for everything that had gone wrong today, but it helped. In ten minutes I was at Damen and back in the wet heat.

A new coffee bar had opened, I noticed, making three, one for each of the three streets that came together at that corner. I stopped for an espresso and to buy a *Streetwise* from a guy named Elton who worked that intersection. Over the months I'd been renting nearby we'd struck up a relationship of the "Hi, how's it going" kind.

When I moved my operation to Bucktown two years ago, the only liquid you could get by the glass was a shot and a beer. Now the bars and palm-readers of Humboldt Park are giving way to coffee bars and workout clubs as Generation X-ers move in. I could hardly criticize them: I'd helped start that gentrifying wave.

The Loop building where I'd rented since opening my practice had fallen to the wrecker's ball more than a year ago, taking with it not just inlaid mosaic flooring and embossed brass elevator doors, but the malfunctioning toilets and frayed wiring that had kept the rent affordable. After the Pulteney's demise I couldn't find anything even close to my price range downtown. A sculpting friend convinced me to rent space with her in a converted warehouse near North and Damen, on Leavitt. I signed before the area started to be trendy and had been savvy enough—for once—to get a seven-year lease.

I miss being downtown, where the bulk of my business lies, but I'm only ten minutes away by L or car. The warehouse has a parking lot, which I couldn't offer clients before. And a lot of the queries I used to have to do on foot—trudging from the Department of Motor Vehicles to Social Security to the Recorder of Deeds—I can handle right in my office by dialing up the Web. The one thing I don't automate is my answering service: people in distress like a real person on the line, not a voice menu.

Inside my office I sternly turned my back on the futon behind my photocopier and powered up my computer. I logged on to LifeStory and submitted the name and social security number of the man Darraugh wanted to put in charge of his paper division.

Most investigators use a service like LifeStory. Data on things you imagine are private, like your income, your tax returns, those education loans you welshed on, and how much you owe on that late-model four-by-four—not to mention your moving violations in it—are all available to people like me. In theory you have to know something about the person, like a social security number and perhaps a mother's maiden name, to get this information, but there are easy ways around that, too. When I first went on-line two years back, I was shocked by how easy it was to violate people's privacy. Every time I log on to LifeStory I squirm—but that doesn't make me cancel my subscription.

The menu asked me how much detail I needed. I clicked on FULL BACKGROUND and was told that it would be a forty-eight-hour turnaround for the report—unless I wanted to pay a premium. I took the slow cheap route and leaned back in my chair to look through my notes. The rest of the assignment would keep until tomorrow, when I'd be—I hoped—more alert. I checked with my answering service to see if anything urgent had come in and then, before calling it a day, phoned over to the morgue.

Dr. Bryant Vishnikov, the medical examiner and the only pathologist I know personally, had left at noon. When I explained that I was an investigator working for Max Loewenthal over at Beth Israel and wanted to know about the Jane Doe we'd sent in this morning, the morgue attendant tried to persuade me to wait until morning when Vishnikov would be in.

I could hear the television in the background, loud enough to make out Chip Caray's patter about the Cubs. It's amazing how little actual information about the game in progress sportscasters give—I couldn't even tell who was at bat.

"The Cubs will still be here tomorrow, and maybe you will be too, but I can't wait that long," I told the attendant.

He sighed loudly enough to drown out the squawk of a chair scraping back from the desk.

"They haven't done the autopsy yet," he announced, after I'd held for four minutes. "She came in too late for the doc to start on her, and he didn't want anyone else working on her, apparently."

"What about her ID? Did the cops have any luck with AFIS?"

"Uh, yeah, looks like we got an ID."

He was making me pay for forcing him to work while on shift. "Yes? Who was she?"

"Nicola Aguinaldo."

He garbled the name so badly I had to ask him to spell it. Once he'd done that he came to a complete halt again.

"I see," I prodded. "Is she so famous I should recognize the name?"

"Oh, I thought maybe that was why you were so anxious—escaped prisoner and all."

I sucked in an exasperated breath. "I know it's hard, having to work for a living, but could you pretty please with sugar on it tell me what came in with the print check?"

"No need to get your undies in a bundle," he grumbled. "I only got four people waiting to look at their loved ones."

"As soon as you tell me how long Aguinaldo's been running, you can turn your charm on the public."

He read out the notes in a fast monotone and hung up. Nicola Aguinaldo had slipped out of a hospital in Coolis, Illinois, on Sunday morning, when the shift changed. The women's correctional facility there had taken her in to treat what they thought might be an ovarian abscess, and Aguinaldo had left with the laundry truck. In the next forty-eight hours she'd made it back to the North Side of Chicago, run into some villain, and gotten herself murdered.

Signor Ferragamo, I Presume

THE ATTENDANT HADN'T included Aguinaldo's last known address in his summary, but that might not have been in the report, anyway. I looked in the phone book, but no one with that name lived anywhere near where Mary Louise and I had found her. Not that that meant anything—if she'd fallen afoul of some pimp or dealer, she might be far from home. It's just that someone escaping from jail usually heads for relatives.

I sucked on a pencil while I thought it over and went back to my computer. None of the usual software turned up an Aguinaldo. I'd have to find her through the arrest-and-trial report, and they're not easy to locate. Since I don't have access to the AFIS system, it would mean searching trial records one at a time, without even a clue on an arrest date to guide me. Even with a Pentium chip that could take me a few weeks. I called Mary Louise again.

"Vic! I was going to get back to you after dinner, when I can hear myself think, but hold on while I get the boys their pizza."

I heard Josh and Nathan in the background shouting over whose turn it was to choose a video, and then Emily, with adolescent disdain, telling them they were both stupid if they wanted to see that bore-ime Space

Berets tape one more time. "And I don't want any pizza, Mary Louise, it's too fattening."

"I suppose Lacey Dowell never eats pizza," Josh yelled.

"No, she eats the blood of obnoxious little boys."

Mary Louise called sharply to Emily to hang up the phone when she got the bedroom extension. In another moment the fighting in the background was switched off.

"I was out of my ever-lovin' mind the day I thought fostering three kids would be a simple management problem," Mary Louise said. "Even with Fabian paying enough for good home help, it's relentless. Maybe I'll switch from law to social work so I can counsel teenagers on how grueling it is to be a single mom.

"Anyway, the news on Lemour is kind of disturbing. Terry says he has a bad rap, even among cops, that there've been around a dozen complaints against him over the years for excessive violence, that kind of thing. But what's more troubling is that Rogers Park lost the incident report. Terry asked them how they knew to come to you if they didn't have the report, and they didn't have a good answer for that. I didn't get the names of either of the officers on the scene last night, did you?"

I felt ice start to build around my diaphragm. No, I hadn't done anything that elementary. We could track down the paramedics—they should have a copy of the report. That would be another time-consuming search, but an uneasy impulse was making me think I'd better make the effort.

"Before you go, there's one other thing," I said. "The woman we found is dead—poor thing had some kind of advanced abdominal injury. She was on the run from Coolis. Could you find out when she was arrested, and why?" I spelled *Aguinaldo* for Mary Louise.

I didn't want to dive into Nicola Aguinaldo's wreck, but it felt as though someone had climbed up behind me on the high board to give me a shove.

Even after Detective Lemour's idiotic hints that I'd been driving drunk this morning, it hadn't occurred to me to call my lawyer. But if Rogers Park had lost the incident report I needed Freeman Carter to know what was going on. If a lazy detective decided to slap a manslaughter charge on me, Freeman would have to bail me out.

Freeman was on his way out of the office, but when I gave him a thumbnail sketch of the last twenty-four hours, he agreed it was too serious to turn over to his intern. After I told him Rogers Park claimed to have lost the incident report, he had me dictate a complete account into his phone recorder.

"Where is your car, Vic?" he asked before hanging up.

"The last I saw it, it was hugging a fireplug in Edgewater."

"I'm late. I don't have time to play games with you. But if the State's Attorney demands it when I talk to him in the morning, I expect you to produce it. And for Christ's sake don't get on your charger and gallop around town confronting the cops. You've turned this over to me and I'm promising to take care of it. So don't do anything rash tonight, okay, Vic?"

"It all depends on your definition, Freeman, but I think the most I'm up to is trying to find something to drive around town in."

He laughed. "You're doing okay if you can keep your sense of humor. We'll talk first thing."

After he hung up I tried to think what further steps to take. I called Lotty Herschel, whom I've known since my undergraduate days. She's in her sixties now, but still works a full schedule both as a perinatalogist at Beth Israel and running a clinic for low-income families on the west fringe of Uptown.

When I told her what was going on she was horrified. "I don't believe this, Vic. I'll ask Max what happened to the young woman when she got to us, but I don't think that will shed any light on why you're being harassed in such a way."

Her warmth and concern flowed through the line, making me feel better at once. "Lotty, I need to ask a favor. Can I come over for a minute?"

"If you can hurry. In fact, Max and I are going out in half an hour. If you don't have a car can you take a cab to me?"

It was close to seven when a cab decanted me on north Lake Shore Drive. For years Lotty lived only a short walk from her clinic, on the top floor of a two-flat she owned. When she turned sixty-five last year, she decided that being a landlord was an energy drain she didn't need and bought herself a condo in one of the art nouveau buildings overlooking the lake. I still wasn't used to dealing with a doorman to see her, but I was glad she'd moved into a place more secure than the fringes of Uptown—I used to worry about her, small woman alone in the early-morning darkness, every user on Broadway knowing she was a doctor.

The doorman was beginning to remember me, but he still made me wait for Lotty's permission before letting me pass. Lotty was waiting for me when the elevator reached the eighteenth floor, her dark, vivid face filled with concern.

"I'm on my way out now, Victoria, why don't we ride down together and I'll give you a lift home while you talk."

Driving with Lotty is almost more adventure than I wanted at the end of a difficult day. She thinks she's Sterling Moss and that urban roads are a competitive course; a succession of cars with stripped gears and dented fenders hasn't convinced her otherwise. At least the Lexus she was driving now had a passenger-side air bag.

"The paramedics would have filed a report at the emergency-room admitting station," I explained as we drove across Diversey. "I want a copy of that—I'm hoping it will include the names of the officers on the scene, and maybe even a copy of the police report, which the Rogers Park station says has disappeared."

"Disappeared? You think they lost it on purpose?"

"That ape Lemour might have. But reports get mis-filed every day; I'm not going to be paranoid about this —yet. Could you keep your hands on the wheel even if you're alarmed or annoyed?"

"You can't come to me for help, Vic, and then start criticizing me," she snapped, but she looked back at the road in time to avoid a cyclist.

I tried not to suck my breath in too audibly. "The other thing is, I'd like the dress Aguinaldo was wearing when she died. Cheviot Labs needs to inspect it to see whether there are signs of any car—especially my car— in the fabric. They wouldn't tell me at the morgue if her clothes came over with her, but I'm betting they're still at the hospital, assuming they're not in the garbage. Could you get Max to track them down? Or ask him for permission for me to call the ER staff? It'd have to be tonight, I'm afraid—the longer we wait, the more likely the clothes will be pitched."

She turned left at Racine after the light had changed —in fact after the eastbound traffic had started to roar through—but I didn't say anything, in case she became cranky enough to cut in front of a bus or a semi.

"We can do it by phone in Max's car. If I can get his attention away from Walter Huston and his horse." Her tone became sardonic: Max has a passion for old Westerns which seems utterly at odds with his other passion, Chinese porcelains. It's also at odds with Lotty's tastes.

"So you're off to watch a Western just because your man likes them." I grinned at her as she pulled up in front of my building. "Well, Lotty, it's taken you over sixty years, but you're finally learning to be graciously submissive to male authority."

"Really, Vic, must you put it like that?" she snorted, then leaned across the seat to kiss me. "Please don't move rashly on this investigation. You're in a swamp, my dear; it's important that you test each step before putting your full weight on it. Yes?"

I held her for a moment, drawing comfort from her embrace. "I'll try to move cautiously."

"I'll call you in the morning, my dear, after I've spoken to Max." She squeezed me briefly and put the car into gear again. "Remember, you're coming to dinner at my place on Monday."

Mr. Contreras was waiting for me on the front stoop. He had spent the day on the phone tracking down cars and badly wanted to talk about them. He'd located an old Buick in Park Ridge that he thought would be the best bet and arranged with the seller for us to look at it tonight—which meant a nice long ride on public transportation, since a cab to the suburbs would run at least forty dollars.

When Lotty roared through that intersection, it had occurred to me I probably left skid marks on the road. Just in case, and just in case no one had obliterated them, I wanted to get up there to photograph them while some daylight remained. Mr. Contreras, always eager for a piece of real detection, called the car owner to say we'd be a little late so that he could help me inspect. I took the dogs for a quick walk around the block and collected my camera and a magnifying glass.

We rode the Red Line up to Berwyn, which was only five blocks from the accident. The golden light of a summer sunset made the streets appear less tawdry than they had in the middle of the night. A group of boys pedaled by, some sitting two to a bike, and we passed a few skateboarders, but no Rollerbladers—in-line skates belong to the yuppie world further south.

At the corner of Balmoral a group of girls was jumping rope. I noticed two Mad Virgin T-shirts on girls whose dark hair was pulled back under fringed scarves. Global Entertainment's tendrils reached even into the immigrant communities.

When I inspected the street I realized I'd wasted time on a fool's errand. The fireplug I'd hit was slightly bent, and even after almost eighteen hours you could still see a trace of rubber in the road where I'd stood on my brakes. But there was no sign of where Nicola Aguinaldo had lain. She hadn't been dead when we found her: no one outlined her body in chalk. I photographed the tread marks and the fireplug, using a flash since the light was dying.

The girls stopped their jumping to stare at me. "You know Morrell, miss?" "Take my picture too, miss?"

"Put me in the book too, miss. Morrell talk to me, not to her."

They began posing and shoving each other out of the way.

"Who's Morrell?" I asked, wondering if a cop had come around pretending to be writing a book.

"Morrell, he's a man, he's writing a book about people who ran away from jail."

I stared at the speaker, a girl of about nine with a braid that reached to the top of her shorts. "Ran away from jail? Does that mean—did he come here today?"

"No, not today, but most days. Now will you take my picture?"

I took shots of the little girls alone and together and tried to get them to tell me about Morrell. They spread their hands. He came around, he talked to some of the parents, especially Aisha's father. They didn't know who he was or where to find him. I gave it up and went back to inspecting the street, getting down on my hands and knees with the glass while Mr. Contreras stood over me to make sure no one hit me.

"You lose something, miss?" "You trying to find your ring?" "Is there a reward? We can help."

I sat back on my heels. "You know a woman was hit here in the road last night? I'm a detective. I'm looking for any clues about her accident."

"You really a detective? Where's your gun?" one demanded, while another said, "Women can't be detectives, don't be a fool, Sarina."

"Women can be detectives, and I am one," I announced.

The girls started inspecting the area around the curb for clues. I found something like dried blood on the asphalt where I thought Nicola Aguinaldo had lain and photographed the spot from several different angles, then scraped a bit onto a tissue. It wouldn't be very convincing if I had to talk to a judge or jury, but it was the best I could come up with.

The girls decided this meant Sarina was right—I must be a detective, they'd seen someone do the very same thing on television. After that they offered me a variety of items, from an empty Annie Greensleeves bottle to a Converse high-top. I solemnly inspected their findings. In the midst of the detritus, a piece of metal caught my eye as it had theirs: "This is gold, isn't it, miss, is it valuable? Do we get a reward?"

It wasn't gold but heavy plastic. It was new, and its shine had attracted the girls—it clearly hadn't lain long in the gutter. It was shaped like a Greek omega, but it wasn't a charm, more like some kind of signature from a handbag zipper, or maybe a shoe. I thought I should recognize the designer, but I couldn't place it off the top of my head.

Mr. Contreras was getting restive: he really wanted to get out to Park Ridge to look at the car he'd picked out. I pocketed the emblem and put the rest of their findings in the garbage.

"Who is the oldest?" I asked.

"Sarina's twelve," they volunteered.

I handed a girl in a fringed scarf one of my cards and three dollars. "The money is for all of you to share; it's your reward for helping me hunt for clues. The card is for your friend Morrell. When he comes again, will you give it to him? It has my name and phone number on it. I'd like him to call me."

The girls clustered around Sarina. "What's it say?"

"Ooh, Sarina, she is a detective, it say so right here."

"She going to arrest you, Mina, for talking back to your mama."

Their comments faded as we rounded the corner to the L. Mr. Contreras filled me in on the Buick Skylark we were going to see. "He's asking seventeen hundred, but it's got ninety-eight thousand miles. You can probably bring him down a couple a hundred, but maybe you want your buddy Luke to go over a car before you buy it—all these computers and whatnot it ain't so easy to tell what's going on inside an engine these days."

"Yeah, my buddy Luke." I thought bitterly of our conversation this afternoon. "He's likely to demand the mortgage on my apartment before he lifts a finger to help. After getting my estimates from Luke I'm beginning to think I should rent something for a few weeks. Even fifteen hundred seems way more than I can afford for temporary wheels, and if it's that beat up I'll have trouble reselling it."

The old man deflated visibly: he'd spent all day on the project and politely deferred pushing it while he helped me on my silly Sherlock Holmes imitation. Guilt is not an adequate reason for bad business decisions, but I couldn't bear to see him so woebegone. We picked up falafel sandwiches and Cokes at a storefront underneath the L tracks and trudged up the stairs for the first leg in our journey.

By the time we got to the seller's apartment, I was so fed up with public transportation I was ready to pay almost any price to get rolling again. The Red Line to Howard. The old Skokie Swift—now the Yellow Line—and then the real time-eater, the wait for the suburban bus to take us five miles further west, to a stop close enough to the guy's place that we could walk.

"You know, if we don't buy the car and take possession tonight, we may end up camping in that forest
preserve we passed," I told Mr. Contreras as we started
walking. "The sign says the last bus leaves the Gross
Point depot at nine-thirty, and it's a quarter of now."

"Cab." He was puffing a little from the heat and the
walk. "I'll treat you to a cab back to the L, cookie."

When we finally reached the seller's apartment, we
saw the car wasn't as bad as I'd feared. Rust over most
of the driver's door and around the trunk made it look
depressing, the tires were worn, but a ten-mile drive to
the airport and back didn't reveal anything amiss in the
engine. The seller was a kid who'd graduated from
Champaign in engineering this spring. He bought the
Skylark used when he started school, drove it hard for
five years, and wanted to unload it now that he'd
landed a real job with serious money. All the time we
talked about his beater, he couldn't stop looking at the
Ford truck he'd bought to celebrate entering the job
market at a hundred thousand a year. Without much
real haggling we got the Skylark for twelve hundred.

Mr. Contreras overwhelmed me by pulling twenty
carefully folded twenties from his inside pocket: "My
contribution to the family car," he insisted, when I tried
to demur. I offered to let him drive home, but he
refused.

"I don't see so good at night anymore, cookie. Matter of fact, I been worrying about it some."

"Then let's get you to the doctor," I said. "You can't
neglect your eyes. If you need new glasses or have cata-
racts or something, now's the time to take care of
them."

"Don't make me out to be an old man," he snapped,
locking the seat belt. "You're as bad as Ruthie, wanting

to push me into an old-age home. I can still see good enough to make out that gizmo you took from them girls on the street. What was it, anyway?"

I'd forgotten about it during our long ride and pulled it out of my shirt pocket for his inspection. He couldn't place it any more than I could, but when we got home —in twenty minutes versus the eighty-seven we'd spent on the way out—I dug a copy of *Mirabella* out of the stack of papers in my recycling box. I went through it page by page studying the ads and on the inside of the back cover struck gold—or painted plastic. A pair of Ferragamo loafers were standing back to front against a rose silk scarf, and a pair of omegas like the one the girls had found were stitched into the strap across the instep.

"*Va bene,* Signor Ferragamo," I said aloud. A horse-shoe, not an omega. The Ferragamo logo. I'd recognized it because I tried on some Ferragamo pumps a few weeks ago: my beloved red Bruno Magli's had finally become so worn that not even old Señor Delgado out on Harlem could patch the sides enough to attach new soles.

I'd decided I couldn't afford shoes that cost almost three hundred dollars this summer—a wise decision, considering the expenses I was racking up right now. It was hard to imagine that the immigrants living along Balmoral and Glenwood could afford them either. I suppose someone might have gone into debt for an up-scale logo, but I went to bed wondering where in the metropolitan area someone was looking in annoyance at a shoe or handbag with a damaged strap.

Habeas Corpus?

MARY LOUISE CALLED me early in the morning. "Vic, I'm running to get Nate to day camp, so this'll be quick: there isn't much, anyway. Aguinaldo was working as a mother's helper for someone named Baladine out in Oak Brook. She'd been there two years when she stole a gold necklace worth forty or fifty thousand dollars—it had gems in it too, bitty diamonds or rubies. They pressed charges—"

"The Baladines?" I interrupted. "As in the Robert Baladines?"

"Robert, Eleanor, and their three children. Do you know them?"

"No, darlin', he's so big I don't even think of him as competition. He runs Carnifice—you know, the billion-dollar PI firm, only when they get that big they're called 'Security Providers,' or something."

"Well, be that as it may, Mrs. Baladine loved that necklace—Robert gave it to her when little Robbie was born, blah, blah, so she pressed charges in a serious way. The defense tried to plead Aguinaldo's blameless previous life and the fact that she was the sole support of a mother and two kids of her own, but we were being tough on immigrants that month and Aguinaldo got five years. She'd been a model prisoner for fifteen months, had worked her way into the clothes shop, which is a premium gig at Coolis, when she escaped. Last known address on Wayne, about two hundred yards from where we found her." She read out addresses and phone numbers both for Aguinaldo's home and the Baladines.

"Now I've got to scoot—Natie's frantic he'll miss the opening ceremony, and he's gotten real into raising the flag and playing reveille. Who knows—maybe he'll want to join the army or be a cop when he grows up."

"Or maybe play the bugle. I'll get him one for his birthday."

"You dare, Vic, and he'll practice under your window every morning at six!"

It wasn't quite eight when she hung up. Too early to expect a report from Freeman. I thought I'd give Vishnikov a chance to take off his jacket and finish his coffee, or whatever his morning office ritual was. I did a full workout in my living room, including a session with my weights. I even took the trouble to put the weights back in the closet before trying the morgue. Vishnikov was in the dissecting room and didn't want to be interrupted. I left a message and took the dogs out.

The air was still thick with humidity, but it was early enough that the heat wasn't unbearable. I ran the dogs to Lake Michigan and back, a nice three-mile stint. The cops have started a major roundup of leash-law violators, even ticketing people whose dogs are swimming from the rocks along the lake, but I managed to get Mitch and Peppy in and out of the water without a citation.

"Lemour may be on me like my underwear, but he's

apparently not an early riser," I told the dogs on the way back.

I tried Vishnikov as soon as I got in, but he still wasn't taking calls. I wanted to go out to Oak Brook and talk to Eleanor Baladine about Nicola Aguinaldo, and I wanted to get up to Aguinaldo's home in Uptown, so the faster I got to my own office and did some work that would generate income, the faster I could get to an investigation that might help save my hide. The only thing more important than doing my real work was getting hold of the dress Aguinaldo had been wearing. As soon as I got to my office I called Lotty.

"You were in luck, Vic: the administrator in charge of the ER in the mornings is so meticulous a follower of regulations that he's wasted on Beth Israel's small protocols. He bagged and labeled the clothes. Do you want to pick them up?"

"No. I don't want anyone claiming I could have tampered with them. I want him to messenger them over to Cheviot Labs. With a note on where they've been since coming off poor little Ms. Aguinaldo's body yesterday. Shall I call Max and ask for that? Or can you?"

She said it would be quicker if she handled it. "And on the other matter, the report the paramedics filed, Max is asking Cynthia to fax you a copy." She hung up on my thanks: she was in the middle of a ferocious patient schedule.

One of the things I invested in when I moved to my new building was a set of detailed maps of most of the states and an art-supply cabinet for storing them. I pulled out the counties of rural Georgia where one of Continental United's trouble spots lay, hoping that I wouldn't have to go there in person to see why so many tire punctures occurred on County Road G. As I drew a line on the map from Hancock's Crossing, where Continental's warehouse sat, to the intersection of County G and Ludgate Road, Freeman Carter's secretary called.

"Freeman wants to talk to you, Vic. He has an opening at twelve-fifteen if you can stop by his office."

I thanked her and turned back to my maps. I was betting either a driver or a dispatcher owned a service station on that corner: it had to be someone who could make sure trucks used a particular route which they probably strewed with nails. The drivers then had no choice but to hike up the road to the station for their tires. I called the director of human resources whom I'd met with yesterday, and asked him to fax me copies of the repair bills. It would be annoying to have to go down and confront these people in person; I hoped I could figure it all out from the paper trail.

Vishnikov returned my call as I was getting ready to leave for my appointment with my lawyer. "Vic! What's up? Need help hiding a body?"

"It may come to that, if a police ape named Lemour harasses me any further. But this is about a body you already have—Nicola Aguinaldo. She died yesterday at Beth Israel in the OR and came in too late for you to work on."

There was a pause on the other end. "That's funny: I remember now, she came in at the end of the morning. I took a quick look at her—there was something unusual about her, so I wanted to do the autopsy myself, but she wasn't—hold on while I check."

He put the phone down. I heard chairs scraping, a murmur of voices, and then a door shutting. I waited a good five minutes before Vishnikov came back.

"Vic, this is one of the more infuriating moments in

my tenure here. Some jag-off released the body last night. I can't even find out who—a form was filed but not signed."

"Released to the family?" I was puzzled. "When I called last night, they didn't have a next of kin listed."

"The form says the girl's mother claimed it. How the hell they released it—well, that's neither here nor there. I've got to go. I need to—"

I spoke quickly, before he could hang up. "What was it about her body that made you want to look at it yourself?"

"I don't remember now. I'm too goddamned angry to think about anything except getting hold of the bastard who let this body out of here without authorization." He slammed the receiver in my ear.

This was the first time I'd heard Vishnikov blow up in the four or five years I've worked with him. I wondered if Lemour had somehow engineered removal of the body, before an autopsy proved I hadn't hit her, or maybe proved she hadn't been hit by a car at all. I began to wonder if Lemour had killed her himself and was trying to find someone else to blame. When he couldn't pin it on me he got a buddy in the morgue to quietly let the body go.

The Beth Israel fax had come in while I was talking to Vishnikov. I stuffed it into my briefcase and dashed out to the L to ride down to Freeman Carter's office in the Loop.

Freeman rented a suite that held the requisite mahoganies and objets d'art of lawyers in the financial district. He rose to greet me when his secretary sent me into his inner office. His summer suit had been tailored to fit his tall body and even to make him look a little broader through the chest, and his white-blond hair had been cut as carefully as the suit. He makes a good impression in court, which I like, and has the brains to back it up, which I like even more.

"Vic, I talked to Drummond at the State's Attorney and he made some calls." He perched on the corner of his desk. "Rogers Park has lost the incident report but they asked the officers who came to the scene to reconstruct it. They say you refused to take a sobriety test—"

"That is an outright lie." I felt my cheeks flush. "They didn't ask for blood, but they breathalyzed me and I walked a line and did all that stuff for them. Freeman, I don't drink and drive, and all I had all night long was three Pellegrinos."

"They got to the scene too late to witness the accident, so they're not accusing you of hitting the Aguinaldo woman. But the State's Attorney is saying if you'll own up to the hit-and-run they won't jeopardize your PI license or standing with the bar by a criminal prosecution."

I was so furious the blood drummed in my ears. "This is so outrageous I can't even comment on it. I will not perjure myself because a couple of cops are too lazy to conduct a proper investigation."

"Whoa, there, Vic. I don't blame you for being angry, but let me finish. I told Drummond that was unacceptable—but if they're claiming you refused a blood test, I need to be one hundred percent sure of the ground I'm on."

"When I'm stupid, careless, or criminal I don't walk away from it, but in this day and age where presidents and senators lie as a matter of course, I don't expect anyone's word of honor means much." I tried to regain my composure. "However, I am telling you the unvarnished truth about Nicola Aguinaldo. Not a courtroom truth. Talk to Mary Louise. She's not under my thumb, and she was at the scene."

He reached behind him to push the intercom button. "Callie, Vic's going to give you some phone numbers when she leaves. Mary Louise—what is it?—Neely. I need her to come in ASAP to give me something like a deposition. Go over my schedule with her and find what fits."

He turned back to me. "It would be very helpful if you produced your car for forensic inspection. Where is it, Vic?"

I gave a tight smile. "It's over at the Cheviot Labs. When they've done all their tests and taken pictures, the police can have it. You know, yesterday morning when Lemour and his partner came over, at first it seemed pretty much like a routine inquiry, following up to a manslaughter. For which the cops usually just go through the motions if there isn't a witness to ID the car. I had my car towed because Lemour seemed so aggressive it got me worried. Half an hour later he threatened me on the street, which told me I was right to be concerned."

Freeman gave a twisted smile. "Vic, this is so like you, to take matters into your own hands. The police are claiming your car as evidence in a manslaughter investigation. Can you do me, your long-suffering counsel, a huge favor and produce it by the end of the day? I would be most grateful. Tell Callie—she'll arrange with Drummond for police technicians to pick it up from Cheviot Labs. And for God's sake, don't start a vendetta against Lemour. You can make better use of your time. I've got to run now: I have a conference at the federal building and I want to grab a sandwich."

As he headed for the door I said, "Before you go, Freeman, did you know the dead woman was a nanny out at the Baladines' in Oak Brook before her arrest? I presume it's the same Baladine who heads Carnifice Security. Is he pushing on the State's Attorney in some way?"

"Can you tell Callie that, too? She'll add it to your file."

"Also, which is really interesting, the dead woman's body was released from the morgue in the middle of the night last night. Before Vishnikov could do the autopsy. Who better than a police detective to arrange something like that?"

"Vic, don't go on a witch hunt after Lemour. Whoever this woman was, and whatever Lemour or even Baladine is doing with her, she is not worth your career. And not to be crude, you haven't got the resources, either financial or in muscle, to take on someone Baladine's size, let alone the Chicago cops. Got it?"

I tightened my lips but followed him to his outer office, where he stopped to rattle off a string of instructions to Callie—most of them about other clients. He finished with my affairs.

"Vic has a few things for you—and she's going to tell you where her car is so you can call Gerhardt Drummond over at the State's Attorney and let him in on the secret—isn't that right, Vic?" He gave me a malicious grin and trotted out to the elevator.

When I finished telling Callie Mary Louise's phone number and the rest of the stuff, I headed out. Down in the building lobby I stopped to call Mary Louise myself, to explain what Freeman wanted, but only got her machine. She was on the go a lot, between the kids, her

work for me, and her classes. I gave as concise an explanation as I could and told her to call me on my cell
phone if she had any questions.

I frowned at the fast-food stalls in the lobby. You
used to be able to get a bowl of homemade soup or a
deli sandwich in the mom-and-pop diners that dotted
the Loop. The new buildings had moved all their shops
inside, to so-called plazas, where they control the take,
then brought in chains that drove the coffee shops out
of business. I picked up something called a Greek salad
—I guess because it had two olives and a teaspoon of
feta on it—and went back to my car.

Mary Louise had given me the Baladines' home number this morning. I sat in my car, trying not to spill oily
lettuce on my lapel, and phoned Oak Brook. If Robert
Baladine broke my legs or bombed my office I'd let
Freeman chant "I told you so" over my hospital bed a
few hundred times.

A woman with a heavy accent answered. After some
prodding she put me through to Eleanor Baladine. "Ms.
Baladine? This is V. I. Warshawski. I'm a Chicago
detective. Did you know that Nicola Aguinaldo had
escaped from prison?"

The silence at the other end was so complete, I
thought for a moment the connection had gone. "Escaped? How did she do that?"

It was such a strange answer that I would have paid
good money to know what went through her mind in
the seconds before she spoke. "I'll tell you what I know
when I see you. We need to talk as soon as possible.
Can you give me directions to your house? I have your
address, but the suburbs are a mystery to me."

"Uh, Detective—uh, does it have to be this afternoon?"

Bridge club? No, not for the contemporary rich woman. Tennis, or something more recherché. Her Artist's Way group, I bet.

"Yes, it does. The faster I get information, the sooner I can figure out where she was headed when she left Coolis. I understand she was with you for two years. I'd like to find out what you knew about her . . . associates."

"She was a maid. I didn't gossip with her about her associates."

"Even if all you ever said to her was, 'Change the baby's diaper,' or 'Make sure you vacuum under the beds,' you must have had some references before you hired her." I tried to sound reasonable, not like an irritable old leftist.

"Oh, very well." She sighed mightily but gave me detailed instructions: the Eisenhower all the way to the end of the expressway, out Roosevelt Road to the winding side streets of one of the area's most exclusive small communities.

8

Poolside Chat

HALF AN HOUR later, as I turned onto Gateway Terrace, I thought that *community* was a strange word for a collection of houses that isolated people so thoroughly. Each house—if that's what you call something with twenty rooms and four chimneys—was set so far back behind trees and fences that you saw only fragments of facades or gables. There weren't any sidewalks, since no one could possibly walk to town—or rather, mall—from this distance. I passed a handful of kids on bikes and was passed in turn by a Jaguar XJ-8 —top down to showcase a woman with blond hair whipping behind her—and a black Mercedes sedan. That was all the street life Gateway Terrace offered me before I reached number fifty-three. Quite a contrast to the crowded, littered streets of Uptown.

I stopped the battered Skylark at the gate and looked for a way in. A large sign told me the premises were protected by Total Security Systems (a division of Carnifice Security) and that the fence was electrified so not to try to climb over it. I wondered if one of those spikes at the top had caused the damage to Nicola Aguinaldo's abdomen. She ran away from Coolis to this house, seeking help from her old boss, impaled herself, and they dumped her near her apartment, waiting for someone like me to come along who could take the fall for her injuries.

As I was scanning the property I became aware that someone on the other side was inspecting me. A round-faced boy of ten or so stepped forward when he realized I'd spotted him. He was wearing jeans and a T-shirt with the Space Berets—Global's big action toy—on it.

"Hi," I called through the fence. "I'm V. I. Warshawski, a detective from Chicago. Your mother is expecting me."

"You're supposed to phone the house," he said, coming closer and pointing to a recessed case with a phone in it.

The steel case was so sleek I'd overlooked it. As my hand moved toward the cover it slid back with a whisper, but before I could reach for the phone inside the boy opened the gates for me himself.

"I'm not really supposed to do this, but if you're with the Chicago police I guess it's okay. Is there something wrong with Nicola?"

I was startled, and wondered if his mother had complained to him. "What makes you think that?"

"The only time the cops were here before was when Mom had them arrest Nicola. Or does she want you to take Rosario this time?"

I asked him to wait a second while I moved my car away from the middle of the entrance. He said he'd ride up to the house with me and hoisted himself into the passenger seat. He was a plump boy, rather short for his age—which was somewhat older than I'd first guessed—and he moved clumsily, as children do when they've been teased about their size.

"This doesn't look like much of a cop car." It was an observation, delivered in a flat voice.

He had a forlorn dignity that made me unwilling to lie to him. "I'm not a cop. I am a detective, but a private one, a PI. And I have come with some questions about Ms. Aguinaldo. It sounds as though you liked her?"

"She was okay." He hunched a shoulder. "Has she done something else wrong?"

"No. Not that I know of, anyway, and even if she has it doesn't matter, or not to me."

We had reached the top of the drive. It forked so that you could go to the garage—big enough for four cars—or the house—big enough for forty residents. I pulled over to the edge, behind a Mercedes Gelaendewagen, the $135,000-dollar model. The vanity plate read GLOBAL 2. I wondered what GLOBAL 1 was attached to. Maybe a Lamborghini.

I wanted to ask the boy about Aguinaldo, but it didn't seem right to question him without his mother's knowledge. And without telling him that she was dead. Or maybe I was being chicken—who knew how a sensitive child would react to the news of his ex-nanny's death.

"So why are you out here?" he demanded.

I made a face to myself. "Ms. Aguinaldo escaped from prison last week. Before she could—"

"She did?" His face brightened. "Cool! How did she do it? Or do you think I'm hiding her?"

On the last question he turned sullen. Before I could answer him, a girl came running from the garage side of the house, yelling "Robbie" at the top of her lungs. She was seven or eight, with water plastering her hair and bathing suit to her body. Where her brother was chunky and blond, she had dark hair and was slim as a greyhound.

My companion stiffened and stared straight ahead. The girl saw the car and ran over to us.

"Robbie! You know Mom will have a fit if she sees you in there." To me she added, "He's supposed to walk instead of riding. You can see he has a weight problem. Are you the Chicago cop? You're supposed to go around back; Mom's waiting for you there. She sent me to tell Rosario to open the gate when you got here, but I suppose Robbie already let you in."

Robbie left the car while she was piping out her report. The girl was young enough to parrot adult comments without editing; the Baladines must have reported Robbie's weight problem to strangers so often that it seemed natural to her to tell me about it. I wanted to say something reassuring to him, but he had slipped around the other side of the house.

"You know, there are worse things in life than being overweight," I pointed out as I followed the girl past the garage.

"Yes, like stealing and getting sent to jail. That's what Nicola did, so we had to get Rosario instead. I was only six when they arrested Nicola, so it was still all right for me to cry. I cried when Fluffy got hit by a car, too."

"You are sensitive, aren't you," I said in admiration.

"No, that's for crybabies. I don't do it anymore, but Robbie cried over Nicola and he was almost eleven. He even cried when Fluffy killed a bird. That's only nature. Mom! She's here! She gave Robbie a ride from the gate to the house!"

We had arrived on the far side of the garage, where a four-lane twenty-five-meter pool and a tennis court offered the Baladines a chance to unwind after whatever rigors a day might hold for them. The pool and court were fringed with trees that created pleasing shade against the heat.

Two women were leaning back on padded chaises, eyes shielded by outsize sunglasses. Their swimsuits showed off bodies made perfect by total devotion to their care. They looked up when the girl and I appeared, but continued a desultory conversation with each other.

A third woman, also showing the kind of body that wealth and leisure afford, stood in the shallow end of the pool. She was coaching two little girls who were splashing along the lane next to her. Twin boys were jumping into the water at the deep end, chasing each other with plastic weapons. Several had been dropped at the edge of the pool. Space Berets action figures. I'd seen them at Mary Louise's—both her boys collected them.

"Not so much motion with your kicks, Utah," the woman in the pool commanded. "Rhiannon, don't lift your arms so high coming out of the water. One more length, both of you, with less wave action. Jason and Parnell"— here she raised her voice to a shout—"if you don't stop making so much commotion you're getting out until we're done here."

She stood with her back to me while Utah and Rhiannon did another twenty-five meters, working hard to keep their splashing to a minimum. My guide watched critically.

"Utah's my sister. She can do better than me when I was her age, but my form is improving. I'm definitely better than Rhiannon. Want to see?"

"Not today," I said. "If Utah's your sister, are you Wyoming or Nevada?"

The girl ignored me and dived into the pool, so

smoothly that she barely caused a ripple. She surfaced a third of the way down her lane. Her form was definitely better than mine.

The woman boosted Utah out of the pool, then hoisted herself out with one smooth push from her upper arm. A fourth woman, dark and round as a Gauguin portrait, came out of the shadows and wrapped a towel around the smaller girl. She silently handed another towel to the mother, then walked off with Utah.

"I'm Eleanor Baladine. I hope this is important, because you're interrupting my training program."

"The Sydney Olympics?" I asked.

"I know you think you're being funny," she said coldly. "Robert and I don't know how good our girls may get, but they could have a shot at a team in ten years. Especially Utah—although Madison is looking better all the time. And Rhiannon Trant is shaping up fast, even though she only started last summer."

Rhiannon Trant? Daughter of Edmund, Murray's new owner? That explained the Global plate out front —I'd thought it stood for Baladine's plans for world domination. "That's good. It would be a shame if they only swam for fun."

"No one swims for fun. You either compete or you aren't motivated enough to get in the water. I missed an Olympic spot by six-tenths of a second. I don't want my girls to lose out like that."

She broke off to call out an instruction to Madison. One of the women in the chaise longues, feeling Rhiannon was being neglected, sat up to call encouragement to her. If she was Edmund Trant's wife, no wonder gossip columnists like Regine Mauger were slobbering over her. It wasn't just her gold hair and tan, but the way she moved, even in a beach chair, and the little twitch of humor at her mouth, as if laughing at herself for caring about her daughter's ability to compete in a neighborhood pool. She made me feel as wide and clumsy as young Robbie.

"I'm V. I. Warshawski." I approached the pair in the chaise longues. "I'm a detective who has some questions for Ms. Baladine about Nicola Aguinaldo."

Eleanor Baladine rushed over. "My children's old nanny, you know, the one we had to send to Coolis for robbery—"

"Burglary, wasn't it?" I interrupted. "Or did she break in and use a weapon?"

"Excuse me, Detective." Baladine poured rich sarcasm over her words. "Not being used to the criminal element, I don't understand these distinctions."

"How did you hire Ms. Aguinaldo to begin with?" I asked.

"Through an agency. We all use it—Help Across Borders—they're usually utterly reliable. They assured me Nicola's immigration status was in order and vouched for her references. She was very good with the children, which I suppose wasn't surprising since she had one of her own—"

"I thought it was two," I interrupted.

"Maybe you're right. This was several years ago; the details are vague to me now. Madison! Work with the kickboard and concentrate on your hips! You're using way too much leg motion. You're a seal with little flippers: let's see them move."

"She lived here? With her children?"

"Certainly not. I'm not running a day-care center, and the person who works here has to concentrate on that: work."

"So how often did she see her own family? And how did she get to them?"

"I always gave her Sundays off, even though it was often inconvenient for us. Except when we traveled, when I had to have her along. Do you have children, Detective? Then you don't know how hard it is to travel with three little ones. The girls are always getting into something, and my son tends to be secretive and wander off where no one can find him. In an effort to avoid anything approaching exercise." Her eyes stayed on the pool; she was moving her hands up and down like little seal flippers, as if trying to get Madison to move properly.

The other two women threw in their own murmured complaints about how hard it is to manage children on the road. "They need their own little routines and friends," one explained.

And pools and ski slopes and who knows what else. "And to see her children every Sunday, someone drove her to the train?"

Mrs. Baladine took her eyes from her daughter long enough to stare at me in some hauteur. "Since the robbery for which Nicola was arrested was over two years ago I can't imagine what bearing her transport has on the situation."

"I'd like to know who could have picked her up when she fled Coolis. She can't have walked all the way to Chicago from there. Did some man fetch her on her days off? Or a woman friend? Or did you or Mr. Baladine drive her to the train?"

"We couldn't take that kind of time. Sometimes Robert gave her a lift if he was going into Oak Brook for a meeting, but she usually picked up the Metra bus at the bottom of Gateway Terrace. Once or twice he drove her all the way home, when he had to be in the city. I knew it was a long trip for her, so I let her spend the night in town and took on getting the kids ready for school myself Monday mornings."

"That was quite a sacrifice on your part." I tried to conceal my contempt, since I wanted information from her, but she wasn't stupid, and she bristled at my words.

I continued hastily. "She'd never stolen anything before she took that necklace, is that right? Did you ever get any sense of what drove her to do that?"

"She was poor and we were rich. What other reason would there be?" She was watching the pool again, but a stiffness in her posture made me think she knew more than that.

"I'm trying to find out who was in her background. If some man who badly needed money was controlling her, or if she had started to use drugs . . ." I let my words trail away suggestively.

"Yes, that's it, Eleanor," the third woman put in eagerly. "She must have known a lot of guys who could have attacked her. Didn't one of them come out here one weekend?"

"Attack her?" I asked. "Who said anything about that?"

The woman looked toward Eleanor Baladine, or at least moved her dark glasses toward her, and mouthed, "Boo-boo," then jumped to her feet, squeaking, "Jason and Parnell are getting much too rambunctious. It's time I got them out of the pool and home. You're a *saint*, Eleanor, to let them come over here when you're trying to coach."

"What was a boo-boo, ma'am?" I asked. "Letting

me know you'd already heard about the attack on Ms. Aguinaldo, even though it hasn't been made public?"

She laughed. "Oh, me and my big mouth. My husband says he can't ask me the time of day because I'll give him a dinner menu instead. I have no idea why that came floating out."

"And what do you say?" I asked Eleanor Baladine. "Did she tell you about the attack on Ms. Aguinaldo? Or did you tell her?"

"Listen here, Officer Whoosis, I've had about all the snooping into my private affairs I'm going to tolerate. Nicola turned out to be the worst kind of immigrant, lying, stealing, filling my son's head with superstitions. I was frankly glad to see her go to jail. If she escaped and got hurt, well, I hate to say it, but she probably had it coming."

"I don't think anyone had these injuries coming. She was murdered. In an extremely foul way. Someone kicked or punched her hard enough to perforate her small intestine, then left her in the road. She died when fecal matter filled her abdomen. It was an unbelievably painful death. If you knew about this before I got here, well, it makes me want to know a lot more about relations between you and your husband and Ms. Aguinaldo."

The children had climbed out of the pool. The girls were huddling within range of their mothers, but the twin boys were pelting each other with the Space Berets. The dark woman reappeared to drape Madison in a towel. The child grabbed her hand.

Mrs. Trant put her arms around Rhiannon. "The injuries sound dreadful, Detective, but maybe we could discuss them some other time."

Eleanor was made of sterner stuff. "I want the name

of your captain, and your name, too, Officer Whoosis. Just because we live in the suburbs doesn't mean my husband doesn't have powerful connections in Chicago."

"I'm sure he does, Ms. Baladine, head of Carnifice and all. As I've said a number of times, my name is V. I. Warshawski." I pulled a card from my handbag. "And I'm a detective. But private, not with the Chicago police."

Eleanor's eyes blazed and her chest expanded enough that she could have crossed the pool without stopping for air.

"Private detective? How dare you? How dare you insinuate your way onto my property to ask impertinent questions? Leave at once or the police will be here. Real police, who will have your behind in jail for trespassing so fast your head will spin."

"I'm not trespassing: you invited me onto your property."

"And now I'm uninviting you. Get out of here. And don't give my son a ride anywhere or I'll have you charged with kidnapping. You are undermining my efforts to get him to lose weight."

I couldn't keep back a laugh. "You are a mighty strange woman, Mrs. Baladine. Your former nanny is murdered and what you care about is your son's waistline. So he's not as addicted to lettuce and workout machines as you and your pals—but he seems like an attractive boy. Don't keep running him down in front of strangers. And do keep my card. Whether I'm public or private, Ms. Aguinaldo is dead and I'm investigating. If you change your mind about letting me in on what you know about her personal life—give me a call."

Eleanor dropped my card on the pavement, started

to grind it with her bare heel, then thought better of it. She clapped her hands and turned to the girls. "Madison, Rhiannon, back in the pool. I want to see a two-lap race. Winner gets a bowl of frozen yogurt."

As I passed the corner of the garage I heard Mrs. Trant say, "I think Rhiannon's had enough for one day, haven't you, darling?"

Out of the Mouths of Babes

As I was fumbling with the release mechanism to the gate, Robbie emerged from the shrubbery. His mother might inveigh against his lack of athletic ability, but he knew how to snake through the undergrowth like Natty Bumpo.

I stopped the car and got out. We faced each other in silence. All I could hear was the birds telling each other about choice worms or approaching cats. The house was so remote I couldn't make out even a faint echo of Eleanor Baladine's coaching, or the shrieks from the boys in the pool.

The longer the silence lasted, the harder it would be for him to break, so I spoke first. "I'm sorry I didn't have a chance to tell you about Nicola's death before your sister showed up."

He flushed a painful red. "How did you—you didn't tell Mom I was listening, did you?"

I shook my head. "I didn't know you were there— you're much too skilled in the undergrowth for a city slicker like me to hear."

"Then how did you know I heard you talking to her?"

I smiled. "Deduction. They teach us that in detective

school. It must be hard to live with three such determined athletes as your mother and sisters. Is your father a mad swimmer, too?"

"Tennis. Not that he was ever a champion like Mom —she has a gazillion trophies, just never anything from the Olympics, so we're supposed to do it for her. I tried, I really did, but—but when they keep calling you butter —butt—"

"Nicola didn't do that, did she?" I cut in before he embarrassed himself by bursting into tears.

He gave a grateful half smile. "Nicola, she didn't speak much English. Some Spanish, but her real language was Tagalog. That's what they speak in the Philippines, you know; that's where she came from. She always said it was better to read and know many things from books than be able to swim. Without an education she could only be a nanny or clean houses. She taught me how to know the stars so I could track at night. I got a book of constellations in Spanish and English, which made Mom crazy; she thought Nicola should learn English instead of me Spanish. Maybe Nicola called me butterball in Tagalog."

That seemed to be an attempt at a joke, so I laughed a little with him. "Who were the women who were there today?"

"Oh, they're friends of Mom's. Mrs. Trant, her daughter and Madison are in the same grade. And Mrs. Poilevy. Parnell and Jason Poilevy. I'm supposed to play with them because their father is important to my father, but I can't stand them."

Poilevy. The Speaker of the Illinois House. He'd been standing next to Edmund Trant at the party Tuesday night.

"Tell me about the necklace," I suggested to Robbie.

"What about it?"

"Do you know if it was really valuable? Do you think it was really missing?"

"You mean, did Mom only pretend it was gone so she could make a scene about Nicola?"

Say what you will about today's children—all those crime shows they watch make them understand the double-cross young. "Something like that."

"You don't know how tough Mom is. If she wanted Nicola gone, *phht,* out the door she'd go. No, Nicola took it all right." He frowned. "She sold it at a place near where she lived. When Mom raised the roof and called the cops and everything, the Chicago police found it at this—some kind of jewelry resale shop."

"Pawnshop," I suggested.

"Yeah, that's what it was. Pawnshop. And the man from the pawnshop picked out Nicola from a photograph. And I remember Dad saying"—here he flushed painfully again—"' Stupid spick only got twelve hundred dollars for a fifty-thousand-dollar necklace.' "

"Do you know why she stole the necklace to begin with?"

"Her little girl had asthma and it got real bad, she had to go to the hospital, only Nicola couldn't pay the bill, I guess. I heard her asking Mom for a loan, and, well, it was thousands of dollars, I guess Mom couldn't possibly loan her that much money, it would be years before Nicola could pay it off. I gave her five hundred dollars—the money I've saved from my grandparents' birthday checks—only then somehow Dad found out, he stopped the checks, that was when he and Mom made me—"

He pulled at his T-shirt, so that the Space Berets

stern faces distorted into sneers; when he spoke again it was in such a rapid monotone I could barely make out the words. "They made me go to this camp for fat kids where you had to run all day and only eat carrots for dinner, and by the time that was over, Nicola was arrested and on trial and everything. I never saw her again. I thought if she ran away from jai . . . only now she's dead. Who killed her? Did you tell Mom she got kicked to death?"

If I'd known this sensitive boy was listening I wouldn't have been so graphic with Eleanor. "The doctor who tried to save her life at the hospital said he thought she'd been punched or kicked, but no one knows who did it. I'm hoping I can find that out. Did she ever talk to you about any of the people in her life, anyone she was afraid of, or owed money to?"

"It's only that she was—she wasn't very big and she was afraid of people hitting her; once she thought Mom was mad enough to throw something at her, she —it was horrible, she was begging her not to hurt her. I wish—" His face crumpled and he began to cry. "Oh, shit, oh, shit, only crybabies cry, oh, stop."

Before I could offer any words of comfort he vanished into the shrubbery. I got back in my car, then, wondering if he might be lurking within earshot, got out again.

"I'm going to leave one of my business cards behind this post," I said loudly. "If anyone finds it who wants to call me, my number's on it."

The grounds were so carefully groomed there were no pebbles or branches to weight the card. I finally tore a twig from the shrubbery and placed it behind the gate-release post with my card. As I released the gate I

heard a motor revving behind me. The Mercedes Gelaendewagen appeared, going fast. It overtook me before I finished turning onto Gateway Terrace. Mrs.
Trant was at the wheel. She and Mrs. Poilevy still had
on their heavy glasses, which made them look like the
menacing action toys at the pool's edge.

The Skylark huffed after them but couldn't keep
pace. Before I reached the first intersection the Mercedes had disappeared.

In a few minutes I was back on the main roads,
where strip malls and office towers made the Baladine
home seem a remote Eden. Buildings of unrelated size
and design are plunked haphazardly on the prairie out
here, as if their haste to fill the vast space makes devel-
opers dig it up at random. It reminded me of a giant
box of chocolates, where someone had eaten bits off
dozens of pieces in a greedy desire to consume the
whole thing at once.

In the distance the orderly Chicago skyline appeared.
I swung onto the expressway—Arthur seeing Avalon
through the mists and eagerly returning. Not that the
pockmarked apartments and burned-out lots lining
the inbound Eisenhower were any more delightful than
the western suburbs.

A roar in the Skylark's exhaust made it hard for me
to think about the Baladines. I hadn't gotten what I'd
gone out there for: the name of anyone who might have
hurt Nicola Aguinaldo. And what had I learned? That
the very rich are different from you and me?

Certainly they're different from me. The neighborhood where I grew up was a lot more like Uptown than
Oak Brook. Every kid on my block knew what a pawnshop was; we were often the ones our parents sent with

the radio or coat or whatever was going up the spout to pay the rent.

By the same token I didn't know what life with a full-time nanny was like. Did they talk about their private lives to their young charges? You couldn't live intimately with people for two years without sharing many intimacies, I suppose, if you found a language in common.

Had Nicola preyed on young Robbie's sympathies? A sensitive overweight boy would be an easy mark in this house of obsessed athletes. Maybe Nicola got tired of Mom—I certainly had after twenty minutes—and decided to steal both her son's affections and her jewelry. Not that I was investigating this long-gone burglary, but I wondered if Nicola Aguinaldo really had an asthmatic daughter.

And what about Dad? Robbie had been awfully quick to get the implication of Eleanor Baladine making an excuse to fire Nicola. And those friends of the Baladines knew something—there was a whiff of concealed knowledge in the stiffening, the glances. Had Robert started playing with the help on those days off when he drove her to Chicago? When she ran away from prison did she think he would come to her rescue —leave Eleanor for a Filipina immigrant? Could he perhaps have killed her to keep her from messing with his happy home?

The rush hour was building. The drive home took almost twice as long as the one out, and the exhaust got louder in the long backup off the Eisenhower to the northbound Kennedy. By the time I pulled up in front of my apartment, my bones were vibrating from it. Definitely not a car I wanted to spend the rest of my life in.

Mr. Contreras was out back with the dogs, working

over his tomatoes. I called from my back porch and Peppy came up to see me. Mitch was gnawing on a tree branch and barely lifted his head.

As I changed into jeans Peppy followed me around the apartment, making it clear she expected to come with me. "I'm going to Uptown, girl. What if someone assaults me and you're left in the car for days? Not that a car on that block gets left for long. And I'd have to leave the windows open—anyone could come by and steal you or hurt you." I couldn't withstand the longing in her amber eyes. After taking my gun from the safe and checking the clip and the safety, I leashed her up and called down to my neighbor that I was taking her with me on an errand.

As I parked between a rusted Chevy and an empty pickle jar, I wondered what went through Nicola Aguinaldo's mind when she made that long trip home on Sundays. Suburban bus to train, train to Union Station, walk to State Street, L to Bryn Mawr, the six blocks over to her apartment on Wayne. Over two hours, even if all connections went smoothly. And when she got home, instead of a pool and manicured grounds for her children, she'd find a tiny glass-strewn square of hard-packed dirt in front of her building. If she had fallen in with some scheme of Baladine's, maybe it was in the hopes of buying her children's way out of Wayne Street.

The girls who'd helped me canvass the street last night were jumping double-dutch when I pulled up. I picked the pickle jar out of the gutter before someone could run over or throw it. I didn't see a garbage can so I tossed it into the open rear window of the Skylark. Peppy stuck her head out, hoping that meant I wanted her. The girls caught sight of her and stopped jumping.

"Is that your police dog, miss?" "Does he bite, miss?" "Can I pet him?" "Will he stay in the car?"

"It's a girl dog who is very gentle; she'd love to say hi to you. Shall I let her out?"

They giggled nervously but approached the car. Peppy has perfect manners. When I let her out of the back, after dancing for a minute to show her pleasure at being released, she sat and extended a paw to the girls. They were enchanted. I showed them how she would take a dog biscuit from my mouth, our noses brushing gently.

"Can I do that, miss?" "Did you raise her from a baby?" "Ooh, Derwa, she likes you, she licked your hand!" "Mina, that police dog going to bite you!"

"Do any of you remember Nicola Aguinaldo?" I asked as casually as I could. "I'd like to talk to her mother."

"Did she steal that gold thing we found?"

"Don't be stupid," another girl with thick braids and a head scarf snorted. "How could she steal something when she was already in jail?"

"That's right, the missus didn't like the way the mister looked at Sherree's mother, that's right, so she pretended Sherree's mom stole something," a third put in.

Someone objected that Sherree's mom really had stolen a necklace and she was a thief, but one girl said, "That's dirty talk, about Sherree's mom and the mister; you shouldn't be saying stuff like that."

"Well, it's only the truth! It's not saying that Sherree's mom did something dirty, not like Mina's mom, you know—"

A hand reached across and slapped the speaker. Before the fight could escalate, I snapped at them to be quiet.

"I'm not interested in what anyone's mother thinks, says, or does—that's her private business. I need to talk to Sherree's grandmother. Will one of you show me where to find her?"

"They moved," Sarina, the oldest, said.

"Where?" I asked.

They looked at each other, suddenly wary. In the world of illegal immigrants, detectives who ask questions about the family are never benign. Not even Peppy or the beat-up Skylark could make me seem less than an educated Anglo—and hence attached to authority.

After some dickering they agreed that I could talk to one of their mothers. Mina was nominated: she'd lived across the hall, and her mom had looked after Sherree when the baby died.

"What baby?"

"Sherree's little sister," a small girl who'd been silent before spoke up. "She coughed and coughed, and Señora Mercedes took her to the hospital; that was when—"

"Shut up!" The big girl with the long braid smacked her. "I told you you could play with us if you kept quiet —well, here you are blabbing your big mouth off, same as always."

"I am not!" The little one howled. "And Mommy says you have to look after me anyway."

"Mina!" I cut in, not sure which one I was addressing. "Let's go talk to your mother and leave these two to sort out their problem."

A girl with short curly hair looked at me. During the discussion she had hovered on the edge of the group, an outsider with the in crowd.

"I guess you can come up." She wasn't enthusiastic.

"But my mom's afraid of dogs; you can't bring your dog inside."

Half a dozen shrill voices promised to look after Peppy, but I thought it would be more prudent to return her to the car. Even a beautifully mannered dog can turn fractious with strangers, and childish strangers also couldn't control her if she decided to follow me—or chase a cat across the street.

Found in Translation

"My mom doesn't speak much English," Mina warned me as she took me inside.

"Neither did mine." I followed her up the narrow stairs, where the smell of old grease and mold vividly brought back the tenements of my own childhood. "We spoke Italian together."

"My mom only speaks Arabic. And a little English. So you'll have to talk to me unless you know Arabic." As we climbed the stairs she took a fringed scarf out of her jeans pocket and tied it around her curls.

Mina's mother—Mrs. Attar to me—received me in a living room that I also knew from my childhood. I used to sit in places like this when my mother took me with her on social calls in the neighborhood: overstuffed furniture encased in plastic, a large television draped in a piece of weaving from the Old Country, a thicket of family photos on top.

Mrs. Attar was a plump, worried woman who kept her daughter planted firmly next to her. Even so, she insisted on offering me hospitality, in this case a cup of thick sweet tea. Hers might be a seat of poverty, but her manners sure beat those in Oak Brook.

I drank the tea gratefully: the heat outside became overwhelming in the overstuffed room. After thanking her for the tea, and admiring the weaving on the television, I broached my subject. I hoped Mina would do an accurate job with the translation.

"I have some bad news about Nicola Aguinaldo. She ran away from prison last week. Did you know that? She died yesterday. Someone hurt her very badly when she was on her way to this apartment building, and I would like to learn who did that."

"What? What you are saying?" Mrs. Attar demanded.

Mina snapped off a string of Arabic. Mrs. Attar dropped her hold on the girl and demanded information. Mina turned back to me to translate. That role was familiar to me as well. My mother's English became fluent with time, but I could still remember those humiliating meetings with teachers or shopkeepers where I had to act as interpreter.

"The girls say you looked after Sherree when the baby was in the hospital. Was that after Nicola was sent to jail? I know the baby was sick before."

When Mina translated, first for me and then for her mother, she said, "My mother doesn't remember Sherree staying here."

"But you remember, don't you?" I said. "You agreed with your playmates when they brought it up."

She looked at me slyly, pleased to be in control. "There are so many kids in this building they probably got confused. Sherree wasn't here."

Mrs. Attar ripped off a question to her daughter, probably wanting to know what our side conversation was about. While they talked I sat back on the crinkling plastic and pondered how to get Mrs. Attar to talk to me. I didn't care whether she'd ever looked after Sherree Aguinaldo. What I needed was the address where the grandmother had moved with Sherree, or the names of any men Mrs. Attar might have seen with Nicola Aguinaldo.

I looked Mrs. Attar in the eye, adult to adult, and spoke slowly. "I'm not with the government. I'm not with Children and Family Services. I'm not with INS."

I opened my handbag and spread the contents on the cluttered coffee table. I laid out my credit cards and my private-eye license. Mrs. Attar looked puzzled for a moment, then seemed to understand what I was showing her. She scrutinized my driver's license and the PI license, spelling out my name from card to card. She showed it to her daughter and demanded an explanation.

"You see?" I said. "There is no badge in here."

When Mrs. Attar finally spoke to me, she said in halting English, "Today is?"

"Thursday," I said.

"One ago, two ago, three ago is?"

"It'd be Monday, Ma," Mina cut in in exasperation, adding something in Arabic.

Her mother put a light hand over her daughter's mouth. "I tell. Men comes. Early early, first prayers. Is —is—"

She looked around the room for inspiration, then showed me her watch. She turned the dial back to five-thirty.

"I wake husband, I wake Mina, I wake sons. First wash. Look outside, see men. I afraid. Woman here, have green card, I find."

"Derwa's mom," Mina put in, sulking because she wasn't controlling the drama any longer. "She's legal; Mama got her to ask the men what they wanted. They were looking for Abuelita Mercedes, so Mama went and woke her—they're not Islam, they don't have to get up at five-thirty like we do."

"Yes, yes. Abuelita Mercedes, much good woman, much good for Mina, for Derwa, take with Sherree when I working, when Derwa mother working. All childrens call her 'Abuelita,' meaning 'Grandmother,' not only own childrens. I take him—"

"*Her,* Mama; if it's a woman it's her, not him."

"Her. I take her, I take Sherree. Men coming here"— she stabbed at her chair, to indicate this very room—"I say, she my mother, these my childs all."

"And then?"

"Leave. No good stay here. Men go, more men come, no good."

I assumed she meant Abuelita Mercedes had to move before more INS agents showed up looking for her. "Do you know where she went?"

A sigh and a shrug. "Better not know. Not want problem."

I asked Mrs. Attar if she knew of any men Nicola had dated. Mrs. Attar only shrugged again—she couldn't help. When I asked about Mr. Baladine—the boss who sometimes drove her home—Mrs. Attar lifted her palms in incomprehension. Nicola was a good mother—it was the only reason she went out to work among rich strangers, to make money for her two little girls. She came home every week to see them; she was never late, she never had time for men. Mina smirked a little at this, which made me wonder if the kids would tell a different story.

"America no good place. Baby sick, mother no money, mother go jail. Why? Why peoples no help?"

She turned to Mina to put her ideas more completely. In Egypt a mother could take her sick baby to a clinic where the government would care for it, then there was no need for the mother to steal to pay the bills.

"Now mother dead, and why? Only want help baby. America very no good."

I couldn't think of a convincing rebuttal. I thanked her for her time and tea and let Mina take me back outside. Her friends had vanished. I tried to ask her about Nicola Aguinaldo, whether Mina had ever noticed any men visiting her or knew of talk on the streets about her, but the child was hurt at her friends' defection. She hunched her shoulder angrily and told me to mind my own business. There didn't seem to be much else I could do, so I got into the rattling Skylark and drove off.

I stopped in the park at Foster to give Peppy a walk. The police were sweeping the area in their three-wheeled buggies, slowing when they passed anyone with a dog, so I kept her on her leash. She didn't like it —especially since the squirrels weren't similarly constrained—but unlike her son she doesn't yank my arm off when she's tied up.

Aguinaldo had run away from Coolis without knowing that her mother had fled their apartment. And then? Had she come home, found her mother gone, and called Baladine for help, only to be beaten up? Or met up with some old boyfriend in the neighborhood with the same disastrous results?

"Those women around the pool knew something, but what? About Aguinaldo's escape, or her injuries, or her relations with Robert Baladine? We're no closer to having anything on Aguinaldo's private life than we did this morning," I said, so severely that Peppy flattened her ears in worry.

"And that smirk Mina Attar gave, when her mother said Nicola had no time for men, it could have concealed anything—the other kids implied Mrs. Attar had plenty of time for men, so Mina might have been smirking at her mom. Or maybe Mina knew something about Nicola that she wasn't saying. It was the look of someone who felt she knew someone else's guilty secret, that's for sure."

And what about this guy Morrell whom the kids had mentioned, the one interviewing people who had escaped from prison? Could he have played some role in Aguinaldo's escape, or in her death?

Who had claimed Aguinaldo's body? Abuelita Mercedes, the neighborhood grandmother? If so, how had she learned that Nicola was dead? From Morrell? Who was he—a social worker? A journalist? I didn't think he could be from INS. And I didn't think he was a cop—he'd been coming around before Nicola's death.

I jerked Peppy away from a dead gull. I wished Vishnikov had done the autopsy when Nicola's body arrived on Wednesday. If she'd gone to the hospital in Coolis for an ovarian cyst, maybe that had caused her internal problems, although the Beth Israel surgeon thought she'd been hit or kicked. The external injuries had been fresh when I found her, and that broken arm looked as though it had just occurred, as if she'd been struck by a car. If so, was there a boyfriend who beat her up? My mind circled back to Robert and Eleanor Baladine.

I could imagine a lot of scenarios where a man might have sex with the live-in nanny, from unregulated desire through hostility toward his wife or rivalry with his son. But would he have prosecuted Nicola for theft as a way to protect himself? Would she have turned to him for help when she escaped from prison? And then—and then what?

He was clearly friends with Edmund Trant, the head of Global Entertainment's media division, or at least the two wives were friends. Along with the wife of the Illinois House Speaker. That was cozy for a couple of important businessmen, to know their wives schmoozed with the wife of the state's key power broker.

I wondered what Murray knew about relations between Edmund Trant and Robert Baladine. Or Trant and Speaker Poilevy, for that matter. I bundled Peppy into the backseat of the Buick and went home.

Clean—On the Outside

I CAUGHT MURRAY at home. "Murray, hi, V.I. here. Quite a job you did Tuesday night—I saw even *The New York Times* condescended to notice Chicago and give you a couple of lines."

"Thanks, Vic." His tone was cautious.

"Even I got a little mention," I persisted. "Was it you who talked to Regine Mauger about me? Crumbs from the Global table would sure be tasty. Maybe it would only take one Global crumb to replace my car."

"Christ, Vic! Give me a break. Do you think I suggested something like that to Regine? Someone gets under her skin and she goes after them like a horsefly. I don't know what you did to annoy her—maybe you called up and persecuted her in her own home. She huffed up to me at the Glow, demanding to know who you were and who got you an invitation."

"I wonder who told her about that eons-old fling you and I had." I sounded earnest and puzzled; when he stammered over a response, I added, "Sorry, I didn't call to tease you. I'm glad you got a good response to your gig. I really called because of something odd I stumbled on—just about literally—on my way home from the party."

I gave him a brief summary of my accident. "I

haven't seen a mention in the papers, even though she broke out of Coolis on Sunday. But I learned something curious today. She was an illegal Filipina immigrant. Who used to be Robert Baladine's nanny—his kids' nanny, anyway—before she went to jail. Don't you think that's worth a line or two of type, Baladine being head of Carnifice Security and all?"

"Illegal immigrants who escape from prison and die aren't the kind of story I cover, Vic. I can mention it to the City Desk, but if it happened Sunday—well, today's Thursday, after all."

I ignored the coldness in his voice. "You know Eleanor Baladine is a mad swimmer? She missed a chance to swim in the Olympics and is determined her children will do it for her. I went out there this afternoon and watched her lashing kids around the pool. Besides her own they included Edmund Trant's daughter and Jean-Claude Poilevy's sons. By the way, if you heard the names Utah and Madison, would you imagine you were being given street directions or hearing about two little girls?"

"If you're trying to imply that Edmund Trant and Jean-Claude Poilevy got together with Robert Baladine to kill Baladine's ex-nanny, you're so far over the edge that no one can pull you back, Warshawski. I have to run—I'm going to be late for dinner."

"Sandy Fishbein or Alexandra Fisher or whoever it is can wait five minutes without hurting your television prospects. The Rogers Park police lost the incident report and now they're saying I was driving drunk and refused a blood test. They want me to take a fall on a hit-and-run in exchange for immunity from prosecution. Don't you think that's queer?"

He was silent for a long moment. "It's unusual. But

it doesn't make me think Baladine is in a conspiracy with Trant and Poilevy to get you."

I fidgeted with the phone cord. "I don't think anyone's out to get me—I mean, not because I'm me. But I do think someone with a heavy hand is leaning on Rogers Park and the State's Attorney to make a tidy end to the case. Because I happened along and called an ambulance I was nominated for the tidy ending—they couldn't know housekeeping has always been my weakest point. Poilevy could be leaning on the State's Attorney as a favor to Baladine, you know, to keep anyone from asking questions about his relations with his kids' ex-nanny. Stranger things have happened in this town. They might have rushed in to charge me, except I'm a detective, my passenger was an ex-cop, and I sent my car to a private lab for forensic work. Along with the clothes Aguinaldo was wearing when she died."

"Vic, it's not that I don't love you, but I'm late, and I don't have a clue why you're telling me all this."

I suppressed a sigh of impatience. "What do you know about Trant and Poilevy's working together, or Poilevy and Baladine, that would tell me whether it's Poilevy pulling this particular lever?"

"Nothing. And I'm not stirring up water around Edmund Trant. For any consideration you can think of. Not even the chance to watch Eleanor Baladine chase him around the pool with a whip."

"Because you know he's Mr. Clean? Or because you're squeamish about taking on your great-grandboss?"

"My great-grand—oh." When he spoke again, it was without the irritation he'd shown before. "Look, Vic. Maybe I'm being chicken. Okay, I am chicken. But you know how hard I tried to peddle my ass after Global bought the *Star*. In nine months I got three offers, and they weren't for serious journalism: hardly anyone's doing that now. I'm forty-six. If I start bird-dogging Trant or his friends I could find myself on the street—with no one wanting to hire a guy who guns for his own boss. So you think I'm a sellout for going on the tube. You want to lord it over me, o queen of the incorruptibles, be my guest, but—there's plenty to investigate in this town without my taking on Trant."

"I don't want to lord it over you. But—here's one thing I've been worrying about. What if Baladine was sleeping with the help and set her up—initially, I mean. Maybe he gave her the necklace, then pretended she stole it."

The more I said, the stupider it sounded, so the faster I talked. "Then she runs away, she needs money, she calls the one person with money she knows—Baladine—"

"Do you have one shred of evidence for this?"

Embarrassment made me hug my knees to my chest, but I bluffed past it. "Well, the three women in Oak Brook sure knew something about Aguinaldo—they knew she'd been assaulted before I mentioned it, and you guys hadn't printed a line of type about her. Not only that, her body disappeared from the morgue before Vishnikov could do the autopsy."

"Vic, this isn't like you. You haven't done your homework," Murray said dryly. "Carnifice runs Coolis for the State of Illinois. So Baladine knew Aguinaldo had escaped, because he heads the company that runs the prison. And he probably got an ID on her from the morgue same as you, only faster. So it's not surprising the ladies already knew. Sorry, Vic. This is a nonstarter. Although I could talk to Trant. I hear the Hollywood operation can use a boost, and that story has Keanu Reeves and Drew Barrymore written all over it. Unless someone's paying you a big fee for fishing in this pond, I'd pull my line in."

He hung up before I could respond. My cheeks were stained crimson. Anger or embarrassment? Or both. Running opposite the how-dare-he track in my mind was his uncomfortable final remark. Why the hell was I taking time to ask questions when I had no fee, no client, and a wrecked car to add to my overhead?

I'm only a few years younger than Murray. I couldn't blame him for not wanting to take on his boss —especially on the insubstantial grounds I'd suggested. It's true Murray has a condo in Lincoln Park and a new Mercedes convertible, compared to my spartan four rooms and beat-up Buick, but you feel fifty coming toward you and start getting nervous about how you're going to afford old age. At least, I do at times.

Murray's scoffing nettled me, but it embarrassed me, too. In the morning I went soberly about the business I was being paid to conduct, taking time only to call Cheviot Labs for a report on the Trans Am. They were giving my car a clean bill of health. I was nervous enough about the pressure from the State's Attorney to ask them to messenger over a copy of the report before they gave the car to the cops, and I found an empty folder for the paramedics' report Max had faxed to me. It was labeled *Alumni Fund,* from when I'd agreed to help raise money for my law school class. I'd done it mostly to help build connections among firms that might need a professional investigator, although when I automated, I'd discovered that most of the information was out of date. I'd type a proper label later, but for now I would attend to my own business. I would not pursue any other ideas, including a thought I'd had about going down to the Ferragamo boutique to see if they knew what garment that little logo had come from.

I printed the LifeStory report on the job candidate I was investigating for Darraugh Graham. I called banks and previous employers and put together a nice little dossier. I went back to my maps of rural Georgia.

At two a messenger arrived from Cheviot with their forensic report on my car. A man named Rieff had signed it. After a thorough inspection of the Trans Am's front end, he said he found no traces of organic matter in the paint, wheels, or grille except for insect carcasses. Rieff was willing to stand up in court and pronounce the Trans Am clean outside, if not in. For this work the lab asked the modest fee of $1,878.

I wrote out a check, then faxed the report to my lawyer's office with a crisp note telling him to get the State's Attorney off my back. Freeman called a little later to tell me that privately the state was persuaded by the Cheviot report, but they weren't going to admit that publicly because, as Freeman said, "You were such a pain in the ass about turning the Trans Am over to begin with. The cops are going to make you pay by holding on to your car."

Rogers Park still hadn't found the incident report, but Freeman thought he'd persuaded them to back away from harassing me about Nicola Aguinaldo's death. Mary Louise had helped, by having Finchley call over to the station and letting them know I essentially had a police witness on my team.

"Thanks, Freeman. Out of curiosity, are the cops do-ing anything else to find who killed Nicola Aguinaldo, now that they've decided I'm not an easy arrest? And are they doing anything to find her body? No one at her old address knows where her mother is living these days."

"Vic, that's none of your business. I told the State's Attorney that we had no compelling interest in her death and that if they let you alone you'd leave her alone. I don't know what got that bee buzzing in their brains to begin with, but I don't think you have anything else to worry about on this. So leave Aguinaldo's death to the cops. You know the story on hit-and-runs as well as I do: with seven hundred murders a year in this town, manslaughter has to take a backseat. You don't need to stand there like Aimee Semple McPherson haranguing sinners if they don't put round-the-clock teams on finding who hit her."

He paused, as if inviting my response; when I didn't say anything he added, "I'm going to Montana for the weekend to do some fly-fishing with a client, so try not to get arrested until Tuesday, okay?"

"I guess that's funny, so I'll laugh, but next time you make a promise in my name to the SA, talk to me first." I hung up with a snap.

So all that excitement with Detective Lemour and my car had been a tempest in a teapot? But someone had killed Nicola Aguinaldo. And those women in Oak Brook knew she was dead before I told them. Okay, Murray was right: one of them was married to the head of the company that ran Coolis for the state, and the woman had been his kids' nanny. So probably he had been notified ahead of the rest of the world. But in the absence of an autopsy, and with no news reports on Aguinaldo, how had those women known she'd been assaulted?

"Don't touch it, Vic. Leave it alone or it will come back and bite you," I admonished myself.

I went back to the Georgia problem with a dogged intensity. I was deep in a reverse directory on the computer, looking for people who lived near the garage that was outfitting Continental United's trucks with new tires, when the phone rang.

It was a woman, with a low smooth voice like cream. "I'm calling from Mr. Baladine for I. V. Warshawski."

So Aguinaldo's death was going to bite me without my touching it. My stomach tightened. I shouldn't have discounted the mad swimmer's threat to tell on me to her powerful husband.

"I. V. Warshawski was Isaac Bashevis Singer's pen name when he wrote for the *Daily Forward* in the thirties. I'm V. I., the detective. Which of us do you want?" Even at forty-plus, nervousness still makes me mouth off.

The cream didn't lose any of its smoothness. "Is this Ms. Warshawski? Mr. Baladine wants to see you this afternoon. Do you know where our offices are?"

That sounded like a command; if nervousness makes me flippant, commands make me ornery. "I know where your offices are, but I don't have time to drive to Oak Brook this afternoon."

"Can you hold, please."

I put the speakerphone on so I could hear her when she returned and obstinately went back to my reverse directory. Dance music wafted to me from Carnifice's on-hold program, followed by a description of Dr. Jekyll and Mr. Hyde. "When you're not home, is your children's nanny Dr. Jekyll or Mr. Hyde? Carnifice Security's Home Security Division can show you how to monitor your nanny on the job. We can trace her references before you hire her, too. Call us for an estimate." They added an 800 number.

The dance music returned, followed almost immediately by the cream. "Mr. Baladine can see you at five today."

"I could be free at *my* office at five if he wants to sit on the Eisenhower all afternoon. Unfortunately I don't have time to do that. How about tomorrow?"

"Mr. Baladine has to be in Washington tomorrow. Can you tell me a time that you could get to Oak Brook today?"

I didn't want to make that long drive just to be chewed out, but I'd love to meet the guy, as long as I didn't have to face rush-hour traffic to do so. "How about seven?"

She put me on hold again, this time only long enough for the start of a spiel on Carnifice's bodyguarding service. If I could make six-thirty, Mr. Baladine would appreciate it.

I said I'd do my best to earn the big man's appreciation and turned thoughtfully back to my computer. Before going on with this dull problem in Georgia, I logged on to LifeStory and asked what they had on file about Robert Baladine. Yes, I told the machine, I was willing to pay a premium for short turnaround.

The Lion's Den

CARNIFICE HEADQUARTERS WERE what you wanted in your security provider if you were a rich parent or wealthy multinational: enormous Persian carpets floating on polished parquet, desks and cabinets that a lot of rain forest had been hacked down to provide, doors opened by magnetic card or guard only, a beautiful young woman who took you from the guard in the lobby to your destination. It was quite a contrast to Warshawski Investigations, where the lone PI or her part-time assistant brought you into a converted warehouse.

My young escort smiled politely when I commented on the ambience, but when I asked how long she'd been at Carnifice, she said that company policy forbade her answering any questions.

"Not even to tell me the time or the weather?"

She only smiled again and opened Baladine's door for me. She mentioned my name, perfectly pronounced, to the woman who sat enthroned in the antechamber, then left, although not, to my disappointment, walking backward.

"Ah, Ms. Warshawski. I'll let Mr. Baladine know you're here." The woman's skin and hair matched her smooth rich voice; the bias-cut dress she wore would have paid the Trans Am's repair bill and left something over for gas.

The great man kept me waiting twelve minutes—exactly the amount of time that I was late. A perfect system of punishments, no doubt learned in running private prisons around the country. I wandered around the room while I waited, looking at photographs of a lean, tanned man with various sheiks and presidents, and at the exhibits of memorabilia, ranging from a Presidential Medal of Freedom to a mock-up of the women's correctional facility at Coolis. I was particularly interested in that, since it made escape seem impossible. The back abutted the Smallpox Creek, but there were no windows or gates on that side. Three layers of razor-wire fencing looped around the front.

"Are you interested in prison security, Ms. Warshawski?"

The lean, tanned man of the photos was standing behind me. I turned and shook his proffered hand. He was fifteen years older than his wife, as I'd learned from my afternoon's research, but looked well able to keep up with her in the pool, or any other arena.

"Only at Coolis, Mr. Baladine—I wondered how a small person like Nicola Aguinaldo could circumnavigate all those fences and guard boxes and so on."

"Ah, yes, poor Nicola. I understand she faked an illness and was taken to the Coolis Hospital, where it was easier to escape. An unhappy life and, I gather, an unhappy death." He put a hand on my shoulder and shepherded me toward his own office. "Claudia, can you bring us something to drink? I understand you like Black Label, Ms. Warshawski."

"Not when I'm negotiating the Eisenhower. Mineral water will be fine, thanks." Since I'd investigated him I shouldn't have been surprised that he'd done the same to me.

His private office was filled with more photographs and trophies—and exotic hardwoods and carpets and art. A diploma issued by the Naval Academy held a prominent place near his desk, next to a photograph of a much younger Baladine on board a destroyer, shaking hands with Nixon's Secretary of Defense.

"Yes, I was in Vietnam in the sixties. And then had my own ship for a few years."

"That was before you joined Rapelec's defense division, wasn't it?"

I said it without looking at him: I didn't want to overplay my hand by scanning his face for any surprise at my research into his life—which had not garnered his drinking preferences. Still, I'd learned that at Rapelec he had moved rapidly from a job in systems procurement to managing their submarine division, and then to heading the manufacture of all rapid-deployment weapons, before the end of the Cold War shrank the importance of the unit. Carnifice brought him in as CEO five years ago. Their private prison business was one of the divisions that had grown the most rapidly under his command.

Claudia brought a bottle of Malvern water and poured for both of us, with a murmured reminder that his conference call with Tokyo would be coming through in half an hour.

"Thanks, Claudia." He waited for the door to shut. "A picture like that probably doesn't inspire you in the same way as it does me, since I gather you and I were on opposite sides in Vietnam."

Okay, he had a staff of three thousand plus to go looking at everything from my drinking habits to my college protest activities, but it still made me uncomfortable. I knew I would have to work hard to keep my temper—since his research had probably also told him that was a vulnerable spot on my heel.

"I was on the side of Washington and Jefferson," I said, "perhaps the side of naïveté and idealism. And you?"

"Certainly I've never been naive. Either about America's external enemies or her internal." He gestured me to a seat next to a coffee table made out of some kind of gold burl.

"And so it was a natural progression for you. To move from killing Zimbabweans to incarcerating Americans. Although exactly why Zimbabwe was an American enemy I'm not sure."

At that his face did twist in brief surprise: Rapelec's arming of the South African secret forces' raids into Zimbabwe during the eighties had been the most deeply buried item I'd found in my afternoon's research. I didn't think it had anything to do with Nicola Aguinaldo's death, but it did shed some insight into Baladine's character.

"Unfortunately, in matters of national security it's not possible to be idealistic. I always think that's a luxury for people who aren't willing to dirty their hands. But perhaps we should move to matters of more immediate importance. My wife was most upset by your questioning her yesterday under pretense of being a detective."

I shook my head. "No pretense. I am a detective. I'm licensed by the state of Illinois and everything."

He smiled condescendingly. "You know you're splitting hairs: she never would have admitted you, let alone spoken to you, if she hadn't believed you were with the Chicago police."

I smiled back. "You should be pleased with me, Baladine—it shows I'm not afraid to get my hands dirty."

He frowned briefly. "I'd prefer you demonstrated that someplace other than with my family. Particularly with my son, who has an unfortunate streak of naïveté of his own and is an easy prey for anyone willing to take advantage of his vulnerability."

"Yes. I suppose one always thinks one's own family ought to be off-limits, no matter how much one claims to inhabit the world of real politik. It's what makes it so confusing, don't you think? Everyone has a family, even Gadhafi, that they think should be off-limits. Everyone has a point of view, and who is to judge which point of view is more reliable or more worthy of protection?"

"And what point of view were you trying to protect by harassing my wife?"

He kept his tone light, but he was upset that I'd one-upped him in a philosophy discussion—he controlled his hands, but he couldn't control a pulse in his temple. I made sure that the breath of relief I exhaled went out very softly indeed.

"My own, Mr. Baladine. With all the money you spent finding out about my whisky preferences, I'm sure you must have put a dollar or two into learning about the State's Attorney's attempt to arrest me for a hit-and-run involving your former nanny. Or was he doing that at your and Jean-Claude Poilevy's request?"

He laughed with a practiced humor that didn't reach his eyes. "I'm honored you have that much respect for my power, but I don't think Nicola's death was any-thing but an unfortunate accident. She ran away from jail; she got hit by a car. I can't even say I'm sorry: she was a liar and she was a thief. My strongest feeling is annoyance, because my hyper-emotional son is having another tiresome episode over her death."

"Poor Robbie," I said. "Not the son for a manly man. Maybe he was swapped at birth with an artist's child."

Irony was wasted on him; he made a face. "I sometimes think so. His kid sister is twice the man that he is. But you didn't bother my wife to find out whether J.C. and I were framing you, because you didn't know we were friends until you ran into Jennifer out there."

He was rattled by my investigation, or he wouldn't have the chronology so pat in his mind. "I had hoped your wife could tell me something about Ms. Aguinaldo's private life, but she apparently had no interest in a woman who was the most intimate caregiver of her children. Maybe you delved deeper?"

"What's that supposed to mean?" He picked up his water glass but eyed me over the rim as he spoke.

I crossed my legs, smoothing out the crease in the silk—I'd taken time to go home to change before trekking out here. "Carnifice provides in-home surveillance and a reference service for nannies. I assume you employed it when you hired Nicola Aguinaldo."

"It's the old truth about the shoemaker's children, I suppose: we relied on the credentials of the agency we had used in the past. It didn't occur to me that Nicola was illegal. And I knew about her children, of course, but I wasn't interested in any private life she might have had on her days off, as long as it didn't spill over into my family." He forced a smile. "Into my private point of view."

"So you don't know who she would have run to for

help when she escaped last week? No lovers, no one who might have beaten her up?"

"Beaten her up?" he echoed. "I understood she was hit and killed by a car. One other than yours, of course."

"Funny," I said. "Your wife and her friends knew she'd been attacked. If they didn't learn it from you, where did they hear it?"

Once again I could see the pulse jump at his temple, although he put his fingers together and spoke condescendingly. "I'm not going to try to untangle a game of who said what to whom. It's childish and not good investigative work, as I often tell our new operatives. Perhaps I spoke to my wife before I had all the information from the Cook County State's Attorney and the Chicago police. The latest word from them is that she was killed in a hit-and-run."

"Then you should get your team to talk to the doctor who operated on her. Even though her body has disappeared, so the medical examiner can't perform an autopsy, the ER doctor at Beth Israel saw that she'd been killed by a blow that perforated her small intestine. Inconsistent with being hit by a car."

"So all you wanted from Eleanor was a lead on Nicola's private life. I'm sorry we can't help you with that."

"Woman worked for you what—two years?—and you know nothing about who she saw on her days off, but in one afternoon you nail down my whisky preferences? I think you care more about your children's welfare than that."

He chuckled. "Maybe you're more interesting to me than a diaper-changing immigrant."

"She seemed to make a deep impression on your son. That didn't concern you?"

Again his mouth twisted in slight distaste. "Robbie cried when the cat caught a bird. Then he cried when the cat had to be put to sleep. Everything makes a deep impression on him. Military school might help cure that."

Poor kid. I wondered if he knew that lay in his future. "So what did you want with me that entailed my making the journey all the way out here?"

"I wanted to see whether you would make the trip."

I nodded but didn't say anything. His point: to prove he was big and I was small. Let him think he had made it successfully.

"You've been an investigator for sixteen years, Vic." He shifted deliberately to my first name: I was small, he could patronize me. "What keeps you going when your annual billings barely cover your expenses?"

I grinned and stood up. "Idealism and naïveté, Bob. And curiosity, of course, about what happens next."

He leaned against the padded leather of his armchair and crossed his hands behind his head. "You're a good investigator, everyone agrees with that. But they say you have a funny kink in you that keeps you picking up stray dogs and that stops you from making a success of yourself. Haven't you ever thought about giving up your solo practice and coming to work for—well, an outfit like mine? You wouldn't have to worry about overhead. You'd even have a fully funded retirement plan."

"This isn't a job offer, by any chance?"

"Something for you to think about. Not an offer. What would you do if outfits like Continental United stopped tossing you their small jobs? We handle their big ones already; they might agree to roll everything into one package with us, after all."

My constant nightmare, but I made myself laugh, hoping the smile reached my eyes. "I'd cash in my CD's and go live in Italy for a while."

"You don't have enough CD's to live on."

"Your people have been thorough, haven't they? I guess I'd hang out in the alley and share a bone with the rest of the strays. Maybe chew on your old shoes—you know, if you've got a Ferragamo loafer missing its little tag and you're thinking of throwing it out anyway."

He stared at me without speaking. Before I could poke any deeper, Claudia came in to say that his Tokyo call was waiting for him.

I smiled. "Catch you later, Bob."

"Yes, Ms. Warshawski. I can guarantee our paths will cross."

The young woman who'd brought me up was waiting in the hall to escort me back down. To keep me from getting lost? Or to keep me from filching some of Carnifice's high-tech gadgetry and using it to steal their clients? I asked her, but of course company policy forbade her telling me.

Saturday at the Mall

THE LAST DREGS of light were staining the western sky pink when I got home. I took the dogs for a walk, then sat chatting in the backyard with Mr. Contreras until the mosquitoes drove us inside. All the time we were discussing whether the Cubs could stay alive in a race for the playoffs, whether Max and Lotty would ever get married, if a lump on Peppy's chest required a trip to the vet, I kept wondering what the real story of Nicola Aguinaldo's death was.

Something about it worried Baladine enough to pull me out to Oak Brook and alternately threaten and bribe me. Maybe his only agenda was to flex his muscles in my face, but I thought he was too sophisticated for simple acts of thuggery. Had my last idle remark, about his shoes, really caught him off guard, or was it my imagination?

And who had claimed Nicola Aguinaldo's body so pat? Was it her mother—or had it been Baladine, trying to prevent Vishnikov from performing an autopsy? That seemed hard to imagine, since the body wasn't claimed until late Wednesday night, and Vishnikov might well have made his examination as soon as Aguinaldo's remains arrived.

"Whatcha thinking about, doll? I asked you three

times if you wanted any grappa, and you're staring into space like there was UFO's flying past the window."

"That poor young woman in the road," I said. "What is so important about her? You'd think she was a fugitive Iraqi dissident or something, the way she's become the focus of so much attention."

Mr. Contreras was glad to talk it over with me, but after an hour of thrashing out the events of the week I didn't feel I had any more insight into what was going on. I finally told him I'd have to sleep on it and stumped slowly up to bed. It wasn't even ten o'clock, but I was too worn out to do anything but sleep.

Saturday I woke so early that I was able to get a proper run in before the heat settled on the city. I even took the dogs swimming and still was out of the shower by eight.

Of the women around the Baladine pool two days ago, the most approachable seemed to be Global magnate Teddy Trant's wife. Maybe I could catch up with her someplace in the morning.

It was a pain having all my computing capability at the office. If Carnifice took over my little operation, I suppose Baladine would pay me enough to install a terminal at home. Until then I had to trundle down to Leavitt to look up the Trant family. I didn't want to spend the time or money on the kind of search I'd done on Baladine yesterday—all I wanted was Mrs. Trant's name and home address. Her first name was Abigail, she used her husband's last name, and they lived four miles northwest of the Baladines with their nine-year-old daughter, Rhiannon. I packed binoculars, picked up a couple of daily papers and a copy of *Streetwise* from Elton, and once again pointed the Rustmobile toward the Eisenhower and the western suburbs.

As soon as I got to Thornfield Demesne I realized the Skylark was badly suited for surveillance. For one thing it stood out hideously against the Range Rovers and other all-terrain vehicles needed to navigate the perilous ground between mansion and mall. More to the point, you can't park on these leafy winding roads in front of the gated communities out here. The demesne's entrance was protected by a guard station that would have put the old Berlin Wall to shame. Not only that, a private security patrol—probably from Carnifice—periodically sent out a cruiser, no doubt to pick riffraff like me up and throw us back across the border.

I drove to a curve in the road about fifty feet from the entrance and pulled my maps out—I could probably pretend one time to the security patrol that I was lost. With the maps propped up on the steering wheel, I tried using my binoculars, but all I could see were tree leaves. If I was really going to survey the place, I needed a horse, or maybe a bicycle. I was on the point of driving to the nearest mall to see if I could rent one—preferably a bike, since I'd never been on a horse—when I had a bit of luck. The great wrought gates of the demesne opened, and the Mercedes Gelaendewagen with the GLOBAL 2 plates shot out.

I wrenched the Buick into a clumsy U-turn and followed at a discreet distance. Once we got onto a main road I let a few cars get in between me and Abigail. To my relief she drove past all the entrances to the Oak Brook shopping mall—I couldn't imagine trying to engineer a meeting with her in there. We'd gone south a couple of miles when the Mercedes turned at a sign announcing the Leafy Vale Stables. It looked as though I could get my wish for a horse after all.

Fortunately, the leafy vale lay on the far side of the

stables and house; I could see the Mercedes clearly from the road. I parked on the verge and watched as the little girl from the Baladine pool jumped out of the passenger seat. Abigail Trant climbed out and escorted her toward one of the buildings. The child was wearing riding clothes, but the mother had on knee-length shorts and a body-hugging top. Mother seemed to be giving directions to a woman who cocked her head deferentially. Abigail Trant kissed her daughter and climbed back into her sports utility tank. I drove a little further and backed the Rustmobile onto the verge where I could turn in either direction. The Mercedes turned toward Oak Brook.

My heart sank when she headed into the mall. It's one thing to strike up a conversation over the produce counter, quite another in the middle of the couture salon at Neiman Marcus. I followed her gamely, parking a few cars beyond the Mercedes on the east side of the mall, and trailed behind her to the Parruca Salon. Parruca had a grand set of double doors. They were lined on the inside with red leather. I was able to detect that when a doorman opened them and greeted Abigail Trant by name. The doors closed as she asked after him with the graciousness of the true grande dame.

Short of pretending to be the new shampooer, I could hardly follow her while she had her weekly hair appointment. I wondered how long beautification took. At least long enough for me to wander into the maze of shops in search of a bathroom and a tall iced tea.

After half an hour I came back outside and waited with my newspaper. There wasn't anyplace to sit, since you're not supposed to be outside a mall—you're supposed to be inside buying. As the sun rose toward the middle of the sky, the shade cast by the buildings became a thin wedge. I pushed my shoulders against the stone wall separating Parruca from the sportswear shop to its south and tried to pay attention to the problems besetting Kosovo.

Teenagers swarmed past me, chattering about hair, clothes, boys, girls. Solitary shoppers strode past, their faces set in grim lines, as though buying were an onerous duty. Every now and then the doorman opened Parruca's red leather doors to decant a client or admit a new one. Finally, when my shirt was so soaked with sweat that I thought I'd have to slip into the sportswear shop to get a fresh one, Abigail Trant came out.

"We'll see you next week, Mrs. Trant," the doorman said, gracefully pocketing her tip.

I unglued my shoulders from the wall. Her honey-streaked hair was carefully combed into the right suggestion of windblown disorder, her makeup painted on with a subtle hand, her nails a gleaming pearl. To approach her in my sweaty sunburned state seemed almost sacrilegious, but I did it anyway.

She was startled but didn't run shrieking for a security guard. Yes, her pleasant face showing no disdain, she certainly remembered my visit to Eleanor Baladine's pool two days ago. But it was all she could do to keep track of her own daughter's nanny—she certainly didn't know anything about Eleanor's.

"And you know, Teddy and I didn't move back to the Chicago area until eighteen months ago, so that girl who was killed the other day wasn't even around then. I'm afraid I can't answer any questions about her."

"Can you take ten minutes for a cup of coffee and answer a few other questions?"

A dimple appeared briefly at the corner of her

mouth. "I've never been interrogated by a detective—
maybe it will help me understand how to respond to the
girls I'm sponsoring for the You Can Do It Foundation.
Many of them seem to have been arrested before reaching high school, although usually for shoplifting." She
looked at her wrist. "I have just about fifteen minutes
before my next engagement."

The coffee bar was so mobbed we didn't bother
waiting for drinks but perched at the high counter. Mrs.
Trant readily stepped me through a few basics—she had
grown up not too far from here, gone to school with
Jennifer Poilevy, had been thrilled when Global sent her
and her husband back from Los Angeles to the
Midwest.

"L.A. is a difficult place to raise a child. Everyone is
on perpetual display, and the kids get sucked into that
precocious environment far too young. Out here Rhiannon can simply be a child."

With her swimming exercises, her horse, and all
those other accoutrements of the simple life. But I
wanted help, so I kept my sardonic observations to
myself.

"It doesn't seem as though Eleanor Baladine's children have that same freedom," I said. "Although I
guess the girls are following her swimming regimen
pretty enthusiastically."

"I admire Eleanor, I really do. She's lucky to have a
gift that absorbs her so completely. And she's wonderful to take Rhiannon under her wing, especially since
Rhiannon's started to outperform Madison. But I think
it's a mistake to push children too hard. When they get
to adolescence that can come back to haunt you, you
know."

I grunted noncommittally. "You said that you grew

up with Jennifer Poilevy. Was Eleanor Baladine part of your childhood as well?"

Looking briefly at her watch, Abigail Trant explained she'd gotten to know Eleanor before they moved to Oak Brook when their husbands started doing business together four years ago. "BB was solving a lot of Global's security problems, and the two of them seemed to hit it off. And of course, Jean-Claude Poilevy has been incredibly helpful to us since we moved out here."

I could imagine how helpful the Illinois Speaker could be to someone with money to fling in his direction—zoning regulations bent, tax breaks for Global, a special deal on the mansion in Thornfield Demesne. "I know the prison notified Baladine as soon as Nicola Aguinaldo got away, so Eleanor knew all about her death before I showed up. Do you have any hunches about why she was so rattled?"

Abigail shrugged. "It's hard when violence comes close to your children, and the girl had been her children's nanny."

I smiled in a way I hoped invited bad-girl chat. "But really—I know she's your friend and you've known her for years—watching her with her son, she doesn't strike me as the warmly concerned mother."

Abigail smiled back but refused to play. "BB is such an athletic man, and his naval service was the most important part of his life. It's understandable he wants his only son to follow his path, and that may blind him and Eleanor to how hard they are on him. And it's a tough world for a boy these days, it would be better if he could develop the ability to compete in it. If that's all you need to know, I have to get going. We have twenty people coming to dinner and the caterer is going to need directions from me."

She slid from her stool; I followed and said, "BB called me out to his office last night to threaten to put me out of business for asking questions about how his kid's old nanny died. Do you have any idea why?"

She paused next to her stool. A teenager demanded to know whether we could make up our minds—were we going or staying—other people are waiting for seats, you know. The rudeness made Abigail Trant lean a hand on her stool and say we'd be through in a minute. The teenager gave an exasperated sigh and swung around, deliberately hitting Trant with her bag.

"Mall brats," Abigail Trant said. "Why Rhiannon is not allowed to hang out here—I don't want her acquiring these manners. Tell me a little about your business. I gather you're not as big as Carnifice."

Thank heaven for mall brats—Trant would be in her Mercedes by now if she hadn't wanted to stomp on the kid. I gave her a thumbnail sketch of the difference between Warshawski Investigations and Carnifice Security. Something about it piqued a genuine interest from her—she forgot about the time and asked me how I'd gotten into detection, what special training I'd needed, how long I'd been doing it.

"Do you enjoy having your own business? Doing all the work yourself, do you ever have time for a private life?"

I admitted a private life was hard for me to maintain. "Since I have to work for a living, I'm happier working for myself than I would be in a big outfit like Carnifice. Anyway, I like knowing that it's my work that's solved a problem."

"Do you think BB could put you out of business?"

I hunched an impatient shoulder. "I don't know. But I'm curious to know why my asking questions about his kid's old nanny makes him want to."

She tapped the wooden counter with one pearl-colored nail. "I don't think there's any special mystery about the dead girl. I think it has to do with BB's personality. You came to his house, you interrogated his wife and his son, and it makes him feel that you proved he was vulnerable. He's threatening you so he can feel better about the fact that a private detective with a very small company could penetrate his security systems." She looked at her watch and gave a little gasp. "The time! I really have to run now."

She threaded her way expertly through the crowds of shoppers. Everything about Abigail Trant depressed me —her polished good looks and manners, the fact that she had stiffed me half a dozen times with perfect good manners, and the possibility she could be right about Nicola Aguinaldo. She was only thirty-five, but she could dance rings about me—no wonder she was entertaining important guests in Oak Brook and I was taking my sweaty body back to my un-air-conditioned car.

Crumbs from the Table

WHEN I GOT back to the city I was too worn out by the heat to go to my office. I'd been planning on buckling down on my project for Continental United, but I went home and showered and lay down.

As I dozed through the midday heat my conversation with Abigail Trant kept coming into my dreams. In some of them she was sweetly commiserating because my work interfered with my social life. In others she was standing on the sidelines as BB Baladine threatened me. I woke for good from a nightmare in which Baladine was choking me while Abigail Trant said, "I told you he didn't like to be threatened."

"But I wasn't threatening him," I said aloud. "It was the other way around." And what was I supposed to do, back away from Baladine because he interpreted any approach as aggression? Anyway, maybe Abigail Trant was right about Baladine's character, but I thought there was more to the story than that—some issue about Nicola Aguinaldo, either her life or her death. Perhaps when she escaped from prison she approached Baladine and he interpreted that as a threat, knocked her out, then ran over her. As he got back into his car the emblem came off his loafer. My research said he was a Porsche man. I wondered if his Carrera had been in a body shop lately.

It was all a load of speculative nonsense. Except for the fact that Nicola Aguinaldo was dead. I wished I could talk to her mother. Why had Abuelita Mercedes disappeared so suddenly just at the time her daughter died? Maybe if I went back to Aguinaldo's neighborhood I could find the mysterious Mr. Morrell, the man asking questions about people who escaped from jail. I made myself an espresso to cut through the dopiness I felt from dozing in the heat, and got dressed again.

I dumped my sweaty jeans in the hamper and chose my outfit carefully—Abigail Trant had made me feel like a grubby hulk. I laughed at myself, a little shamefaced, but still put on clean linen slacks with a big white shirt, even dabbing on lipstick and powder. The result didn't approach Ms. Trant's perfection: a polished appearance is like any other skill—you have to work at it a lot to be good. Maybe weekly visits to Parruca's would help, too.

Saturday is errand day in Uptown just as in Oak Brook, but the girls here were doing chores, not taking riding lessons. When I rang Mrs. Attar's bell, a sullen Mina, huffy at having to dust, came to the door. The girls had mentioned someone named Aisha; it was Aisha's father Morrell was talking to. After some grumbling, Mina directed me to the other girl's apartment, two doors up the street.

Aisha's father was home, looking after a small boy who was wearing only a diaper. The man greeted me with unsmiling reserve and didn't move out of the doorway. In stilted but passable English he demanded to know what business of mine it was whether he had a daughter named Aisha? When I explained my errand,

the man shook his head. He was afraid the neighborhood girls liked to tease strangers. He didn't know anyone named Morrell. His wife might have known a
woman named—what was it? Abuelita Mercedes?—but
she was at the market; the name meant nothing to him.
And now if I would excuse him he was very busy. I
handed him a card, with a request to call me if he ever
heard from Mr. Morrell. It fluttered to the floor in front
of him, where I left it.

It was humiliating to be mistaken for an INS officer.
Or an agent of a foreign secret-police force. I didn't
know which would be worse.

There might have been something more profitable I
could have done with the rest of the afternoon, but I
went home and worked on personal projects, matting
some prints I'd picked up at a flea market. One of the
pictures showed a young woman about Aguinaldo's
age. She was partly dressed, in a kind of camisole, and
was staring at a window; what I liked about the picture
was the reflection of her face in the glass.

I started wondering about the shirtdress Aguinaldo
had been wearing. The lab's report had explained only
how they'd tested the outside of the fabric for automo-
bile traces. Maybe the inside of the shirt could tell me
something about how Nicola Aguinaldo had died.

I was actually feeling edgy enough to try the lab. Of
course no one was answering on a Saturday afternoon.
I worked my way through the voice menu and left a
message in the mailbox of the guy who had signed the
report on the Trans Am.

Sunday morning I went out with the dogs for another early swim, keeping an eye open for Lemour.
Back home I told Mr. Contreras I would take Peppy to
the office with me for company. I assured him I'd be

back by four: he and the dogs and I were joining Mary
Louise and her foster sons for a picnic. Mary Louise
and I get together once a week to go over work; this
week we'd decided to combine it with a family outing.

"Okay, doll, okay. You got a water dish down there?
It's too hot for the princess to go all day without
drinking."

I bit back a sharp retort. "Her comfort is my main
object in life. And my office is air-conditioned. I hope
no animal-rights people are out throwing yellow paint
on her today, because she just won't give up that big
old fur coat, not even in June, will you, girl?"

Peppy grinned in happy agreement and clattered
down the stairs with me, her tail waving a pointed put-
down at Mitch, left at home with my neighbor. At my
office she ran first to Tessa Reynolds's studio. Tessa is a
sculptor. These days she was working with marble; the
dust made her short dreadlocks glitter under her bright
lights. She waved a muscular forearm at me, gave the
dog a quick scratch, but was too deep in her work to
take a break.

If Tessa wouldn't stop to talk I had no choice but to
go to work myself. While my computer came up I
pulled out my phone books and started calling everyone
in the metropolitan area named Morrell. I didn't try
anything smart—just the unvarnished truth: V. I. Warshawski, private investigator, looking for the man asking questions of immigrants in Uptown. Of course half
the people weren't home, but those who were either
didn't know what I was talking about or affected
not to.

"Enough, Warshawski, get to the stuff you know
you need to do," I muttered, inserting a CD-ROM with
a cross-directory for Georgia phones and addresses.

Checking phone numbers was mindless work; my thoughts kept creeping back to Aguinaldo. Baladine said she'd faked an illness to get sent to the hospital. Mary Louise said the prison had reported an ovarian cyst. Did Baladine know that was faked? Or that the report was a fake?

When I was with the public defender, my clients found it impossible to get medical care. One man with lymphoma had a tumor constricting his diaphragm and died in solitary for causing a disturbance when he tried to summon help. It was hard to believe that Coolis was so tender of their charges that Aguinaldo could have faked illness. And once she'd fled the hospital, how had she gotten to Chicago so fast?

I put down my notes on Georgia and went to the cupboard to pull my Illinois county maps. Peppy, lying under a table, half-sat up to see whether I was leaving. She lay down again when I returned to my desk.

The hospital in Coolis sat on the northwest end of the town, the prison side, where growth was fastest. If Aguinaldo had left in a supply or laundry truck, they would have gone out the service road, which followed Smallpox Creek. I squinted through my magnifying glass to bring up the details. Assuming she'd hopped off the truck before it reached the town center, she had limited choices—she could follow Smallpox Creek on foot north to Lake Galena or try to hitch a ride on Route 113, which led from the hospital past the prison as well as northeast away from the town.

There was only one crossroads between the hospital and the prison, Hollow Glen Road, which intersected again with 113 a mile north and another state road a mile south. It might be worthwhile to see if someone picked her up—assuming Robert Baladine hadn't been waiting at Hollow Glen Road in his Porsche. Those queries were ones that only the police or state marshals had the resources to undertake. I put the map down in frustration.

I went back to my paying client's work and forced myself to stay with it, copying numbers into a file, then laying them across a blowup of the area where Continental United's trucks were coming to grief. I was hard at it when Tessa popped her head around my door.

"Your friend Murray is outside—he rang my bell by mistake. Shall I let him in? He's brought some talent with him."

My brows shot up in surprise, but I followed her to the front door. Murray was outside with Alex Fisher. She had on skintight jeans and a big mesh shirt, which revealed not only her Lycra tube-top but the sharp points of her breastbone. As she and Murray came in, I glanced at Alex-Sandy's feet, but of course if she owned Ferragamos with a missing emblem she wouldn't have them on.

Murray stopped to talk to Tessa. "Sorry you couldn't make it to the Glow Tuesday night. You missed a great evening."

Tessa gave him the kind of polite brush-off she'd learned from her years jetting around the world with her wealthy parents. I always envy someone who doesn't have to go to the jugular. As I promptly did.

"Sandy—sorry I didn't recognize you right away Tuesday night. You looked a lot different when you were urging us all to the barricades back in law school."

She flashed an empty smile. "I'm Alex now, not Sandy—another one of the changes in my life."

She surveyed my office with frank interest. I'd divided my share of the warehouse into smaller spaces with pasteboard partitions, not because I need a lot of rooms but because I wanted some human scale to the place. Aside from that and good quality lighting, I hadn't invested heavily in furnishings.

Alex-Sandy seemed to be preening herself, perhaps imagining her own office by contrast, when her eyes widened at a painting on the partition facing my desk. "Isn't that an Isabel Bishop? How did you come by it?"

"I stole it from the Art Institute. Do you want to sit down? Would you like something to drink?" An elderly woman whose grandson had been stripping her assets gave me the Bishop in lieu of a fee, but that didn't seem to be any of Alex-Sandy's business.

"Oh, Vic, you always had a bizarre sense of humor. It's coming back to me now. Do you have Malvern water? It's hideously hot out—I'd forgotten Chicago summers."

"Malvern?" I stopped on my way to the refrigerator. "Did you introduce BB Baladine to that, or the other way around?"

"I didn't know you knew Bob. I think it's something we probably both learned from Teddy Trant. He spends a lot of time in England. Do you have any?" It was said smoothly, and it was even plausible.

She sat on a stool next to the table where Peppy was lying. The dog had gotten up to greet her and Murray, but something in my tone must have sounded a warning, because she crawled under my desk.

I offered Alex-Sandy a choice of tap water or Poland Springs, which is cheap and no different from the foreign imports as far as I can tell. Murray took iced tea, which Tessa makes fresh and drinks by the gallon when she's working. We share a refrigerator out in the hall and write scrupulous notes about who's taken what from whose shelves.

"Murray says you've become a private investigator," Sandy said when I'd sat at my desk. "It seems like strange work for someone with your education. Did you get tired of the law? I can totally understand that, but my own fantasies run more to retiring to a ranch."

"You know how it goes, Sandy—Alex—middle age comes on and you revert to your roots. You left the barricades for the boardroom; I couldn't stay away from my cop-father's blue-collar work." I turned to Murray. "Sandy was always on my butt for not joining protest movements with her. She kept telling me that a blue-collar girl—whatever that is—should be in the forefront of organizing struggles."

"You have to learn to move on from those old battles. These are the nineties, after all. Anyway, Murray suggested your name when we were mulling over how to help Lacey with a sticky situation."

A crumb from the Global table. Maybe Murray had been as embarrassed as I by our conversation the other night and was trying a subtle amend. I could see him at dinner with Alex-Sandy. At the Filigree, or perhaps Justin's, the hot new hole on west Randolph, Murray leaning across the table toward Alex's modest cleavage: *You know, V.I., you know what a prickly bitch she's always been. But she did the legwork on a couple of the stories that built my reputation and I hate to leave her standing in the dust. Isn't there something Global needs that would give her a break?*

"Global has a gazillion lawyers, detectives, and strong-armed types to protect their stars." I wasn't hungry enough yet for a crumb, I guess.

"It's a little trickier than that," Murray said, "at least as I understand it. Since you were at the Glow on Tuesday, maybe you saw the problem."

"Lucian Frenada," Alex said briskly. "He and Lacey had a boy–girl kind of understanding twenty years ago, and he won't accept that it's over, that Lacey's moved on and he has to also."

I stared at her blankly. "And?"

"And we want you to make that clear to him, clear that he has to stop harassing her, calling her, or hunting her out in public." Alex spoke with an irritability that definitely hadn't changed from her old harangues.

"I don't do bodyguard work. I'm a one-woman shop. I have people I call on for support, but if you want guaranteed protection you need to go to an outfit like Carnifice."

"It's not a bodyguard kind of situation." Alex looked around for a table and put her drink on the couch next to her. "She says she's not afraid of him, but that he's embarrassing her."

I made a face. "Murray, if this was your idea of a favor, take it somewhere else. If she's not afraid of him, she can talk to him. If he's bugging her, the studio has the muscle to make him back off."

"You didn't used to be stupid in law school," Alex snapped. "If it was that simple we'd be doing it. They were childhood friends, stood up for each other when the rest of the street harassed them for being geeks. She can't bear for his feelings to be hurt, because he rescued her at least once from some serious bangers in the stairwell. Beyond that, the guy is a kind of model enterprise-zone leader. If it looks like a big corporation is persecuting him, we'll have a lot of hostility in the

Spanish press, and of course that would be damaging for Lacey's image."

Murray was fidgeting with his glass. Something about the picture was making him ill at ease, whether Alex's condescension or my snappishness or the assignment as a whole I had no way of knowing.

"He owns a business?" I asked. "What kind?"

"Gimmicky clothes," Murray said. "Uniforms for kids' teams, specialty T-shirts, that sort of thing. He started out doing the soccer uniforms at St. Remigio's and moved on. He employs a lot of people right there in the neighborhood. On their old street he's the second-biggest hero, right behind Lacey."

"So what do you want me to do? Burn down his factory so that he has so much to worry about he leaves Lacey alone?" To my annoyance, Alex-Sandy seemed to be considering this smart-ass suggestion. "Lacey's going back to Hollywood, he's staying here, it's not a problem."

"It's image, Vic," Alex snapped. "Lacey's going to be in town for eight weeks—they're shooting *Virgin Six* here this summer. We can't have him harassing her, and we can't put him down hard. Why don't you look into his affairs, see if he's cut some corners someplace, see if we can't offer him a little quid pro quo: leave Lacey alone and we won't report you. If you turned up something, Global would be very grateful, and they have the resources to express their gratitude."

I leaned back in my chair and studied them. Murray had stopped playing with his glass in favor of mutilating his napkin. Gray balls of wet paper were falling on his jeans. Alex was staring at me with an arrogant impatience that I found exasperating.

"I'm not manufacturing evidence of a crime or misdemeanor, even if it means so much to Global they give me the residuals for *Virgin Six*."

"Of course not, Vic." Alex bristled. "I'm not asking for that—but for you to fish. What's your usual fee?"

"A hundred an hour plus nonoverhead expenses."

She laughed. "I'd forgotten how honest you always were. Most people double or triple a number when a studio lawyer comes to visit."

Meaning a hundred was so low it had to be the truth.

"We'll double your fee if you'll make this a priority. And throw in a high five-figure bonus if you come up with something we can use. Here are Frenada's addresses and phone numbers."

"Not so fast, Sandy." Like Aisha's father this morning, I let the proferred paper fall between us. "I need to think it over, and I'd have to talk to Ms. Dowell to see if she has the same take on the story you do."

Alex-Sandy pursed her lips. "We'd rather Lacey wasn't involved."

My jaw dropped. "If she's not involved, then what on God's green earth is all this fuss about?"

Murray coughed, a deferential sign so out of his normal character that my irritability increased. "Vic, let me put it bluntly. You can talk to Lacey, of course, and get her read on Frenada. What we're trying to avoid, or what Global is trying to avoid, is any hint that they're beating up on Lacey's old friends.

"No one wants you to manufacture anything. And no one who knows you would imagine that you ever would. As I made clear to Alex when we were talking about this last night. But if you do find something that the studio can use as a bargaining chip with Frenada, then we'd—they'd—prefer Lacey didn't know it was because of Global that things got resolved. And we don't want it in the papers."

"Seems to me Teddy Trant can decide that," I said, not trying to keep sarcasm out of my voice.

"Teddy only controls one paper and one television station, and anyway, the business side doesn't dictate to the editorial," Alex-Sandy said.

"Yeah, and the pope has no effect on the parish churches around here. I'll think about it and let you know. Of course, if I agree to work on it, Global signs the contract. Not you. And not Murray as your front man." I barely kept "your stooge" from popping out.

"Come on, Vic, you know me. And Murray's a witness."

"We're going to flap our little Phoenix neckties and shout the Chicago fight song to prove our loyalty to each other? We went to law school on the South Side of Chicago, not to Eton. Maybe the South Side has stuck to me more than the law, but one of the things Professor Carmichael pounded into our heads was the importance of written contracts for business agreements."

Her wide mouth flattened into a hard line, but at last she said, "Think it over. I'll call you tomorrow morning."

"I'm not making a decision that fast. I have some urgent projects in hand that I have to finish before I can consider yours. Which is why I'm working on a Sunday. By the way, Murray, what made you drop by here today? You can't possibly have expected to find me in."

Alex answered for him. "Oh, we stopped at your apartment first, but the old man said you were here. I'll call you tomorrow."

"I can't wait to hear his description of you. As

Murray can tell you, it's likely to be colorful and unstinting."

Why did I have to show hackle every time my fur was ruffled? No sooner had I asked myself that pointed question than I called to Murray, who was following Alex-Sandy through the door, "Was it Justin's or Filigree where you cooked this up?"

He turned and cocked a sandy eyebrow at me. "You wouldn't be showing some jealousy there, would you, Warshawski?"

15

Family Picnic

I STARED AT the computer for a while, but I couldn't summon any enthusiasm for the Georgia trucking problem. Murray's last remark rankled. Which meant there might be a grain of truth to it. Not that I was jealous of women he dated, danced, slept with. But we'd worked together for so long we had the shared jokes and shortcuts of old comrades. It did hurt to see him more in tune with someone like Alex Fisher-Fishbein than me. I had character, after all. All she had was power, money, and glamour.

Murray was an investigative reporter. He had the same sources I did—sometimes even better ones—for uncovering dope on entrepreneurs around town. Maybe he was offering Frenada to me as a chance to make some real money. Or because he felt guilty for selling himself to Global. Maybe I should be grateful, but all I felt was queasy.

Alex's reason for coming to me instead of the studio's usual security detail made a kind of sense, but not enough. When I'd talked to Frenada briefly at the Golden Glow, he'd seemed personable, quiet, not a masher. Still, one is forever reading about serial killers who seemed quiet and normal to their neighbors. And it's true, I myself had watched Frenada accost Lacey in the middle of the Golden Glow. If he was really a stalker, then Alex was being pretty cavalier about danger to Lacey. If he wasn't, then Global had some agenda that was going to get me in a pack of trouble if I took on their dirty work.

Frenada had said at the party that maybe I could help him—that something odd was happening in his office. My own upheaval around Nicola Aguinaldo had driven my conversation with him far from my mind. Now I wondered if Global was already doing something to discredit him. If he'd stumbled on their plan, and Global realized it, Alex might be trying to bring me in as fresh bait on the line.

I logged on to LifeStory and requested a check on Frenada, not so much because I'd decided to take the job as to look for some context around the guy. To understand his character, I'd do better to talk to the people who knew him, but I couldn't afford to spend time with his employees or his priest or whoever in Humboldt Park if I wasn't going to take the job.

As I tried to make up a list of tasks for Mary Louise and me to split on the Georgia inquiry, I couldn't help thinking of Alex's remark, that if I did the work she wanted, Global had the resources to express their gratitude. A bonus in the high five figures. I wondered how high. Fifty thousand would not only get me a new car but let me build a cushion, maybe hire someone full-time instead of relying on Mary Louise's erratic hours. Or what if it were seventy or eighty thousand? Murray was driving a powder-blue Mercedes these days; I could pick up that red Jaguar XJ-12 I'd seen in the ads on Wednesday.

"And that's how they catch their fish," I admonished

myself out loud. "If you can be bought for the price of a used car, V.I., then you're not worth owning."

I worked hard for another couple of hours, stopping only once, to go out for a sandwich and to let Peppy relieve herself. After that I didn't look up until Tessa came in around three-thirty.

"Mary Louise hasn't been in for a while," she commented, perching on the couch arm.

"You keeping an eye on the premises?"

She grinned. "No, doofus. You aren't the only detective around here: when Mary Louise comes in she always tidies up the papers. I'm taking off. Want to go for a coffee?"

I looked at the clock. I told her I'd have to take a rain check so I could get back to pick up Mr. Contreras. I started my system backup program and began hunting through the heap on my desk for the report Max had faxed over from Beth Israel: I wanted to discuss it with Mary Louise. I'd forgotten stuffing the papers into the folder labeled *Alumni Fund* but came on it by the sophisticated method of going through all the folders I'd stacked up lately.

I pulled out the report the paramedics had filed with the hospital. It described where they'd found Aguinaldo, what steps they'd taken to stabilize her, and the time they'd delivered her to Beth Israel (3:14 A.M.), but not the names of the officers who'd talked to Mary Louise and me in Edgewater. I wondered if I needed to know badly enough to pay for Mary Louise to talk to the ambulance crew and see if they remembered the guys. But I didn't know how else to start finding out whether Baladine or Poilevy had been pulling the strings that made the cops come after me.

"I'm going to take a shower. And neatly put away

all my tools," Tessa added pointedly as I dropped the folder back on the heap of papers: if Mary Louise were working on it she'd have typed up a label on the spot and stuck it in the drawer with other pending cases.

"Yeah, you always were teacher's pet. It ain't going anywhere, but I am." I shut down my system for the day and stuffed a second copy of the backup program in my briefcase. It was the second thing my old hacker friend had taught me—always keep a copy of your programs off the premises. You never think your office is the one that will be burgled or burned to the ground.

Tessa, her hair heavy from her shower, was locking her studio when I came into the hall. She had changed into a gold sundress of some kind of soft expensive cotton. I wondered if a ten-thousand-dollar wardrobe could make me look as good as her or Abigail Trant. The two came from similar worlds—fancy private schools, fathers successful entrepreneurs. Probably the only difference was their mothers—Tessa's had broken through the white male barricades into a major law career.

"Not to be a feline, but I always thought Murray liked softer women than that bionic specimen he brought in today," Tessa remarked as she set the alarm code. "He was kind of preening when he introduced us, so I take it they weren't making a business call?"

"Not the Bionic Woman—a Space Beret." When she looked puzzled, I said, "I can tell there aren't any small boys in your life. That's Global Studio's movie-cartoon-comic-book and megabillion-dollar action figure. The woman is one of their lawyers. When we were in school together she was Sandy Fishbein and led sit-ins. Now that she's Alexandra Fisher and sits on boards, I get confused about how to think about her or what to call her. She's seduced Murray, and now they're trying for a ménage à trois with me."

"I never trust a woman who gets all her muscles at the health club and only uses them as an accessory to her wardrobe," Tessa announced, flexing her own arms, sinewy from years of hammering on stone and metal.

I laughed and waved at her as she climbed into her pickup—one of those fancy modern ones with leather seats, air-conditioning, and perfect suspension. Seen next to it, the Skylark looked more decrepit than ever. I felt another unwelcome twist of jealousy. I wouldn't have traded either of my parents for the wealthiest tycoons in the West, but every now and then I wished my legacy had included more than the five-room bungalow whose sale after my father's death barely covered his medical bills.

The thought of Abigail Trant made me wonder if she'd played a role in sending Alex and Murray to me. Something about my operation had roused her full interest. Maybe she'd gone to Teddy. Playing with his tie as they dressed to receive their important guests: *Teddy, you know that woman that BB is so riled about? I think she's worth helping. Let's send her some work.* So maybe I should think about the offer more carefully. At least find out if Frenada really was harassing Lacey Dowell.

When I got to the apartment I ran upstairs to call Mary Louise's house. Emily answered, saying Mary Louise had already left for our picnic.

"That's okay. It's your expertise I want right now. Do you know where Lacey Dowell is staying while they're shooting *Virgin Six*?"

"You're not trying to prove she committed some kind of crime, are you?" Emily demanded.

"No. Someone was saying an old friend of hers was harassing her. I want to talk to her doorman and see if it's true."

She thought it over and decided it was an innocuous enough reason to reveal her heroine's whereabouts: a suite at the Trianon, a luxury hotel on the tip of the Gold Coast that overlooks the cardinal's residence on one side and Lake Michigan on the other. A nice change from the corner of North and California, where Lacey had grown up.

"Thanks, honey. You're not coming out with us this afternoon? Mr. Contreras is going to provide the food."

She mumbled something about having to see her father. "He's got a new girlfriend. He wants us to be friends before I leave for France."

"You don't have to do it if you don't want to," I reminded her.

"Yeah. I guess. Anyway, I'm flying on Wednesday, so I might as well tell him good-bye."

I don't suppose you ever outgrow the hope that your parent, however vile and violating he may have been, will magically turn into someone who cares about you. I turned sadly to join Mr. Contreras and the dogs in my car.

In the event, I had a pleasant outing. We joined Mary Louise and the boys in a forest preserve on the northwest side. Over a meal Mr. Contreras had created with boys in mind—fried chicken, potato chips, chocolate cupcakes, and marshmallows—Mary Louise and I went through the list of jobs that had come in this week. I had a half dozen background checks that were her main contribution to my work and a few other odds and ends, but I really wanted to talk to her about Alex-Sandy's offer and my meeting with Baladine.

"You don't need me to tell you not to touch that Global assignment," she said. "I hope your pal Murray isn't signing on for some real sleaze with them: that job sounds pretty bogus. As far as I can tell, your only reason for taking it on is to see what Murray is up to—and that's not enough reward for maybe getting hung out to dry by one of the biggest laundries in America."

I sat back on my heels, blushing—I didn't know I was that transparent. "It's not only that. What if Abigail Trant stuck an oar in to try to keep Baladine from swallowing me up?"

Mary Louise snorted. "What if she did? Are you supposed to fall over and slobber on her manicured toenails? Come on, Vic. This isn't a job, it's a setup. You know that as well as me."

She was right. Probably right. I didn't need the aggravation of being spun around by an outfit as slick as Global.

"But the Aguinaldo business is different," I said. "That's having a direct effect on me, what with that creep Lemour, and the State's Attorney panting for me to take a fall. Will you check with the paramedics to see if they can remember the officers who came to the scene that night?"

"I can do it, but it's a question of money, Vic. You pay me, remember, so even if it's pro bono for you, it's not for me. I think it's an unnecessary detail right now, given your budget. You have plenty else going on. You told me the evidence from Cheviot Labs on your car got the SA to back off. Let it go for now. I'll make those Georgia phone calls for you in the morning, but you know as well as I that there's a trip south of the Mason–Dixon line in your future: I can't leave town with those two monsters on my hand." She gestured toward Nate and Joshua, playing Frisbee with the dogs.

She bit her lip, the way people do when they're deciding to say something you don't want to hear, then burst out, "Vic, there's a kernel of truth in what Baladine said to you. About you going after strays all the time—only I call them wild-goose chases. You gnash your teeth over how you're always hard up for money, but you've got the contacts and the skills to build a big agency. It's just there's something in you that doesn't want to go corporate. Every time it's about to happen you get involved in a story like Aguinaldo's, and *phht,* there goes your chance to grow your business."

"Grow my business?" I faked a punch at her. "You sound like a business-school manual."

She started shadowboxing me, and pretty soon we were chasing each other around the park, the dogs in hot pursuit and the two boys screaming with excitement from seeing grown-ups act like children. When we flopped back on the grass, gasping for breath, the conversation moved in a new direction.

Nonetheless, her wisecrack felt as though it were coming close to some truth that I wasn't willing to face in myself. I wondered about it as I was driving home with Mr. Contreras and the dogs. Maybe Alex Fisher was right, that my blue-collar roots defined me. Would it make me feel guilty to enjoy a material success that my parents hadn't achieved? In fact, that might have saved my mother's life? She had died of cancer, a uterine cancer that metastasized because she hadn't sought treatment when her symptoms first appeared.

Mr. Contreras's conversation made it possible to defer any more serious self-examination. "Those two boys are awful cute, and the little one might make an athlete. They see anything of their old man?"

"Meaning that growing up with only a foster mother may make him a sissy?" I asked, but when he started coughing with embarrassment I let him off the hook and told him that Fabian was not exactly the athletic type. "He's got a new girlfriend, some student half his age. Maybe she's idealistic enough to think she wants to take on his first wife's children, but I don't know that they'd be better off."

A Friend of the Family

THE SUN WAS still well above the midsummer horizon when we got back to the city. It was early enough and light enough to go down to the Trianon to check on Lacey. I knew Mary Louise was right, that touching anything Global was involved in was an invitation to disaster, but I needed to find out if they were actively trying to set me up. I dropped my neighbor and the dogs at the apartment and went south, first to my office to tack together a letter authorizing me to make inquiries, then on to the Gold Coast.

The doorman at the Trianon sent me to the head of the hotel's security detail, since he was in checking his duty rosters for the upcoming week. I couldn't believe my luck when I was ushered into the office: Frank Siekevitz had been a rookie who rode with my dad for a year right after my mother died. With the ethnic insularity of some Chicagoans, Siekevitz had clung to a mentor named Warshawski. That made him doubly delighted to see me; we spent a half hour catching up not just on our lives, but on the contemporary situation in Poland.

"You didn't lose that big diamond tiara of yours at our reception for the French president, did you, Vicki?" he asked with a wink.

I'd forgotten the tiresome way my father's colleagues all use a nickname I hate. "I wish. No, I'm an investigator, private, not public."

"Yeah, private, that's where the money is. You're smart to do that. Plus you don't face the hours or the dangers you do on the force. I'm a hundred percent happier now that I'm doing private security."

Yep. That was my life. Filled with money and safety. I explained frankly that Global had hired me to keep Lucian Frenada from harassing their big star and that I wondered how much of a pest he really was. After consulting with the doorman, Siekevitz said that Frenada had been around once, on Thursday, but Lacey had brought him to her suite, where he stayed for over an hour. He had phoned twice, and she had taken both calls. Their switchboard kept a list of the people phoning her just in case a question of harassment arose.

Siekevitz actually let me look at the phone log—he knew Tony would want his little girl to get all the help she needed. "Not that you were very little when I met you, Vicki, playing forward on that high-school team of yours. My, my. Tony was that proud of you. He'd love to know you walked in his footsteps."

I gave a sickly smile, wondering what my father would really make of the life I was leading these days, and bent over the log. Teddy Trant called every day. Sometimes Lacey spoke to him, sometimes she told the operator to say she was in the health club. Regine Mauger, the *Herald-Star*'s gossip columnist, was the only person whose calls she absolutely refused to take. I felt meanly pleased by that.

When I asked if I could speak with the star myself, Siekevitz shook his head regretfully. "She went off to California for a few days, since they weren't ready to start shooting. She'll be back Thursday, from what I hear. Of course the studio is keeping the suite for her. It's only eight thousand a week. For Hollywood that's the same as a buck for you or me."

We chatted another few minutes about his private life. No, he'd never married. Never met the right woman, he guessed. He escorted me to the entrance, where I gave the doorman a ten for his pains. I walked across the park to my car: I hadn't wanted to raise doubts in the hotel staff's minds by letting them see the wreck I was driving.

As I drove home through the soft purple of early night, I thought sourly that Alex was trying to set me up. But why? Lacey Dowell clearly didn't feel bothered by Frenada. As for Murray's role in the errand, he was in so far over his head that my exasperation was tempered by sadness. Even though I wanted to see him and tell him what I'd learned from Siekevitz, I didn't want to go looking for him: it would be too painful to find him with Alex Fisher. Anyway, I didn't know where Chicago's movers shook these days—or nights. Murray used to be a regular at Lucy Moynihan's place on Lower Wacker, but that was a journalist's watering hole; television personalities drink elsewhere.

Cruising around town looking for him would really waste time I didn't have. I went virtuously home and bundled my dirty clothes into the washing machine in the basement. The phone was ringing as I let myself back into my apartment.

"Ms. Warshawski?" It was a man and a stranger. "My name is Morrell. I understand you want to talk to me."

An hour later I was sitting across from him at Drummers, a wine bar in Edgewater. Morrell was a slender man about my height, with light curly hair. That was as much as I'd been able to tell from watching him walk up the street toward me.

At the fringe of the pavement an older couple ate a late dinner, hunching toward each other to talk across the noise of the tables full of boisterous young people. I felt a twinge of envy for the woman, white-haired in the streetlight, her hand resting on the arm of the old man. Meeting a stranger for a drink because of an investigation made me feel very lonely.

I had tried to explain what I wanted to know over the phone when Morrell called, but he said he would only answer my questions if he could see me in person. He was calling from Evanston, the first suburb north of Chicago; Drummers was a halfway point between us.

"You're really a private investigator?" he asked when the waiter had brought our drinks.

"No, it's my hobby," I said, getting cranky. "My day job is wrestling alligators. Who are you, besides the man talking to people who've run away from jail?"

"Is that what the children said?" He laughed softly. "What I really want to know is who is paying you to ask questions about Nicola Aguinaldo."

I took a swallow of cabernet. It was vinegary, as if it had sat open in the bar too long. Served me right for ordering pricey wine in a neighborhood that only three years ago had been proud to serve Mogen David by the bottle.

"I'd be a mighty poor confidential investigator if I told a complete stranger who was hiring me to do a job. Especially a stranger who is asking questions about an immigrant who died in an unpleasant and, as it turns out, suspicious way. Perhaps you're an undercover INS

agent? Perhaps even an agent of the Iraqi secret police
—what are they called? Ammo or something?"

"Amn," he corrected. "Yes, I see the problem."

He tapped a finger on his coffee cup and finally decided he'd have to reveal something if I was going to
talk. "My interest is in political prisoners. I've written
on that subject off and on in various places for over a
decade. My work has appeared in places like *The New
Yorker,* but a lot of what I write is for organizations
like Americas Watch or the Grete Berman Institute.
They're the ones who commissioned this particular
book."

I'd vaguely heard of the Grete Berman Institute—a
man whose mother died in the Holocaust had endowed
it to help torture survivors recover. "This particular
book being about?"

He ate some of the nuts on the table. "I'm curious
about the life political refugees can make, whether they
find unusual obstacles or sources of strength in starting
out fresh in a new place. If a man—or woman—was a
professional in their home country, they're often wel-
comed by an academic institution, here or in Europe.
Anyway, professionals are the kind of people who most
often have the resources and contacts to emigrate once
they've been released from prison. But what of someone
outside that professional milieu who leaves home?
What happens to him then?"

The waiter stopped with the stock inquiry; I asked
him to take the cabernet away and bring me a glass of
Black Label, neat. "I see. Aisha's father."

"Yes. Aisha's father. What led you to him?"

I smiled. "I grew up in an immigrant neighborhood
much like Aisha's and Mina's. There's no such thing as
a secret among the children, especially if it involves

someone like you—or me—coming in from the outside."

"Yes, I always worry about who the children will talk to, but if you swear them to secrecy it only makes them behave more suspiciously to strangers. I heard about you from them. That you were a cop who came around with a police dog. Looking for Señora Mercedes."

I took a sip of whisky. "If you came home with me I'd introduce you to the police dog. She's an eight-year-old retriever with the incurable friendliness of all goldens. I wasn't trying to sniff out Señora Mercedes with her. Or I was, but not with deportation in mind. Her daughter ran away from the prison wing of Coolis Hospital a week ago today and ended up dead a few hundred yards from her old front door."

"And what's your interest in the young woman?"

"I found her lying in the road Tuesday night. She died a few hours later in the operating room at Beth Israel, of advanced peritonitis caused by a severe blow to the abdomen. I'd like to know how she got from Coolis to Balmoral and who inflicted that desperate injury on her."

"Are you usually this quixotic, Ms. Warshawski? Spending your life investigating deaths of poor immigrant prison escapees?"

His mocking tone nettled me, as perhaps he intended. "Invariably. It makes a nice change from wrestling alligators, to meet people as uniformly civil and helpful as you."

"Whoof." He sucked in a breath. "I apologize: I earned that. I'm not often in Chicago. Who could I talk to who knows your work?"

That was fair. Why should he give confidential information to a stranger? I gave him Lotty's name and asked him for a reference in return. He knew Vishnikov from forensic work the pathologist had done in South America for the Berman Institute.

The older couple behind me paid their bill. They strolled across the street to the car, their arms around each other. I felt more forlorn than ever.

"If you know Vishnikov, maybe you can remind him about Nicola Aguinaldo's body. It's disappeared from the morgue. Tomorrow I hope to find out what it would cost to do an analysis of Aguinaldo's clothes, if the private lab that looked at them still has them, but it would be so much easier if I knew where her body was. If her mother has it, how did she learn her daughter was dead? She left the old apartment the morning of the day I found Nicola. Some official-looking men came around and scared the neighborhood, as I'm sure you must know."

I paused and finally Morrell gave a grudging half nod.

"So who were the men?" I continued. "State marshals sent by the prison to look for Nicola? INS agents, as the neighbors suspected? Private agents of a large security firm? At any rate, since Señora Mercedes vanished, the men haven't been back. So they were looking either for Señora Mercedes or her daughter. If one of your contacts in that neighborhood would tell you the mother's whereabouts, maybe you'd be the man to talk her into getting the autopsy done."

Morrell didn't say anything. I became aware of the waiter and bus crew hovering around our table. It was eleven o'clock; the only other people still at a table were a young couple buried in each other's necks. I fished a ten out of my wallet. The waiter swooped on it while the crew quickly cleared the table.

Morrell handed a couple of singles to me. We walked down the street together toward Foster, where we'd both parked. Drummers was only seven or eight blocks from where I'd found Aguinaldo's body, but it might as well have been seven or eight miles.

"I wish I knew someone who could tell me about Aguinaldo's life before she was arrested," I burst out as Morrell stopped at his car. "Did she have a boyfriend who beat her up when she came home, then left her to die in the street? Or was it her wealthy employer—she thought he would help her when she ran away from jail, but he hurt her instead? Someone in that building on Wayne knows, at least knows who she was sleeping with."

He hesitated, as if debating whether to speak. Finally he pulled out a card and gave it to me.

"I'll talk to Aisha's family and see if they know anything about Señora Mercedes. I've never met her personally. If I learn anything that may be helpful to you I'll call you. And you can reach me through the number on the card."

It was the local number for the press agency that represented him. I put it in my hip pocket and turned to cross the street.

"By the way," he said casually, "who *is* paying for you to ask these questions?"

I turned to face him again. "Are you asking in a more subtle way if INS is bankrolling me?"

"Just wondering how quixotic you really are."

I pointed across the street. "See that late-model wreck? I'm quixotic enough for that to be the car I can afford to drive."

I climbed into the Skylark and turned it around, with a roar of exhaust that made me sound like a teenage boy. Morrell's Honda moved sleekly to the intersection ahead of me. He must make some money writing about torture victims; the car was new. But what did that prove? Even a person with strong principles has to live on something, and it wasn't as though he was driving a Mercedes or a Jag. Of course, I had no idea what his principles were.

Spinning Wheels, Seeking Traction

IN THE MORNING I went to my office early: I had a meeting with potential new clients at eleven, and I didn't want my personal searches to make me late. I looked Morrell up on the Web.

He had written a book about psychological as well as physical torture as a means to suppress protest in Chile and Argentina. He had covered the return to civilian government in Uruguay and what that meant for the victims of torture in a long essay in *The Atlantic Monthly*. His work on SAPO forces in Zimbabwe had won a Pulitzer prize after its serialization in *The New Yorker*.

Zimbabwe? I wondered if he and Baladine had met there. Although Baladine probably hadn't actually gone to southern Africa. He would have directed operations from the Rapelec tower on east Illinois Street, or perhaps met their South African customers in London.

The *Herald-Star* had interviewed Morrell when the Chile book came out. From that I learned he was about fifty, that he'd been born in Cuba but grew up in Chicago, had studied journalism at Northwestern, and still followed the Cubs despite living away from home most of his adult life. And that he only went by his last name; the reporter hadn't been able to dig his first name out of him. Although they had his initials—C.L.—he wouldn't divulge the name.

I wondered idly what his parents had called him. Maybe he'd been given some name commemorating a great battle or economic triumph that was so embarrassing he dropped it. Was he Cuban, or had his parents been there with a multinational or the army when he was born? Maybe they'd named him for some Cuban epic, like the Ten Years War, and he'd shed it as soon as he could. I was tempted to hunt through old immigration or court records to come up with it, but I knew that impulse was only frustration at not being able to get a sense of direction.

To change sources of frustration, I turned to the LifeStory report I'd requested on Frenada. I'd invested in a priority turnaround—not the fastest, which sets you back a few grand, but overnight, which was expensive enough. I saved the report to a floppy and printed it out.

Frenada's personal finances were simple enough for a child of eight to decipher. He had an interest-bearing checking account, where his expenses more or less equaled the thirty-five hundred dollars he took home from his business each month. The business, Special-T Uniforms, was nine years old. It had grown from annual receivables of six thousand to over four hundred thousand.

Frenada was writing regular tuition checks to St. Remigio's Catholic school for two children—not his own as far as I knew. At least there was no record of a marriage, or any indication of a child-support agreement. He averaged seven hundred dollars a month each on his American Express and MasterCard, for the ordinary business of living. He held a certificate of deposit for twenty thousand dollars. He was paying a mortgage on a $150,000 two-flat in the Irving Park neighborhood, and he had a life-insurance policy worth a hundred thousand dollars, with three children named Caliente listed as the beneficiaries. Besides that munificence, he drove a four-year-old Taurus that he'd just about paid for.

No holdings in the Caymans, no portfolio of stocks or options. No residue of the drug trade, no unusual income of any kind that might indicate blackmail. Frenada was either extremely honest, or so clever that not even LifeStory's paid informants could track his holdings.

So what did Murray and Alex-Sandy think was buried here? If it was a juvenile crime, I wasn't interested in digging that far into his past. Maybe he'd done a quasilegal deal to get preferred treatment in orders or to obtain financing. That didn't seem any different from Baladine and Rapelec in Africa, except the scale was smaller.

I reached Murray in his office. "I can't take on this Frenada assignment. Since you came along with Alex to try to hire me, I assume I can tell you without needing to talk to her."

"Yeah, I'll tell her. Any particular reason?"

I stared at the floor, noticing the dust bunnies that had gathered around my copier. "I'm busy these days," I said after too long a silence. "An inquiry like this would take more resources than I have."

"Thanks for trusting me, Vic. I'll tell Alex you're too busy."

His anger, more hurt than rage, made me say quickly, "Murray. You don't know what Global's real agenda is here, do you?"

"Alex talked the situation over with me on Friday," he said stiffly. "If it sounds incredible to you, then it's because you don't understand the way Hollywood operates. Everything is image for them, so the image becomes more real than the actual world around them. Lacey's success and Global's image are intertwined. They want—"

"I know what they want, babe," I said gently. "I just don't know why they want it. In the matter of the actual world, I talked to the house dick at the Trianon. I don't know if he'd be as forthcoming with you as he was with me, but you might check him out."

We hung up on that fractured note. Poor Murray. I didn't think I could bear to witness his vulnerability if Global took him to pieces.

Mary Louise came in around ten, after she'd gotten Nate and Josh off to day camp. She was going to make phone calls to Georgia for me while I pitched my wares to a couple of lawyers who were looking for a firm to handle their investigations. Such meetings often lead nowhere, but I have to keep doing it—and with enough enthusiasm that I'm not defeating myself walking in the door.

"You call this Alex woman to say you weren't playing Global's game?" Mary Louise asked as I gathered presentation materials into my briefcase.

"Yes, ma'am, Officer Neely." I saluted her smartly. "At least, I told Murray."

The phone rang before I could leave; I hovered in the doorway while Mary Louise answered. Her expression became wooden.

"Warshawski Investigations . . . No, this is Detective Neely. Ms. Warshawski is leaving for a meeting. I'll see if she can take your call. . . . Speaking of the devil," she added to me, her finger on the HOLD button.

I came back to the desk.

"Vic, I'm disappointed that you won't take the job for me," Alex said in lieu of a greeting. "I'd like you to think it over—for your sake as well as Lacey's—before I take your no as final."

"I've thought it over, Sandy—Alex, I mean. Thought it over, talked it over with my advisers. We all agree it's not the right assignment for me. But I know the house detective at the Trianon; you can trust him to look after Lacey for you."

"You talked to Lacey after I expressly asked you not to?" Her tone was as sharp as a slap in the face.

"You're piquing me, Sandy. What would Lacey tell me that you'd rather I didn't hear?"

"My name is Alex now. I wish you'd make an effort to remember. Teddy Trant really wants you to take this job. He asked me personally to offer it to you."

So maybe Abigail was putting a finger in my pie. "I'm excited. I didn't think the big guy knew I was on the planet. Unless BB Baladine told him?"

That made her huffy. "He knows about you because I recommended you. After Murray gave you a glowing buildup, I might add."

"I'm grateful to both of you, but the answer is still no."

"Then you're making a big mistake. Think it—"

"That almost sounds like a threat, Sandy. Alex, that is."

"Friendly advice. Although why I bother I don't know. Think it over, think it better. I'll leave the offer open until noon tomorrow." She broke the connection with a snap.

"Murray can do better for himself than that" was Mary Louise's only comment when I repeated the conversation before taking off.

My presentation went well; the lawyers gave me a small job with the prospect of bigger ones to follow. When I got back at four, Mary Louise had completed her calls and typed up a neat report for me to send over to Continental United in the morning. Altogether a more productive day than I'd had lately.

I finished my share of the report and went over to Lotty's. We try to get together once a week, but tonight was our first chance for a relaxed conversation in over a month.

While we ate smoked salmon on her tiny balcony, I caught Lotty up on the little I knew of Nicola Aguinaldo's story. When I told her about Morrell, Lotty went into her study and brought out a copy of *Vanishing into Silence,* his book on the Disappeared in Chile and Argentina. I looked at the photograph on the jacket flap. Of course I'd only seen Morrell by candlelight, and he was seven or eight years younger in the picture, but it was obviously the same man. He had a thin face and was smiling slightly, as if mocking himself for posing for a photograph.

I borrowed the book from her—I wanted to get an idea of how Morrell thought, or at least what he thought. After that, Lotty and I talked idly about other matters. Lotty's is an intense, sometimes stormy presence, but in her home, with its polished floors and vivid colors, I always find a reassuring haven.

Lotty's workday starts at six. I left early, my mood benign enough to take on dull household tasks: I put my laundry away, cleaned the mold out of the bathtub, washed down the kitchen cabinets and floor. The bedroom could use a vacuuming, but my domesticity spreads only so far. I planted myself in front of the piano and began picking out a fughetta with slow, loud fingers.

It's possible, as the detective at the Trianon had said yesterday, that my dad would have loved to see me follow in his footsteps, but I knew my mother would not. She wanted me to live a life of erudition if not artistry, to inhabit the milieu the second World War had destroyed for her—concerts, books, voice lessons, friends who lived for music and art. She had made me learn both piano and voice, hoping I would have the vocal career the war had taken from her. She certainly would have resented anyone who called me a blue-collar girl.

I moved from the fughetta to warming up my voice, which I hadn't done for several weeks. I was finding my middle range when the phone rang. It was Morrell.

"Ms. Warshawski. I'm in the neighborhood. Can I come up for a minute?"

"I'm not ready for company. Can't we do this on the phone?"

"I'd rather not. And I won't be company—I'll be gone so fast you almost won't know I was there."

I'd changed into cutoffs for my housework, and my arms and legs were streaked with dirt. So be it. If he wanted to drop in on me unawares, he had to take me as I was. I went back to my middle voice and let Mr. Contreras and the dogs answer the bell when Morrell rang.

I waited a minute before going out to the landing. My neighbor was interrogating Morrell: "Is she expecting you this late at night, young man? She never mentioned you before that I ever heard of."

I laughed a little but ran down the stairs in my bare feet before the woman who lived opposite Mr. Contreras came out to complain about the noise. "It's okay. He's got some information for a case I'm working on."

I introduced Morrell to Peppy. "This is the police dog. The big guy is her son. And this is my neighbor and good friend, Mr. Contreras."

The old man had been looking hurt that I hadn't told him about Morrell earlier, but my introduction appeased him slightly. He took the dogs back inside the apartment after only a very small discourse on how I needed to let him know what strangers to expect when the police were on my butt.

Morrell followed me up the stairs. "I suppose with a neighbor like that you don't need a security system. Reminds me of the villages in Guatemala, where people seem to look out for each other more than we do here."

"He drives me crazy half the time, but you're right: I'd feel mighty lost without him."

I ushered Morrell to the stuffed armchair and sat astride the piano bench. In the lamplight I saw that his thick hair was streaked with white and the laugh lines around his eyes were more deeply grooved than in his book-jacket photo.

"This really will take only a minute, but my years in South America make me nervous about giving confidential information over the phone. I managed to find Nicola Aguinaldo's mother. She didn't know her daughter was dead. And she definitely doesn't have her body."

I looked at him narrowly, but there's no real way to tell whether people are lying to you or not. "I'd like to talk to Señora Mercedes myself. Can you tell me where you found her?"

He hesitated. "She's not likely to confide in a stranger."

"She confided in you, and last night you assured me you'd never laid eyes on her."

His mouth twitched in the suggestion of a smile. "I've talked to a couple of people about your work, and they were right: you are a very astute observer. Can you please take my word for it, that Señora Mercedes doesn't have her daughter's body?"

I picked out a minor triad in the bass clef. "I'm getting fed up with people pushing me toward Aguinaldo with one hand and pulling me away from her with the other. There's something wrong with how she died, but you seem to be joining the group of break-dancers writhing on stage, saying, 'Watch,' 'Don't watch.' I need to find someone who knows about Aguinaldo's private life. Her mother may not, but her kid might. Children know a lot about what their mothers get up to."

He drummed his fingers on the chair arm, thinking it over, but finally shook his head. "The trouble is, the more people who talk to Señora Mercedes, the riskier her position becomes."

"Riskier how?"

"Deportation. She wants to stay in America so that her surviving granddaughter can get an education and make something more of herself than being a nanny or a factory hand. I can try to find out something for you, if you'd like. . . ." His voice trailed away, leaving it as a question.

I agreed somewhat grumpily. I hate leaving a crucial piece of an investigation in someone else's hands, especially when I don't know anything about his skills.

He got up to leave but stopped to admire the piano.

"You must be a serious musician to keep a baby grand in your living room. I play some, but not on anything this nice."

"My mother was a serious musician. One of her old friends keeps this in shape for me, but I never made it past Thompson's fourth book." I loved action too much, even as a child, and my hours of practice were a misery when I longed to be running or swimming.

Morrell gave the same self-mocking smile he'd shown in his photo and sat down to try the piano. He ran through part of a Chopin nocturne with unusual feeling for an amateur. When he saw "Erbarme dich" on the music rack, he started to play and I began to sing. Bach produces a certain kind of balm. When Morrell got up to go, with an apology for showing off, I felt calmer but no more certain than I was earlier whether he was telling the truth about Nicola Aguinaldo's mother. But if she didn't have the body, where was it?

Perhaps those researchers who want you to listen to Bach or Mozart to boost your brain are right, because when he left I had an idea for the morning. It wasn't the best idea I ever had, as it turned out, but that wasn't really Bach's fault.

I went down to Mr. Contreras's when I heard the front door shut. As I'd expected, my neighbor was waiting up to see how long I kept a strange man in my apartment.

"How would you like to go on a wild-goose chase with me tomorrow?" I asked him before he could comment on Morrell. "Be a grieving grandfather whose darling baby ran away from jail and died a sad death?"

He revived instantly.

18

These Walls Do a Prison Make

THE NEXT MORNING, while Mary Louise sat at my desk organizing files, I collected my maps and set out with Mr. Contreras and the dogs for the long drive across the state to Coolis. The muffler was rumbling more loudly than ever. The air-conditioning didn't work, so we had to ride with the windows open and our teeth rattling.

"That muffler wasn't this bad when we picked up the car," Mr. Contreras observed when we stopped at the Elgin toll plaza to throw in our quarters. "Guy must have stuck it on with duct tape to sell this heap."

"Let's hope the thing holds together until we're back in Chicago."

The dogs kept their heads out the windows, periodically switching sides as we moved into the real country and they picked up the scent of the river. West of Rockford we pulled over at a rest area for lunch. Mr. Contreras was a willing but uncertain partner in the outing; while the dogs swam in the Fox River we went over his lines until he felt confident enough to fly solo.

Even with that long break, by keeping the Rustmobile roaring at its top speed—around seventy—we managed to get to Coolis a little after twelve. It was a pretty town, built in a valley of two small rivers feeding the Mississippi: the big river lies ten miles to the west. Coolis had been a lead-mining hub in the 1800s, but was close to death when the state decided to build its new women's prison here.

I'd never known who in Coolis had enough money or clout to grease Jean-Claude Poilevy's wheels, but as we drove through town to the prison, we passed Baladine Hardware, followed by Baladine Lincoln–Mercury. I could see BB as a boy at Baladine Hardware, playing with the combination locks and fantasizing about someday playing with really big locks and keys. As a friend of Poilevy's, Baladine would have had the inside track anyway on where the legislature awarded the prison contract, but the decision to build in his family's town must have taken a major contribution to the Republican party coffers.

Illinois seems like a large place when you look at a map, stretching four hundred miles from Wisconsin to Missouri, but it's really just a cozy little hometown, where everybody knows everybody else and nobody tells secrets outside the family. Businesses pay money to politicians to get even greater amounts of money pumped back to them via state contracts, and while some of it may be scuzzy, none of it's illegal—because the guys who have their hands in one another's pockets are writing the laws.

The prison stood two miles west of town; scraggly strip malls had grown up along the route. Signs warned drivers against hitchhikers, since they might be escaped prisoners and should be considered dangerous. Women like Nicola Aguinaldo, for instance, might bleed all over you; that would be bad.

Even Mr. Contreras grew quiet when we passed the front gate. Three layers of high fencing, with razor wire along the tops and current running through the outer-most, separated us from the prison. It looked in some ways like a modern industrial park, with its low white buildings laid out in a kind of campus—except that the windows were mere slits, like the arrow holes in a medi-eval castle. Also like a castle, watchtowers holding armed guards covered the perimeter. A kind of reverse castle, where the guards thought the enemy lay within rather than without.

Although the land around the prison was dotted with wildflowers and trees, inside what wasn't concrete had become hardscrabble from too many marching feet and too little care. In the distance we could see some women playing what might be softball; as they ran they kicked up dust eddies.

"Umph." Mr. Contreras let out a grunt after I turned around and headed back into town. "If you wasn't des-perate before you landed in that place, you sure would be after you'd been there a day or two. If that didn't cure you of a life of crime nothing would."

"Or it would get you feeling so hopeless you'd feel you didn't have any choices." My neighbor and I do not think as one on most social issues, but that doesn't stop his wanting to be involved in helping me tilt at whatever windmill I'm charging on a given day.

The hospital lay inside the town boundary, off the main road leading to the prison. Behind it ran Smallpox Creek, flowing northwest to the Mississippi, although not at any great pace. We let the dogs out again to cool off in the water, then checked the side roads around the hospital. Just as my maps had shown, you could either go directly to jail or into town from the hospital, but you didn't have any other choice for escape than the creek. After driving the route long enough to memorize it we returned to the hospital and parked.

Coolis General had started as a small brick building. With the arrival of the prison and wealth, two enormous wings had been attached, giving it the appearance of a dragonfly. We walked up a long path, past beds of summer flowers, to the entrance, which was in the old part, the body of the insect. Signs directed visitors to the Connie Brest Baladine Surgicenter, to radiology, and to patient information.

"Howdy," Mr. Contreras said to the bored woman at the information desk. "I need to talk to someone about my granddaughter. She—well, she was a patient here up to last week, and things didn't turn out too good for her."

The woman braced herself. I could see *what to do if family threatens a malpractice suit* running through her mind as she asked Mr. Contreras for his granddaughter's name.

"Nicola Aguinaldo." He spelled it for her. "I ain't saying we blame the hospital or anything, but I sure would like to know how she come in and how she left and all. She—well, she got herself in a little bit of trouble up in Chicago, and she was over here in Coolis, in the jail, when she took sick."

Once he got past his initial nervousness, he was in full stride. I began to believe that Nicola Aguinaldo really had been his granddaughter, with the family that worried about her, but you know how it is with today's young people, you can't ever tell them nothing. The woman at the desk kept trying to interrupt him—she wanted to explain that she couldn't talk to him about patients, especially not when they were prisoners, but she finally gave up and summoned a superior.

In a few minutes a woman about my own age showed up. If she'd been sprayed with polyurethane she couldn't have been glossier or more untouchable. She introduced herself as Muriel Paxton, the head of patient affairs, and invited us to follow her to her office. The back of her crimson suit barely moved as she walked, as though she'd figured out how to use her legs without involving her pelvis.

Like all modern hospitals, Coolis General had spared no expense on their administrative offices. Radical mastectomies may be done now as outpatient procedures, but heaven forbid that management skimps on any attention to comfort. Muriel Paxton enthroned herself behind a slab of rosewood that clashed with the red of her suit. Mr. Contreras and I, feet sinking to our ankles in the lavender pile on the floor, sat in faux-wicker side chairs.

"Why don't we start with your names." Ms. Paxton held a pen like a dagger over a legal pad.

"This is Nicola Aguinaldo's grandfather," I said, "and I'm the family lawyer."

I spelled my last name slowly. As I hoped, the presence of a lawyer kept Ms. Paxton from demanding Mr. Contreras's name—he didn't want to call himself Aguinaldo, and he'd told me on the way over if he was going to take part in this scheme he didn't want his name taken down.

"And what seems to be the problem?" The administrator's smile was as bright as her lipstick, but no warmth came with it.

"The problem is, my little girl is dead. I want to know how she could have got out of here with no one the wiser."

Ms. Paxton put the pen down and leaned forward, a

motion learned in media training school: lean forward forty-five degrees to show concern. It wasn't reflected in her eyes.

"If a patient wants to check out, even if it's not in her best medical interest, there's little we can do to stop her, Mr. Uh—"

"Huh, that's a laugh. She come over from the jail, in chains like as not, and you say she can check herself out if she wants to? Then I bet the waiting list from the jail over to here must be five miles long. How come we never was told she had female problems? How come when she called home she never said nothing about that, that's what I'd like to know. You tell me you can let someone waltz away from this hospital without their family knowing they was even in here to begin with?"

"Mr. Uh, I assure you that every precaution—"

"And another thing, who even did the diagnosis—some prison warden? She didn't have nothing wrong with her that we ever heard of. Not one person from this hospital got in touch with us to say, 'Your baby is sick, do we have your permission to do surgery?' or whatever it was you was planning on doing. What happened—did you mess up on the surgery and—"

I had briefed Mr. Contreras as best I could over lunch, but I needn't have worried: with the bit in his teeth not much short of a bullet can stop him. Ms. Paxton kept trying to interrupt, growing progressively more angry at each failure.

"Now, now," I said soothingly. "We don't know that they did surgery, sir. Can you look up Ms. Aguinaldo's record and let us know what you did do?"

Ms. Paxton jabbed her computer keys. Of course, without a subpoena she shouldn't tell us anything, but I was hoping she was angry enough to forget that part of her training. Whatever she saw on the screen made her become very still. When she finally spoke it was without the fury that I had been counting on to push her to indiscretion.

"Who did you say you were?" she demanded.

"I'm a lawyer and an investigator." I tossed my card onto her desk. "And this is my client. How did you come to let Ms. Aguinaldo out of the hospital?"

"She ran away. She must have feigned her illness as an excuse for—"

"You calling my baby a liar?" Mr. Contreras was indignant. "If that don't beat the Dutch. You think because she was poor, because she went to jail trying to look after her own little girl, you think she made up—"

Ms. Paxton's smile became glacial. "Most of the prisoners who seek medical care either have injured themselves on the job or in a fight, or they are malingering. In your granddaughter's case, without the permission of the doctor in charge I am not at liberty to reveal her medical record. But I assure you she left here of her own free will."

"As my client said earlier, if anyone can walk out of here of her own free will, you must have a prison full of people trying to injure themselves in order to get moved to the hospital."

"Security is extremely tight." Her lips were opened only wide enough to spit the words out.

"I don't believe you," Mr. Contreras huffed. "You look at that machine of yours, you'll see she was just a little bit of a thing. You brung her over in a ball and chain, and you telling me she sawed it off?"

In the end, he got her angry enough that she phoned someone named Daisy to say she had a lawyer here who needed proof that you couldn't get out of the prison ward. She swept out of her office so fast that we almost had to run to keep up with her. Her high heels clicked across the tile floors as if she were tap dancing, but she still didn't move her hips. We trotted past the information desk, down a corridor where various hospital staff greeted Ms. Paxton with the anxious deference you always see displayed to the bad-tempered in positions of power. She didn't slow her twinkling tapping across the tiles but did nod in response, like the Queen of England acknowledging her subjects.

She led us behind the hospital to a locked ward separated from the main hospital by three sets of doors. Each was opened electronically, by a man behind thick glass, and the one behind you had to shut before the one in front of you could open. It was like the entrance to the Fourth Circle in Dante. By the time we were in the prison ward I was pretty much abandoning hope.

Like the rest of Coolis General, the ward was built out of something white and shiny, but it had been created with the prison in mind: the windows once again were mere slits in the wall. So much for my idea that Nicola had jumped out a window when the staff's back was turned.

A guard inspected Mr. Contreras's pockets and my handbag and told us to sign in. Mr. Contreras cast me an angry look, but signed his name. When I filled mine in below his, I doubted whether any state employee could have found him by his signature—it looked like *Oortneam*. Ms. Paxton merely flashed her hospital badge—the guard knew her by sight.

Inside the third door we were met by Daisy—Nurse Lundgren to us—the ward head. She looked coldly at Ms. Paxton and demanded to know what the problem was.

"These people are concerned with the escape of that color—that girl, that young person who got away last week." Ms. Paxton's realization that the colored girl's grandfather and lawyer were present flustered her. "I want them to see that this ward is very secure. And that however the girl got away it wasn't through any negligence on our part."

Nurse Lundgren frowned. "Are you sure you want me talking to them? The memo from Captain Ruzich was very clear on the subject."

Ms. Paxton smiled with more menace than a mere frown could convey. "I'm relying on your discretion, Daisy. But the grandfather has driven all the way from Chicago. I'd like him to see that we do take proper precautions when prisoners are entrusted to our care."

"Very well," the nurse said. "I'll take them onto the ward. I expect you have enough work of your own without needing to come with us."

Ms. Paxton seemed to be of two minds whether to fight Lundgren in front of us but finally swiveled on her motionless hips and stalked away.

"How many escapes have you had from the hospital?" I asked as we followed the nurse into the locked ward.

"Five," the nurse said. "But that was before this wing was built. It used to be fairly easy to jump out a window, even if it had bars, because the girls knew how to finagle their way into the cafeteria or some other place they weren't meant to be."

I glanced in a room as we passed. It was empty; Lundgren didn't object when I asked to inspect it. It had the tiny arrow holes of the prison, and no bathroom: Lundgren said the women had to use a bathroom in the hall, which was kept locked and was opened by a

correctional officer. The hospital couldn't afford to
have hiding places in the room where an inmate could
either lie in wait to attack—or kill herself in private.

In the next room a woman was lying in bed, sleeping
heavily, wasted as my mother had been by her cancer.
Across the hall a young woman with dark curly hair
was watching television. It was only when I looked
closely that I saw she was handcuffed to the bed.

"How are you feeling, Veronica?" Lundgren called
as we passed.

"I'm okay, Nurse. How's my baby?"

Veronica had given birth early that morning. She'd
be returned to the prison in another couple of days,
where she could keep her infant for four months. Coolis
was progressive that way, the nurse explained, releasing
the lock on the door that separated the nurses' station
from the ward. She cut short a flirtation between one of
her subordinates and the corrections officer assigned to
guard the hall, telling her junior to pay attention to the
ward while she talked to us.

"It's hard for them to work here—it isn't like real
nursing, and then they get bored when the ward is as
empty as it is right now."

She led us into a tiny room behind the nurses' station
that held a table, a microwave, and a small television. It
was the one room on the floor with actual windows,
but as these were made of wire-enforced glass they
didn't offer much of a view.

Lundgren took us through the statistics of the floor
without any hesitation. There were twenty beds, but
they never had more than eight or ten of them filled,
except one disastrous occasion when there was a major
food-poisoning outbreak at the jail and some of the
patients with heart trouble came close to dying.

As to how easy or hard it was for an inmate to get to the hospital, she wasn't privy to prison decisions, but in her experience, women were pretty sick before they were brought over. "Girls are always trying to get over here. The hospital food is better and the routine is easier to take. In jail there are counts every six hours, and lockdowns and all the rest of it. For someone serving a long sentence the hospital can seem like a vacation. So the prison makes it hard for anyone to malinger."

"And Nicola Aguinaldo? How sick was she when she came here?"

Her lips tightened, and her hands moved uneasily in her lap. "I thought she was quite ill. So ill I was surprised that she was able to move enough to leave."

"What was the problem?" Mr. Contreras demanded. "Was it some kind of woman problem? That's what the cops told me, but she never said nothing about that to her ma—"

"A doctor didn't actually examine her before she left. I was told by the prison nurse that they suspected an ovarian cyst. But before a doctor could see her, she was gone."

"How did that little bit of a thing get away from you and the guard and everyone?" Mr. Contreras demanded.

Lundgren didn't look at us. "I wasn't on duty when it happened. I was told she used her small size to follow behind the laundry cart, on the side away from the guard, and that she probably concealed herself in the cart when the janitor stopped to talk to someone. In theory the laundry would be inspected before leaving this ward, but in practice they probably let it go through without poking at it: no one wants to touch soiled linens. A number of the women have AIDS."

"And you believe Aguinaldo escaped that way?" I asked, keeping my voice neutral. "Wasn't she cuffed to the bed?"

Lundgren nodded. "But these girls have nothing to do all day long except figure out how to use a hairpin on their handcuffs. It happens now and then that one of them gets loose, but since the ward is locked it doesn't do them much good. I don't think there's anything else I can tell you. If you'd like some time alone in the chapel before you set out, I can have an orderly show you to it. Otherwise he'll escort you to the main entrance."

I left my card on the table when we got up to leave. "In case something else occurs to you that you'd like me to know about, Nurse."

On the way out, Mr. Contreras exploded with frustration. "I don't believe it. A laundry cart, huh? Things ain't bigger than a minute, and not even Nicola was that tiny. I want you to sue them. Sue them for—what was it you said—not taking due something?"

Veronica, the woman who'd had the baby, managed to be in the hall, cuffed to the orderly, who was escorting her back from the bathroom. "You know Nicola? What happened to her?"

"She's dead," I said. "Do you know why she was in the hospital?"

Nurse Lundgren appeared next to us. "You can't be talking to the patients, ma'am. They're inmates even if they're in the hospital. Veronica, you're well enough to parade the hall, you're well enough to get back to the house. Jock, you can take these visitors out to the main entrance. Show them where the chapel is before you come back."

Veronica looked momentarily furious, then, as if her

powerlessness were something she'd just remembered, her shoulders sank and her face crumpled into despair.

Jock gave permission to the man behind the glass wall to release the doors. At the entrance to the main hospital wing, he pointed down a hall to the chapel.

19

Power Dining

So WHAT DO you think, doll?" Mr. Contreras asked as he buckled himself into the seat. "That nurse seemed mighty uneasy. And how would a little thing like that girl was get out of a place like that?"

I didn't have an answer. Nurse Lundgren seemed competent, and even, for the setting, compassionate. I agreed she'd seemed uncomfortable, but it would be easy for me to read into that what I wanted to. Maybe she was troubled at the loss of a patient rather than covering up special knowledge of Aguinaldo's escape.

We drove over to Smallpox Creek to let the dogs cool off again before the drive home. Mr. Contreras, suddenly seeing Nicola Aguinaldo as a person, not an illegal immigrant or a criminal, was subdued during the ride. We got home a little before six. Mary Louise had shoved a packet underneath the locked inner door with a report on her day's work. She had delivered our report to Continental United; the human resources vice president had called to say they were delighted with our work, but that they thought they would have to send someone down to Georgia to check on things in person. And that someone would likely be me—unless Baladine persuaded the company to turn all their work over to Carnifice.

I didn't want to hang about the back roads of Georgia, waiting for someone with a tire iron to hit me on the head. On the other hand, if I stayed in Chicago I might start doing unlucrative things like tailing Morrell, to see if a man worried about committing himself on the phone might drive to Nicola Aguinaldo's mother's home.

A man named Rieff phoned from Cheviot Labs at eleven, Mary Louise had written in her round schoolgirl hand. *He says he can provide a printout of what is on Aguinaldo's dress, but he does not know how meaningful it is. It was a long T-shirt with Lacey Dowell as the Mad Virgin on it. A label said it was a specialty shirt but did not identify where it was manufactured. There are traces of sweat, which are presumably Aguinaldo's, but without a DNA sample he couldn't say. There is a trace of cigarette ash around the inside of the neck. He is not charging for that information because the analysis was already done when they inspected the dress last week, but if you want to know what brand of cigarette, that will cost around two hundred extra.*

Cigarette ash around the inside of the neck? I wondered if Aguinaldo was a smoker, and how hard or easy it was to drop ash down your own neckline if you smoked.

I turned back to Mary Louise's notes. *At two o'clock Alex Fisher phoned. She wanted to know if you had thought over her offer any more. I said you were out of town for the day and would get back to her in the morning; she urged me to push you to take the job, it would mean a lot for your agency one way or another however you decided. Vic, what does this woman want?*

She'd underscored the question several times. I was

with her there: what did Alex want? What was Teddy Trant going to do to me if I didn't dig around in Frenada's affairs? Put a V chip in my TV so I was forced to watch nothing but Global programs? If Abigail Trant had persuaded her husband to give me some work, was that enough reason for him to be surly at my refusal to accept it?

Of course the other connection to Global was Lacey Dowell. She, or at least her face, kept cropping up. Now she was on the shirt Nicola Aguinaldo had on when she died. Was Global's big star involved in something so ugly the studio wanted to pin it on Frenada? But there was nothing to link Lacey with Nicola Aguinaldo, at least as far as I could tell.

Maybe I should try to see Lucian Frenada. I had entered the phone numbers Alex Fisher gave me into my Palm Pilot. When I called his home, a machine told me, in Spanish and English, that Frenada regretted not answering my call in person, but that he was perhaps at his factory and would get back to me if I left a message.

I thought it over, then got up abruptly and went downstairs. If Frenada was perhaps at his factory I could see him in person. My back was stiff. A nagging sensible voice—Mary Louise's or Lotty's—told me if I had to poke at this wasp's nest at all to do it in the morning. Or at least to take my gun, but what was I going to do with it—pistol-whip him into telling me what secret Trant wanted me to find?

There is no direct route from my place to Frenada's factory. I snaked south and west, through streets filled with small frame houses and four-plus-one's, past boys skateboarding or in small gangs on their bikes, now and then crossing pockets of lights around bars and pool halls. As I passed the fringes of Humboldt Park, the streets revved up with boom boxes and low-riders but died away again at the seedy industrial corridor along Grand Avenue.

A freight line cuts northwest through the area, making for oddly shaped buildings designed to fill odd lot sizes right up to the embankment. A train was rumbling past as I pulled in front of a dingy triangular building near the corner of Trumbull and Grand.

Lights blazed through open windows on the second floor. The outer door was shut but unlocked. A naked bulb glared just inside the entrance. Drunken letters in a notice board listed a wig manufacturer and a box maker on the ground floor. Special-T Uniforms was on two. As I climbed concrete steps slippery with age, light glinted on long falls of hair in a display case. It was like walking behind the guillotine after dark.

The noise coming down the stairwell sounded as though fifty guillotines were all whacking heads in unison. I followed light and sound along a metal walkway and came to Special-T's open door. Even though it was nine at night, nearly a dozen people were working, either cutting fabric at long tables in the middle of the floor or assembling garments at machines along the wall. The racket came partly from the sewing machines, but mostly from the shears. Two men positioned layers of cloth at the end of the tables, clamped them in place under a pair of electric shears, then wielded a control box to release the blades.

I watched, fascinated, as the shears whicked through the fabric and the men carried pieces over to the sewing-machine operators. One person was sewing letters to the backs of shirts, another attaching sleeves. At least half the crew was smoking. I thought of the cigarette ash smudged into the neck of Nicola Aguinaldo's dress.

Maybe it had come from the person who made the garment, rather than from Aguinaldo herself.

Lucian Frenada was standing at one of the cutting tables next to a stocky man with thin black hair. They seemed to be discussing the proper placement of a pattern stencil. I walked over to stand in his range of vision —if I touched him to get his attention he might be startled into landing under one of the fabric scythes.

Frenada looked up, frowning. *"Si? Le puedo ayudar en algo?"*

I held out my card. "We met at Lacey Dowell's party last week," I shouted over the noise of the machinery.

The man next to him stared at me with frank curiosity: was I a girlfriend so enamored that I would pursue Frenada into his shop? Or was I with INS, about to demand that all hands produce their papers? Frenada touched his arm and said something in Spanish, then pointed at the floor, ankle-deep with scraps of cloth. The man passed a command on to one of the cutters, who stopped his work to start sweeping.

Frenada took me to a cubbyhole at the rear of the floor, which was protected enough from the floor noise to allow conversation. Fabric samples and patterns festooned the top of a metal desk; production schedules were taped to the door and the sides of an old filing cabinet. The only chair had a motor on it. Frenada leaned against the door; I perched gingerly on the edge of the desk.

"Why are you here?" he demanded.

"You mentioned Tuesday night that something odd was happening at your shop."

"Do you usually sell your services like this, door to door?"

My cheeks and neck grew warm with embarrassment, but I couldn't help smiling. "Like encyclopedias, you mean? A reporter I know has been asking questions about your business. And I remembered what you said, so I wanted to see Special-T for myself."

"What reporter? What kind of questions?"

"Wondering what secrets you were hiding here at Special-T." I watched him steadily, but he looked only puzzled, and somewhat scornful.

Another freight train began to thunder behind the building, drowning Frenada's reply. While I waited to be able to hear him, I looked around the office. On his desk, underneath one of the fabric swatches, I saw a glimpse of a slogan I knew from Emily Messenger's wardrobe: *The Mad Virgin Bites.*

The train passed, and Frenada said, "Secrets? I can't afford such things. I thought you meant—but it doesn't matter. My business runs on a shoestring; if something a little strange happens, then I have to accept it as an act of God."

"Lacey reassured you when you saw her on Thursday?"

"Did she—who told you—"

"No one. It was a deduction. That's what I do—get facts and make deductions. They teach it in detective school." I was babbling, because of the Mad Virgin T-shirt.

Frenada looked around his office and caught sight of the shirt. He got to his feet and moved me toward the door.

"My business has nothing to do with Lacey. Nothing at all. So keep your deductions to yourself, Miss Detective. And now, by another gracious act of God, I have a large order to get out, the largest I have ever been blessed with, the uniforms for a soccer league in New Jersey, which is why you find me here so late at night." He hustled me out through the shop floor to the metal walkway, waiting until I reached the stairwell landing before he turned back inside.

I put the Rustmobile into noisy gear and started for home. My route took me past St. Remigio's church and school, where Lacey Dowell and Frenada had been students twenty years ago. Lacey had learned acting there, and Frenada had started his business by making the school's soccer uniforms. I slowed down to read the times for daily mass from the signboard, wondering whether I might go in the morning, meet the priest, learn something about Frenada. But if Frenada had told his confessor why he had a Mad Virgin T-shirt half-buried under his fabric samples, I didn't think the priest would share it with me.

Was that the secret that Trant wanted me to find? Was Frenada making bootleg Virginwear clothes in his little factory and selling them in the old 'hood? In that case, it was a legitimate inquiry. Although I expected Trant used something like Burmese or Honduran slave labor for his own production, in which case I was just as happy for Frenada to sell pirated shirts employing local workers at living wages.

Sal had called while I was at the factory, wanting to see if I'd like to catch Murray's second program and get some dinner. I took the L down to the Glow so I could drink: it had been a long day and I didn't want to drive anymore, anyway. The usual crowd of tired traders was drinking, but they let me switch from the Sox on GN to Global—after all, it was only the third inning and the Sox were already down four runs.

After his debut with Lacey Dowell I wondered what

Murray could find to titillate the viewers, but I had to agree with Sal: the second show at least nodded in the direction of respectable journalism. He'd taken a sensational local murder, of a prominent developer, and used it as the springboard for a look at how contracts are awarded in the city and suburbs. Although too much of the footage showed the man at Cancun with three women in string bikinis, Murray did wedge in fifty-seven seconds on how contracts get handed out in Illinois.

"Some of it was respectable, but he was too chicken to mention Poilevy by name," I grumbled when the show ended.

"You want egg in your beer?" Sal said. "Guy can't do everything."

"I wish he'd covered the women's prison at Coolis. That'd be a great place to showcase a cozy pair of dealmakers. I'm surprised it's not called Baladine City."

"Vic, this may make sense to you, but it's Greek to me."

"Ever since that wretched party you threw here last week, I've been running around in circles. Like my dog Mitch chasing his tail, come to think of it—exhausting and about as meaningful." I told her what I'd been doing. "And don't tell me it's none of my business, because it is, even if no one is paying me for it."

"Get off your high horse, St. Joan." Sal poured me another finger of Black Label. "It's your time and money; do what you want with it."

That encouragement didn't cheer me as much as it might have, but dinner at Justin's in the west Loop—where the owner knew Sal and whisked us past a dumbfounded line of beautiful Chicagoans—made me much happier. At least until I caught sight of Alex Fisher halfway through my tuna in putanesca sauce.

I couldn't help staring. Alex was at a table with Teddy Trant and a bald man with the kind of shiny face all Illinois politicians take on after too much time snuffling around in the public trough. Jean-Claude Poilevy in person. If Trant would rather eat with him and Alex than the exquisite Abigail, there was something seriously wrong with his taste.

When we got up to leave, Alex and her convoy were still talking over coffee. Sal tried to dissuade me, but I went to their table. Trant was as perfectly groomed as his wife, down to the clear polish on his manicured nails.

"Mr. Trant," I said. "V. I. Warshawski. I wanted to let you know I appreciate your willingness to send me some work. I'm sorry I couldn't take it on for you."

Alex gave me a look that could have done laser surgery on my nose, but Trant shook my hand. "Global tries to do business with local firms. It helps us anchor ourselves in cities we're new to."

"Is that why you've been talking to Lucian Frenada?" It was a guess, based on the Mad Virgin decal I'd glimpsed at Special-T earlier in the evening, but everyone at the table froze.

Poilevy put down his coffee cup with a clatter. "Is that the guy you were—"

"Lucian Frenada is the man who's been harassing Lacey." Alex cut him off quickly and loudly.

"Sure, Sandy, sure. It's not a bad story, even if it has a few holes around the edges. Alex, I mean. She changed nicknames in the last twenty years," I added to Trant. "We were such good pals when she was Sandy, I keep forgetting she's Alex now."

"What do you mean, holes around the edges?" Poilevy asked.

"I did a little looking. I talked to Lucian Frenada. I talked to the head of security at Ms. Dowell's hotel. Maybe the studio is overreacting to the scene between Frenada and Ms. Dowell at the Golden Glow last week —understandable with an important star—but I can't find any evidence that Frenada's been hanging around her."

"That isn't what I asked you to investigate," Alex snapped.

"No, but you haven't been asked to pay me anything either, have you."

Sal came up behind me and put a hand on my arm. "Let's go, Vic. I've got to get back to the Glow—it's my night to close."

I reminded Alex and Trant that they knew Sal from last week's party. We all said meaningless nothings, about Murray's debut, about Sal's bar, but I would have given a month's billings to know what they said when Sal and I moved out of earshot. I turned to look when we got to the door; they were bent over the table like the three witches over a pot.

20

Child in Mourning

WHAT WITH THE drive to Coolis and the long night hopping around town, I was glad to crawl into bed. I read a little of Morrell's book on the Disappeared in South America, stretching my legs between clean sheets to pull the kinks out of my spine.

The phone rang as I was drifting off. I groaned but stuck out an arm and mumbled a greeting. There was a pause on the other end, then someone garbled my name in a hurried voice just above a whisper.

"Yes, this is V. I. Warshawski. Who is this?"

"It's—This is Robbie. Robbie Baladine. I was at the gate, you know, when you came last week, you know, when you talked to my mom about—about Nicola."

I came fully awake in a hurry, turning on the light as I assured him that I remembered him well. "You're the expert tracker. What can I do for you?"

"I—It's not for me, but Nicola. I want—want to go to her funeral. Do you know when it is?"

"There's a problem about that," I said carefully. "The morgue seems to have lost her body. I don't know how that happened, but until they find it there can't be a funeral."

"So he was right." His young voice was filled with a

kind of bitterness. "I thought he was making it up to—to tease me."

"Your dad?"

"Yeah, old BB." He was forgetting to whisper in his anguish. "Him and Eleanor, they've been so mean about Nicola. Since she died and all. When I said I wanted to go to her funeral, they said why, so I could stand around with all the emotional spicks and bawl to my heart's content, and then finally BB said there wouldn't be a funeral because no one could find the body and to—to shut the fuck up."

"I'm sorry, honey," I said inadequately. "I guess your dad worries about whether he's a tough enough man, and so he's always on guard against any strong feelings. I don't suppose it's much comfort to you now, but can you imagine him as someone who is incredibly weak and scared so he acts like a bully to keep other people from guessing how scared he is?"

"You think that could really be true?" There was wistfulness in the young voice, a hope that his father's meanness wasn't due to his own failings.

I thought of Baladine, casually helping with the dismemberment of African newborns, getting his hands dirty, and wondered if my diagnosis had any basis in reality. Maybe he was someone who enjoyed torture for its own sake, but I gave Robbie a hearty assurance I didn't feel.

"Your father is a cruel man. Whatever the reason for his cruelty, will you try to remember that his sadism is about him, about his needs and weaknesses, and not about you?"

I talked to him for a few more minutes, until he'd recovered enough equilibrium for me to turn the conversation. There were two questions I wanted to put to him before we hung up. The first was about Nicola's smoking. Oh, no, Robbie said, she never smoked, not like Rosario, their nanny now, who was always sneaking off behind the garage for a cigarette, which made Eleanor furious, because she could still smell the smoke on her breath even after Rosario swallowed a zillion peppermints. Nicola said she had to save all her money for her children; she couldn't waste it on cigarettes or drinking.

My second question was whether his dad owned any shoes with horseshoe emblems—and if he did, were any of the emblems missing. Robbie said he didn't know, but he'd look.

It made me feel like a creep, asking Robbie to spy on his own father—but I suppose it also made me feel like I was paying BB back for his frothing over his son's masculinity. If he'd been proud of his sensitive child I might not have done it. But if he could be proud of a sensitive child, he wouldn't be doing other stuff.

Before Robbie hung up I asked, as casually as I could, how he'd gotten my unlisted home number: it wasn't on the business card I left him last week.

"It was in BB's briefcase," Robbie muttered. "Don't tell me I'm a criminal to go snooping in his case, it's the only way I know when he's planning something awful, like that camp for fat kids he sent me to last summer. I checked it out, and he had this whole file on you, your home number and everything."

My blood ran cold. I knew Baladine had done research on me—he'd made that clear enough on Friday—but it seemed worse, somehow, his carrying the information around with him.

"Doesn't he keep his case locked?"

"Oh, that. Anyone with half a brain knows all you

have to do is plug in his ship's ID, the biggest number in his life."

I laughed and told him he was plenty smart enough to keep up with his dad if he could remember not to let BB get under his skin. In case I ever needed to burgle Baladine's briefcase myself, I got Robbie to give me his father's ship number. On that note he seemed to feel calm enough to hang up.

I finally went to sleep, but in my dreams Baladine was lugging Nicola Aguinaldo's body through Frenada's factory, while Lacey Dowell leaned heavy breasts forward, clutching her crucifix and whispering, "Her hands are dirty. Don't tell her anything, or the vampire will get you."

In the morning I had a call from the operations manager at Continental United, asking me to come in to discuss my report. He thanked me for writing so clearly that everyone could understand it: too many firms cloak the obvious in meaningless jargon, he said. Maybe it was my ability to write a clear English sentence that kept Continental coming to me, rather than my superior analytic skills.

They didn't want to fire the dispatcher without concrete evidence, the operations manager added, or without knowing whether the plant manager was in on the scam.

"If you want to spend the money you'll have to have someone on the spot doing surveillance," I said. "It'll take two people. One to handle the truck, one to operate a camera. And it has to be people who aren't at the plant, because you don't know how many employees on the ground are involved, or at least aware."

As I'd feared, they nominated me as the one to handle the camera. And they figured their fleet manager in

Nebraska could pose as a truck driver, as a walk-on for someone out sick. They were losing so much money on that route, not just from replacing tires but from lost delivery time, that they wanted me to "do what it takes, Vic; we know you're not going to pad a bill for the heck of it."

I was sort of flattered, although, remembering Alex-Sandy's scorn for my low fees, I wondered if it was more a description of a low-rent outfit than a compliment. My man made a call to Nebraska; the fleet manager would meet me in Atlanta tomorrow night. A nice bonus for me if we wrapped it up quickly.

From Continental United's offices I went to the Unblinking Eye. They carry surveillance matériel as well as running a more prosaic film and camera business. I talked to the surveillance specialist about the kind of equipment I ought to use. They had some marvelous gadgets—a still camera that fit in a button, one that was disguised in a wristwatch, even one in the kid's teddy bear if you wanted to watch the nanny. Too bad Eleanor Baladine hadn't trained one on Nicola Aguinaldo. Or maybe she had—the Baladines probably had every up-to-the-moment security device you might want.

I settled on a video camera that you wore like a pair of glasses, so that it followed the road as you drove. You needed two people to operate it, since it required a separate battery pack, but that was okay: the Continental fleet manager would wear the glasses while I operated the equipment. I saw no need to plunk down four grand of Continental's money to own the camera, but took it on a week's rental.

The Unblinking Eye is on the west edge of the Loop. It didn't seem that far out of the way to drive the extra

fourteen blocks to the morgue to see if Nicola Aguinaldo's body had turned up. Since Vishnikov starts
work at seven I wasn't sure he'd still be there this late in
the afternoon, but he was actually walking to his car
when I pulled into the lot. I ran over to intercept him.

When he saw me he stopped. "The girl who died at
Beth Israel. Is that why you're here?"

Her body hadn't turned up; he had lost track of the
inquiry in the press of other problems, but he'd get
back to it tomorrow. "As I recall, the release form
wasn't signed. It's the trouble with these job sinkholes
the county runs. Most of our staff is good, but we always have some who are there because their daddies
hustle votes or move bodies for the mob. I've turned her
disappearance over to the sheriff for an investigation,
but a dead convict who was illegal to begin with
doesn't rank very high—family isn't in a position to
make a stink, and anyway, if they've been able to conduct a funeral they're not going to want to."

"I don't think this family has held a funeral. I
haven't seen them myself. In fact, I don't know where
they are, but a guy named Morrell has been interviewing immigrants in Aguinaldo's old neighborhood. He
says you know him, by the way."

"Morrell? He's a great guy. I know him from my
work on torture victims in the Americas. He pulled me
out of one of the worst traps I ever walked into, in
Guatemala. Nothing he doesn't know about the Americas and torture. I didn't realize he was in town. Tell him
to call me. I have to run." He climbed into his car.

I leaned in before he could shut the door. "But, Bryant—Morrell talked to Aguinaldo's mother. She didn't
even know her daughter was dead, so she definitely
doesn't have the body."

He stared at me in bewilderment. "Then who does have it?"

"I was hoping you could help on that one. If the form wasn't signed, is there a chance the body is still in the morgue? Maybe the tag got taken off or changed. The other possibility is that a Chicago police officer named Lemour got the body. Do you think there's any way to find out?"

He turned the ignition key. "Why would—never mind. I suppose it could have happened. I'll ask some more questions tomorrow." He pulled the door shut and shot past me out of the lot.

I walked back slowly to the Rustmobile. I wished Vishnikov hadn't turned the investigation over to the sheriff's office. If anyone was covering up for the disposal of Nicola's body, the sheriff's office was probably knee-deep in how it was done. But I had enough going on without trying to run an inquiry at the morgue.

I went home to take the dogs for a swim and to let my neighbor know I'd be in Georgia for a few days. I also called my answering service, telling them to hand any problems over to Mary Louise until Monday.

I drove up to O'Hare with Mary Louise and the boys to help put Emily on the plane to France. She was scared and excited but trying to cover it with a veneer of teen cool. Her father had given her a camcorder, which she used with a studied offhandedness. At the last minute, when he saw she was really leaving, four-year-old Nate began to bawl. As we comforted him and his sniffling brother, I thought again of poor Robbie, unable to express his grief over his dead nanny without his father tormenting him.

We took the boys out for an evening show of *Captain Doberman*—another Global moneymaker. Over ice cream afterward, Mary Louise and I discussed odds and ends.

"Emily wanted me to promise I wouldn't let you get Lacey in trouble while she was away." Mary Louise grinned. "I think it was more like a subtle hint that she wanted every word of any conversation you and Lacey have."

"I haven't seen Lacey, only her old childhood friend Frenada. Over at his Special-T—" I broke off. "Mary Louise, you left me a note about the report from Cheviot on that shirtdress they found on Nicola's body. You wrote down that the label said it was a specialty shirt. Could it have been *Special-T*?"

I spelled out the difference. Mary Louise looked chagrined and said she would check with the engineer at Cheviot Labs in the morning. She asked if I wanted her to go over to Frenada's shop and talk to him while I was away, but we decided that could wait until I got back from Georgia.

It was past ten when I got home, but I wanted to pack my gun before going to bed. It's a time-consuming business, and in the morning I'd be too rushed to get it done to FAA specs. I laid packing and cleaning materials on the dining room table and took the gun apart, placing two empty magazines in the carton—the cartridges have to be packed separately. I was cleaning the slide when the phone rang.

It was Rachel from my answering service. "I'm sorry to call so late, Vic, but a man named Lucian Frenada is trying to get in touch with you. He says it's really urgent and he doesn't care if it's midnight, if you don't call him he's going to get the police to find you and bring you to him."

I blinked—that was a curious coincidence. When the

phone at the factory didn't answer, I reached him at home.

He was so furious he could hardly get out a coherent sentence. "Did you plant this story? Are you behind this effort to defame me?"

"Do you know that I have no clue what you're talking about? But I have a question for—"

"Don't play the innocent with me. You come to my plant with insinuations, and twenty-four hours after I refuse to hire you, this—this slander appears."

"Which slander? Innocent or not, I don't know what it is."

"In the paper, tomorrow's paper, you thought I wouldn't see it? Or not so early?"

"Okay, if we have to do it by twenty questions, let me guess. There's a story about you in tomorrow morning's paper, is that right? About you and Lacey? You and that Virgin T-shirt? Do you want to tell me, or do you want to hold while I go out and find a newsstand with the early edition in it? I can be back in half an hour, probably."

I don't know whether he believed me or not, but he didn't want to wait for me to call him back. He read me from Regine Mauger's column in the early edition of the *Herald-Star*: "*A little bird at the State's Attorney says Lucian Frenada, who's been hanging around Lacey Dowell all week like a sick pit bull, may be using his T-shirt factory to smuggle cocaine into Chicago from Mexico.*"

"Is that it?" I asked.

"Is that it?" he mimicked bitterly. "It is more than enough. She calls me a sick pit bull, which is a racist slur anyway, and then accuses me of being a drug dealer, and you think I shouldn't be angry? My biggest order of my life, the New Jersey Suburban Soccer League, they can cancel if they think I'm a criminal."

I tried to stay patient. "I mean, is that the only story on you in the paper? Regine Mauger can print anything as a rumor. A little bird told her. I don't know if anyone at Global—I mean the *Herald-Star*—fact-checks her. But if they ran a news story, that means they have actual evidence."

"No one could have evidence of this, because it isn't true. Unless they made it up." He was still angry, but calmer. "And I am thinking you could have been a little bird yourself, out of revenge."

"Then you aren't thinking at all," I snapped. "If I want to stay in business the last thing I'll do is run smear campaigns on people who spurn my services. That word gets around fast. The next thing I'd know, all my clients would have left me for Carnifice."

"So if you didn't plant that story, who did, and why?"

I let out a compressed breath. "You want to hire me to find out, Mr. Frenada, I'll be glad to talk it over. Otherwise, since I'm leaving town in the morning, I need to get to bed."

"That would be funny, wouldn't it—I call to chew you out and end up hiring you. The trouble is, I am so vulnerable, I and my small company." His voice trailed away.

I knew that feeling. "Do you feel like telling me the odd thing you mentioned last week, or why you had a Lacey Dowell shirt in your plant?"

"I—they came—I made a couple on spec." He floundered for words. "It didn't get me anywhere. Global uses offshore labor, it's much cheaper than anything I can produce."

"Why didn't you want to tell me last night?"

He hesitated. "For personal reasons."

"To do with Lacey?" When he didn't say anything I added, "You didn't make the shirtdress Nicola Aguinaldo was wearing when she died, by any chance?"

He became totally quiet, so much so I could hear the tree toads croaking from the back of the house. Frenada gave me a hurried good night and hung up.

So he did know something about Nicola Aguinaldo's death. That was a sad and startling thought, but it wasn't as urgent for me at the moment as my own fury with Murray. Was that what he told Alex Fisher-Fishbein I would do—plant evidence of a cocaine ring at Special-T Uniforms? And then, when I didn't jump at their offer, he and Alex decided to move matters on by putting a rumor in the paper?

I called Murray. He wasn't at home—or at least he wasn't answering, and he wasn't at the office. I tried his cell phone.

"Vic! How in hell did you get this number? I know damned well I never gave it to you."

"I'm a detective, Ryerson. Getting a cell phone number is child's play. It's the grown-up stuff that has me baffled. What was the point of that charade you and Alex Fishbein acted out in my office last week?"

"It was not a charade. It was a serious offer to give you—"

"Some crumbs from Global's richly spread table. But when I didn't snatch the bait you took an easier tack and planted a story in that prize bitch Regine Mauger's ear. The last time she checked a source was probably 1943, but it doesn't matter if a column devoted to innuendo gets the facts wrong."

"How do you know they're wrong? How do you

know he isn't smuggling coke in through his shirt factory?"

"So you did plant the story with her!" I was so furious I was spitting into the receiver.

"No, I didn't," he shouted. "But I read my own damned paper to see what they're printing. And yes, I usually get the early edition as soon as it's out. If you've made yourself the guy's champion you are going to have egg all over your smug face. And I for one will not be sorry to help plaster it there. My story will run on Friday, and it will sizzle."

"What are you talking about?" I demanded. "Did going on TV make you feel checking facts was for little people? I looked into Frenada's finances when you and Sandy Bitchbein came around last week. He's clean as a whistle."

"Clean as a whistle? One that's been in the sewer for a week. I did a priority check on Frenada when I learned Regine was running this little tidbit. Guy's got money parked all over the globe."

"Bullshit," I screamed. "I looked him up on Life-Story on Sunday and he doesn't have a dime except the pittance that little T-shirt factory makes for him."

"No." Murray was suddenly quiet. "You didn't. You couldn't have. I just ran a check on him, a priority-one, two thousand bucks to turn it around in ten hours, and it's not true. He's got three accounts in Mexico that are worth a million five U.S. dollars each."

"Murray. I ran the check. I did at the deepest level of numbers. That's why I turned down Bitchbein's offer."

"Her name is Fisher. Why you have a knot in your ass about her—"

"Never mind that. Don't let her wave so many

Golden Globes in front of you that you're too blinded to see the facts, Murray. And by the way, if you're planning on leading your story with, 'There was egg all over smug V. I. Warshawski's face,' don't, because there won't be. I'm leaving town in the morning, but as soon as I get back I'll fax you a copy of that LifeStory report. If I were you, I'd hold off running your sizzle until you've seen it."

I hung up smartly and went back to packing my gun. I'd been feeling irritable about going to rural Georgia, but taking on some punks putting nails under truck tires was beginning to sound downright wholesome compared to what I was looking at here in Chicago.

I was too tired, and too agitated by Murray to figure out what was going on with all these people. If Frenada manufactured the dress Nicola was wearing when she died, how had she gotten it? Had he given it to someone at Carnifice? Given it to Nicola herself? Or to Alex Fisher?

And then there was Global. They wanted me to expose Frenada, then miraculously came up with a rumor about him and cocaine when I wouldn't do the job. I wished I'd known that when I saw Trant and Poilevy last night. It could have made the conversation livelier, although I suppose Alex would have kept them from saying much.

My brain swirled uselessly. It was way too much for me to figure out with the minute information I had. I snapped the gun case shut and filled out the forms I needed for the airline. Put jeans and some sweatshirts in an overnight bag with the gun and a small kit of basic toiletries, then packed the surveillance camera, some blank cassettes, and a charger for the unit together with my maps in a briefcase. That should get me through a few nights away. A book for the flight. I was working my way through a history of Jews in Italy, trying to understand something of my mother's past. Maybe I'd get as far as Napoleon by the time I came home.

21

We Serve and Protect

I SPENT THE next several nights on the back roads of Georgia, sitting in the passenger seat of a fully loaded thirty-ton truck. The fleet manager, who looked authentic with a beer gut hanging over oil-stained jeans, had ambled in as a replacement for a sick driver; I was his girlfriend who hopped on board once the truck left the yard, but with plenty of people to see it happen. To make a long story short, it gave us the right veneer of venality, and we were able to rope in the dispatcher without much trouble. He fingered three buddies and the plant manager. And it was all on film, which made it tidy. Continental United promised an appropriate expression of gratitude—not the kind of bonus I might have snared from Alex Fisher, but enough to pay the Trans Am repairs and cover my mortgage for a couple of months.

When I got home Saturday afternoon, I felt refreshed, the way one does from executing a job well. And the job had been so straightforward, none of the tangled web of weirdness of Baladine and Frenada and Global Entertainment.

Despite my pleasure at being away from all those strange people, the first thing I did, after greeting Mr. Contreras and the dogs, was skim the *Herald-Star* for the last few days to see whether Murray's story on Frenada and the drug ring had run. To my relief it hadn't. Murray apparently still had enough journalism left to wait for the facts. I would reward this good behavior—or try to guarantee its continuation—by going down to my office right now to fax him the Life Story report on Frenada. I wanted to check my mail, anyway.

After taking the dogs to a pocket-size park in the neighborhood, I told my neighbor to fire up the grill, I'd be home for chicken and tomatoes in an hour. I picked up my briefcase, the camera and videocassettes still inside it, and drove the two miles south, humming "Voi che sapete" under my breath.

My happy mood disappeared as soon as I reached my office. I actually was halfway across the room before my brain registered the disaster. The deranged upheaval of papers on the floor wasn't because of me: someone had taken the place apart. Had dumped papers out of drawers with a wanton hand. Unzipped covers from the couch cushions and left them on the floor. Poured a cup of coffee over the papers on the desk. I gaped dumbly for a long moment, not moving, not thinking.

Street vandals. Druggies who'd seen I was away and taken advantage. But the computer and printer remained. Anyone looking for quick cash or the equivalent would have taken those, and anyway, the average druggie wasn't sophisticated enough to bypass the number pad on the front door.

I felt ill, an uncontrollable shiver rising along my back. The violation was too extreme. Someone had been in my space, had come in brazenly, made no effort to conceal it. Were they looking for something, or was this like smashing up hospitals in Zimbabwe—trying to terrify the civilian populace and destabilize the government?

My first impulse was like anyone's—call the cops, get away from the sickness as fast as possible. But if there was some signature in the mess that would tell me who had been there, I'd miss it if I let the cops look first. I sat on the arm of the couch, shaking, until I could control my legs enough to walk, then slid a bolt home on the inside of my office door. Someone— Baladine?—had proved he could get past the number pad on the front door without any trouble, but he'd have to break the inner door down to get past that bolt.

I zipped the cushions back into their covers. Even if I disturbed some vital piece of evidence, I needed to sit down. I wanted water too, but that meant going to the hall, to the refrigerator, and I didn't want to open my door until I felt safe inside my building.

What did I have that someone might want? Besides my computer, of course. My Isabel Bishop painting was the only valuable in the office. I got up and looked at the partition facing my desk. The painting had been tossed to the floor. I didn't touch it. The glass would show prints if any had been left.

Even Tessa absorbed in work would have responded to the racket made by this wantonness. Would the intruders have hurt Tessa? Again I wanted to run to the hall, run to look in her studio, but fear kept me locked inside.

I finally pulled my cell phone from my handbag and phoned Tessa's home. She lived with her parents in their Gold Coast duplex. Her mother answered, the rich contralto that worked magic in courtrooms around the country vibrating the airwaves.

"Victoria. How are you? I didn't recognize your voice."

"No, ma'am. I've had a bit of a shock. I just got in from out of town and found my office vandalized. I wanted to make sure Tessa was all right."

Mrs. Reynolds made the proper statements of alarm and concern but reassured me about Tessa. She had picked her daughter up at the studio for a cup of coffee around noon. Tessa was off for a weekend's sailing with friends, and Mrs. Reynolds, back from a busy week in Washington, had wanted to see her alone for a few minutes.

"When the police come, have them examine her studio to make sure nothing's wrong in there. I've never liked her being that close to Humboldt Park. I don't care how big her lats are, as she keeps telling me, or how good you are in a fight, you two young women need to be in a safer part of town."

"You're probably right, ma'am," I agreed, as the easiest way to end the conversation.

I leaned back on the couch and shut my eyes. Imagined lying in Lake Michigan with the sun overhead until my breath was calm enough for me to think about my situation. If this were Baladine's work it could be an attempt to terrorize me, but if he were also looking for something what would it be? I thought through my conversations during the last week, with Frenada, with Alex. With Murray. The last name came most reluctantly to mind.

I'd told Murray about my LifeStory report on Frenada, that I had proof he was clean. But this was not Murray Ryerson's work. It could not be. Murray was a journalist. The story and the chase, wherever the road led you, that was what mattered to him. Global couldn't have destroyed that in him in a few weeks, he was better than that. Really, he was.

I was saying the same thing over and over in my mind, as if standing in front of the bench pleading his case. I needed to find the hard copy, if it was still there, although with the leisure to search my absence had guaranteed them, the intruders could have turned over every piece of paper in the room.

I shut my eyes and tried to remember what I'd done with the LifeStory printout. I'd stuffed everything into a desk drawer, because I knew Mary Louise was going to be in using the desk, and unorganized stacks of files drove her mad. I opened the drawer. Many of the papers had been pulled out, exposing a box of tampons I kept there. They were rolling around in the drawer, and I automatically stuffed them back into the box. They wouldn't go in, so I picked up the carton, forgetting for the moment about evidence.

Inside was a plastic freezer bag filled with white powder. I stared at it, my numbed mind moving like a dog in quicksand. Cocaine. Maybe heroin—I wouldn't know one from the other. Someone wrecked my office and planted drugs in it. I didn't want to send it to a lab for testing, and I didn't want to explain it to the cops. I didn't want to explain it to anyone.

I leapt to my feet in a sudden frenzy and searched every drawer in the room, every light fixture, every crevice. I found two more bags—one taped inside the printer and the other tucked into a rip in the fabric underneath the couch.

I unbolted the door and ran down the hall to the bathroom, flushing and flushing until the powder was gone, until the bags—cut to pieces with Tessa's cuticle scissors—were gone, standing under the shower in my clothes, running hot water over me until I thought any treacherous trace of powder was gone. I got out and changed into a clean set of Tessa's work clothes. Hung my wet ones from a hook behind her studio entrance. A bubble of incipient hysteria made me want to leave a note on the refrigerator in our *I took* column. *I took one pair of cuticle scissors and a pair of khakis and a T-shirt. Will replace ASAP.*

Back in my office, I picked up the cell phone and called the cops. While I was waiting for them I put on a pair of latex gloves and looked gingerly through my papers. I had put the Frenada report in an old file, but I couldn't remember which. I could only remember thinking Mary Louise would have typed a fresh label at once. The squad car still hadn't shown when I came on the folder labeled *Alumni Fund.* The Frenada printout was still in there, along with the paramedics' report Max had faxed me from Beth Israel.

The police come slowly to this end of Wicker Park. On an impulse born of fear, I stuffed all the papers into a manila envelope, addressed them to Mr. Contreras, and went down the street to the mailbox at the corner of Western and North.

Elton was standing there with his usual ingratiating smile: *I will not hurt you, I am your friend, help me out.* He started his usual patter:

"*Streetwise*, miss. Get your update on hot bands in Chicago this weekend. Find a nice place for your boy-friend—oh, evening, Vic. You been away?"

I gave him a five and took a paper. "Been away. Someone broke into the office while I was gone. You notice anyone strange hanging out the last few nights?"

Elton scrunched up his face in earnest thought but shook his head regretfully. "But I'll be on the lookout

now, Vic, you can count on that. God bless you, Vic.
. . . *Streetwise,* sir. Now, how about a list of all the
hot new bands in this area, place to take your best
girl . . ."

Blue strobes were dancing toward me along North
Avenue. I hurried back up Leavitt and got to my office
as a blue-and-white pulled up. A young pair stepped
out, black woman, white man. The perfect TV cop-
show pair. I showed them mutely what I'd come on.

"You didn't touch anything, did you, ma'am?" the
woman asked, following me into the office.

"I—uh, I put the covers back on the couch." Somehow that seemed the worst thing. "I tried not to touch
any papers, but I'm not sure. Anyway, my prints are on
everything. Mine and my assistant's."

The male half of the team was on his radio sum-
moning additional troops. It's something cops love to
do. The work has so much tedium that when one of
them finds something, the others all get invited to look.
In ten minutes they had a whole battalion in place.

I was answering questions from the pair who took
the call—was anything missing, had the lock been
forced, how long had I been out of town—when a
plainclothes team arrived. A thin, triumphant voice demanded to know if the crew had searched the premises.

"I don't think the perp is on the premises, Sergeant,"
the woman said.

"Not for the perp, for drugs. We've got information
that Warshki is dealing."

Craning my neck, I saw Detective Lemour. He was
wearing the same brown polyester suit he'd had on the
first time I saw him, unless he'd bought a closetful on
sale at Wal-Mart.

I stood up. "Sergeant Lummox. What a coincidence. I didn't know you worked burglary."

"It's Lemour, and I don't work burglary, I work violent crimes. I told you I'd be on you like your underwear, but you went on across that line, Warshki, the one we knew you danced on, and we've got you dead to rights."

"What are you talking about, Lemming? Since when is it a crime in this town to be the victim of a major break-in?"

The woman on the team coughed to cover a laugh, while her male partner stood as solemnly as if he'd been embalmed.

"It's not a crime, if it really happened." He showed his row of little pike's teeth in a vindictive smile.

"If it really happened? Sergeant, I trust you have a tech unit on the way here to take prints, because if you don't I am going to be raising a serious complaint with the police review board. And if you accuse me in front of witnesses of dealing in drugs, then I will also sue you as a private citizen for slander."

"You do that, Warshki, but I have a red-hot tip that you've got a half kilo of powder right here on the premises. And you schmucks can stop grinning behind your hands and search this office. Now."

For the next twenty minutes, seven uniformed people turned my office over. The papers that the original invaders hadn't tossed joined the landfill in the middle of the room. I sat with my arms crossed, my lips tight with anger—and my heart thumping erratically. What if I had missed a niche? I hadn't climbed a ladder to deal with the ceiling fixtures—I'd only checked the lower ones, the spotlights and lamps that I'd installed when I moved in.

I was fuming with an impotent rage, wishing I could get him on film, when I remembered the surveillance camera in my briefcase. I picked it up from the floor next to the couch and pulled the glasses out. Lemour watched me closely, but when he saw I was only putting on glasses he turned his head away. In that brief moment I reached into my case and fumbled with the battery pack. After two nights in the dark roads of Luella County I could load it blindfolded. I put in a new tape and started recording, following the team's destructive swath through the room, but focusing mostly on Lemour.

Lemour himself went to my printer and pulled out the cartridge. When he didn't find the bag of powder he dropped the cartridge, leaving a sooty trail on the floor, and banged the printer on its side. Twelve hundred dollars of Hewlett Packard's best work. I hoped it would survive mauling.

Scowling with fury, he marched to the couch and yanked me to my feet. He ran a hand underneath, found the slit in the bottom, fumbled inside it. When he came up empty he bared his pike's teeth in an ugly grimace. He ordered two of the uniforms to turn the couch over. He ripped the fabric completely off the bottom and started prodding the interior.

At that point I pushed past him and went to the desk to beep my lawyer. "Freeman," I said to his machine. "It's V. I. Warshawski. The cop who was harassing me last week is in my office. I had a break-in; he came around accusing me of dealing drugs. And now he's ripped my couch and is wreaking havoc with my papers. If you get this message I'd appreciate your earliest possible response."

Lemour's thin lips were a line of rage. He shoved the

uniforms out of the way and yanked the phone from my
hand, then slapped my face hard with his open palm. I
kept my arms at my side through an effort of will so
intense that my shoulders ached.

"You think you're smart, don't you, Warshki?" he
hissed.

"Phi beta kappa my junior year at Chicago. That's
usually for smart people, Lemming." I was taking
singer's breaths, pushing air to the front of my mouth,
keeping my voice light so that no cracks of fury showed
in it.

He slapped the other side of my face. "Well, you're
not as smart as you think you are. If I have to take this
room apart brick by brick, I will find where you put
that stash. I know it's here, you smart-assed broad.
Cuff her while you finish searching," he added to the
woman who'd answered my original call.

She couldn't look at me. Her dark face turned
purply-black with shame as she locked my wrists together; she muttered, "I'm sorry," through lips that
barely moved.

The glasses had slipped off my face at a cockeyed
angle. She settled them back on my nose. My neck
ached. Tension. Or maybe whiplash from the force of
Lemour's blows.

The crew went through the room, then the hall and
the bathroom. Brick by brick. Lemour watched, patches
of red on his white cheeks, spittle forming around his
mouth. I kept my video glasses on him as best I could
with my arms hooked to a radiator coil.

When the team didn't find the drugs, I thought
Lemour was going to go over the brink and choke me.
He may have thought so too, but his cell phone rang
before he could do it.

"Lemour," he snarled. "Oh . . . no, sir, it wasn't . . . we did, sir, all three places . . . bitch must've . . . I did, sir, but I couldn't be here twenty-four hours a day . . . I could still bring her in . . . I see. You can?" His pike's teeth showed in an unpleasant grin. "I'll look forward to that, sir."

He put the phone back in his pocket and turned to me. "Your lucky day, Warshki. My—boss says if you swallowed the evidence I can't hold you, although I'd like to bring you in and choke it out of you. You can go home. You—Holcomb, is it? Uncuff her and let her go."

While the officer undid the lock, she whispered that her mother was an upholsterer, that she'd bring her over in the morning and get her to repair my couch, no charge. I was too tired and too angry to do anything but nod my sore neck. I leaned against the wall, my arms crossed, until the last of the battalion had left. I barricaded the door from the inside and sat on the couch. The mess in the room was now so unbearable I couldn't imagine ever being able to work in this space again.

22

Night Crawlers

Mr. CONTRERAS ROUSED me from my stupor, calling on my office phone, his voice rough with anxiety: at four-thirty I'd said I'd be back in an hour for dinner, and here it was almost eight. When I told him what had happened he insisted on flagging a cab and coming to the office. Nothing I said could dissuade him, and in my fragmented state I didn't try too hard. When he knocked on the door fifteen minutes later, I shocked both of us by bursting into tears.

"This is terrible, doll, this is terrible. Who could've done such a thing? That cop, that creep that wanted to arrest you last week? And he hit you? You can't take that. You gotta tell someone. Call the lieutenant. Call Detective Finchley."

I blew my nose. "Yeah. Maybe. What I'd like is to get some kind of padlock for the doors. Whoever broke in bypassed the code on the front door. They can break down padlocks too, but they'll be more obvious from the street if they're doing that."

One of the chains had opened a big all-night home supply store not too far from my building. The old man rode over with me and helped pick out locks and tools. When we got back I was still so jumpy that I insisted on inspecting both my office and Tessa's studio to make sure no one had arrived in my absence.

While Mr. Contreras set to work installing the locks, I made a half-hearted effort to organize the wreck. The Isabel Bishop I handled with latex gloves, putting it in a plastic bag to give to Mary Louise on Monday. I wanted her to get it dusted for fingerprints and to have someone in the department run a check on AFIS. I also figured I could pay her to put files in order: it would be so much easier for her than for me, since she was not only more organized, but not so emotionally invested in the destruction.

I did restore the couch, screw in the light bulbs that the vandal cops had removed, picked up obvious garbage, scrubbed coffee stains from the little bit of carpet. My mother's engraving of the Uffizi Gallery had been knocked over and the glass cracked. I bit my lip but put it in the bag with the Isabel Bishop. I wasn't going to break down over this. The picture wasn't damaged underneath; the glass could be replaced.

The printer cartridge Lemour had dropped on the floor was leaking carbon. I threw it out, cleaned out the printer, and installed a fresh cartridge. I held my breath and turned on the machine. I hit the TEST button, and a page of beautifully executed font samples ran out the mouth. I felt better. One small vessel saved from the inferno.

When Mr. Contreras grunted with satisfaction that he'd got the place pretty well bolted down, my office still looked like the *Titanic* after the iceberg. Who would have thought the old room had so much paper in it?

Mr. Contreras praised my progress—more visible to

him than me—and I dutifully praised his handiwork, which was actually quite impressive. With a handful of inexpensive tools he'd installed a serious lock system. Nothing is impregnable, but this would take long enough to smash that Elton or someone might wander along and interrupt the intruders. I took time to call Tessa's mother to explain what I'd done and to leave a message for Tessa—I'd drop off a spare key before she got back from her sailing trip.

As we walked to the car, Elton popped out of the shadows. "Saw you had the cops with you, Vic. They find anything?"

"*Nada.* But the sergeant who came is in on the fix. If you see anyone—don't call 911, because the cops may be the perps. Call—can he call you?" I asked Mr. Contreras. "I'm not home enough."

My neighbor wasn't pleased at my involving him with a street person, but he grudgingly agreed that I could write his phone number on one of my business cards and hand it to Elton. "Call collect," I recklessly committed my neighbor. Illinois Bell charges thirty-five cents—it's even harder for the homeless to come up with correct change than for the rest of us.

When we got home I insisted first on inspecting the Rustmobile to make sure no contraband had been slipped into the trunk. Then I brought Mitch and Peppy up to the third floor with me while I made a circuit of my apartment. I was ashamed of my jumpy vulnerability, but every time I thought of those bags of white powder, the skin on the back of my neck crawled.

My neighbor put fresh charcoal on the grill outside his back door and started cooking chicken. Before going down I called Lotty, hoping for sympathy—and a prescription for my sore neck. She gave not just sympathy but alarm, trying to persuade me to spend the night in the safety of her eighteenth-story apartment. I thought I'd be happier in my own home, among my own things, but told her I'd keep the dogs with me until things simmered down.

"As far as your neck goes, my dear—aspirin and ice. Ice now and before you go to bed. And call me in the morning."

I felt irrationally bereft when she hung up. She'd offered me a bed—why did I want technical medicine instead of love? Ice, when the left side of my neck was sore to the touch? What did Lotty know about neck injuries, anyway. I stomped into the kitchen, filled a freezer bag with ice, and pressed it against the sore area, as if determined to prove her wrong. Instead, by the time Mr. Contreras phoned up to say the chicken was cooked, I could move my head more easily. Which made thinking more possible as well.

The cassettes that I'd made of Lemour in my office— I needed to do something with those. A copy for my lawyer, and maybe one for Murray. Would he run a story on the break-in? Was I testing him, to see whose orders he was following?

After dinner I went back upstairs and hooked the cassette pack up to my VCR and ran the tape. Knowing I had sat passively while Lemour grew ever more demented made me feel the violations of the afternoon all over again. My stomach clenched. I could hardly bring myself to keep watching. When I heard the call that made Lemour let me go, though, I sat up and played it back several times.

His caller kept cutting him off. Perhaps he didn't like

Lemour's thin nasal voice. But maybe he didn't want Lemour revealing too much on an open line. Lemour's evil grin, and the way he said he'd look forward to that —whatever *that* was—made it clear they had some more elaborate frame in store. Although what could be more elaborate than drugs planted in my office I didn't know. Maybe I should go to Lotty's after all.

I stopped the tape again when Lemour said it was my lucky day, I could go home. He paused before saying his "boss" had ordered my release. A cop does not refer to superiors as bosses; he calls them by title—lieutenants or watch commanders—whatever the highest rank happens to be. So who was on the phone? Baladine? Jean-Claude Poilevy?

Maybe a really sensitive machine could pick up the voice of the person speaking to Lemour. I could talk to the engineer at Cheviot Labs about that, but it would probably have to wait until Monday. Just in case the guy came in on weekends I left a message on his voice mail.

I locked the tape in my closet safe and went back downstairs to collect the dogs. With an aspirin on top of my long day—my long week—I was asleep as soon as I turned out the light.

Two hours later the phone pulled me up and out of a deep well of sleep. "Ms. Warshawski? Is that you?" The hoarse whisper was barely audible. "It's Frenada. I need you at once. At my plant."

He hung up before I could say anything. I held the receiver to my ear, listening to the silence at the other end. My mind had that deceptive clarity that the first hours of a sound sleep bring. Frenada didn't have my home phone number: when he called to scream about

Regine Mauger's blurb in the *Herald-Star*, he got me through my answering service. Perhaps he used caller ID and had picked up my number when I called his home.

I turned on my bedside light and looked at my own ID pad. *Caller unidentifiable.* The person had either blocked the call or was using a cell phone. I went into the living room. Mitch and Peppy had been sleeping next to the bed, but they followed me, crossing in front of each other so that I had a hard time moving.

I nudged them out of the way and found my brief-case where I'd left it, next to the television. I dug out the Palm Pilot and looked up Special-T Uniforms. When I phoned the plant, the number rang fifteen times without an answer. His home phone gave me only his bilingual message.

"So what should I do, guys?"

Mitch looked up at me hopefully. *Go for a run* seemed to be his advice. Peppy lay down and began methodical work on her forelegs, as if to say, *Take a bath and go back to sleep.*

"It's a setup, don't you think? Lemour's handler made him release me. So that they could trap me at the plant? Leaving me with egg all over my smug face, as Ryerson informed me Wednesday night? Or was this really Frenada, in serious trouble? In which case, why didn't he call the cops, instead of me?"

The dogs looked at me anxiously, trying to figure out my mood from my voice. Maybe Frenada's experience with the cops was the same one I'd had this evening, so that he didn't feel he could rely on them.

A wiser person would have followed Peppy's advice and stayed home. Maybe I am that wiser person

now—experience does change you—but in the middle
of the night, with that sensation of looseness that made
me think I was still thirty and able to leap tall buildings
at a bound, I pulled on my jeans and running shoes, put
my gun back together and stuck it in a shoulder holster
under a sweatshirt, put my PI and driver's licenses in
my back pocket with a handful of bills, and made my
cautious way down the back stairs. To their annoyance,
I left the dogs behind—if I got involved in a shooting
war I didn't want them complicating the battle.

Lemour thought he could get me, but I would make
a monkey of him. That seemed to be the gist of
my thinking, if acting solely on impulse can be called
thinking.

I drove past the plant at Grand and Trumbull. A
light was shining through one of the rear windows on
the second floor. In case Lemour had set a trap, I didn't
slow down but turned south at the next intersection. I
parked three blocks away.

Saturday nights on the fringes of Humboldt Park are
not quiet. The streets in this industrial section were
empty, but sirens and dogs keened a few blocks away. I
even heard roosters crowing. Someone was running a
cockfight nearby. A freight train squeaked and hooted
in the distance. As it drew near, its rackety *clank-clank*
drowned out other sounds.

When I got to Frenada's building I scouted it as
closely as I could in the dark. I paused outside an old
delivery van, listening intently at the rear doors to see if
it was a stakeout vehicle, although it was hard to hear
anything above the thundering of the freight train.

I stood across the street from the entrance for ten
minutes, waiting for some sign of life. Or was I waiting

for my courage to build enough for me to enter a rick-
ety building alone in the dark? The longer I stood, the
more inclined I would be to go home without looking
inside. And what if that really had been Frenada on the
phone? And what if he really was in trouble, bleeding,
dead? Then what? I took a deep breath and crossed the
street.

The front door was unlocked. *It's a trap, Vic,* the
sensible voice whispered, but I slid sideways through
the opening, gun in hand, palm clammy against the
stock.

Inside the entrance, the dark wrapped around me
like a living cloak. I could feel it grabbing at my neck,
and the soreness, which I'd forgotten, came back. I
moved cautiously to the stairwell, fighting the impulse
to turn tail and run.

I climbed the slippery concrete stairs, pausing on
each riser to strain for noises inside. Outside, the freight
thumped and squeaked into the distance. In the sudden
stillness I could hear the sirens and car horns again,
making it hard to focus on the building. I hugged the
stairwell wall, trying to make no sound myself, hoping
the hammering of my heart was audible only to me.

At the top landing I could see a bar of light under
Special-T's door. I moved faster, as if light itself meant
safety. At the door I knelt down to look through the
keyhole but saw only the legs of the long worktable. I
lay flat, trying not to think of the filth of decades
against my face (how many men had spat on this floor
when walking out at the end of the day?), my eye
pressed against the thin slit of light. All I saw were bolts
of fabric and some wadded-up paper. I waited a long
time, watching for feet, or for a shadow to move. When

nothing happened I stood up and tried the handle. Like the outer door, the one to the shop floor was open.

A clothes shop is probably always chaotic, but Special-T looked as though someone had tossed the place through a wind tunnel. Whoever had rampaged through my office had been here as well. The long tables in the middle where the cutting took place had been cleared; fabric, shears, and pattern stencils lay in a heap around them. Along the wall, the sewing machines stood with their covers unscrewed. A single light over one of the machines was the one that I'd seen from the street.

I moved fearfully toward a small room at the back, expecting at any second to come on Frenada's body. Instead, I found more signs of upheaval. The vandals had taken the room apart with a ruthless hand. The intruders had been looking for something: drawers stood open, their contents dangling over the side to spill on the floor. A piece of loose tile had been pulled up and tossed to one side. Invoices, dressmaking patterns, and fabric samples made a gaudy stew on the floor. The bulbs had been removed from the desk lamp.

I was certain that there must be bags of powder on the premises, but it wasn't a search I wanted to make alone and in the dark. I looked in Frenada's office for the Mad Virgin shirt I'd seen on Tuesday. When a quick inspection of the tangled heap of cloth and paper didn't reveal it, I moved to the hall. I'd see if Frenada was in the john or at the back by the freight elevator; if he wasn't on the premises I was out of Dodge.

The toilet was in the hall that ran outside Special-T's door. A supply closet was next to it; the freight elevator was at the end farthest from the stairs. I had looked inside the closet and found nothing more disgusting than a mop that needed a good bath in disinfectant, when I heard the scuffling sound of a door opening, of many feet trying to sneak silently up concrete stairs. A second later a train began to wheeze and crank its way up the track: if they'd waited only a heartbeat longer I'd never have heard them.

23

A Run to O'Hare

I SLID OUT of the supply closet. No cover there. Where? No way to scale the wall, no way up to those windows. I ducked into the freight elevator. The train rattled the walls, drowning any sound of my pursuit. If they'd started up the stairs, it wouldn't take them long to look in here. Even if I had a key to start the elevator, while it toiled downstairs a dozen men could wait outside the door and pick me off like a duck in a crate.

Fool. Damned cocky fool to plunge into this building when the whole evening was painted with red warning signs, stay away, don't touch. Someone knew me too well, knew that I'd weigh the risks and take them anyway. Set the tiger trap. If I was a real tiger I could have leapt from shop floor to window and been on my way.

I looked around the elevator cage. The service hatch stood open. I measured the distance: about four feet over my head. I wasn't a tiger, and I'd get only one chance on these forty-plus muscles. A light bounced off the hallway wall. I crouched, swung my arms, and jumped. My hands clawed at the edge of the opening. Left hand on a nail, grab hard with my right while I move the left, claw for purchase, fingers digging into splintery wood, biceps bulging as they hoist my weight.

The freight train screeching past covered my scramble through the hatch, my rasping breath.

Above me a skylight filtered in starlight, showing ghostly shapes of cables and the wooden slab that covered the hatch. I slid it across the opening. The cage shook with the thundering of the train but settled down as the noise receded. I started hearing voices, words muffled by the shaft, then one directly under me.

"She should be here."

My stomach heaved, felt as though it might split itself open.

"Did you see her leave home?" Lemour's unmistakable squeak.

"No, but her car's gone. She must have gone out through the alley before we thought of putting a watcher out back. And there's no answer on her phone."

"Then we beat her here. Maybe she stopped for help. I'll get someone into the broom closet, someone in Frenada's office. You wait here."

The voices faded. I was sitting on a piece of metal. Now that I knew I must not move, I became aware of every surface detail—an edge like a razor cutting into my left buttock, the cable under my right foot that would twang if my sore muscles buckled.

I took slow careful breaths, the air scraping against my dry throat. I was terrified that I might have to cough. I inched my neck slowly back so that I could see the skylight. Some rungs were bolted to the wall leading up to it. If I could get to them without the man in the elevator hearing . . . Tilting my head back increased the strain on my throat, and a large cough built in my lungs. I held it as long as I could, desperately swallowing but unable to produce enough saliva to coat it. Just as I could hold it no longer the cage began to shake again. For a brief flash of terror I thought the watcher was following me up the hatch, but as the cough exploded in my chest, another train began to rumble behind the building.

Grabbing the cable in front of me, I eased myself to my feet. My left thigh trembled. I'd been bracing myself with it, not realizing until I started to move that it held my weight. I flexed my leg cautiously; even with the train as cover I couldn't afford a loud noise here in the shaft.

As soon as the worst cramping subsided, I stepped to the edge of the cage and tugged on the rung above my head. It seemed secure. Holding it firmly I pushed with my right leg on the rung in front of me. It held as well. I stepped off the edge of the cage and began hoisting myself up. Like in Ms. McFarlane's gym class back in high school, when we had to climb ropes. *Why,* one of the girls had demanded, *we're never going to be firefighters.* If I got out of here—when I got out of here —I'd go back to South Chicago and tell today's know-all adolescents: *The day may come when you're as stupid as me, when you've backed yourself into an ambush and need to climb out of it.*

A short climb, only fifteen feet. Five rungs to the skylight. Step, hoist, and then a final yard into space to reach a tiny platform for the work crew to sit on. You couldn't be a very big machinist and work in this space. And why didn't the skylight open? Didn't they ever need to get out on the roof? I couldn't see a latch. Was this window simply decorative?

The train continued to rattle underneath. I pulled my gun from my shoulder holster and smashed the stock, hard, against the glass. It crashed down the shaft. No one could overlook that sound. I knocked the glass clear from frame. Pulled my sweatshirt over my head and erupted through the window as the watcher underneath me shouted for backup.

I scrambled onto the flat tar roof and ran to the edge. A cop car was parked on Trumbull, blue strobes inviting, warning bystanders. Another covered the west end of the building. I backed away and ran to the other side. The freight tracks curved behind the building. The train rocking slowly through the turn cut off any escape on that side.

In the middle of the roof a head popped through the broken skylight. "Freeze, Warshki!"

I fell to the flat tar as Lemour fired. Swung my legs over the side. Extended my body by my fingertips. Lemour ran toward me. I twisted as far to the right as I could and dropped.

Like falling off a bike. The boxcar moved forward underneath me; I fought to keep upright but landed hard on my left hip and forearm.

I lay that way, rocking with the train, so happy at my escape that I almost relished the pain in my side. A badge of the adventure. I wasn't too old to leap tall buildings after all. I grinned stupidly in the dark.

I lay that way for about ten minutes, watching streetlamps and tree branches rock past. As my euphoria at escaping died down, I began to worry about what to do next. I couldn't ride this train out of town. Or I could, but what would I do then? A stay in a cornfield overnight. Persuade someone to give a beat-up, disheveled specimen a ride to the nearest town. Some small-town Wisconsin cop finding me with a gun on me and not believing I had any right to it. Even worse was the possibility that Lemour was following the train. I stopped grinning and sat up.

I had no idea where I was. The city as familiar to me as the bones and markings of my face had changed into a mass of signal lights and looping tracks. I felt alone in the swirling dark. The train was gathering speed, hurling through strange seas toward strange land. A southbound freight rattled past, shaking me so hard I lay down again.

A plane floated over me, a giant grasshopper, its lights bulging eyes. Lying on my back I could see the belly light, the landing gear. O'Hare. So at least we were somewhere near the city.

The train suddenly braked, with a jolting screech that rocked me back again on my sore hip. I didn't take time to curse or feel my bruises but scrambled crablike to the front of the car, found the ladder and climbed down. The train was still moving, although slowly. I jumped free of the slicing wheels, rolling with the motion of the train, landing on grass, rolling downhill, my gun digging into my breast, until I came to rest against a concrete wall.

I got on my hands and knees, but when I heaved myself to my feet I felt a tearing in my side that took my breath away. I leaned against the wall, tears smarting in my eyes. Gingerly, I touched the area under my holster. An edge of pain cut through me. A broken rib? A badly torn muscle? If Lemour had persuaded someone to stop the train, I couldn't stand around waiting to heal. I had to keep moving.

When I started to walk the gun bore into the sore area. I used the wall as a brace and held my left arm up to unbuckle the holster. Checking the safety on the

Smith & Wesson, I stuck it in my pocket and fastened the holster loosely around my waist.

The sleeves of my sweatshirt had gaping tears from the glass in Special-T's skylight. The rest of me was covered with oily mud. Blood was caked along my neck and arms—cuts I hadn't known I was getting were starting to bother me. I hobbled along as fast as I could, straining my ears for sounds of pursuit above the rocking of the train.

Bright lights above the wall I was using for support showed me every detail of the ground—refuse of fast food tossed from cars, Coke cans, plastic bags, even shoes and clothes. I limped my way along the wall to the bottom of the embankment. The street sign said MONTROSE AVENUE. Lying on the boxcar, I had thought I'd been traveling an hour or more and pictured myself in some unknown suburban landscape, but I was still inside the city. The unknown landscape suddenly turned on its side in my brain and I knew it. The concrete wall was a barricade between me and the Kennedy expressway. The roar I was hearing didn't come from the train, which had moved on, but from traffic.

I followed the exit ramp up, looking nervously behind me but not seeing Lemour. Each step was now a prolonging of fatigue and pain. I made it across the expressway bridge to the L stop, where I fed singles into a ticket machine, then slumped onto a bench waiting for a train.

It was four-thirty now and the summer sun was beginning to turn the eastern sky a muddy gray. When a train screeched in twenty minutes later, the cars were half full, bringing home the night crews from O'Hare, sending early shifts into town to work coffee bars and diners. I found an empty seat and watched people sidle away from me. No one wants to catch poverty or grime from a stray homeless person. In my filth and tatters I looked worse than most.

I dozed my way downtown, changed to the Red Line, and dozed my way back north to Belmont. If someone was staking out my place I was past caring. I staggered the five blocks home and fell into bed.

24

Annoying the Giants

THE GUN HAD dug a deep bruise into my side when I tumbled from the boxcar. I'd be sore for four or five days, but if I was careful I'd be okay. Ditto for my left hip. The bruising there went down to the bone, so it would take longer to heal, but nothing was broken and none of the glass cuts in my arms needed stitches. Lotty dispensed that verdict at her clinic Sunday afternoon, her lips flat, her black eyes large with a misery that hurt me more than anger.

"Of course, being careful, taking it easy, those are concepts beyond you, as I know to my sorrow. Still, I understand what these glib radio psychologists mean when they talk about enablers." She put her ophthalmoscope away with a snap and turned to wash her hands. "If I would have the courage to stop patching you up, perhaps you would stop breaking yourself into pieces. You are foolhardy, which, in case you didn't know, means to be daring without judgment: I looked it up this morning. How long do you think you can go on this way? A cat has nine lives, but you have only the one, Victoria."

"You don't have to tell me; my body's doing it for you." I found myself shouting. "My arms are sore. My hamstrings ache. I can hardly walk across the room. I'm getting old. I hate it. I hate not being able to count on my body."

"So you are going to follow Joan of Arc into the flames before your body fails you and you have to admit you're mortal?" Lotty gave a twisted smile. "How old was your mother when she died?"

I stared, startled by the unrelated question, and subtracted dates in my head. "Forty-six."

"And she was ill for two years? It's a hard feeling, to know you will live longer than a mother who died young, but it is not a crime to do so," Lotty said. "You'll turn forty-four next month, won't you? You don't need to push yourself past the brink so that you burn up in the next two years. You could have found a dozen ways to learn whether Mr. Frenada was inside his building last night. Make that the intelligent use of your energy, figuring out how to conserve your strength for those times when using your body is your last resort, not your first one. Don't you think that's what your mother would want for you?"

Oh, yes, probably. Surely. My mother's intensity had a blast-furnace quality, but she didn't prize brute strength above finesse. She'd died of a metastasis from the uterus that became apparent after a miscarriage, when the bleeding wouldn't stop and I'd brought her pads and changed my own in terror each month for years, wondering when it would happen to me, when I would drain away from the inside. Perhaps Lotty was right. Perhaps I was draining myself from the inside out of some survivor's guilt. If that was the case, my mother most surely did not want that from me, but life.

Lotty insisted on taking me home with her. I wanted to make phone calls, see if Lacey Dowell knew where Lucian Frenada was: I hadn't been able to raise him at his home or shop when I tried before coming to Lotty's clinic. I wanted to talk to Murray about how he'd gotten word that Frenada was running cocaine. I even had a manic idea about calling Baladine and accusing him of engineering the dope stashes.

Lotty refused to listen to my impassioned plea for a phone—she pushed me to her guest room and pulled the jack out of the wall. I fumed for around thirty seconds, but the next thing I knew it was ten o'clock Monday morning and I was more hungry than angry.

Lotty had left a note for me: the doorman knew I was staying and had orders to let me back into the building if I went out for a walk. I should take it easy for a few days. The building had a sauna and a gym on the third floor—the spare key to her front door tucked into the envelope would open the gym. *Help yourself to fruit and bread. And, Victoria, for my sake if not yours, don't leap again without looking very carefully.*

After an orange and a piece of toast I went down to the gym. It was really only a small workout room, with weights and an exercise bike, but I was able to work off some of my stiffness. A half hour in the sauna sent me back to bed. When I got up again, around one, I made a hot meal out of eggs and fresh tomatoes. The calls I'd wanted to make yesterday didn't feel so urgent today, but I took the phone out onto Lotty's balcony and started with Mary Louise.

When I finished describing Saturday's debacle at my office, she said, "So you really did find drugs there. And if Lemour planted them, then you can't call the cops."

"I do have a videotape of Lemour in the act, which I guess I could take to the State's Attorney. Trouble is, I don't know anyone there personally these days, and anyway, I'm afraid Lemour might be able to make even

that evidence disappear. If I thought Murray would or
could do anything, I'd give it to him, but these days I'm
not sure I can count on him. How about showing it to
Terry Finchley?"

She hesitated. "I've got these children I'm responsible for. I can't put my life on the line for some case
you're inventing."

I sat up with a jolt that made my side ache. "Mary
Louise, where do you get off with that kind of statement? You were with me when all this started. In fact, if
I remember correctly, it was your panic that made me
wreck my car. Which has been impounded by the cops
and may well never surface again. Exactly what about
that am I inventing?"

"Okay, not making up," she muttered. "And I'm
sorry about your car. If I had the money I'd repair it for
you. But it's the same story with you every time. You
can't bear to be scared or beaten, so if someone threatens you, you have to take them on, no matter how big
they are. Terry warned me about that when I started
working for you, he said he saw you do it over and over
again and that no one's life is worth that much principle. And in this case you're trying to take on giants.
Don't you see? Don't you know?"

I clutched the phone so hard my sore palms began to
throb. "No. I don't."

"Oh, Vic, use your brain. That didn't take a beating
Saturday night. You're trying to go nose-to-nose with
Robert Baladine. Who's his best friend? Who got him
that contract out in Coolis? And who can bury a body,
no questions asked, faster than you can say 'Jimmy
Hoffa'? Why didn't you take that nice little assignment
Alex Fisher dangled in front of you?"

"What on earth? You yourself advised me not to

touch it. And if you think I want to be bought by some—"

"I know. You're too damned holy to be bought off by a Hollywood slimeball. One thing you'd better believe—I'm not putting Josh and Nate at risk. Thank God Emily's in France and I don't have to worry about her. If you keep poking at this hornets' nest, I'm resigning and flying out of town with the boys."

You can't quit, you're fired. That's the standard line in such cases, but I only thought it, didn't say it. When I cooled off I'd regret it—Mary Louise is good for my little operation. But I hadn't cooled off yet, and our good-byes were unfriendly. Especially after she said she didn't have time to help put my files back together. She had exams, she was doing some work for a law firm that might let her take an internship, she had the boys in summer camp, she couldn't possibly spend a week cleaning up the kind of wreck I was describing.

At first I was too angry to think, but I made myself calm down, hobbled around the apartment, studied Lotty's art collection. Including an alabaster figurine of Andromache that I'd recovered for her by the same methods she and Mary Louise were criticizing in me today. No, dwelling on that was only making me angry all over again.

I drank a glass of water and went back to the balcony to stare at the lake. At the edge, the line where lake meets sky, a cluster of sailboats looked like bits of white paper glued to a child's collage. I wanted to be on that remote horizon, but I had no way to reach it.

What didn't I see and know about Baladine? Of course it was Poilevy who got him that contract out in Coolis, you didn't have to be Sherlock Holmes's smarter brother to figure that out. But bury a body, no questions asked, as Mary Louise had said, meant Poilevy had mob ties in Du Page County. One of her old pals must have warned her about him while I was in Georgia—probably Terry Finchley.

It also didn't take a genius to figure that Detective Lemour could do mob work on the side, not after what I'd seen of him on Saturday. And he could do it in the suburbs. Chicago cops were required to live inside the city limits, but no ordinance forbade their moonlighting in the collar counties if they wanted to. We'd had two police superintendents with ties to the mob in recent years, and I guess you have to start somewhere.

Lemour must be on Poilevy's payroll. No, not Poilevy's. The House Speaker wasn't going to get his hands dirty in a way that a reporter like Murray—like Murray used to be—could uncover. Lemour was on someone's payroll. But I already knew that. It was obvious Saturday afternoon when his unnamed boss had phoned, told him to let me go.

What I couldn't make sense of was how all this had mushroomed out of Nicola Aguinaldo's death. What did Lucian Frenada know that mattered to Baladine or Poilevy? Something about the Mad Virgin T-shirt dress Aguinaldo was wearing when she died. Would Lacey Dowell know? And would she tell me if she did?

I looked up the Hotel Trianon number. The operator asked me to spell my last name, put me on hold for a moment, and then said Ms. Dowell wasn't available. Had Ms. Dowell returned from Santa Monica I asked.

"All I can tell you is that Ms. Dowell isn't available." She hung up crisply.

I lay back on the floor. I'd become a non-grata person since talking to Frank Siekevitz in the Trianon's security department last week. Had Lacey put me on her index, or had Alex Fisher done it for her? I sat up and redialed the hotel and asked for Siekevitz.

"Vicki!" He was embarrassed. "I'm sorry, but the lady doesn't want to talk to you. She put it in writing."

"She did, Frank? Or did the studio?"

"That I can't tell you. But you don't want to go bothering her if the studio wants you to stay away, do you?"

"Actually, I do. I need to talk to her about something pretty important."

"Nothing's that important, Vicki, believe me."

"So it was the studio."

He gave an uncomfortable laugh and hung up gracelessly. I wanted to limp to the Trianon as fast as my trembling hamstrings would carry me, but Mary Louise's comments haunted me. What would running to the hotel do for me, anyway? Frank would stiff me harder in person, because the giants, as Mary Louise had called them, had left nothing to chance. They had threatened him or cajoled him.

The giants knew our strengths and weaknesses. I'd realized that Saturday night: they knew I would rise to the bait, that I'd be daring without exercising judgment. Joan of Arc, Lotty'd called me. What no one around me would believe was that I really didn't want to lift the siege of Orleans. I wanted to keep on doing nice little investigations for Continental United until I made enough money to fund my Money Purchase Pension Plan and bought me a little house in Umbria, where I'd make Orvieto Classico and raise golden retrievers.

In frustration, I turned on the television, looking for news, fearing actually to hear news about Frenada. The Global channel had local coverage at four. It was the usual tabloid stew of sex and violence: an overturned truck on the tollway with flames and car wreckage, Mrs. Muffet and Mr. Tuffet exclaiming that they heard the explosion, they thought my God it's World War III. Nothing on Frenada—or me, thank goodness.

When the ads started I turned off the sound, but after a truck climbed the Grand Canyon and a cleanser removed oily stains from a white blouse, a map flashed on the screen, showing a dotted line connecting Mexico and Chicago. Then Murray's face loomed over it. I hastily switched on the sound but heard only, "Tuesday night at nine. Chicago's hottest news, from the inside out, with Murray Ryerson."

After that I kept the station on for another half hour, watching a tedious rerun of some sex comedy and about twenty commercials, until the Mexico map finally reappeared. "Enterprise zones. The perfect route for small businessmen hoping to make it to the top. But sometimes those businesses are taking federal seed money and using it to grow cocaine. Go inside Chicago with Murray Ryerson and find out how Mexican immigrants are using such innocuous-seeming businesses as a uniform factory as a cover for drug deals. Tuesday night at—"

I switched off the set before the tag line ended. Joan of Arc or no, on my own against the giants or not, I couldn't lie here on Lotty's living room rug while Global used Murray to destroy Frenada's reputation. I started a reflexive finger on the phone buttons, about to call Murray and shriek at him, when I realized it would be one of those conversations that begin with "what the hell do you think you're doing" and end with both parties slamming the phone down.

I frowned for a moment, then went into Lotty's little home office. She's never felt the need to add automation to her home, but she has a typewriter. I'd used just such a primitive instrument until a couple of years ago. I scrounged in her drawers for a large envelope, typed LACEY DOWELL, TRIANON HOTEL. SCRIPT CHANGES. BY MESSENGER in caps across it on the diagonal. In the left corner I typed Global's Chicago address. It would be better, of course, if I had a laser printer and could manufacture something resembling their corporate logo, but this would have to do.

Dear Ms. Dowell, I wrote.

Do you know that on Tuesday night, Global television is going to run a story denouncing Lucian Frenada as a drug smuggler? Do you know why they want to do this? Do you approve? Finally, do you know where Mr. Frenada is? I am a private investigator who has been caught up willy-nilly in his affairs, and I am virtually certain that evidence against him has been manufactured. If you know any reason why the studio would do such a thing, I will wait downstairs to talk to you, or, if you prefer, you may call me.

I included my home and office numbers, put the note in the envelope, and sealed the whole thing with packing tape. I wrote a note for Lotty, telling her I was going home and would call her tonight, and rode the elevator down to the lobby, where I got the doorman to summon a cab.

25

Reaching Out To—A Friend?

No ONE BARS you from an upscale hotel as long as you're properly dressed. I had the cab swing by my apartment and wait while I put on my wheat-colored pantsuit and some makeup. The midsummer heat continued as June inched into July; the rayon rubbed unpleasantly against my cuts and bruises, but the bellman inside the Trianon's entrance accepted the envelope and a ten with a respectful promise to see that it was taken up to Ms. Dowell's suite at once. I sat in an alcove off the main lobby, flipping idly through newspapers, but although the bellman assured me he'd hand-delivered my packet, no message came down for me.

Short of checking into the hotel, there wasn't any way I could get upstairs without Lacey's summons: the Trianon had someone stationed between the desk and the elevators to monitor traffic. I watched a discreet pantomime take place between the front-desk staff and the monitor, subtle nods allowing the blessed to pass into paradise. If I wanted to get upstairs, Lacey had to call me.

I read pages of Washington scandal, which I usually avoid; I read about the bodies hauled off the sidewalks after the weekend's drive-bys—which I also usually skip —and even the sad ending of an unidentified man in his late thirties who'd been pulled out of the water at Belmont Harbor, but no word came for me from on high. I was starting to feel frustrated, which made my sore muscles ache more ferociously.

Maybe after another night's rest a different way of probing at Frenada and Global would come to me, but for now all I had energy for was collecting my car—which I hoped was still sitting three blocks from Frenada's headquarters. As I pushed myself out of the padded armchair, someone I recognized sailed through the revolving door like the *Merrimac* descending on a wooden frigate. Alex Fisher had such a head of steam that she ignored the doorman holding the side door wide for her. She also ignored a younger woman who was running to catch up with her.

"I can't wait around for you," Alex snapped in a ringing voice.

"I'm sorry, Ms. Fisher, I was paying the cab." The young woman panted; she was pasty-faced and out of shape, probably from too many late nights dining on pizza while waiting for commands from the studio.

I had slipped behind a pillar to watch, but Alex was so wrapped up in her own business that not even a marching band could have distracted her. When the hall monitor tried to detain her, Alex jerked away and pushed the elevator call button. I was admiring her forthright tactics when Frank Siekevitz suddenly appeared at her side.

I couldn't hear what the security director said, but Alex announced that Lacey Dowell was expecting her, this was urgent, and would he get out of the way. Frank murmured something else, his posture so deprecating that I cringed. The hall monitor used a phone, and in another minute Alex and her satellite were allowed to pass.

I sat back down, hoping Lacey might decide I could help her after all, but when Alex and her attendant reappeared, no one had asked for me. I couldn't resist following Alex outside.

"Vic!" Her greeting was half surprise, half venom. "I thought you—what are you doing here?"

So Lacey hadn't told her I'd written to her: interesting. "Yeah, I know, I was supposed to be dead or in jail or something, but here I am. Lacey doing okay?"

"If you're trying to see her, you can't." Alex waved off a doorman offering her a taxi.

"She's not the only guest at the Trianon. I was having tea with my aunt. She's a permanent resident."

"You don't have an aunt who can afford this place."

"You haven't read the LifeStory report on me very thoroughly, Sandy," I chided her. "As a matter of fact I do have a rich aunt. Actually, I have a rich uncle. He's very big in the food industry. And his wife could afford to live here if she wanted to. By the way, where did you get the cocaine you planted on me?"

Alex became aware of her satellite, who was frowning in an effort to follow our conversation. She gave an unconvincing laugh and said she didn't know what I was talking about.

"It has that Hollywood feel to it, the kind of thing Gene Hackman would turn up in *French Connection Three*. Did you get Teddy Trant to talk to his screenwriters, have them come up with an absurd plotline, then turn it over to Baladine and his tame goons to act out?"

"Vic, why didn't you take that assignment I dug up

for you? It would have saved everyone a lot of grief."
Her green eyes were dark in the twilight.

"Was it a bribe or a distraction?" I asked.

"There are worse things on the planet than bribes. I
didn't remember you as so uncompromising in law
school."

"No, that was you back then," I agreed. "Hot politics and stubborn intransigence. If you weren't part of
the solution you were part of the problem. Although
maybe in that regard you haven't changed so much."

She bit her lower lip, swollen from collagen injec-
tions. "Well, you were always stubborn, that's for
damned sure. But you weren't ever right about everything. As you'll find out now if you don't back off.
Felicity, can you get a cab over here? We have a lot of
work to do tonight."

Felicity scuttled over to the doorman, who blew
grandly on his whistle. The lead car in the taxi line
pulled forward.

"Back off? From what?"

"Don't play the naive fool with me. I have you pretty
well pegged by now. Come on, Felicity. Are you waiting
for the Second Coming?"

"Poor Felicity," I said. "If her mama knew she'd be
working for you, Sandy, maybe she would have named
her Anxiety instead."

"And you know damned well that regardless of what
my *mama* called me, my name is Alex—Vicki." On that
shot Alex threw herself into the car, Felicity handed the
doorman a dollar, and the two of them took off.

I stood in the drive, watching the street long after
the cab's taillights had disappeared. I know I'm not
right about everything, but she'd made it sound like

something specific. Was it the same as the egg Murray was going to smear all over my smug face?

I was too tired and too sore to figure it out this evening. The doorman who'd taken in my letter to Lacey was urging me out of the drive and into a cab. I followed him meekly, although it was the fifth driver he whistled up who agreed to take me—when the first four heard the address I wanted, they shook their heads, willing to lose their place in line to avoid Humboldt Park. I didn't blame them, exactly, but I could understand why people on the West Side get so frustrated at being denied service. The guy who finally took me to my car barely waited for my feet to touch the street before screeching into a U-turn and heading back to the Gold Coast.

The Rustmobile fit into the neighborhood so perfectly that no one had removed the tires in the two days I'd left it there. The roar from the exhaust blended in with the vibrating low-riders. Definitely a better car for me than a Jaguar convertible or some other high-rent import. No one looked at me as I went back down Grand. I stopped in front of Special-T's front door. No lights shone tonight, but I wasn't going in for another look—I wasn't in shape to escape a second trap.

I parked several blocks from my apartment. Now that Alex could tell Lemour I'd surfaced, I needed to watch out for ambushes. No one was lying in wait so far; I stopped to chat with Mr. Contreras and the dogs. My neighbor had received the LifeStory report on Lucian Frenada that I'd mailed Saturday afternoon. I'd forgotten to tell him about it, but I explained its importance to him now.

"You want me to keep it for you, doll, I'll be glad to."

"Remember how you got shot a couple of years ago when you were helping me out? I don't want to involve you like that again. Anyway, I need to make a bunch of copies so I can get it into the public arena as fast as possible."

He protested his willingness to take on any punk his size or bigger, but I took the report upstairs with me. I wished there was someone I could talk to—about the LifeStory report, or the putative connection between Baladine and Officer Lemour, or even the story Murray was running on Frenada. I hadn't realized how dependent I'd grown on Murray over the years. This was the first major investigation I'd taken on that I couldn't discuss with him, or tap into his vast knowledge of local corruption. And I badly needed help. This wasn't even an investigation. It was some kind of demon's cauldron I'd fallen into. I was bobbing around with the newts' eyes and bats' wings, and I wasn't going to have too much more time to figure out the brew before I drowned in it.

I suddenly thought of Morrell. He didn't have Murray's local connections in politics, but he had an entree into Nicola Aguinaldo's world. Vishnikov vouched for him. And I didn't think anyone knew I'd been talking to him.

I looked up his home number on my Palm Pilot, but as I was dialing I remembered his own nervousness about talking on the phone. If BB Baladine was really riding my ass, he could have a tap on my line or even a remote device to pick up anything I said in my building. That might explain why I hadn't seen any obvious surveillance on the street: if they knew they could track me at home, they could jump me on my way out, without having to leave a man in place twenty-four hours a day.

I don't like having to be paranoid about everything I say and do, but I switched on a Mozart CD on my stereo and the Cubs on television and sat between them with my cell phone. It was hard for Morrell to understand me over the interference, but once he did he readily agreed to meet me for a drink.

If I was right about Baladine not doing on-site surveillance, then I could probably leave again as long as I was quiet about it. I waited until the roar from Wrigley Field rose to a fever pitch, both on the streets behind me and on the set in front of me, and slipped out my door in bare feet, carrying my sandals to avoid making noise on the upper landing. An hour later I was back at Drummers, in Edgewater.

When I described my exit to Morrell, making a comic story of it, he didn't laugh. "That's the trouble with living in fear of the cops: you don't know if you're being a fool or taking sensible precautions."

"My dad was a cop and a good honest man. And so were his friends. Some of them are still on the force."

I thought of Frank Siekevitz. My dad trained him. The three of us used to go to baseball games together. Siekevitz wept at my dad's funeral and vowed in a tribute that made others cry to remain true to Tony's principles. Now he was backing away from me because Global Entertainment had leaned on him.

Maybe that was what was really keeping me from taking my story to my dad's oldest friend on the force. I was afraid deep down that Bobby Mallory would turn away, too. Not bought—no one could buy him—but any man with six children and a dozen grandchildren is vulnerable. Of course, everyone has a hostage to fortune. If someone kidnapped Lotty, or threatened to hurt her—

"Where are you, Vic?" Morrell asked.

I jumped at his voice. "In a place where I feel terrified and alone. That's why I called you. I need an ally, and I need one who doesn't have an easy lever to pry him apart. Unless—do you have children or lovers?"

He blinked. "Are you asking me to risk myself for you because I'm alone in the world and no one cares if I die? Why should I do that?"

I felt my cheeks stain crimson. "No reason I can think of. Unless you think I could teach you something useful, like how to jump off a building onto a moving freight train."

"Probably not a skill I can use: most of the places I'm fleeing don't have buildings high enough to jump from. Anyway, don't you do financial investigations? Why were you jumping onto a train?"

I gave him as complete a rundown of the past two weeks as I could manage. He interrupted with the occasional question, but for the most part he sat quietly, chin in hand, dark eyes watching me.

"That's why I'm eager to talk to Nicola Aguinaldo's mother," I finished. "I need someone who can tell me who her daughter would run to—or from. Nicola worked for Robert Baladine, and he's definitely on the visiting team. Would she have gone to him and ended up being beaten or kicked for showing up? It matters terribly that her body's disappeared, and I'd like to know that Abuelita Mercedes really didn't bury it without an autopsy."

Morrell put a warning hand on my arm; I hadn't noticed the waiter hovering nearby. I ordered a double espresso and a little gorgonzola–pear pizza. Riding the rods Saturday night had taken away my appetite. I certainly didn't feel like drinking. No Philip Marlowe I, downing a pint of rye every time I got injured.

When the waiter had left I said, "When Nicola died she was wearing not a dress but a long T-shirt, a Mad Virgin T-shirt. I think Lucian Frenada made it, and that doesn't make a lot of sense to me, either. How did she get it after making her break from Coolis? They can wear civilian clothes in jail, but not that kind of flimsy minidress."

After the waiter brought our food, Morrell asked me what had happened to make me think someone might be monitoring my apartment. "The last time we talked you weren't very forthcoming. Now you're rattled and want to make me an accessory, if not an ally."

I grimaced. "You weren't Chatty Cathy, either. I was willing to let it go because I thought I could get information on Aguinaldo some other way. But I haven't been able to, and anyway, so much is going on I can't seem to focus on any one problem. And then, when I got back from an out-of-town assignment this past Saturday, I found that someone was trying to frame me in a major way."

I went into more detail about the dope I'd found in my office and the chaos I'd seen at Special-T Uniforms. "I haven't been able to get hold of Frenada since the phone call—which presumably didn't come from him at all. I did go to see Lacey Dowell today—which sent her hotfoot to Global's lawyer, instead."

When I finished, Morrell nodded to himself several times, as if digesting what I'd told him. "Abuelita Mercedes really doesn't have her daughter's body. If her assailant got the body released, it's probably been buried or cremated by now; I don't think we can expect to find it."

I agreed. "The jobs are county patronage; it would be easy for a man whose clout owed Baladine or Poilevy a favor to misdirect a body if that was required. I did talk to Vishnikov the other day, and he said he'd check to see whether the body was still there but had been mislabeled. Maybe if my pals know Vishnikov is mounting a major investigation, they'll tip their hands. But the person I'd most like to talk to is Abuelita Mercedes. I would dearly love to ask her about her daughter's acquaintances."

He shook his head. "You sound like dynamite right now, to be blunt. I don't want you leading some menace to her doorstep. She fled her old apartment because someone was asking after her. Remember? You told me that yourself, and she confirms it."

I ate a slice of my cold pizza. "What if they weren't from INS or the state? What if they were the people who killed Nicola, come to make sure she hadn't talked to her mother? No matter how much Abuelita Mercedes denied having heard from Nicola, they'd never believe her. Have you asked her yourself? If Nicola talked to her before she died, I mean?"

Morrell's lips twisted in a half smile. "Bryant Vishnikov warned me that you'd wear me out if I got involved with you. No, I haven't asked her that, and yes, I'll make time to get back to Señora Mercedes in the next day or two."

"Did Vishnikov tell you I'd consulted him about you as well? He didn't give me a character reading, though."

"Maybe there's nothing people need to be warned about when they meet me," he said with a sly smile.

"Or maybe too much to be covered in a single phrase. What does the C.L. stand for?"

"Good grief. Have you really been investigating me? I didn't think any record still existed of those initials. My parents didn't speak English, and they longed for America as for the promised land. They named me in the hopes I'd fit in when we finally got here and instead gave me something that got me beat up regularly. It would have hurt their feelings if I'd changed my name, so I use only my surname. Think of me as someone like Madonna or Prince."

I imagined lying in bed with him, whispering "Morrell" instead of—what name could have been that embarrassing? Maybe they'd named him for name brands, like Clorox and Lysol. I blushed at my fantasy and hurried back to business.

The list of things that needed doing depressed me. I was like a tetherball, gyrating erratically from one side to another, depending on who was punching me. My physical stamina was limited and my emotional energy was not much greater.

"There's one other thing I'd like to ask of you," I said abruptly. "I don't think it will wear you out, but who knows? I have a videotape of the police goons in my office. I'd like it taken to Cheviot Labs, to an engineer named Rieff who's been doing some work on Aguinaldo's dress for me. I was going to send it to him tomorrow, but I want copies made first. I'm too nervous about how much of my phone conversations may have been overheard. I'm thinking my assailant heard me talking to my client about my out-of-town trip and used the opportunity to plant drugs in my office. If they heard me leave a message for Rieff Saturday night they'll go to him, or intercept me, or do something to keep the tape from him. The other thing is a copy of a report on Lucian Frenada's finances. Global is going to slam him on—on Murray Ryerson's show tomorrow night, but I have evidence that he's not living in luxury off the drug business. I want a million photocopies so it's public."

"Fine." Morrell held out a hand. "I'll take care of those. What do you want me to do with the copies?"

"Of the videotape? One to my lawyer, the original to Rieff to see if he can pick up who Lemour was speaking to on his cell phone. One to Murray Ryerson. And the report on Frenada, that should go to all those people, and a bunch of reporters I know—I can make up a list for you."

"How'd you videotape Lemour when he had you cuffed?"

"Carnifice Security isn't the only high-tech player in the detective world." I told him about the video glasses as I scribbled a media list on the back of an old parking receipt.

"I once helped photocopy details of torture conducted by the Brazil secret police," Morrell said. "It was a project organized by the Archbishop of Rio. We had a terrifying time, sneaking into the office after hours to see the records, copying them, returning them without anyone getting caught out or squealing. We could have used glasses like those. You going to be okay getting home?" he added as the waiter brought a check. "You'd be welcome to stay with me—I've got a spare bedroom."

It was appealing, the idea of not having to worry about who might be lying in wait outside my door. Besides, there was my fantasy, lying with his long fingers on my body—on my sore body, but maybe he had a lover of some sex and wouldn't find an exhausted forty-plus detective sexy, anyway.

Lotty had almost been killed once, helping me in a crisis, and Mr. Contreras had been shot. Conrad had left me after a similar episode. I couldn't bear to have one more person maimed on my account, even one I didn't know well. I thanked him but turned my roaring Skylark south toward home.

26

If You Can't Swim,
Keep Away from Sharks

I HAD CALLED Lotty from a pay phone on my way home
to tell her I was still alive and to ask her to phone me
with only the most innocuous questions. She wasn't
best pleased at being awakened—it was past eleven—
and took in my request with a terse wish for me to stop
being so melodramatic. Melodramatic and foolhardy.
Those were hard words to take to bed.

When I left Mr. Contreras, he sent Peppy up with me
for comfort. I hoped she brought enough that I could
keep at bay my nervous fantasies about someone scal-
ing the side of the building to break into my bedroom.

As I switched off the light the phone rang. I sucked
in a breath, wondering what new threat might lie at the
other end of the line, but I answered. "Warshawski's
twenty-four-hour detective service."

"Miss Warshawski?"

It was a child's voice, high-pitched with its own
nervousness. "Yes, this is V. I. Warshawski. What is it,
Robbie?"

"I've been calling you and calling you tonight. I
thought you'd never answer. First I was just going to
tell you about BB's shoes—you know, you asked if any
of them had horseshoe buckles or something, and I
don't think so—but this is worse, it's about that man,

that man they showed on the news. He was—" I heard
a click and the line went dead.

I squinted at my caller-ID pad and dialed the number
on it. It rang fifteen times without an answer. I hung up
and tried again, making sure I'd entered the right numbers. After twenty rings I gave up.

One of his parents must have heard him talking to
me and cut off the phone. I pictured the mad swimming
Eleanor standing over the phone, listening to it ring
when I called back. Or they turned off the sound and
watched a light flashing red until I hung up, while Robbie protested, crying, his father mocking him for his
tears and making him cry harder.

A week ago I might have driven out to the Baladine
home, middle of the night or not. But only someone
who had daring without judgment would do that. Or
someone whose hamstrings weren't so sore that she
couldn't run if she had to. Anyway, before leaping into
action I should find out what man Robbie had seen
on the news. There wasn't any local television coverage
this time of night, but if it was important—or grisly—
the radio would carry the story.

"It's midnight and hazy in Chicago, seventy-nine at
O'Hare, eighty-one at the lakefront, going down to a
low of seventy, with another muggy scorcher in store
for us tomorrow. Sammy Sosa capped a sparkling June
with his twentieth home run, the most in a month in
major league history, but the Cubs dropped another
one at Wrigley today, going two and eight over their
last ten games."

I drummed my fingers impatiently through another
update of the Starr chamber's slow grind; through the
pious hypocrisies of the House Speaker and the

President's sincere bombast, through more mass murders in ex-Yugoslavia and riots in Indonesia.

"In local news, the drowning victim found late yesterday at Belmont Harbor has been identified as local Hispanic entrepreneur Lucian Frenada. It is not known when or how Frenada came to be in the water; the sister with whom he lived had reported him missing Saturday morning. Mrs. Celia Caliente says she does not know what would have taken her brother to Belmont Harbor, but that he was unable to swim. In other local news, accused killer—"

I snapped off the set. Lucian Frenada was dead. That's why he hadn't been answering his phone. I wondered how you got a man who didn't know how to swim into the lake. I wondered how long it would be before I joined him.

I pulled on a shirt and tiptoed into the living room. If Baladine had one of those fancy listening devices tuned on my building, could it pick up the faint tap of Peppy's toenails as she followed me? I slipped a finger between two slats of the blind and squinted at the street.

This part of Racine is close to the trendy bars of Wrigleyville, which means we get a lot of people trying to find parking. Even late on a Monday night, occasional knots of young men, made loudly cheerful by beer, swayed up the street. I stood for twenty minutes but didn't see the same people pass twice.

If I boldly went out the front door, collected my car, and drove to Oak Brook, would I be followed? And more to the point, what would I do when I got there? Climb the security fence on my quivering legs, get arrested for trespassing, try to claim I was responding to an SOS from a twelve-year-old boy whom his successful and beautiful parents would paint as emotionally unstable. Prone to self-dramatization. And maybe they were right. Maybe it was only my animus to Eleanor and BB that made me take their child seriously.

I tried the Baladine mansion one more time, but the phone still rang unanswered. I climbed back into bed, lying rigidly, waiting for the sounds of traffic, of crickets, of drinkers laughing their way up the street, to resolve themselves into menace. There is no worse feeling than not knowing if you are truly alone in your own home. To my surprise, when Peppy pawed at my arm to rouse me, it was eight-thirty.

I rolled over and looked into her amber eyes. "Woof. Sorry, old girl. Bruises and too much of whatever anti-inflammatory Lotty gave me, and I even sleep through fear. Let's get you out and fetch the paper."

Ever since Peppy and Mitch learned that bringing in the paper netted a dog biscuit, they like to collect them for the whole building. This morning we were up so late that only my own *Herald-Star* was still on the sidewalk. Mr. Contreras sent Mitch out to join us, but Peppy drove him off with a serious growl and presented the paper to me, golden plume waving grandly. The encounter made me laugh out loud—a good thing, since the rest of the day was singularly lacking in humor.

I unfolded the paper in the vestibule outside Mr. Contreras's door. The *Herald-Star* put Frenada's death on the front page, under the headline DRUG LORD DROWNS.

Late yesterday, police identified the man pulled out of Belmont Harbor early Sunday morning as Lucian Frenada, owner of Special-T Uniforms in Humboldt Park. Frenada had become the subject of intense investigation by *Herald-Star* reporter Murray Ryerson, who taped an exposé on the use of Frenada's small business as a cover for a drug smuggling ring. This story will air tonight at nine on GTV, Channel Thirteen.

Police who raided Special-T late Saturday night discovered five kilos of cocaine inside the cardboard rolls used for shipping uncut fabric. While Frenada hotly denied any connection to the Mexican drug cartels, his bank accounts told a different story. Police speculate that he may have committed suicide to avoid arrest. Frenada grew up in the same Humboldt Park building as movie star Lacey Dowell, widely known by her fans as the Mad Virgin for her role in those movies. Dowell couldn't be reached for a comment on her old playmate's death, but studio representative Alex Fisher says the star is devastated by the news. (*Murray Ryerson and Julia Esteban contributed to this report.*)

The story ended with a tearful denial by Frenada's sister, Celia Caliente, who said her brother had no money and that it was a struggle for him to meet his share of the mortgage on the two-flat they jointly owned. The story ran with a photo of Lacey Dowell as the Mad Virgin next to a picture of her at her First Communion. Their irrelevance to Frenada's death underscored the titillative purpose of using them. *Buy this paper and get an intimate look at Lacey Dowell.* I thrust it from me with so much irritation that Peppy backed away in alarm.

"What's up, doll?" My neighbor had been watching me read.

I showed him the story and tried to explain why it bothered me so much. The one thing Mr. Contreras picked up from my incoherent rant was that Murray was framing Frenada. He didn't care whether it was because Global was feeding Murray the story or not—Mr. Contreras has always disliked Murray, even more than the men I date. I've never been sure why, and now, to my own exasperation, I found myself feebly defending Murray to the old man.

Mr. Contreras was pardonably incensed. "Either he's acting like a scumbag, no matter what the reason for it, or he's not. Don't go being his ma or his scoutmaster, telling me he's a good boy at heart, because someone with principles don't carry on this way, and you know that as well as me, cookie. He wants the limelight, he wants that TV show they got him doing, and he's looking the other way. Period."

Period indeed. I knew all those things were true, but Murray and I had been friends for so many years it hurt like any other loss to see him move away from me. Away from truth. I made a sour face at my own arrogance: I was hardly the avatar of truth.

Mr. Contreras was still fuming, hands on hips. "So whatcha going to do about it?"

"I'm going to work out and eat breakfast." I felt too defensive to share the rest of my morning's agenda.

I assured Mr. Contreras I wouldn't go to the park alone: Mitch and Peppy were happy to be my guardians. I did my stretches, then tested my legs with a modest run. I stuck my Smith & Wesson in a fanny pack. It bounced uncomfortably against my abdomen as I jogged, but the bruise in my side was still too tender for me to carry a shoulder holster.

I could only manage three very slow miles, but I was happy to be in motion again. While I jogged, I kept the dogs closely leashed, much to their annoyance. They kept tugging at me, testing the muscles in my side. I turned around frequently to see who was coming up on me, but we did a little circuit of the harbor where the cops had found Lucian Frenada without anyone trying to shove me off the rocks.

On the way back to the car I called Morrell from a pay phone. I started to ask him about the LifeStory report, but he cut me short.

"You're calling from a pay phone, but I'm on my home phone. I don't think you can take any chances with these people. There's a coffee shop two blocks north of where we ate last night. East side of the road. I'll be there in half an hour."

"Cops and robbers," I muttered to the dogs. "Or paranoids and orderlies. This is ludicrous."

Yesterday I'd accused Alex-Sandy of getting a Hollywood scriptwriter to devise the plot to frame me with cocaine in my office, but today I felt I was acting out a B movie myself, playing at spies, with a guy so nuts he wouldn't use his first name. I drove up to Edgewater and cadged a container of water for the dogs while I waited for Morrell. When he arrived, he looked more worried than wild, but who knows what face paranoia turns to the world. I asked if this charade was really necessary.

"You're the one who called me last night worried about eavesdroppers. As to whether it's necessary— that's the misery of this kind of situation. You don't know if you're being watched or making it up. The psychological toll rises so high that you almost welcome a chance to give in, just to have the uncertainty end. Which is why it's important that teammates keep each other's morale up."

I felt chastened and took the manila envelope he was

carrying with a mumbled thanks. "I know I came to you first, but it seems nuts to be playing James Bond in my own hometown."

He bent over to greet the dogs, who were whining for attention. "That's quite a collection of bruises you've got. They from your jump on Saturday?"

I hadn't had time to change out of running shorts and top. They revealed large patches of greeny purple on my legs and torso, as if Jackson Pollock had been spray-painting me.

"Well, you weren't running away from a phantom." He straightened up and looked at me, brown eyes somber. "I know living in Central America has distorted my judgment, and I try to correct for it when I come home. But you see how easily the lines between police and power get blurred, especially in a country like America, where we're always on full alert against enemies. After fifty years of the Cold War, we've gotten into such a reflexive posture of belligerence that we start to chew up our own citizens. When I come home I like to relax, but it's hard to put aside the habits that help me survive nine months out of twelve. And in this case—well, you did find drugs in your office. And Lucian Frenada is very dead."

Robbie Baladine's late-night call came back to me with a jolt. "There's something odd about that death. Can you call Vishnikov, ask him to do the autopsy himself? Just in case SMERSH did use some poison known only to Papua natives before putting Frenada into Belmont Harbor."

He grinned. "You'll be okay, Vic, as long as you can joke about it." He looked a little embarrassed, then added, "You have beautiful legs, even with all those bruises on them."

He turned hurriedly toward his car, as if paying a compliment might leave him open to a hand grenade. When I called out a thanks, he smiled and sketched a wave, then suddenly beckoned me over to the car.

"I forgot. Since we're playing at James Bond we need a more efficient way to keep in touch. Are you free for dinner tonight? Do you know a restaurant where we could meet?"

I suggested Cockatrice, part of the restaurant explosion in Wicker Park. It was walking distance from my office, where I hoped to spend the afternoon cleaning up files. First, though, I needed to run some errands.

27

Hounding a Newshound

MURRAY WASN'T AT the *Herald-Star,* but he rated a personal assistant now, so I got to speak to a human voice instead of a machine. When I told her I had important information on the Frenada story—and gave her enough details to convince her I wasn't one of the horde of nutcases who always have important information on breaking stories—she said Murray was working at home.

"If you leave your number, I'll give it to him when he calls in for his messages," she promised.

I told her I'd call back later and didn't leave a name. I pulled on clean jeans and a scarlet top and took the Smith & Wesson out of the fanny pack. I balanced it on my palm, trying to decide whether to take it or not. In my present mood I might use it on Murray, but that was a risk he'd have to take: I felt more secure with the weapon. I put it in a leg holster, where I could get to it if I acted like a contortionist. The straps dug into my calf.

No one stopped me on my way to the Rustmobile. I kept checking my mirror on the way to Lake Shore Drive, but if I was being tailed it was expertly done. I detoured downtown to my bank and left a copy of the report on Frenada in my safe deposit box. Heading back north, I swung by Tessa's mother's palace on the Gold Coast long enough to leave spare padlock keys with the doorman so that Tessa could get into our building.

I didn't bother to look for parking on the streets near Murray, since there never is any. I left the Skylark in the alley behind his building, underneath a sign that said: WARNING, WE CALL THE POLICE TO TOW UNAUTHORIZED VEHICLES. Let them.

Murray lives in one of those six-flats with wood-burning fireplaces, tessellated marble floors in the entryways, and all the other stuff you get if you can afford a Mercedes convertible. The bells were brightly polished brass set into cherry paneling.

When Murray's voice came through the intercom, I pinched my nose and said, "Florist. Delivery for Ryerson."

We all imagine we're so special that an unexpected gift of flowers doesn't seem surprising. Murray released the lock and waited for me in his doorway. Sinéad O'Connor was wafting out from the living room behind him when I got to the second floor. The surprise in his face when he saw me did not seem to include delight.

"What the hell are you—"

"Hi, Murray. We need to talk. Is Alex-Sandy here?"

He didn't move from the doorway. "What do you think this is? A public library with regular visiting hours?"

"That's very good. I'll have to use that. Like the next time you come around unannounced with Alex Fisher-Fishbein to con me into framing someone for you. What did you say to her: 'Let's sprinkle some crumbs from the Global table in front of Warshawski, she's so perennially hard up she'll jump on them like a carp on live bait?' "

His face darkened. "I tried to do you a favor. Just because you're in some twenty-year-old catfight with Alex—"

"Darling Murray, when I'm in a catfight you see the gashes a jaguar leaves. But it's hard for even a jungle cat to do much against a shark. Are you her partner or her patsy?"

"I've listened to you mouth off a lot of bull to a lot of people over the years, but this is the most offensive thing I've heard you say yet."

"Did she tell you Global planned to toss my place? And did she mention whether they were sowing or reaping?"

His scowl got uglier, but he moved out of the doorway. "You'd better come in and tell me what happened before you go off half-cocked to Alex."

I followed him into the living room and sat uninvited on one of the couches. He picked up a remote gadget and shut off his stereo, a cute system about as thick as my finger, with silvery speakers like rockets tucked into the corners of the room.

He leaned against the wall: this wasn't a social visit and he wasn't going to sit. "Okay. What happened to your place?"

I eyed him narrowly, even though I know you can't read the truth in most faces. "Someone planted three— large—bags of coke in it while I was out of town last week."

"Don't bring it to me. Call the cops."

"I did that very thing. A specimen named Lemour, who apparently freelances for BB Baladine, or maybe

Jean Claude Poilevy, beat me and tried to have me arrested. That was when he couldn't find the stuff. And he knew exactly where it was supposed to be." I smiled unpleasantly and cut off Murray as he started to speak. "I ran a secret camera during the search."

His scowl didn't lighten, but a shade of doubt came into his eyes. "I'd like to see the film."

"So you shall. I'm having your very own copy made for you. And today, because we've been pals for a long time and I hate to see you turn into a fawning sycophant for the studio, I am hand-delivering to you the LifeStory report I ran on Lucian Frenada two days before Global decided he needed to be discredited."

Murray's eyes blazed with fury at my studied insult, but he snatched the envelope out of my hand and sat down opposite me. While he examined the report I looked at the mess of papers on the glass-topped table. He'd been fine-tuning his script for tonight when I arrived: even upside down it was easy to make out Frenada's name.

After a couple of minutes Murray dug out another report from the pile in front of him—his copy of Frenada's finances—and began a page-by-page comparison. When he finished, he flung both of them onto the table.

"How do I know you didn't forge this?"

"Feeble, Murray: the creation date is embedded in the report. What I want to know is what Frenada knew about BB Baladine—or Teddy Trant—that made the studio come after him."

"He was harassing—"

"No." I cut him off sharply. "He was not hanging around the hotel. He came there once, and Lacey met with him for an hour in her suite. Frank Siekevitz, the

Trianon's security chief, may be changing his tune now, but he told me that a week ago. I'll be honest—Lacey has refused to talk to me—but I don't believe that crock about Frenada harassing her. I think Global wanted me and Frenada both out of the picture. They'd give me so huge a fee for getting dirt on him that I couldn't speak against them—and he'd be discredited. I know nothing that could interest, or harm, the studio, so why they're riding me so hard I don't understand. Whether Frenada did is another matter, but one we're not too likely to find out at this juncture. But one thing I will stake my reputation on is that he was not in the drug trade."

Murray's full lips tightened in a thin line. I realized I wasn't used to seeing his mouth—in all the years I'd known him he'd covered it with his beard. His face looked naked now, with a kind of bewildered petulance replacing his anger. It made me uncomfortable and I felt myself softening—into his ma or his scoutmaster. Mr. Contreras's admonition came back to me and made me laugh.

"Yeah, it's really funny. Maybe I'll get the joke in a year or two," Murray said resentfully.

"I was laughing at myself, not you. What are you going to do with this?"

He hunched a shoulder. "Cops found five kilos of coke in his office Saturday night."

"Put there by the same hand that planted them on me. Unless you think I, too, am running drugs in from Mexico?"

"Nothing you do would surprise me, Warshawski. Although it wouldn't be like you to do something that actually turned a profit. Where is the stuff you found?"

"St. Louis."

"St. Louis? Oh. You flushed it."

The Chicago sewers flow into the Chicago River. To keep the lake clean, we reversed the current of the river so that our sludge—properly treated, of course—flows backward, into the Mississippi. I suppose eventually it reaches New Orleans, but our rivalries are local—we prefer to think we're dumping on St. Louis.

"In that case, you've got no proof. I don't know what to make of this report. It's the only thing that contradicts my story. It may be that new evidence came in between when you asked and when I did."

"In forty-eight hours?" I lost my temper again. "If you go on the air tonight with this slander against Frenada I am going to persuade his sister to sue the studio and you for every dime you have."

His anger flared up as well. "You are always right, aren't you? You have one flimsy piece of counterevidence and you come galloping in like some damned Amazon, quivering with omnipotent self-righteousness, and based on your say-so I'm supposed to abandon an investigation I've worked hard on. Well, take your story to the *Enquirer,* or put it on the Web. A lot of people out there love conspiracies. And unless Frenada's sister is a major enemy of yours, don't egg her on against the studio: Global breaks bigger people than Celia Caliente like crackers over soup."

"That what they're threatening you with?"

His face turned the color of Lake Calumet brick. "Get out! Get out and don't come near me again."

I got to my feet. "I'll give you a hint for nothing. The story on Frenada and Global isn't about drugs. I'm not sure, but I think it's about T-shirts. Mad Virgin T-shirts. We could have a nice little coup together—if Global didn't own you. I mean, the paper, of course."

He put a hand between my shoulders and pushed me

toward the door. When he slammed it behind me, I dearly wanted to put my ear to the keyhole to see if I could hear him on the phone: would he go straight to Alex? I was glad I thought better of it: as I started down the stairs his door opened.

I turned to look at him. "Second thoughts, Murray?"

"Just wondering if you were really leaving, Vic."

I blew him an airy kiss and continued down the stairs. At the bottom I wondered what I'd really gained from the encounter. It's a mistake to try to interrogate someone when you're angry. But at least that cut both ways with Murray this morning.

My car was still in the alley when I got there. One of the few pluses of a difficult day.

28

Friendly Warning

I WAS EXPLAINING to a woman from a temporary agency how to match invoices and case reports when the call came. "Collect for V. I. Wachewski from Veronica Fassler," the operator said.

I thought for a minute but couldn't place the name. "Sorry. I think she's mistaken."

"Tell her from Coolis, she met me at the hospital," a voice at the other end gabbled frantically, before we were cut off.

Veronica Fassler. The woman who'd had the baby and was shuffling along the hall chained to the orderly when Mr. Contreras and I left. So much had happened in the last week that I barely remembered the event. I wondered how she'd gotten my name and number, but that wasn't important—I'd been strewing my cards wholesale around the hospital.

"Oh, yes," I said slowly. "I'll accept the call."

"I been in line thirty minutes and there's people behind me still waiting. You asking questions about Nicola, right?"

Nicola Aguinaldo. Somehow I'd also lost track of her in the last few days.

"Did you know something about her?" I asked.

"Is there a reward?"

"The family doesn't have much money," I said. "If they could find out how she managed to get out of the hospital, it might be worth a hundred dollars."

"Out of the hospital? I only know how she went. On a stretcher. That ought to be worth a whole lot more than how she left."

"Female difficulties, I understand." I sounded prim.

"You call pounding a CO on the chest with your bitty fists and getting burned 'female difficulties,' you have a different body than me, miss."

"Burned?" Now I really was bewildered: I didn't remember seeing burn marks on Nicola's body, but there was no way of finding out now.

"You don't know anything, do you? With a stun gun. The CO's all carry them to keep order in the workshop. No one would've guessed they'd ever need one on Nicola."

"That's what took her to the hospital?"

"What about the reward, before you pry any further."

"Did you see the CO burn her?"

A silence on the other end told its own tale. Before the speaker could bluster into some lies, I said I thought that much information was valuable, probably worth fifty dollars.

She paused again, marshaling her tale, then said in a rush, "Nicola took the gun—the stun gun—from the guard, turned it on him, and he got so mad he gave her a lethal dose. Stuns the heart, you know, just like the electric chair, if they turn up the juice. So the guards thought she was dead and rolled her body out of the hospital themselves to make it look like she didn't die there. They wouldn't want an investigation. That's what happened."

"I like the story; it's a good one. But it's not how she died. Where shall I send the fifty?"

"Fuck you, bitch, I'm calling to help, aren't I? How do you know when you wasn't there yourself?"

"I saw Nicola's dead body." I didn't want to tell her what injuries caused the death, because then she'd embroider some story to account for them. I told her it would be worth another fifty to me if she could get me the name of someone at Coolis who'd known Nicola well.

"Maybe," she said doubtfully. "She didn't speak much English, but the Mexican girls didn't hang with her on account of she was from China."

I was startled, but then decided it was just garbled geography, not some unusual fact about Aguinaldo I hadn't heard before. "You said she got injured in the workshop?"

"You know, where we do prison work. She was in the sewing shop. My friend Erica, her roommate Monique was working there the day the CO took after Nicola."

"Maybe I could talk to her roommate."

"And let her get the reward money when I've done all the work? No thanks!"

"You'd get a finder's fee," I encouraged her. "The roommate would get an informer's fee."

Before I could push any harder, the line went dead. I called the operator to find out if she could reconnect me, but she told me what I already knew: you can call out from jail, but no one can call in.

I sat back in my chair. So the prison had lied about the ovarian cyst. Possibly had lied, if I could believe Veronica's tale. The idea of Nicola Aguinaldo attacking a guard seemed utterly improbable, but it was obvious when Veronica had started lying—when she blurted out the tale about the guards putting Nicola's dead body out of the hospital. Of course, she'd had a week to prepare a realistic story. You don't have to be behind bars to be a con artist, but the odds are more in your favor there. In my days as a public defender I'd encountered every variation of injured innocence known not just to man but to woman as well.

I needed more information on Coolis, on what Nicola had been doing the day before she went into the hospital. I'd have to make another trip out there, in my guise as a lawyer in good standing with the Illinois bar —which I am, but I wouldn't advise anyone to retain a lawyer who hadn't practiced in over a decade.

In the meantime I had more obvious tasks right in front of me. The woman from the temporary agency was standing next to me with a heap of computer printouts that needed sorting.

We were halfway through those when Tessa bounced in. She'd wrapped red beads around her locks and pulled them back in a kino cloth.

"What's going on around here, V.I., that you put up that ridiculous set of . . . ?" Her voice trailed away as she took in the chaos. "Good grief! I knew you were a bit of a slob, but this is way outside your usual housekeeping. Unkeeping."

I made sure the woman from the agency was clear enough on her work to leave her alone for a while and took Tessa into her studio to talk. She frowned when I finished.

"I don't like being so vulnerable here."

"Me either," I said with feeling. "If it's any comfort, I don't think my marauders would bother you."

"I want to get a better lock system installed. One

that's more secure than those padlocks you have out front. And I think you ought to pay for it, since it's due to you that the place was vandalized."

I expelled a loud breath. "You're going to choose it and I'm going to fund it? No, thanks. You chose a number-pad system that seemed relatively easy to bypass."

She frowned again. "How did they do that?"

I shrugged. "The pad itself hadn't been tampered with, so my best guess is with UV-sensitive ink. They spray the pad, then after you go in they shine an ultraviolet light on the pad. The keys you've touched are clean, see. Then they just have to try those numbers in different combinations until they get the right sequence. If that's the case we could reset the combination—but we'd have to remember to touch every number on the pad each time we went in. A magnetic card lock would be less vulnerable—but you have to remember to carry the card with you all the time. Anyone can break a padlock, but you have to stand there with equipment, which makes you more vulnerable to a passing squad car. Or to Elton. He's keeping an eye on the joint for us."

"Oh, for God's sake, Vic! An alcoholic street dweller!"

"He's not usually falling-down drunk," I said with dignity. "And his drinking doesn't stop him from using his eyes. Anyway, I'll ask Mary Louise to look into it. If she has time."

My voice trailed away into doubt. Mary Louise seemed more than just too busy to work for me right now. She seemed scared.

Tessa was too absorbed by her own needs to notice my hesitation. "Daddy thinks I should—we should—

get a system like Honeywell's, that notifies a central computer of an unauthorized break-in."

"Your daddy could well be right. But the guys who came in here wouldn't have triggered anyone's alarm system."

We thrashed it around inconclusively, until the woman from the agency came to get more direction.

I tried the Baladines a couple of times during the afternoon, but only got Rosario, the maid, who said, Robbie not home, Robbie away, Missus away. The third time I called I asked for one of the precocious swimming daughters. I remembered they had names like street signs, but it took me a while to come up with Madison and Utah. The intersection where bad deals are done.

I didn't introduce myself in case there was a parental warning out on me. Madison had seemed alarmingly forthcoming in her remarks when I was out there two weeks ago. She didn't disappoint me today.

"Robbie isn't home. He ran away, and Mommy's out looking for him. Daddy is furious, he says when he finds Robbie he'll make sure he toughens up, we've been soft on him too long."

"He ran away? Do you know where he'd go?" I hoped there was a sympathetic grandmother or aunt someplace who might stand up for Robbie.

That's why Eleanor had taken off, Madison explained, to go to her mother's in case Robbie was hiding there. "We're going to France on Saturday, and Robbie better be back before then. We're renting a castle with a swimming pool so me and Utah and Rhiannon can practice. Do you know we're having a swimming meet here on Labor Day? If Rhiannon beats me in the backstroke, I am going to be so sick. Robbie would never beat me, he's too fat, he can't do anything with his body. Like last summer when he fell over his feet playing football at our cousin's. He got his feet tangled up in his shoelaces. He looked so funny, me and my cousin Gail laughed our heads off. Robbie was up all night crying. That's something only weak girlie girls do."

"Yes, I remember," I said. "You didn't even cry when a fire truck ran over your cat. Or did you cry because the nice shiny engine had a smear on it?"

"Huh? Fluffy didn't get hit by a fire truck. That was Mom; she ran over her with the car. Robbie cried. He cried when she killed a bird. I didn't."

"You're going to be a credit to Dr. Mengele one of these days."

"Who?" she screeched.

"Mengele." I spelled the name. "Tell BB and Eleanor he has an opening for a bright young kid."

I tried not to slam the phone in her ear: it wasn't her fault her parents were bringing her up to have the sensitivity of a warthog. I wished I could take some time off to look for Robbie, but I had more to do here than I could figure out. Such as what to do about Veronica Fassler's call from Coolis. In the morning I'd take another trip out there, but for right now I could try to get the doctor who'd operated on Nicola Aguinaldo at Beth Israel.

Before calling the hospital I looked inside my phone to see if the folks who broke in had planted a bug in it. When I didn't find anything unusual in the mess of wires, I went out behind the warehouse to inspect the phone junction box. There I found that the wires had been stripped and clipped to a secondary set of cables, presumably leading to a listening station. I tapped on them thoughtfully. Probably best that I left them in place. It wasn't a sophisticated system, but if I dismantled it, Baladine would get something less primitive, harder to find, and harder to circumvent.

Back inside, I let Andras Schiff play Bach on my office CD. I don't know if those old spy movies are right, that radios block listening devices, but the *Goldberg Variations* might at a minimum educate the thugs—who knows? I sat next to the speaker with my cell phone and called the hospital. The woman from the agency stared at me curiously, then turned a huffy shoulder: she thought I was trying to keep her from listening to me.

Max Loewenthal's secretary, Cynthia Dowling, came on the line with her usual efficient friendliness.

"I can't remember the ER surgeon's name," I said. "I should, since it's Polish, but all I remember is that it had a hundred zees and cees in it."

"Dr. Szymczyk," she supplied.

When I explained what I wanted, she put me on hold and tracked down the report. Of course Dr. Szymczyk hadn't done an autopsy, but he had dictated information while he was working on Aguinaldo. He had described necrotic skin on the abdomen but hadn't mentioned any serious burn wounds. He had noted a couple of raw spots above the breasts that didn't seem connected to the blow that killed her.

Raw spots. Those could conceivably have been caused by a stun gun, so maybe Veronica Fassler hadn't been spinning a complete lie. I would bring fifty dollars for her with me to the prison in the morning.

I worked desultorily with the woman from the agency, but it was hard for me to focus on files. For some people, putting papers in order is a wonderfully soothing act, but I could make so little sense of the world around me that I couldn't make sense of my scattered papers either.

Late in the afternoon, as I was trying to remember what year and what file records about Humboldt Chemical belonged to, my office buzzer rang. I stiffened and had my gun in hand when I went to the front door. I was astounded to see Abigail Trant, her honey-colored hair and softly tinted face as perfect as when I'd met her two weeks ago. Her Mercedes Gelaendewagen was double-parked on the street outside. When I invited her in, she asked if I'd talk to her in her vehicle instead. I wondered briefly if she had been dragooned into acting as a decoy but followed her to her trucklet.

"Do you know that Robbie Baladine has disappeared? If you know where he is, can you send him home?"

I blinked in surprise but assured her I hadn't heard from him for several days. "Did Eleanor or BB send you to talk to me?"

She looked straight ahead, ignoring an angrily honking line of cars behind her. "I came on my own initiative, and I am hoping you will honor my speaking confidentially to you. We are flying to France with the Baladines on Saturday, along with the Poilevys, so Eleanor discussed Robbie's disappearance with me in a frank way, as it is affecting their travel plans. They both feel that you have encouraged Robbie to be disobedient. I don't know if that is the reason, but BB has been talking furiously about wanting to put you out of business or thoroughly discredit you in some way. Knowing something about his methods, I didn't want to call you—he might well be monitoring your phone calls. I think I told you when we met that he doesn't like to feel anyone is getting the upper hand with him: for some reason he thinks you are taunting him or undermining him in some way."

I gave a snort of mirthless laughter. "He's been making it almost impossible for me to run my business."

A car shot around her from behind, giving her the finger and a loud epithet. She paid no attention.

"I had suggested to Teddy that Global try to make use of your agency, that it would be a good thing to support local talent. But he said you refused to take the assignment."

My jaw dropped so suddenly that my ears popped. "You were behind that? Mrs. Trant—that was extremely gracious of you. The trouble is, the assignment as it came to me from Alex Fisher was to frame someone, a man named Lucian Frenada who was drowned over the weekend. I couldn't take it on."

She sighed. "That's so typical of Alex. I wish Teddy didn't rely on her advice so much—I think she often leads him astray."

What a good wife, letting herself believe her husband was the innocent victim of bad advisers. But I wasn't going to ride her: she had gone out on a long limb for me with no reason for doing so. I asked her what made her put in a word for me with her husband.

She looked at me for the first time. "Do you know that the only money I've ever worked for was exercising horses for people when I was a teenager? I love my life and I love my husband, but I've often wondered what I would do if he—and my own family—lost everything. Would I be able to cut my own path, the way you have? Helping you out is like—like—"

"A sacrifice to the gods to keep them from putting you to the test?" I suggested when she fumbled for words.

She flashed a radiant smile. "That's it exactly. What a beautiful way of phrasing it! But in the meantime, if you hear from Robbie, send him home. Even if he's not always happy there, his parents really have his best interests at heart. And I don't think you can win against BB. He's too big, and he has too many powerful friends."

I couldn't argue with that. I hesitated over my words before speaking again, then said, "Mrs. Trant, you've gone out of your way to help me. So I don't like putting you on the spot. But have you noticed whether any of—well, the men you see socially, BB or Poilevy for instance—would you notice if one of them had lost a medallion from a Ferragamo shoe?"

"What a strange question. I suppose that means you must have found one? Where, I wonder? Are you allowed to tell me?"

"In the street near where Nicola Aguinaldo—the Baladines' old nanny—died."

She smiled again but without the radiance. "It's not the kind of thing I notice, I'm afraid. Now—I'd better take off. It's an hour on the Ike this time of day, and we're entertaining some studio execs. I'll certainly pay special attention to everyone's feet tonight. Don't forget about Robbie, will you? He should be at home."

That seemed to be my exit line. I thanked her for her warning. And for trying to help my little agency. Maybe that was why Baladine hadn't murdered me, I thought as I went back into my office. Maybe Teddy had told him that Abigail would be upset if they killed me. She knew about the shoe, though. I was willing to bet my meager pension plan on it.

29

Help Me, Father, for I Know Not
What I'm Doing

At FIVE-THIRTY I sent the woman from the agency home. I didn't want to pay overtime on a job that would take at least sixteen or twenty more hours to finish. And I wanted her to leave while enough commuters were filling the sidewalks that no one would shoot at her, thinking it was me.

Tessa was still working in her studio. She put down her mallet and chisel after I'd been standing in her line of sight for six minutes. Artistic geniuses can't break their concentration, I know. I told her I was worrying about her safety while Baladine was gunning for me.

"I'm going to take my computer home. It's the only thing I need from my office for the immediate present. And then I'll get word out that I'm not operating out of here. We could install a small video camera at the entrance concealed in one of your metal pieces; that would provide a record of anyone who broke in. For an extra five hundred or so we could even get little monitors so we could watch the entrance. And we could install a five-digit number pad with a breaker that froze it if someone tried more than three times in ten minutes to open it. With those you should be pretty safe."

She wiped her face with a used towel, leaving a film

of glittery dust on her cheeks. "Oh, damn you for being so noble, Vic. I was all set to chew your ass into tiny pieces. Now what am I supposed to do?"

"If you'd chew up BB Baladine it would be more helpful. I know everyone thinks I'm in this mess because I'm too impulsive, but honestly, all I did was stop to help a woman in the road."

"That means something to you, I suppose. Get me a video camera installed tomorrow, and a new number pad, and leave your damned computer here. By the way, my daddy is insisting that someone from his staff meet me when I leave here at night."

"Ah, that would be your mother's next candidate for the father of her grandchildren?"

She grinned. "She's hoping. His name's Jason Goodrich—sounds solid enough, doesn't it? He's one of those software whizzes who gurgle in code coming out of the womb."

"More to the point is whether the boy knows how to disarm a man holding an automatic. But if you're happy, I'm happy."

I went back to my office to call Mary Louise. When I asked her if she would have time to take care of the office security, she hemmed and muttered something about her midterms.

"Pete's sake, Mary Louise. This isn't asking you to go into the Georgia mud for a month. It would be a big help if you could take care of the setup. I don't want to discuss what I want on the phone, but I can come over tonight or tomorrow morning and explain it."

"No!" she snapped. "You're not to come anywhere near this place."

"What on earth is going on?" I was hurt more than baffled. "What have I done to you?"

"I—you—Vic, I can't do any more work for you. You take too many risks."

"You made it through ten years in the department, but I take so many risks you can't even go to the Unblinking Eye for me?" I slammed the phone down so hard my palm smarted.

Was I really more dangerous to work for than the Chicago police? I fumed, pacing the room. If she could go down dark alleys after drug dealers, why couldn't she at least go to the camera store and arrange for a video monitor for me? And all she'd say was she wasn't going to put the children at risk. As if I were asking her to use them as human shields.

I came to a halt by my desk. Of course. Someone had threatened the children. That was what had happened. My hand hovered over the phone, then I thought better of it. If BB was monitoring my calls, then he'd assume Mary Louise had squealed. Then he might really go after the children. I felt trapped, and horribly alone. I sat with my head in my hands, trying not to cry.

"Vic! What's wrong?" Tessa was leaning over me, her face lively with concern.

I rubbed a hand through my hair. "Nothing. I'm feeling sorry for myself, which is a disastrous indulgence for a detective. You taking off?"

"My appointed knight has arrived. It's time for me to go, or have my mother show up with the FBI."

She gestured toward the door and a man came in. He was tall and dark, almost as dark as Tessa herself, with fine-drawn features and the easy manner you get growing up with a lot of money. I could see why Mrs. Reynolds thought he looked like good husband material.

"Don't sit here brooding alone," Tessa said. "We'll

take you down to the Glow or some other place where you can be with friends."

I pushed myself upright. The soreness in my legs was fading, that was one thing to be thankful for—a tribute to my daily workouts, or maybe just my DNA.

"It's not such a good idea right now for you to hang out with me." I tried not to seem melodramatic, and sounded pompous instead. "Anyway, I'm going to see a priest, so I'll be in good hands."

"A priest?" Tessa echoed. "Vic! Oh, you're pulling my leg. Well, don't stay alone here too late, hear?"

I followed her to the door and watched her and her escort leave. He was driving a navy BMW sedan, an easy car to keep an eye on if you were tailing. Just as well I'd turned down a ride.

I watched the street through the small pane of wire-filled glass for five minutes or so. Who knew if I was under surveillance or not? I walked down to the corner, leaving the Rustmobile in the lot.

Elton was hawking *Streetwise* near the L stop. I stopped to buy a few; his red-streaked blue eyes looked at me with lively curiosity. "I see some dudes hanging around today," he whispered with hoarse importance. "*Streetwise,* miss, *Streetwise,* sir—read about the mayor and the homeless on Lower Wacker—they was driving some kind of late-model tan car, maybe a Honda. Fact of the matter they're driving down Leavitt now. Coming up behind you. *Streetwise,* sir, thank you, sir."

I scuttled up the L stairs, frantically fishing in my wallet for singles to stuff into the ticket machine. Below me the tan Honda stopped. I grabbed a ticket and ran up to the platform, shoving my way through a knot of commuters who swore at me for my rudeness. A south-bound train was getting ready to leave. I stuck a hand into the shutting panels, earning another yell—this time from the trainman—and watched the platform with a sick franticness until the doors hissed shut and we were under way.

I rode the train all the way into the Loop, where I got out and walked slowly around Marshall Field's, admiring the beachwear in the State Street windows and the garden furniture at the north end of the store. The setting sun made a mirror of the glass; I watched the people behind me. No one seemed to be paying me any special attention.

I climbed back up the L stairs and picked up the Blue Line outbound: I'd had a tiny inspiration while I was indulging in misery in my office. It took me to the California stop, in the heart of Humboldt Park. I walked the six blocks to St. Remigio's.

St. Remigio's was a Victorian brick monster, dating to the turn of the last century when Humboldt Park had a large Italian population. Whoever Remigio had been, his miraculous powers hadn't extended to protecting the building: the great arched windows in the sanctuary were boarded over, and the old wooden doors were fastened with massive chains.

Despite the lateness of the hour, small boys were racing after a soccer ball in the heavily fenced schoolyard. A stocky man with sparse white hair punctuated their screams with shouted directions in Spanish. After a minute or two he saw me at the locked gate and came over, asking in Spanish what I wanted.

"Ando buscando a el Padre." I stumbled through the phrase in my schoolgirl Spanish.

He waved an arm toward the back of the church and said something so fast that I couldn't follow it. Before I could ask for a repetition, two little boys ran over to tug at his arm and demand—as far as I could tell—a ruling on some dispute. I was immediately forgotten in the more important business of the moment.

I walked past the front of the church and found a narrow walkway leading to the rear. Chunks of pavement were missing, but someone had made a gallant attempt to spruce up the area. Scraggly rosebushes surrounded a dejected-looking statue that I assumed was St. Remigio himself. I picked an empty bottle of Four Roses from behind him and looked for a garbage bin. Finally, not wanting to present myself to the priest carrying a bottle, I tucked it into my handbag and rang a bell labeled FATHER LOU.

After a longish wait, when I was thinking the soccer coach might have been explaining that Father Lou was away, a harsh squawk startled me. I hadn't noticed the intercom to the left of the door.

"This is V. I. Warshawski. I want to talk to the priest about one of his parishioners." I didn't think I could explain my errand intelligibly at a shout through a speaker.

After another long wait, the dead bolt snapped back and an old man in a T-shirt and slippers stood in the doorway. His upper body and neck had the thickness of a weight lifter. He looked at me as if assessing whether to pick me up and throw me off the stoop.

"Father Lou?"

"Are you with the police or the press?" He had the gravelly voice of the old Irish South Side.

"No. I'm a private investigator—"

"Whether you're private or public, I won't have you digging around in that boy's past, trying to prove some slander about him." He turned back inside and started to shut the door.

I put out a hand to brace the door; it took all my strength to keep a big enough crack open for me to cry out, "I'm not slandering Lucian Frenada. I've been trying to stop the *Herald-Star* from running their story on him and drugs. I've been trying to talk to Lacey Dowell, because she knows something about the true reason he was killed, but she won't talk to me. I was hoping you might know something."

The pressure on the other side eased. Father Lou reappeared in the entrance, frowning. "If you aren't digging up dirt on Lucy, what's your involvement?"

"Please. Can we sit down? I can explain the whole story to you, but not standing out here in the heat with one foot in the door hoping you won't shut it on me."

"This is my rest time," the priest grumbled. "Everyone around here knows not to bother me from six to seven. It's the only way an old man like me can keep running a big parish."

That must have been what the soccer coach was trying to tell me—the priest is back there, but don't interrupt his nap. I was starting to mutter an apology when he added, "But Lucy's death—I can't sleep anyway. I might as well talk to you."

He led me into a wide dark vestibule. Despite his age he moved easily, his walk a graceful bounce. Dancers' legs, boxers' legs.

"Mind your step. I don't put lights on in the hall— have to save every nickel in a poor parish; don't want the cardinal shutting us down because we're too expensive."

Father Lou unlocked a small side room, furnished with the heavy remains of the previous century. Eight chairs with ornate legs stood primly around a heavy table. A blackened painting of Jesus in a crown of thorns hung over an empty grate.

The priest motioned me to one of the chairs. "I'm going to make tea. Make yourself comfortable."

I did my best in the wooden chair. The flowers carved into the back dug into my shoulder blades. I shifted forward. On the table a plaster statue of the Virgin smiled at me sadly. Her lips were chipped and the paint had flaked from her left eye, but the right one stared at me patiently. She was wearing a cloak of faded taffeta, painstakingly trimmed in handmade lace.

Father Lou returned with a battered metal tray holding a teapot and two cups as I was fingering the fabric. "A hundred years old, that lace, we have it on the altar, too. What did you say your name was?"

When I repeated it he tried to talk to me in Polish. I had to explain that I knew only a handful of words, gleaned from my father's mother; my own mother, an Italian immigrant, spoke to me in her language. At that he switched to Italian and grinned with delight at my surprise.

"I've been here a long time. Baptized Italians here, married Poles; now I offer the mass in Spanish. Neighborhood's always been poor; wasn't always this dangerous. Parish council suggested soccer. Seems to be good for the little kids, lets them run off some of that energy."

"But you were a boxer?" I was guessing, from his gait.

"Oh, yeah. I boxed for Loyola in the forties, then I found my vocation but kept boxing. I still run a club here. St. Remigio's remains the school to beat—gives the boys something to be proud of. We can't play football against those big suburban schools. We can't get enough equipment for eleven boys, let alone fifty or sixty the way they do. But I can outfit boxers. Lucy was one of my best. I was that proud of him."

His jaw worked. For a minute he looked like a tired old man, his pale eyes filming over, then he shook himself, an unconscious motion, shaking off one more punch.

He looked at me aggressively, as if to make sure I didn't try to pity him for his weakness. "The police came around suggesting Lucy was running drugs through his factory. They wanted me to spy on him. I told them what I thought of that. Then the papers and the television. Mexican boy makes good, so he must be selling drugs. All that innuendo—I saw what the *Herald-Star*'s been saying. This boy who drove an old car so he could pay his sister's children's fees here at Remigio? They couldn't leave him alone."

He stopped to drink some tea. I had some too, to be polite. It was light and flowery and surprisingly refreshing in the heat.

"When did you last talk to him?" I asked.

"He came here to mass once or twice a week. I'm thinking it was last Tuesday. He filled in as a server when he saw that the kid who was supposed to do it hadn't shown. They used to laugh at him when he was fourteen, when I talked him into coming here, do some training and serve at the mass—little altar boy, that's what they called him—but then he started winning boxing matches, and the tune they sang on the streets changed in a hurry.

"I'm getting sidetracked. I don't like to think about him being dead, that's all. It's easy to say people are with Jesus when they die, and I even believe it's true, but we need Lucy here. I need him, anyway. Jesus wept when Lazarus died—He's not going to condemn me for crying over Lucy."

He picked up the statue of the Madonna and twisted it around, smoothing the taffeta cape over her hips. I sat still. He'd speak when he was ready, but if I prodded him he might turn pugnacious again.

"So—he still came to mass. When he started his shop, Special-T, he could have gone someplace farther away, a safer neighborhood, but he liked to stay close to the church. Felt his life had been saved here. He went from being a lookout for the Lions, selling nickel bags, to citywide lightweight champ. Then my old school, Loyola, working nights at a downtown hotel to put himself through college, but he left those Lions and drugs behind for good when he boxed for me. I make it clear to all the boys: they can't get in the ring with Jesus and drugs at the same time."

There wasn't any hearty piety in his voice, just the facts. No one looking at those forearms, or the stern set to his jaw, could doubt Father Lou's ability to stand up to a gangbanger.

"Anyway, I'm thinking it was Tuesday, but maybe it was Wednesday, I can't be sure. But we had a cup of coffee and a donut after the service."

"Was he worried then?"

"Of course he was worried, all this—this crap about him and drugs!" the old man shouted, smacking the table hard enough to make the Virgin wobble. "And what's it to you, anyway?"

"If it's any comfort, I think someone was setting him up with the drugs." Once again I went through the long story of Nicola Aguinaldo, of Alex Fisher and the studio asking me to look into Frenada's finances, and the two very different reports on them.

"It's disgusting," Father Lou said, "disgusting that you could go pry into the boy's private business like that."

My cheeks grew hot. I didn't try to defend myself—I know it's a breach of privacy, and I wasn't going to give that pathetic adolescent bleat that everyone did it.

Father Lou glared at me, his jaw working, then said, "Still, I suppose it's a good thing you saw the accounts the way they really were. How could it happen, the report being changed like that, so that you get one version, that reporter friend of yours another?"

"I've thought a lot about that," I said. "That's one of the reasons I came to see you. You read from time to time about hackers trying to move money from a bank into their accounts; the security stops them when they try to take it out. I don't think it would be so hard for someone with a lot of sophisticated resources to break into a system and make more money appear than was really there. But what will happen if the user tries to withdraw it? If Lucian Frenada's sister is his heir, can you get her to try to take the money out? That will prove whether it's really there or just a shadow."

He thought it over. He didn't react quickly, but he was thorough, asking a series of questions designed to make sure Frenada's sister wouldn't be in any danger if she tried to get the money.

"Okay. I won't say yes or no tonight, but I'll talk to Celia in the morning. I want you to promise me you won't bother her. Are you a Catholic? Do you have a pledge that you honor?"

I shifted uncomfortably on the hard chair; my mother, fleeing Fascist Italy because of religion, didn't want that to define her daughter's life in the New

World. "I'll pledge you my word. When I give it I do my utmost to keep it."

He grunted. "I guess that'll have to do. And the other thing you wanted from me?"

I took a breath and said in a rush, "Lacey Dowell. She knows something about Frenada, about his shirts, why he made those Mad Virgin T-shirts and then pretended he hadn't. She won't talk to me."

"Magdalena. I never can think of her by that silly stage name. You think I can make her give up her story?" His full mouth twisted, whether in amusement or scorn I couldn't tell. "Maybe. Maybe. You being a detective and all, I suppose you know what fancy hotel she's staying in while she's in town. She sure avoids the old neighborhood, unless she's got a team of cameras following after her."

30

The Mad Virgin's Story

FATHER LOU WAS gone about twenty minutes. When he came back he said if I could wait he was pretty sure Magdalena would be along to the church sometime this evening.

I suddenly remembered Morrell, waiting for me at a restaurant on Damen, and asked for a phone. Father Lou took me into his study, a shabby but far more comfortable room than the parlor we'd been using. Boxing trophies were scattered about shelves stuffed with old papers. The desk, with a simple wood crucifix over it, was stacked with financial reports and old sermons. He didn't have many books; I noticed a collection of Frank O'Connor short stories and, to my surprise, one by Sandra Cisneros—trying to keep up with parishioners, he explained when he saw me looking at it.

He had an old black rotary phone, heavy and clunky to hands used to plastic Touch-Tones. He listened in unashamedly as I made my call—I suppose to make sure I wasn't going to set a mob heavy on Frenada's sister—but when he heard me ask the maître d' for Morrell he brightened.

"So you know Morrell," he said when I hung up.

"You should have told me that sooner. I didn't know he was back in town."

"He got thrown out of Guatemala," I said. "I don't know him well."

Father Lou had met him during the Reagan years, when American churches sometimes gave sanctuary to El Salvadoran refugees. St. Remigio's had sheltered a family that fled to Humboldt Park, and Morrell had come to do a story on them.

"Does a lot of good, Morrell. Not surprised he got thrown out of Guatemala. He's always covering underdogs of one kind or another. If you were meeting him for a meal I suppose you must be hungry."

He took me down a long unlit corridor to his kitchen, a cavern of a room, with a stove even older than the rotary phone. He didn't ask me what I wanted, or even what I wouldn't eat, but fried up a pan full of eggs with an expert hand. He ate three to my two, but I kept even with him on the toast.

When Lacey still hadn't arrived at nine, we watched Murray's show on a set in the parish hall. It was so old that Murray's face danced around in a wavy line of reds and greens. The report was subdued and lacked Murray's usual punch: he'd apparently been rattled by my information, however angrily he'd tossed me out this morning. Most of the report focused on the Mexico-Chicago drug route, with only ninety seconds on Lucian Frenada, "an up-and-coming entrepreneur whose untimely death means a lot of questions with no answers. Was he the point man for a drug ring, as the five kilos of coke found in his shop last week suggest? Was he murdered by associates he'd run afoul of? Or was he the innocent bystander his sister and other friends claim?"

Murray segued from that to footage of the shop, footage of the coke inside a bolt of T-shirting, and some old footage of Lacey and Frenada in front of the very church where I was sitting. "Father Lou Corrigan, who trained Lucian Frenada as the city champion light-weight boxer in this building, wouldn't talk to Channel Thirteen, either about Frenada or his other prizewin-ning student, Lacey Dowell."

He went on with details of Lacey's life, showed foot-age of his two-week-old interview with her, and closed with a summary that seemed lame to me. Father Lou was furious, but I thought it was a much more muted report than Murray would have made without my in-put. Of course, the priest had known Frenada for thirty years. It was a personal story to him.

We were back in his study, still thrashing it out over a second pot of tea, when the doorbell rang, a harsh, loud buzzing that fitted the priest's own voice. He pushed back from the chair and moved out to the hall on his light dancing step. I followed: if Lacey was bait in a Global trap I didn't want to be sitting under a crucifix waiting for it.

The star was alone, her cloud of red curls tucked inside a motorcycle helmet. No one would have known her in her nondescript jeans and jacket.

She put an arm around the priest. "I'm so sorry, Father Lou. Sorry about everything."

"Oh? And what do you have to be sorry for, miss? Something that you and I should talk about privately in a confessional?"

Her head jerked up and she squinted over his shoul-der down the hall. When she saw me she moved away from Father Lou, and away from her sad drooping. "Who is that?"

"That's a detective, Magdalena," the priest said. "She's private, but she's got some questions about Lucy you would do well to answer."

Lacey turned toward the door, but Father Lou grabbed her left wrist in a businesslike grip and pulled her forward. "Your old playmate, and I have to call you to get you to come talk to me about him. That tells its own tale, Magdalena."

"Isn't this rather melodramatic?" Lacey said. "Midnight meetings in the church?"

"Why not?" I put in. "The whole of the last two weeks has been B-grade garbage. Did you talk to Alex Fisher about coming here? Is hers going to be the next knock on the door?"

"Alex doesn't know I'm here. She's making me nervous these days."

"This something that came on you suddenly after you saw the news about Frenada?" I demanded.

"Girls—ladies, I mean. Let's go sit down. More light, less heat."

Father Lou put a muscular arm around each of us and propelled us back to his study. He came up to about my nose, but I wouldn't like to test the strength in those arms. He poured cold tea into three cups and set the pot down with a firm smack on the tray.

"Now, Magdalena, you'd better tell me everything you know about Lucy's death." He spoke with an old authority over her.

"I don't know anything about his death. But—oh, I don't even know where to begin. I'm so confused."

She blinked tears away from her large blue eyes, but I didn't feel moved to pity, and Father Lou apparently didn't either. He fixed her with a hard stare and told her to save her dramatics for her movies. She flushed and bit her lip.

"What about the cocaine," Father Lou said. "Do you know anything about the drugs that were planted in his shop?"

"Planted? That isn't what happened." She shook her head. "I was shocked. I'd talked to Lucy at my hotel, oh, weeks ago, and he never breathed a word about it. Of course he wouldn't necessarily, but—but—it was unexpected, anyway."

"How do you know they weren't planted?" I asked. "Is that what Alex told you? After I wrote you that Global was doing the broadcast tonight?"

"How do you know—she didn't—" Lacey stammered.

"Alex?" Father Lou said. "Oh, the girl from Hollywood. Don't lie about this, Magdalena. If she talked to you about it, I want to know."

Lacey's wide mouth contracted into a sulky pout. "When I read this Warshawski woman's note, I called Alex. Don't bite me: I know her, and I don't know Warshawski from a pit bull. Someone like me gets a million people a day saying they have special news or they can protect me from some weird shit or other. I thought Warshawski wanted to scare me into hiring her detective services."

"That isn't implausible," I said. "But it doesn't explain why it rattled you so badly you had to call Alex about it. I wrote Ms. Dowell that Global was going to smear Frenada on television," I added to the priest. "I wanted to talk to Ms. Dowell about it. Since I couldn't get a phone call in to her, I wrote her and waited in the lobby in case she wanted to talk to me. Half an hour later Global's Doberman showed up, very agitated."

"What did she tell you, Magdalena?" Father Lou demanded.

"She—Alex—she came to the Trianon and told me it was true, she even showed me a photograph they had of a kilo of cocaine inside a fabric bolt Lucy brought in from Mexico." Lacey looked pleadingly at the priest. "If you think I wouldn't come here because I'm cold-hearted, you're so wrong. I didn't want to have to talk about Lucy with you if he was dealing drugs. You never could hear one bad word about Lucy. Not even when he was a lookout for the Lions when he was eleven. If you want to believe it was a plant, go ahead, but Alex warned me, warned me that Warshawski would try to get me caught in a smear campaign. And she warned me not to talk about it. It's one thing for Hugh Grant or some other male star to get in trouble with sex and drugs, but when a woman does it, especially one getting to be my age, she looks like slime. Alex said it could kill me if it got around." Lacey looked at me. "I suppose you were hiding behind the potted palm in the lobby."

"You took her word for it without asking anyone else?" Father Lou said. "Your old comrade, who saved you from getting beat up, and you didn't even question what a television show was going to say about him? Did you see what they did to him tonight, that boy who worked day and night to keep a roof over his sister's head after her husband was killed?"

"Alex had a photo," Lacey said, but she looked at her hands.

"That's true, Ms. Dowell," I said. "That's very true."

Lacey flushed. "She had a photo; I saw the cocaine in a photo."

"They set him up," I said. "You live in a world of doctored images; you know how easy it is to make a picture look like the truth. And how did you know the kilo in the bolt of cloth was even in Frenada's shop? But it's not the coke per se I care about. What I'm trying to understand is why they needed to shut him up. Was it something to do with the T-shirts? Why did he have a Mad Virgin T-shirt in his office?"

"It can't be anything about the T-shirts," she said. "That's not a story at all. Here's what happened. Lucy and I didn't stay close, but we keep—kept in touch. He sent me that story that ran in the *Herald-Star* about him two years ago, how he was the model of the up-and-coming minority entrepreneur. Then when we decided to shoot *Virgin Six* here, of course it was a big story. Lucy saw it. He wrote and asked if I would get the studio to give him a contract for some of the Mad Virgin T-shirts, a Chicago commemorative or something. So I told him I'd talk to Teddy Trant, which I did, and Teddy gave me a sarcastic brush off. And I let it drop."

"You were never a shuffler, Magdalena. You didn't care about Lucy enough to stand up for him?" The priest looked at her over the rim of his teacup.

"We were in the middle of a difficult contract cycle. I know—I should have thought more of Lucy, but I'm thirty-seven; in another few years unless I'm really lucky I won't be able to be a star. And anyway, Father Lou, I moved away more than twenty years ago." She held out her hands, the gesture she often made to her old lover halfway through the Virgin movies.

"But he made some shirts on spec?" I said.

"I guess he must have. Suddenly, the day before I was flying out, Teddy called me and asked for Lucy's number. He wanted to look at the factory or something."

"Then at Murray's party at the Golden Glow two weeks ago, why did you get so angry with Frenada?"

"Were you there?" she said. "Behind another potted palm or something? Teddy said he looked at Lucy's stuff. He said it wasn't up to Global standard. But Lucy claimed Teddy stole one of his shirts. I said that was nuts, we—the studio—manufacture zillions of them, why would Teddy steal one? Lucy threatened to make a scene right there, and I hate being humiliated in public that way. I had him thrown out. And then I felt terrible. I did, Father Lou, I really did. I called him and apologized and invited him up to my hotel for lunch. We talked and talked and he said one of the shirts he'd made really was missing. I couldn't get him to let it drop, so I told him I'd mention it to Alex, but really I thought one of his workers must have stolen it; it's the kind of thing people take."

"Yes, that is possible," Father Lou said. "What did you say to this woman Alex or to your boss?"

She knit her fingers. "I didn't see how I could say anything to Teddy. He'd already assured me he didn't have the shirt. He said something horrible about Lucy, anyway, and I had to remind him that I'm Mexican, too. But I told Alex and she said to stop fussing about it, if Lucy was missing a shirt she'd send him one. But of course that wasn't the point."

"What was so special about his shirts?" I asked. "The fabric? The picture?"

"Honestly, I don't know," she said, spreading her hands again. "I think Lucy was upset because Global didn't give him the contract, and it distorted his judgment."

"Where does Global make its spin-offs—shirts and dolls and whatnot?" I asked.

"I've never asked. All over, I suppose."

"Third World countries? America?"

She shook her head impatiently. "I don't know."

"You collect the royalties, but you don't ask for fear of what they'll tell you?" I said.

"I've sat here long enough with you thinking I'm a cockroach in the sink." She uncoiled her legs and sprang out of the chair. "I'm out of here."

Father Lou reached the door ahead of her and barred her way. "You can leave in a minute, Magdalena. I'm glad you came tonight. I think you'll sleep better, having told the truth, as I'm sure you've done.

"We're having the funeral mass tomorrow," he added, when she didn't say anything. "I expect you to be there. It will be at eleven. Lucy left his sister's children provided for—he had a life-insurance policy—but they could use another bit of cash to pay their school fees. And it would be a graceful gesture if you gave a scholarship to the school in his memory."

Her face was stormy, but after staring at the priest for a long minute she muttered agreement. He let her go. A few minutes later we heard a motor roar into life. Her motorcycle. I'd have to ask young Emily what kind of bike Lacey Dowell rode around town. I was betting on a hog.

Twenty thousand dollars to St. Remigio's instead of three Hail Marys? That's what it sounded like to me.

"I'm tired; I'd like to go to bed," he said. "Did she tell you what you need to know?"

I wasn't sure—I still didn't understand why the shirt

Frenada made was so important. And I wasn't as sure as Father Lou that I'd heard the truth. When I left the rectory I wondered how much time I had before I joined Lucian Frenada in a pine box. Maybe Father Lou would offer a funeral mass for me, heathen that I was.

31

A Day in the Country

EVERYTHING WAS MAKING me nervous. I was afraid to go home because I didn't know if someone would jump me. I was afraid to go to my car for the same reason. I was afraid to send Mr. Contreras down to my office to fetch the car in case Baladine had planted a bomb under the hood. In the end my nervousness made me angry enough that when I got off the L, I went home the direct way: up the sidewalk, into the front door. Nothing happened, and perversely enough that made me even edgier.

In the morning I took the train down to my office and threw a rock at the hood of the car. It bounced off. The car didn't blow up, but a couple of boys who were lounging across the street scuttled into the alley: it's scary to share the street with a crazy woman.

The woman from the temporary agency was waiting for me inside: Tessa had arrived unusually early and let her in. I got the woman started on organizing papers before calling the Unblinking Eye to discuss a surveillance system for the building. Since Tessa and I really had only one entrance to protect, we didn't need more than two screens, one for each of our work spaces. Although it was still money I didn't have, it wasn't as big a hit as I'd feared. The Unblinking Eye would do the installation in the morning and pick up their rental camera from me at the same time.

After that I buckled down at my computer, researching court cases, trying to find Veronica Fassler. It's a needle-in-a-haystack job: there's no index of cases by defendant. I tried to guess the year she'd been convicted, since she said she'd been at Coolis longer than Nicola Aguinaldo, and finally, with some luck, found her case, dating back four years. Fassler had been caught with five grams of crack on the corner of Winona and Broadway, and justice had followed its inexorable course of three to five years. A year for every gram. It seems odd that the U.S. is so reluctant to go metric, except in measuring the minute amount of crack it takes to send someone to prison.

I also did a search for information on Coolis. I had ignored stories when it was under construction, since I wasn't with the public defender any longer. I started with *Carnifice gets contract for new facility*. The *Corrections Courier* said it was *a novel idea, combining jail and prison in northwest Illinois, typical of the innovative approach to vertical integration that is Carnifice Security's hallmark*. Because of overcrowding in Cook and Du Page County jails, women arrested and unable to post bond would be housed in a special wing of Coolis. That way they could just move down the hall to the prison once they were convicted—since being in jail for a year or more while awaiting trial greatly increased your chance of conviction. If you couldn't afford bond you must be guilty, I guess.

Because you go from jail to trial, jails are supposed to be close to the courts—a condition obviously not being met at Coolis. An article in the *Herald-Star* described how House Speaker Poilevy overcame that little obstacle. The year Coolis opened, he held a special legislative session on crime. Fifteen of sixteen bills zipped through the state legislature that session. One designated a particular courtroom to be part of Cook County on Mondays, Tuesdays, and Wednesdays, part of Du Page on Thursdays, and split between Lake and McHenry on Fridays. A couple of public defenders from each county could carpool with the State's Attorney, spend a few nights in Coolis, and save the state the cost of busing large numbers of women from the jail to their local county court.

I could see why Baladine was so tight with Poilevy—the House Speaker worked Springfield as if it were legerdemain, not legislation he was engineering. What I couldn't figure out was where Teddy Trant and Global Entertainment came into the picture. The financial papers didn't shed any light on the problem.

The only story the *Wall Street Journal* ran had questioned whether Carnifice was making the right kind of investment in a women's multipurpose correctional facility. The *REIT Bulletin,* in contrast, praised the move highly and gave the project a triple-A rating for investors.

Women prisoners make up the fastest growing segment of the fast-growing U.S. prison population, the *Bulletin* said. A twelvefold increase in women in prison in the last decade . . . seventy-five percent with children . . . eighty percent commit nonviolent crimes—possession, prostitution . . . theft usually to pay rent or other bills, unlike men doing it for drugs or thrills.

I skimmed the stories and finished with *Model workshops in prison: Coolis is of, for, and by the prisoners.* Prison workshops in Coolis allowed prisoners to earn as much as thirty dollars a week manufacturing food and clothes for consumption in the state prison system. The computer produced a blurry picture of smiling inmates in a prison kitchen and two serious-looking women operating monster sewing machines. Carnifice had invested a lot of money in the workshops when they built the prison; they lobbied unsuccessfully to overturn an Illinois law that prohibited sales of goods outside the prison system. In fact, that was the only bill that failed Poilevy's special crime session.

"The labor unions have a stranglehold on this state," Jean-Claude Poilevy grumbled when he was unable to muster the votes to overturn the law. "They make it impossible for efficient use of industrial facilities in order to protect their own fiefdom."

While I waited for the articles to print, I logged back on to LifeStory. I should have done this days ago, but my cocaine adventures had put it out of my mind. I wanted to see what kind of report I would get on Lucian Frenada this time around and contrast it with the first. I pulled up my original report so I could double-check the parameters I had specified.

When it came on the screen I thought I was hallucinating: instead of the modest bank accounts and two credit-card balances I'd seen ten days ago, I got pages of detail: bank accounts in Mexico and Panama; eighteen credit cards with charges on each ranging as high as twenty thousand a month for travel and jewelry; a home in Acapulco and one in the Cote d'Azur. The list went on and on in a mind-numbing fashion.

I was so bewildered I couldn't even think for a few minutes. Finally I went to my briefcase and took out the wallet of backup disks I carry between home and office. I found the floppy with the Frenada report on it and opened the file. The simple figures were the ones I'd shown Murray yesterday morning.

I sat bewildered for a long time before I could think at all. It slowly came to me that when the vandals broke into my office last week, they'd gone into my computer and altered my files. They'd somehow loaded bogus numbers into the LifeStory files and downloaded them onto my machine.

I wondered whether they had messed around with any of my other documents—altered my case records, my tax data—they could have done anything. Once again the sense of violation made me feel sick. Someone had helped themselves to what was almost an extension of my mind.

I'd started the day determined to drive out to Coolis to try to see Veronica Fassler as soon as I found her trial record, but I was too upset to deal with the prison system this morning. I wished I could find my old hacking buddy, Mackenzie Graham. He could have told me how someone had managed to screw around with the LifeStory data, but he was somewhere in East Africa with the Peace Corps these days.

I opened up several old case files but then decided I didn't want to find evidence of a stranger's hands and feet in my life. I zeroed out my disk. *Are you sure you want to do this?* The system asked me twice and then seemed to shrug its electronic shoulders. *Okay, but you will lose all your files.* I wiped it clean and reloaded the system from my backup disks, reloaded all my data, offering Mackenzie a million thanks for forcing me to the unwonted discipline of daily off-site backups.

I spent the rest of the day working assiduously with the woman from the agency. By five we had eighty-two neat piles of papers for which she could type folder labels in the morning. I told her what to do in the morning when the Unblinking Eye came to install our surveillance camera and monitors, then lugged my computer to my car and drove it home. I didn't know where to set it up that would be really safe, but my apartment was less vulnerable than the warehouse, because at least here someone was usually around.

I took my computer to the third floor and sat in my bathtub for half an hour, listening to Bach, trying to relax. It would have helped if I knew what my opponents wanted. Besides to drive me crazy with uncertainty. By and by I poured myself a whisky and went downstairs to see my neighbor. I wanted to persuade him to lie low until this miserable business had come somehow to an end. When he came to the door, I put a hand over his mouth and led him through his apartment to the back. A couple on the second floor was entertaining on the back porch. The reassuring clink of glasses and friendly laughter drifted down to us. Under its cover I told Mr. Contreras how someone had frightened Mary Louise into backing away from me and that I didn't want the same people terrorizing him.

"I don't want you to be a sitting target for BB Baladine," I whispered urgently. "What if he comes around trying to find who went with me to Coolis? For all I know they had a security camera taking pictures of us—I wasn't very bright. I bolted headlong into trouble without stopping to think. I'm worried I put you at risk as well. You were right not to want your name on the record."

"It ain't like you to scare easy, doll."

"It isn't very often that I come across a man who thinks bayoneting newborns is all in a day's work. Will you do me a favor and go to your daughter's until, well, until this Aguinaldo business gets sorted out?"

Of course he wouldn't. Aside from the fact that he and his only child had as much in common as a dog and a fish, he wasn't about to turn tail. Didn't I ever listen to him when he talked to me about Anzio?

"Listen!" I screeched, forgetting to whisper, so that the party above us momentarily grew quiet. "You were twenty-something at Anzio. You may have the will you had then, but you don't have the strength. And if this guy figures out the relationship between us, which he will if he puts any energy into the matter, then he'll know it was you with me at the Coolis hospital, not Nicola Aguinaldo's grandfather."

We argued for an hour, but all he would agree to was to deny any relationship with me if someone came around asking. Oh, Ms. Warshki, she lives in the building, but she's a young woman, we know each other to say hi coming in the door at night. Of course, if someone questioned the rest of the tenants, one of them was bound to say that the old guy and I were pretty tight. The woman on the ground floor, for instance, who complained about the noise the dogs made when I came in late. Or even the party above us tonight: Mitch and Peppy, bored with lying in the yard, went up to the second floor to investigate. I followed just in time to grab Mitch before he helped himself to a plate of hummus. Those neighbors certainly would remember Mr. Contreras and me barbecuing together in the backyard.

"Okay, I won't open the door to no one I don't know while you're away from home, but even if I ain't the guy I was at twenty, I can still look after myself without running off to Hoffman Estates like a scared mutt." That was the best I was going to get out of him.

Thursday morning I got up early, took the dogs for a long swim, and headed out to Coolis. Even though I wasn't stopping for lunch, without Mr. Contreras the ride seemed to take longer than it had last week. Still, I pulled into a visitors' lot at the prison a little before noon.

I had dressed professionally, in my wheat rayon trouser suit. The drive in the un-air-conditioned car had left my white shirt wet around the armpits and neck, but I thought the front still looked pressed and clean enough for my mission. I carried the briefcase my dad gave me when I graduated from law school. It's almost twenty years old now, the red leather worn pinky-white around the edges. To preserve it I use it sparingly, but today I needed to feel his presence in my life.

The prairie sun pounded on me as I walked across the asphalt to the first checkpoint. In the distance I could hear grasshoppers whirring in the high grasses, but in the prison compound no trees or grasses mediated the heat, which shimmered from the pavement in knee-high waves. The white stone was so bright that my eyes watered behind my sunglasses.

I stopped at the first checkpoint, held out my ID, explained I was a lawyer here to see one of the inmates. At the second my briefcase was examined for weapons. I waited forty minutes there for an escort to the prison entrance. The CO who finally came for me was a short, plump woman who joked with the guard but didn't say anything to me.

At the entrance the door slid slowly open on its pneumatic trolley. We then faced an inner door, which would open only when the one behind us had wheezed shut again. Inside, I was escorted to yet another guard station, where I explained my business: I was a lawyer, here to see Veronica Fassler.

I was sent to a waiting room, a small windowless space with plastic chairs on top of worn linoleum and a television mounted high on the wall. Oprah shouted down at me and the three other women in the room.

Two of the waiting women were black, the only faces of color I'd seen since entering the prison compound; all three stared ahead with the weary passivity of those accustomed to being of no account to the world around them. A corrections officer looked in periodically, I suppose to make sure we weren't stealing the furniture. When I asked her to turn down the volume, since none of us was watching the program, she told me to mind my own business and retreated again.

Around one-thirty the older of the black women was escorted to the visitors' room. Two more people arrived —a Hispanic couple, middle-aged, nervous, wanting to know what to expect when they saw their daughter. The white woman continued to stare stolidly ahead, but the second black woman began explaining the procedure, where you sat, what you could talk about. It was hard for the pair to follow her underneath the noise of the television. As she repeated something for the third time, the corrections officer returned to escort me to the warden's office.

CAPTAIN FREDERICK RUZICH, WARDEN, the plaque on the door announced. The CO saluted smartly; the captain dismissed her and invited me to be seated. Despite his military title he was wearing civilian clothes, a pearl tropical worsted with a navy tie. He was a big man; even sitting he seemed to loom over me. With his gray hair and eyes he looked almost colorless, certainly terrifying.

"I understand you want to see one of our prisoners, Miss . . . uh . . ."

"Warshawski. Yes. Veronica Fassler. She's serving a five-year sentence for possession and—"

"So you're familiar with her case. I wondered if you were coming out here on a fishing expedition." He smiled, but with so much condescension that it became an insult.

"No one comes to a prison hunting for clients, Captain. The legal-aid money doesn't even cover gas and tolls from Chicago. Do you take a personal interest in every lawyer–client consultation here at Coolis?"

"The important ones I do. Have you talked to Veronica's regular lawyer about her case? I would have expected him to be here with you or at least to call ahead to let us know a different arrangement had been made."

"Ms. Fassler asked to see me when she called my office. And her representation arrangements are with me, not between the prison and other counsel. Or between me and the prison."

He leaned his massive torso back in the chair, his hands clasped behind his head, the smile lurking at the corner of his mouth. "Be that as it may, we had orders to transfer her. She's in another part of the prison system. So you made your trip out here for nothing, Detective."

I stared steadily at his smirk. "It's true I'm a detective, Captain. But I'm also a lawyer, in good standing with the Illinois bar. Where was Ms. Fassler sent?"

"I wish I could tell you that, but I can't because I don't know. Carnifice Security sent someone in with a van and moved her and the infant yesterday morning, and that's all I can tell you." His gray eyes were transparent, like a guppy's, which made it hard to look at them.

"Why was she moved? She didn't know anything about it when she phoned me."

The superior smile lingered. "There's always a problem in the prison when a prisoner has a baby. The logistics are hard here. No doubt too many of the other inmates complained."

"What a humane place this is, where the women's complaints are taken so seriously by the staff." I was not going to let him goad me into losing my temper, but I couldn't help myself pushing on him a little. "But a man like you who likes to be in charge, I can't believe you just salute and say yessir when your bosses tell you to move out a prisoner to an unknown destination. Especially in a private prison, where it affects your bed count and your margins."

The smile hovered at the corner of his mouth. "Whatever you want to believe, Warshawski, whatever you want. How did the Fassler woman get your number to begin with?"

"Probably from the yellow pages. That's how most people find me."

"Wouldn't have been on your visit to the hospital asking questions about Nicola Aguinaldo, would it? When you came out with her—grandfather, was that what you called him?—making inquiries. Was that as a detective or as a lawyer?"

"When a lawsuit is threatened, it's usually because a lawyer's present."

"And usually someone with standing is present." His smirk turned into a full-fledged grin. "You claimed the man was the girl's grandfather, but she doesn't have a grandfather. At least not an American. And that was definitely an American you brought out here."

I clasped my hands around my right knee in a pretense of thoughtful relaxation. "Is your information about Ms. Aguinaldo's family from BB Baladine or the INS? It's hard for me to believe BB pays much attention to the families of the illegal immigrants he hires. Not enough to know whether an American serviceman might have been in the Philippines during World War Two and have a Filipina granddaughter."

Poor Mr. Contreras: he would have protested mightily if he knew I was imputing that kind of immorality to him. He might have had sex with a local woman in his army service days, but he wouldn't have left her alone with a child.

"If he cared so much about the girl I'm surprised he never tried to visit her here."

"Family relations are a never-ending mystery, aren't they?" I said affably.

"If this grandfather really exists I'd like to talk to him, especially if he's bringing a suit against the hospital." He wasn't sure whether to believe me or not, but at least his lingering smirk disappeared.

"If he decides to file the suit, the hospital's lawyers will be allowed to interview him for discovery. Until then, if you have any questions for him, you can direct them through me. By the way, it would lessen the chance of a lawsuit if I could get him more concrete information about what made you send Ms. Aguinaldo to the hospital in the first place, and how she was able to escape from what is clearly a tightly secured ward."

"The information I have from my staff is that she had female difficulties. You'd probably know more than me what that meant." The sneering smile played again around the corners of his mouth.

"Ovarian cysts or cancer, which wasn't present when the doctors in Chicago opened her."

That not only effectively destroyed his smile but caused him to forget himself: he blurted out that the body was missing, that no autopsy had been performed.

"You do keep a lively interest in your prisoners, even after death," I marveled. "It's true her body disappeared from the morgue before they could perform an autopsy, but the surgeon in the emergency room where she was sent did a detailed report on her abdominal cavity after he failed to save her life. He wondered if the peritonitis might have been caused by an ovarian or uterine rupture and looked specifically at those organs."

Of course I was making all that up, but it didn't matter. I was convinced that whatever had sent Nicola Aguinaldo to the hospital, it hadn't been an inflamed ovary. At any rate, for the first time since I'd come into his office, I'd made Ruzich uneasy. What was it he was afraid an autopsy would have shown?

"Why don't you let me see the model workshop where Ms. Aguinaldo was working when she took so ill she had to go to the hospital? If I can assure her grandfather that it's a safe environment, it might make him less inclined to sue."

He scowled, an ugly expression but easier to watch than his smile. "Definitely not. You have no reason to be involved in that part of my operation."

"Not even if that's where Ms. Aguinaldo's injuries occurred?" I suggested softly.

"She was not injured there, despite the wild rumors Veronica Fassler was spreading. Yes, Ms. Warshawski, we monitor all those phone calls. We have to. It's the best way to keep track of drug and gang traffic between the cities and the prison. I'm sorry you made that long drive for nothing, but there's nothing else for you to do here. Unless you'd like to come up with the name of another prisoner to pretend you represent." Ruzich pushed his intercom and demanded that a CO escort me from the building.

32

Midnight Caller

I TRIED TO think over what I'd learned from meeting the warden, but the long wait I'd had before seeing him meant I hit Chicago at rush hour. In the time I sat on the tollway, it was hard to think of much of anything except floating in Lake Michigan with a cold drink in my hand.

They had moved Veronica Fassler as soon as they overheard her conversation with me. Whether she had been sent to another of Illinois' women's prisons or out of state or was simply in solitary at Coolis didn't matter. What mattered was that Fassler knew something about Nicola Aguinaldo's death that the prison didn't want me to find out.

I couldn't force my mind beyond those elementary deductions. When I got home, eager to get out of my rayon trousers, it was hard for me not to bark at Mr. Contreras, bustling into the hall with the dogs. Apparently the only effect last night's conversation had on him was to make him redouble his vigilance as the guardian of my gate.

I leaned against the railing, scratching the dogs' ears. I couldn't very well embroil him in my affairs and then refuse to talk to him, but while I told him about my day my hot, swollen feet occupied most of my mind.

Partway through my recital, the woman who lives across the hall from Mr. Contreras opened her door. "I have a presentation to an important client tomorrow, and I don't need your dogs and your conversation going on in the background while I try to finish it. If you two have that much to say to each other, why don't you move in together? It would give the rest of the building some much-needed peace and quiet."

"Living together don't guarantee peace for the building," Mr. Contreras said, his color heightened. "Maybe no one ever told you, but when you and your husband or boyfriend or whatever he is get to shouting at each other, even I can make out every word, and my hearing ain't a hundred percent these days."

Before the quarrel could build, I pushed myself upright and said I needed to take a cold shower and change out of my business clothes. The woman muttered something that ended with "show some consideration" and slammed her front door shut. Mitch barked sharply, to say he didn't like her attitude, but I persuaded Mr. Contreras to take him inside and let me get some rest.

I lay in the tub for a long time, long after the grime of the drive and the prison were out of my skin and hair, trying to figure out what Baladine was up to. Maybe he only wanted to discredit me, possibly with a spectacular arrest for drug possession, rather than kill me outright, but in a way it didn't matter.

I couldn't keep on this way, not knowing where the next menace might come from. Whether Baladine was carrying on a war of nerves, or he wanted me dead or arrested, or all three, I couldn't run a business when I was afraid to be both in my office and in my home. I couldn't turn to my oldest friends for fear of jeopardizing their lives or families. Murray, who I'd worked with for so many years, was carrying a bucket for the other side this time. Mary Louise had been frightened into leaving me alone.

If only I could get the story together I might be able to find a way to make it public. It had something to do with Coolis and something to do with Frenada's factory, although how those two places came together on Nicola Aguinaldo's frail body I didn't understand. I needed to get in touch with Morrell and insist that he take me to Aguinaldo's mother before Baladine succeeded in whatever his plan was.

When I finally climbed out of the tub it was dark outside. I could hear the steady popping of firecrackers as people in the area geared up for the Fourth of July, coming up on Saturday.

When I was a child my father used to take me for a walk on the Fourth, telling me a thrilling version of the War of Independence, stressing the role of General Kosciuszko and other Poles in the American Revolution. My mother always followed my father's tale with a reminder that it was Italian explorers who found the New World and made it possible for the English and Poles to leave Europe.

In the afternoons we'd make a picnic with my father's pals on the force and my mother's vocal coach and his daughter. My mother would make my favorite dessert—an Umbrian rice pudding with currant jelly and sweet wine sauce—and I'd race around screaming with the other children, playing baseball and wishing I had a big family instead of just my one cousin, Boom-Boom.

I wondered what the Baladines taught their children

on the Fourth of July. Perhaps something instructive about free markets.

I took that bitter thought to bed with me. Despite my fatigue I couldn't relax. Coolis, Aguinaldo, Frenada chased through my mind, sometimes with Baladine in pursuit, sometimes Alex Fisher. I was just deciding I'd do better to get up and pay bills than lie churning over these profitless ideas when my front doorbell rang.

No one in Chicago pays calls at midnight if they have your well-being in mind. I pulled my jeans on and grabbed my gun from the closet safe before calling down through the intercom.

A voice quavered, "It's me. It's Robbie Baladine."

I stuck the gun in the back of my jeans and went downstairs. Sure enough, Robbie Baladine was standing, by himself, on the other side of the door. His plump cheeks were dirt-stained, and he looked exhausted. I opened the front door at the same time that Mr. Contreras came into the hallway with Mitch and Peppy: he probably thought Morrell was paying another late-night call.

When the dogs bounded forward to greet him, Robbie stood stock still and turned white. Yelling at the dogs to stay, I caught the boy as he started to crumple. I caught him before he hit the floor. His deadweight hit my low back and hamstrings like a pile driver.

"Put the dogs inside, will you?" I panted to Mr. Contreras. "And let's get this young man warm."

Robbie hadn't quite fainted. While my neighbor dragged the reluctant dogs back to his apartment, I helped Robbie to the bottom of the stairwell and made him sit with his head between his legs. He was shaking with suppressed sobs. His skin was clammy, his sweat acrid with the smell of fear.

"I'm such a weakling, aren't I, fainting at the sight of a dog," he gasped.

"Is that what happened? Mitch is a pretty big dog, and he took you by surprise. And you look done in. Don't worry about it."

Mr. Contreras returned with an old sweater and helped me wrap it around Robbie's shoulders. "This a friend of yours, doll? He needs hot cocoa. You stay here with him; I'll heat up some milk."

The door opposite Mr. Contreras's opened and the woman making the important presentation stormed out in sweat clothes. "Did you buy this stairwell to use as your living room?" she demanded. "If not, could you entertain upstairs so that people like me who work for a living can get some rest?"

Behind Mr. Contreras's door, Mitch took exception to our neighbor's hostility and let out a sharp bark.

"Think you can manage the stairs?" I said to Robbie. "If this woman gets any more excited she'll have a stroke, and then we'll be up all night carting her to the hospital and you'll never be able to tell me why you came or how you got here."

"I'm only asking you to show some consideration," the woman said.

I didn't think Robbie needed the added stress of me getting into a fight, so I bit back the various remarks that sprang to mind and concentrated on helping him up the stairs. When I turned my back on her, the woman gasped and ran back inside her apartment. It was only when we reached the second landing that I realized she must have seen my gun. I laughed a little to myself: that might be the last time she pissed to me about noise in the building.

We went slowly; by the time we reached my door

Mr. Contreras was huffing up behind us with a tray and three cups of cocoa. The old man is at his best in dealing with the halt and lame. I left him roughly coaxing Robbie to drink some cocoa while I took my gun back to my bedroom.

"You must think I'm pretty weird, coming here like this and fainting and everything," he said when I came back.

I pulled the piano bench next to the armchair. "I don't think anything about you, but I'm about to burst with curiosity. Your sister said you'd run away. How did you get to Wrigleyville?"

"Is that where we are? By Wrigley Field? I've been here with my dad." Some of the strain eased out of his face—if I lived in known territory it couldn't be as scary as he'd been thinking. "I came how Nicola used to—I took my bike to the bus and rode the bus to the train. But then I got lost trying to find you and I didn't have enough money for a cab or anything, so I've been walking and walking, I bet I've walked five miles. That would make BB and Eleanor delirious with joy if they knew I got that much exercise in one afternoon."

"Who are BB and Eleanor?" Mr. Contreras asked.

"Parents," I explained briefly. "Baladine's nickname at Annapolis was BB-gun Baladine."

"He loves it," Robbie said. "He's such a he-man, it proves it when people call him that. Only—only I'm not. He hates that. Or hates me; he wishes Madison and Utah had been the boys and me the girl, he said if I was a girl he could dress me in—in pink ruff—ruffles."

His teeth began to chatter. I moved over to the arm of the chair and forced some cocoa into him, giving Mr. Contreras a warning sign to keep quiet. I was afraid even a man as benign as my neighbor might appear threatening to this very tired child.

"You're exhausted," I said in a matter-of-fact voice. "You're probably dehydrated too, from walking so much. That's why your body is acting up on you. Everybody's does when they're overtired and then have to deal with a strange situation: it happens to me, which is how I know. Finish this cocoa before you try to say anything else."

"Really?" He looked at me hopefully. "I thought— thought it was only because I was a—all the names he calls me."

I supposed Baladine stood over him and called him a faggot or queer or other names that pass for insults with someone like him. "Name-calling is a horrible kind of torture, especially when it comes from your parents. It leaves you without any defenses."

He gulped the drink and kept a death grip on the cup as the best way to hold on to his wayward feelings. When he seemed calm enough to speak, I asked why he'd come to me.

"That was probably the stupidest thing of all, me coming to you, because what can you do? Only, when I saw he was going to send me to—to boot camp, I thought I couldn't take another time like that, like when they made me go to the camp for fat kids, that was horrible enough, but at least everyone else was overweight too, but boot camp, that's like when all the other kids get to haze you for being queer or different somehow. Like my cousins, when I have to go spend a month with them, they play football, they're supposed to toughen me up."

I blinked. "Is this a definite plan?"

"Oh, yes." He looked at me bleakly. "Don't tell me it's wrong to snoop in his briefcase, it's the only way I know what he's up to, and I saw the fax from this place in South Carolina—of course anyone who does anything with prisons or army stuff, they fall over themselves for a chance to help out BB and this guy, he's the head of this military school and they run a summer boot camp. So he faxes BB that they'll be expecting me Saturday night, I can start Monday morning. BB and Eleanor can put me on a plane to Columbia when they take off for France. Not that I wanted to go to France with those ghastly Poilevy twins and my sisters, watch them swimming all day long to get ready for Mom's swim meet. She's doing this thing for charity on Labor Day, and of course she wants Madison to beat everyone. But I'd rather clock Madison and Rhiannon Trant in the pool than go to military camp."

"But you disappeared two nights ago, didn't you? Where have you been in the meantime?"

He looked at his hands. "I hid out in our grounds. When BB and Eleanor went to bed I'd go sleep in the cabana. Only the gardeners found me this morning and I was afraid they'd tell Eleanor."

"Your folks are looking for you—that's how I know you left home. Do you think they would call the police, or will they rely on Carnifice's private security force?"

"I'm so stupid, aren't I, I didn't think about that," Robbie muttered. "I only thought I should get away as fast as I could. Of course if he wants me he'll sic his whole team on finding me. Not that he really wants me, but no one is supposed to outsmart BB Baladine."

"I think you're pretty smart," I said comfortably. "You hid out right under your parents' noses for two days. You found me, and that's not so easy for a suburban kid who gets driven everywhere, to navigate a city like Chicago at night.

"Here's the problem. I don't mind putting you up, but your father is on my case in a serious way, and if he came here looking for you I wouldn't have any way to keep him from taking you: you're a minor child and I have no legal relationship to you. Is there anyone you can go to who would stick up for you with your dad? A teacher, or an aunt? Your grandparents?"

He shook his head, miserable. "I'm like this really weird person in my family. Even my grandmother keeps telling BB he's too soft on me. If I ran away to her she'd probably put me in handcuffs and take me to military camp herself."

Mr. Contreras cleared his throat. "He could stay with me, doll. I got that sofa bed."

Robbie turned white but didn't say anything.

"Is it the dogs?" I asked. "They look ferocious because they're huge, but they're pretty gentle."

"I know it's sissy to be scared of dogs," he whispered, "but it's one of the—BB—some of his clients work with rottweilers, he thought it would be funny—it made everyone laugh—Nicola, she tried to get the dogs to leave and one of them bit her."

"What did he do?" My hand on his shoulder had clenched reflexively into a fist, and I had to force the fingers to relax.

"He brought them home with him. Also the handler. It was kind of when he started running Carnifice. *This will kill you or cure you,* that's what he's always saying to me. So he sort of, well, he didn't really sic the dogs on me, tell them to attack me, just to corner me, in the family room, I was watching television, they stayed there and stayed there and I—I couldn't help it, I had to go to the bathroom so bad—"

His shoulders started to heave again. I kept my arm around him but drank some cocoa myself to try to keep my own stomach from turning inside out on me. Family night at the Baladines. Fun for everyone.

"Now listen here, young man," Mr. Contreras spoke roughly. "I been a soldier, I been a machinist, I spent my life with men who could take your daddy apart and line up all his arms and legs in a row and not even work up a sweat, and let me tell you that is not how a real man acts, setting a dog on his kid."

"Damn straight," I said. "Why don't we bring the dogs up here for the night and let Robbie sleep downstairs with you? That way if BB shows up he'll get an earful of Mitch but no son."

Robbie cheered up at that. I helped him back down the stairs to Mr. Contreras's and held the dogs while he went inside. The old man said he reckoned Robbie could wear one of his pajama shirts to sleep in tonight and they'd get him some blue jeans and T-shirts in the morning.

"I know you're really tired, but could you answer one question for me before you go to bed?" I was unfolding the sofa bed while Mr. Contreras brought in clean sheets. "What were you wanting to tell me when you phoned me last week?"

He'd forgotten about it in the stress of his journey. That phone call to me was what made BB and Eleanor decide to send him to military camp, but it had lost its importance to him. He blinked his eyes anxiously, then suddenly remembered.

"You know that man who got pulled out of Lake

Michigan? I'm pretty sure he came out to see BB. With
Mr. Trant, you know."

"Teddy Trant from Global? Are you sure?"

"Come on, doll. Boy's asleep on his feet. This will
wait until tomorrow."

"You're right. Sorry, I wasn't thinking," I said, but
Robbie, taking off his military shirt with a sigh of relief
and putting on one of Mr. Contreras's violently striped
pajama tops, said, "Of course I recognize Mr. Trant,
and I'm pretty sure it was the guy I saw on television
with him. He was really, really angry, but I couldn't
hear what he said and, well, they kind of locked me in
the nursery with Rosario and Utah. On account of
Mom said I was—a little snoop—who'd go telling tales
out of school. But I woke up in the middle of the night
because they were standing under my window and Mr.
Trant was saying that should solve the problem for the
time being if only Abigail—Mrs. Trant, you know—
didn't start getting helpful ideas again."

"Okay, Victoria. Boy's going to bed now. No more
detecting tonight."

"Ms. Warshawski, thank you for letting me stay
here, and you too, sir, only I'm sorry I don't know your
name, and I'm sorry about the dogs, about making
them leave. Maybe—maybe tomorrow I won't be so
chicken around them."

I squeezed his shoulder. "Get a good sleep. Like the
man said, tomorrow is another day."

It was only as I started back up the stairs that I remembered my fears about BB bugging my apartment. I
hoped I was wrong, but my stomach turned cold as I
imagined what Baladine might do next.

33

Thrown in the Tank

LEMOUR ARRESTED ME as I unlocked my front door Friday afternoon. He flung me against the stone railing and yanked my purse from my shoulder. A Du Page County deputy sheriff who was with him tried to calm him down and was thrust roughly aside.

When Lemour had the cuffs locked, he flashed a warrant under my nose for the arrest of one Victoria Iphigenia Warshawski, acting upon information and belief that she did unlawfully and without the permission of the parents seize and hold against his will Robert Durant Baladine, a minor child not her own.

Mr. Contreras erupted with the dogs. Mitch broke away from him and launched himself at Lemour. The detective punched his head. Mitch yelped and huddled on the ground. Lemour started to kick him, but I threw myself between his foot and the dog. We went over in a heap of leash, detective and me, with Peppy joining in to mew worriedly at her son.

"That's it, Warshki," Lemour panted from the pavement. "I'm adding resisting arrest to the kidnapping charge. You'll be lucky if you're home in time for Christmas. And I'll have this dog put to sleep for assaulting me."

Homebound commuters began to crowd around to

see what the show was. One young woman said she thought it took a lot of nerve to beat a dog and then threaten to put it to sleep.

"He's obviously perfectly friendly and he's on a leash, aren't you, good doggy." She scratched his ears, carefully avoiding looking at me.

"Shut the hell up unless you want to be arrested for interfering with the police," Lemour said savagely.

She backed away as the sheriff's deputy once more muttered an ineffectual intervention.

My hands were cuffed behind me. I'd fallen hard on my side and lay there on the walk, the wind knocked out of me, my right cheek smarting from grazing the concrete. Mitch climbed to his feet and shook himself like a boxer who's taken a bad blow but is ready to go back in the ring. Peppy licked him anxiously. He's a big ugly dog, half black Lab, half golden Peppy, and I've never been crazy about him, but right now his attempts to grin, wag his tail, show there were no hard feelings, made my eyes smart.

I rolled forward onto my knees. Mr. Contreras anxiously helped me up, keeping one eye on Lemour, who was brushing concrete crumbs from his suit, his face patchy-red with rage. When he got to his feet the dogs started toward him.

"Mitch, Peppy! Stay!" I was gasping for breath, but the dogs for once paid attention and sat. "Get them inside before Lummox here loses his head completely and shoots them," I said to Mr. Contreras. "And take my handbag before this cretin steals my wallet. Can you call Freeman for me? Also, will you get a message to Morrell? I'm supposed to meet him for a picnic tomorrow. In case I can't get out on time, will you call and tell him? His number's in my electronic diary, there in my bag."

Mr. Contreras was looking so bewildered I wasn't sure he'd heard me, although he did pick up my handbag from where Lemour had dropped it. I started to repeat myself, but Lemour, furiously trying to straighten his tie, grabbed my arm and jerked me down the walk. He tried to throw me into the back of the squad car, but he wasn't big enough to get the right leverage. The Du Page sheriff's deputy took my left arm and whispered something apologetic as he pushed me behind the cage.

"Uh, Doug, uh, can you give me the key? I need to lock her to the seat, and she can't ride with her arms behind her."

Lemour ignored him and climbed behind the unmarked car's wheel. The sheriff's deputy looked at me uncertainly, but as Lemour started the engine he quickly shut the door on me and got into the passenger seat. Lemour took off so fast that my head banged into the metal cage.

Rage was building in me. I knew I had to keep it down. I was helpless—physically and in the situation—and if I let my fury ride me I'd give Lemour the opening he wanted to pound me into the ground. When he stopped at the light on Addison, I maneuvered my body so that I was sitting sideways in the narrow space with my legs stretched out across the width of the backseat. My shoulders were beginning to ache horribly.

The day had started so well, too. When I got back from swimming with the dogs, young Robbie was up and willing to make timid overtures to Peppy. Mr. Contreras prepared his breakfast specialty, French toast, and Robbie relaxed visibly as the old man urged seconds on him: perhaps it was the first time in his life his every mouthful hadn't been monitored and criticized.

I drove north to Morrell's place in Evanston. In the theme of Spy–Counterspy, I wrote out a note explaining my visit to Coolis yesterday and how imperative it was that I talk to Señora Mercedes. Morrell frowned over my message, then finally decided—whether because of my dogged determination, my impeccable logic, or my nice-looking legs—to take me to see Nicola Aguinaldo's mother. We rode the L, since that was the easiest way to check for tails, first in and out of the Loop and then over to Pilsen on the city's near southwest side.

When I met Abuelita Mercedes I realized I'd been carrying the unconscious stereotype of her title of "granny"—I'd been expecting an old woman in a kerchief, with round red cheeks. Of course, a woman whose daughter was only twenty-seven was still young herself, in fact only a few years older than I. She was short, stocky, with black hair curling softly around her ears and forehead and a permanent worry crease worked between her brows.

Tagalog was her first language, but she could get by in Spanish, which Morrell spoke fluently—although his was the Central American version, not always in sync with Filipino Spanish, he explained. Abuelita Mercedes's English was limited to a few social phrases, which she used upon his introducing us: *Señora Mercedes, le presento a la Señora Victoria.* He assured her that I was a friend worried about Nicola's death, as well as a lawyer committed to justice for the poor.

Sherree, Nicola's surviving child, greeted Morrell with an eager cry of *"Tío!"* but she chattered away in English to him. After a formal reception, with strong black coffee and little fried donuts, we began to broach the subject of Nicola's death.

With Morrell translating Señora Mercedes's Spanish and Sherree reluctantly assisting with a Tagalog phrase or two, Nicola's mother made her halting way through Nicola's story. She explained that she knew very little of what had happened to her daughter in prison. Señora Mercedes couldn't afford a phone, so it wasn't possible for her to talk to her daughter except at very wide intervals: she would get permission from a neighbor, often Señora Attar, to use her phone, so that Nicola could call collect on a prearranged day. But then it depended on whether she was able to get a letter in to Nicola or whether Nicola could get phone privileges on that day.

She had to write in Spanish, which neither she nor Nicola wrote well, since anything she wrote in Tagalog was automatically turned back. Even so, the Spanish letters were often sent back. Coolis, out in the rural white countryside, had only one or two Spanish-speaking guards, despite the large number of Hispanic inmates. They often refused to let Spanish-language mail in or out, with the excuse that Señora Mercedes could be providing gang information to her daughter.

Now that Sherree was in third grade she wrote English—very good in English—but Nicola hadn't written English well enough to send out detailed news.

When the baby died, oh, that was terrible. Señora Mercedes couldn't go to Coolis: she didn't have a green card, she didn't know what papers you had to show, and what if they arrested her when she was visiting her daughter? Then, too, everything cost money, the bus fare to Coolis, it was all too much. So she sent a letter in Spanish, Sherree sent a letter—the priest helped her write it in English, this was before Señor Morrell became a friend or he would surely have helped—but she never heard from her daughter again, she didn't even know if Nicola learned the news about the baby's death before she died herself, and now here was poor Sherree, no mother, no sister, father dead in the Philippines.

Sherree seemed to have heard this lament before. She frowned over the dolls she was playing with and turned her back on her grandmother as Señora Mercedes went into detail about the baby's death. The poor baby, the cause of so much misery, needing money for the hospital, causing Nicola to steal, but then, those employers, so mean, not letting her get away to be with her own baby in the hospital, not lending her money, it was wrong of Nicola to steal, but Señora Mercedes could understand why she did it. And then, five years in prison? When men who did far worse crimes were there for much less time? Here in America it was all terrible. If not for the money, for the chance to have Sherree get a good education, they would never stay.

We took a break to let Señora Mercedes recover her poise before I asked what I most wanted to know: about Nicola's work in the prison shop. That was good, her mother said, because she got paid two dollars and fifty cents an hour. It was for sewing, sewing shirts, and Nicola was very fast, her little fingers so—so nimble, yes, that was the word, the best on the floor, the bosses at the prison said. It was piecework, but Nicola was so fast she made the top rate.

What kind of shirts? I asked, but Señora Mercedes had no idea. Of course she'd never seen her daughter's work. Even if she had visited her daughter, she would not have seen her work. Shirts, that was all she knew. She pulled out a letter from Nicola to show me.

With Morrell leaning over my shoulder to help translate, I stumbled my way through the text, which had
been heavily censored:

My dear Mama,

   I am well, I hope you and Sherree and Anna are
well and happy. I am working now in the sewing shop,
where I can make very good money. We sew (*crossed
out*), I make more than anyone else in an hour, the
other girls are jealous. For a higher rate you can work
the (*crossed out*), but it is too heavy for me.
   You must not worry about me, even though I am
small (*two lines heavily crossed out*). Señora Ruby is
a sweet old lady who takes care of me, and now that
people see she looks after me the big women (*crossed
out*). The food is good, I eat well, I say my prayers
every day. Please give many many kisses to Sherree
and to Anna.

Nicola

Anna had been the baby's name. There were six letters in all, all Nicola had been able to send in fifteen
months, and most of them with large sections excised.
   When we moved onto more delicate ground—
namely, Nicola's love life—Señora Mercedes either
knew nothing, or there was nothing to know. When did
Nicola have time to meet a man? her mother demanded. She worked six days a week for those cruel
people. She came home on Sundays and spent the day
with her own children. Nicola worked, Señora Mercedes worked on the night shift at a box factory, all so
that Sherree and Anna could have a good life. A man

named Lemour? No, Señora Mercedes never heard Nicola mention him. And Mr. Baladine, Nicola's employer? Nicola didn't like him but the money was good and she tried not to complain. Sherree, busy on the floor with her dolls, didn't seem to have anything to add to the story.

We had been talking for two hours. Morrell took us down the street to a tacqueria for lunch. Over burritos and fried plantain Señora Mercedes told me about the day that Nicola died.

"I didn't know she was dead until the next day. My own daughter. Because on Monday the marshals came and Señora Attar, a good woman even if a different religion and a different language, woke up and saw them before they could arrest me and Sherree. She told these officers I was her own mother. What a good woman! But of course I had to move away at once."

I interrupted Morrell's translation to ask for a detailed description of the men. There were two. And how were they dressed? In suits. Not in uniforms?

"What's the point?" Morrell asked, when I pushed for as accurate a description as possible.

"If they were state marshals, they would have been in uniform. INS, who knows, but these men sound expensively dressed. I don't think they were with the law, except the one unto themselves."

"*Qué?*" Señora Mercedes demanded of Sherree. "*Qué dicen?*"

Sherree refused to look up from the dolls, who she'd brought to the tacqueria and that were now climbing on top of each other in a fearful tangle of arms.

"The lady thinks they were not with the law, but perhaps men who had an evil intention toward Nicola and her family," Morrell said in Spanish.

That was as far as we could take matters. Señora Mercedes had seen Señor Baladine drive her daughter home, perhaps four times during the years she worked for him, but he always stayed in the car, she had no way of recognizing his face. If he had been at her home the day before Nicola died, she didn't know. I would have to dig up photos of Baladine and Trant to see if Señora Mercedes recognized either of them.

We left the taqueria with copious thanks for the señora's time. Morrell bought Sherree a frozen mango on a stick from one of the pushcarts we passed on the way back to their apartment. On the L north, Morrell and I went over the conversation from as many angles as we could but couldn't squeeze any more out of it.

As for Nicola's body, that, too, remained a mystery. Morrell said he'd talked to Vishnikov, who hadn't been able to track it down. Vishnikov had also reported on Frenada's autopsy: the man had died by drowning—the water in his lungs made that clear.

"Frenada was out at the Baladine estate the night before he died," I said. "Robbie Baladine saw him there. I'd love to know whether the water in his lungs came from a swimming pool or Lake Michigan."

Morrell pursed his mouth in a soundless whistle. "I'll ask Vishnikov. I don't know if it's too late or not—the morgue released the body to Frenada's sister yesterday afternoon. Now, since I've been a good collaborator, taken you where you wanted to go, found out what news there was to learn about Lucian Frenada, will you do something for me?"

"If it's in my power, sure."

"Join me for a Fourth of July picnic tomorrow. I'll supply the food. We can use the private beach up the street from me—I know one of the families who live there."

I laughed. "That task sounds well within my capabilities. Thank you."

I was still smiling when I got home and walked into Lemour's arms. It was a long time before I smiled that freely again.

34

Fourth of July Picnic

I SPENT FRIDAY night at the Rogers Park police station. When we got there I was fingerprinted and searched. Strip-searched while Lemour looked on. His eyes were glistening, his lips white with spittle. All I could do was hold myself aloof. The dissociation that all prisoners practice. I would become expert at it in the weeks ahead.

The police have rules governing interrogation, but if they breach them it's hard to do anything about it— especially on a Friday night before a holiday with your lawyer who-knows-where. I tried to insist on my right to phone counsel, but Lemour and the charge officer ignored me.

I was put in an interrogation room where I sat for hours, without water, while Lemour screamed meaningless questions at me. When would I confess to cocaine possession? How had I gotten hold of Robbie Baladine? Alternating questions and punches. Every now and then he would leave and a uniformed man would come in and say, *Tell him what he wants to know, honey; it will only get worse.*

At first I kept repeating that I would answer questions only in the presence of my attorney. I kept praying for Freeman's appearance. Had Mr. Contreras understood my plea to call him?

After a time I stopped speaking altogether. Lemour's fury mounted, until a final blow knocked me to the floor. I'm not sure what happened next—the charge sergeant pulled Lemour out of the room and came back for me.

"You sleep it off," he advised. "It'll look better in the morning."

"What will?" I muttered through bruised lips. "The charge of police brutality against Lemour?"

The sergeant took me to the station lockup, where half a dozen other women were waiting. One of them looked at me with shock that was half admiration. "What'd you do to Lemour, girl, refuse to pay him his shakedown? I seen him go insane more than once but never nothing like he did to you tonight."

I tried to say something, but my mouth was too swollen for me to speak. She banged on the cage demanding water. By and by a matron brought a paper cup of tepid tap water. I swallowed as best I could and sat down, gingerly rubbing my sore head and shoulders. I tried to thank my benefactor, but only parodies of words came from my bruised mouth.

I spent a sleepless night. One woman was chain-smoking, the one next to me on the floor spewed curses as the ashes floated on her, while a third roommate moaned over the fate of her baby. Roaches paraded across us all night. We were transients; they owned this room.

In the morning a matron came into the cage, forcing all of us to our feet. The lights in the room were too bright, but when I shut my eyes the room around me spun in nauseating spirals. I held on to the wall for support and felt my stomach heave. I didn't want to throw up, not on myself, not in public, but I couldn't hold it in.

"Jesus Christ, you whores come in here with a load on and then foul up the cell. Come on, wash it off, put these on, let's get going."

I was cuffed to another woman who'd also been sick. We were taken to a tiny toilet where we cleaned ourselves as best we could. I put my head under the sink tap and let water run through my hair and mouth until the officer dragged me away.

"You there, Warshki, get moving."

"I need a doctor." I coughed hoarsely. "I have a concussion."

"You need clothes. Put these on. You're riding out to Coolis."

"Coolis?" I couldn't raise my voice above a whisper. "Not Coolis. Only arrested, not convicted."

The policewoman pulled me away from the sink. "You have a bad fall or a rough john or what last night? Put this shirt on."

The shirt was a bright yellow that made my eyes smart. On the back was stamped IDOC—Illinois Department of Corrections. "Your detective Lemour, he's got to be the roughest john in Chicago. This was all his handiwork. I'm not going to Coolis. I'm waiting for my attorney. Post bond."

"Look, Warshki, I don't have time for games. I got four girls to get on a bus, including you, and you're not in shape to do anything but say yes, ma'am. It's a holiday today, no bond court; your lawyer if he calls will be told where you are. Coolis has the overflow jail for Cook and Du Page County, and we are filled to the brim with all you girls turning tricks up and down the city, so you get a bus ride in the fresh country air, which is more than I'm allowed on the nation's birthday, let me tell you."

I put the shirt on. I didn't know what other choice I had. I had been so sure Freeman would be here this morning to post bail that I was too disappointed to react. Only four of us out of the cage were being sent to Coolis—did the others get a free pass, and if so, why?

The matron cuffed me back to my bathroom partner and marched us out to the street, where an old white bus painted with the Department of Corrections logo waited. Our escort exchanged a few jovial words with a guard as she handed us over to the state. I got my watch back and the six dollars I'd had in my jeans, but my keys were a potential weapon and were handed to the guard in a sealed envelope together with my paperwork.

Rogers Park was the last stop for the bus, which had picked up women from various lockups on the west and north ends of town. There were twenty-nine of us altogether. The guard pushed me into a seat, attached leg and hand shackles to me, connected them to a central pole, and signaled to the driver to take off.

As we lurched west to the expressway, the diesel smoke and the hard seats made my empty stomach heave again. A pregnant woman two seats in front and on my left begged the driver to stop, in halting accented English. No one paid any attention. She threw up, trying to cover her mouth with her manacled hands.

"Can you stop?" I called through my bruised lips. "There's a sick woman in here."

No response from the armed guard.

I shouted again. Several prisoners stamped their feet. A guard yelled through the loudspeaker that they would halt the bus and make us stand at attention on the side of the road for an hour if the noise continued. Everyone subsided, including me—I didn't want to be the one who made this group of women stand in the midday sun.

"Fucking assholes," the woman next to me muttered as the bus waited in line to get on the tollway. "Don't let you go to the john, then bounce you around hard enough to make you pee over yourself."

She wasn't talking to me, and I didn't answer. She'd kept up a stream of invective since the guard attached us. She was twitching, her eyes a telltale yellow. As the day wore on, flecks of spittle appeared around her mouth, but she couldn't stop talking.

At noon we halted for a rest stop at the place where Mr. Contreras and I had our picnic with the dogs two weeks ago. We were unshackled two at a time, the bathroom closed to the public while we were escorted in. It was hard to walk past the people stopping for food or walking their dogs, their jaws gaping, trying not to show how avidly they were staring.

We were given fifteen minutes to relieve ourselves and buy something at the vending machines. I used one of my six dollars to buy a can of juice, which I had to drink in quick gulps under the intense glare of a guard: they would confiscate any metal we tried to sneak onto the bus.

While we waited for the driver, some of the women exchanged small talk with the guards. When we were finally loaded back on, the smart talkers got to move closer to the front, away from the diesel fumes. I got to move closer to the back. My reward for trying to speak up for the pregnant woman.

It was three when the bus pulled in through the main

gates at Coolis. A heavily armed force supervised our unbuckling from the pole and emergence into the prison yard. I ended up behind the pregnant woman. She was small and dark, like Nicola Aguinaldo, and deeply ashamed of the vomit down her front. She tried timidly to ask for help but none of the guards responded. They were busy counting us and comparing lists. It was here that the sheep and the goats were separated—some bound for prison, some for jail.

"This woman needs help," I said to one of the guards near me.

When he ignored me I repeated myself, but the woman next to me hissed and stepped on my left foot. "Shut up. They only start over from the beginning each time they're interrupted, and I need to use the john."

A smell of urine now came from the pregnant woman and she began to weep. The guards ignored her and began the count again. Finally, when the heat of the sun and the long wait made me wonder if she might faint, they started calling us forward. My traveling companions disappeared one by one into the building. Another half hour went by. I badly needed a toilet myself, but they were taking us in alphabetical order. There were three of us left when they called me.

"Warshki."

I shuffled forward in my chains. "Warshawski, not Warshki."

I should have kept quiet—speech was their license to kill. They sent me back to wait, took "White" and "Zarzuela" while I compressed my thighs as best I could for the chains. And finally was called again. Not "Warshki" this time but "Warshitski."

At the door I was unlocked, printed again, sent under double escort to an interior room where I once again took off all my clothes, squatted, coughed, tried to remove myself from the burn of shame at my exposure, and the dribble of urine I couldn't help releasing. A guard barked me into the shower, where hair and a whitish film of soap covered the floor and sides. I was given a clean IDOC uniform, the pants too short on my long legs and riding too tightly in the crotch, the shirt big enough for three of me. At least it covered my waist so I could leave the pants unzipped.

On this far side of the gates my shackles were finally removed. A guard took me through a series of locked corridors to the jail wing. At five I joined the line to the refectory and had a Fourth of July special: hard-fried chicken, overboiled green beans, corn on the cob, and cooked apple slices on something that looked like cardboard. It was too tough to cut with the plastic utensils we were issued, so most of the women picked it up and ate it by hand.

I was eating the corn when I felt something on my leg. I looked down and saw a roach working its way toward my food. I smacked it off in revulsion, then saw that the floor and table were covered with them. I tried to stand, but a guard quickly came over and slapped me back down. Even though I hadn't eaten since the lunch Morrell bought me yesterday in Pilsen, I couldn't face the food. I kept flicking roaches, real and imagined, from my legs and arms until the guards were willing to escort us back to our cell blocks.

At nine I was locked in an eight-by-twelve room with another woman, a black woman young enough to be my daughter, who told me she'd been arrested for possessing crack. We were given bunk beds, metal frames bolted deep into the wall with a thin mattress, a nylon sheet, and a blanket on each. A toilet and sink formed out of a single piece of stainless steel was buried in the concrete floor. There is no privacy in prison—I would have to learn to perform intimate functions in the open.

Like the shower, the sink was caked with hair and mold. I didn't know how to get soap or cleansers to make it palatable to brush my teeth—but then, I didn't have a toothbrush either.

My cellmate was angry and jumpy and smoking heavily, which made my head ache. If I had to live with it for more than a day I'd ask her to stop, but it was the kind of request that could escalate into a fight in here, and I didn't want to be fighting other prisoners. My quarrel was most assuredly not with them.

I was exhausted, I was sick to my stomach, my shoulders were sore, but I couldn't sleep. It terrified me to be locked inside a room, subject to the whims of men —or women—in uniform. All night I lay rigid on a narrow mattress as prayers and shouts hurtled through the corridor. I am strong, and a skilled street fighter, but the misery and madness around me kept swooping toward mob hysteria. Like telephone poles dipping past a train, swooping down, veering away just as you were sure they would hit you. Every now and then I dozed off, but then a cell door would slam, a woman would scream or cry out, my neighbor would mutter in her sleep, and I would jerk awake again. I was almost happy when a corrections officer came around at five to rouse us all for breakfast and the day's first head count.

35

A Little Game on a Small Court

ALL DAY SUNDAY I tried signing up for phone privileges, but I wasn't able to get a time slot until Monday afternoon. All day Sunday I fumed uselessly about my incarceration. I was furious at being locked up—as were many of the people around me. The level of rage was so high that the building could have exploded at any time. Everywhere we went guards watched us behind double-thick glass, or behind TV monitors, tracking the furies and the fights before the corridors turned incandescent.

The calmest women were those who'd been in the jail wing for some months, waiting for trial. These were the people who either had been denied bail—or more commonly didn't have a thousand or fifteen hundred dollars to post it. For half a dozen or so women, this marked the second Independence Day they'd spent in jail. They had gotten used to the routine and were more or less at ease with it, although they worried about their children, their lovers, sick parents, whether they'd still have a place to live if they got off the charge that had brought them here in the first place.

A jail is a place where someone awaits trial. A prison is where you go if you've been convicted and sentenced. Coolis was the great experiment in combining the two places for cost-saving reasons. And while the jail was technically separate from the prison, one of the ways Carnifice saved money was by combining as many functions as possible. We jailbirds ate with the prisoners and used the same common room for recreation.

On Sunday afternoon a guard took me down there for my hour of recreation. It was a multipurpose room, with an exercise area separated from the entertainment unit simply by a difference in floor—green linoleum for the common room, bare concrete for exercise. The entertainment side included a television set attached to the wall and a long deal table with cards, checkers, and some jigsaw puzzles. A handful of women were watching some inane game show, turned to top volume, while three others yelled ribald insults at each other over a game of hearts.

I went to the exercise area to work the worst knots out of my shoulders and legs. The room didn't have much in the way of equipment, but it did have a basketball hoop and ball. I began shooting. At first my shoulders resisted and I had trouble making my hook shot, but after a while the muscles loosened up and I got into a rhythm. Shooting baskets is a narcotizing, private kind of routine. Dribble, shoot, retrieve the ball, dribble, shoot, retrieve. I began to relax for the first time since Friday afternoon. The blare of the television and the shouted insults of the women playing cards receded.

"You're pretty good." One of the women in front of the television had turned around to watch me.

I grunted but didn't say anything. I play most Saturdays through the winter with a group of women who've been together for fifteen years. Some of the young ones were in tough collegiate programs—I've had to get better to keep in the game with them—but mostly I play for the pleasure of feeling my body move through space.

"Play you one-on-one," she persisted. "Dollar a point."

"Play you one-on-one for nothing," I panted, not breaking stride. "I don't have one thin dime in my possession."

"No shit?" she demanded. "Your family, they haven't sent you nothing for a prison account?"

"No shit. Anyway, I only got here yesterday." I jumped up and pulled an errant shot off the backboard.

She got off the couch and came to stand next to me. Other women in the room urged us to a game: "Come on, Angie, she can give you a real game for a change." "No way, my money's on Angie." "Not me, I been watching Cream there, I put five bucks on Cream." I noticed my cellmate on the fringes of the crowd, shivering and rubbing her arms.

Angie snatched the ball away from me and posted up. I jumped as she shot and batted the ball down. She elbowed me hard in the side and grabbed the ball back, shot, and scored. When I rebounded she came in low, trying to head-butt my stomach. I twisted away and shot over her head. The ball caromed around the rim, then went through. She grabbed the rebound, kicking me savagely on the shin as she passed me under the basket. I went in below her guard as she was shooting and knocked her arms up in the air. She swore and gave me an undercut to the chin. I twisted away and grabbed the ball. We weren't playing for baskets but for dominance.

The calls from the sideline grew louder. Out of the corner of my eye I saw uniforms of the corrections officers on the fringes of the crowd, but I didn't dare take my eye off Angie or the court. My sore shoulders, my weak stomach, all that had to be put to one side. Shoot, grab, feint, duck, rebound, shoot again.

Sweat was blurring my eyes. Angie was a good athlete. She was strong, and she was some years younger than me, but she wasn't well-conditioned and she didn't have disciplined technique, either as a fighter or a player. I was keeping up with her and giving her back blow for blow. Moves I'd learned on the streets of South Chicago thirty years ago came to me as if I'd last been jumped on Commercial Avenue yesterday.

The crowd was beginning to roar every time I shot. That made Angie fight uglier but more wildly, and I had less trouble keeping the ball from her. I was driving to the basket when I saw light glint on metal in her hand. I dropped to the floor, rolled over onto my back, and scissor-kicked Angie's feet out from under her. When I jumped up to kick away her weapon, Angie was lying under the basket. A knife cut out of an aluminum can lay next to her.

The women in the crowd began a confused yelling, urging us on to fight. Some of them were Angie's followers, wanting a real brawl; others wanted me to put a stop to her once and for all: "Stick the knife into her now while she's on the ground," I heard one person call out. A guard stepped forward and picked up the knife, while another put a headlock on me. I knew how to break that hold, and with my adrenaline still high was about to, but remembered in time that I mustn't fight back. The guards carried stun guns on their belts; they had plenty of other weapons, not the least the power to keep me in Coolis longer than I wanted to stay.

"Bitch planted that on me," Angie muttered.

One of the CO's who'd been cheering loudest said he

was writing us both up. If you're written up in jail it adds to the charge sheet when you finally get your court date. If you're already in prison it can send you into solitary and deducts from your "good time" for early release.

As I stood motionless with my head under the CO's arm, facing Angie, who was similarly corralled, a woman spoke up from the middle of the crowd. Everyone in the room, CO's and inmates both, quieted down at once. The woman said that there hadn't been any fighting, just basketball, and where that knife came from she didn't know, but she could swear I hadn't pulled it.

"That's right," several voices affirmed. "You were there, Cornish, you saw. They was playing one-on-one. Angie musta tripped in her own sweat."

Cornish was another CO who'd been watching the game, if that's what you could call my outing with Angie. He asked the first speaker if she was sure, because if she was he wouldn't issue either of us a ticket on account of the holiday weekend.

"Uh-huh, I'm sure. Now I'm going to get me a pop. It's a hot day." She was a tall woman, with skin the color of toffee and thick graying hair pulled back from her head in a knot. As she moved toward the vending machines in a corner of the room, the crowd parted, like the Red Sea.

The guard who'd been clutching me let me go. A couple of women came over to slap my palm and tell me they'd been with me from the start. Others, perhaps members of Angie's gang, gave me an evil eye and some pretty inventive insults.

CO Cornish grabbed my arm and told me I needed to get back to my cell to cool down. And what was my name? Warshawski? "You're new, right, oh, in the jail wing. Then you shouldn't be down here for prisoners' recreation. Jail-wing recreation is in the mornings." I opened my mouth to say I'd been ordered down here at three, but shut it again. Don't trouble trouble, my mother always warned me, and trouble won't trouble you.

A woman CO, one of only two or three I'd seen since arriving, was appointed to escort me back to the jail wing. "Lucky for you Miss Ruby spoke up when she did. Otherwise you'd have found your bail request doubled for sure."

"Miss Ruby? Who is she?"

The CO snorted. "Miss Ruby thinks she's Queen of Coolis because she's been in prison a long time, at Dwight eight years before they opened this place. She cut her husband into little pieces and put him in different garbage cans around Chicago, claimed it was self-defense if you can believe that, but the judge didn't buy it and gave her thirty years. Now she's a churchgoer, and the lieutenants and some of the CO's treat her like she's holy. And she has a lot of influence on the young girls, so it doesn't pay to go up against her."

We had reached my wing. The CO signaled to the guard behind the control panel to let me through. She stood on one side of the airlock and watched it close around me. When the door on the other side opened to decant me onto my floor, she took off again.

The wing had a shower room in between the cell block and the guard station. I knew the guards had cameras trained on the showers, and they also could come in on unannounced inspection, but I needed to rinse off my sweat and blood: Angie had given me some pretty serious bumps. When you're in the middle of a

fight—or game, for that matter—you don't notice the
cuts and blows. It's only later, when the adrenaline is
wearing off, that you start to ache.

I didn't have any soap. I had learned this morning
that even the most basic toilet items like toothbrushes
and shampoo had to be purchased from the commissary
and that I had to have money deposited in a trust account at the prison before I could buy anything. It was
a nice little racket, like a company store for sharecrop-
pers. You're there, you're a captive market, and they
can charge you whatever they damned well want. Even
if my five remaining dollars would have covered the
cost of basic toiletries, I was told I couldn't open my
trust account until after the holiday weekend.

I dried myself with the threadbare square of gray
toweling I'd been issued when I arrived yesterday and
put my pants back on. They smelled pretty unpleasant,
but at least they fit.

At five we were all ordered into our cells for a head
count and then escorted down to the dining hall. I
hadn't realized yesterday that you had some control
over what went on your tray and that salads were available on request. Tonight I asked for a salad and extra
bread and rolled lettuce up into a sandwich, which I ate
while walking to the table. I tried to eat some of the
overcooked meat and beans on my tray but still
couldn't deal with the roaches. I suppose if I had to stay
here any length of time I'd learn to overlook them, but I
was still too finicky in my ways.

Within five minutes of my sitting down I'd been identified as the woman who "took out Angie." A woman
across from me told me I'd better look out, Angie was
one of the West Side Iscariots and they were panting for
revenge. Another one said she heard from her girlfriend

that I used karate to wipe out Angie and could I teach her how to do it. One woman, with a dozen braids done up in colored ribbons, said Miss Ruby told a lie to save my hide, but three others spoke up hotly.

"Miss Ruby never told no lie. She spoke the truth, she say Cream here did not pull a knife, and she say Cream and Angie just playing basketball, not fighting, which is the gospel truth, right, Cream?"

"It was the most physical basketball game I ever played," I said, which somehow satisfied her.

The woman with braids said, "No, it's true—Angie, she dissed Miss Ruby, stole her shampoo out of the shower, so Miss Ruby, she was lying in wait to teach Angie a lesson, that's why she stood up for the new girl. Even though she's white."

That started a hot argument, which raged as if I weren't there at all: was I white or Spanish or black? The one who'd nicknamed me Cream insisted I was black. With my olive skin and dark curly hair I could have been anything; since there were very few white faces at the tables, they assumed I was part of the majority culture, although most of them decided I must be Spanish.

"Italian," I finally explained. There was more argument, over whether Italy was part of Spain. I let it flow past me—I wasn't there to conduct geography lessons. In fact, I had a feeling that the less I flaunted my education, the better off I might be.

They also wanted to know how old I was, and when I told them, the one with the ribbons in her braids exclaimed I couldn't be, her mother wasn't that old and I looked younger than her mother. I realized with a jolt that the women around me were terribly young. Only a handful could have been my age, let alone as old as

Miss Ruby. Many didn't seem to be out of their teens, certainly not over twenty-five. They probably yearned desperately for their mothers, or some mother: no wonder they clung to Miss Ruby and argued jealously about who she favored and what she was doing.

I couldn't see Miss Ruby in the dining hall, but they put us through in three shifts of three hundred. Even if she'd been in my shift I might not have been able to spot her in the throng. When I asked after her, they told me she was probably eating in her room: women with enough money or status could buy special food from the commissary. They said it was so expensive most of them did it only for their birthdays, but there was almost always someone wanting to buy a meal for Miss Ruby.

My cellmate ate on the shift after mine, so I had the room to myself for forty-five smoke-free minutes. When she came in, I saw my prowess against Angie had affected her: she accorded me a nervous respect, and when I asked her not to smoke after lights out, she didn't wait for us to be locked in for the night but quickly stubbed her cigarette out on the floor.

Her nervousness made me aware that I was big enough and strong enough to seem menacing. It took me back uncomfortably to the year after my mother died, when I went wild on the streets of South Chicago. I had always been big for my age and I had learned early—partly from my hockey-playing cousin Boom-Boom, partly from experience—how to defend myself in the rough neighborhood where we grew up. But the year I was sixteen I roamed the streets looking for fights. It seemed as though after Gabriella died, I couldn't feel anything unless I was feeling physical pain. After a while even the biggest boys stayed away from me: I was too crazy, I fought with too much insanity. And then I was picked up, and Tony found out and somehow helped me get over it. But I'd felt that same surge of maniac rage on the court with Angie, and I didn't want it taking me over: I might be able to terrorize my jailmates, but I didn't like what it would do to me in the process.

I leaned over the top bunk and asked my roommate her name and whether she had a trial date. Solina, and no trial date yet. With a patient interest I wasn't really feeling, I pried her story out of her, got her to relax over the narrative of her babies, her mother, the father of the children, how she knew she shouldn't be doing crack but it gets hold of you, it's hard to let go of it, and all she wanted was a good life for her children.

At nine the loudspeaker interrupted us. It was time for the day's final count. We stood in our cells next to our beds while the CO's looked in, asked our names, checked them on a board, and locked us in for the night. Once again the hiss of the magnetic lock made my stomach turn over. I climbed to the upper bunk as the lights went out and prayed that Freeman would get a message from Mr. Contreras, track me down, and be waiting for me first thing in the morning with a check for my bail.

Fatigue finally pushed me into an uneasy sleep, in which I kept feeling roaches on my face and hands. Sometime in the night the slamming of a door jerked me awake. I heard a woman scream. My heart began to race again: I was locked up and could do nothing, for myself or anyone around me in peril.

I thought of Nicola Aguinaldo, lying in a bunk like mine on the prison side of Coolis. How much more helpless even than I she must have felt, with no lawyer to bail her out, no powerful friends, alone in a strange country, getting commands in a language she barely understood. At least in her last letter to her mother she had said that—I sat up in bed. Nicola had told Abuelita Mercedes not to worry, that Señora Ruby was taking care of her. Miss Ruby, the powerful protector of young inmates.

I'd been a fool to howl over the injustice of being sent to Coolis. I was right where I needed to be: in the heart of Carnifice territory, where Nicola Aguinaldo had last been seen alive. I turned on my side on the narrow bunk and fell deeply asleep.

36

Bail? Why Leave Such Cool Quarters?

WHEN FREEMAN CARTER arrived Tuesday morning, he was appalled at my decision not to post bail. "I agree two-fifty is outrageously high: that's because it's Baladine and Carnifice. I couldn't get the judge to lower it. But Vic, there is every reason to post it and no reason to stay in here. Frankly, you smell awful and you look worse. That makes a hell of a bad impression on a jury."

"I won't smell so bad when you've deposited money into an account for me here and I can buy soap and shampoo," I said. "And I'm not going to stay in here until my trial—only until I find out what I want to know."

That made him explode. "You pay two hundred dollars an hour for my advice, which you proceed to flout, but I'm going to give it to you anyway. Get out of here. If you stay in here on some cockamamie scheme to rout out corruption in Coolis, you will be hurt worse than you have ever been before in your life. And if you then call on me to glue whatever's left of you back together, I will not be a happy man."

"Freeman, I won't claim my brain is in top gear right now. Being locked up is distorting, I agree. But for the last three weeks I've been ducking missiles that

Carnifice and Global Entertainment have been launching at me. I was sure you'd understand if you watched the video I asked Morrell to send you, the one showing Baladine's tame cop looking for coke he'd planted in my office. For once in my life I did not go out of my way seeking to make an enemy: they came and found me."

We were sitting in a special meeting room for attorney visits. It was utterly bare except for two plastic chairs separated by a table that was bolted to the floor. We had to stay in our respective chairs, or the guard watching us through a glass panel would remove me. Supposedly the room was soundproofed, but for all I knew they were taping everything we said.

When I talked to Freeman Monday afternoon, during my fifteen-minute slot for phone calls, I insisted he bring a camera with him to photograph the fading remains of Lemour's attack on me. He'd harrumphed a bit on the phone but came with a Polaroid. When he saw the marks on my face and arms, his eyes widened with anger and he took a dozen shots. He was already planning the complaint against Lemour, but it made him even less able to understand why I wanted to stay at Coolis.

I pushed my palms together, trying to marshal my words. "It all started when I stopped to help Baladine's ex-nanny three weeks ago. Until I find out why that matters so much to him and to Teddy Trant, I don't think there's going to be much left of me even if I do leave Coolis. The answer is here, at least the answer to what happened to the nanny, to young Nicola Aguinaldo. If I had money in a trust account and some bills for feeding the guards, I should be able to learn what I

need to know about her in a couple of weeks. Maybe
less."

He thought I was quixotic as well as insane, and he
argued persuasively: I may have thought I wasn't going
out of my way to needle Baladine, but why didn't I
leave well enough alone as he'd asked me when he was
dealing with the State's Attorney about my car last
month? And prison was a destructive environment. It
wore on you physically as well as mentally, warped
your judgment and your ethics.

"You know that as well as I, Vic: you did your share
of criminal pleadings in your days with the public defender."

"I know it from being here four days. I got entangled
with the leader of the West Side Iscariots on Sunday and
I've been watching my back ever since. I hate it here.
I'm lonely. Even if the food wasn't horrible, the dining
hall is so covered with roaches you have to keep brushing them off your legs while you're at the table; every
time the locks shut on our rooms at night, my stomach
twists up so hard I can't sleep; there's no privacy, even
on the toilet." To my dismay I could hear my voice
cracking on the edge of tears. "But if I let you bail me
out, the only thing that will save me is to close up my
business and hide out someplace. Even if my self-respect
would permit that my finances won't."

"You can't convince me those are your only two
choices, but I can't stay to argue. I have to get back to
Chicago for a court appearance." He looked at his
watch. "Anyway, you've already made up your mind to
be pigheaded, so there's no point in my arguing with
you. Tell me what you want, both in bucks and in permitted goods, and I'll send Callie over to your home to
collect things. I've got an intern who can ferry things

out here for you and do the basic paperwork on the money."

Besides the clothes I was permitted (two bras, two pairs of jeans, three underpants, five shirts, a pair of shorts, and a modest set of earrings) I told him what I most wanted was to see Morrell. "I want to see any friend who will make the drive—I listed Lotty and Mr. Contreras and Sal on my visitors' sheet—but will you ask Morrell to come out here as soon as possible? As far as the money goes, I'd like three hundred dollars put into a prison trust account."

I picked my words carefully for the rest of my request. "I know it's a felony to bring cash in for someone in prison, so I'm not going to ask you to do it. If I could get four hundred dollars in bills, though, it might come in handy. Will you mention the idea—and the risk —to Lotty?"

I wanted money in hand in case I needed to bribe some CO's or inmates or both. In theory, there was no cash at Coolis: you got issued a photo-ID card with a computer chip when you were admitted. Any money in your account was programmed onto the chip and then deducted when you used the card, whether in vending machines, at the commissary, or doing laundry. The idea was you wouldn't have gambling or bribing or drug sales if you kept out the cash, but in my four days here I'd already seen plenty of bills changing hands— and not always very secretively.

Freeman frowned and said in his most austere tones that he would speak to Lotty, but only to advise her of the felony nature of my request.

He finished making notes in his quick, tiny script and packed up his papers. "Vic, you know my steadiest advice as your counsel is for you to post bail and come home. If you decide to listen to me, a call to my office will get someone out here on the instant."

"Freeman, before you go, do you know why I'm here? I mean, instead of at Cook County? Was this some shenanigan of Baladine's?"

He shook his head. "I have to confess I wondered about that, but once you were arrested, even with Lemour involved, you moved out of Baladine's orbit. The simple truth is, Cook County is always filled to capacity, and on the Fourth they started splitting at the seams. Women arrested at precincts on the far North or West Sides were automatically shunted out here. Anyway, Baladine is out of the country. He's taken his family on some exotic vacation."

"I know: to the South of France. Is Robbie with them? I don't know what became of him after I left the house on Friday morning."

Freeman told me that Baladine had wrested Robbie from Mr. Contreras in the middle of the night Saturday. The old man ("He's been living with you too long," Freeman said in an unnecessary aside) had tried to hold off a warrant from a Du Page County sheriff's deputy. He only gave in when Robbie said he couldn't stand it if they arrested Mr. Contreras; he would leave if the sheriff promised not to hurt the old man. Robbie's father had taken him to South Carolina, to boot camp, before flying out to join the Poilevys and the Trants with the rest of his family in the Pyrenees.

"I tried to talk to Baladine, but his staff wouldn't give me his number overseas. They say he left strict orders that even though he has the kid back he's not doing a deal with you," Freeman added.

"Freeman—if they don't know I'm here don't tell

them. If anyone asks, let them think I posted bail and am lying low."

He gave me a queer smile, half loving, half exasperated. "As you wish, Donna Victoria of the Rueful Countenance."

He tapped on the window to let the guard know we were finished. I was searched, the guard spending more time than necessary on my bra, and taken back to the jail wing. Now that I was alone I felt unbearably desolate. I lay on my bunk, a strip of towel over my eyes against the light, which stayed on from 5:00 A.M. until lights-out at nine, and let myself give way to misery.

37

In the Big House

THE NEXT FOUR weeks were the hardest of my life. I hunkered down and tried to learn the ropes at Coolis—how to avoid being beaten up by my sisters in chains, how to butter up the CO's without having to have sex with them, how to keep myself busy enough that the pervasive helplessness and boredom wouldn't drag me so far down I couldn't function.

I wanted to talk to Miss Ruby, to thank her for her help on Sunday, but mostly to find out what she could tell me about Nicola, and about getting work in the clothes shop. I let everyone I talked to know that I'd like to meet her, but except for a couple of times in the dining hall, where the CO's kept us firmly in place at the table, I didn't see her after that first day.

Freeman's visit did bring a material change in my physical comfort. True to his word, he sent his intern out with money for my account, along with my clothes allotment. The intern had a stack of legal documents for me to read and sign. In the middle of them was a letter from Lotty. She begged me to post bail in lines of such loving concern I was hard put to stick to my resolve about staying, but in a postscript she added, *I helped Freeman's secretary pack your clothes and mended various tears.*

"She especially wanted you to know about a hole in the waistband to your shorts," the intern said primly.

Lotty was no seamstress. When I got back to my cell, I surreptitiously picked apart an inch of the waistband seam. Tightly folded bills almost matched the khaki of the fabric. I pulled out a twenty before stitching the seam shut again—it was the safest place to store money, and washing wouldn't hurt it any.

With my prison trust account set up, I was not only able to buy a toothbrush and soap at the commissary but also some cleanser to scrub out the sink–toilet unit in my cell. The cash I would keep for bribes, once I knew to whom and how to administer them.

Except for being able to buy overpriced, poor-quality shampoo and soap, my first trip to the commissary was a disappointment. The women around me had talked about what they planned to do on their expeditions as if their weekly thirty-minute trip was an outing to Water Tower Place. I suppose the women found the trips exciting because they made a break in the routine. They were also our main contact with the outside world, which we could experience through magazines like *Cosmo* or *Essence*. *Soap Opera Digest* was also popular.

Besides magazines and toiletries, you could buy canned or packaged food, cigarettes, and artifacts made by inmates throughout the Illinois prison system. A large number of male inmates seemed to like to embroider. We could get handkerchiefs, place mats, head scarves, even blouses with intricate designs of birds and flowers, brought in from Joliet and points south.

Also available were Mad Virgin T-shirts and jackets —the average age of the prison population was, after all, Lacey's target audience, and many of the inmates

were fans. Curious, I inspected the labels. They read
Made with Pride in the USA, so I didn't think Nicola
Aguinaldo had bought the shirt she died in here. The
commissary also stocked spin-offs from other Global
favorites, including Captain Doberman and the Space
Berets, which women liked to buy for their children.

On my first outing I bought cheap lined writing paper—the only paper the commissary carried—and a
couple of ballpoint pens. When I asked the clerk if they
had plain paper or roller-ball pens, she snorted and told
me to go to Marshall Field's if I didn't like the selection
here.

When I got back to my cell, my roommate, Solina,
apathetically watched me scrub the basin. She had been
at Coolis only a week longer than me, and the fact that
the sink was filthy when she got here meant it wasn't
her job to clean it up.

"We'll take turns," I said, my voice bright with menace. "I'm getting it spick-and-span, and that means tomorrow, when it's your turn, it will be easy for you to
clean up."

She started to say she didn't have to obey orders
from me, then remembered my prowess against Angie
and said she'd think about it.

"We can control so few things in here," I said.
"Keeping the place clean means at a minimum we can
control the smell."

"Okay, okay, I already got the point." She stomped
out of our cell down the hall to watch television on a
small set belonging to an inmate who'd been awaiting
her trial date for eleven months.

I had to laugh to myself, picturing the friends who've
complained about my slovenly housekeeping over the

years—they'd be astounded to find me laying down the law on hygiene to my roommate.

Besides making it possible for me to bathe, Freeman had also delivered my message to Morrell. On Thursday near the end of my first week, I got summoned to see him in the visitors' room.

My arrest had stunned him. He hadn't even known about it until he saw a paragraph in the *Tribune* on Sunday—Mr. Contreras, never fond of communicating with the men in my life, had been too rattled to call Morrell. Like Freeman, Morrell talked to me persuasively about all the reasons to leave Coolis, but unlike Freeman, he could see a point to my staying.

"Are you learning anything helpful?"

I grimaced. "Not about Nicola, so far. About the way people without power turn on each other because they feel too helpless to see who's really to blame for their day-to-day misery—I'm learning way too much about that."

I leaned forward to talk more privately, but an alert CO made me back away the requisite arm's length—if we touched, Morrell might pass drugs to me. After five minutes of glaring scrutiny the CO decided I wasn't trying anything too heinous and turned her attention to another inmate. Only a handful of women got visitors on weekdays; it was hard to speak privately.

"There's a place called the Unblinking Eye where you can get a particular kind of watch–camera," I said in a prison-yard mumble as soon as the CO turned her attention away. "If you buy one for me and bring it on a Saturday or Sunday when there's a mob here, we ought to be able to make a switch."

"Vic, I don't like it."

I smiled provocatively. "I don't think they'll do anything to you if they find you with it—except bar you from visiting me."

He gave an exasperated sigh. "I'm not worried about that but about you, you fool."

"Thanks, Morrell. But if I ever manage to get into the clothes shop, I may see something that I should document. And frankly, there's plenty else to record here between the inmates and the guards."

Morrell gave me another quizzical look and said he'd see what he could do. He switched the talk to neutral matters—my neighbor, who was so distraught at the idea of me behind bars that he wouldn't make the trip to see me. He gave me news of Lotty, of the dogs, of all the people whose welfare I cared about and couldn't attend to. He stayed an hour. I felt a wrenching desolation when he left. I went down to the rec room, where I shot baskets for an hour, until I was wet with sweat and too tired to feel sorry for myself.

When I went back upstairs to shower, the CO at the entrance, a man named Rohde, seemed to react oddly. He looked at me, then got on the phone. I had to wait five minutes before he let me in, and then it was only when two other CO's joined him. I wondered if they had somehow monitored my conversation with Morrell and were going to put me on report, but Rohde watched me go past the guard station without saying anything. Still, he seemed to have an air of suppressed excitement about him, and he was joined behind the double-glass walls by the other two men. The video cameras were trained on the shower rooms as well as all other common areas, but I had already figured out which shower head cut the camera angle so that it could only catch me if I stood directly under it. If he'd called his buddies for a peep show, I figured I knew how to avoid providing it.

I was jumped almost before I got into the shower room. Two women, one from the front, one from the rear. Rohde's manner had put me on guard, otherwise they might have destroyed me. I dropped my supplies and towel and kicked, all in one motion. I was lucky; my foot caught the woman in front square on the patella, and she grunted and backed away.

The one behind me had my left shoulder in a steel grip. She was pulling me toward her. I gasped—she had something sharp that sliced across my right shoulder. I hooked my feet around her ankles and used her own force to catapult her forward. The wet floor made it hard to get a purchase and I slipped and fell with her. I chopped across her right wrist before she could recover and forced her to let go of her weapon.

The one I'd kicked was closing in on me. I rolled over on the moldy floor and got up into a crouch. She flung herself at me before I could kick the weapon away. She had her hands around my neck. I held on to her shoulders for leverage and swung both knees into her stomach. She squawked in pain and let go of me.

The woman with the weapon was behind me again. I was winded; I'd already been working out for an hour and didn't know how much longer I could keep fighting. When she lunged at me I ducked. It was the wet floor that did the rest. She lost her footing, scrabbled to gain it, and careened so hard against the concrete wall that she stunned herself. Her partner saw her fall and suddenly shouted for help.

The guards appeared so fast I knew they must have

been on their way as soon as the woman knocked herself out.

"She jumped me! She jumped Celia, too, and knocked her out!"

Rohde grabbed me and held my arms behind me. Polsen, the CO who'd joined him at the video monitor, stood nearby but didn't touch my assailant.

"Nonsense," I panted. "Celia is lying there with something in her hand that gave me this cut on my neck. And as for you, whoever you are, if you were waiting to take a shower, where the hell is your towel or your soap? As you two CO's know, because you were watching all this on your monitor."

"You stole them from me."

"Those are my things on the floor there. Where are yours?" I demanded.

At that point CO Cornish appeared. He was the fairest-minded of the CO's on our wing.

"You fighting again?" he asked me.

"The woman on the floor there cut me with something when I came into the shower room," I got my story in quickly. "She still has the razor or whatever she used in her right hand."

The woman was beginning to stir. Before Rohde or Polsen could move, Cornish bent over and pulled a strip of metal from her.

"She belongs on the prison wing. As does the other one. I'm putting all three of you on report. Warshawski, if I catch you in one more fight you're going into segregation. And you two, off you go to your own quarters. How did you get in here, anyway?"

Rohde was forced to let me go. He and Polsen escorted my assailants off the floor. Cornish looked at my neck and told me to go to the infirmary for a tetanus

shot. It was the closest he was going to come to acknowledging that I'd been jumped, but it eased the injustice of the whole situation slightly.

"I'd like to wash off first," I said.

Cornish waited in the hall while I picked up my
shampoo and towel from the filthy floor. I took off my
shirt and bra and washed off under the shower most
remote from the video monitor. Cornish took me in an
elevator down to the basement, which I'd never seen,
and waited while I got my shot. The woman on duty
put some antibiotic ointment on the wound in my neck.
It hadn't gone deep enough to require stitches, which
was fortunate, since she didn't have the equipment to
put me back together.

Cornish took me back to my cell and told me to be
very careful where I walked at night. Everyone on my
wing seemed to know about the attack. In fact, they
seemed to have been warned away from the showers
when I came up from my workout.

"You're in trouble now," Solina said, gloating.
"Rohde's fucking one of the Iscariots. He got those two
to jump you out of revenge for Angie. And he put
money on them."

When we stood at attention for our predinner head
count, Rohde handed me a ticket. He had written me
up for instigating a fight that injured two other inmates.
My hearing would come in a month, after the captain
had reviewed the charge. Great. Now Captain Ruzich
would realize I was one of his inmates. As I studied the
ticket I got my one gleam of hope: Rohde had put my
name down as *Washki*. Maybe the fact that none of the
CO's could pronounce my last name, let alone spell it,
would save my butt.

Miss Ruby stopped me after dinner and told me she

was disappointed in me, that she didn't think fighting was the right way to solve my problems inside. "The women tell me you're old enough to be a mother to most of them. This isn't the way to look after the young ones or set them an example."

I pulled down my T-shirt to show her the oozing wound in my neck. "Should I have turned the other cheek until I was cut to ribbons?" I demanded. She gave a snort that was half a gasp but wouldn't stay to discuss the point.

After that I began to wonder if the attack in the shower would make it impossible for me to learn anything about Nicola. I even began to wonder if Baladine knew I was here, if he'd e-mailed the warden from France and told him to stage the attack. Only the realization during the next few days that none of the CO's treated me any better or worse than the rest of the inmates made me decide that was a paranoid fantasy.

The fight in the shower grew as it was told around the prison. I had moves like you saw in the kung fu movies. I had given the two Iscariots subtle blows that stunned them and then pulled a knife to finish them off when the guards intervened. Some of the women wanted to attach themselves to me as a protector, but others, especially the real gangbangers, thought they wanted to fight me. I managed to talk my way out of several confrontations, but it added to my tension to have to be on my guard during recreation time or in the dining room. Any time I saw signs that anger was about to spill over into combat, I'd leave the area and return to my cell.

Fights were always breaking out, over things that might seem trivial to you if you'd never had this experience, the experience of being crammed behind bars with a thousand other people, without privacy, at the mercy of whatever whims the guards might feel that day. Someone stole someone else's body lotion, or pushed in front of her in line, or spoke disrespectfully of a relative, and fists and handmade weapons flashed out in an instant.

People also fought over clothes. You got a replacement bundle only every five years in prison, so a torn shirt or lost button mattered terribly. Women paired off as lovers and had lovers' quarrels. Various street gangs besides the Iscariots marked territory and tried to control such things as the flow of drugs.

After my fight in the shower room, my roommate became more nervous around me than ever. At least fear made her cut down on her smoking and made her halfheartedly clean out our sink every few days, but I learned she had begged for a transfer, terrified that I would jump her in the night.

Her attitude changed dramatically on my second Thursday, when I returned from my workout to find her bunched up in bed howling with misery.

"Caseworker is trying something with my children," she screamed when I asked what was wrong. "Moving them to foster care, saying I'm unfit; even if I get out of here I can't keep them. I love those children. No one can say they ever went to school without socks and shoes. And that caseworker, did she ever come watch me cooking dinner for them? They eat a hot meal every night of the week."

"You don't have a mother or sister who could take them in?"

"They're worse off than me. My mother, she's been high since the year I start first grade, and my sister, she's got eight children, she don't know where they're at from one end of the week to the next. My aunt down in Alabama, she'd take them if I send them, but the caseworker won't listen to me about my aunt. And who will give me money for my children's bus fare if the caseworker's against me?"

I leaned against the wall—of course we didn't have a chair. "You could write again, showing that you have a proper home for them to go to and pledging your willingness to go into rehab as part of a plea bargain."

She looked at me suspiciously. "What do you know about plea bargains and rehab? And how can someone like me who can't afford a lawyer, how can I get into a rehab program? You think they grow on trees for poor people? The only rehab for someone like me is doing time."

I sidestepped how I knew about things like plea bargains and concentrated on how she could find one of the few remaining publicly funded drug programs. The good programs have long waiting lists, of course. I wondered whether Solina was a serious addict who would promise reform to get out of prison time but not really try to quit: drugs were readily available in Coolis, as in many jails and prisons, and some of her more violent mood swings, with periods of agitated withdrawal, told me that Solina had found her way to an in-house crack supplier. But drafting a letter for her would give me something to do, besides shooting baskets and occasionally practicing my singing.

Solina was touchingly awed by the finished letter. We didn't have access to computers or typewriters, but I printed it carefully for her on the cheap lined paper available in the commissary. She read it over and over, then took it down the hall to the cell where she spent most of her day and showed it to the group around the television. A number of inmates studied law books in the library and filed complaints and appeals for themselves or their friends, but most came to Coolis with such minimal literacy that they couldn't put their learning into appropriate language.

The word of that letter and my special knowledge spread fast: over the weekend, women began visiting my cell with requests for letters—to the State's Attorney or their public defender, to different welfare agencies, the children's caseworkers, the employer, the husband or boyfriend. If I would write they would get me anything I wanted—cigarettes, reefer, coke, crack, I didn't do drugs? Then alcohol, chocolate, or perfume.

If I didn't accept payment I'd look like a patsy or a phony. I said I'd write a letter in exchange for fresh fruit or vegetables—much harder to come by in Coolis than drugs.

It was my letter-writing that really saved my hide in Coolis. The women I helped began constituting themselves into an informal set of watchdogs, warning me when trouble was lurking.

My letters also began to make it possible for me to ask questions about Nicola and the clothes shop.

38

Prisoners in Cell Block H

WHETHER YOU WERE in jail or prison, if you were at Coolis for more than two weeks you had to work. A woman lieutenant named Dockery, who was strict but considered fair by most of the inmates, made up job rosters. The newest arrivals got kitchen or cleaning duty, the lowest paid and least popular. Kitchen duty, as far as I could make out, had to be the worst, working with grease and heat and heavy pots, but cleaning the showers and other common rooms would come a close second.

The most coveted jobs were in telemarketing and hotel reservations. The pay was the best and you didn't have to lift anything heavy. But that kind of work only went to prison inmates. In management's eyes, those of us in jail awaiting trial wouldn't be around long enough to go through the training—or, more to the point, for our names to move to the top of the long waiting list for the cushiest jobs.

Of course what I was most interested in was the clothes shop. When I was in line at the dining hall or working out in the rec room, or in my cell writing letters for women, I kept trying to find someone who worked there or who roomed with someone who worked there. Everyone had a different story about it, and no one wanted to work there.

"But I knew one woman, Nicola, she wrote her mom that the pay was really good," I said one day in the rec room when several women were watching me shoot baskets.

They didn't play themselves, but they were hoping someone who did play would show up—watching and betting on games was a popular pastime. One of the women asked who Nicola was.

"She was that girl from China who ran away," one woman said.

"She wasn't from China, it was some other place over there, like maybe Japan," someone named Dolores chimed in.

"Philippines," I suggested, jumping up for the ball as it banged off the rim. "I know her mother, and she said Nicola wrote she was really happy to have a job in the clothes shop."

"Of course, if she wrote it in a letter home," Dolores snorted. "They don't let you say nothing bad about it, or it won't get past the censors. One woman, she worked there, she was crying all the time, they treat you too rough there."

The third woman said they only took foreign girls in the shop; they worked them to death and then brought in more foreign girls as replacements.

"Oh, don't be stupid," Dolores said. "They use foreign girls because they know foreigners won't complain in case their children get deported."

"Yes, but don't you remember Monique? She was from Haiti, and she said the back room was foreign girls on death row. They're all in segregation, and the

CO's bring them over in the morning in a locked van to work and then take them back at night."

It was a startling notion, but I said I didn't think there was a death row at Coolis.

"Maybe not," the friend said stubbornly, "but still, there's something spooky over there. Maybe it's because they don't let Americans work there. It's all Mexicans and Chinese and—where did you say Nicola was from? Uh-oh—Polsen's looking at us queer; better go to our cells for head count."

This last she muttered out of the corner of her mouth in the prison mumble everyone mastered in their first few days. CO Polsen was always looking at women "queer," when he wasn't outright touching or threatening to touch us.

Polsen was one of the CO's that I tried to avoid, but of course the guards had enormous power in our lives. If they took a dislike to you they wrote you up—gave you a ticket, which could result in anything from a loss of commissary privileges to a stint in segregation. Women they liked they brought gifts for, ranging from better cosmetics than you could get in the commissary to drugs. But the women they liked had to pay a price for that attention. Rohde, sleeping with one of the Iscariots, wasn't the only CO having sex with the inmates.

One of the hardest things to take during my time at Coolis was the constant sexual harassment. It was verbal, it was physical, it was incessant. Many of the CO's, not just Rohde, put their hands on your ass when you were waiting in line for dinner. When they searched you after you had a visitor, they would linger a long time on your breasts. I had to learn to hold myself very still, very aloof, not act on the impulses of a lifetime to break an arm or separate a rib. If I saw something blatant I tried to photograph it with my wrist-camera, but it was the language as much as the behavior that was demeaning. It was hard to accept the abuse passively, and it fueled both my rage and my fear.

Morrell brought me the wrist-camera from the Unblinking Eye on my second Sunday in Coolis. In the crowd of women and children in the visitors' room, we managed to exchange my wristwatch for the camera model. I now had a watch that could take pictures, although I hated seeing mine go out the door with Morrell—my father's mother gave it to him when he graduated from the police academy fifty-five years ago.

The tiny camera had cost over fourteen hundred dollars. Freeman was paying my bills while I was locked up, but I wondered how I'd ever pay him back—my prison time wasn't a good advertisement to clients.

At least the camera made me feel a modicum of control over the crazy world I was inhabiting. I started taking pictures of some of the worst outrages I saw, but I would have needed the video model I took to Georgia to capture the verbal abuse.

"Looking good, Cream," CO Polsen said as I came into the rec room a few days later. "Like to see you in shorts. I bet that pussy of yours has seen plenty of action, so I'd fit right in."

I moved past him without breaking stride or looking at him: Polsen had constituted himself an enemy, and right now the only defense I could come up with was to pretend he didn't exist.

The problem had really begun over my fight in the shower: he'd been watching on the monitors and felt cheated by my taking out my assailants before anything serious got under way. But his hostility was exacerbated the night after I got my camera, when I was running a load of laundry. The laundry room lay beyond the rec room, so I was watching TV with some of the women while I waited on my clothes.

Polsen was one of the CO's on duty. He abruptly called Dolores out of the room. The sudden slackness in her face and her dragging posture as she obeyed made me get up a few minutes later and follow after her into the laundry room.

Polsen was behind the door trying to pull down her jeans. Dolores was struggling to keep them up, hissing, "No, please don't do this, please don't do this, I'll tell the lieutenant," and he was laughing and saying she was dirt, no one believed her lies, but that if she did say something, he'd see she got into segregation so fast it would make her head spin. I had been practicing with my wristwatch and used it now, wishing I could tape him as well. Polsen looked up and I turned quickly and moved my clothes out of the washer. He let go of Dolores, who ran from the room back toward the prison wing. Polsen gave me a look that liquefied my hamstrings.

When I returned to the common room, the women in front of the television shrank from me: they all knew why Polsen had called Dolores away, and they had watched from the shadows the byplay that took place when I went into the laundry. None of them wanted Polsen to think they supported me.

Back in my cell I wrote down a verbatim account of Polsen's language and what I'd seen, with the date and the time. I interleaved the pages with a copy of *Cosmo*, which I'd bought at the commissary as a cover for my notes. When Freeman's intern came out the next day to tell me my trial date was set for the last week in September, I managed to slide the magazine to her in a flurry of exchanging documents. I asked her to take the magazine away with her and keep it for me. I wasn't sure what use I'd make of my notes, but I didn't want to leave them in my cell—we'd already been locked down twice for searches in my short time at Coolis.

Before she left, the intern asked if I was ready to post bail. It was hard to say no, but I wanted to get a look at the clothes shop. I said I'd give it one more week before throwing in the towel.

I was pretty sure at least one CO was going into rooms on our wing after lights out—it was the only explanation I could think of for the banging doors and cries that sometimes woke me in the night. But none of the women ever said anything. There were several pregnancies in the prison, I noticed, among women who had been inside for over a year—in one case six years.

When I asked about it during my letter-writing sessions, the women clammed up. One of them whispered to me in line at dinner later that someone named Cynthia spent a year in solitary for filing a report on a CO who raped her. The prison said she made up the charge to try to shorten her time. After that, people were more afraid than ever to complain. Usually, too, if they got you pregnant they gave you drugs. "They say, oh, your cycle out of balance, you take these. Then you sick for three days, a week, and you lose the baby."

Chemically induced abortions, in a country that banned RU-486. How enterprising of the Department of Corrections. I wondered who made the diagnosis and who dispensed the drugs, but we had gotten our trays and my informant scuttled across the floor to join her friends.

If Polsen decided to come into my cell after lights-out, what would I do? The thought made me lie tense in bed that night and for some nights after.

39

An Audience with Miss Ruby

AT THE START of my third week I was assigned to a kitchen shift, a miserable job, especially in summer. We lugged fifty-pound pots of food between stove and steam table, carried out mounds of refuse, slipped in grease on the filthy floor, got covered with burns from careless cooks flinging hot food around. The work paid sixty cents an hour. My coworkers were sullen and sloppy and made it harder to keep from getting injured.

The only job action available to Coolis workers was refusal to work. This led to a ticket, and enough tickets sent you to solitary confinement, but usually after your stint in segregation you got a new work assignment. Turnover was high in the kitchen, but I couldn't afford time in segregation, so I grimly kept at my post.

"This isn't a vacation resort," the CO in charge would say if a woman complained of a burn or a sore back. "You should have thought of that before you thought a life of crime was fun. You're not here for your health, but to learn a lesson."

I had already learned that such medical care as existed was hard to come by. When a woman had hot grease spilled down her arm, the CO in charge of the kitchen upbraided her for crying over nothing. The next day she didn't come in to work; I learned from the comments of the other women that her arm had become a mass of pustules in the night. She had been treated by the in-house "doctor," a CO who had studied prenursing for a year at the local junior college before getting into Coolis.

The stench of the overboiled food and the sight of roaches and mouse droppings took away most of my appetite; if it hadn't been for the fruit my clients brought me I don't think I would have eaten. After a week in the kitchen I was so exhausted it was hard to remember why I'd decided to stay in jail instead of posting bail. I was lying on my bunk Friday night, trying to make up my mind whether to call Freeman and ask him to bail me out on Monday, when Solina came in to say that Miss Ruby had sent word over that she wanted to see me.

On my first day at Coolis, Cornish had sent me back to my cell with a reprimand because jail inmates were supposed to use recreation facilities at a different time than the prisoners, but I'd learned early that was a regulation the CO's enforced only if they wanted an excuse to write you a ticket.

The main reason I hadn't seen Miss Ruby in the rec room since Independence Day was her work schedule. She had one of the cushy jobs, the phone reservation desk for the Passport chain of motels and rental cars. While most prison jobs ran from nine to three, the reservation lines had to be staffed twenty-four hours a day. She'd been on the noon-to-six shift, and I hadn't known to look in the rec room for her in the mornings.

A day earlier I'd written a letter to Rapelec Electronics for a woman, explaining why she was not able to take part in her job-training program and requesting that an opening be kept for her in September. The woman paid me with a box of six local tomatoes, the best food I'd eaten since my arrest. I took two of them as an offering and went with the woman who'd brought the message from Miss Ruby; Jorjette had grown up with one of her granddaughters.

It took some doing to get the guards to let Jorjette and me into the rec room in the morning. CO Cornish, on duty that morning, worked closer to the rules than Rohde or Polsen did on the afternoon shift. Jail inmates didn't have recreation privileges until 3:00 P.M.

"Vic going to show me her basketball shot," Jorjette whined. "You know everyone say she the best, she beat Angie. And we got kitchen duty in one hour; we gotta go now if we're going at all."

"We could do it another time," I said. "Although another time I probably won't have any tomatoes. Do you grow them yourself, Cornish?"

I held one out for him to look at. He admitted that gardening was his hobby but that his tomatoes hadn't ripened yet.

"You have one hour down there, girls," he finally said, accepting the tomato as he signaled to the man behind the bulletproof glass to release the lock on the jail-wing door.

When we got to the rec room, a woman CO I didn't know was on duty. She was watching Oprah with a handful of women on the couch. Miss Ruby sat in the middle of the group, her iron-gray hair freshly cut and curled, shell earrings three or four times regulation size in her ears.

Her eyes flicked at Jorjette and me when we came in and pulled up chairs nearby, but she gave no sign of noticing us until Jorjette approached her during a commercial break and asked nervously how Miss Ruby was doing today.

Miss Ruby inclined her head, said as well as anyone could in this heat, too hot to go outside, but she longed for a breath of fresh air. Jorjette said, well, it was pretty hard on everyone but she knew Miss Ruby's joints suffered real bad in the heat. Maybe she'd like a nice fresh tomato, to remind her of the fresh outdoor air?

"Cream here brought it for you special."

Miss Ruby accepted the tomato and jerked her head toward the far end of the deal table. The CO stayed on the couch watching Oprah, and the handful of other women left us alone: Miss Ruby wanted privacy, Miss Ruby got privacy.

"I can't make up my mind about you, Cream," she said when we were seated. "Are you a fighter or a Good Samaritan? First you beat up a couple of gangbangers, but now I hear you spend your spare time writing letters for the girls. Some of them think you're an undercover cop."

I blinked. Of course in a way that was the truth, but I didn't know Miss Ruby and I couldn't trust my secrets to a stranger, especially one who seemed to be plugged in to the gossip pipeline as thoroughly as Miss Ruby was.

"If I'd known my life history mattered here, I'd have written it up on the bathroom wall," I said. "I was arrested same as everyone else."

"And that would be for what crime, I wonder?"

"You know the sad old story about the man who leaves his wife for a cute young thing? And the first wife, who worked hard and put him through school and scrimped so he could build his business, she gets left with the shirt on her back and not much more? And he gets the kids, because how can she give the kids a decent home when she doesn't have any money and she has to be out at work all day?"

"I heard a bunch of versions of that story in my time." She kept her eyes straight ahead, talking in a prison mumble out of the corner of her mouth.

"My twist on it is I figure the guy for about the meanest bastard in Chicago. So I take the oldest child. A boy, who's overweight and sensitive, and Daddy likes to beat on him, make him cry, then beat on him some more for crying like a girl. Daddy had me arrested for kidnapping."

"Uh-hunh. And you couldn't make bail. Everyone says you got a real lawyer, not a PD. Not to mention, of course, your fancy education that lets you write all those letters."

"Guy's got a lot of important friends. The judge set bail at a quarter of a million. If your friends ran a financial check on me they could tell you why I couldn't pull together that much money overnight."

"And how'd you learn to fight like you do, taking out two big women in the shower?" she demanded. "Not to mention Angie, which I watched you do."

"Same way Angie did," I said softly. "On the streets of Chicago. Ninety-first and Commercial to be exact. But I was lucky. My mother wanted me to have an education, and she made me study when the other girls on my street were getting pregnant or doing drugs."

Miss Ruby thought this over. "I don't know whether to believe you or not. But I hear you've been asking questions about a young woman who used to be here. I hear you've been saying you want to talk to me about her. And so here I am, talking to you, wondering how you know her and if that's the real reason you're at Coolis."

I sidestepped the comment. "I never met Nicola Aguinaldo. I know her mother. Señora Mercedes is grateful to you for looking after Nicola."

"Hmm. She's not very grateful in person."

"She doesn't have any money. And she doesn't have a green card. She's afraid to come out here in case they inspect her documents and report her to INS, and she can't write in English. But Nicola's last letter to Señora Mercedes brought her great comfort, because Nicola told her mother you were keeping an eye on her."

Miss Ruby inclined her head slightly in acknowledgment. "And how did someone like you come to be friends with Nicola's mother?"

I smiled. "I didn't say we were friends, but that I know her. Before my own arrest I was trying to help Señora Mercedes find out what happened to Nicola. You know that she died?"

Miss Ruby gave another brief dip of her chin.

"All the women say you know everything that happens in this prison. I want to know what happened to Nicola. How did she get to the hospital?"

"If you're not a cop yourself, they put you here to talk to me." She spoke with finality but didn't try to move away from me.

"Cops don't give a rat's toenail for who killed a poor little girl who didn't even have a green card to her name."

"So who did put you in here?"

"You know who Robert Baladine is?" When she shook her head no, I explained that he owned Coolis and that Nicola had worked for him before she was arrested. "He's the man I was talking about, and he's got way more power and money than I ever will. He likes the idea of me being locked up in his prison."

She finally looked at me directly, thinking over my story, which had the unusual virtue of being mostly true —even if it might leave her thinking Baladine was my ex-husband. "Nobody knows what happened to Nicola. I heard a lot of different stories, and I don't know which is true. The CO's said she had female difficulties and went into the hospital, where she ran away. Someone else said she got tangled up in one of the big machines in the clothes shop and got killed and the guards were scared they'd be punished for not turning the machinery off in time, so they dumped her body in Chicago. And some girls are saying she beat up on a CO, which is silly, because she wasn't much bigger than a minute, let alone those men."

"She actually died in Chicago," I told her.

Miss Ruby liked having inside information, more than a whole bushel of tomatoes, and she questioned me closely on Nicola's death. After I told her what I knew—omitting how I'd come on Nicola to begin with —I asked how she came to take Nicola under her wing.

"Too many of these girls here don't have any respect for any other human being on the planet. Nicola came from a country where old people are treated with respect—someplace near Japan, which is probably the reason why. She saw how my shoulders and neck bother me after talking on that phone for six hours, and she used to rub the knots out for me. Of course I tried to help her in a few little ways myself."

While Miss Ruby talked, I wondered if perhaps Nicola had never made it to Coolis Hospital. Maybe Captain Ruzich had her taken to Chicago directly from the prison. No, that didn't work—the floor head at the hospital's prison wing clearly had known about Nicola. Unless she'd been primed to say Nicola had been on the ward when she wasn't?

"I need to find someone who will tell me what went on in the shop the day Nicola left here. Or I need to get a job working over there."

Miss Ruby grunted. "You can't get girls to talk about what goes on in the clothes shop. Of course everyone around here is more or less scared, the guards can take away your commissary privileges or your phone calls or put you in seg. But the girls in the clothes shop, they don't talk to anyone. And of course, for the most part they don't speak English anyway."

"So if I wanted to get into the clothes shop, I'd have to be a foreigner."

"First, you have to lose at your trial. The jail girls, they get kitchen duty and other ugly stuff, but they don't ever get the jobs that pay anything decent."

"I really need to see the inside of that shop," I said, looking across the room. CO Polsen was in the doorway, eyeing me in a way I didn't like, but I willed him out of my mind. "How much would it cost, and who could arrange it for me?"

"What's your real business here, Cream?" Miss Ruby asked softly.

I continued to look ahead, speaking as she did, out of the side of my mouth. "I want to see Robert Baladine destroyed. If I can learn what happened to Nicola, I may find a way to make him . . . well, sorry he ever crossed my path."

"If revenge is what you want to eat for dinner, you're going to get yourself a bad case of indigestion. It never pays, believe me, Cream. I tried that meal for a lot of years, before Jesus showed me a better way."

She paused, as if waiting for me to say amen, sister, or ask for her conversion story, but even for her help I couldn't pretend to a faith I don't own.

Disappointed at my lack of interest, she finally said, "No one wants the jobs in the clothes shop; the stories on how they treat the girls over there are too unpleasant. So I never heard of anyone bribing her way in before—usually they're crying to get out. And most of them sleep and eat together, too. So if you want to get in, well, Lieutenant Dockery, she's in charge of the work details, and no one ever gave her a bribe in their life: she's strict but fair. But Erik Wenzel—he's in charge of the shop—he's another kettle of fish. And he's not a CO, he's some manager they hired, like they do for my reservations work—someone who knows how the job is supposed to be done. Give me a day or two. I'll see what I can find out."

She tapped my arm with a manicured finger. "You don't know how to behave here, Cream. Maybe you're the toughest bitch on your block in Chicago, but that makes you a challenge to the CO's: they want to break you. There are no secrets in Coolis. And the CO's know them, too. There's always some girl willing to tattle to them in exchange for some favor, a better work assignment, or real makeup—you notice how most of the girls here are black, but the makeup in the commissary is made for whites? Which, by the way, you can wear with your skin, but most of us can't. So if you can come up with some carmine nail polish and lipstick for me, it would make me move faster on your strange request.

"Anyway, what I'm trying to tell you, Cream, Troy Polsen is a bad man, but don't go beating him up. The satisfaction you'd get wouldn't be worth it. You'd land in segregation, and you'd never get out of it, so you'd go to your trial in prison clothes, and you know how that will look. Watch yourself, Cream."

Polsen yelled to Jorjette and me that we were due in the kitchen. "You're not on vacation here; move those lazy buns."

"Exquisite manners," I murmured. "It's either that or the cuisine that keeps me coming back. I appreciate the warning and the offer of help, Miss Ruby. I don't want to look a gift horse in the mouth, but . . ." I let my voice trail away suggestively.

"Why am I helping you? You don't need to know everything about my life." She smiled suddenly. "This I'll tell you for nothing: I have a big bone of curiosity. My mama always said it would be the death of me, but I want to know what goes on in that shop myself. I have to spend another eight years in this building. I hate there being stuff about it I don't know."

Polsen came over and yanked me roughly to my feet. "Come on, Princess Di, they want you at Buckingham Palace."

As he shoved me toward the corridor I couldn't help wondering if my own bone of curiosity would be the death of me.

40

Sewing Circle

MANNACCIA!" I SWORE. *"Puttana machina!"*

My fingers had once more slipped on the stretchy fabric so that the armholes puckered up. While I used the little clippers to pull the threads out, I flexed my shoulders, trying to ease out the knots in my neck as well. None of the women around me stopped or looked up. They were tied to the whirring machines, working on jackets and leggings, their fingers moving so fast the movement of arms, fabric, and needle was a blur of motion.

"Hey, you, Victoria!" Erik Wenzel suddenly stood in front of me. "I thought you said you knew how to run this machine. *Sabes usar esta máquina.*"

When they spoke Spanish, the men always used the familiar form of *you.* I said in Italian how insufferable Wenzel's manners were, then added in Spanish, *"Sí, sí, se usarla."*

"Then act like you can *fabricar.*" He snatched the shirt from my fingers, ripping it in two, and slapped my head. "You've destroyed this shirt so it can't be used. *La arruinaste!* It comes out of your pay. *No te pago por esta!*"

It had taken almost my whole four hundred dollars cash to get here; so far all I'd learned was that in a prison shop the foreman can do whatever he damned well wants. Miss Ruby managed somehow to spread the money among CO Rohde in the jail wing, his counterpart in the prison wing, and one of Erik Wenzel's subordinates who put together the work rosters for the clothes shop. She told the man that I was a fragile immigrant far from home and she thought kitchen work might kill me. Miss Ruby got a Revlon lipstick and compact, and they weren't easy to come by either.

I hoped I never had to depend on sewing to pay my bills. I thought it would be a cinch to run one of those machines, and I thought it would be a holiday after the misery of working in the prison kitchen, but after four days all I had to show were a permanent knot in my shoulders and neck, bruised and bleeding fingers from getting in the way of the needle, and three dollars and twenty-four cents in earnings, which wouldn't be paid into my trust account until the end of the week.

We got paid by the piece: nine cents for T-shirts, which were the easiest to assemble, fifteen cents for shorts, thirty-three for the heavy denim jackets. Some of the women were so fast they could make nine or ten jackets an hour. One of my neighbors was turning out thirty-two T-shirts an hour.

When I started, one of the women was detailed to show me how to assemble a shirt. She put one together at lightning speed, unwilling to slow down her own production to show a newcomer the ropes. I had followed her moves as best I could. By the end of the second day, I had worked out how to do eighteen an hour, but of those only ten or so met the quality-control standards; the ruined ones got deducted from my pay. And if Wenzel was angry at a woman—as he was with me—he would deliberately destroy a garment and then deduct the cost from her pay. One thing about prison labor: there is no shop steward or Labor Department to take a grievance to. If the foreman is pissed off at you and wants to spit at you or slap you or destroy your output, there's not a lot you can do about it.

In a twist of irony, we sewed little tags into the shirts that read *Made with Pride in the USA*. So I had learned one thing—that the shirts in the commissary were made in the prison, although the ones we sewed were all plain white. Maybe they were shipped to one of the men's prisons for the Mad Virgin or Captain Doberman to be embroidered onto them.

In an adjacent room, women operated heavy shears to cut out the pieces to the garments we were sewing. A pair of runners went between the cutting room and the sewing room, bringing us the raw materials for construction.

We got two ten-minute breaks in our six-hour shift, with half an hour in the dining hall, but most of the women except the smokers preferred to work through their breaks. As Miss Ruby had said, the crew here were all foreign, primarily Hispanic but with a handful of Cambodian and Vietnamese women.

Also as Miss Ruby had said, most of the women in the clothes shop were housed together. They arrived in a group in the morning, were escorted to the dining hall or commissary in a group, and were taken off together to a separate floor at night. I hadn't been moved over to their quarters, but I was closely monitored now by the CO's. So closely that I decided I had better speak only Italian, or my fractured Spanish, from now on, even in my cell.

My withdrawal from English made Solina and the

crowd begging for letters at first tearful, and then furious. In revenge, Solina started smoking heavily in the cell, as if hoping to provoke me into yelling at her in English instead of Italian. She fell asleep each night with a cigarette burning on the floor beside her, when I would climb down to make sure it was out—I didn't want to go through everything I was enduring only to suffocate in a cigarette fire.

It seemed absurd to think that I could fool the CO's into thinking I wasn't really an English speaker, but I hoped to keep the pretense in place long enough to learn something about Nicola's end. CO Polsen was the likeliest to get me into trouble. When he was on duty in the afternoon, responsible for taking me over for recreation after my work shift ended, he showered me with foul language. When he did that, I treated him as if he were part of the ambient air, but if he tried touching me I would shout loudly—still in Italian—and keep shouting until I could move away from him to a public space. It wasn't a great defense, but it was the only one I could think of. I hoped I learned something useful soon, because I didn't know how much time I'd have before either the women or Polsen decided to take me apart.

In the shop I trailed around with the smokers during our brief breaks, trying to ask them about Nicola or about the clothes—where did they go when we finished them? Illinois law said that anything manufactured in the prisons had to be for prison consumption, but I'd never seen any of these plain shirts or jackets for sale in our commissary. And our—or at least my coworkers'— output was enormous.

It was the size of the production, and the fact that no English speakers were working in the shop, that kept me going, despite my hacked-up hands and the fury that the foreman Erik Wenzel kept unleashing on me.

The other thing that kept me going was a room down the hall where our goods were sent when they were done. Every hour Wenzel and CO Hartigan, the subordinate who'd taken my money from Miss Ruby to give me my assignment, collected our output, inspected it, wrote on a card how much was usable, and stacked the finished goods on a giant trolley. One of the Cambodian women pushed the trolley down the hall to the next room.

My second morning, during the smoking break, I sauntered after her. When the door opened to admit the trolley, I saw a kaleidoscope of lights, machines, and people. Before I could look more closely I was flung hard to the ground. I rolled over, ready to kick my assailant. I actually had my legs scissored, pulling in to strike, before I remembered myself. Wenzel stood over me, his face red with fury, and ordered me back to the workroom in a mix of English and Spanish. His Spanish wasn't any better than mine, but it included an array of crude words for female anatomy that startled me. He wrote me a ticket, my third since coming to Coolis. My tickets could get me put in segregation at any moment, since they were all for offenses that could be construed as physical assaults.

My glimpse into the room had been so fleeting, I couldn't make sense of what I'd seen. How secret could it be if the Cambodian women were allowed into it? Yet my coworkers were so fearful of talking about it that it must be very secret indeed. The only women who worked back there had been given life sentences—that was all I could glean. No one ever talked to them— they were housed in a separate part of the prison.

When I persisted in trying to ask about the room the next morning, the smokers backed away from me in a cluster, as if I were a wolf going after a flock of pigeons. CO Hartigan was a heavy smoker himself; the women eyed him nervously when I talked to them.

"Tu preguntas demasiado," one of the women finally whispered to me when Hartigan had gone into the cutting room to deal with a machine that had stopped working. "No *sigas preguntando por Nicola.* Do not keep asking about Nicola. She learned that her baby was dead, and she wanted to go to Chicago to bury the child. Of course no one would let her leave, but she was mad with grief and began pounding on Wenzel with her tiny hands. He and Hartigan shot her with those guns of theirs that fire electricity, and then they laughed and made sport with her. Now, ask nothing more. For us she never existed, and the guards will punish you severely if they know you are inquiring about her. And they will punish me if they think I remember her."

Her hoarse Spanish was hard for me to follow, but before I could ask her to repeat anything she flinched and tried to duck back into the workroom. CO Hartigan grabbed her arm and then one of her breasts, which he twisted until she gasped in pain.

"You're not talking out of turn, are you?" he asked the woman. "Remember: we know where your little boys are. *Sabemos donde son tus niños.*"

Her eyes were streaming and she spoke pantingly. "Only tell woman, she no have money, no get my cigarette. She lazy, not working, why I think she pay back someday?"

I knew her quick wits were protecting herself, not me, and the look she gave me was one of loathing. Hartigan let her go and slapped me for good measure: I was a lazy cunt, he said, and they weren't going to give me a free ride forever.

Once again I controlled myself in the nick of time. Rage and helplessness were so bottled and boiling inside me, I knew I had to leave Coolis soon; even if the guards didn't harm me I was destroying myself. If I didn't learn something soon that I could use against Baladine, I would forfeit my only chance to understand what was going on in the clothes operation. I had a pretty clear picture at least of why Nicola had gone to the hospital, even if I didn't know how she'd died in Chicago, but it wasn't anything I could use to get her killers arrested.

I didn't want to think about what might have lain behind the woman's phrase that the guards "made sport" with Nicola. I only knew I had to move fast before either my language fraud or my ineptitude with the sewing machine landed me in trouble. How fast I'd have to move was made clear to me on my return to the jail wing that afternoon, when I got a summons to see a visitor.

Morrell stood up on my entrance, an old-fashioned courtesy so remote from the mores of Coolis that I blinked back tears. It was a Thursday; as always midweek, the visitors' room was almost empty.

Morrell squeezed my fingers, a fleeting pressure that the CO in the room overlooked. "You need to leave as soon as possible, Vic."

I agreed, thinking of the abuse I was enduring, and started to detail some of the language and actions of the CO's and the work shift managers.

Morrell cut me short. "That's appalling, Vic, but that isn't what I mean. Things have come unraveled on the outside. Since Baladine left Chicago shortly after your arrest, he apparently didn't know what had happened to you. He's coming back from Europe tomorrow. He knows—or will know when he lands—that you're here. And while you're in Coolis he has the power to have you treated more harshly than you want to imagine."

I shivered involuntarily. "How do you know this?"

He gave a glint of a smile. "I'm a journalist, I have press credentials. I've started being very attentive to Alex Fisher at Global, told her I'm working on a book about the security business."

To my chagrin I felt a stab of elemental jealousy. In the midst of my potpourri of misery and fear, I was picturing the contrast between Alex, with her clear, smooth skin and Rodeo Drive wardrobe, and my own bedraggled condition. Like seducing Murray wasn't good enough for her, she had to take Morrell, too. I muttered something farouche about her being able to make sure he got a good movie deal for his book.

"In that case I'd better get a contract before she reads it. She thinks highly of you, by the way, and says it's a pity your stubbornness gets in the way of your success. I've told her you were out of town, vacationing until your trial, and I don't think she's double-checked that news. And since she's extremely busy, she's been happy to palm me off on her poor overworked assistant. Who's not sophisticated enough to keep news to herself. Like the urgent e-mail Baladine sent Alex yesterday demanding to know your whereabouts after making bail. It will take them this long"—he snapped his fingers—"to learn you're in here. Have you found out what you wanted to know?"

I shook my head. "I've learned some things, but not enough. It seems reasonably clear that Nicola died of injuries she got here, although I don't think I can ever prove that. There's some reign of terror that goes on with the women in the clothes shop where she worked —the foreman today threatened the children of a woman who was talking to me. Whether that's random —there's a lot of vile abuse that goes on here, most of it sexual assault—or whether there's something specific they don't want the women talking about, I don't know. It's mighty peculiar that the only women who work back there can't speak English."

Morrell tapped the table impatiently. "Vic, do I have your permission to go to Freeman and tell him to bail you out as fast as possible? He might be able to appear for you in a Chicago court tomorrow instead of waiting through the weekend."

I rubbed my face, overwhelmed with a desire to lay my head down on the table and cry my heart out. Everything I'd been doing seemed so futile, ever since the night I'd stopped to help Nicola Aguinaldo. My career was in shambles, I was demoralized from my weeks in Coolis, I didn't know any more than I had a month ago about why BB Baladine was gunning for me.

"Yeah, tell Freeman to bail me out. I don't have much time left in here before everything comes unglued for me in here, anyway. Everyone on the jail side knows I speak English, that I was even writing legal letters for some of the women. It won't be long until that word gets over to the creep who runs the clothes shop, and then I'll—well, the best-case scenario is I'll be assigned back to the kitchen."

"Vic, I don't know whether you're heartbreakingly gallant or only out of your mind, but you're worth a dozen of Alex Fisher, with her stock options thrown in besides. Don't do anything too foolish before Freeman

can post bail." His lips brushed the back of my hand
and he was gone.

CO Polsen wasn't on duty; the woman guard patted
me down in a perfunctory way and sent me to my cell
to be counted before dinner. I brushed the back of my
hand against my cheek. I had one last chance to learn
something tangible at Coolis. I don't know if it was
gallantry or insanity that was driving me, but the only
plan that came to me made me so cold that I lay shivering under my blanket while Solina and her friends
marched in formation to the dining hall.

41

Photo Op

IN THE MIDDLE of the night, when I couldn't sleep, I wrote a letter to Lotty. A light in the corridor came through the grated window at the top of our door, projecting a small grid of light on the wall behind our toilet, enough for me to make out the shape of my words on the page without being able to read them.

I wanted Lotty to know how important she'd always been to me, since my student days at the University of Chicago when I'd been not only young but rawly unsophisticated. She took me under her wing and taught me basic social skills I'd missed growing up in a rough neighborhood with a dying mother. Somehow over the years she'd moved from being a kind of fulfillment of my mother to a more equal friend, but she'd never lost her importance for me.

If I am foolhardy, daring without judgment, *I wrote,* it isn't because I don't love you, Lotty. I hate to bring you grief, and if I am seriously injured you will grieve. I don't have an answer to the conundrum. Not the old masculine swagger that I couldn't love you as much as I do if I didn't love honor more. Something more restless drives me, a kind of terror that if I don't take care of things myself I will be left with a terrible helplessness. More than anyone I've ever known, you've kept that helplessness at bay. Thank you for your years of love.

In the morning I quickly put it in an envelope without reading it over. On my way to breakfast I handed it over to CO Cornish for the outbound mail.

The condemned woman's last meal: cornflakes, powdered orange juice, watery coffee, a piece of soggy toast. At nine, CO Cornish brought me to the gate of the prison's work wing. There we were counted again and marched down the hall to our assignments. One group was escorted to the room of phone banks, where Miss Ruby and other well-spoken inmates took hotel reservations for families crossing America on their summer vacations. The rest of us were taken farther down the hall to the sewing room. We stood at attention while we were counted for a third time, this time by Wenzel and Hartigan, and then sent to our machines.

Before I could start on the pile of pieces I had left over from yesterday, Hartigan grabbed my arm. "You!" he spat at me in English. For one heart-stopping minute I thought maybe Baladine had already tracked me down and given orders to treat me in some unspeakable way.

Apparently it was only my ineptitude as a seamstress that made Hartigan grab me. In a graphic mix of Spanish and English he explained I was being demoted to a cutter. The pay there was a flat dollar-thirty an hour, did I understand?

"*Comprendo,*" I said through lips thick with anger.

For the next three hours, with one ten-minute break, I stood in the cutting room, pinning stencils to thick stacks of cotton, then holding the stacks in position as automatic shears sliced through them. It was back-breaking work, made harder by Hartigan's periodic eruption into the room to yell, "*Vamos, más rápido!*"

All last night as I had lain sleepless on my bunk and in the morning as I moved the heavy plastic stencils onto the fabric, I kept rehearsing in my mind what I wanted to do. My chance came at lunchtime. We were allowed to put aside the stencils and turn off the shears just as the Cambodian woman gathered up the previous hour's sewing output onto the trolley. While everyone else moved into formation for lunch, I followed the trolley down the hall in the other direction. As people chattered and milled around stretching their sore arms, neither Wenzel nor Hartigan noticed I was going the wrong way.

The Cambodian woman rang a buzzer in the door. When it opened I followed her inside. In the confused medley of light and noise that greeted me, I couldn't make anything out at first: giant machines, women in Corrections Department smocks, the ratcheting of conveyor belts. It was a major production plant. I moved to a conveyor belt carrying T-shirts.

Lacey Dowell's face stared up at me. Her red hair was artlessly tangled, her lips half-parted in a mischievous smile. The smile was repeated half a dozen times as shirts passed in front of me on the belt. Hot lights overhead made me start to sweat; I realized they were there to dry wet ink—two women operating a giant press on my right were stamping decals onto shirts the Cambodian woman was unloading from the trolley. At a second belt facing me, another pair were stamping Space Beret insignia onto denim jackets.

At the far end of the belts other women pulled the garments off, folded them, and fed them to someone operating a commercial iron. Another pair laid ironed clothes in boxes. I watched in frozen fascination, until a shout behind me galvanized me. I began snapping the stem of my wrist camera, taking pictures as fast as I could, of Lacey's face, of the belt, of women pressing decals onto shirts and jackets.

A man grabbed my arm, yelling, "What the hell are you doing in here? Where did you come from?"

I darted away, trying to snap a picture of the machines themselves, of the workers, of anything where I could get a clear view. The man who'd yelled out at me began to chase me. I ducked under a conveyor belt and skittered on my hands and knees toward the entrance. The women feeding shirts to the iron stopped working and huddled against a wall. Clothes began to pile up and then fall to the floor.

My pursuer tripped on the T-shirts and bellowed for backup. CO Hartigan came through the door on the run. Jackets and shirts tumbled from belts and got tangled in the machinery. Sirens howled and the clanking machines ground to a halt.

I ducked under Hartigan's outstretched arm and pushed open the door, with some foolish hope of pretending I'd gotten turned around and ended up in the room by mistake. Wenzel was on the other side of the door. He seized my arms. I slid my legs around his ankles and with the fury that had been boiling in me for a month, took his feet out from under him. He fell backward, still holding me, but his grip loosened as he fell, and I pulled away, rolling on my side and coming up in a crouch.

Hartigan was facing me, pulling a gun. I twisted away, then suddenly lost control of my limbs. I was shot through the air as from a cannon and careened headfirst onto the pile of jackets. I couldn't breathe. I couldn't move. The skin on my chest stung. My legs were wet, and I smelled urine and burning cloth. My arms and legs jerked spastically.

Hartigan stood over me, a smile of exultant sadism on his face, and lifted one large booted foot. I managed to wrench myself sideways just before he kicked me. His boot sank savagely into my ribs, and then into my skull.

When I woke I was in a dark room. My head pounded violently. I tried to lift a hand to feel my head but I couldn't move my arms. My ribs ached and my stomach heaved. I shut my eyes and passed out again.

I felt a hand on my arm and someone saying, Is she alive? I wanted to pull my arm away but I still couldn't move it. I was alive, someone else confirmed, but I wasn't going anywhere, they could take off the manacles.

"Someone like her will fool you, Hartigan," the first voice said. It belonged to CO Polsen. "Wenzel has a concussion from the blow she gave him. Leave her chained up, that way you'll be sure."

It was the fall, I wanted to say. I took his legs out from under him and he fell. But my jaw hurt and I couldn't speak. Later someone brought me water. I was so grateful tears spurted out the sides of my eyes.

My cousin Boom-Boom had dared me to climb the crane, I tried to tell my mother. And why had I done it, she demanded in Italian. *Do you need to do everything that crazy boy does? What are you trying to prove, that you're a cat who has nine lives?* My father told her to let me be, I had a concussion and two broken ribs and that was punishment enough. *And my punishment,* my mother shouted in English, *if she's taken from me in one of these crazy exploits you and your brother laugh at, I will never survive it.*

I thought it would be safe now to open my eyes, because my father would be smiling down at me, but when I opened them I was in a cell—not the one I shared with Solina—one with a single bed in it. I heard a sharp snap. The pounding pain had subsided to a muted throb and I could move my head. I saw the door, with a window in the top and an eye bulging as it peered at me. There was a second snap as a shutter slid across the window, leaving me once more in darkness.

I kept dozing off into phantasmagoric dreams, where I was eight or nine or ten, with my mother as she made me practice scales until my arms hurt so much I begged her not to make me do music anymore, or with Boom-Boom at a Fourth of July picnic where the fireworks made my head ache and tears run down my cheeks. The fireworks smelled, too, like some kind of horrible un-cleaned toilet.

The snapping shutter roused me periodically. I could move my arms now, but the pain in my ribs and gut was so great I didn't move them much. I was alternating between drenching sweats and chills so violent they caused a rattling at my feet. I thought my bones were clanking, but when I tried to sit up to look at my feet, the pain in my stomach stabbed me brutally. I cried out and lay back down. Once when the shutter opened I had a flash of awareness: my legs were manacled together. It didn't matter—I was in too much pain to walk anywhere. I shut my eyes again.

Someone asked again if I was still alive. I knew the voice, but my mind floated off. She's not in good shape, a second man answered. She stinks, the first voice said. She'll be in back, Polsen, you won't smell her once you get her inside. Wenzel can't drive; you'll have to come along. Put on some gloves and a mask. Change her shirt; we don't want to get into the mess we had with the other one, having to come up with a clean shirt because this one's got burn marks on it.

CO Polsen. He was tearing off my shirt; he was going to treat me the way he had that other woman, and I was powerless to stop him. I would not cry I would not give him the satisfaction I would not cry when he touched the raw skin on my breasts. I was jerked upright, and the pain across my abdomen was so ferocious I blacked out. Then I was sick and my father was carrying me, but he was too rough, he was hurting me, my head and my stomach.

"No, Papa," I begged. "Put me down."

That made him laugh, and I cried for my mother but she couldn't hear me. When he finally put me down it was on something hard, not my bed. *"Mio letto,"* I sobbed. *"Voglio mio proprio letto."* He slapped my face and shut the door on me, and I remembered it hurt his feelings when I spoke Italian, because he didn't speak it himself. "I want my own bed," I repeated in English, but it did me no good, he started shaking the room from side to side so that my sore ribs and stomach bounced against the hard floor.

I kept passing out. I would come to when an extra-fierce jolt flung me against the floor. At some point the jolting stopped and the door opened. I had another brief moment of clarity: I was in a panel truck, lying on packing cartons. A couple of men approached me. I couldn't protect myself as they seized me. They tossed me on the ground and slammed the van door shut. Polsen called me a stupid cunt and said this would teach me to mind my own business and then they left me on the ground and returned to the truck. The back door swung open as they drove off and several boxes bounced onto the road.

I saw now how Nicola Aguinaldo got out of prison and made it back to Chicago. And died.

42

Slow Mend

I LOOKED UP and saw the machine that made decals ready to push into me. My arms were manacled to the bed and I couldn't lift them to guard my face. A man leaned over me. I didn't want CO Polsen to know I was scared, but I couldn't help crying out. The man called me "cookie" and seemed to be weeping. I shut my eyes and fell back asleep.

The next time I woke I realized the machine was the arm holding an IV drip. I wasn't wearing manacles but had lines running into both arms and an oxygen tube in my nose. A woman was feeling my left wrist. She had on a yellow sweater and smiled when she saw me watching her.

"You're all right, you know. You're with friends, so don't worry: you're not in prison and you're going to recover."

I looked at my wrist. It was empty. I didn't have my watch, my father's watch that he'd worn for twenty-five years.

I croaked something and she said, "Your watch didn't come over from the hospital with you. I'll ask Dr. Herschel about it."

This seemed so disastrous to me that I began to cry. The woman in the yellow sweater sat down next to me and wiped my eyes, since I was having trouble moving my arms. The fingers on my right hand were in splints, but both my arms were so sore it seemed like too much work to lift them to wipe my eyes.

"We'll do everything we can to get your watch back to you. Now that you're awake I want to see if you can drink something. You'll recover faster if you can start to eat on your own. As soon as you drink a bit of this, I'll call the hospital about your watch." She cranked the bed up, and I swallowed something sweet.

I croaked again.

"You're in the Grete Berman Institute. Recovering from your injuries."

I knew I had heard of the Grete Berman Institute, but I couldn't remember what it was. I went back to sleep, puzzling over it, but after that I began recovering, drinking more each time I woke, staying awake for longer intervals. Sometimes the man who called me "cookie" was there, and I finally remembered it was Mr. Contreras. I tried to smile and say something so that he'd know I knew him and appreciated his being there; I could just manage to say "Peppy," which made him start to cry again.

Once when I woke, the woman in the sweater handed me my father's watch and helped me strap it onto my wrist. I was relieved to have it back but still felt upset, as if I were missing something of even greater importance. The woman in the sweater urged me to drink miso broth. I was getting stronger—in a few days I'd be able to have rice, and then I'd be strong enough to remember what was troubling me.

I was too tired to think. I gave up worrying about the watch and drifted between waking and eating and struggling upright: the wound in my abdomen made

sitting up an exquisite pain. It was only three days, in
fact, between my first waking up and my shaky progression from bed to chair and a tour of the hallway, but
the pain and the painkillers stretched time's passage in
odd ways.

On the day that Mr. Contreras helped me into a
chair so that I could eat my rice and watch the Cubs,
Lotty came in. Sammy Sosa had just hit his forty-sixth
home run, but Mr. Contreras muted the television and
with rare tact left us alone.

When Lotty saw me out of bed and in a chair, she
burst into tears and knelt with her arms around me.
"Victoria. I thought I was going to lose you. Oh, my
dear one, I am so thankful to have you back."

Close to her I could see how much gray was in her
hair; for some reason that made me cry as well. "I
thought you would chew me out."

She blinked back her tears. "Later. When you're
strong enough to fight back."

"She mustn't have too much agitation, Dr. Herschel," the nurse said.

Lotty pushed herself to her feet. Despite the gray
hair, she still moved with easy agility. I smiled foolishly
at her. She didn't stay long but the next evening she
returned with Morrell. The two together told me my
story.

A state trooper had found me on the Belmont exit
ramp to the Kennedy around three on Sunday morning.
The boxes that tumbled out of the back of the truck
when CO Polsen drove off had saved my life: a motor-
ist, swerving to avoid them, noticed me lying in the
road and called the cops. The state troopers rushed me
to Beth Israel, where Dr. Szymczyk—the same surgeon

who'd been on call the night I found Nicola Aguinaldo
—patched me together.

I had been luckier than Nicola on several counts.
When Hartigan kicked me, I'd managed to twist away
enough so that my ribs took the main force of his blow.
He had badly bruised my intestine and I had developed
a severe infection, which accounted for my fever, but
when the state trooper found me, the wound had only
just begun to perforate the peritoneum. Nicola already
had such advanced peritonitis when I came on her that
she didn't have much chance for survival.

And then, unlike Nicola, I was in good physical condition and I was used to defending myself, so that despite the jolt from the stun gun—which was what
Hartigan shot me with—I was able to shield myself
from the worst of his blows. I had apparently managed
to put my hands over my head, so that the kick that
knocked me out broke the fingers in my right hand but
didn't do serious damage to my skull.

"You were lucky, Vic," Lotty said. "But you also
don't have the habit of victims."

"But how did I end up here instead of in the hospital? The Grete Berman Institute is for torture victims,
isn't it? That isn't really me."

"I didn't think you should be moved from Beth Israel
until you were more stable, but Morrell persuaded me
that the man Baladine could get access to you in a hospital if he was looking for you. I wanted to bring you to
my home, but the Berman Institute is secure and fully
staffed, so I finally agreed to let you be moved here as
soon as you were out of surgery. But besides that,
you—" Her voice cracked and she steadied it. "You
were in a helpless situation, at the mercy of the law,

shot with an electric weapon, beaten, and then chained to a bed. I think you were tortured, Victoria."

"She needs to rest now, Dr. Herschel," the nurse intervened.

Over the next several days, as I got back on my feet and began to get some exercise in the Berman Institute gardens, Morrell put together the rest of the story for me. He had called Freeman Carter when he got back to Chicago from Coolis that last Thursday, urging him to try to get me a bail hearing in Chicago on Friday; Morrell told Freeman he was worried that Baladine might not let me survive the weekend. Freeman was skeptical at first, but Morrell managed to persuade him.

Freeman spent all day Friday shaking up the judicial system trying to find me. It was three on Friday afternoon before the head of the circuit court granted Freeman permission to post my bail in a Chicago courtroom and have me released that afternoon instead of making us wait until a circuit judge rode out to Coolis on Monday.

At that point, although no one outside the prison knew it, I was already chained to a bed in the segregation wing, with a rising fever. Freeman couldn't get anyone at Coolis to admit to my whereabouts and finally was told that they lacked the administrative personnel to process my release after 5:00 P.M. on Friday, that Freeman would have to come back on Monday.

Freeman went to the state appellate court and got an emergency writ requiring my immediate release. The prison then told him I had faked an injury at my work station and they had put me in the hospital. On Saturday, as my fever rose, they played a shell game with Freeman, passing him between the prison and the hospital, each saying the other had possession of my body.

Of course neither Freeman nor Morrell knew what discussions took place at the prison end of things, but the most likely guess was that the staff panicked. Perhaps they thought I might die, and Freeman was making it clear they would face intense scrutiny if they didn't produce me in good shape. They probably figured they could repeat what had sort of worked for them with Nicola Aguinaldo: dump me in Chicago—where I'd either be hit by a car or die of my wounds—and put out word that I had managed to escape. Morrell showed me the *Herald-Star*'s report.

PRIVATE EYE, HELD ON
KIDNAPPING CHARGE, FLEES COOLIS

For the second time this summer, a woman managed to run away from the experimental jail–prison complex operated by Carnifice Security in Coolis. This time, though, the hue and cry is much louder: the woman in question is notorious in Chicago, being private eye V. (Victoria) I. (Iphigenia) Warshawski. Warshawski had been arrested on charges of kidnapping the son of Carnifice chief Robert Baladine and spent a month in the jail wing at Coolis after failing to post bail.

She was not an easy prisoner, Warden Frederick Ruzich said, often getting involved in fights with other inmates and ignoring orders from corrections officers, whose job includes trying to smooth the adjustment for women new to the Coolis system.

How Warshawski managed to escape may never be known. Her body was found at the foot of the Belmont ramp to the Kennedy. Although she is still alive, she suffered severe brain damage and may never speak again. Dr. Charlotte Herschel, Warshawski's physician at Beth Israel Hospital, says Warshawski is able to breathe on her own, which gives them hope for some partial recovery. She has been moved to a nursing home, but Dr. Herschel declined to tell reporters where.

Warshawski is best known for the work she did in tracking down the murderer of social activist Deirdre Messenger last year, but her successes in investigating white-collar crime have earned her respect from many quarters in Chicago, including the Chicago Police Department.

Robert Baladine, the president of Carnifice Security, is angry at lapses in security at the Coolis complex, which have made escape begin to seem like a routine matter for the inmates. He promised a thorough investigation of security measures at the prison. Illinois House Speaker Jean-Claude Poilevy (R–Oak Brook) says the legislature granted a number of tax breaks to Carnifice to get them to take on the women's prison and expects them to live up to their side of the bargain. (*See Murray Ryerson's story on Page 16 for a summary of Warshawski's most notable cases.*)

The story included a map of Illinois, with a blowup of the northwest corner showing the town of Coolis, the prison, and the roads running to Chicago.

I put the newspaper lethargically to one side. I didn't even care what Murray had to say about me. I had remembered recently what was troubling me about my watch, and it left me feeling so futile that it was affecting my recovery.

"That mini-camera that got me these wounds—it's

disappeared," I muttered to Morrell. "I don't know if they took it off me when they put me in segregation or if it just got lost at the hospital, but it's gone."

Morrell's eyes widened. "V. I.—they were supposed to tell you when they gave you back your father's watch. I have it. I took it to the Unblinking Eye to get the pictures developed. I didn't mention it because they keep telling me not to get you excited, and I thought you'd bring it up when you were ready to look at the pictures. They'll be ready in another day or two."

After that I felt giddy with relief. "Did you and Lotty really think I might never talk again, or was that wishful thinking?"

Morrell grinned. "Alex Fisher from Global kept pumping me, so I thought I'd play it safe. When I told Freeman what she and I said, he thought it was such a good idea that he put it out in a press release. The only people who know the truth besides him and Dr. Herschel are Sal and of course your neighbor. Dr. Herschel thought it would be intolerably cruel to Mr. Contreras to imagine you in such straits. And it gives us some wiggle room to figure out what to do with Baladine and Global Entertainment."

Yes. Baladine and Global Entertainment. I wanted to do something about them, but right now I couldn't imagine what. My first week at the Berman Institute I was too tired and too sore to think about what I'd been through. As I grew stronger physically, I was bewildered by my wild mood swings. At one moment I'd be euphoric over my escape and the knowledge that I had managed to smuggle out pictures; the next I'd see a stranger coming toward me and think it was one of the corrections officers, Polsen or Hartigan. I'd start feeling unbearably helpless, as I had in Coolis, and would find myself moving away as fast as I could, my legs wobbly, as if I expected to be hit again with fifty thousand volts of electricity.

The institute treated many people who had been held longer and in greater duress than I. I felt guilty for taking up room that someone from Rwanda or Guatemala could have used, but the psychologist who met with me twice a week told me the institute didn't see it that way.

"Do you think our doctor shouldn't treat your broken hand because someone else has breast cancer and needs more intense medical attention? You deserve to make the best recovery you can from your experience."

"But the other people here didn't choose to be tortured," I burst out. "I chose to stay at Coolis. If I'd followed my lawyer's advice and made bail, none of the rest would have happened."

"So you blame yourself for your misfortunes. But many of the people here torment themselves in the same way: if I had not gone back to my home that morning, if I had followed my mother's wishes and gone to see her, if I had not signed that petition. We wish we had power over our fates, and so we blame ourselves when something goes wrong. You wanted to stay in Coolis to try to understand what happened to a poor young woman you tried to help. I think that was noble. And you cannot blame yourself for the fact that men—and women—with unlimited power over the lives of others used that power in very sadistic ways. If Coolis were run along humane lines—well, your young friend would not have died to begin with."

I tried to accept his advice, but my dreams were still so shocking that I often dreaded going to sleep. I knew if I could only rest properly, I would recover more rapidly.

"What will help you sleep?" he asked the next time we talked.

"If I could stop feeling so humiliated. I know I can't shut down Coolis. I can't change any prison anywhere in America. All these degradations will go on and on for any woman who lands there, the sex talk and the rape and whatever else. The law makes it almost impossible for a woman to lodge a complaint, and even if she does, the guards have so much power they can stop her voice."

Freeman Carter was filing lawsuits for me—one against the Chicago Police Department for the violence committed against my person and against my office by Douglas Lemour. The other was against the Illinois Department of Corrections for my injuries there. Bryant Vishnikov was studying the OR films of my injuries and thought he might be able to prove they'd come from a particular set of boots. Such as those of the man Hartigan out at Coolis.

"But these cases will take years to work through the courts," I told the Berman psychologist. "By that time I could be out of business and too broke for a settlement to help me. I want Robert Baladine to pay a price now for siccing his bent cop on me and for having me arrested on a trumped-up charge. I want that cop out of the force, and I want Baladine publicly exposed. And of course I need him off my back if I'm ever going to run my business again." Miss Ruby had told me if I wanted to eat revenge it would give me indigestion, but it seemed to me passivity was making me sicker than revenge ever would.

The psychologist didn't exactly endorse my wish: he told me he thought it was helpful to imagine a recovery of my own power and see where that left me.

A recovery of my own power meant I needed to recover my physical fitness. I began working out in greater earnest. Four weeks after I was found on the expressway, I ran a wobbly mile, but after that my strength grew measurably every day. On the Thursday before Labor Day, as the El Niño heat finally subsided into a bearable warmth, I felt ready to move on.

43

Planning Session

I'D DECIDED IT was time to move on, but I wasn't sure where to go. My own apartment would leave me a sitting duck as soon as Baladine learned I'd surfaced. For the same reason, I resisted Lotty's invitation to come home with her: I'd rather be killed than endanger her life one more time in one of my exploits.

It was Morrell who suggested that I spend a week or two in Father Lou's rectory. I kept asking him to make sure he'd discussed it with Father Lou and that the priest understood the potential risk; Father Lou in the end sent me a terse note saying I was welcome as long as I didn't smoke. The kids around the school were used to strange families moving in and out as the priest offered refuge to people who'd been evicted or were seeking sanctuary; they wouldn't blow my cover through idle chatter around the neighborhood. And so the Friday before Labor Day I moved from the modern, warmly furnished rooms of the Berman Institute to a narrow bed under a crucifix and a bathroom holding a badly stained tub and toilet. It was still a big step up from Coolis.

During the weeks I was healing, Morrell or Lotty came to see me almost every day. Lotty brought flowers that well-wishers, believing I was in a brain-damaged stupor, sent to her office. Darraugh Graham, my most important client, sent a miniature orange tree and a note that said if I ever felt able to get back to work he was eager to continue to do business with me. I was touched, and relieved as well, although Morrell, collecting mail from my office, found an ominous number of letters from clients canceling my services. (*We find a large firm such as Carnifice better meets our security needs at this time. . . .*)

Mr. Contreras visited me regularly while I was at Berman. Once he learned he could bring Mitch and Peppy, he'd bundle the dogs into the Rustmobile and drive down, careful to follow Morrell's instructions to keep anyone from tailing him. The dogs helped my recovery. When I ran around the gardens behind the institute with them, I started feeling more like myself.

A bouquet of anemones came with a note from Abigail Trant, wishing me a speedy recovery from all my ailments. After her surprise visit the week before my arrest, I wasn't exactly startled, but I was very pleased.

I saw Mrs. Trant's name in the papers from time to time, especially as the swim meet Eleanor Baladine had organized drew near: the *Herald-Star,* in its new role as shill for Global Entertainment, actually treated the event as front-page news. The meet was to raise money for several children's programs dear to Abigail Trant, Jennifer Poilevy, and Eleanor Baladine. The three women were photographed around Eleanor's pool, looking like beauty queens in their sleekly fitting swimsuits. Tickets were a thousand dollars; anyone with a child under thirteen who wanted to compete should get in touch with Alex Fisher at Global.

Another evening Lotty arrived with an outsize bouquet of scarlet and gold flowers and a letter from Murray Ryerson.

Dear Vic,

I can't believe you're really lying in a stupor. Half of it's denial, and the other half is my sources: they can't find you in any of the nursing homes in the area. So maybe Lotty Herschel will bring you these flowers and my letter.

I'm sorry you were arrested. I'm sorry you spent time in the big house. I don't know how you got out without posting bail, but my compliments: that took some doing. I'm sorriest of all I blew up at you over Frenada's finances. I don't know who or how that strange data got into his LifeStory report, but it was bogus. When his sister tried to access one of the accounts, it turned out there was nothing there. For reasons I haven't been able to find out, Carnifice may have wanted to discredit Frenada. At any rate they certainly have the technical wizardry to plant phony data on Frenada.

Anyway, I want you to know that I tried to do the right thing. I tried to tape a follow-up to my show explaining that I had received erroneous information about Frenada. The station wouldn't allow the tape. I tried to print a story in the *Star,* but the editor blocked it. I've been asked to take a vacation for a few weeks to see if "I can regain a sense of proportion."

If you're alive and well, give me a call. On the other hand, if you're really in danger of your life, V.I., I wish I could see you to tell you I'm sorry. And beg you not to die. I don't think I could keep working in Chicago if you weren't part of the landscape.

Murray

I pinned one of the flowers to my blouse and danced around the Berman gardens with it. I had a moment's euphoric impulse to phone Murray, to relieve his own anxiety. We had worked out some amazing stunts together in the past. But I couldn't afford to take risks right now, even for an old friend. Murray's course this past summer had been too rocky for me to trust him based on one letter.

The day I heard from him was the same day that Morrell brought in the pictures I'd taken at Coolis. There were thirty-three: I hadn't had time to shoot the whole roll. A few showed scenes in the jail, like the time CO Polsen was trying to pull down Dolores's jeans, or the pustular burn on the arm of a woman in the kitchen. Where I'd had time to focus, however surreptitiously, the quality was good enough to make out detail.

Many of the two dozen I'd taken in the back room were blurred because of my nervous flying around the space, but there was one clear shot of Lacey's face on a T-shirt, with a man in an IDOC uniform standing behind it. I had two shots of women operating the stamping machines. And somehow, at the end, I'd photographed Hartigan standing over me with the stun gun pointed down at me. I didn't remember taking it; perhaps his shooting or kicking me had inadvertently clicked the shutter. He was foreshortened by my lying on the floor, with his head, bloated and shining in sadistic pleasure, looming larger than his body. The gun appeared in one corner.

Looking at the picture made me start to sweat. I had to take a walk around the Berman gardens before I could sit down again with Morrell. I felt embarrassed by my weakness.

"What do these pictures show, Vic? Besides the idea of a certain amount of sadism in the prison, I mean."

I'd had a lot of time to think during my recuperation, and I spelled it out slowly, putting the events in order as much for myself as for Morrell. "A prison is a great place to run a factory. Labor is cheap and it's captive: you never have the danger that a union will form or that anyone will protest work conditions. Even if you're paying the workers more than you would in Southeast Asia, you still save money because you don't have any capital costs. The state provides the physical plant. The state buys the machinery. Shipping to the world's biggest market is cheaper than from Thailand or Burma, especially if you're close to the main shipping routes out of Chicago. So Coolis started producing shirts and jackets for Global Entertainment."

He frowned. "It sounds disgusting but not a reason to try to kill you for finding it out."

"Illinois law. You can only make things in prison for sale in the prison system. Baladine and Teddy Trant at Global are good friends. When Baladine started running Carnifice Security and got the bid to build and run Coolis, the two of them probably saw what great potential there was in the captive workforce. The two men are very tight with the Speaker of the Illinois House. Poilevy ran a special legislative session exclusively on crime a couple of years ago. I think he probably promised Baladine that for enough money sprinkled around the right way he could overturn the law, but labor balked. Usually they do pretty much what the Speaker says, but they wouldn't budge on this one, because they'd face a rebellion from the rank and file if they undercut real jobs in the state."

Morrell fiddled with the photographs. "I still don't get it. Did Baladine have his nanny arrested simply to send another body to the prison factory?"

"No. That was one of those things. Nicola was arrested for stealing. She was tried, and sentenced, and ended up in the clothes shop because she was small with quick little fingers and because she didn't speak much English and the prison tries to keep discussion of the operation to a minimum. They intimidate the women who work in the clothes shop and try to keep them separate from the rest of the prison population. I discovered early on that women were scared to work in the clothes shop, even though they could make better money for piecework than they could at some of the other gigs.

"Then Nicola learned her little girl had died of asthma, the same little girl whose hospital bills put her in so much debt that she stole the necklace to begin with. She wanted to see the dead child herself and bury her, and they laughed at her. She lost her head and pounded her little fists on this guy's chest—" I flicked my middle finger against Hartigan's face. "He shot her with a stun gun. He kicked her. Her intestine perforated. They shut her in segregation, then they got scared and sent her to the hospital. I'm guessing the hospital said she needed expensive surgery to fix her up and even then she might well die. They thought if they dumped her body near her apartment, they could pretend she'd run away and been killed at home."

My voice became drier and drier, more and more impersonal as I tried to keep from feeling anything about the narrative. Morrell put a hand in mine, giving me a chance to draw away if I wanted to: it's one of the things they train you in at the Berman Institute. Let people have plenty of room to get away if they're nervous about being touched. I squeezed his fingers gratefully, but I needed to get up, to be in motion. We went back to the garden and talked while I restlessly moved around the late-flowering bushes.

"When they got Nicola to Chicago they saw that the stun gun had singed her shirtfront. In case the medical examiner noticed the burn holes during an autopsy, they stripped off her clothes and put on a Mad Virgin T-shirt—I'm pretty sure one that Lucian Frenada had made on spec for Global."

I explained to Morrell what I had learned about Frenada and Trant the night I'd been at Father Lou's, right before my arrest, that Frenada had made some shirts for Global and had argued both with Lacey and Trant over what became of them.

"He claimed Trant had stolen one, and Lacey laughed it off. I did, too—why would a Global boss steal a shirt when he could get a dozen of them free anytime he wanted? But the ones Trant could get all had a label reading *Made with Pride in the USA*, a kind of *Arbeit macht frei* label we had to sew into the necks of the T-shirts we made. Why they wanted a Mad Virgin T-shirt on Nicola I don't know—maybe Trant had a crazy idea that they could finger Frenada for the murder if anyone was asking questions. Everything they did had a B-movie feel to it; it was just the thing that a studio executive would come up with. Or maybe it was Alex Fisher's idea.

"When they thought I was dying they took my damaged shirt off in the cell and put on another one. They made some comment about it at the time. Even though I kept blanking in and out, I was aware of what was going on, although at the time, it didn't make sense."

Before my arrest, I had wondered if Frenada had something to do with Nicola Aguinaldo's death, but during a wakeful night at Coolis I remembered the sequence of conversations we'd had. It was when I asked him how a shirt he made came to be on her body that Frenada suddenly became quiet, then hung up on me. The night that Robbie saw him in Oak Brook, Frenada had gone out to confront Trant and Baladine. The trouble was, I couldn't prove that Baladine killed Frenada—I could only guess it. I asked Morrell if Vishnikov's autopsy had turned up anything unusual.

"Oh, that's right: we've had so much else to talk about I forgot about that," Morrell said. "Frenada definitely died by drowning. Vishnikov says he had a blow on the side of the head that could have come from slipping on the rocks by the harbor—he got it before he died, and that might have been why he went into the water. Other contusions had appeared postmortem."

I scowled. "He was out at the Baladine estate the night he died. Robbie saw him there and later overheard a most suggestive remark from Trant, something about that taking care of the problem. I think they drowned Frenada in the pool and carted him off to Lake Michigan, but I guess that didn't show up on autopsy."

Morrell shook his head. "After you asked me to go back to him, Vishnikov did a really thorough study of every organ in the body, but he says there's no way to prove whether he drowned in fresh or chlorinated water."

I started shredding the wilted flower in my buttonhole. "If I can't pin something substantial on that bastard, I'm not going to be able to work again. I can't prove he killed Frenada. I can testify to someone somewhere about the shirts, but I can't prove they're running a factory out in Coolis either. That is, I can't prove they're selling the shirts and jackets and whatnot outside the prison system, not without a huge amount of effort."

"What would it take to prove it?" Morrell asked.

"Oh, the grubby kind of detective work we used to do in the days before we could check everything out online. Watching for service vans like the one that carted me off, follow them, see which ones contain Global products, where they get dropped off. You could probably bribe the drivers and shorten the process, but it would still take weeks. And then there'd be hearings, and somehow during that time I'd have to come up with money to live on, not to mention money to fund the investigation. It would be easier if I could get Baladine to confess."

Morrell looked at me in astonishment. "You don't really think you could do that, do you? That kind of guy won't. His self-image, his need to be the top dog—"

While he was talking I was imagining the way Baladine had come after Frenada and me: trying to plant cocaine in both our shops, arresting me for kidnapping, planting phony data on the Internet about Frenada's finances. Baladine wasn't just a high-tech operator; he liked to get his hands dirty. But I began to see a way in which I could use his technology to make the confession happen. Was I going to be foolhardy once again? To be daring without judgment? In a way, I didn't care. I had been through the fiery furnace; I had been badly burned, but I had survived. No harms that befell me in the future could be as bad as the ones I had already endured.

"I have an idea." I interrupted Morrell abruptly. "But I'm going to need a little help."

44

Diving in with the Sharks

THE BALADINE INVITATIONAL swim meet drew a respectable crowd. Morrell dropped me twenty yards from the
front gate. It stood open but was protected by uniformed members of Carnifice Security's private security
division. I joined a line that spilled into the road, standing between a couple of small girls arguing over a gym
bag and two well-coiffed men discussing baseball. We
crawled forward as guards checked tickets with a
handheld scanner. They ran the scanner over my media
pass and looked into my briefcase but saw only videocassettes and a notebook. Another man handed out
maps and programs. He directed me toward the pool,
where a special tent had been set up for media, with
refreshments.

"And you can use the bathroom off the kitchen,
ma'am. The public and swimmers are using the facilities
in the cabana."

It felt good to be called "ma'am" by a member of the
Carnifice organization. I thanked him genially and min-
gled with the crowd going up the drive. I wasn't exactly
in disguise, but hoped that a wide-brimmed hat and the
fact that no one expected to see me would protect me. I

skirted the drive, clogged with SUV's and the occasional actual car, and moved around to the back of the house, where the crowd was thicker.

In the media tent I got the press packet marked for Morrell but ducked back outside before I had to get into idle chitchat with anyone. Alex Fisher's hapless assistant was there; I didn't want her questioning me on where Morrell was. Besides, I had recognized several reporters I knew, and it would take only about three sentences before they'd realize it was my face behind the big hat and sunglasses. I planned to talk to them all soon enough, but it would be disastrous if they saw me now.

Thirty-two children were entered in the contest, I read in my packet. The meet was divided into different heats for children of different ages and abilities. Swimming was scheduled to start at one, but the Carnifice and Global sponsors had plenty of entertainment lined up for both before and after. Lacey Dowell was supposed to make an appearance, and the first three Virgin films were being shown in a tent behind the garage.

The event had grossed sixty-seven thousand dollars to be shared by three charities dedicated to children with disabilities, inner-city children, and children's athletic programs. Carnifice Security and Global Entertainment had each contributed ten thousand dollars. It was a nice mediagenic event, and plenty of media was swarming about.

"Jennifer! They want us inside in five minutes to do a press conference."

It was Eleanor Baladine, speaking so close to me I jumped. She was on the other side from me of a large shrub with spiky leaves. I sipped my Malvern water thoughtfully and kept an eye on the flash of turquoise linen, which was all I could see of her.

"I'm annoyed with Abigail," Eleanor continued. "She says Rhiannon got tired of swimming when we were in Limoux and doesn't want to compete. I wish she had said something before we had the programs printed: I tried telling her how bad it looks for one of the organizers to withdraw her own daughter from competition. I thought it was ridiculous the way she kept running off with her daughter to Toulouse for little shopping trips, as if they were girlfriends together. My girls were in the pool six hours a day and loved every minute of it."

"But you're so intense, Eleanor," Jennifer Poilevy said. "Not everyone has your drive. Of course your girls inherited your competitive spirit. It's a shame about poor Robbie, but I do wish you and BB had brought him to France with you. He might have kept the twins from terrifying me with their climbing and jumping. Half the time we were there, I was scared they were going to be brought in on stretchers."

"We certainly never have to worry about that with Robbie," Eleanor said dryly.

"Eleanor—there you are." Baladine had come up to the women from the other side of the house. The sound of his voice woke in me such a frenzy of hatred and of helpless rage that I had to move away before I blew my cover by leaping through the shrubbery and strangling him.

Before I got out of earshot I heard Baladine say, "Did your sister say anything about visiting Robbie at Camp Muggerton on Friday? Major Enderby called to say the boy's Aunt Claudia took him out for dinner and got him back after lights-out."

My stomach jumped. I hadn't expected the camp commandant to check up on a family visitor. That meant I had to move as fast as possible.

I scurried past the media tent into the kitchen, since the bathroom we media folk were allowed to use was there. Rosario the nanny was washing glassware while caterers assembled monstrous platters of shrimp, mushroom tartlets, and other delicacies. The contrast to the kitchen at Coolis, where roaches crawled over congealing piles of grease, and women swore at each other as they lugged dented pots around, made my anger start to boil again. When a waiter offered me a tray of salmon tartare with a perfect circle of caviar in the middle, I turned him away with more fury than manners.

The bathroom stood next to a swinging door leading into the body of the house. I pushed on it—anyone could make a mistake—and a Carnifice guard sprang to life in the hall beyond. He saw my green media badge and said, "House is off-limits to guests, ma'am. If you're looking for the bathroom it's next to this door. And don't you want to be at the press conference? It's starting in two minutes."

I murmured an apology and slipped into the bathroom. The first swim heat would start immediately after the press conference. It was the one for the littlest children, in which the Baladines' younger daughter was competing. Both Eleanor and BB would be at the pool for that, or at least Robbie had seemed to think so. "They'll both want to see the girls beat everyone else, or if they lose, BB and Eleanor will want to show them everything they did wrong. They love that kind of stuff."

He told me that at dinner Friday evening. When he came into the visitors' room at Camp Muggerton on lagging steps, his head down, I felt an uncomfortable parallel to the visitors' room at Coolis, but when he saw me his face lit up.

I had been afraid he'd blow my cover out of surprise, but after a moment's confusion he said, "Oh, I thought —oh, it's you, Aunt Claudia."

Over chicken and mashed potatoes at a diner in Columbia, he begged me to take him away. I wished I could but told him that would put real teeth into his father's kidnapping charge and I might not manage an acquittal.

He started crying, apologizing between sobs, but Camp Muggerton was a miserable place, the hazing was horrible, he couldn't get anything right, he was always last at everything. And they were on strict orders about his diet, did I know that?

I knew that—Major Enderby had stressed it when I was sent to his office for a visitor's pass. The major was pleased to see a family member paying a visit: most of the boys were home for the holiday weekend, and young Robert felt left out, having to stay in camp, but Commander and Mrs. Baladine thought it better he not be put in the way of the temptation of a big party. I gave my most dazzling smile and nodded gravely when the major told me Robbie was not allowed fat or sweets of any kind—so no Big Macs and shakes, ma'am.

I said that Robbie's weight was a trial to the whole family and everyone wondered where it came from. Certainly not my sister's and my side, although Commander Baladine's mother had been a plump little woman.

I told Robbie about the conversation while helping him decide whether he wanted caramel or chocolate

sauce on his sundae. He had lost weight, his soft chub-
biness replaced by something worse, a kind of gaunt
hunger.

"You've lost weight too, Ms. Warshawski. Was that
because of being in jail? Was jail as horrible as this
camp? You don't want ice cream?"

I'm not much of a sweets eater, but I got a cone to
keep him company. As we ate our ice cream, Robbie
sketched a plan of the Baladine house for me—where
Baladine's study was, where the controls for the house
security system were, and where the surveillance cameras were trained. I had explained I wanted to know
because it had to do with Nicola's death.

"But I want to use the information to—well, in part
to get your father to stop trying to destroy me and my
business, and in part to pay him back for the miseries I
endured in the prison he runs. I want you to think carefully before you betray your parents to me."

His tear-streaked face contorted in angry hurt.
"Don't start preaching the Ten Commandments to me
like they do here. I know I'm supposed to honor my
father and mother, but how come they never think of
me? It's like there's something horrible wrong with me,
I know they wish I'd disappear on them, I wish I could,
I wish I was strong enough to kill myself."

I gave him what awkward consolation I could—not
that deep down his parents really loved him, but that
deep down he was a fine and unusual person and that
he needed to hold on to that idea. After we had talked
for a time, I was relieved to see him start to look happier. I asked him if he wanted more time to think over
what I wanted to do, but he said it was fine with him, as
long as Utah didn't get hurt.

"She's kind of a brat, but I like her."

"I don't think anyone's going to get hurt. Not physically, anyway, although I'm hoping your father may have to find a new job, perhaps in a different city. That may be hard on your mother."

He ate another ice cream while he helped me draw up plans of the interior of the house. Afterward we sat and talked, about life and what could lie in store for him after he outgrew Eleanor and BB. I hadn't noticed the shadows drawing in on the town; we were going to be late for taps. I bustled Robbie into the rental car and drove like mad for the camp.

Before dropping him at the guardhouse I gave him a handful of twenties. "This is enough for bus fare from Columbia back to Chicago, if you decide you can't stick it out here any longer. Sew it into the waistband of your shorts, but for pity's sake, don't use it until I know if your dad is going to drop the kidnapping charge. Or until after my trial, whichever comes first."

The escape hatch seemed to breathe a little bit of optimism into him. I apologized to the guard for making my nephew late and begged him not to blame Robbie: I had gotten lost, and that wasn't the boy's fault. I had thought another dazzling smile would take care of matters, but now here was Major Enderby calling the Baladines to tell them Aunt Claudia had violated lights-out.

I waited in the kitchen bathroom until I heard the loudspeaker heralding the start of the swim meet. The bathroom had a second door, locked right now, that led into the maid's room. It took about fifteen seconds to pick that lock. I moved quickly, in case Rosario was getting a break while the swimming started, only stopping for a moment in front of a tin icon to the Virgin of Guadalupe, which was nailed over the prim single bed.

I whispered a little plea for protection, although perhaps the Virgin would feel that not even Baladine's iniquities warranted protecting an intruder.

The back stairs led to Utah's and Madison's bedrooms and their playroom. On the other side of the playroom was a hall leading to Baladine's home office. I studied the location of the monitoring cameras in the bedrooms, playroom, and hall on my pencil map and ducked around the lenses, creeping into Baladine's office on my hands and knees.

Robbie said the system was voice- and motion-activated. My hands and knees rustling on the carpet wouldn't turn it on, but a cough might.

Inside Baladine's office, I crawled along the edge of the room and came to the desk from behind. Lying flat, I stuck up an arm and found the switch for his in-office video monitor and turned it off. I got to my feet and held my breath. After a couple of minutes, when no security guards appeared, I relaxed enough to look around.

I found myself listening tensely for noise. The house was well soundproofed, and the cheers from the pool came through as only a faint echo. I might have half an hour; I needed to control my nerves and make the most of it.

The room held everything a manly man wanted in his home office, from the buttery black leather couch in a window alcove to the electronics on the zebrawood desk, which included a shredder, a fax, a scanner, and a videophone.

I switched on the computer, covering my hand with a Kleenex—I thought it would be impossible to explain away rubber gloves if someone came in on me. The system came up and asked for a password. Baladine's ship number was what Robbie thought his father would use. When that didn't let me in I tried the name of the ship. Bingo. To get into Carnifice files I needed another password. I tried the ship ID again, but the machine preferred his service dates.

I called up the home-security system and set the hall camera to appear in a split screen of the computer. That would give me a little advance warning if Baladine was coming. I checked the doors on the far side of the room. One led to a closet, another to a bathroom, and a third to the far hallway.

I logged on to the e-mail server and called up the list of clients. Five of my own former clients had little stars by their names; Darraugh Graham had a question mark. I had memorized what I wanted to say and typed quickly, nervously proofreading and correcting my text. Did I want to send to the entire recipient list? I did.

Next I typed in my own media list and composed another message. When I'd e-mailed my media list I breathed more easily. I deleted all the messages, both from the out-box and from the trash file, so that Baladine wouldn't know from looking at his mailbox that someone had been using the server. Even if he found me now, I'd done enough to cause him some discomfort.

Just as a precaution I copied his home-security file onto a floppy, copied his client list onto another floppy, then, while I was still logged on to his network, started looking through his in-box for any messages that might be about me.

The searches had taken too much time. I was sweating, wondering if I'd better pack up and go, when I saw Baladine and Alex Fisher appear on the hall camera. I turned off the machine, grabbed my floppies, and dived into the closet at the back of the room. My heart was pounding so hard, I thought the closet door must surely vibrate in rhythm with it.

The two came into the room, talking in such low tones all I could make out was the murmur of their voices. Sweat began soaking my shirtsleeves as I imagined a telltale floppy or tissue alerting them to an intruder.

I didn't know whether to laugh or scream when I realized that Baladine and Alex hadn't come up to look at his computer, but to grab time together while Eleanor was focused on the pool, although I had one bad moment when Baladine spoke loudly enough for me to hear, saying he didn't remember switching off his office camera. After twenty minutes of frenzied thrashing on the leather couch and the murmured endearments of one barracuda for another, a hand grasped the closet doorknob.

It opened a crack, but Baladine said, "No, no, my dear, bathroom's the other door—that's just a supply closet."

Alex, sloppy Alex, didn't close the door all the way. "I need to get back downstairs, BB. I just got beeped—that means Lacey Dowell's limo is coming up the drive, and Teddy will want me on hand for her. She's been temperamental since Frenada died, and we don't want her going off half-cocked to some reporter."

"Like Ryerson?" Baladine said.

"Ryerson was a newspaperman from day one. I shouldn't have let him persuade Teddy he could handle television—he was in way over his head. Although we still haven't found anyone who can handle that 'Behind Scenes in Chicago' segment. Anyway, as the man said, enough of this lovemaking—on with your clothes."

"Want to see the replay on television while you dress?"

"You have a camera back here? God, I thought Teddy Trant was infatuated with his body, but not even he videos himself in the act."

"I'm infatuated with your body. This is so I can watch it over and over."

"Right, BB. I'll take that. I don't need to see myself on the Net, and you're just the kind of guy to make that kind of use of a tape."

They had a few more minutes grappling, with Baladine laughing and then cursing at her for being a damned bitch. I wasn't an Alex fan, but I hoped that meant she'd wrested the tape from him. Then a sound of hand on flesh and a furious outburst from Alex. I put my eye on the crack in the door. Baladine had Alex's left arm twisted back and was putting pressure on her wrist. Her face was contorted in pain and she dropped the tape.

He laughed and said, "I thought you'd see it my way, my dear. But don't worry, I won't share you with the Internet. The world at large can't appreciate you the way I do."

She swore at him but finally left when Eleanor phoned up to say Lacey was here and they were trying to find Alex. The door shut behind her. Baladine washed off noisily in the bathroom, humming "Anchors Aweigh." In another minute he was gone as well.

By then I was so shaken that I was tempted to quit with what I had—but I didn't know when I'd ever have another chance like this one. I turned off his personal camera again and went back to the computer. Shutting it off without exiting properly had made it unhappy; I had to wait an extra five minutes while it examined all its files. While it cycled through itself, I looked around for the tape he'd just made. He'd left it on the bathroom sink. I shrugged and slipped it into my pocket.

Finally I got back to Baladine's e-mail server and went to his in-box. In June, on the date I'd been in Georgia, I found someone calling himself *Shark* at AOL reporting on *successful drop-off.*

Subject out of town. 3 packs of Colombian Gold successfully deployed in location 1, 4 others at location 2.

My stomach so tight that my incision started to ache, I copied all of Baladine's correspondence with Shark. I logged off the Web and went into his data files to search for any material about me, or Shark. I found his detailed report from LifeStory and reports on the surveillance of my apartment. These files identified Shark as D.L. Not that I needed an acronym to tell me it was Douglas Lemour, but I was pleased that Baladine hadn't felt a need for real secrecy.

As recently as three days ago, D.L. reported a cruise around my neighborhood to make sure I hadn't surfaced. He was also looking at Lotty's place off and on *as the safe house the subject usually chooses.* I scrolled quickly through the rest of the file and came to an expense report. Five thousand dollars to D.L. for security work. It didn't seem like enough of a payoff for the amount of misery he'd caused me.

My heart was starting to beat too hard to focus on the screen. I copied the file and shut the system down. It was high time I was gone.

On a shelf in the closet where I'd waited out Alex and Baladine, he kept cassettes from the video monitor. After his byplay with Alex, I was curious to see them. I pulled one from the last month Nicola had worked here, another from six months previously. I peeled off the labels, stuck them on the blank cassettes I'd brought with me, and put the blanks in the empty slots.

I was halfway down the hall when I remembered Frenada. I counted dates frantically on my fingers. Even though I didn't have a third blank to use as a replacement, I ran back to the study and took the tape for two weeks before July Fourth. As I was leaving the second time, I remembered to switch Baladine's vanity recorder back on. I hurried down the hall again, through the girls' playroom, past acres of Barbies and stuffed animals, and down the stairs to the kitchen. I stopped briefly in Rosario's room to thank the Virgin of Guadalupe.

I'd been upstairs ninety minutes—nerves had made it seem even longer. I slipped outside and down the drive without anyone stopping me. Morrell was waiting for me at the bend in the road. His face was pinched with anxiety, but I felt lighter-hearted than I had in months.

45

Fugitive

MORRELL ARRIVED EARLY the next morning with the papers and a couple of cappuccinos—Father Lou breakfasted on sweet tea and bacon sandwiches and didn't keep coffee or fruit in the rectory. I'd already been up for a few hours when Morrell arrived. Game-day nerves, I suppose.

Father Lou had been up for hours, too. He started Labor Day as he did every day, with mass. This morning he startled me considerably by asking me to serve, since none of the children in his acolytes group had appeared. When I told him I'd never even been baptized, he grunted and said he supposed some hairsplitter would consider that a barrier, but would I at least keep him company by reading the lesson.

I stood in the Lady Chapel of the enormous church and read from the book of Job about how God desires humans to see the light. As Father Lou began the prayers for the mass, he prayed first for the souls of Lucian Frenada and Nicola Aguinaldo, for the working people of Chicago, for everyone who worked hard and had little to show for it. Along the way he surprised me by asking for light on my enterprise, to see whether it was good to let it prosper. I thought again of Miss

Ruby, warning me that revenge didn't make a good meal.

At the end of the mass I stood in front of a wood statue of the Virgin of Guadalupe, stubbornly arguing my case in my head. Even if it was revenge, didn't I have a right to live and work in this town? I said as much to Father Lou while he fried bacon in the cavernous kitchen.

He grunted again. "Not saying you don't, my girl. Turning the other cheek isn't the only advice Our Lord gives people. Just saying you need to remember you're not Almighty God sitting in judgment on Robert Baladine. Not why I asked you to read the lesson, though—wasn't trying to teach you a lesson." He laughed heartily at his little pun. "I wanted some company. It's a big cold church to celebrate mass in by myself."

Morrell's arrival cut the theology discussion short. He dropped the papers in front of me with a coffee and a bag of Michigan peaches.

"Triple Crown, Warshawski. All three Chicago dailies, not to mention the gorilla from New York."

I snatched the stack from him. The gorilla was on top and began with its usual rotund phrases.

CONFUSION REIGNS
AT CARNIFICE SECURITY

Oak Brook, Ill.— The Illinois prairie in this upscale community west of Chicago has been replaced by smooth sod and cool white marble, but inside the Carnifice office tower, life is anything but placid on

this Labor Day. Robert Baladine is emphatically con-
tradicting an e-mail message received by Carnifice clients yesterday announcing his resignation as chairman
and CEO of Carnifice Security, while his staff scurries
to explain how a third party could have breached the
security provider's own defenses to post messages on
Mr. Baladine's e-mail server.

These messages bear the unmistakable "finger-
print" of Mr. Baladine's personal e-mail address.
They say, in part, that impending publicity about alleged misconduct at the Coolis correctional facility
that Carnifice runs is forcing Mr. Baladine to resign
(*see Page C23 for the complete text of the e-mail received by Ajax Insurance in Chicago*). The misconduct is an alleged use of the Coolis correctional
facility to manufacture T-shirts and jackets for the
Global Entertainment company. This is in violation of
Illinois law, which forbids sale of prison manufac-
tures outside the state prison system. Congressman
Blair Yerkes (R–Ill.) has called for a complete investigation of the prison to see whether there is any truth
to the allegation. "I have known BB Baladine since we
hunted together as boys, and I utterly repudiate the
suggestion that he has lied."

In the meantime, more disturbing to Carnifice clients is the possibility that an outsider could penetrate
Carnifice's own computer. It means that confidential
—often highly volatile—data entrusted to the security
firm is at risk for dissemination across the Web. As
Ajax Chairman Ralph Devereux said, "From our
standpoint, we're left with two equally unpleasant
possibilities: either Robert Baladine is lying about his
resignation, or a hacker has been able to bypass all of

Carnifice's security measures. Either way, the instabil-
ity of the company's head honcho leaves us wondering whether Carnifice is the right company to handle
our most private matters."

Various papers and television stations also received
e-mail from the Carnifice server, describing the manufacturing relationship between Carnifice and Global
at the Coolis prison site. Because the source of the
report could not be verified, it is not clear whether the
information is accurate or whether it comes from a
disgruntled Carnifice employee. Efforts to view the
prison shop have been rebuffed by Coolis authorities,
but state lawmakers are demanding an inquiry.

Mr. Baladine would not return phone calls to this
paper, but Global Entertainment spokeswoman Alexandra Fisher says Global is considering the possibility
that a local private investigator with a grudge against
Baladine may have perpetrated the vandalism. The investigator, V. I. Warshawski, spent a month at Coolis
after Mr. Baladine had her arrested on kidnapping
charges. Although Ms. Warshawski escaped with
what physician Dr. Charlotte Herschel calls brain-
threatening injuries, Ms. Fisher says no one actually
knows the detective's whereabouts. Finding the solo
investigator is Carnifice Security's first priority. (*See
Page B45 for coverage of some of Ms. Warshawski's
investigations into industrial espionage.*)

Father Lou was reading the report in the *Sun-Times,*
which gave the story the most attention of any of the
Chicago papers. The *Herald-Star,* as a Global paper,
ran a one-paragraph story in the business section that
sounded as though there'd been a brief snafu in the
Carnifice e-mail server. The *Star* didn't mention the

Global T-shirt connection at Coolis. The *Tribune* ran a half column in the middle of Marshall Field's big Labor Day advertising spread.

"So now what?" Morrell asked when I'd finished reading. "Wait for the Carnifice clients to drop like flies and come running to Warshawski Investigative Services for help?"

I made a face. "They're busy doing damage control at Carnifice. And the CEO of Warshawski et cetera had better surface if she wants any clients. I think the next thing is a media show. For which we need secure space. That, I think, will get BB so furious that he's likely to come for me in person. I want to put together a little tape of all my bits and pieces of pictures. Make some bullet-point slides—everyone feels they've gotten real information if you give it to them in bullet points. And I want a VCR so I can watch Baladine's home videos. He was taping himself having sex with Alex Fisher yesterday. It struck me as funny that the guy keeps his old home-security tapes, so I took three."

Father Lou stared at me in disgust. "Man photographs himself having intercourse? Did the girl know?"

"She tried to get the tape from him, but he wouldn't let her." I didn't feel like explaining that I had it now. I wasn't sure what I was going to do with it.

"Got a VCR in the school you can use," the priest said. "I'm still not sure whether you're doing the right thing, not sure I should encourage you since you stole the tapes you want to look at, but the man Baladine seems to do people a variety of harm. Set it up for you, then I have to meet with members of the parish council. Got a bunch of kids coming, cleaning out the crypt before school starts tomorrow. Parish picnic this afternoon. Lots to get done."

I ran down to my room and picked up the tapes I'd taken from Baladine's closet yesterday. The three of us walked through the church to a door that connected to the school. The dark vaulted space was full of life as a group of boys shouted to each other behind the altar: "Bet you it's full of bones." "Yeah, Carlos here is going to faint when he sees one of those arms coming after him, ain't you, man?"

Father Lou interrupted them with a good-natured shout that they needed to be more afraid of him than of any bones and he'd be back in a minute to make sure they were clearing out the old hymnals. He undid the dead bolt and led us into another long unlit hallway. He walked quickly in the semidarkness. Morrell and I kept tripping on things like loose tiles as we tried to keep pace. Father Lou took us up a back staircase to the school library. There he reluctantly decided he needed light to see what he was doing and turned on one dim desk lamp.

When he saw that Morrell and I knew how to set up the VCR, he went back downstairs to see how his hooligans were doing in the crypt. I started with the tape for the week that Frenada died.

We got a series of disconnected frames from the voice-activated system of Rosario waking Utah and Madison, of Eleanor starting work with them in the pool and then turning off the camera. And then Frenada was poolside with Trant and Baladine. The little red date in the corner identified it as June 26, the night Frenada died. Trant said he understood Frenada was telling people that he, Trant, had stolen a T-shirt and he was tired of hearing about it. Baladine must have turned the camera off at that point because the next scene was the following day with Rosario in the nursery.

I sat back in my chair. "No proof, but very suggestive," I said to Morrell. "Let's get some copies of this before I send it back to the Baladines."

He grunted agreement, although he pointed out there wasn't enough there to get Baladine arrested, let alone convicted. I agreed and put in the first of the Nicola tapes to see if it might give us something more concrete.

The tape was dated about six months before Nicola's arrest for theft. We watched Nicola waking Utah and Madison, a sleepy Utah clinging to her nanny while Madison chatted vivaciously about the many things she was doing better in at school than anyone else. We saw Eleanor and BB kissing briefly as he left for the office on a "don't know how late I'll be tonight, sweetheart" line and Eleanor in the nursery adjuring Nicola not to baby Utah. "She's almost three. It's time you stopped carrying her everywhere." When Nicola said brokenly that she didn't understand, Eleanor told her not to play stupid and plunked Utah from Nicola's arms onto the floor. Utah began to howl. As soon as Eleanor left the room, Nicola picked her up and began soothing her in a language I didn't know, presumably Tagalog.

It was unnerving to watch Nicola Aguinaldo alive, even in the grainy production of the home video. She was petite, so small that next to Eleanor Baladine she looked like a child herself. In Eleanor's presence she became as waxen as one of the children's dolls, but alone with the little girls she grew more relaxed. Robbie came in and began playing with Utah. He spoke Spanish to Nicola, who teased him about his accent and got him to laugh back at her. I had never seen Robbie happy. Talking in Spanish to him, Nicola became vivacious, almost beautiful. Eleanor called up to say the school bus was there.

The tape covered a two-week period. Scenes broke off abruptly as people either moved out of camera range or turned off the camera. A conversation Eleanor was having with a gardener ended suddenly as Baladine called Nicola to his study. We watched her enter and stand with a face drained of expression. When she quietly took off and folded her clothes, she seemed to treat it as the same kind of chore that putting away Madison and Utah's clothes was. Baladine himself did not undress. It was unbearable, and I couldn't watch. When Morrell heard me crying he switched off the machine.

"I can't show that to a roomful of reporters," I muttered. "It's too indecent."

"Do you want me to watch the other reel and summarize it for you?" he asked.

"Yes. No. I think I'd better see for myself."

The second reel was similar to the first, except for the scene in Baladine's study. This time Nicola was begging for money for her child's hospital bills and Baladine was telling her impatiently that he paid her a good wage and that she had a hell of a nerve to try begging for money on a made-up story. Nicola offered herself to him and he laughed at her. It was a scene of such agonizing humiliation that I finally left the library to pace the school corridor. When I came back, Morrell had finished the tape and rewound it. Father Lou had slipped into the room while I was walking around.

"There wasn't anything on it about the necklace or her arrest. We'll have to imagine that part," Morrell said.

"That poor child," Father Lou said. "What a crucifixion she endured. That man, her boss, he's the one you're after?"

I was as sweaty and depleted as if I'd run a marathon and could only nod.

"I still don't know if you're doing the right thing or not, but I'll help you out. Let you use the library here for your press conference."

I blinked. "But, Father, you know—Baladine not only has a lot of artillery at his disposal, he's not afraid to use it. Women and children don't mean anything special to him. I couldn't possibly guarantee your safety, or the safety of the school. Unless . . ."

"Unless what?" Morrell said sharply when I didn't finish the sentence.

"Unless I get Baladine to come to me first. Before we lay the case out to the media. Especially since we can prove Frenada was at his pool the night he died. If I bring him to me, I won't have to lie here tensely waiting for him to make some kind of move."

"No," Morrell said. "Putting your head on the block for him to chop off is nuts. You know Freeman Carter would give you the same advice."

I scrunched up my mouth in a monkey face. "More than likely. But I'm tired of walking around in terror. Ever since he sicced Lemour on me in June, I've had to watch every step I take, and my time in Coolis has only made me more nervous. If I let him know I've got these tapes and the tape he made of him and Alex, I think he'll come get them. And if I leave the church, he won't do it here where the kids will be in danger."

"Your press presentation is your best route," Morrell said patiently. "Bringing that much publicity not just to his Coolis operation but to his use of a Chicago police officer to plant drugs in your office will force Baladine to stop harassing you. Probably force his board to make him quit, too."

"Abigail Trant told me that he can't stand the notion of being bested. I saw it—or heard it—yesterday: he was furious when Alex got the tape from him. He hurt her to get it back: it wasn't a game to him. There's no telling what he might do."

"Think about it overnight," Father Lou suggested. "Offer a special intention at mass in the morning. Do some manual labor in the crypt. Nothing like hard work to clear the mind."

So Morrell and I spent the rest of the morning in the chamber underneath the altar, shifting old boxes of hymnals that Father Lou had decided the church would never use again, digging out the costumes the children wore in their Christmas pageant, and uncovering an actual reliquary that the Italians who built the church a hundred years ago had brought with them. This caused an explosion of nervous ribaldry from the boys working with us.

I hadn't resolved matters by three, when Father Lou called a halt to our work so that the boys could attend the parish picnic. Nor did a nap while Morrell joined them in a baseball game in Humboldt Park bring any special vision. I still wanted to call Baladine and tell him I had his videotapes: something like a childhood taunt—come catch me if you can.

The problem remained where I would be when I issued the taunt. At the church I endangered Father Lou and his schoolchildren. In my own home there were Mr. Contreras and the other tenants. Tessa's studio ruled out using my office. And he might be so berserk that he'd go after someone like Lotty out of sheer terrorism, even if I wasn't near her.

All evening long, as Morrell and I worked on my presentation—preparing the photographs in order, figuring out what video sequences to show of Lemour in action against me, where to put Trant and Frenada with Baladine at his pool, discussing whether to use any of the Aguinaldo footage, typing up camera-ready copy in St. Remigio's school computer lab—Morrell and I debated the question. At midnight, when Morrell left with the material—he was taking it to the Unblinking Eye in the morning for production—I was no nearer a solution.

I went to bed and fell into a restless sleep. It was only an hour later when Father Lou shook me awake. "Old man's at the door with a kid and some dogs. Says he's your neighbor."

"My neighbor?" I pulled on my jeans and jammed my feet into my running shoes and sprinted down the hall, Father Lou following on his rolling boxer's gait.

I looked through the peephole at the figures on the doorstep. Mr. Contreras. With Mitch, Peppy, and Robbie Baladine. My heart sank, but I told Father Lou it was, in fact, my neighbor.

"With the kid whose father had me arrested the last time he ran away to me."

Father Lou unscraped the dead bolts and let them in. Mr. Contreras started speaking as the door opened. All I caught was, "Sorry, doll, but I didn't want to use the phone in case they was tapping my line," before the dogs overwhelmed me with their ecstatic greeting and Robbie, painfully thin and grubby, started apologizing: "I know you said to wait until I heard from you, but BB called."

Father Lou shut the door. "Okay. Into the kitchen for tea, and let's sort this out one voice at a time. These dogs housebroken?"

"Where's the car?" I asked, before Father Lou pushed the dead bolts home.

"Sorry, doll, sorry, it's out front, you want me to move it?"

"It needs to go away from here. It's very identifiable, and if Baladine is scouring the city for me, he'll find it."

"Rectory garage," Father Lou said. "Filled with old junk but room for the car. I'll show—what's your name?—Contreras the garage. You take the boy into the kitchen. Put on the kettle."

Robbie and the dogs bounded down the hall with me to the kitchen. Robbie was trying hard not to flinch from Mitch, which seemed more heartbreaking than anything else about him.

"I'm sorry, Ms. Warshawski," he whispered, "but they figured out you weren't Aunt Claudia. They were going to lock me in the punishment barracks. I didn't know when I'd ever get out. And I thought if BB did something else bad to you because you came to see me, I'd have to kill myself. So I ran away. But now I see he can put you in prison no matter what I do."

"Sh, sh, *poverino*. It's okay. You're here, let's deal with that. Tell me the story when Father Lou and Mr. Contreras get back; that way we'll all get the same version and you'll only have to tell it once."

When the two men came in, the kettle was boiling. Father Lou made a large mug of cambric tea for Robbie and black tea with sugar for himself. I poured more hot milk into a mug for myself.

Mr. Contreras impatiently waved away refreshments. "He showed up about an hour ago, doll. He's done in. I didn't know what to do—like I say, I was afraid to use the phone—but I figured if they had any kind of watch on the place, it wasn't good to leave him there. I guess I could have gone up to Morrell, but all I thought was, you'd be in real trouble now if that creep Baladine—sorry, son, I know he's your old man—"

"Let's have it from the beginning, and short," Father Lou said. "Have to say mass in a few hours, don't want to stay up all night."

As short as any story involving Mr. Contreras could be, it boiled down to this: the camp commandant had summoned Robbie and questioned him about my visit. Robbie stuck to the story that I was his Aunt Claudia, his mother's younger sister, but the commandant revealed he had talked both to BB and to the real Claudia Sunday night after the swim meet. All Robbie could do was insist that I was Aunt Claudia. The commandant said Robbie would be sent to the punishment block for a few days until Eleanor arrived in person to talk to the commandant.

"During reveille, while everyone stands at attention, I snuck off. It was only this morning, but it seems like it must've been a year ago. I ran in a ditch alongside the camp and got out the back way and hitched into Columbia. Then I used your money to get the bus to Chicago, but I didn't know where to go except to your apartment. I'm awful sorry, Ms. Warshawski; if this means BB sends you back to jail for kidnapping, I don't know what I'll do."

His eyes were dilating with fear and exhaustion. Father Lou cut off a hunk of bread and smeared it with butter.

"Eat that, son. Cross that bridge when you come to it, but if you stand up in court and tell your story like a man, no one will send her to prison. Time you were in bed. You've had too long a day. You can sleep in in the morning, but you go to school in the afternoon. What year you in? Seventh grade. Get you a uniform—have extras for kids too poor to buy 'em. Worry about everything else later."

Father Lou looked a bit like Popeye, but his voice had the authoritative reassurance that children respond to. Robbie calmed down and followed me docilely to a bedroom near mine. I pulled clean sheets from a shelf and made up the narrow bed.

I heard a barking and yelping in the kitchen and ran back down the hall to find that Mitch had made himself into a hero: he'd emerged from the pantry with a rat in his mouth. Father Lou said in that case the dogs could stay the night. As an afterthought he offered Mr. Contreras a bed, too.

The priest stomped off to bed, leaving me to make up another bed for my neighbor. When he said good night, Mr. Contreras handed me a paper bag. "I been holding this for you since the day you was arrested, doll. I figure you might need it now."

It was my Smith & Wesson, which had been in the handbag I'd flung to Mr. Contreras the day Lemour came to get me.

46

In the Church Militant

MITCH HAD CAUGHT another rat and was barking with joy. "That's a good boy," I mumbled. "Now be quiet and let me sleep."

I put out a hand to pet him and woke up when I was stroking air and the barking hadn't stopped. I pulled on my jeans again and picked up the Smith & Wesson.

I'd gotten used to finding my way through the rectory in the dark and went down the hall in the direction of Mitch's voice. He and Peppy were trying to get into the church from the rectory passage. When they heard me they ran to me and pawed at my legs, trying to get me to open the door leading into the church.

Peppy, scratching on the door, only made impatient grunts in the back of her throat, but I couldn't quiet Mitch enough to listen for sounds from the church. Finally, I clamped his muzzle shut with my left hand, but he thrashed so violently that I still couldn't hear anything. I was trying to picture the geography of the buildings, wondering how to get around to the rear, when Father Lou materialized behind me.

"Think it's your man in there?"

"I don't know. You get many gangbangers breaking in at night?" I whispered back.

"Usually know better. Could call the cops, but it

takes them an hour to show around here. Hold the dogs. I'm opening the door into the church, want to see what's going on without animals running wild in the sanctuary."

He undid the three massive locks to the church door and went inside. Mitch was whining and straining to be after him, and even Peppy was pulling on my arms in angry protest. I'd counted to a hundred, figuring I'd go to one-fifty before I plunged after the priest, when he slipped back through the passage.

"Think they're coming in through the school. Fourth-floor windows don't have bars—must've scaled the wall somehow. I'm going outside to holler them down."

"No!" I let Mitch go. He scampered into the church and made a beeline for the door that connected the nave to the school. "If it is Baladine, he may have someone outside to pick off anyone who leaves the building. If he's coming in through the school he's probably hoping for a surprise attack, but it could still be a feint designed to draw us—me—outside."

There wasn't any light; I felt rather than saw the priest scowling. "Old coal passages connect church, school, rectory through the crypt. Keep them locked to stop the kids horsing around down there. I can come into the school behind him through the basement. Know my way in the dark, you don't, you stay here. Don't want any shooting in the church; do your best if they come in. Calling the cops on my way; hope they get here sometime before we're all dead."

By tacit consent we left Mr. Contreras asleep. Father Lou went down the hall to the kitchen, and I went into the church. I didn't know what time it was, but it was still too early for any light to come in through the church's dirty east windows. The red sanctuary lamp gave off the only light. I fumbled my way to the sanctuary, trying to orient myself by the lamp and by Mitch, who was barking sharply at the door to the school.

I bumped into Peppy and almost screamed. She wagged her tail against my legs. I clutched her collar and let her guide me. At the steps to the altar I could follow the altar rail toward the raised podium used for sermons on formal occasions.

When we finally reached Mitch he had gotten tired of his frenzied assault on the door and was lying on his haunches. I felt his raised hackles when I touched him, and he jerked his head impatiently away from my hand. The door was too thick for me to make out the sounds he was hearing on the other side. I took it for about five minutes, then retraced my way to the altar. A massive wood and marble carving rose behind it. When I worked my away around to the back, where the crypt entrance was, the altarpiece itself blocked most of the glow from the sanctuary lamp.

The trapdoor to the crypt was unlocked. I climbed stealthily down the narrow spiral stair, Peppy following me on uncertain feet. She mewed unhappily, and I hoisted her down after me one step at a time.

At the bottom I was in a well of such intense blackness that I had no way of orienting myself. I risked the switch at the foot of the spiral stairs. It showed me the passages that I'd overlooked when I was working down here this morning, one on the north to the rectory and another opposite that connected to the school. I flicked off the light and made my way through the south door to the school basement.

Clutching Peppy's collar, I let her guide me again,

until she found a staircase. We crept up, pausing after each step to listen. I heard the humming of machinery, but no human sounds. At the top I pushed open the door. Father Lou had come this way earlier and left it unlocked.

We were in the school kitchen; a streetlight made it possible to see the big stoves and refrigerators. I went through a swinging door into a hallway and suddenly could hear voices. Keeping my hand on Peppy, now more as a warning to her to be silent than because I needed her navigation, I moved toward the sound. Father Lou was outside the door that led from the school into the church.

"If you thought your son was with me you'd have knocked at the door like an honest man," Father Lou was saying. "You're breaking into a school. I don't know what valuables you thought a poor school in a neighborhood like this has, but I have you red-handed, and the cops will take it from here."

Baladine laughed. "A police detective is stationed outside. If the cops ever show up, he'll tell them he's got the situation under control. I'm sure there would be a lot of mourning in the neighborhood over your death, but wouldn't you rather get out of my way than die defending that stupid Warshawski woman and my tiresome son?"

My stomach tightened at the sound of his voice, at the reckless superiority of it. At first I thought Baladine was alone, and I was willing to risk a shot, but as my ears and eyes adjusted I realized he had at least two other men with him. I could make out only their ghostly shapes, but Father Lou's bald head reflected what light there was. He was the short ghost whose arms were perhaps pinned by two larger wraiths. Baladine was behind him. I lowered my gun; I couldn't possibly get a clear shot.

"I know you got into the school building from inside the church, Padre," Baladine said in the same patronizing voice, "because my man has the outside covered. So be a good fellow and let us into the church, and I promise you'll be alive to say mass in the morning."

"Jesus wants me tonight, tonight's when He'll get me," Father Lou said. "If not, not your decision, young man."

Baladine laughed. He was making a smart-alecky comment back when I heard a worse sound than Baladine's voice: a muffled outburst on the other side of the door. I couldn't make out the words, but the cadence told me Mr. Contreras had woken up. He wanted to know what was going on, did Mitch have someone cornered on the other side? He was fiddling with the bolts.

In the instant that everyone's attention slackened, Father Lou gave one of his captors a punch that knocked him over. I yelled at top volume to Mr. Contreras to leave the door alone and sped back down the hall to the basement stairs. I saw a red marker dancing on the floor, trying to find me. For one crazy moment I thought it was another sanctuary light. Then a gun spat fire at me as the red marker danced after me. Baladine had a laser sight. A death marker, not sanctuary. It terrified me so much that I hurled myself through the swinging door into the kitchen, Peppy running with me. In the light from the streetlamp I found the stairs and stumbled down them so fast I tripped over my feet and ended in a heap at the bottom. Behind me a shot echoed along the hallway. I prayed it hadn't hit Father Lou. Or Mr. Contreras.

Peppy landed on top of me. We scrambled to our feet in a confused mess of dog and woman and moved as fast as possible toward the crypt. Behind me I could hear doors slamming as the pursuit looked for the exit I'd taken, and then I saw a flashlight finger on the stairwell. It gave me the view I needed of the basement. I was heading away from the crypt door. I righted myself, called Peppy to me, and managed to get us both inside. I slid the bolt home as another shot sounded.

My legs were shaking as I climbed back up the spiral stairs. Above me the church was still dark, but when I got to the top I could see a light bounce along one of the aisles. I waited behind the altar. I was trying to figure out from the sound what was going on, when I heard Baladine's voice.

"Warshawski? I've got the priest and the old man. Come on out. Your life for theirs."

"Don't do it, doll." Mr. Contreras was panting. "Don't do it; run for help, I been around plenty long enough. Shouldn't have opened the door, anyway."

I slipped around the edge of the altarpiece, keeping low so that the altar itself shielded me from sight. I made my way to the old preaching tower and climbed up into it. From there I could see that the light in the aisle was coming from a flashlight. It was hard to see what lay behind it, but Father Lou and Mr. Contreras seemed to be attached to each other. One of Baladine's thugs had a gun trained on them. I couldn't hear or see Mitch.

"Your quarrel's with me, Baladine," I called. "Let the men go. When they're safely inside the rectory, I'll come out."

The flashlight swung around in my direction. Baladine couldn't see me, but he shone the light along the altar, the laser sight dancing behind it.

"Go open the front door to the church," he finally said to his henchman. "Lemour can come in and earn his keep, since the priest knocked out Fergus. This place is too big to search alone. Don't try anything, Warshawski: I'll shoot your friends at the first wrong move you make."

The underling went down the aisle and scrabbled with the heavy locks. I didn't know what to do next. Peppy was crying to join me in my turret, and Baladine said irritably that he thought they'd shot the damned dog. The red laser sight moved around the sanctuary, trying to pick out a warm target, but the turret was between Peppy and him. He himself was shielded by one of the pillars, or I would have risked a shot at him.

"Aren't there any lights in this damned place?" It was Lemour's reedy voice coming in to the body of the church. "What do you need me for, boss? Hunt out the Warshki bitch? Turn on the lights and we'll get her in no time. Drabek, go in the back and find the switches. I'll cover the altar."

Under cover of Lemour's voice, I slipped out of the little turret. I had chosen it because I could shoot anyone who came close enough to me to attack it, but I realized it was a stupid hideout: all my friends would be dead while I defended myself, and then I'd run out of bullets and die as well. I got down on my hands and knees and crawled down the center aisle until I came to the pews. Making sure the safety was on, I stuck my gun in a jeans pocket and slithered along the floor toward Baladine. I wished I could have ordered Peppy to stay at the turret, but she was anxiously following me.

"I know you're back there, Warshawski, I can hear you. Come out on the count of five or the first bullet goes into the old man."

"It's okay, cookie, don't give up, I can take it, just don't hold it against me that I let the guy in. You know there's never been anyone like you in my life, all seventy-nine years, and I ain't having you take a bullet just so I can see eighty."

Baladine savagely ordered him to be quiet, but the old man was either beyond paying attention or deliberately trying to give me cover. He started recounting the first time he saw me, I was wearing a red top and cutoffs and going after a gangbanger, street punk, but nowhere near as bad as this bastard, pardon his French.

Baladine smacked him, I think with his pistol. When Mr. Contreras fell silent, Father Lou began to sing, in a loud, tuneless voice, a Latin chant. I risked getting to my feet and running toward Baladine. He had one hand on the flash, the other on the gun pointing at Mr. Contreras's head. He was yelling at Father Lou to shut up or be killed when I got behind him and savagely chopped the back of his head.

He dropped the flashlight. His knees buckled, and I grabbed his right arm with all my might. He wrenched his arm free and his gun went off. A window shattered. Father Lou stuck out a foot and kicked the flashlight away, and I grappled with Baladine in the dark. Lemour shouted at the henchman to get the damned lights on, he was going to take care of Warshki once and for all.

Baladine was trying to twist his arm around to get a shot at me. I stayed behind him, pinning his left arm so

he had only his gun hand free: if he wanted to fight he'd
have to drop the gun. He jabbed backward with his gun
arm. I stuck my knee in his back and pulled his left
shoulder toward me. He dropped the gun, which went
off again, and pulled me close to him, bending to flip
me over his head. I held on and we landed on the floor
together. I lost my grip in the fall and he straddled me,
his hands locking around my throat. I brought a knee
up to his groin. His hold slackened enough for me to
get a breath and to try to pull my gun from my pocket.

In the dark next to me I heard a deep angry growl
and felt a heavy furry body lean against me. Baladine
gave a loud scream and let go of my neck. I wrenched
away from him and bounced to my feet. I kicked out as
hard as I could, not able to see him in the dark. I kicked
high, wanting to miss the dog. My foot connected with
bone. Baladine fell heavily against me. I backed away,
ready to kick again, but he wasn't moving. I must have
knocked him out. I scrabbled under the pew and picked
up the flashlight.

Mitch was lying across Baladine's legs. Mitch, bleeding but alive. I couldn't take time to figure out what had
happened, how he'd bitten Baladine—I had Lemour
and his partner to deal with. I shone the light briefly on
Father Lou, but he and Mr. Contreras were handcuffed
together, with their arms behind them. I couldn't free
them now.

Father Lou shouted a warning: Lemour had picked
his way through the pews to my side. I hurled the flashlight into his face and ran back toward the altar.

A bullet whined and smashed into the altarpiece, and
I smelled smoke. I ran behind the altarpiece. Lemour
fired again, this time in front of me. Light flooded the
building, and I was blinded. Lemour, running toward

me, was blinded as well. He tripped across the open trapdoor and fell headlong down the spiral stairs. Glass splintered as he crashed to the bottom.

I braced myself, waiting for the henchman to come after me, when a fireman appeared behind the altar. I thought at first I was hallucinating, or that Baladine had dragooned the fire department along with the police, and lifted my gun.

"No need to shoot, young lady," the man said. "I'm here to put out the fire."

47

For Those Who Also Serve

THE GUNSHOTS WOKE me and I saw the door to the church was open, so I snuck in. I heard everything but I didn't know what to do, because BB was saying he had a cop to cover up for him. Then I thought, well, if the church was burning, the fire department would come, so I set fire to a newspaper in the kitchen and called 911 and told them the church was on fire. Then I was afraid I was really going to burn down the building. Is Mitch going to be okay? What did they say at the vet?"

We were sitting in the rectory kitchen, drinking more cambric tea as Father Lou and I tried to clean up the sodden mess the firemen had left behind.

"Robbie, you're a hero. It was a brilliant idea, but next time you don't have to set fire to the kitchen—they can't tell downtown if the place is really burning up or not." I laughed shakily. "Mitch is going to be okay. The vet said he took the bullet in his shoulder, not the heart, and even though he lost a lot of blood he should make it through."

Peppy had stayed at the emergency vet to be a blood donor for her son. After the firemen finished putting out the kitchen fire, they'd gotten an ambulance for the wounded. Mr. Contreras and Baladine had both been carted off to County Hospital, although Mr. Contreras was protesting it was only a head injury, he'd survived worse than that at Anzio.

Detective Lemour was in the morgue. He'd broken his neck when he landed on the reliquary at the bottom of the stairs. The remaining two men from Carnifice Security had been carried off by a squadrol that the firemen had summoned. One of the officers driving the squadrol had been a student at St. Remigio's six years ago. He was horrified at seeing his priest in handcuffs and was happy to accept Father Lou's version of events: that Baladine had broken in with his two thugs, and that Lemour had died trying to rescue the priest.

"Saves trouble," the priest said when the policeman had left. "Hard to get the cops to believe one of their own is bent. If Baladine denies the story when he recovers, he'll have a lot of explaining to do, why Lemour was with him."

The firemen helped me carry Mitch out to their own car. They gave Peppy and me a ride to the emergency vet and even stayed with me to bring me back to the church an hour later.

"Six o'clock," Father Lou announced now. "Mass. Want to serve, young lady?"

I started to remind him I wasn't even baptized, then saw his fierce look and shut my mouth. I followed him back down the hall to the church. Robbie trailed behind us. There was broken glass in the side aisle, and a piece of St. Veronica's arm had been shot off the high altar, but the church looked remarkably placid in the daylight.

I went into the vestry with Father Lou and watched him robe. He told me what vessels to bring and just to do as he said and I'd be fine. I walked behind him to the

Lady Chapel, where a half dozen women waited, teachers going to mass on the first morning of school.

Father Lou bowed to the altar and turned to the women. "I was glad when they said to me, let us go to the House of the Lord."

48

Meet the Press

This photograph is a close-up of a bruise on my abdomen. A forensic pathologist says he can identify at least the make and size of the boot that made it. There will be a trial, I'm suing the person who kicked me, and I'll make an identification in court, so it doesn't matter now whether he burns the boot or cleans it. The point is, I'm alive, and I can make the identification."

The eleven people whose papers and broadcast stations had decided to send them to St. Remigio's looked at each other with a kind of incredulity that said, is this what she dragged us out here for? I smiled at them, I hoped engagingly. When they had come into the school library where Morrell had set up the screen and the projector, they'd mobbed me, wanting answers to all kinds of questions, ranging from what I knew about Baladine's injuries to where I'd been since getting out of Coolis. I promised they could ask me anything when I finished my presentation.

Murray Ryerson, looking both belligerent and sheepish, was the only one who hung back from the group swarming around me. He said he knew I couldn't be dead, I was too much of a grandstander for that, then planted himself in a corner and made a big play of studying his own paper when I started speaking.

In the back of the room Father Lou sat with a couple of squarely built men whom the priest identified only as being from his parish council, there to help out if the need arose. Also in the back were Mr. Contreras with Mitch and Peppy, Lotty and Max, and Sal. Neither Mr. Contreras nor Mitch seemed any worse for their night in the church, although Mitch had a large bandage wrapped around his belly and shoulder. He was sitting up, grinning crazily at anyone who wanted to pet him. Morrell was off to one side, operating the projector.

It was a week after Baladine's assault on the church. We had decided to go ahead with the show, because there were too many open-ended issues. Baladine was going to recover, and he was already trying to make a case that he had used some fancy equipment to scale the side of the church school, break in through the fourth-floor windows, and attack the priest simply in order to get his son back. I wanted my version in as many hands as possible.

"I'm starting with this picture because in a curious way it's the crux of a difficult case involving Global Entertainment, Carnifice Security, and that perennial chestnut, Illinois politics. I'm alive, talking to you, but another young woman, who received what I believe are identical injuries, was not so fortunate. Nicola Aguinaldo died in the early hours of June seventeenth from a perforated intestine. Her body disappeared from the medical examiner's office before an autopsy could be performed."

We had made a still of Nicola smiling, from a frame of the home video where she'd been talking to Robbie. I explained who she was, using a slide with bullet points, how she'd landed in prison, and how I'd inadvertently found her.

"I don't think we'll ever know what became of her body: her grief-stricken mother was denied the chance to bury it. But my guess is that a political appointee of Jean-Claude Poilevy at the county morgue removed the body on Poilevy's orders so that no one would be able to see what kind of boot kicked in Nicola Aguinaldo's abdomen."

I nodded at Morrell, who clicked up the slide of Hartigan standing over me with the stun gun. The audience gasped with shock.

"He was about six foot two, perhaps two hundred, two-twenty pounds. She wasn't five feet tall and weighed maybe ninety pounds. She didn't have too much of a chance against him. I managed to take this picture with a hidden camera seconds after I'd been shot with fifty thousand volts from a stun gun, right before I was kicked into insensibility." I held up my right hand, which was in a kind of brace; I'd reinjured the fingers fighting Baladine. "Two of my fingers and five of the small bones in the back of my hand broke as I tried to protect my head."

I heard another intake of horrified breath but continued with my presentation in a dry, academic voice. It was the only way I could speak without giving way to emotion. I went through the details of Nicola's daughter's death, what I'd been told by the women at Coolis about Nicola's desperate grief and how she'd pounded on the guard's chest when they laughed at her plea to be allowed to attend the baby's funeral. I couldn't look at Mr. Contreras; he was so upset that I knew my own composure would crack. I heard Peppy whining by his side with shared misery.

Morrell put up another slide. This one had a red flashing header reading *Speculation! Speculation!* We'd decided to use that to separate fact from guesswork. I told them I was guessing that Nicola was dumped on the Chicago streets in the same way I was.

"What takes some of the guesswork out of this is the fact that the guards changed my shirt before they took me out of Coolis. I was concussed, manacled, and running a high fever and not able to defend myself; they tore off my shirt and put on one that wouldn't show the scorch marks from the stun gun." I stopped for water, remembering Polsen touching the burned skin on my breasts. "They made a comment about not making the mistake they had before, where they had to change the victim's shirt in Chicago, so they had clearly done this before. It's just a guess that Nicola Aguinaldo was the person they'd done it to.

"Now here comes more speculation, and mighty interesting it is. The shirt they put on Aguinaldo had been made by Lucian Frenada. You may remember Mr. Frenada's name: his dead body was found floating in Lake Michigan right before the Fourth of July. Everyone who isn't brain-dead knows Frenada was a boyhood friend of Lacey Dowell, because Global has been trumpeting that information on television and in the *Herald-Star* for two months. They grew up together right here at St. Remigio's." I glanced at Murray. He was studying the floor.

Beth Blacksin from Channel 8 interrupted with a question about Lacey, and several other reporters jumped in. I ignored them and explained how Frenada had gone to Lacey and asked for a chance to make some of the Global Entertainment spin-off products.

"Money in movies isn't just made on the screen. When your kid has to have that Captain Doberman

T-shirt or those Space Beret action figures, the cash reg-
isters at Global are ringing. Mad Virgin shirts are very
popular with young teens—they're one of the first
movie spin-off items to find a huge marketing success
with teenage girls. Oversize denim jackets are another
hot seller in Global's Virginwear line.

"When Nicola Aguinaldo's body was found, she was
wearing one of the T-shirts that Lucian Frenada made
as a demo for Teddy Trant at Global. You all remember
the party at the Golden Glow back in June, when
Frenada came and Lacey had him thrown out? He was
demanding to know why Trant had stolen one of the
shirts. Global didn't want to work with him, but
Frenada was highly suspicious that Trant might be going to copy some of his workmanship. Of course everyone thought Frenada was trying any tactic he could to
get Lacey to influence Global into buying from him:
why would a studio head, who could pick up a Mad
Virgin T-shirt anytime he walked into his office, go to
the trouble of stealing one from a small Humboldt Park
entrepreneur?

"But I believe that is exactly what Trant did. He was
at Frenada's shop on the Tuesday night right before
Nicola died. That's a fact. This next is a guess, but I
believe that in some crazy scheme, maybe caused by
watching too many of his own movies, Trant stole one
of Frenada's shirts to put on Nicola, so that if any questions were asked about her death he could direct attention away from Coolis, from Global, and toward an
innocent bystander."

The room was in an uproar. I went back through the
argument, ticking off the points on the slide that high-
lighted them.

When they seemed to be caught up with me, I went

back to Baladine and his fury with me. How Global
first tried to bribe me by hiring me to frame Frenada,
and when I wouldn't play, how Baladine began hound-
ing me, culminating with planting cocaine in my office.

I played the video I'd made in my office. The group
was firing so many questions now that I had to play it
three times before I could go on.

"I don't know if Baladine wanted me dead or discredited—" I began, when Murray piped up unexpectedly from the back of the room.

"He was spinning around. I don't think he could
possibly have told anyone he wanted you dead, but
when some of us at the *Star* caught wind of the discussions going on about your involvement in the case, we
—uh, made it as clear as we could that if anything—uh
—well, a lot of people in Chicago would want to know
why you got—uh—hurt. Also, I got the idea that someone high in the Global organization was lobbying for
you, although Al—my contacts there—never said who
it was. Anyway, I have a feeling—I was not involved in
any discussions about you—but I think he—Baladine—
thought discrediting you was the viable route. I didn't
know about the drugs. And I was as amazed as everyone else here when you were arrested for kidnapping.
And then, why on God's green earth you didn't post
bail—" He broke off midsentence. "I guess you were
being Wonder Woman again. Take us to the limit one
more time, Warshawski."

I blushed but went on with my presentation. "As far
as Frenada goes, I think they wanted him dead: he was
starting to complain to too many people about Trant
taking one of his sample Virginwear shirts. They
thought they could discredit him with drugs; they
planted some in his shop and planted some data on the

Web trying to show he was a high roller. I'm afraid it was something I said that sent him hotfoot out to Oak Brook to try to confront Baladine and Trant the night of June twenty-sixth."

Morrell ran the footage of Frenada with Baladine and Trant at Baladine's pool. He stopped it to make sure everyone noticed the date embedded in the film.

"This film doesn't prove that Baladine and Trant killed Frenada, but it does put the three men together the night Frenada died. Lucian Frenada had told me he couldn't compete with Global's current suppliers because his labor costs were too high. He also had other overhead that someone running a factory in a prison doesn't have to deal with. The state of Illinois paid for the machines that Global gets to use. The state of Illinois pays the rent on the space for the Global factory. You can't get lower production costs for this kind of operation, even if you go to Burma, because you can't beat free space and machinery. And you have a labor force that can never go on strike, never balk at the working conditions, never complain to OSHA or the NLRB. It's a beauty for the bottom line in these days of the global economy."

There was another barrage of questions about the Global–Carnifice shop. "You've been most patient to listen to me for such a long period," I finally said. "There are only a few more things I want to say. All summer, as Baladine and Trent were boxing me in, I kept wondering what was so important about Nicola Aguinaldo that they needed to find someone to take the blame for her death. It wasn't she they cared about, but their manufacturing scheme. It had been operating smoothly, no questions asked, for several years; they didn't want some outsider poking into Nicola's death to upset it.

"Maybe you're wondering how they could run that plant as long as they did with no one noticing. For one thing, they were well connected to the Illinois House Speaker, who's got a lot of power, in and out of Springfield.

"For another, we all assume that whatever goes on behind those iron bars is protecting all us law-abiding citizens—sorry, all you law-abiding citizens; I'm out on bail facing a felony charge." People laughed more loudly than my little joke merited—they needed some kind of release from the horrors they'd been hearing.

"Some of what goes on may be nasty, but as the corrections officers said to me and my sister inmates many times—like when a woman wasn't allowed medical care after getting a major burn on her arm in the kitchen"—I nodded and Morrell flipped up a slide of the arm—"Coolis isn't a resort. Inmates aren't on vacation. We law-abiding citizens don't necessarily want prisoners rehabilitated, but we sure do want them punished. And they get punished in carloads full of discipline."

I finished with the slides I'd taken of CO Polsen assaulting Dolores in the laundry room. The only sound in the room now was Peppy, crying to be allowed to come to me.

"This kind of thing is a daily occurrence. I witnessed it, I was humiliated in similar ways myself. Women have no recourse against this kind of abuse. Illinois law has no serious provision for removing abusive guards or for disciplining them. It can take over a year for a woman prisoner complaining of rape or battery to get a court hearing. During that year she can be put in segregation. She can be repeatedly assaulted. And if her case is found to be without merit, then she is cattle fodder for the corrections officers. That's daily life at Coolis.

"I understand Robert Baladine sent around an e-mail, offering to resign. I don't know if it's true or not, but if it weren't for the fact that Lucian Frenada was—probably—killed in an effort to cover up the Global manufacturing operation, I'd think Baladine should resign not because of Frenada but because of the degradation of prisoners that goes on hourly in a prison that his company built and runs for the state of Illinois."

I'd lost my dry composure. I sat down, shivering, my teeth chattering. Morrell was at my side to put a jacket around my shoulders. Murray had stepped forward along with the rest of the team in the room, but when he saw Morrell behind me, he turned on his heel and left.

Lotty and Sal and Mr. Contreras applauded vigorously, and Mr. Contreras finally let Peppy come up to me. I sank my hands gratefully into her gold fur and tried to calm down enough to answer other questions.

What the reporters most wanted to know, besides their fascination with sex in the prison, was how Baladine came to be injured.

"He says he needed to break into the church to get his son back. I believe Father Lou has made a sworn deposition that Baladine never approached him about his son. Indeed, Robbie arrived at the church only a few hours ahead of his father, who could have phoned or come to the door the way most people might. But someone watching my home apparently saw him arrive, tailed him here to St. Remigio's, and then called

Baladine for instructions. He chose to approach his son in this highly unusual way, and a police officer is dead as a result."

One of the Carnifice Security men who'd been in the church last week had decided to do a deal with the State's Attorney. No one in the State's Attorney's office cared much about Lucian Frenada, or Nicola Aguinaldo—or me. But Father Lou was a local legend. For forty years, any policeman who'd ever boxed grew up knowing him. An assault on him in his church was more than blasphemy. So the guy Father Lou had knocked out, after realizing that the cops were more interested in finding out exactly what punch the priest had used on him than in sympathizing with him, turned on his boss and his partner and told the cops the story of his watch on my building, of seeing Robbie arrive on foot, of calling for instructions.

"Isn't the dead officer the same man who was in your office with the cocaine?"

I smiled. "You'll have to ask the department about that one. I never actually saw the man who died at St. Remigio's: everything took place in the dark."

"And what about Baladine?" Beth Blacksin from Channel 8 asked. "I hear he's undergoing shots for rabies because your dog bit him? Is he suing you?"

"You have it backward," I said. "I'm giving my dog Mitch a series of rabies shots in case Baladine infected him. No, seriously, he shot the dog and thought he'd killed him, because the dog tried to stop him from chaining Father Lou to my old friend and neighbor Salvatore Contreras. When Baladine was strangling me, Mitch somehow made a supercanine effort, dragged himself up on his weak legs, and dug his teeth into Baladine's ass. If Baladine chooses to sue me, my lawyer is looking forward to cross-examining him, but we'll cross that bridge when we get there."

Regine Mauger, the *Herald-Star*'s gossip columnist, got up to demand what right I had to vilify the Trant family. Abigail Trant was a lovely woman who was doing an enormous amount of good for needy Chicagoans, and Regine thought I should be ashamed for attacking her husband in this way.

I didn't tell her I had called Abigail Trant myself the day after the fight in the church. After her efforts to help me, she deserved advance notice of what I was going to say about her husband. She asked only if I was sure. And I said, not about everything but about Trant's being with Baladine and Frenada the night Frenada died. And about the production of Global spin-offs at Coolis.

She didn't say anything else, but two days later she came to see me—again without warning, leaving the Gelaendewagen double-parked on Racine. She was as exquisite as ever, but the skin on her face was taut with tension.

"Rhiannon and I fell in love with France when we were there this summer. I'm taking her back to Toulouse. I've found a wonderful school she can attend there. I don't know what Teddy will do, because I don't know what Global will do when they hear your report."

She hesitated, then added, "I don't want you to think I blame you in any way for—for—the collapse of my marriage. I think the time will come when I will be grateful that my eyes were opened, but right now I can't feel much but pain. There's something else you deserve to know. Teddy came home the night of Global's television debut with the emblem missing from one of his

Ferragamo loafers. Maybe it's weak of me, but the day you asked about the emblem I went home and threw out the shoes."

She left abruptly on that line. I didn't think Regine Mauger needed to report any of that in her coy little phrases.

Mauger and some of the others continued to harangue me. Lotty came forward and announced that as my physician she was declaring an end to my stamina: I was recovering from serious injuries, in case they had forgotten. The group looked suitably abashed and packed up cassette recorders and other equipment. Morrell gave each person a copy of the videotape and slides. The two men sitting with Father Lou grunted and got up to escort the reporters out of the building.

"Now what?" Sal asked when they had gone.

"Now—" I shrugged. "Now I try to patch my business back together. Hope that enough people buy my version of events that some of the misery at Coolis will end, even if no one is ever arrested for Nicola Aguinaldo's murder."

"And what is Robbie going to do?" Sal asked.

I grinned. "Eleanor came to pick him up on Wednesday afternoon. He ran into the church screaming that he was claiming sanctuary, that he would chain himself to the altar and go on a hunger strike. That should have thrilled her, but it only made her angrier. She finally worked out a deal with Father Lou that Robbie could stay on as a boarder and go to St. Remigio's. Father Lou said that for a donation to the St. Remigio scholarship fund and money to repair the damage to the altar, he was willing to tell the state to drop the trespassing charge against Baladine."

Watching Father Lou blandly extort a fifty-thousand-dollar pledge from Eleanor Baladine had been one
of the few joyous moments of the past few months. She
had arrived at St. Remigio's with her lawyer, convinced
that she was going to browbeat the priest with threats
of additional charges of kidnapping, as well as of assault against Baladine—man coming to claim his son is
set on by dogs, rabid detectives, and other scum. She
left without her son and with a signed undertaking to
support him at the school. The sop to her pride was
Father Lou's grave statement that boxing would make
Robbie a truly manly man, and that he, Father Lou,
would personally oversee her son's training.

"The funny thing is, Robbie actually wants to learn
to box," I told Sal. "This boy who couldn't learn to
swim or play tennis to please his parents runs wind
sprints every morning after mass."

I'd moved back home, of course, but for some reason
I found myself getting up early every day and driving
over to St. Remigio's for the six o'clock mass. Robbie
or one of the other St. Remigio boxers would serve.
Father Lou gruffly announced I could read the lesson as
long as I was there. All that week, as I made my way
through the book of Job, I thought about the women at
Coolis. If there was a God, had He delivered the women
into the hands of Satan for a wager? And would He
appear finally in the whirlwind and rescue them?

Scar Tissue

MY VINDICATION BY the Chicago press was something of a nine-day wonder. Clients who'd left me for Carnifice called to say they'd never doubted me and they would have assignments for me as soon as I got off the disabled list. Old friends in the Chicago Police Department called, demanding to know why I hadn't complained to them about Douglas Lemour; they would have fixed the problem for me. I didn't try to argue with them about all the times in the past they'd told me to mind my own business and leave police work to them. And Mary Louise Neely showed up one morning, her face pinched with misery.

"Vic, I won't blame you if you feel like you can never trust me again, but they called to threaten me. Threaten the children. The man who called knew the exact address of Emily's camp in France and told me what she'd eaten for dinner the night before. I was terrified and I felt trapped—I couldn't send the boys back to their father, and I didn't know what else to do with them. I thought if I told you, you'd go riding off half-cocked and get all of us killed." She twisted her hands round and round as if she could wash off the memory.

"You could be right." I tried to smile, but found I

couldn't quite manage it. "I'm not going to sit in judgment on you for being scared, let alone for trying to look after Nate and Josh. What hurt was the way you were judging me. Claiming I was running hotheaded into danger when I was fighting for my life. I had to go into the heart of the furnace to save myself. If you could have trusted me enough to tell me why you were withdrawing from me, it would have made a big difference."

"You're right, Vic," she whispered. "I could have gone to Terry about Lemour; maybe it would have stopped him from trying to plant the coke on you or from beating you when he arrested you. I can only say —I'm sorry. If you're willing to let me try again, though, I'd like to."

We left it at that—that she would open the office back up, get the files in order, take preliminary information from clients while I continued to recuperate. We'd give it three months and see how we felt about the relationship then.

I kept trying to go back to work myself, but I felt dull and drained. I had told the psychologist at the Berman Institute I would sleep better if I stopped feeling so humiliated. By rights, taking care of Lemour and Baladine should have solved my problems, but I still was plagued by insomnia. Maybe it was because my month at Coolis sat like a bad taste in my mouth, or maybe it was because I couldn't stop blaming myself for staying inside when I could have made bail, as if I had deliberately courted what had happened to me. There were still too many nights I dreaded going to sleep because of the dreams that lay on the other side.

The night after my press presentation I'd invited Morrell home with me, but when he started to undress I told him he would have to leave. He took a long look at me and buttoned his jeans back up. The next day he sent me a single rose with the message that he would respect my distance as long as I felt I needed to maintain it but that he enjoyed talking to me and would be glad to see me in public.

The knowledge that I could choose, that Morrell at least would not force himself on me, made sleep come a bit easier to me. I went to a couple of Cubs games with him as the season wound down—thanks to tickets from one of my clients—and saw Sammy Sosa hit his sixty-fourth home run, invited Morrell to my Saturday afternoon pickup game in the park, ate dinner with him, but spent my nights with only the dogs for company.

I kept busy enough. I made endless depositions with attorneys for the state, attorneys for the CO's I was suing out at Coolis, attorneys for Baladine, attorneys for Global. I even had a meeting with Alex Fisher. She thought it would be a good idea if I toned down some of my statements about Global and Frenada.

"Sandy, the reason I call you Sandy, which you hate, is that it's the only thing about you I ever liked. You were a pain in the ass in law school. You wanted to be a firebrand and take the message about racism and social justice to the proletariat, and I made you uncomfortable because I was that odd phenomenon in an upscale law school—a genuine blue-collar worker's genuine daughter. But at least you were who you were—Sandy Fishbein. You didn't try to pretend you were anything else. Then you went off and found capitalism, and had your nose and your lips done, and cut off your name, too."

"That's not what I came to talk to you about," she said, but her voice had lost its edge.

"And another thing. I have a tape of yours. Baladine made it during his swim meet."

"How did you get it?" she hissed. "Did he give it to you?"

I smiled blandly. "He doesn't know I have it. It's yours, Alex. It's yours the day I get concrete evidence that Global has fired Wenzel, the man who managed the Coolis shop, and that he is not working elsewhere in your organization. And the day that Carnifice lets CO Polsen and CO Hartigan go. Without placing them elsewhere."

Her wide lips were stiff. "I have little influence on Global's day-to-day operation, and I do not work for Carnifice."

I continued to smile. "Of course not. And it doesn't look as though Baladine will be at Carnifice much longer, anyway, at least not if the report in this morning's papers can be believed. Between his sending that e-mail announcing his resignation and all the publicity we've generated this week, his board is pressuring him to step down. And Jean-Claude Poilevy, who's always been a survivor, is backpedaling as fast as he can scoot. He says Baladine operated a for-profit shop at Coolis completely without his knowledge, and he's shocked at the tales of sexual abuse in the prison. I think Carnifice would welcome the chance to fire a couple of low-level employees. If they let Polsen and Hartigan go, they can make a big press pitch on how they're cleaning house."

"I can't promise anything, of course."

"Of course not. By the way, you're not the only woman Baladine taped on that couch. He also took advantage of his kids' ex-nanny, the one who died. Not a nice man to be around."

Her throat worked as the implications of that struck

her. She started to ask me what I'd seen and then swept out of my office without saying anything else.

I'd thought about trying to use the Aguinaldo tapes as counters to get Baladine to drop the kidnapping charge, but I hated to exploit her in death as she had been in life. And I was sure by now I could beat the charges in court. In fact, six days later when my trial date came up, the judge dismissed all the charges. He made a stern statement to the effect that he didn't know why the state had charged me in the first place, but since the parents were not present to offer any explanation about why they'd called the police, he couldn't begin to speculate on their underlying rationale. At any rate, the arresting officer was dead, and that was the end of it. A real whimper after all that banging.

When I got home I found a hand-delivered envelope from Alex including copies of the termination orders for Wenzel from Global and Polsen and Hartigan from Carnifice. The three were fired for misconduct in performance of their duties and were not eligible for workers' compensation. I sent Alex her tape but kept the other three in a safe deposit box at the bank.

A discreet report in the paper the next day said that Baladine was suffering from exhaustion brought on by overwork and that the Carnifice directors had accepted his resignation while he received medical care in Houston. His wife was moving to California with her daughters to enroll them in a premium swim program while she took a job coaching the University of Southern California swim team. Good old Eleanor. She sure hated hanging with losers.

And still I couldn't sleep at night. I finally decided I had to go back to Coolis. I had to see the place, to know it had no power over me.

They were harvesting corn as I drove west the next morning. The bright greens of summer had given way to drab tans in the groves along the Fox River, but the weather still held an unseasonable warmth.

As I approached the prison, the place in my abdomen where Hartigan had kicked me tightened. I was coming here of my own free will, a free woman, but the sight of the razor-wire fences made me start to shake so badly, I had to pull over to the side of the road.

Morrell had offered to come with me, but I wanted to prove I could make this journey on my own. I wished now I'd taken him up on his offer. I wanted to turn around and head back to Chicago as fast as I could go. Instead, I made myself drive inside the front gate to the visitors' parking lot.

The guard at the first checkpoint didn't give any sign of recognizing my name. He passed me on to the next station, and I was finally admitted to the visitors' waiting room. It was CO Cornish who was assigned to escort me from there to the visitors' lounge.

He tried to greet me jovially. "Couldn't stay away, huh?"

I grunted noncommittally. I had filed a suit against the Department of Corrections for inflicting grievous bodily harm, and against Polsen and Hartigan by name. Cornish would probably be called as a witness; I didn't need to alienate him.

Miss Ruby was waiting for me in the visitors' lounge. "So you made it out, Cream. Made it out and now you've come back. You're a kind of hero around here, do you know that? The girls know it's because of you they kicked out Wenzel and Polsen and Hartigan. They closed that T-shirt factory too, but I suppose you know that."

I knew that. A report in this morning's financial section announced that Global was returning their sewing operations to Myanmar. I guess it made me happy to know that the Virginwear line was now being made by inmates in Myanmar's forced labor camps instead of inmates in an Illinois prison.

"They're still making things here, but not for Hollywood anymore, so production is way down. It's hard on the women who got let go; they don't speak English and they can only get work in the kitchen now, which doesn't pay as well. But I think they appreciate not having to work in that atmosphere over there. Everyone was too scared all the time. So I guess you are a hero, at that."

"You sound bitter. I didn't set out to be a hero."

"No, but you were undercover. I asked you point-blank and you lied. You might have told me when you came to me asking for help."

"I really was arrested. Just as I told you, because Robert Baladine accused me of kidnapping his son. The cops sent me out here because I got arrested on a holiday weekend. I decided to stay to try to find out what happened to poor young Nicola. I didn't dare tell a soul. Not just to protect myself: you have a lot of influence here with the other women, and even the guards mostly treat you with respect, but you're here and you're vulnerable. I didn't want harm to you to haunt me for the rest of my life."

She thought it over and finally, grudgingly, decided maybe I hadn't abused our relationship. I stayed to tell her the whole story, the story I'd given to the press. She liked having an insider's look at the news, and she especially enjoyed hearing about my confrontation with Baladine and Lemour at St. Remigio's.

"Girl like you who took on Angie and the Iscariots, you were plenty tough enough to go up against a bent cop. Glad to hear about it. Glad to know about it."

Before I left, I handed her a little bag of cosmetics I'd brought with me, buried under a stack of legal documents that hadn't been searched thoroughly. CO Cornish watched me but didn't try to intervene.

"Revlon! You remembered. Moisturizer, cleanser, new lipstick in my favorite color—you're a good woman, even if you did come to me under false pretenses. Now, since it turns out you're really a lawyer and a detective and all those things, maybe you'll write one of your famous letters for me. I've done fourteen years, that's already way over average for murder in this state, but I've got eight more to go. See if you can help me on my parole. I'd kind of like to see my granddaughter before she's a grandmother herself."

I promised to do what I could. Back in the parking lot I stood with my hand on the car door for a long time before opening it. The car was a late-model green Mustang, a replacement for both the Rustmobile and the Trans Am. Freeman had tried to get me back my beloved sports car, but the police first claimed they couldn't find it and then finally had to admit they'd pretty well trashed it. Luke went to the police pound to look at it, but the Trans Am was way beyond even his miraculous fingers. Freeman was suing the city for me to try to recover the price of the car, but I figured I'd be seventy before that case came to judgment.

Lacey Dowell had given me the money for the Mustang. She'd given me enough money that I could probably have bought a used XJ-12 convertible, but that was a fantasy, not a car for a working detective who has to use her wheels in the grime of Chicago.

Lacey came to see me at the end of the filming of
Virgin Six. Father Lou told her that I'd solved Frenada's
murder and that even though Trant and Baladine would
never be arrested for it, she should know that the two
men had killed her childhood playmate.

"I told them at Global that I couldn't work with
Teddy anymore, that I'd stop production if he had anything to do with the movie. I guess I'm still a big enough
star that they cared. They sent Teddy to Chile to head
up their South American operation. But I understand
from Father Lou that you put in a great deal of work on
the case and never got paid. In fact, he told me you
were badly injured as the result of your investigations.
So I felt I should pay your fee, since Lucy and I were old
friends, and we swore a pact when we were ten to help
each other in the face of every danger. I didn't do too
well by him this year: the least I can do is thank you for
looking after him for me."

The check was for forty thousand dollars. Enough to
take care of the bills that had mounted while I was out
of commission. Enough for a car with only six thousand miles on it. Enough to pay some of Freeman's fee.
Money made from T-shirts sewn by women in prisons
here or abroad. It was in my hands, too. I could have
turned it down, but I didn't.

I got into the car when the guard came over to see
what the matter was. I sketched a wave and headed
back to the tollway.

When I reached the city I drove to Morrell's place in
Evanston. I tried to tell him what I'd been thinking as I
drove home.

He cupped my face in his long fingers. "Vic, look at
me. You set an impossibly high bar for yourself to
jump. When you run into it, you bruise yourself and

then blame yourself for the injury. You have to live in the world. It's the unfortunate reality of being alive. Even a monk who abjures the world and the flesh gets his clothes and food provided by someone who's willing to do the dirty work for him.

"You can't save everyone or fix every broken part of this planet. But you do more than most. If Lacey's money comes in part from sweatshops, you still brought some relief to women in prison here in Illinois. And that bastard Hartigan, who kicked you—he's likely to go to prison himself. Even if it's not for the murder of Nicola Aguinaldo, there's a measure of justice there. It's true Trant and Baladine are walking around, but Trant lost his marriage and it looks as though the studio is demoting him in a serious way. You said Lacey told you they're sending him to Chile.

"And look at Robbie Baladine following Father Lou around like a duckling. Share some of his joy in life. You've earned it, you brought it to him. Okay?"

"Okay," I whispered.

I spent that night with him and a number of nights after. And if my sleep was still disturbed, if the images of terror still sometimes woke me, at least I had the comfort of a friend to share my journey.

"No one, male or female, writes better P.I. books than Paretsky."

—The Denver Post

___0-440-23476-X	*Bitter Medicine*	$6.99/9.99
___0-440-20420-8	*Blood Shot*	$6.99/8.99
___0-440-20845-9	*Burn Marks*	$6.99/8.99
___0-440-21332-0	*Deadlock*	$6.99/8.99
___0-440-21399-1	*Guardian Angel*	$6.99/8.99
___0-440-21069-0	*Indemnity Only*	$6.99/8.99
___0-440-21528-5	*Killing Orders*	$6.99/8.99
___0-440-21752-0	*Tunnel Vision*	$6.99/8.99
___0-440-21873-X	*Windy City Blues* *V.I. Warshawski Stories*	$6.99/8.99
___0-440-21335-5	*A Woman's Eye* (Anthology)	$6.99/8.99
___0-440-22325-3	*Women on the Case* (Anthology)	$6.99/8.99
___0-440-22470-5	*Hard Time*	$6.99/9.99
___0-440-33336-6	*Ghost Country*	$13.95/21.95